CRISIS
ON MULTIPLE EARTHS
VOLUME 6

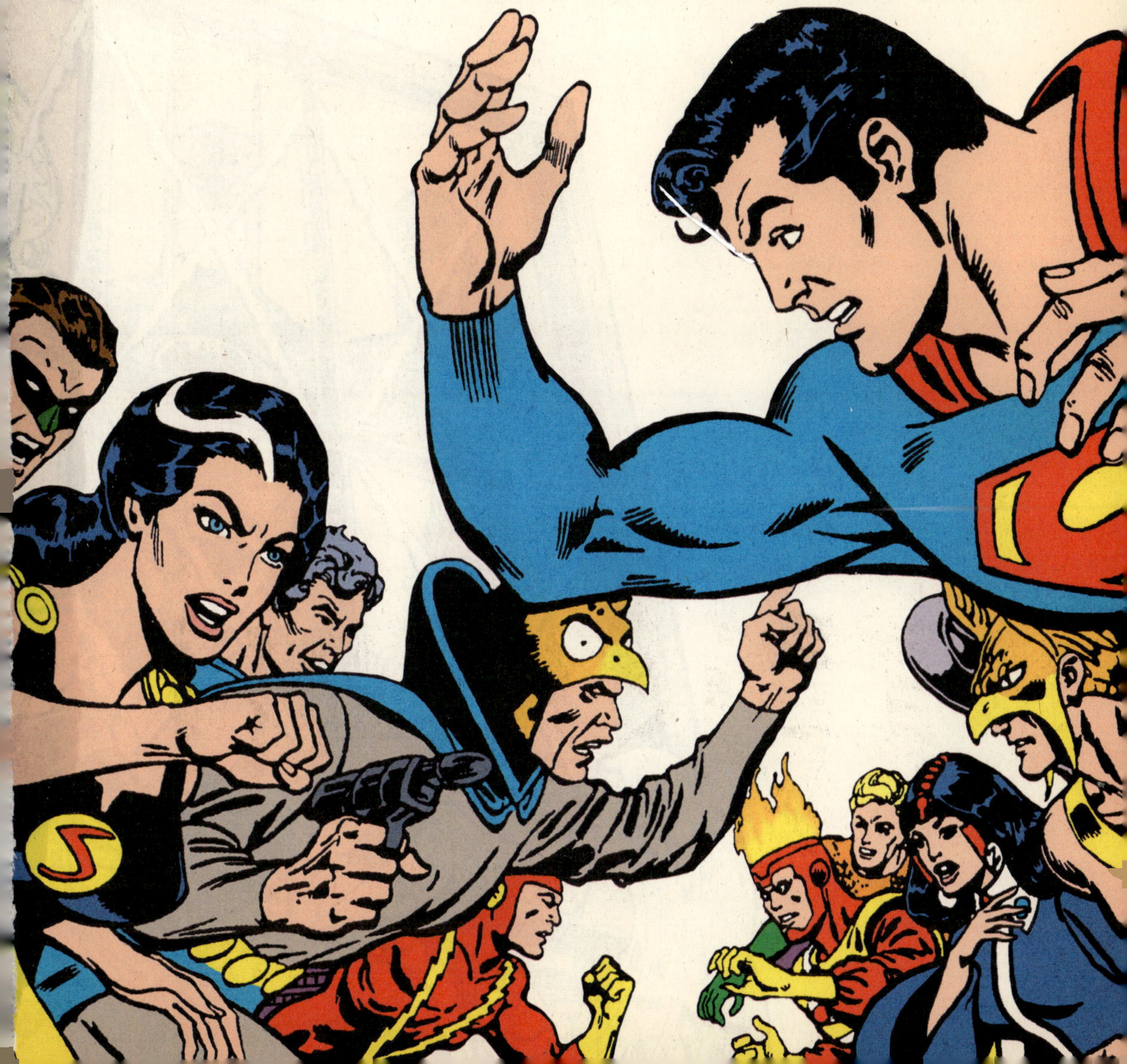

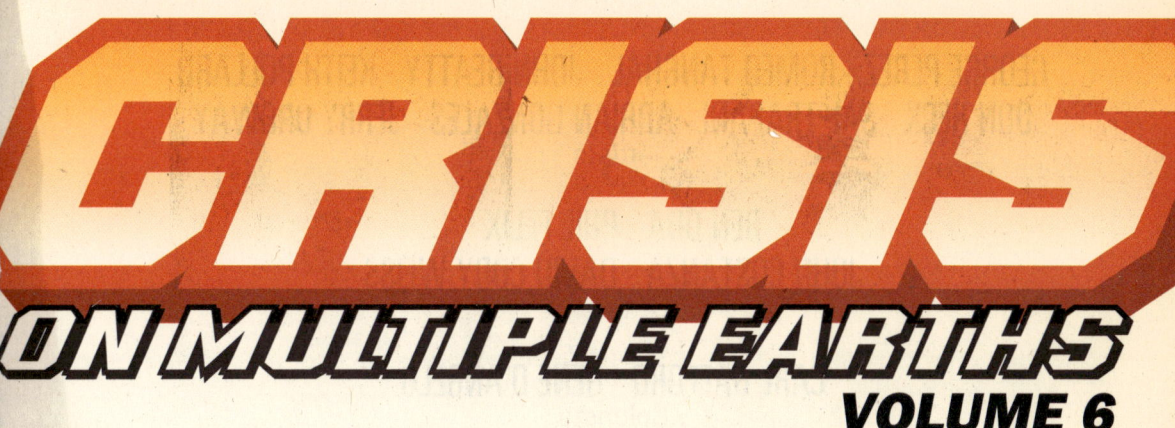

GERRY CONWAY • ROY THOMAS
Writers

**GEORGE PÉREZ • ROMEO TANGHAL • JOHN BEATTY • KEITH POLLARD
DON HECK • SAL TRAPANI • ADRIAN GONZALES • JERRY ORDWAY**
Artists

**BEN ODA • PHIL FELIX •
JOHN COSTANZA • DAVID CODY WEISS**
Letterers

CARL GAFFORD • GENE D'ANGELO
Colorists

GEORGE PÉREZ & MIKE DECARLO
Collection cover artists

CRISIS
ON MULTIPLE EARTHS
VOLUME 6

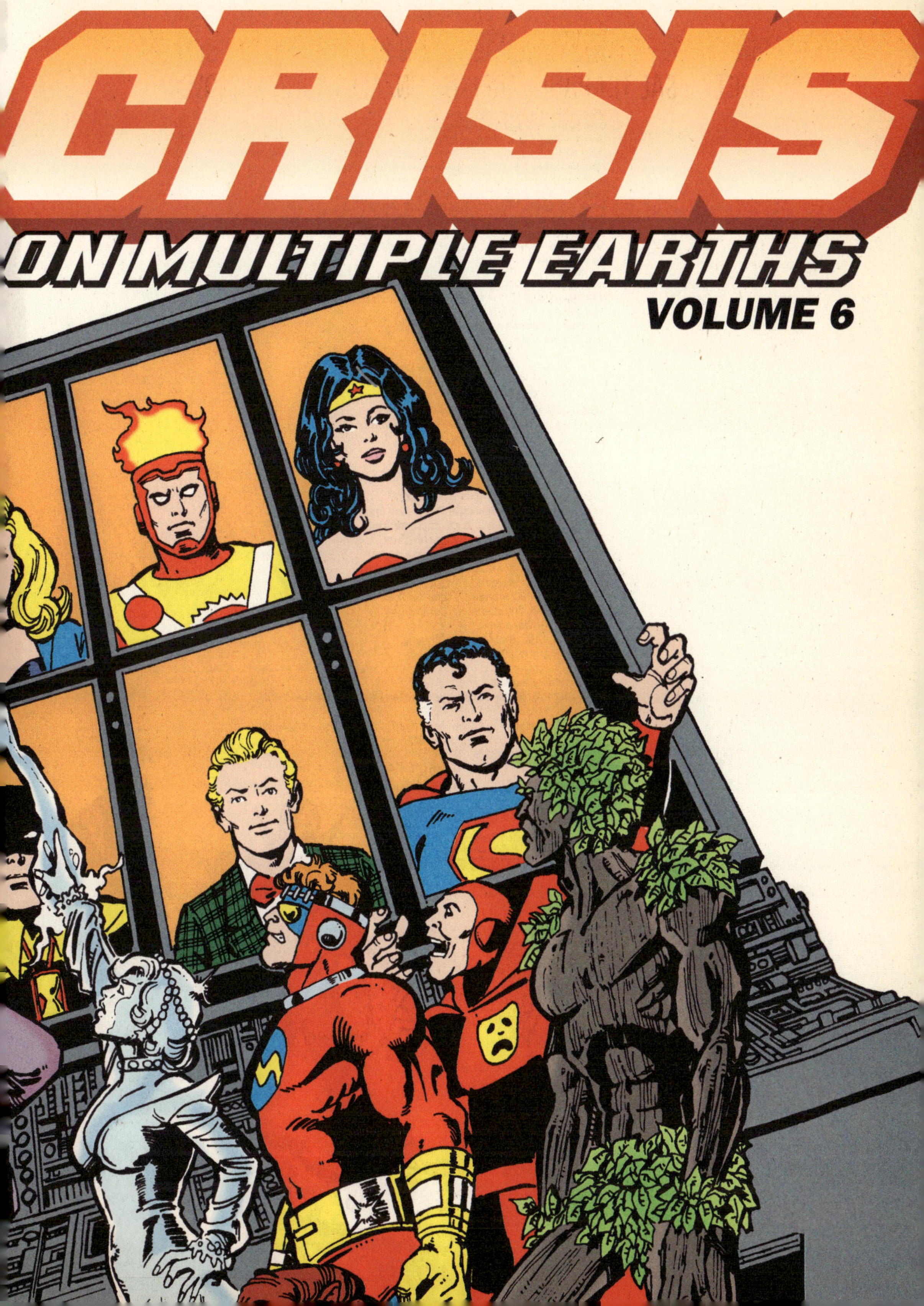

Len Wein Editor – Original Series
Rowena Yow Editor
Robbin Brosterman Design Director – Books

Bob Harras VP – Editor-in-Chief

Diane Nelson President
Dan DiDio and **Jim Lee** Co-Publishers
Geoff Johns Chief Creative Officer
John Rood Executive VP – Sales, Marketing and Business Development
Amy Genkins Senior VP – Business and Legal Affairs
Nairi Gardiner Senior VP – Finance
Jeff Boison VP – Publishing Operations
Mark Chiarello VP – Art Direction and Design
John Cunningham VP – Marketing
Terri Cunningham VP – Talent Relations and Services
Alison Gill Senior VP – Manufacturing and Operations
Hank Kanalz Senior VP – Digital
Jay Kogan VP – Business and Legal Affairs, Publishing
Jack Mahan VP – Business Affairs, Talent
Nick Napolitano VP – Manufacturing Administration
Sue Pohja VP – Book Sales
Courtney Simmons Senior VP – Publicity
Bob Wayne Senior VP – Sales

Cover art by George Pérez and Mike DeCarlo
Color reconstruction by John Kalisz

CRISIS ON MULTIPLE EARTHS VOLUME 6
Published by DC Comics. Cover and compilation Copyright © 2013 DC Comics. All Rights Reserved.

Originally published in single magazine form in JUSTICE LEAGUE OF AMERICA 195-197, 207-209; ALL-STAR SQUADRON 14-15. Copyright © 1981, 1982 DC Comics. All Rights Reserved.

All characters, their distinctive likenesses and related elements featured in this publication are trademarks of DC Comics. The stories, characters and incidents featured in this publication are entirely fictional. DC Comics does not read or accept unsolicited ideas, stories or artwork.
DC Comics, 1700 Broadway, New York, NY 10019.
A Warner Bros. Entertainment Company.
Printed by RR Donnelley,
Salem, VA, USA. 5/3/13. First Printing.
ISBN: 978-1-4012-3822-3

Conway, Gerry, author.
Crisis on Multiple Earths. Volume 6 / Gerry Conway, George Pérez.
pages cm
"Originally published in single magazine form in Justice League of America 195-197, 207-209, 219-220."
ISBN 978-1-4012-3822-3
1. Graphic novels. I. Pérez, George, 1954- illustrator. II. Title.
PN6728.J87C66 2013
741.5'973–dc23
2012046494

TABLE OF CONTENTS

TARGETS ON TWO WORLDS   7
From **JUSTICE LEAGUE OF AMERICA #195** OCTOBER 1981
Cover: GEORGE PÉREZ
Writer: GERRY CONWAY *Penciller:* GEORGE PÉREZ *Inker:* JOHN BEATTY *Letterer:* BEN ODA

COUNTDOWN TO CRISIS!   33
From **JUSTICE LEAGUE OF AMERICA #196** NOVEMBER 1981
Cover: GEORGE PÉREZ & DICK GIORDANO
Writer: GERRY CONWAY *Penciller:* GEORGE PÉREZ *Inker:* ROMEO TANGHAL *Letterer:* BEN ODA

CRISIS IN LIMBO!   61
From **JUSTICE LEAGUE OF AMERICA #197** DECEMBER 1981
Cover: GEORGE PÉREZ & MIKE DECARLO
Writer: GERRY CONWAY *Pencillers:* KEITH POLLARD & GEORGE PÉREZ *Inker:* ROMEO TANGHAL
Letterer: BEN ODA

CRISIS TIMES THREE!   89
From **JUSTICE LEAGUE OF AMERICA #207** OCTOBER 1982
Cover: GEORGE PÉREZ
Writer: GERRY CONWAY *Penciller:* DON HECK *Inker:* ROMEO TANGHAL *Letterer:* BEN ODA

THE MYSTERY MEN OF OCTOBER!   113
From **ALL-STAR SQUADRON #14** OCTOBER 1982
Cover: JOE KUBERT
Writer: ROY THOMAS *Artists:* ADRIAN GONZALES & JERRY ORDWAY
Letterer: BEN ODA

THE BOMB-BLAST HEARD 'ROUND THE WORLD!   137
From **JUSTICE LEAGUE OF AMERICA #208** NOVEMBER 1982
Cover: GEORGE PÉREZ
Writer: GERRY CONWAY *Penciller:* DON HECK *Inker:* SAL TRAPANI *Letterer:* PHIL FELIX

MASTER OF WORLDS AND TIME!   161
From **ALL-STAR SQUADRON #15** NOVEMBER 1982
Cover: JOE KUBERT
Writer: ROY THOMAS *Artists:* ADRIAN GONZALES & JERRY ORDWAY
Letterer: JOHN COSTANZA

LET OLD ACQUAINTANCES BE FORGOT...   185
From **JUSTICE LEAGUE OF AMERICA #209** DECEMBER 1982
Cover: GEORGE PÉREZ
Writer: GERRY CONWAY *Artist:* DON HECK *Letterer:* BEN ODA

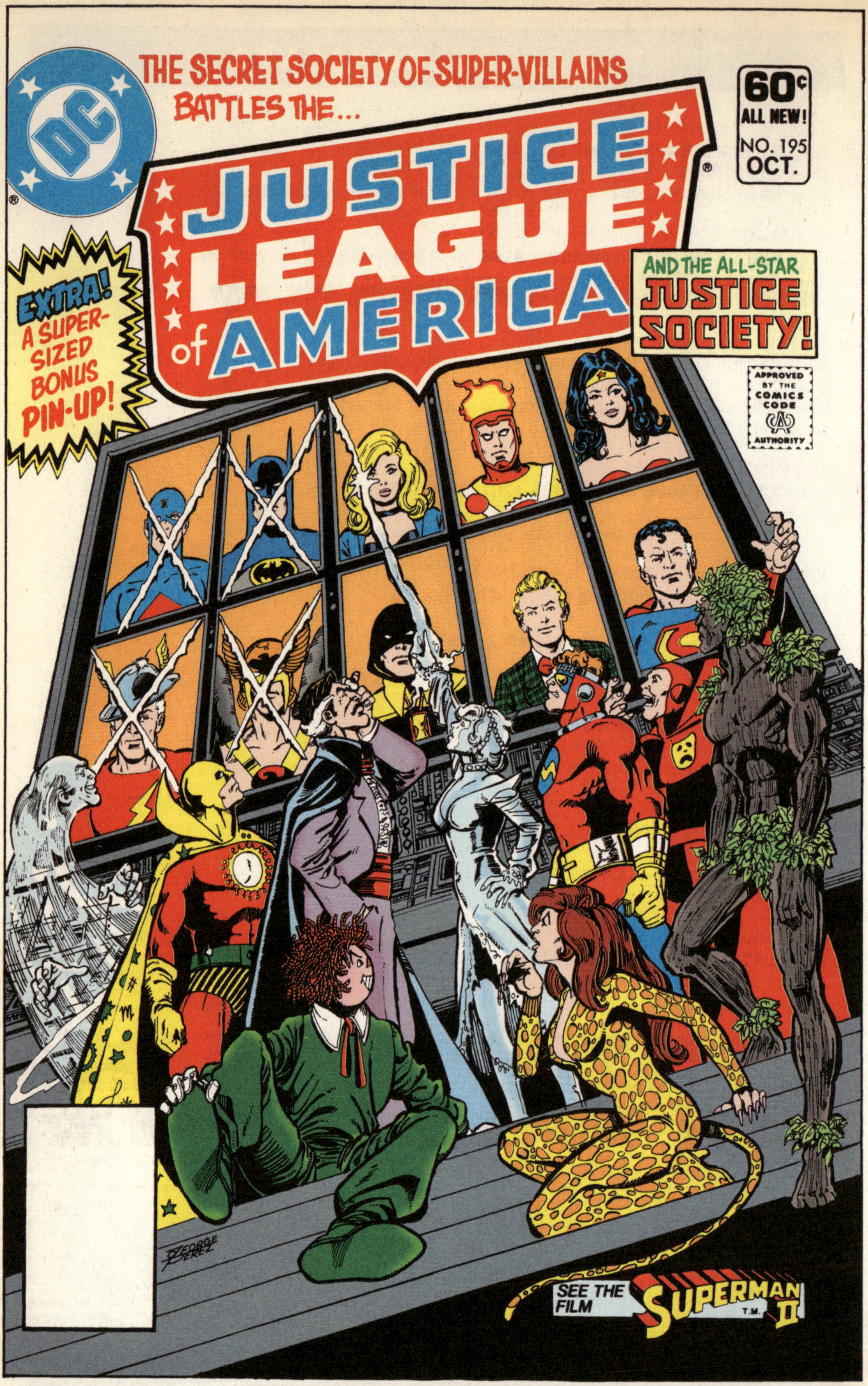
THE SECRET SOCIETY OF SUPER-VILLAINS
BATTLES THE...
JUSTICE LEAGUE of AMERICA
60¢
ALL NEW!
NO. 195
OCT.
AND THE ALL-STAR
JUSTICE SOCIETY!
EXTRA! A SUPER-SIZED BONUS PIN-UP!
APPROVED BY THE COMICS CODE AUTHORITY
GEORGE PEREZ
SEE THE FILM
SUPERMAN II
T.M.

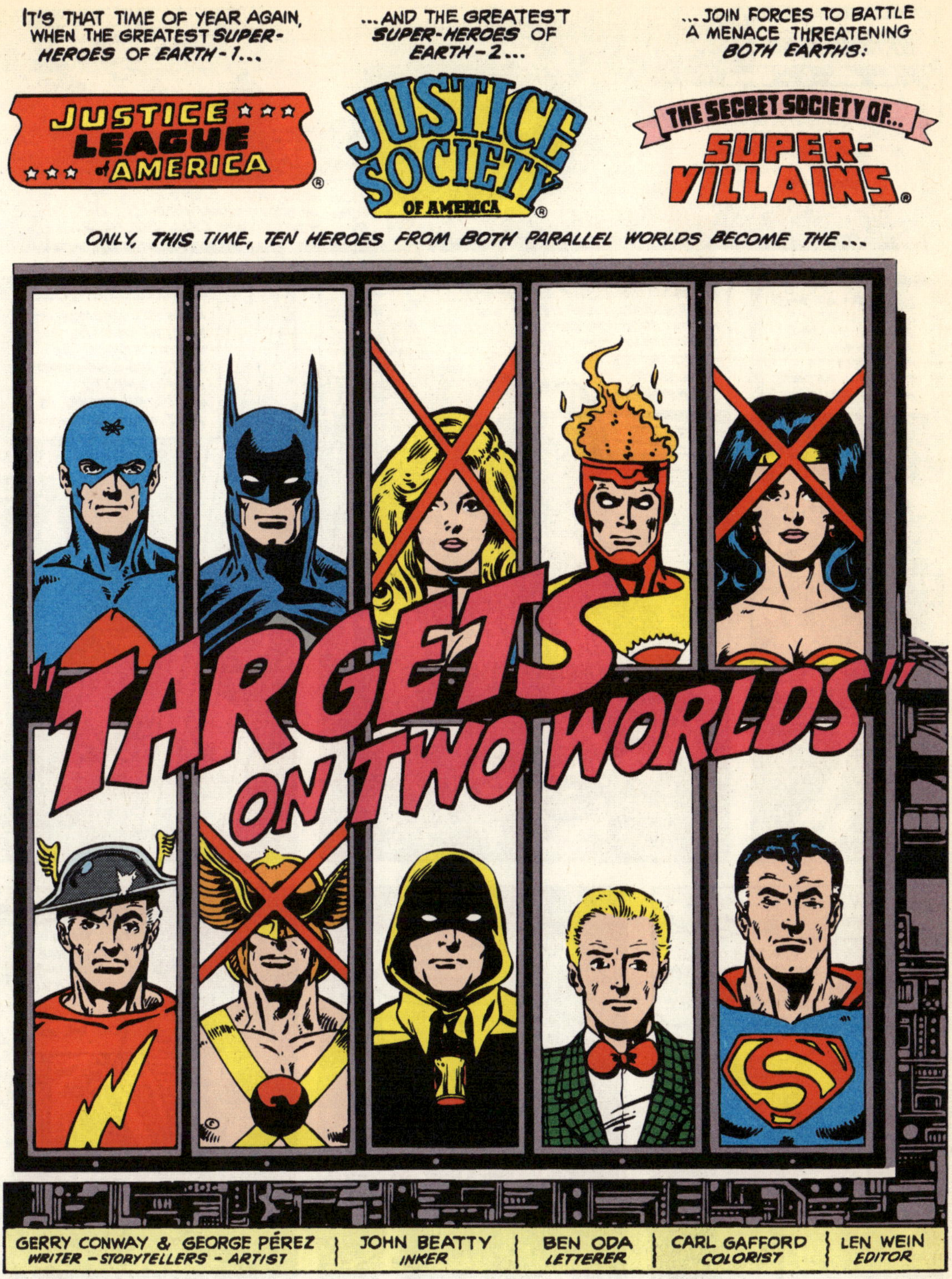
IT'S THAT TIME OF YEAR AGAIN, WHEN THE GREATEST SUPER-HEROES OF EARTH-1...
...AND THE GREATEST SUPER-HEROES OF EARTH-2...
...JOIN FORCES TO BATTLE A MENACE THREATENING BOTH EARTHS:
JUSTICE LEAGUE of AMERICA
JUSTICE SOCIETY OF AMERICA
THE SECRET SOCIETY OF... SUPER-VILLAINS
ONLY, THIS TIME, TEN HEROES FROM BOTH PARALLEL WORLDS BECOME THE...
"TARGETS ON TWO WORLDS"
GERRY CONWAY & GEORGE PÉREZ WRITER - STORYTELLERS - ARTIST
JOHN BEATTY INKER
BEN ODA LETTERER
CARL GAFFORD COLORIST
LEN WEIN EDITOR

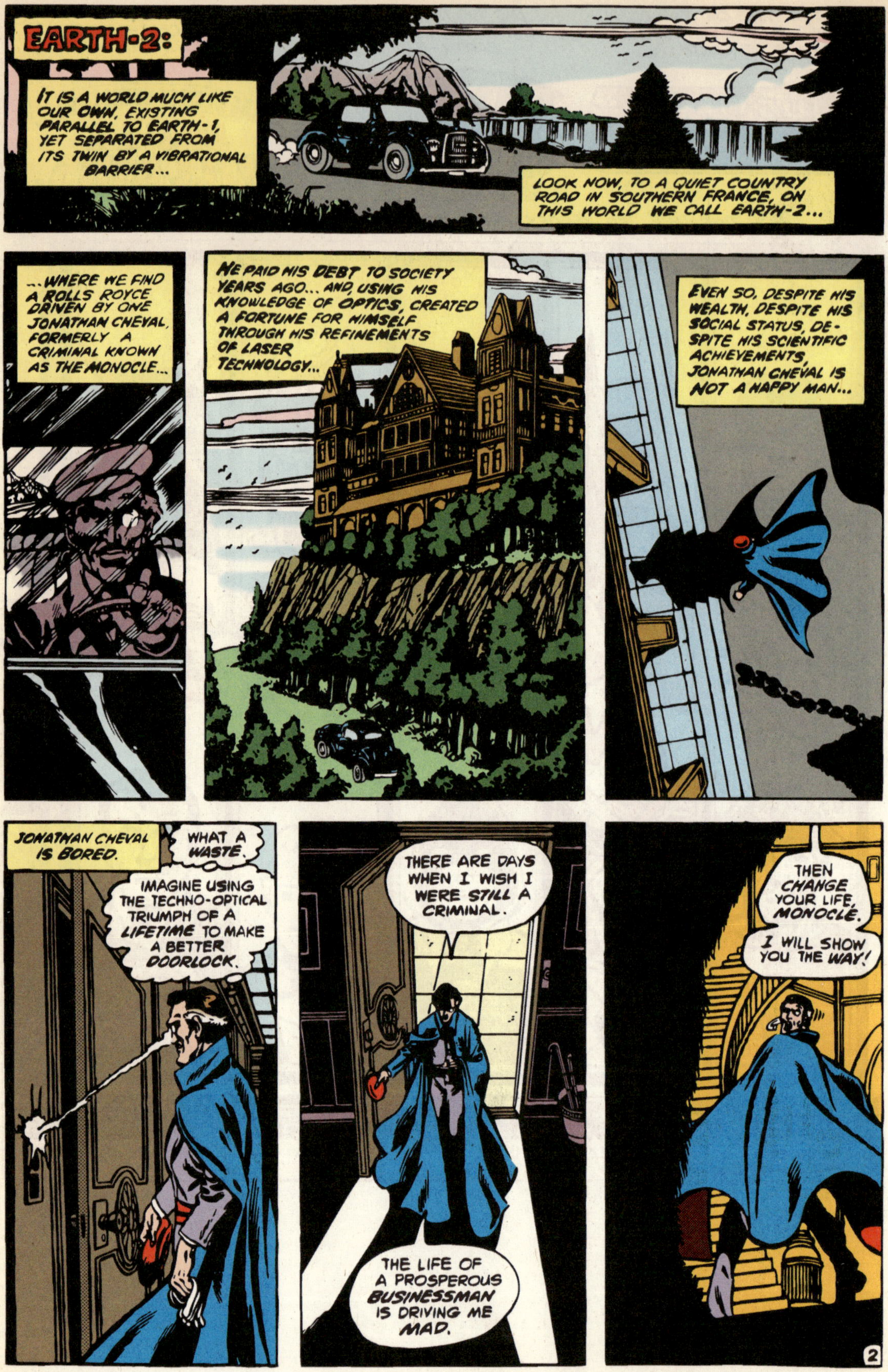
EARTH-2:
IT IS A WORLD MUCH LIKE OUR OWN, EXISTING PARALLEL TO EARTH-1, YET SEPARATED FROM ITS TWIN BY A VIBRATIONAL BARRIER...
LOOK NOW, TO A QUIET COUNTRY ROAD IN SOUTHERN FRANCE, ON THIS WORLD WE CALL EARTH-2...
...WHERE WE FIND A ROLLS ROYCE DRIVEN BY ONE JONATHAN CHEVAL, FORMERLY A CRIMINAL KNOWN AS THE MONOCLE...
HE PAID HIS DEBT TO SOCIETY YEARS AGO... AND, USING HIS KNOWLEDGE OF OPTICS, CREATED A FORTUNE FOR HIMSELF THROUGH HIS REFINEMENTS OF LASER TECHNOLOGY...
EVEN SO, DESPITE HIS WEALTH, DESPITE HIS SOCIAL STATUS, DESPITE HIS SCIENTIFIC ACHIEVEMENTS, JONATHAN CHEVAL IS NOT A HAPPY MAN...
JONATHAN CHEVAL IS BORED.
WHAT A WASTE.
IMAGINE USING THE TECHNO-OPTICAL TRIUMPH OF A LIFETIME TO MAKE A BETTER DOORLOCK.
THERE ARE DAYS WHEN I WISH I WERE STILL A CRIMINAL.
THE LIFE OF A PROSPEROUS BUSINESSMAN IS DRIVING ME MAD.
THEN CHANGE YOUR LIFE, MONOCLE.
I WILL SHOW YOU THE WAY!
2

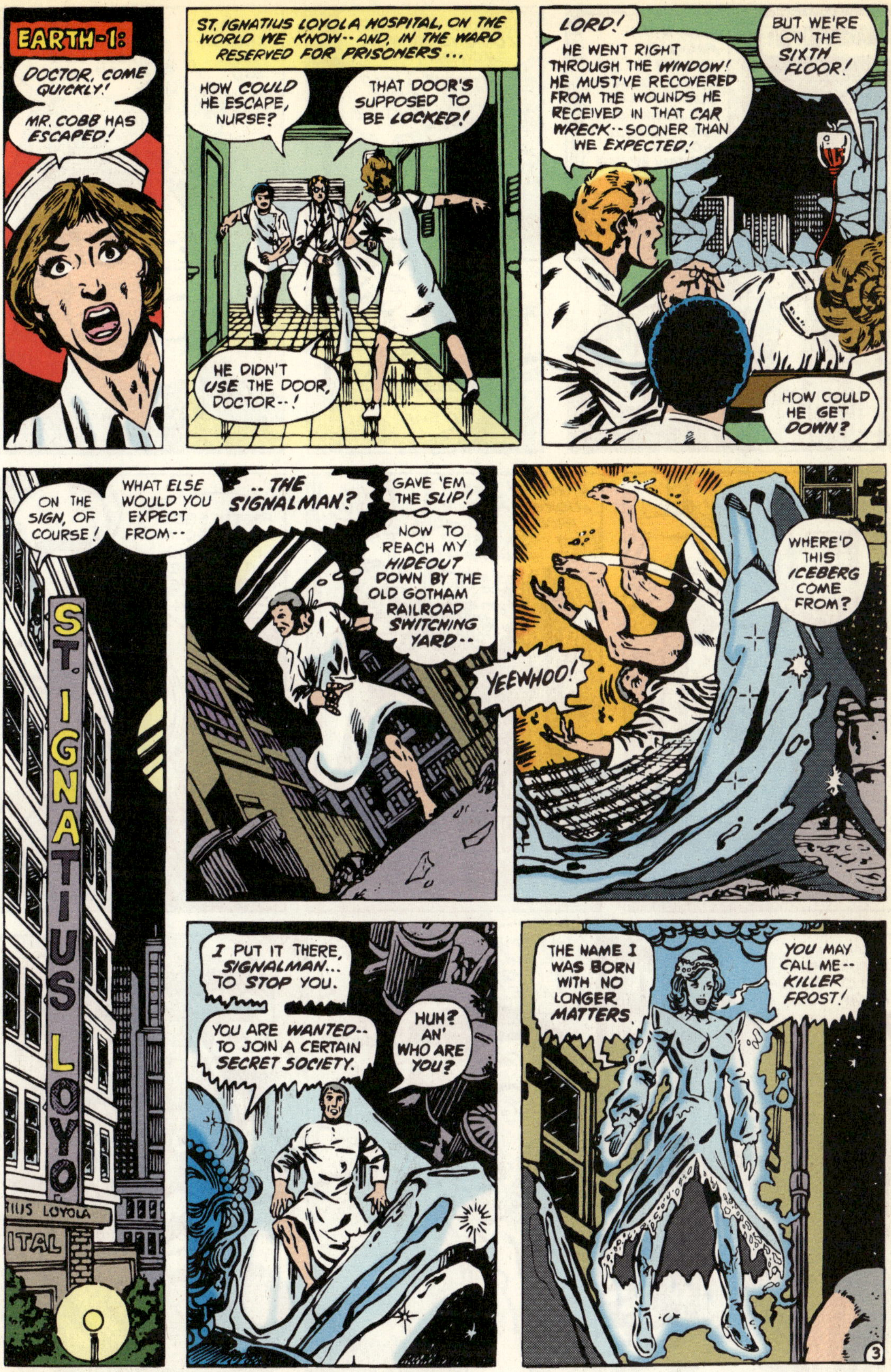
EARTH-1:
DOCTOR, COME QUICKLY!
MR. COBB HAS ESCAPED!
ST. IGNATIUS LOYOLA HOSPITAL, ON THE WORLD WE KNOW--AND, IN THE WARD RESERVED FOR PRISONERS...
HOW COULD HE ESCAPE, NURSE?
THAT DOOR'S SUPPOSED TO BE LOCKED!
HE DIDN'T USE THE DOOR, DOCTOR--!
LORD!
HE WENT RIGHT THROUGH THE WINDOW! HE MUST'VE RECOVERED FROM THE WOUNDS HE RECEIVED IN THAT CAR WRECK--SOONER THAN WE EXPECTED!
BUT WE'RE ON THE SIXTH FLOOR!
HOW COULD HE GET DOWN?
ON THE SIGN, OF COURSE!
WHAT ELSE WOULD YOU EXPECT FROM--
..THE SIGNALMAN?
ST. IGNATIUS LOYO
IUS LOYOLA
ITAL
GAVE 'EM THE SLIP!
NOW TO REACH MY HIDEOUT DOWN BY THE OLD GOTHAM RAILROAD SWITCHING YARD--
YEEWHOO!
WHERE'D THIS ICEBERG COME FROM?
I PUT IT THERE, SIGNALMAN... TO STOP YOU.
YOU ARE WANTED--TO JOIN A CERTAIN SECRET SOCIETY.
HUH? AN' WHO ARE YOU?
THE NAME I WAS BORN WITH NO LONGER MATTERS.
YOU MAY CALL ME--KILLER FROST!
3

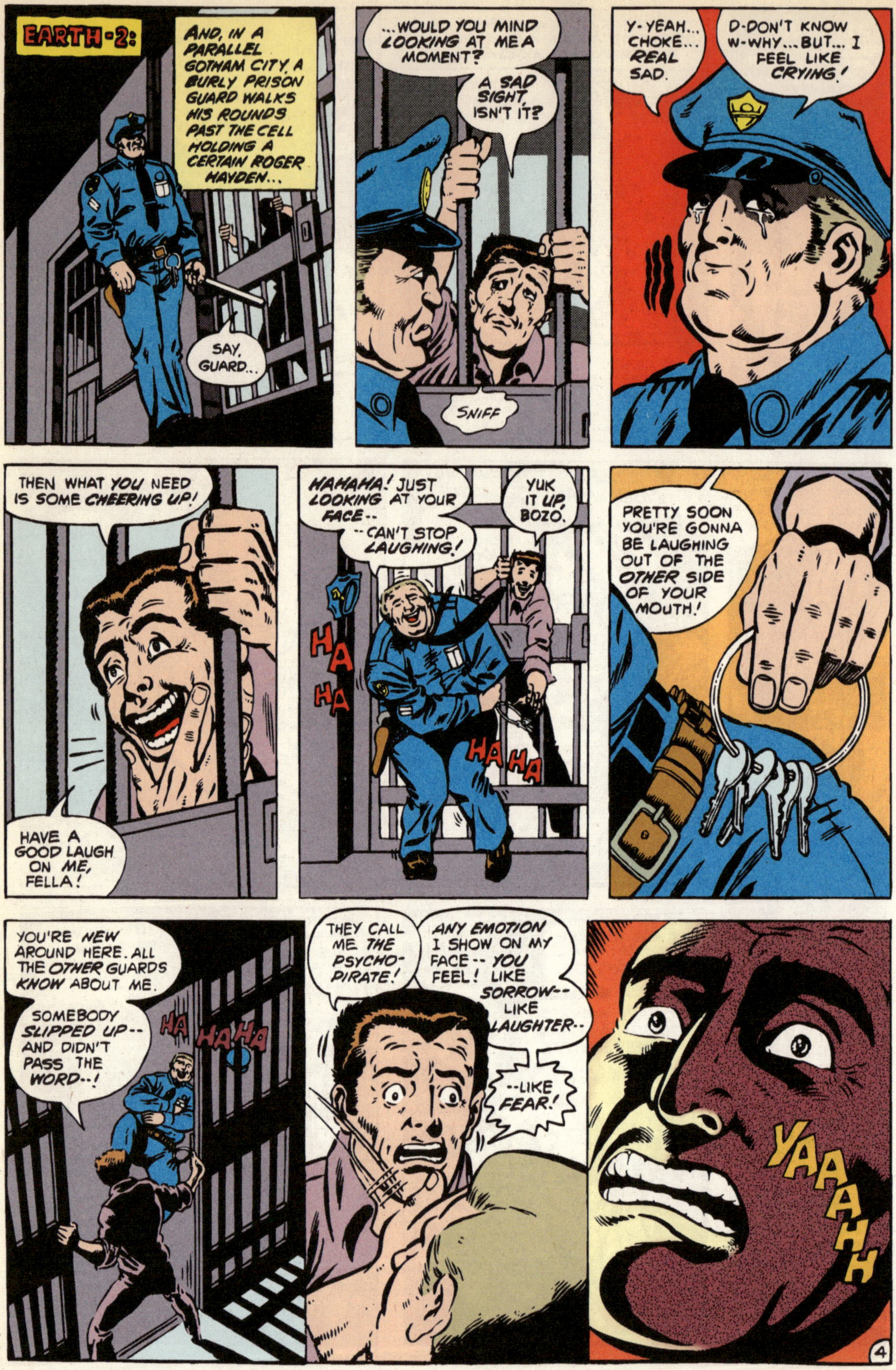
EARTH-2:
AND, IN A PARALLEL GOTHAM CITY, A BURLY PRISON GUARD WALKS HIS ROUNDS PAST THE CELL HOLDING A CERTAIN ROGER HAYDEN...
SAY, GUARD...
...WOULD YOU MIND LOOKING AT ME A MOMENT?
A SAD SIGHT, ISN'T IT?
SNIFF
Y-YEAH... CHOKE... REAL SAD.
D-DON'T KNOW W-WHY... BUT... I FEEL LIKE CRYING!
THEN WHAT YOU NEED IS SOME CHEERING UP!
HAVE A GOOD LAUGH ON ME, FELLA!
HAHAHA! JUST LOOKING AT YOUR FACE--
--CAN'T STOP LAUGHING!
YUK IT UP, BOZO.
HA HA
HA HA
PRETTY SOON YOU'RE GONNA BE LAUGHING OUT OF THE OTHER SIDE OF YOUR MOUTH!
YOU'RE NEW AROUND HERE. ALL THE OTHER GUARDS KNOW ABOUT ME.
SOMEBODY SLIPPED UP-- AND DIDN'T PASS THE WORD--!
HA HAHAHA
THEY CALL ME THE PSYCHO-PIRATE!
ANY EMOTION I SHOW ON MY FACE -- YOU FEEL! LIKE SORROW-- LIKE LAUGHTER--
--LIKE FEAR!
YAAAHH
4

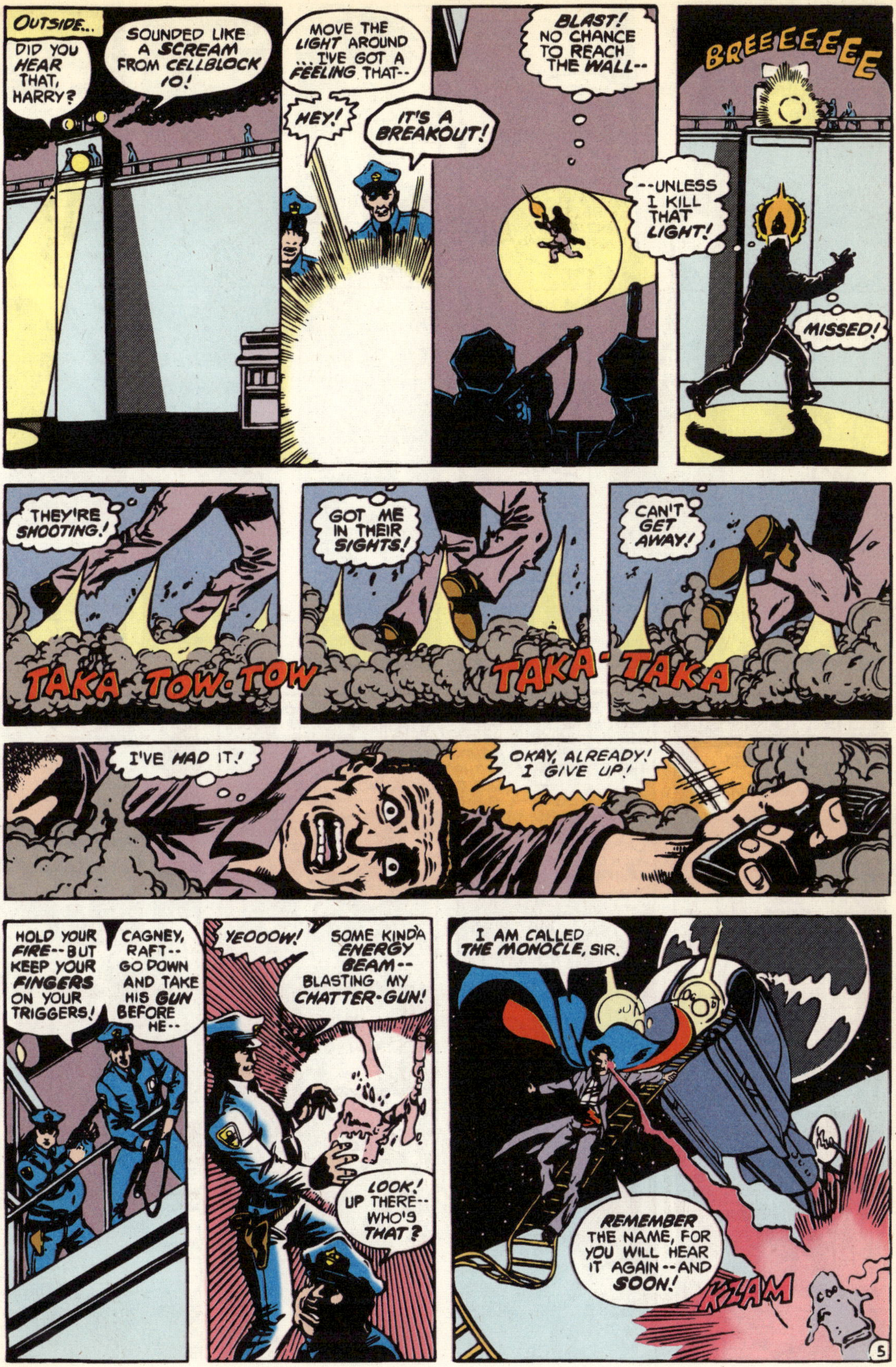
OUTSIDE...
DID YOU HEAR THAT, HARRY?
SOUNDED LIKE A SCREAM FROM CELLBLOCK 10!
MOVE THE LIGHT AROUND ... I'VE GOT A FEELING THAT--
HEY!
IT'S A BREAKOUT!
BLAST! NO CHANCE TO REACH THE WALL--
--UNLESS I KILL THAT LIGHT!
BREEEEEEEE
MISSED!
THEY'RE SHOOTING!
GOT ME IN THEIR SIGHTS!
CAN'T GET AWAY!
TAKA TOW-TOW TAKA-TAKA
I'VE HAD IT.!
OKAY, ALREADY! I GIVE UP!
HOLD YOUR FIRE--BUT KEEP YOUR FINGERS ON YOUR TRIGGERS!
CAGNEY, RAFT--GO DOWN AND TAKE HIS GUN BEFORE HE--
YEOOOW!
SOME KIND'A ENERGY BEAM--BLASTING MY CHATTER-GUN!
LOOK! UP THERE--WHO'S THAT?
I AM CALLED THE MONOCLE, SIR.
REMEMBER THE NAME, FOR YOU WILL HEAR IT AGAIN--AND SOON!
KLAM
5

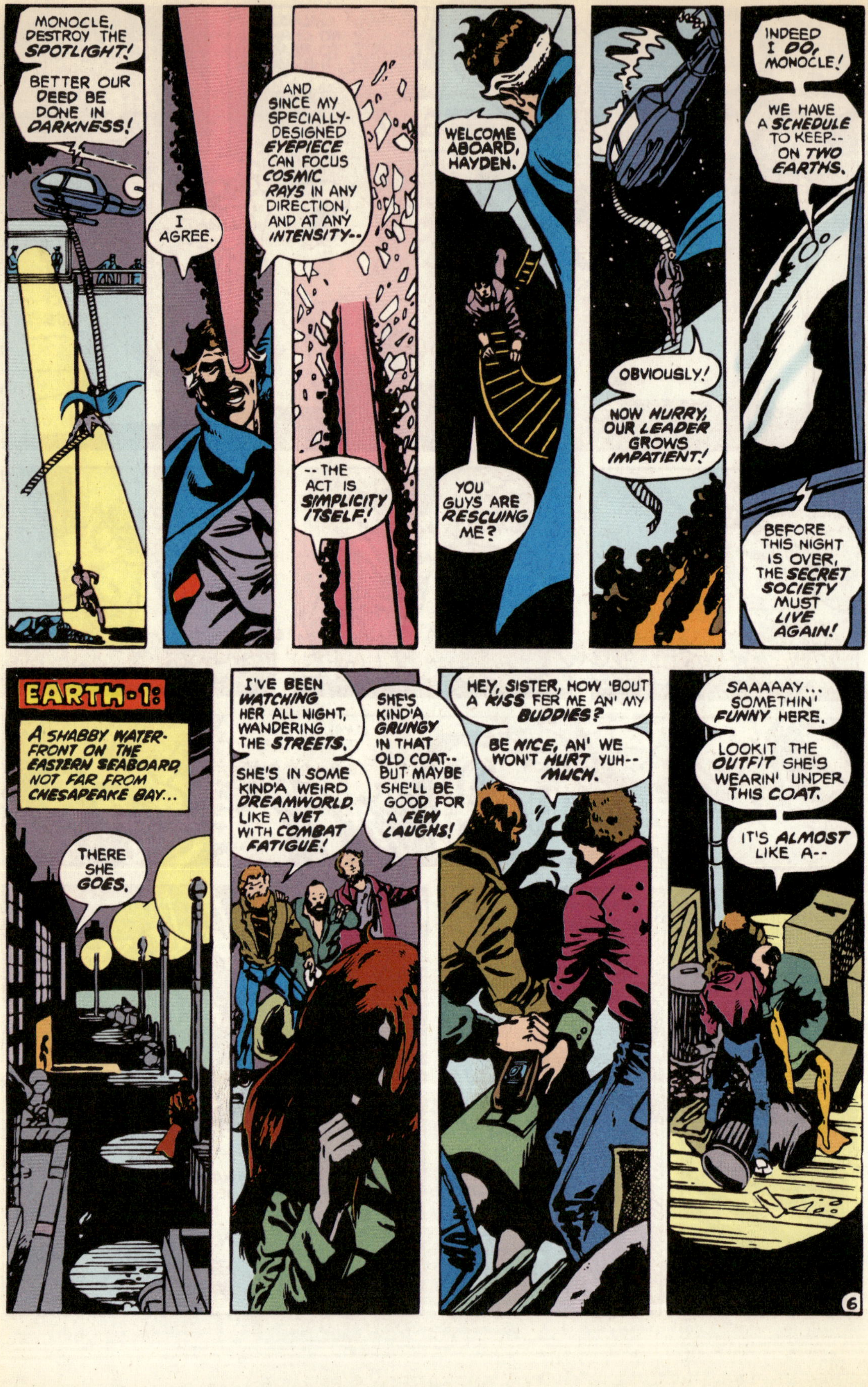
MONOCLE, DESTROY THE SPOTLIGHT!
BETTER OUR DEED BE DONE IN DARKNESS!
I AGREE.
AND SINCE MY SPECIALLY-DESIGNED EYEPIECE CAN FOCUS COSMIC RAYS IN ANY DIRECTION, AND AT ANY INTENSITY--
-- THE ACT IS SIMPLICITY ITSELF!
WELCOME ABOARD, HAYDEN.
YOU GUYS ARE RESCUING ME?
OBVIOUSLY!
NOW HURRY, OUR LEADER GROWS IMPATIENT!
INDEED I DO, MONOCLE!
WE HAVE A SCHEDULE TO KEEP-- ON TWO EARTHS.
BEFORE THIS NIGHT IS OVER, THE SECRET SOCIETY MUST LIVE AGAIN!
EARTH-1:
A SHABBY WATER-FRONT ON THE EASTERN SEABOARD, NOT FAR FROM CHESAPEAKE BAY...
THERE SHE GOES.
I'VE BEEN WATCHING HER ALL NIGHT, WANDERING THE STREETS.
SHE'S IN SOME KIND'A WEIRD DREAMWORLD, LIKE A VET WITH COMBAT FATIGUE!
SHE'S KIND'A GRUNGY IN THAT OLD COAT-- BUT MAYBE SHE'LL BE GOOD FOR A FEW LAUGHS!
HEY, SISTER, HOW 'BOUT A KISS FER ME AN' MY BUDDIES?
BE NICE, AN' WE WON'T HURT YUH-- MUCH.
SAAAAAY... SOMETHIN' FUNNY HERE.
LOOKIT THE OUTFIT SHE'S WEARIN' UNDER THIS COAT.
IT'S ALMOST LIKE A--
6

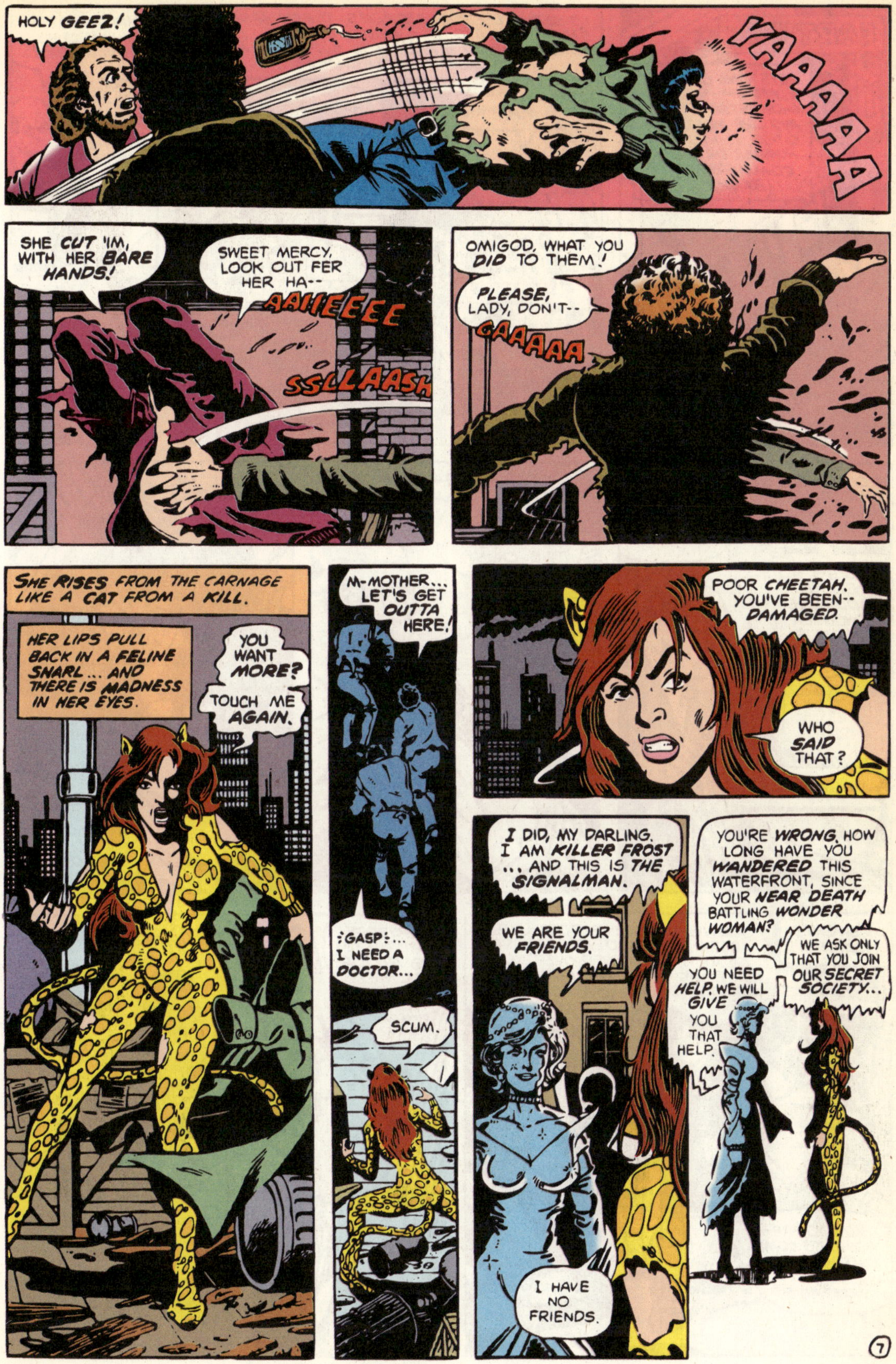
HOLY GEEZ!
YAAAAAA
SHE CUT 'IM, WITH HER BARE HANDS!
SWEET MERCY, LOOK OUT FER HER HA--
AAIIEEEE
SSLLAASH
OMIGOD, WHAT YOU DID TO THEM!
PLEASE, LADY, DON'T--
GAAAAA
SHE RISES FROM THE CARNAGE LIKE A CAT FROM A KILL.
HER LIPS PULL BACK IN A FELINE SNARL... AND THERE IS MADNESS IN HER EYES.
YOU WANT MORE?
TOUCH ME AGAIN.
M-MOTHER... LET'S GET OUTTA HERE!
:GASP:... I NEED A DOCTOR...
SCUM.
POOR CHEETAH. YOU'VE BEEN-- DAMAGED.
WHO SAID THAT?
I DID, MY DARLING. I AM KILLER FROST ... AND THIS IS THE SIGNALMAN.
WE ARE YOUR FRIENDS.
I HAVE NO FRIENDS.
YOU'RE WRONG. HOW LONG HAVE YOU WANDERED THIS WATERFRONT, SINCE YOUR NEAR DEATH BATTLING WONDER WOMAN?
YOU NEED HELP. WE WILL GIVE YOU THAT HELP.
WE ASK ONLY THAT YOU JOIN OUR SECRET SOCIETY...
7

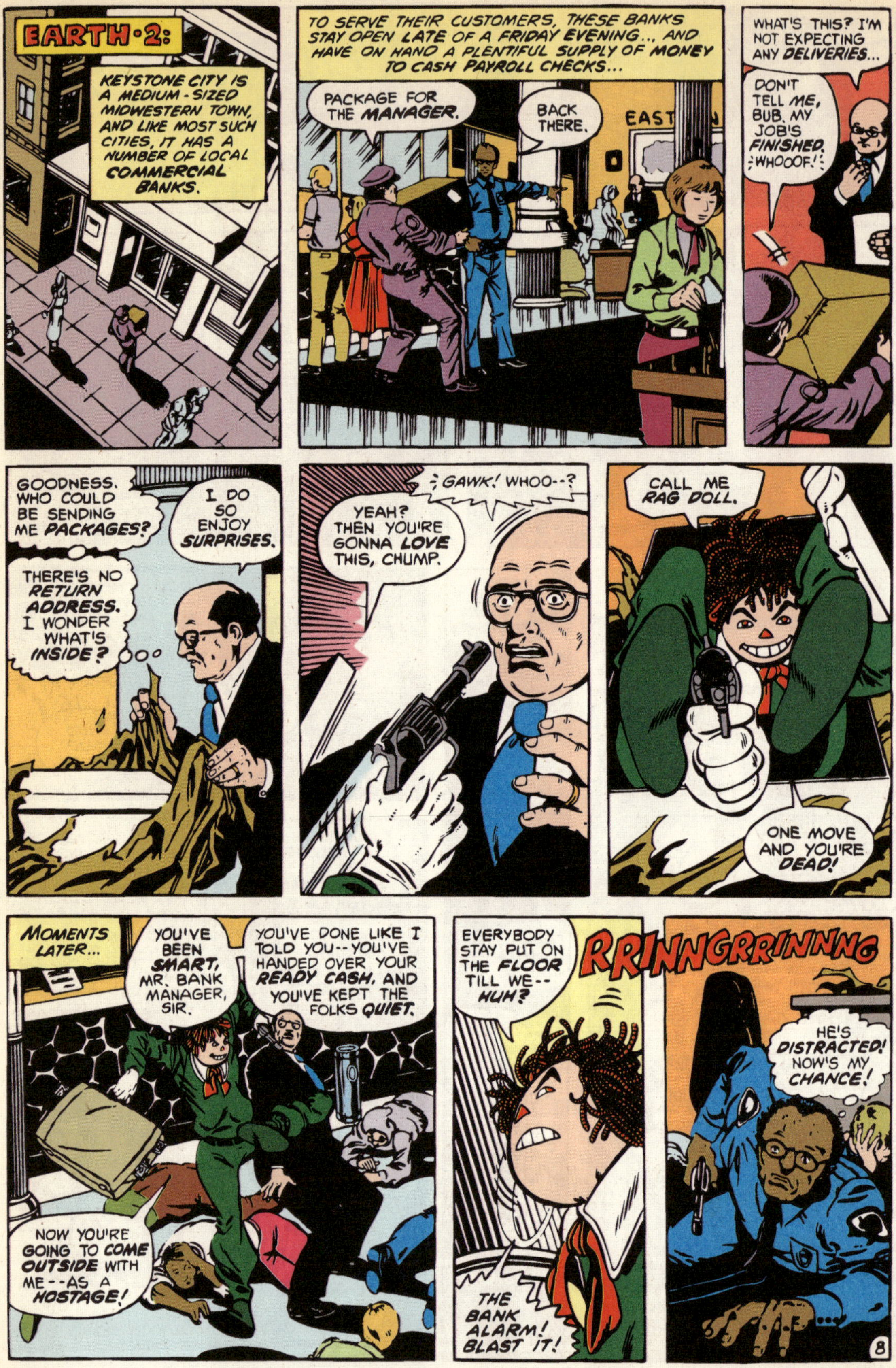

EARTH-2:
KEYSTONE CITY IS A MEDIUM-SIZED MIDWESTERN TOWN, AND LIKE MOST SUCH CITIES, IT HAS A NUMBER OF LOCAL COMMERCIAL BANKS.
TO SERVE THEIR CUSTOMERS, THESE BANKS STAY OPEN LATE OF A FRIDAY EVENING... AND HAVE ON HAND A PLENTIFUL SUPPLY OF MONEY TO CASH PAYROLL CHECKS...
PACKAGE FOR THE MANAGER.
BACK THERE.
WHAT'S THIS? I'M NOT EXPECTING ANY DELIVERIES...
DON'T TELL ME, BUB. MY JOB'S FINISHED. WHOOOF!
GOODNESS. WHO COULD BE SENDING ME PACKAGES?
I DO SO ENJOY SURPRISES.
THERE'S NO RETURN ADDRESS. I WONDER WHAT'S INSIDE?
GAWK! WHOO--?
YEAH? THEN YOU'RE GONNA LOVE THIS, CHUMP.
CALL ME RAG DOLL.
ONE MOVE AND YOU'RE DEAD!
MOMENTS LATER...
YOU'VE BEEN SMART, MR. BANK MANAGER, SIR.
YOU'VE DONE LIKE I TOLD YOU--YOU'VE HANDED OVER YOUR READY CASH, AND YOU'VE KEPT THE FOLKS QUIET.
NOW YOU'RE GOING TO COME OUTSIDE WITH ME--AS A HOSTAGE!
EVERYBODY STAY PUT ON THE FLOOR TILL WE-- HUH?
THE BANK ALARM! BLAST IT!
RRINNGRRINNNG
HE'S DISTRACTED! NOW'S MY CHANCE!
8

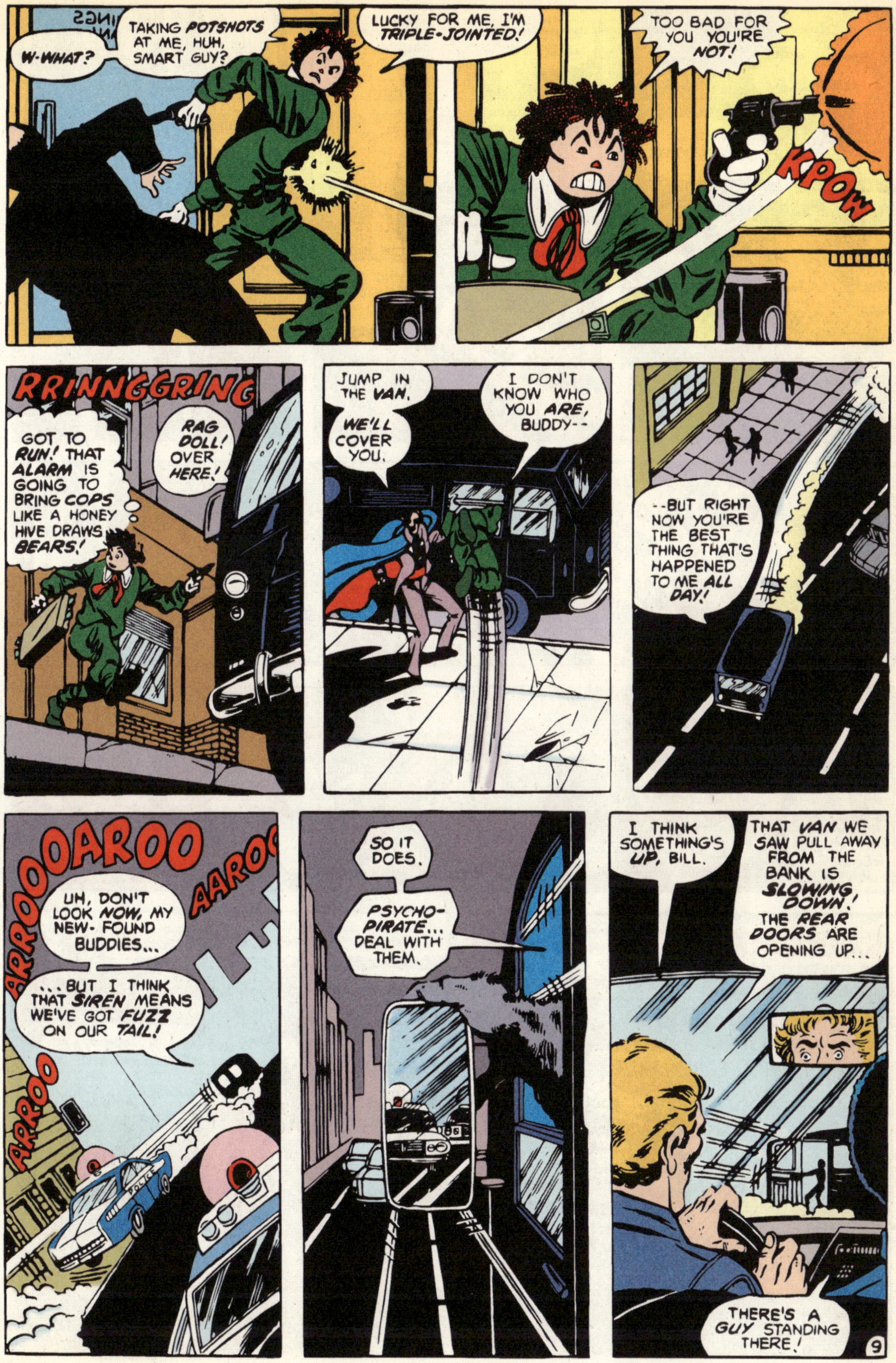

W-WHAT?
TAKING POTSHOTS AT ME, HUH, SMART GUY?
LUCKY FOR ME, I'M TRIPLE-JOINTED!
TOO BAD FOR YOU YOU'RE NOT!
KPOW
RRINNGGRING
GOT TO RUN! THAT ALARM IS GOING TO BRING COPS LIKE A HONEY HIVE DRAWS BEARS!
RAG DOLL! OVER HERE!
JUMP IN THE VAN.
WE'LL COVER YOU.
I DON'T KNOW WHO YOU ARE, BUDDY--
--BUT RIGHT NOW YOU'RE THE BEST THING THAT'S HAPPENED TO ME ALL DAY!
AARROOOOAROO
AAROO
UH, DON'T LOOK NOW, MY NEW-FOUND BUDDIES...
...BUT I THINK THAT SIREN MEANS WE'VE GOT FUZZ ON OUR TAIL!
AARROO
SO IT DOES.
PSYCHO-PIRATE... DEAL WITH THEM.
I THINK SOMETHING'S UP, BILL.
THAT VAN WE SAW PULL AWAY FROM THE BANK IS SLOWING DOWN! THE REAR DOORS ARE OPENING UP...
THERE'S A GUY STANDING THERE!
9

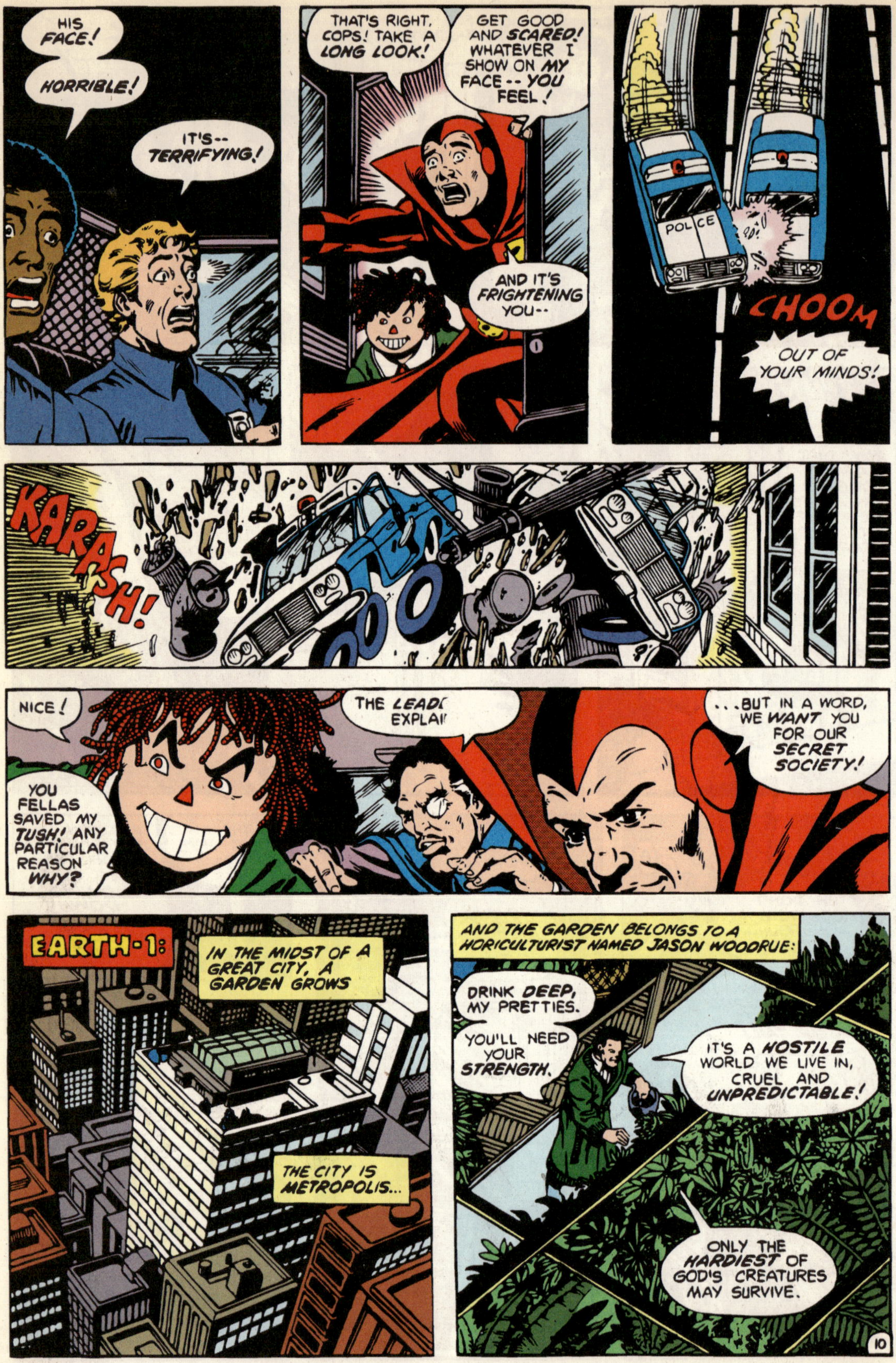
HIS FACE!
HORRIBLE!
IT'S-- TERRIFYING!
THAT'S RIGHT, COPS! TAKE A LONG LOOK!
GET GOOD AND SCARED! WHATEVER I SHOW ON MY FACE -- YOU FEEL!
AND IT'S FRIGHTENING YOU--
POLICE
CHOOM
OUT OF YOUR MINDS!
KARASH!
NICE!
YOU FELLAS SAVED MY TUSH! ANY PARTICULAR REASON WHY?
THE LEADE EXPLAI
...BUT IN A WORD, WE WANT YOU FOR OUR SECRET SOCIETY!
EARTH-1:
IN THE MIDST OF A GREAT CITY, A GARDEN GROWS
THE CITY IS METROPOLIS...
AND THE GARDEN BELONGS TO A HORICULTURIST NAMED JASON WOODRUE:
DRINK DEEP, MY PRETTIES.
YOU'LL NEED YOUR STRENGTH.
IT'S A HOSTILE WORLD WE LIVE IN, CRUEL AND UNPREDICTABLE!
ONLY THE HARDIEST OF GOD'S CREATURES MAY SURVIVE.
10

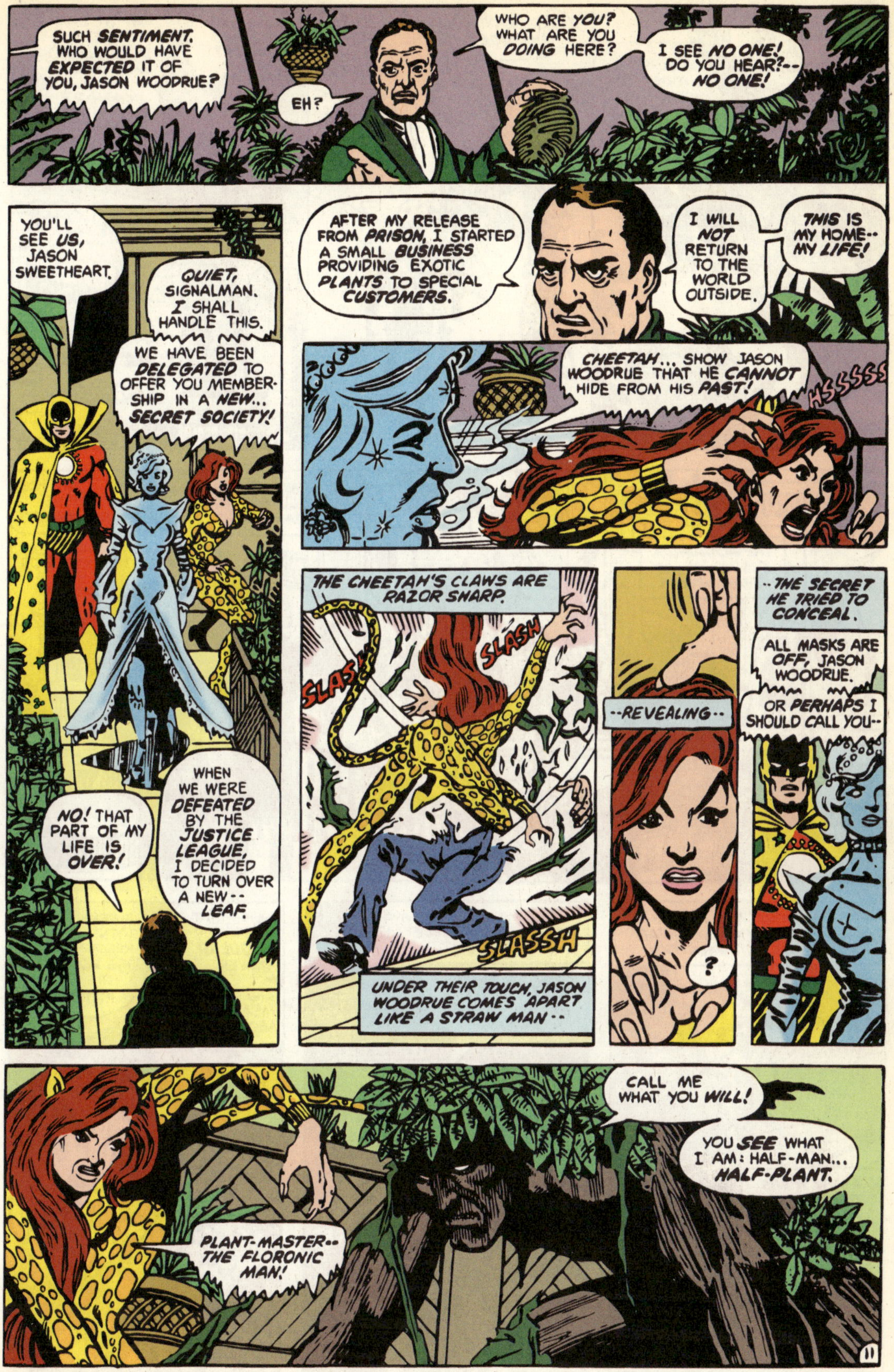
SUCH SENTIMENT. WHO WOULD HAVE EXPECTED IT OF YOU, JASON WOODRUE?
EH?
WHO ARE YOU? WHAT ARE YOU DOING HERE?
I SEE NO ONE! DO YOU HEAR?-- NO ONE!
YOU'LL SEE US, JASON SWEETHEART.
QUIET, SIGNALMAN. I SHALL HANDLE THIS.
WE HAVE BEEN DELEGATED TO OFFER YOU MEMBERSHIP IN A NEW... SECRET SOCIETY!
NO! THAT PART OF MY LIFE IS OVER!
WHEN WE WERE DEFEATED BY THE JUSTICE LEAGUE, I DECIDED TO TURN OVER A NEW-- LEAF.
AFTER MY RELEASE FROM PRISON, I STARTED A SMALL BUSINESS PROVIDING EXOTIC PLANTS TO SPECIAL CUSTOMERS.
I WILL NOT RETURN TO THE WORLD OUTSIDE.
THIS IS MY HOME-- MY LIFE!
CHEETAH... SHOW JASON WOODRUE THAT HE CANNOT HIDE FROM HIS PAST!
HSSSSS
THE CHEETAH'S CLAWS ARE RAZOR SHARP.
SLASH
SLASH
SLASSH
UNDER THEIR TOUCH, JASON WOODRUE COMES APART LIKE A STRAW MAN--
--REVEALING--
?
..THE SECRET HE TRIED TO CONCEAL.
ALL MASKS ARE OFF, JASON WOODRUE.
OR PERHAPS I SHOULD CALL YOU--
PLANT-MASTER-- THE FLORONIC MAN!
CALL ME WHAT YOU WILL!
YOU SEE WHAT I AM: HALF-MAN... HALF-PLANT.
11

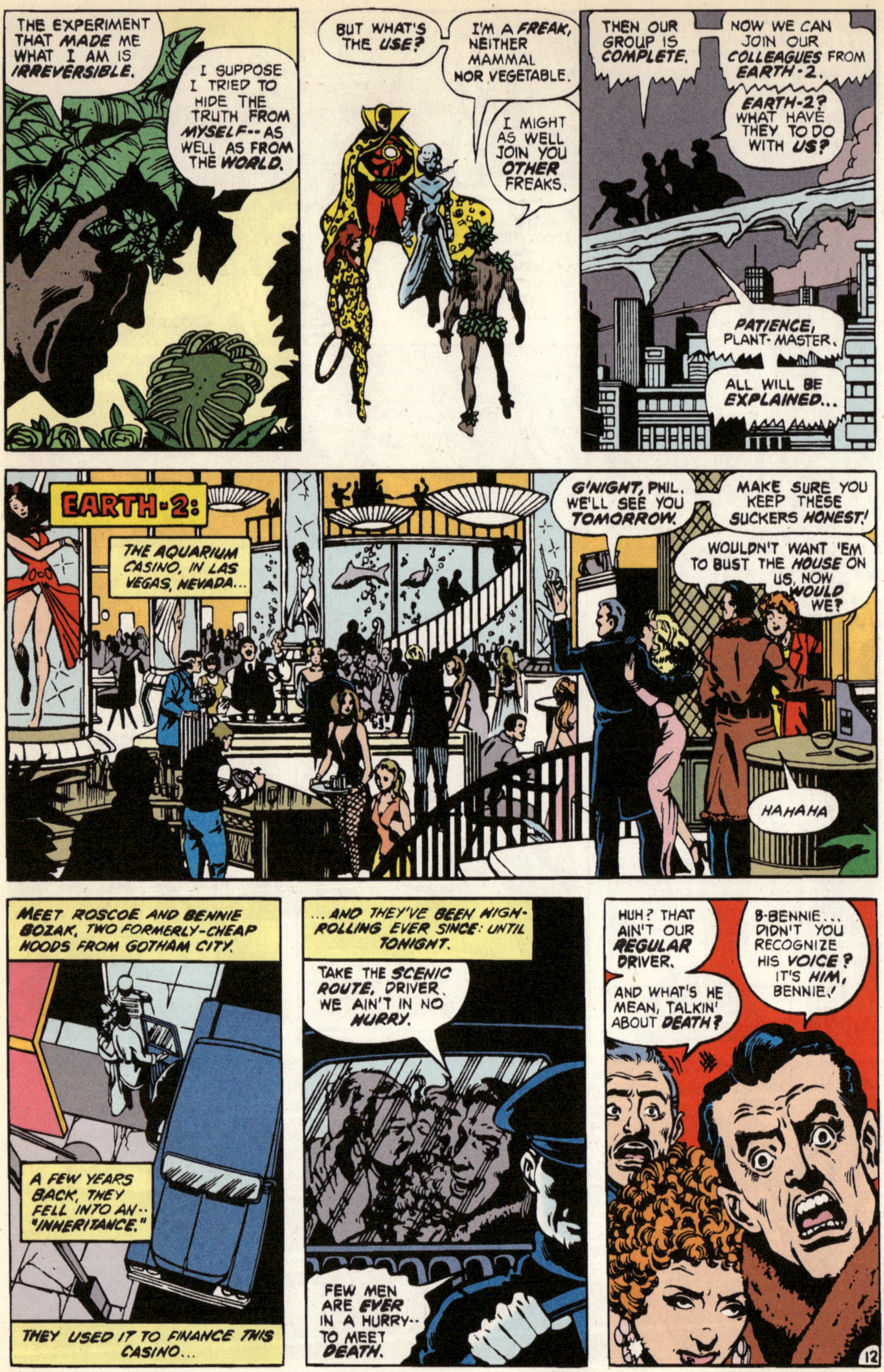
THE EXPERIMENT THAT MADE ME WHAT I AM IS IRREVERSIBLE.
I SUPPOSE I TRIED TO HIDE THE TRUTH FROM MYSELF-- AS WELL AS FROM THE WORLD.
BUT WHAT'S THE USE?
I'M A FREAK, NEITHER MAMMAL NOR VEGETABLE.
I MIGHT AS WELL JOIN YOU OTHER FREAKS.
THEN OUR GROUP IS COMPLETE.
NOW WE CAN JOIN OUR COLLEAGUES FROM EARTH-2.
EARTH-2? WHAT HAVE THEY TO DO WITH US?
PATIENCE, PLANT-MASTER.
ALL WILL BE EXPLAINED...
EARTH-2:
THE AQUARIUM CASINO, IN LAS VEGAS, NEVADA...
G'NIGHT, PHIL. WE'LL SEE YOU TOMORROW.
MAKE SURE YOU KEEP THESE SUCKERS HONEST!
WOULDN'T WANT 'EM TO BUST THE HOUSE ON US, NOW WOULD WE?
HAHAHA
MEET ROSCOE AND BENNIE BOZAK, TWO FORMERLY-CHEAP HOODS FROM GOTHAM CITY.
A FEW YEARS BACK, THEY FELL INTO AN.. "INHERITANCE."
THEY USED IT TO FINANCE THIS CASINO...
...AND THEY'VE BEEN HIGH-ROLLING EVER SINCE: UNTIL TONIGHT.
TAKE THE SCENIC ROUTE, DRIVER. WE AIN'T IN NO HURRY.
FEW MEN ARE EVER IN A HURRY.. TO MEET DEATH.
HUH? THAT AIN'T OUR REGULAR DRIVER.
AND WHAT'S HE MEAN, TALKIN' ABOUT DEATH?
B-BENNIE... DIDN'T YOU RECOGNIZE HIS VOICE? IT'S HIM, BENNIE!
12

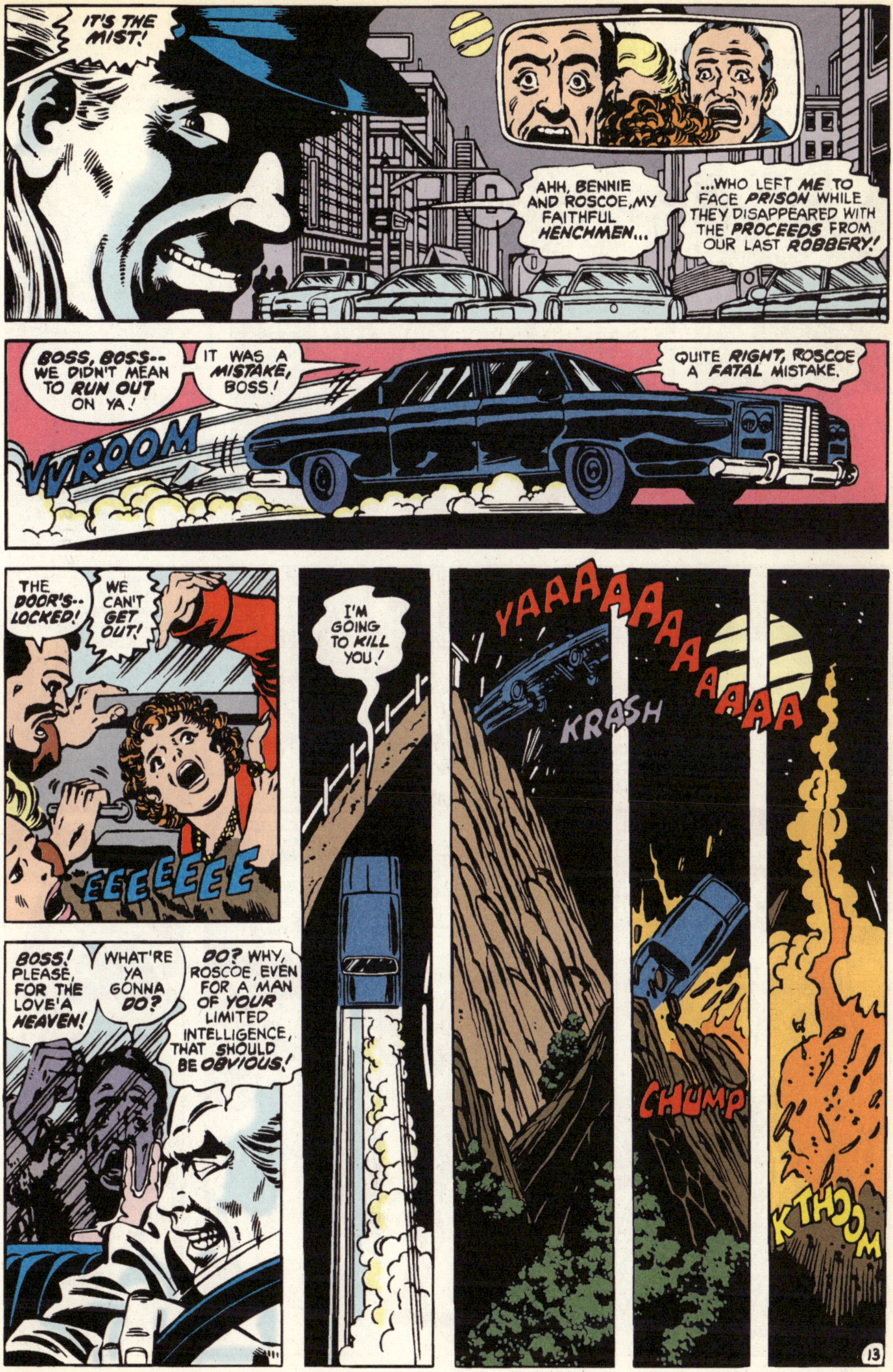
IT'S THE MIST!
AHH, BENNIE AND ROSCOE, MY FAITHFUL HENCHMEN...
...WHO LEFT ME TO FACE PRISON WHILE THEY DISAPPEARED WITH THE PROCEEDS FROM OUR LAST ROBBERY!
BOSS, BOSS-- WE DIDN'T MEAN TO RUN OUT ON YA!
IT WAS A MISTAKE, BOSS!
QUITE RIGHT, ROSCOE A FATAL MISTAKE.
VVROOM
THE DOOR'S-- LOCKED!
WE CAN'T GET OUT!
EEEEEEEE
BOSS! PLEASE, FOR THE LOVE'A HEAVEN!
WHAT'RE YA GONNA DO?
DO? WHY, ROSCOE, EVEN FOR A MAN OF YOUR LIMITED INTELLIGENCE, THAT SHOULD BE OBVIOUS!
I'M GOING TO KILL YOU!
YAAAAAAAAAAAA
KRASH
CHUMP
KTHOOM
13

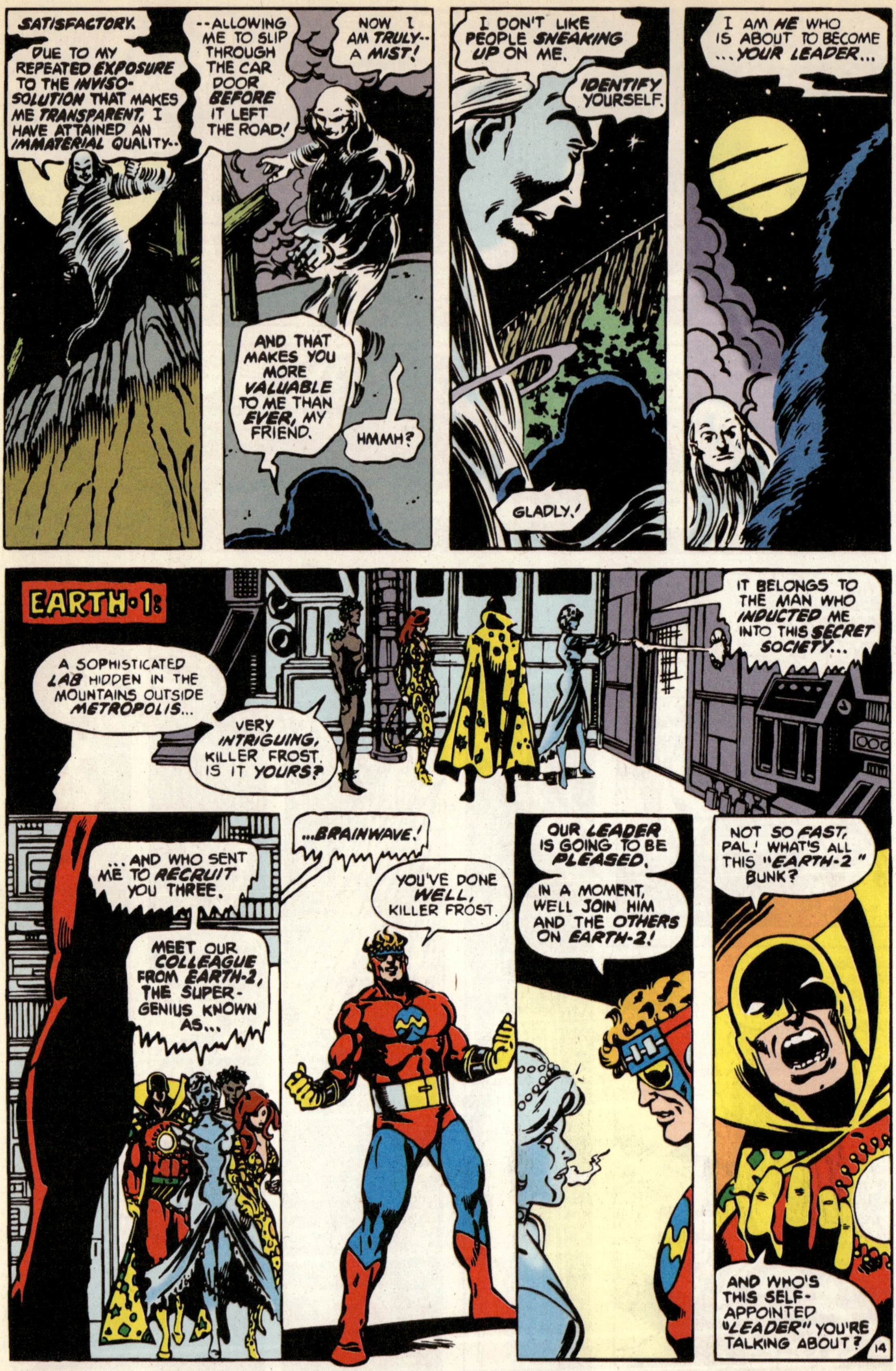
SATISFACTORY.
DUE TO MY REPEATED EXPOSURE TO THE INVISO-SOLUTION THAT MAKES ME TRANSPARENT, I HAVE ATTAINED AN IMMATERIAL QUALITY..
--ALLOWING ME TO SLIP THROUGH THE CAR DOOR BEFORE IT LEFT THE ROAD!
NOW I AM TRULY-- A MIST!
AND THAT MAKES YOU MORE VALUABLE TO ME THAN EVER, MY FRIEND.
HMMM?
I DON'T LIKE PEOPLE SNEAKING UP ON ME.
IDENTIFY YOURSELF.
GLADLY!
I AM HE WHO IS ABOUT TO BECOME ...YOUR LEADER...
EARTH-1:
A SOPHISTICATED LAB HIDDEN IN THE MOUNTAINS OUTSIDE METROPOLIS...
VERY INTRIGUING, KILLER FROST. IS IT YOURS?
IT BELONGS TO THE MAN WHO INDUCTED ME INTO THIS SECRET SOCIETY...
...AND WHO SENT ME TO RECRUIT YOU THREE.
MEET OUR COLLEAGUE FROM EARTH-2, THE SUPER-GENIUS KNOWN AS...
...BRAINWAVE!
YOU'VE DONE WELL, KILLER FROST.
OUR LEADER IS GOING TO BE PLEASED.
IN A MOMENT, WE'LL JOIN HIM AND THE OTHERS ON EARTH-2!
NOT SO FAST, PAL! WHAT'S ALL THIS "EARTH-2" BUNK?
AND WHO'S THIS SELF-APPOINTED "LEADER" YOU'RE TALKING ABOUT?
14

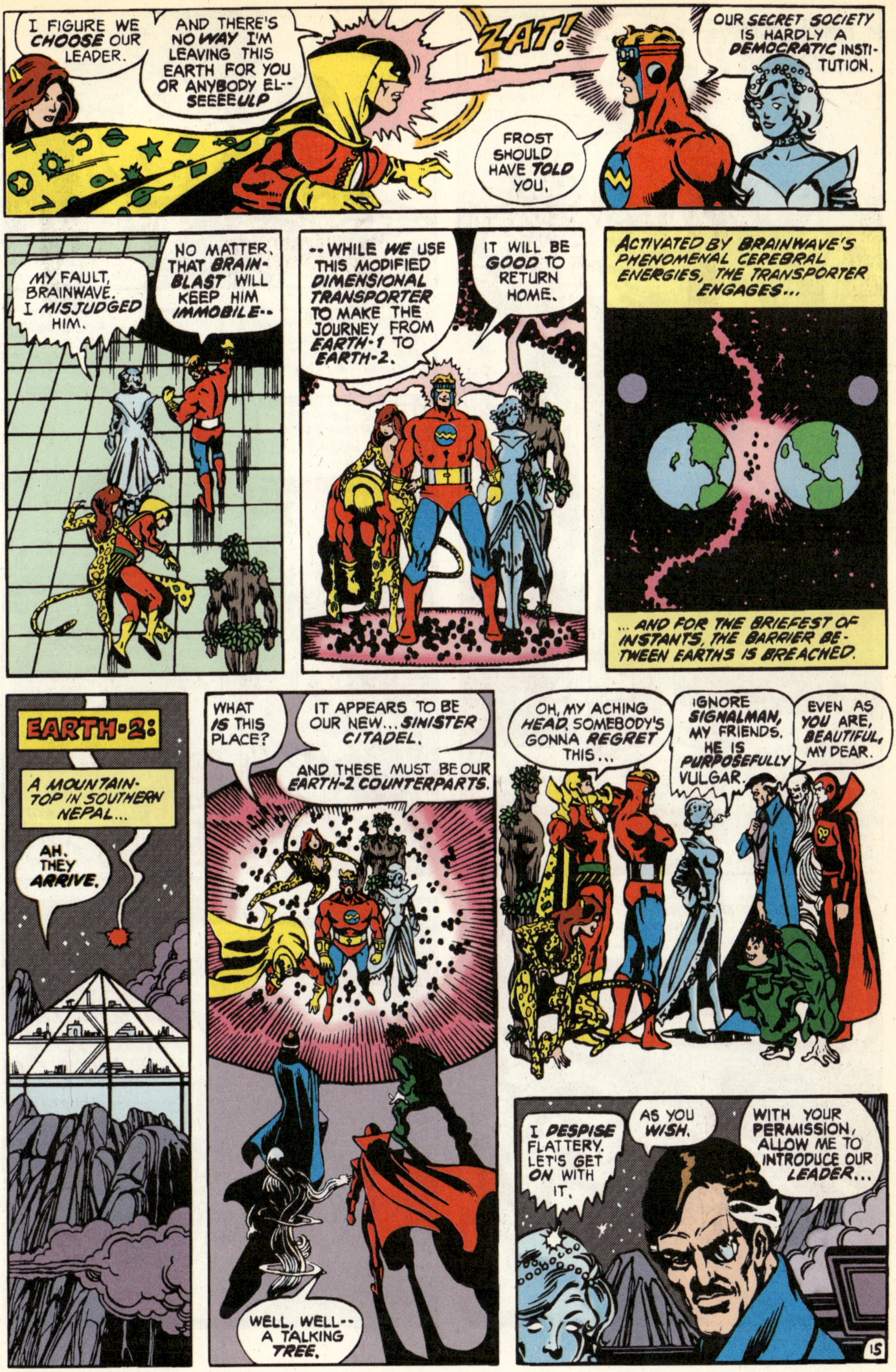
I FIGURE WE CHOOSE OUR LEADER.
AND THERE'S NO WAY I'M LEAVING THIS EARTH FOR YOU OR ANYBODY EL--SEEEEULP
ZAT!
OUR SECRET SOCIETY IS HARDLY A DEMOCRATIC INSTITUTION.
FROST SHOULD HAVE TOLD YOU.
MY FAULT, BRAINWAVE. I MISJUDGED HIM.
NO MATTER. THAT BRAIN-BLAST WILL KEEP HIM IMMOBILE--
--WHILE WE USE THIS MODIFIED DIMENSIONAL TRANSPORTER TO MAKE THE JOURNEY FROM EARTH-1 TO EARTH-2.
IT WILL BE GOOD TO RETURN HOME.
ACTIVATED BY BRAINWAVE'S PHENOMENAL CEREBRAL ENERGIES, THE TRANSPORTER ENGAGES...
...AND FOR THE BRIEFEST OF INSTANTS, THE BARRIER BETWEEN EARTHS IS BREACHED.
EARTH-2:
A MOUNTAIN-TOP IN SOUTHERN NEPAL...
AH. THEY ARRIVE.
WHAT IS THIS PLACE?
IT APPEARS TO BE OUR NEW... SINISTER CITADEL.
AND THESE MUST BE OUR EARTH-2 COUNTERPARTS.
WELL, WELL-- A TALKING TREE.
OH, MY ACHING HEAD. SOMEBODY'S GONNA REGRET THIS...
IGNORE SIGNALMAN, MY FRIENDS. HE IS PURPOSEFULLY VULGAR.
EVEN AS YOU ARE, BEAUTIFUL, MY DEAR.
I DESPISE FLATTERY. LET'S GET ON WITH IT.
AS YOU WISH.
WITH YOUR PERMISSION, ALLOW ME TO INTRODUCE OUR LEADER...
15

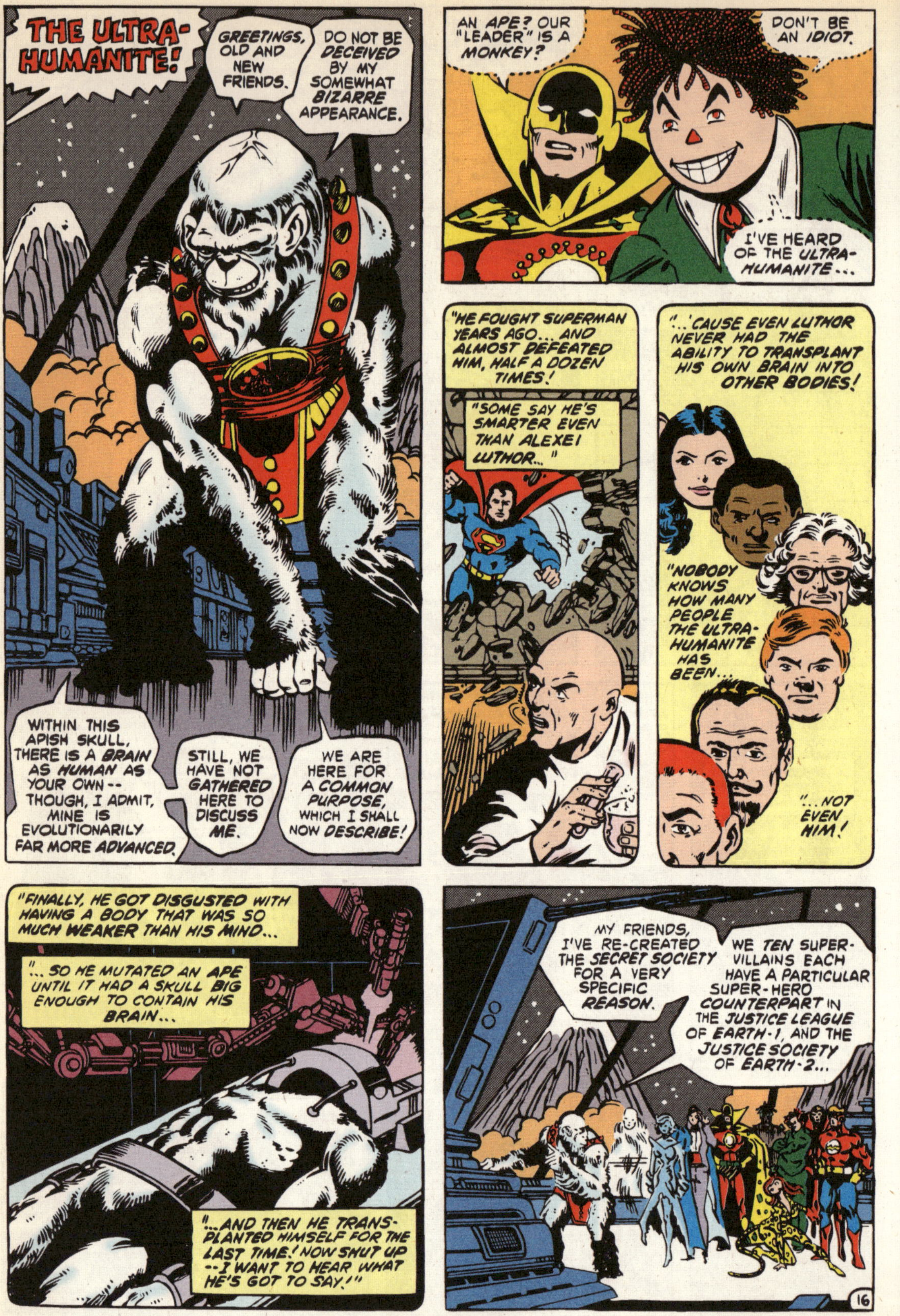
THE ULTRA-HUMANITE!
GREETINGS, OLD AND NEW FRIENDS.
DO NOT BE DECEIVED BY MY SOMEWHAT BIZARRE APPEARANCE.
WITHIN THIS APISH SKULL, THERE IS A BRAIN AS HUMAN AS YOUR OWN -- THOUGH, I ADMIT, MINE IS EVOLUTIONARILY FAR MORE ADVANCED.
STILL, WE HAVE NOT GATHERED HERE TO DISCUSS ME.
WE ARE HERE FOR A COMMON PURPOSE, WHICH I SHALL NOW DESCRIBE!
AN APE? OUR "LEADER" IS A MONKEY?
DON'T BE AN IDIOT.
I'VE HEARD OF THE ULTRA-HUMANITE...
"HE FOUGHT SUPERMAN YEARS AGO... AND ALMOST DEFEATED HIM, HALF A DOZEN TIMES!
"SOME SAY HE'S SMARTER EVEN THAN ALEXEI LUTHOR..."
"...'CAUSE EVEN LUTHOR NEVER HAD THE ABILITY TO TRANSPLANT HIS OWN BRAIN INTO OTHER BODIES!
"NOBODY KNOWS HOW MANY PEOPLE THE ULTRA-HUMANITE HAS BEEN...
"...NOT EVEN HIM!
"FINALLY, HE GOT DISGUSTED WITH HAVING A BODY THAT WAS SO MUCH WEAKER THAN HIS MIND...
"...SO HE MUTATED AN APE UNTIL IT HAD A SKULL BIG ENOUGH TO CONTAIN HIS BRAIN...
"...AND THEN HE TRANSPLANTED HIMSELF FOR THE LAST TIME! NOW SHUT UP -- I WANT TO HEAR WHAT HE'S GOT TO SAY!"
MY FRIENDS, I'VE RE-CREATED THE SECRET SOCIETY FOR A VERY SPECIFIC REASON.
WE TEN SUPER-VILLAINS EACH HAVE A PARTICULAR SUPER-HERO COUNTERPART IN THE JUSTICE LEAGUE OF EARTH-1, AND THE JUSTICE SOCIETY OF EARTH-2...
16

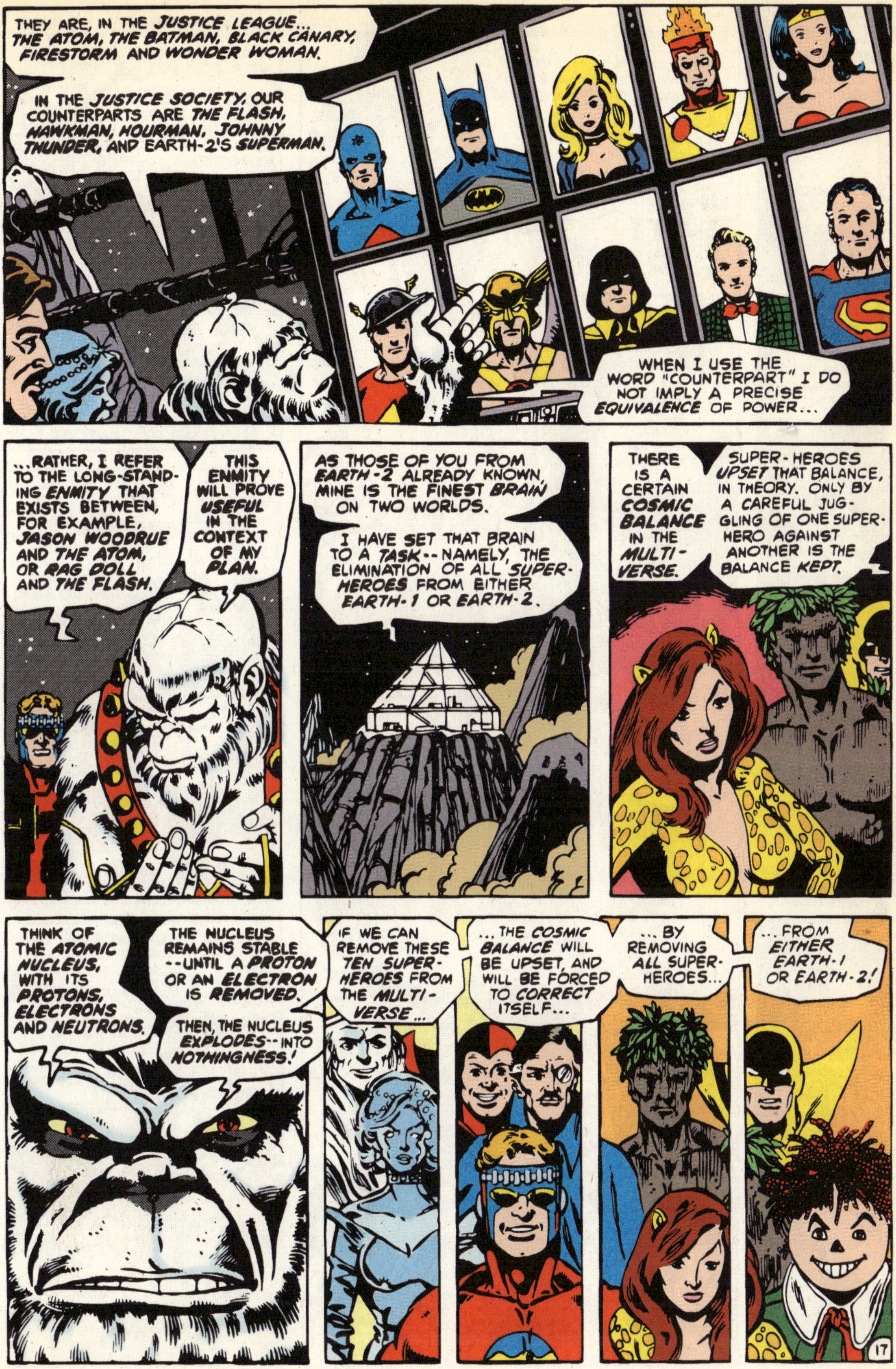
THEY ARE, IN THE JUSTICE LEAGUE... THE ATOM, THE BATMAN, BLACK CANARY, FIRESTORM AND WONDER WOMAN.
IN THE JUSTICE SOCIETY, OUR COUNTERPARTS ARE THE FLASH, HAWKMAN, HOURMAN, JOHNNY THUNDER, AND EARTH-2'S SUPERMAN.
WHEN I USE THE WORD "COUNTERPART" I DO NOT IMPLY A PRECISE EQUIVALENCE OF POWER...
...RATHER, I REFER TO THE LONG-STANDING ENMITY THAT EXISTS BETWEEN, FOR EXAMPLE, JASON WOODRUE AND THE ATOM, OR RAG DOLL AND THE FLASH.
THIS ENMITY WILL PROVE USEFUL IN THE CONTEXT OF MY PLAN.
AS THOSE OF YOU FROM EARTH-2 ALREADY KNOWN, MINE IS THE FINEST BRAIN ON TWO WORLDS.
I HAVE SET THAT BRAIN TO A TASK--NAMELY, THE ELIMINATION OF ALL SUPER-HEROES FROM EITHER EARTH-1 OR EARTH-2.
THERE IS A CERTAIN COSMIC BALANCE IN THE MULTIVERSE.
SUPER-HEROES UPSET THAT BALANCE, IN THEORY. ONLY BY A CAREFUL JUGGLING OF ONE SUPER-HERO AGAINST ANOTHER IS THE BALANCE KEPT.
THINK OF THE ATOMIC NUCLEUS, WITH ITS PROTONS, ELECTRONS AND NEUTRONS.
THE NUCLEUS REMAINS STABLE --UNTIL A PROTON OR AN ELECTRON IS REMOVED.
THEN, THE NUCLEUS EXPLODES--INTO NOTHINGNESS!
IF WE CAN REMOVE THESE TEN SUPER-HEROES FROM THE MULTIVERSE...
...THE COSMIC BALANCE WILL BE UPSET, AND WILL BE FORCED TO CORRECT ITSELF...
...BY REMOVING ALL SUPER-HEROES...
...FROM EITHER EARTH-1 OR EARTH-2!
17

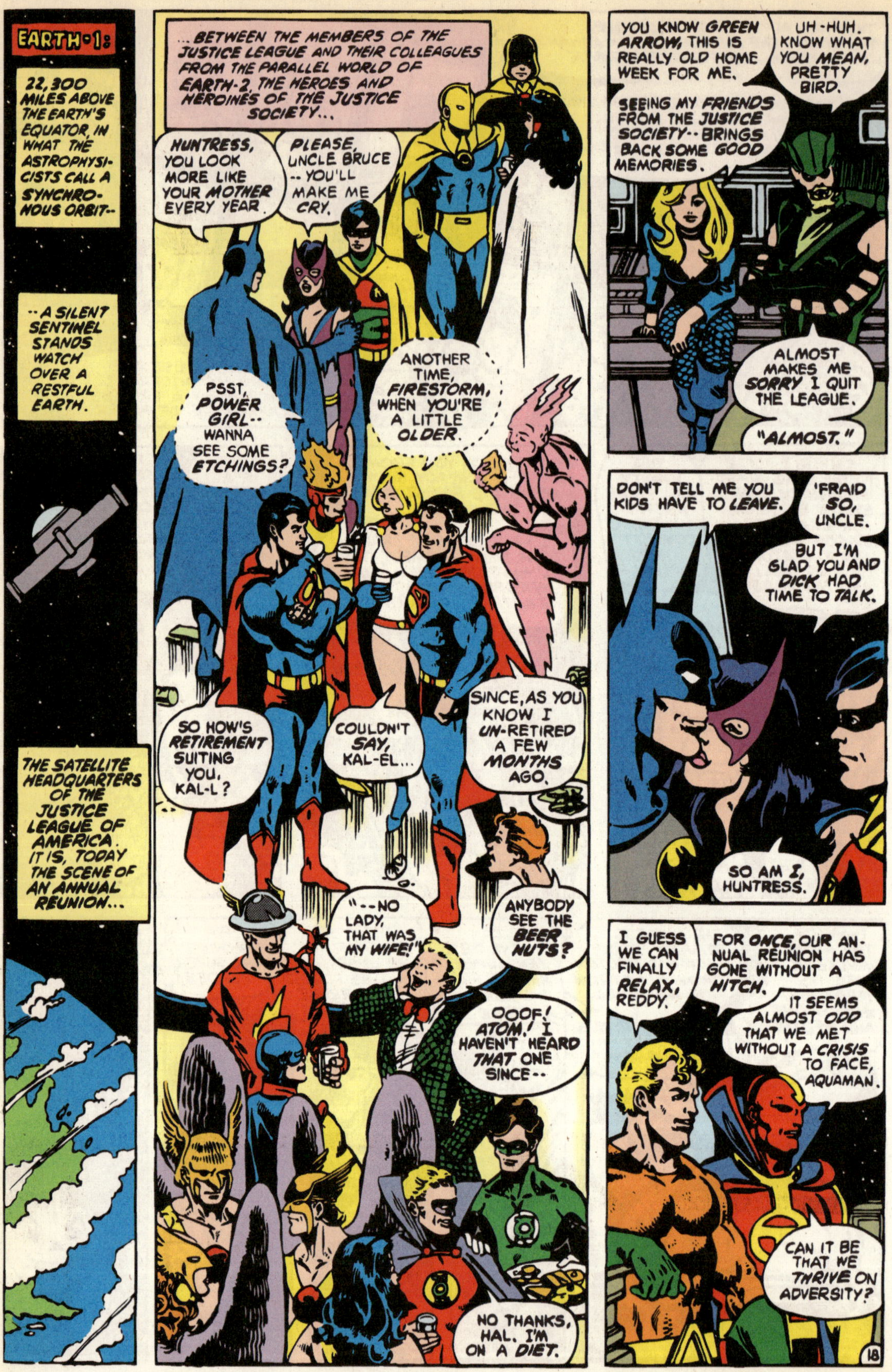
EARTH-1:
22,300 MILES ABOVE THE EARTH'S EQUATOR, IN WHAT THE ASTROPHYSICISTS CALL A SYNCHRONOUS ORBIT--
--A SILENT SENTINEL STANDS WATCH OVER A RESTFUL EARTH.
THE SATELLITE HEADQUARTERS OF THE JUSTICE LEAGUE OF AMERICA. IT IS, TODAY THE SCENE OF AN ANNUAL REUNION...
...BETWEEN THE MEMBERS OF THE JUSTICE LEAGUE AND THEIR COLLEAGUES FROM THE PARALLEL WORLD OF EARTH-2, THE HEROES AND HEROINES OF THE JUSTICE SOCIETY...
HUNTRESS, YOU LOOK MORE LIKE YOUR MOTHER EVERY YEAR.
PLEASE, UNCLE BRUCE -- YOU'LL MAKE ME CRY.
PSST, POWER GIRL-- WANNA SEE SOME ETCHINGS?
ANOTHER TIME, FIRESTORM, WHEN YOU'RE A LITTLE OLDER.
SO HOW'S RETIREMENT SUITING YOU, KAL-L?
COULDN'T SAY, KAL-EL...
SINCE, AS YOU KNOW I UN-RETIRED A FEW MONTHS AGO.
"--NO LADY, THAT WAS MY WIFE!"
ANYBODY SEE THE BEER NUTS?
OOOF! ATOM! I HAVEN'T HEARD THAT ONE SINCE--
NO THANKS, HAL. I'M ON A DIET.
YOU KNOW GREEN ARROW, THIS IS REALLY OLD HOME WEEK FOR ME.
UH-HUH. KNOW WHAT YOU MEAN, PRETTY BIRD.
SEEING MY FRIENDS FROM THE JUSTICE SOCIETY-- BRINGS BACK SOME GOOD MEMORIES.
ALMOST MAKES ME SORRY I QUIT THE LEAGUE.
"ALMOST."
DON'T TELL ME YOU KIDS HAVE TO LEAVE.
'FRAID SO, UNCLE.
BUT I'M GLAD YOU AND DICK HAD TIME TO TALK.
SO AM I, HUNTRESS.
I GUESS WE CAN FINALLY RELAX, REDDY.
FOR ONCE, OUR ANNUAL REUNION HAS GONE WITHOUT A HITCH.
IT SEEMS ALMOST ODD THAT WE MET WITHOUT A CRISIS TO FACE, AQUAMAN.
CAN IT BE THAT WE THRIVE ON ADVERSITY?
18

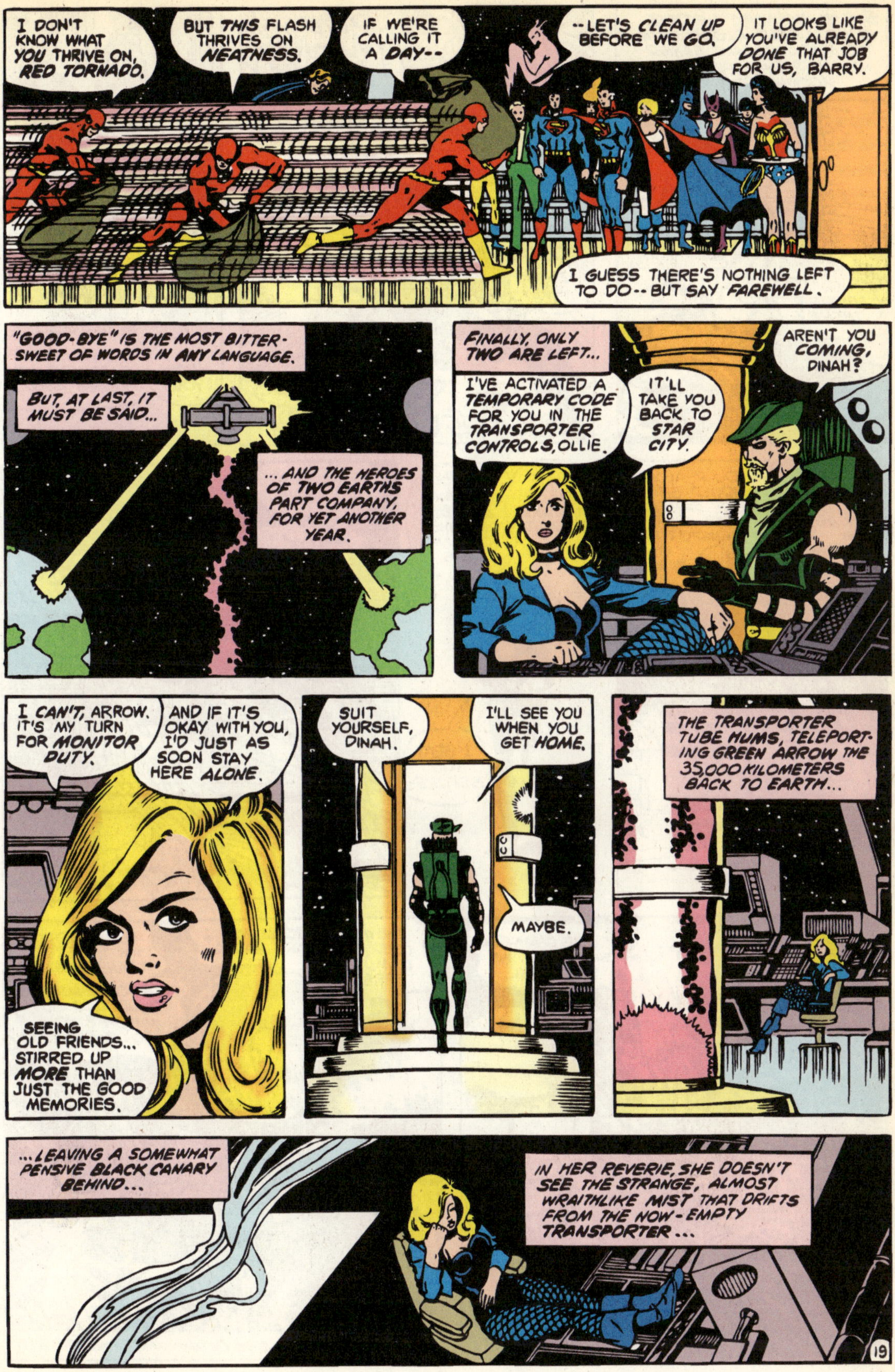
I DON'T KNOW WHAT YOU THRIVE ON, RED TORNADO.
BUT THIS FLASH THRIVES ON NEATNESS.
IF WE'RE CALLING IT A DAY--
--LET'S CLEAN UP BEFORE WE GO.
IT LOOKS LIKE YOU'VE ALREADY DONE THAT JOB FOR US, BARRY.
I GUESS THERE'S NOTHING LEFT TO DO-- BUT SAY FAREWELL.
"GOOD-BYE" IS THE MOST BITTER-SWEET OF WORDS IN ANY LANGUAGE.
BUT, AT LAST, IT MUST BE SAID...
...AND THE HEROES OF TWO EARTHS PART COMPANY, FOR YET ANOTHER YEAR.
FINALLY, ONLY TWO ARE LEFT...
I'VE ACTIVATED A TEMPORARY CODE FOR YOU IN THE TRANSPORTER CONTROLS, OLLIE.
IT'LL TAKE YOU BACK TO STAR CITY.
AREN'T YOU COMING, DINAH?
I CAN'T, ARROW. IT'S MY TURN FOR MONITOR DUTY.
AND IF IT'S OKAY WITH YOU, I'D JUST AS SOON STAY HERE ALONE.
SEEING OLD FRIENDS... STIRRED UP MORE THAN JUST THE GOOD MEMORIES.
SUIT YOURSELF, DINAH.
I'LL SEE YOU WHEN YOU GET HOME.
MAYBE.
THE TRANSPORTER TUBE HUMS, TELEPORTING GREEN ARROW THE 35,000 KILOMETERS BACK TO EARTH...
...LEAVING A SOMEWHAT PENSIVE BLACK CANARY BEHIND...
IN HER REVERIE, SHE DOESN'T SEE THE STRANGE, ALMOST WRAITHLIKE MIST THAT DRIFTS FROM THE NOW-EMPTY TRANSPORTER...
19

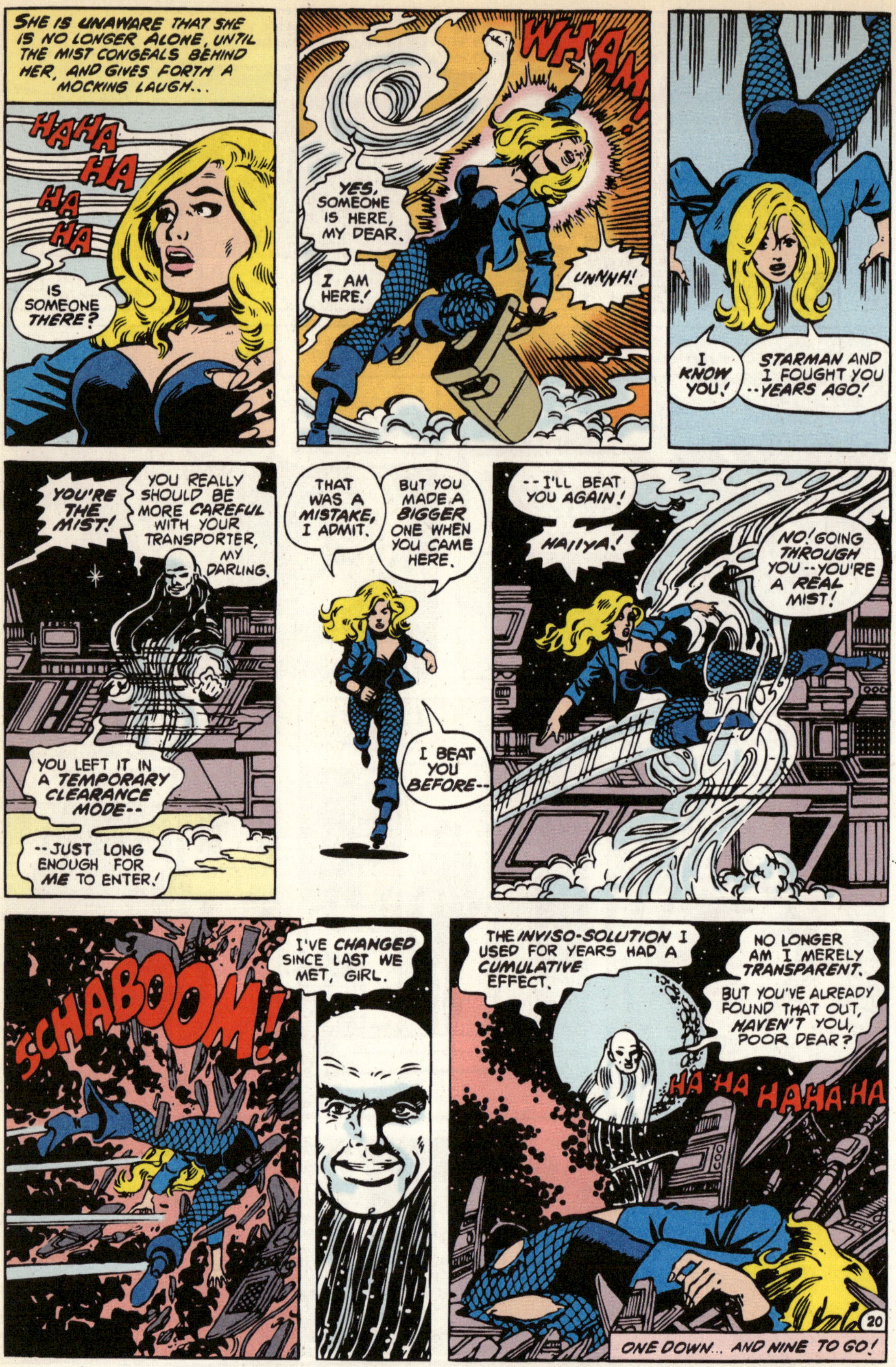
SHE IS UNAWARE THAT SHE IS NO LONGER ALONE, UNTIL THE MIST CONGEALS BEHIND HER, AND GIVES FORTH A MOCKING LAUGH...
HAHA HA HA HA
IS SOMEONE THERE?
WHAM!
YES, SOMEONE IS HERE, MY DEAR.
I AM HERE!
UNNNH!
I KNOW YOU!
STARMAN AND I FOUGHT YOU --YEARS AGO!
YOU'RE THE MIST!
YOU REALLY SHOULD BE MORE CAREFUL WITH YOUR TRANSPORTER, MY DARLING.
YOU LEFT IT IN A TEMPORARY CLEARANCE MODE--
--JUST LONG ENOUGH FOR ME TO ENTER!
THAT WAS A MISTAKE, I ADMIT.
BUT YOU MADE A BIGGER ONE WHEN YOU CAME HERE.
I BEAT YOU BEFORE--
--I'LL BEAT YOU AGAIN!
HAIIYA!
NO! GOING THROUGH YOU--YOU'RE A REAL MIST!
SCHABOOM!
I'VE CHANGED SINCE LAST WE MET, GIRL.
THE INVISO-SOLUTION I USED FOR YEARS HAD A CUMULATIVE EFFECT.
NO LONGER AM I MERELY TRANSPARENT.
BUT YOU'VE ALREADY FOUND THAT OUT, HAVEN'T YOU, POOR DEAR?
HA HA HAHA HA
20
ONE DOWN... AND NINE TO GO!

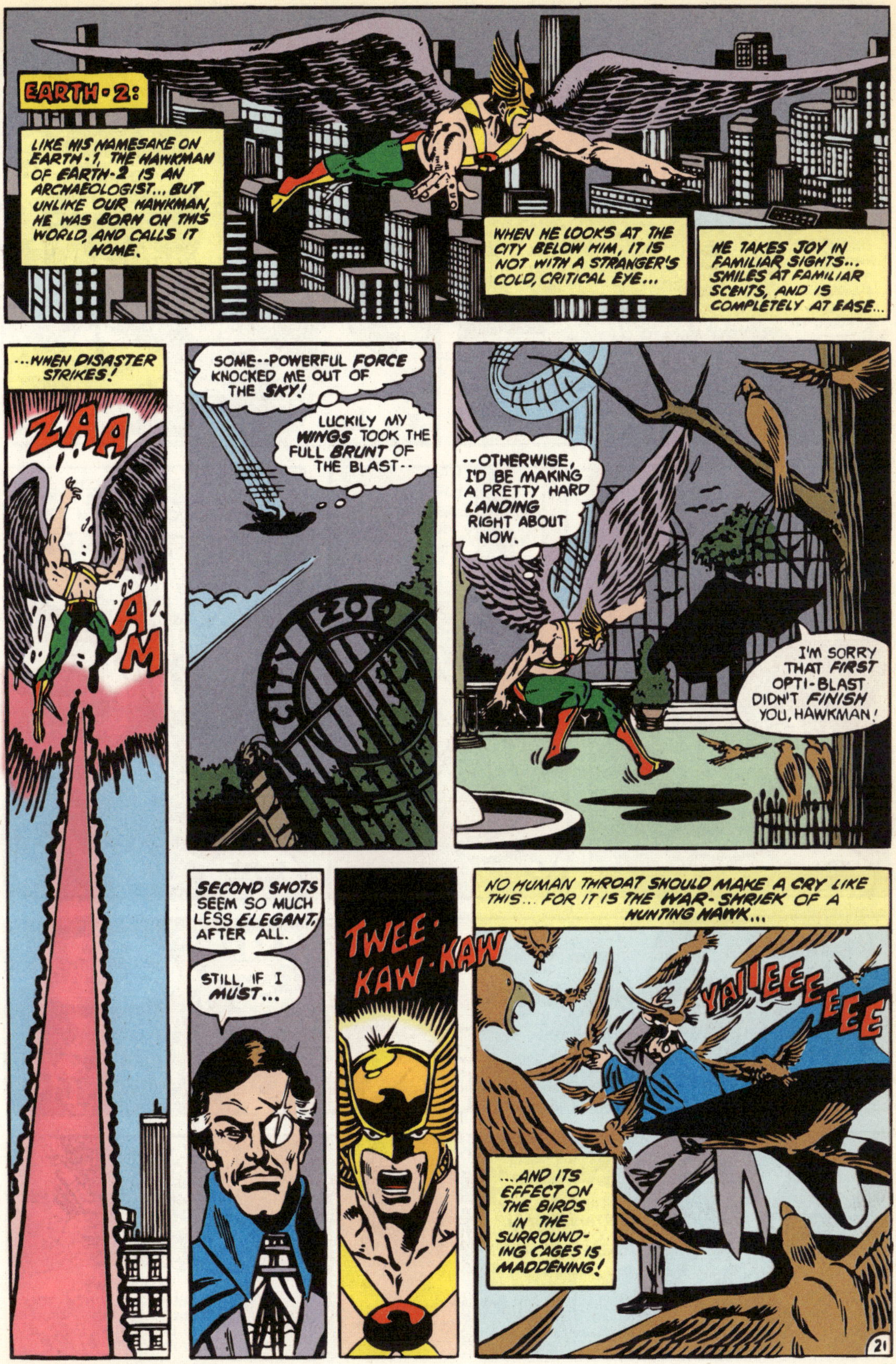
EARTH-2:
LIKE HIS NAMESAKE ON EARTH-1, THE HAWKMAN OF EARTH-2 IS AN ARCHAEOLOGIST... BUT UNLIKE OUR HAWKMAN, HE WAS BORN ON THIS WORLD, AND CALLS IT HOME.
WHEN HE LOOKS AT THE CITY BELOW HIM, IT IS NOT WITH A STRANGER'S COLD, CRITICAL EYE...
HE TAKES JOY IN FAMILIAR SIGHTS... SMILES AT FAMILIAR SCENTS, AND IS COMPLETELY AT EASE...
...WHEN DISASTER STRIKES!
ZAAAM
SOME--POWERFUL FORCE KNOCKED ME OUT OF THE SKY!
LUCKILY MY WINGS TOOK THE FULL BRUNT OF THE BLAST--
CITY ZOO
--OTHERWISE, I'D BE MAKING A PRETTY HARD LANDING RIGHT ABOUT NOW.
I'M SORRY THAT FIRST OPTI-BLAST DIDN'T FINISH YOU, HAWKMAN!
SECOND SHOTS SEEM SO MUCH LESS ELEGANT, AFTER ALL.
STILL, IF I MUST...
TWEE-KAW-KAW
NO HUMAN THROAT SHOULD MAKE A CRY LIKE THIS... FOR IT IS THE WAR-SHRIEK OF A HUNTING HAWK...
YAIIEEEEEEE
...AND ITS EFFECT ON THE BIRDS IN THE SURROUNDING CAGES IS MADDENING!
21

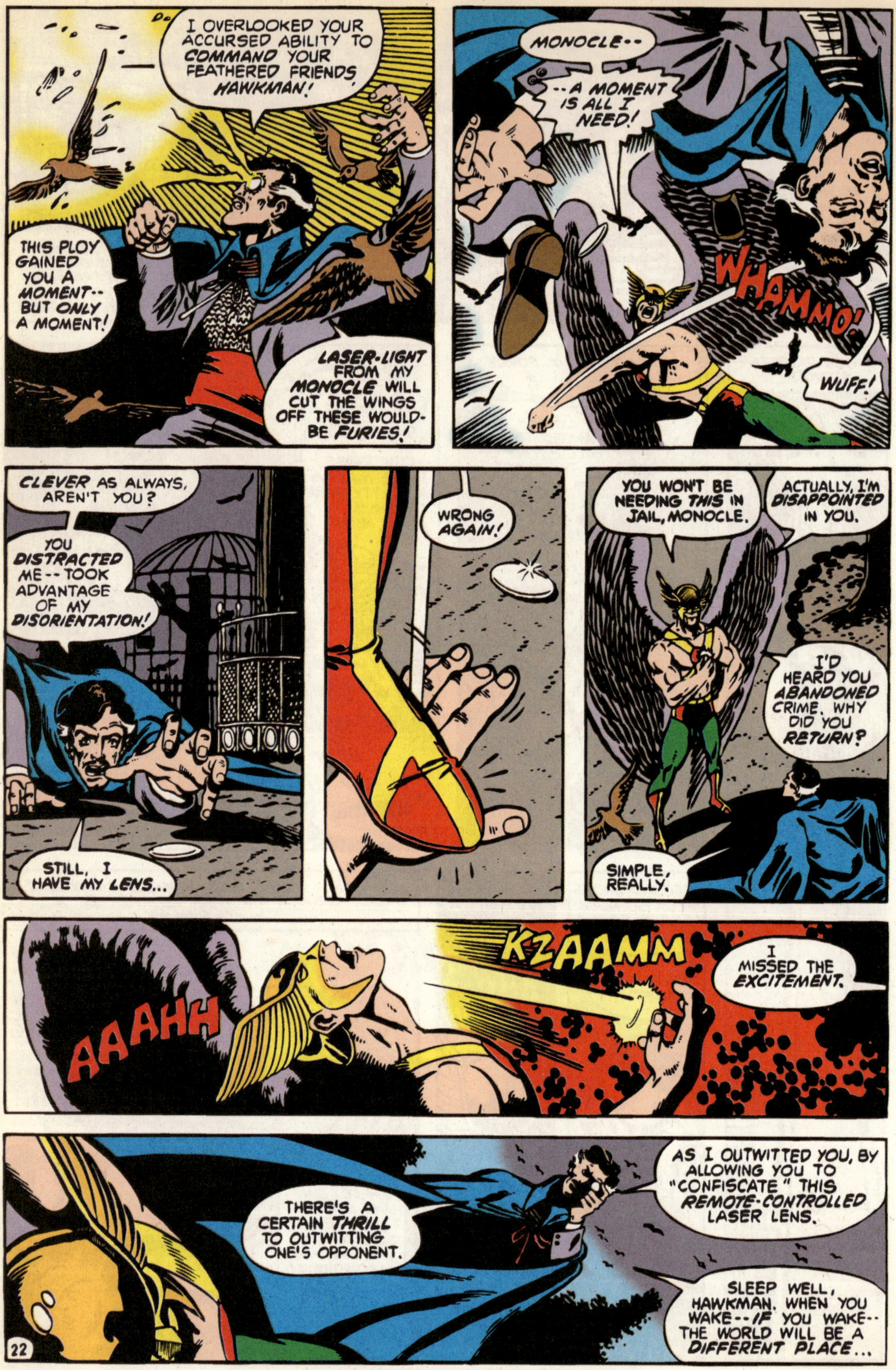
I OVERLOOKED YOUR ACCURSED ABILITY TO COMMAND YOUR FEATHERED FRIENDS, HAWKMAN!
THIS PLOY GAINED YOU A MOMENT-- BUT ONLY A MOMENT!
LASER-LIGHT FROM MY MONOCLE WILL CUT THE WINGS OFF THESE WOULD-BE FURIES!
MONOCLE--
--A MOMENT IS ALL I NEED!
WHAMMO!
WUFF!
CLEVER AS ALWAYS, AREN'T YOU?
YOU DISTRACTED ME--TOOK ADVANTAGE OF MY DISORIENTATION!
STILL, I HAVE MY LENS...
WRONG AGAIN!
YOU WON'T BE NEEDING THIS IN JAIL, MONOCLE.
ACTUALLY, I'M DISAPPOINTED IN YOU.
I'D HEARD YOU ABANDONED CRIME. WHY DID YOU RETURN?
SIMPLE, REALLY.
AAAHH
KZAAMM
I MISSED THE EXCITEMENT.
THERE'S A CERTAIN THRILL TO OUTWITTING ONE'S OPPONENT.
AS I OUTWITTED YOU, BY ALLOWING YOU TO "CONFISCATE" THIS REMOTE-CONTROLLED LASER LENS.
SLEEP WELL, HAWKMAN. WHEN YOU WAKE--IF YOU WAKE--THE WORLD WILL BE A DIFFERENT PLACE...
22

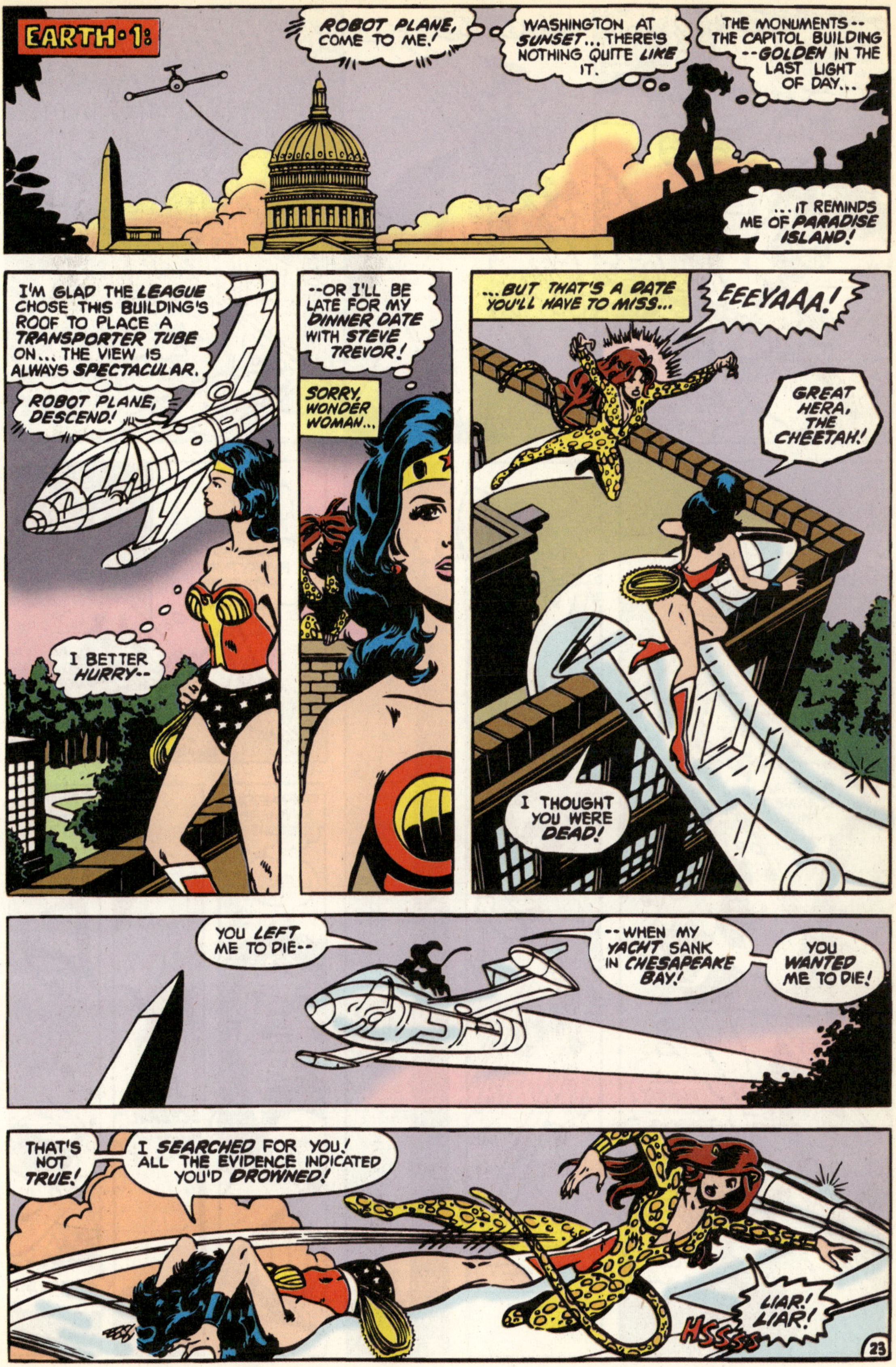
EARTH-1:
ROBOT PLANE, COME TO ME!
WASHINGTON AT SUNSET... THERE'S NOTHING QUITE LIKE IT.
THE MONUMENTS--THE CAPITOL BUILDING--GOLDEN IN THE LAST LIGHT OF DAY...
...IT REMINDS ME OF PARADISE ISLAND!
I'M GLAD THE LEAGUE CHOSE THIS BUILDING'S ROOF TO PLACE A TRANSPORTER TUBE ON... THE VIEW IS ALWAYS SPECTACULAR.
ROBOT PLANE, DESCEND!
I BETTER HURRY--
--OR I'LL BE LATE FOR MY DINNER DATE WITH STEVE TREVOR!
SORRY, WONDER WOMAN...
...BUT THAT'S A DATE YOU'LL HAVE TO MISS...
EEEYAAA!
GREAT HERA, THE CHEETAH!
I THOUGHT YOU WERE DEAD!
YOU LEFT ME TO DIE--
--WHEN MY YACHT SANK IN CHESAPEAKE BAY!
YOU WANTED ME TO DIE!
THAT'S NOT TRUE!
I SEARCHED FOR YOU! ALL THE EVIDENCE INDICATED YOU'D DROWNED!
LIAR! LIAR!
HSSSSS
23

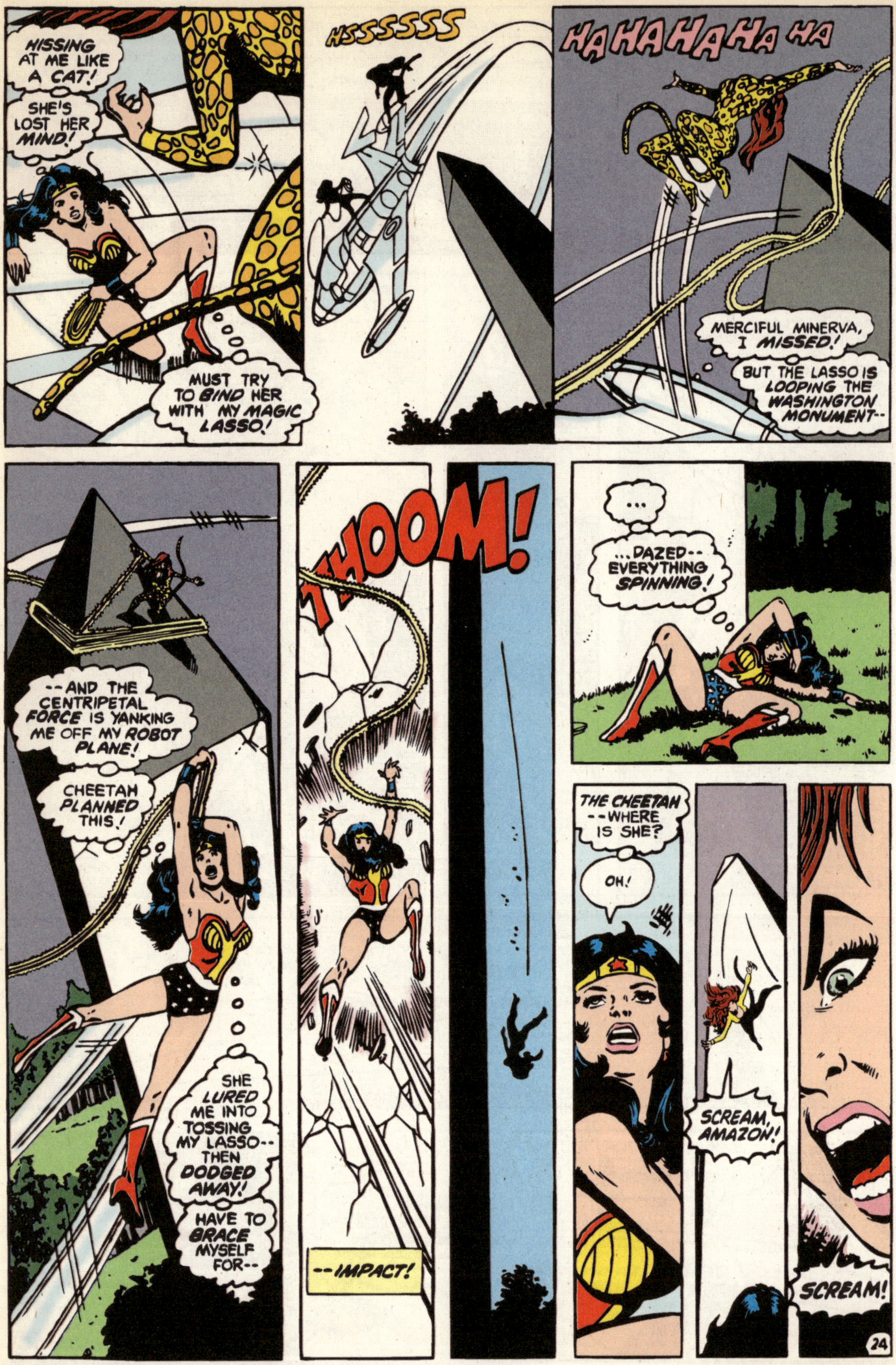
HISSING AT ME LIKE A CAT!
SHE'S LOST HER MIND!
MUST TRY TO BIND HER WITH MY MAGIC LASSO!
HSSSSSS
HAHAHAHAHA HA
MERCIFUL MINERVA, I MISSED!
BUT THE LASSO IS LOOPING THE WASHINGTON MONUMENT--
--AND THE CENTRIPETAL FORCE IS YANKING ME OFF MY ROBOT PLANE!
CHEETAH PLANNED THIS!
SHE LURED ME INTO TOSSING MY LASSO--THEN DODGED AWAY!
HAVE TO BRACE MYSELF FOR--
THOOM!
--IMPACT!
...
...DAZED--EVERYTHING SPINNING!
THE CHEETAH--WHERE IS SHE?
OH!
SCREAM, AMAZON!
SCREAM!
24

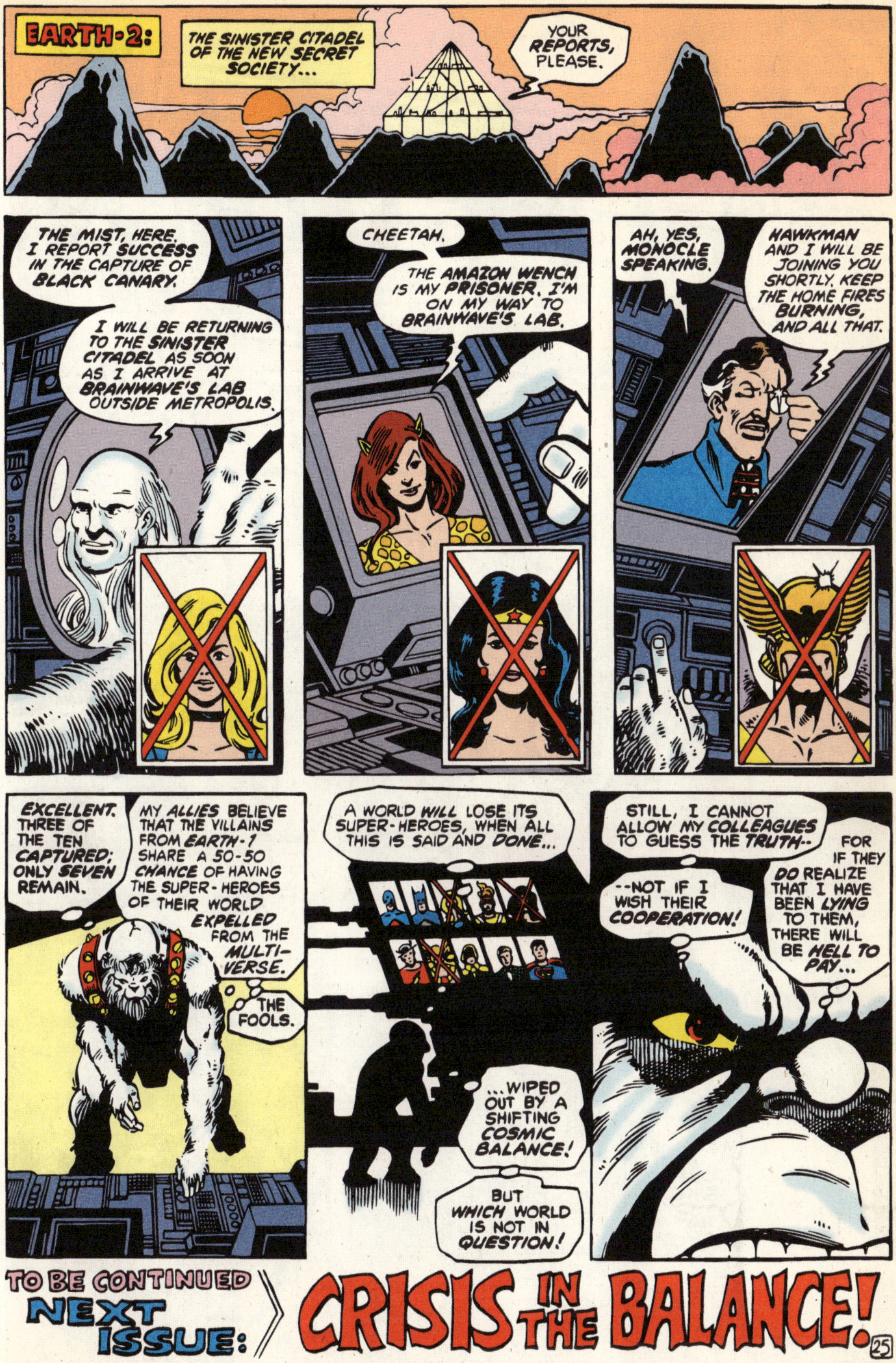
EARTH-2:
THE SINISTER CITADEL OF THE NEW SECRET SOCIETY...
YOUR REPORTS, PLEASE.
THE MIST, HERE. I REPORT SUCCESS IN THE CAPTURE OF BLACK CANARY.
I WILL BE RETURNING TO THE SINISTER CITADEL AS SOON AS I ARRIVE AT BRAINWAVE'S LAB OUTSIDE METROPOLIS.
CHEETAH.
THE AMAZON WENCH IS MY PRISONER. I'M ON MY WAY TO BRAINWAVE'S LAB.
AH, YES, MONOCLE SPEAKING.
HAWKMAN AND I WILL BE JOINING YOU SHORTLY. KEEP THE HOME FIRES BURNING, AND ALL THAT.
EXCELLENT. THREE OF THE TEN CAPTURED; ONLY SEVEN REMAIN.
MY ALLIES BELIEVE THAT THE VILLAINS FROM EARTH-1 SHARE A 50-50 CHANCE OF HAVING THE SUPER-HEROES OF THEIR WORLD EXPELLED FROM THE MULTI-VERSE.
THE FOOLS.
A WORLD WILL LOSE ITS SUPER-HEROES, WHEN ALL THIS IS SAID AND DONE...
...WIPED OUT BY A SHIFTING COSMIC BALANCE!
BUT WHICH WORLD IS NOT IN QUESTION!
STILL, I CANNOT ALLOW MY COLLEAGUES TO GUESS THE TRUTH--
--NOT IF I WISH THEIR COOPERATION!
FOR IF THEY DO REALIZE THAT I HAVE BEEN LYING TO THEM, THERE WILL BE HELL TO PAY...
TO BE CONTINUED NEXT ISSUE: CRISIS IN THE BALANCE!
25

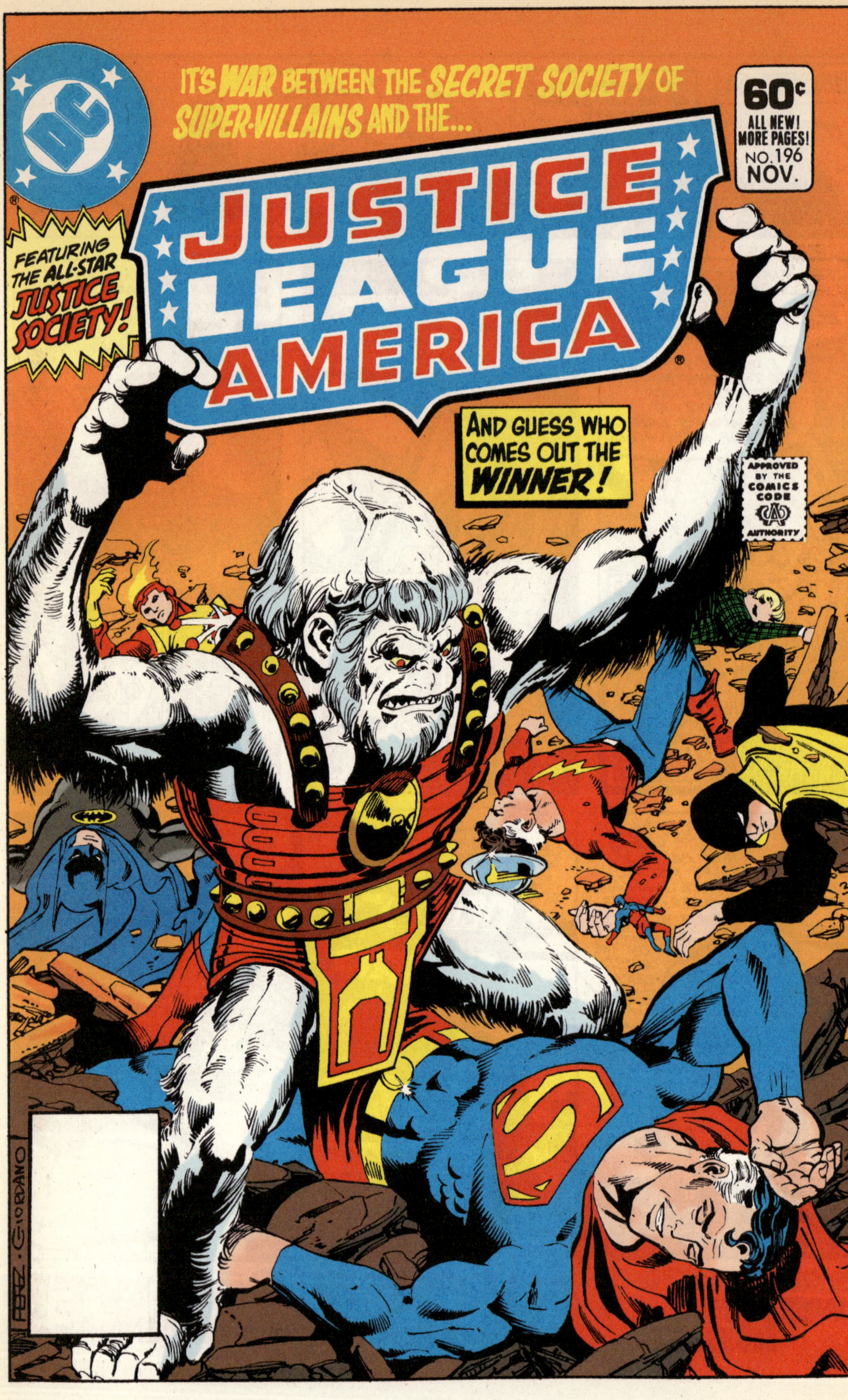

IT'S WAR BETWEEN THE SECRET SOCIETY OF SUPER-VILLAINS AND THE...
60¢
ALL NEW! MORE PAGES!
NO. 196
NOV.
JUSTICE LEAGUE AMERICA
FEATURING THE ALL-STAR JUSTICE SOCIETY!
AND GUESS WHO COMES OUT THE WINNER!
APPROVED BY THE COMICS CODE AUTHORITY
PEREZ·GIORDANO

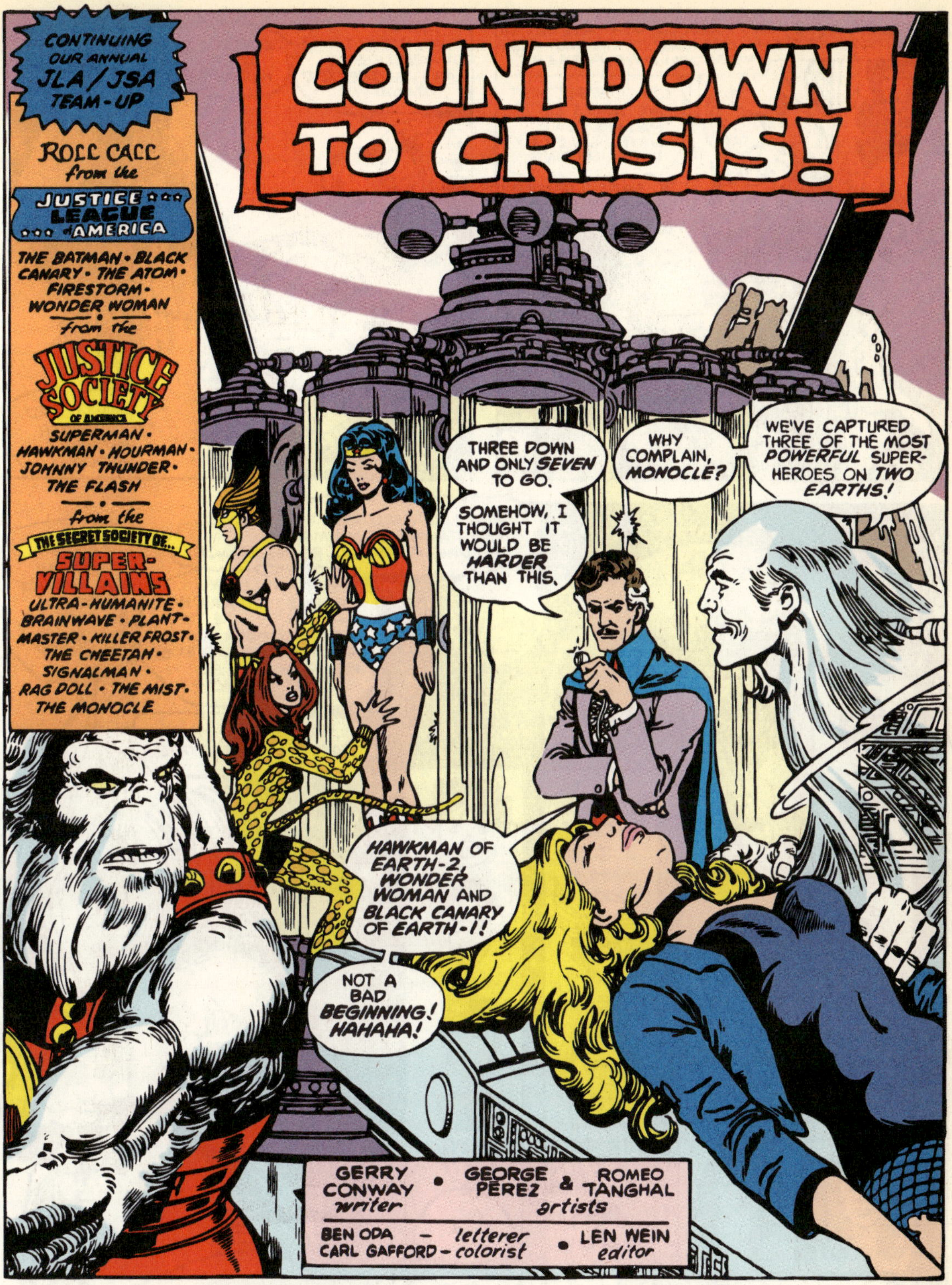
CONTINUING OUR ANNUAL JLA/JSA TEAM-UP
COUNTDOWN TO CRISIS!
ROLL CALL from the JUSTICE LEAGUE of AMERICA
THE BATMAN • BLACK CANARY • THE ATOM • FIRESTORM • WONDER WOMAN
from the JUSTICE SOCIETY OF AMERICA
SUPERMAN • HAWKMAN • HOURMAN • JOHNNY THUNDER • THE FLASH
from the THE SECRET SOCIETY OF... SUPER-VILLAINS
ULTRA-HUMANITE • BRAINWAVE • PLANT-MASTER • KILLER FROST • THE CHEETAH • SIGNALMAN • RAG DOLL • THE MIST • THE MONOCLE
THREE DOWN AND ONLY SEVEN TO GO.
SOMEHOW, I THOUGHT IT WOULD BE HARDER THAN THIS.
WHY COMPLAIN, MONOCLE?
WE'VE CAPTURED THREE OF THE MOST POWERFUL SUPER-HEROES ON TWO EARTHS!
HAWKMAN OF EARTH-2, WONDER WOMAN AND BLACK CANARY OF EARTH-1!
NOT A BAD BEGINNING! HAHAHA!
GERRY CONWAY writer • GEORGE PÉREZ & ROMEO TANGHAL artists
BEN ODA – letterer
CARL GAFFORD – colorist • LEN WEIN editor

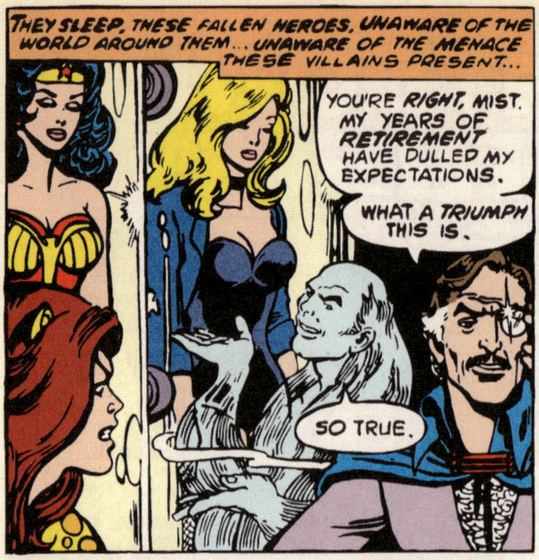
THEY SLEEP, THESE FALLEN HEROES, UNAWARE OF THE WORLD AROUND THEM... UNAWARE OF THE MENACE THESE VILLAINS PRESENT...
YOU'RE RIGHT, MIST. MY YEARS OF RETIREMENT HAVE DULLED MY EXPECTATIONS.
WHAT A TRIUMPH THIS IS.
SO TRUE.
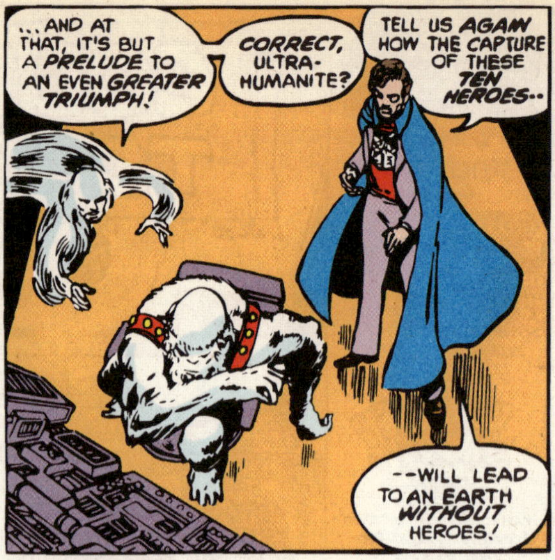
...AND AT THAT, IT'S BUT A PRELUDE TO AN EVEN GREATER TRIUMPH!
CORRECT, ULTRA-HUMANITE?
TELL US AGAIN HOW THE CAPTURE OF THESE TEN HEROES--
--WILL LEAD TO AN EARTH WITHOUT HEROES!
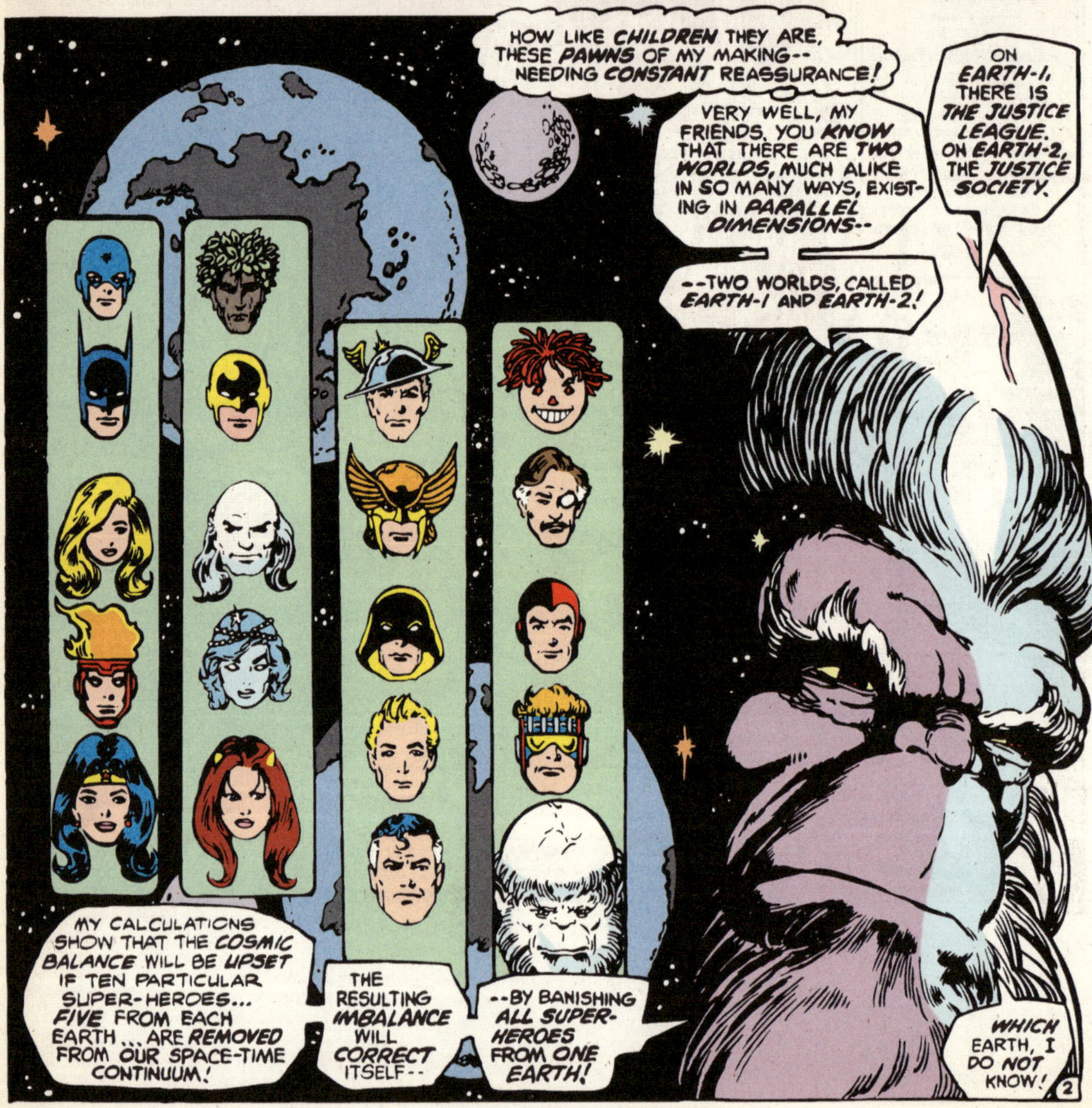
HOW LIKE CHILDREN THEY ARE, THESE PAWNS OF MY MAKING-- NEEDING CONSTANT REASSURANCE!
VERY WELL, MY FRIENDS. YOU KNOW THAT THERE ARE TWO WORLDS, MUCH ALIKE IN SO MANY WAYS, EXISTING IN PARALLEL DIMENSIONS--
--TWO WORLDS, CALLED EARTH-1 AND EARTH-2!
ON EARTH-1, THERE IS THE JUSTICE LEAGUE. ON EARTH-2, THE JUSTICE SOCIETY.
MY CALCULATIONS SHOW THAT THE COSMIC BALANCE WILL BE UPSET IF TEN PARTICULAR SUPER-HEROES... FIVE FROM EACH EARTH... ARE REMOVED FROM OUR SPACE-TIME CONTINUUM!
THE RESULTING IMBALANCE WILL CORRECT ITSELF--
--BY BANISHING ALL SUPER-HEROES FROM ONE EARTH!
WHICH EARTH, I DO NOT KNOW!
2

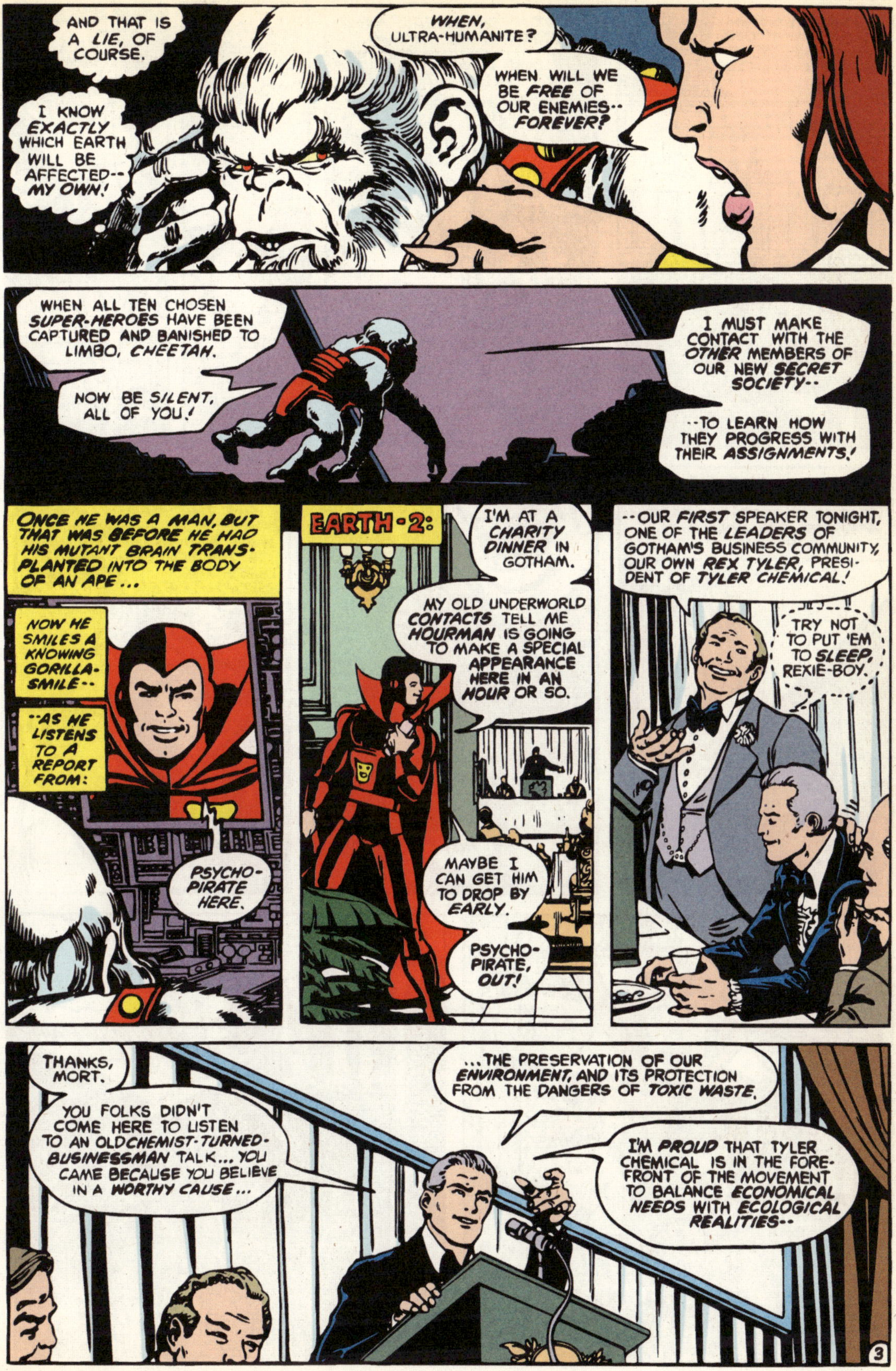
AND THAT IS A LIE, OF COURSE.
I KNOW EXACTLY WHICH EARTH WILL BE AFFECTED-- MY OWN!
WHEN, ULTRA-HUMANITE?
WHEN WILL WE BE FREE OF OUR ENEMIES-- FOREVER?
WHEN ALL TEN CHOSEN SUPER-HEROES HAVE BEEN CAPTURED AND BANISHED TO LIMBO, CHEETAH.
NOW BE SILENT, ALL OF YOU!
I MUST MAKE CONTACT WITH THE OTHER MEMBERS OF OUR NEW SECRET SOCIETY--
--TO LEARN HOW THEY PROGRESS WITH THEIR ASSIGNMENTS!
ONCE HE WAS A MAN, BUT THAT WAS BEFORE HE HAD HIS MUTANT BRAIN TRANS-PLANTED INTO THE BODY OF AN APE...
NOW HE SMILES A KNOWING GORILLA-SMILE--
--AS HE LISTENS TO A REPORT FROM:
PSYCHO-PIRATE HERE.
EARTH-2:
I'M AT A CHARITY DINNER IN GOTHAM.
MY OLD UNDERWORLD CONTACTS TELL ME HOURMAN IS GOING TO MAKE A SPECIAL APPEARANCE HERE IN AN HOUR OR SO.
MAYBE I CAN GET HIM TO DROP BY EARLY.
PSYCHO-PIRATE, OUT!
--OUR FIRST SPEAKER TONIGHT, ONE OF THE LEADERS OF GOTHAM'S BUSINESS COMMUNITY, OUR OWN REX TYLER, PRESI-DENT OF TYLER CHEMICAL!
TRY NOT TO PUT 'EM TO SLEEP, REXIE-BOY.
THANKS, MORT.
YOU FOLKS DIDN'T COME HERE TO LISTEN TO AN OLD CHEMIST-TURNED-BUSINESSMAN TALK... YOU CAME BECAUSE YOU BELIEVE IN A WORTHY CAUSE...
...THE PRESERVATION OF OUR ENVIRONMENT, AND ITS PROTECTION FROM THE DANGERS OF TOXIC WASTE.
I'M PROUD THAT TYLER CHEMICAL IS IN THE FORE-FRONT OF THE MOVEMENT TO BALANCE ECONOMICAL NEEDS WITH ECOLOGICAL REALITIES--
3

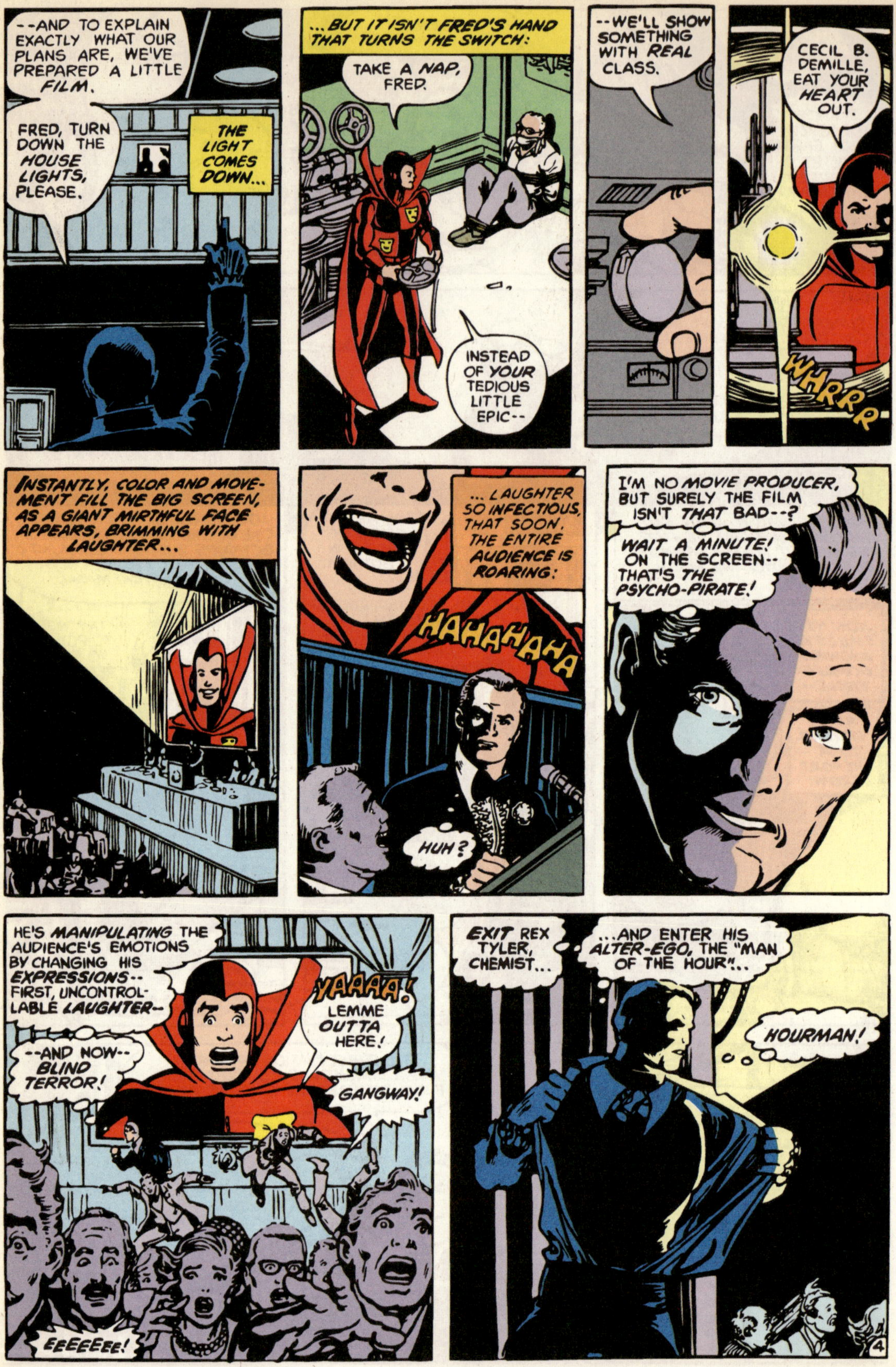
--AND TO EXPLAIN EXACTLY WHAT OUR PLANS ARE, WE'VE PREPARED A LITTLE FILM.
FRED, TURN DOWN THE HOUSE LIGHTS, PLEASE.
THE LIGHT COMES DOWN...
...BUT IT ISN'T FRED'S HAND THAT TURNS THE SWITCH:
TAKE A NAP, FRED.
INSTEAD OF YOUR TEDIOUS LITTLE EPIC--
--WE'LL SHOW SOMETHING WITH REAL CLASS.
CECIL B. DEMILLE, EAT YOUR HEART OUT.
WHRRRR
INSTANTLY, COLOR AND MOVEMENT FILL THE BIG SCREEN, AS A GIANT MIRTHFUL FACE APPEARS, BRIMMING WITH LAUGHTER...
...LAUGHTER SO INFECTIOUS, THAT SOON, THE ENTIRE AUDIENCE IS ROARING:
HAHAHAHAHA
HUH?
I'M NO MOVIE PRODUCER, BUT SURELY THE FILM ISN'T THAT BAD--?
WAIT A MINUTE! ON THE SCREEN-- THAT'S THE PSYCHO-PIRATE!
HE'S MANIPULATING THE AUDIENCE'S EMOTIONS BY CHANGING HIS EXPRESSIONS-- FIRST, UNCONTROLLABLE LAUGHTER--
--AND NOW-- BLIND TERROR!
YAAAAA! LEMME OUTTA HERE!
GANGWAY!
EEEEEEE!
EXIT REX TYLER, CHEMIST...
...AND ENTER HIS ALTER-EGO, THE "MAN OF THE HOUR"...
HOURMAN!
4

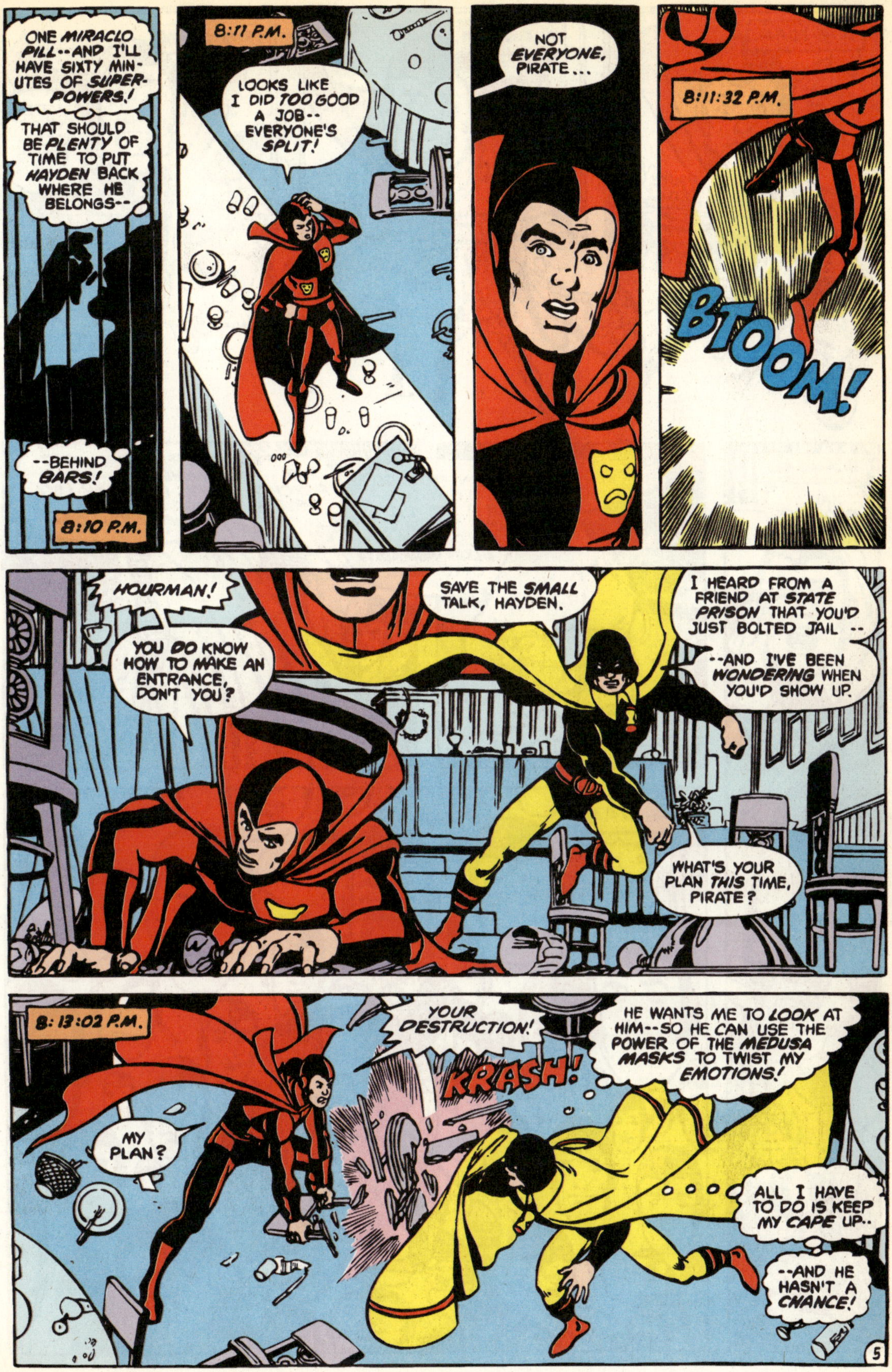
ONE MIRACLO PILL--AND I'LL HAVE SIXTY MINUTES OF SUPER-POWERS!
THAT SHOULD BE PLENTY OF TIME TO PUT HAYDEN BACK WHERE HE BELONGS--
--BEHIND BARS!
8:10 P.M.
8:11 P.M.
LOOKS LIKE I DID TOO GOOD A JOB--EVERYONE'S SPLIT!
NOT EVERYONE, PIRATE...
8:11:32 P.M.
BTOOM!
HOURMAN!
YOU DO KNOW HOW TO MAKE AN ENTRANCE, DON'T YOU?
SAVE THE SMALL TALK, HAYDEN.
I HEARD FROM A FRIEND AT STATE PRISON THAT YOU'D JUST BOLTED JAIL --
--AND I'VE BEEN WONDERING WHEN YOU'D SHOW UP.
WHAT'S YOUR PLAN THIS TIME, PIRATE?
8:13:02 P.M.
MY PLAN?
YOUR DESTRUCTION!
KRASH!
HE WANTS ME TO LOOK AT HIM--SO HE CAN USE THE POWER OF THE MEDUSA MASKS TO TWIST MY EMOTIONS!
ALL I HAVE TO DO IS KEEP MY CAPE UP..
--AND HE HASN'T A CHANCE!
5

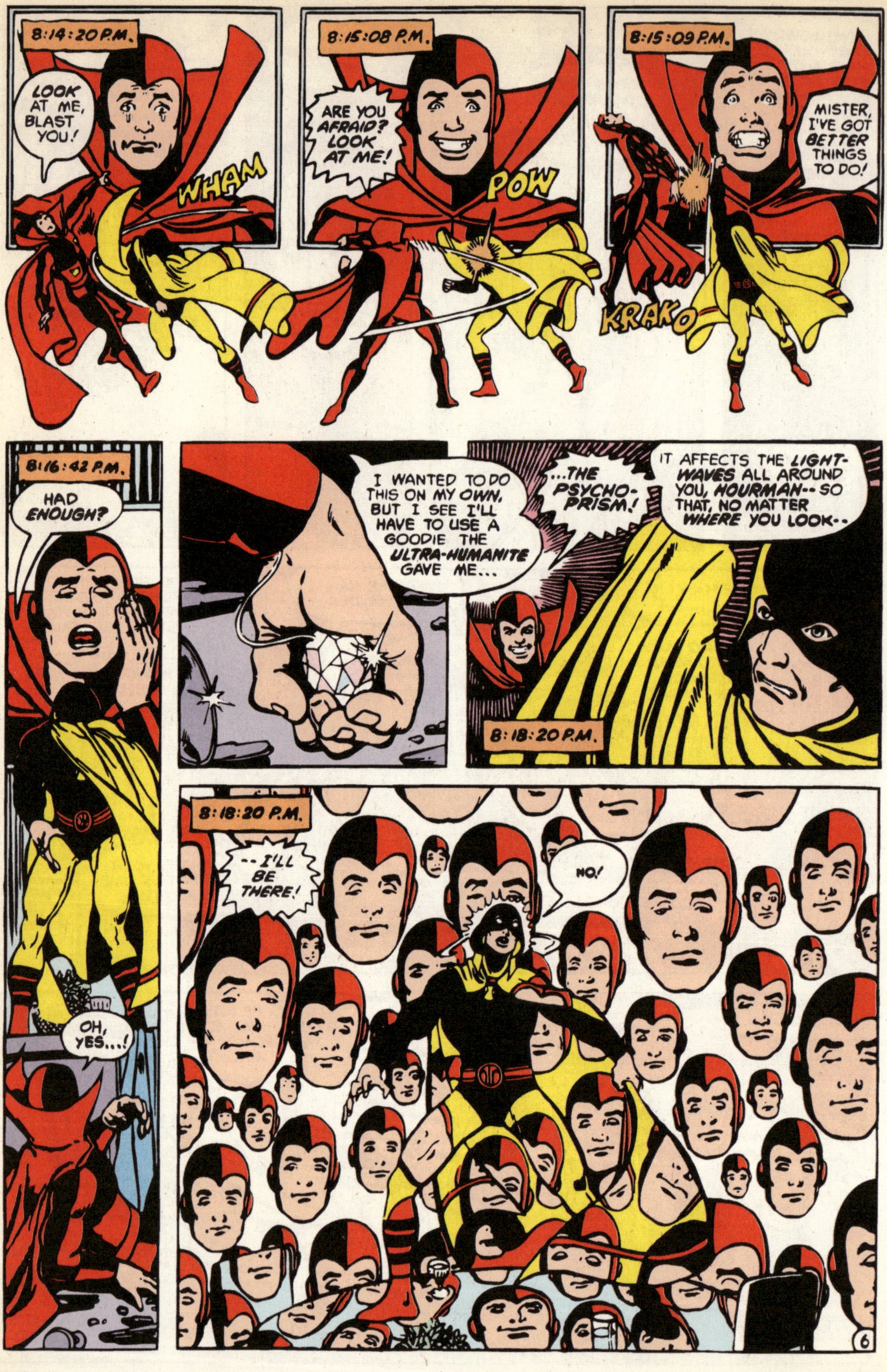
8:14:20 P.M.
LOOK AT ME, BLAST YOU!
WHAM
8:15:08 P.M.
ARE YOU AFRAID? LOOK AT ME!
POW
8:15:09 P.M.
MISTER, I'VE GOT BETTER THINGS TO DO!
KRAKO
8:16:42 P.M.
HAD ENOUGH?
OH, YES...!
I WANTED TO DO THIS ON MY OWN, BUT I SEE I'LL HAVE TO USE A GOODIE THE ULTRA-HUMANITE GAVE ME...
...THE PSYCHO-PRISM!
IT AFFECTS THE LIGHT-WAVES ALL AROUND YOU, HOURMAN-- SO THAT, NO MATTER WHERE YOU LOOK--
8:18:20 P.M.
8:18:20 P.M.
--I'LL BE THERE!
NO!
6

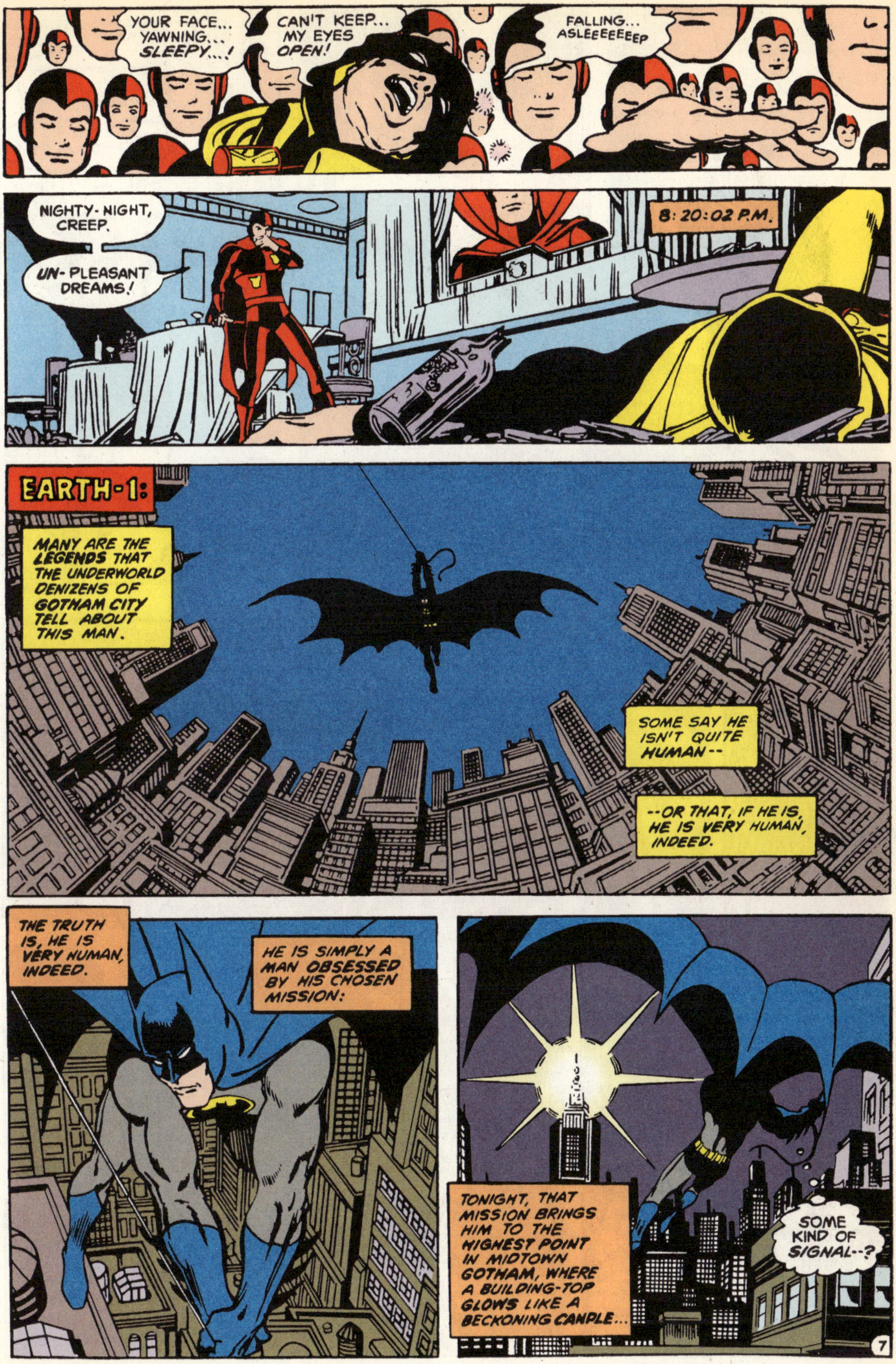
YOUR FACE... YAWNING... SLEEPY...!
CAN'T KEEP... MY EYES OPEN!
FALLING... ASLEEEEEEEP
NIGHTY-NIGHT, CREEP.
UN-PLEASANT DREAMS!
8:20:02 P.M.
EARTH-1:
MANY ARE THE LEGENDS THAT THE UNDERWORLD DENIZENS OF GOTHAM CITY TELL ABOUT THIS MAN.
SOME SAY HE ISN'T QUITE HUMAN--
--OR THAT, IF HE IS, HE IS VERY HUMAN, INDEED.
THE TRUTH IS, HE IS VERY HUMAN, INDEED.
HE IS SIMPLY A MAN OBSESSED BY HIS CHOSEN MISSION:
TONIGHT, THAT MISSION BRINGS HIM TO THE HIGHEST POINT IN MIDTOWN GOTHAM, WHERE A BUILDING-TOP GLOWS LIKE A BECKONING CANDLE...
SOME KIND OF SIGNAL--?
7

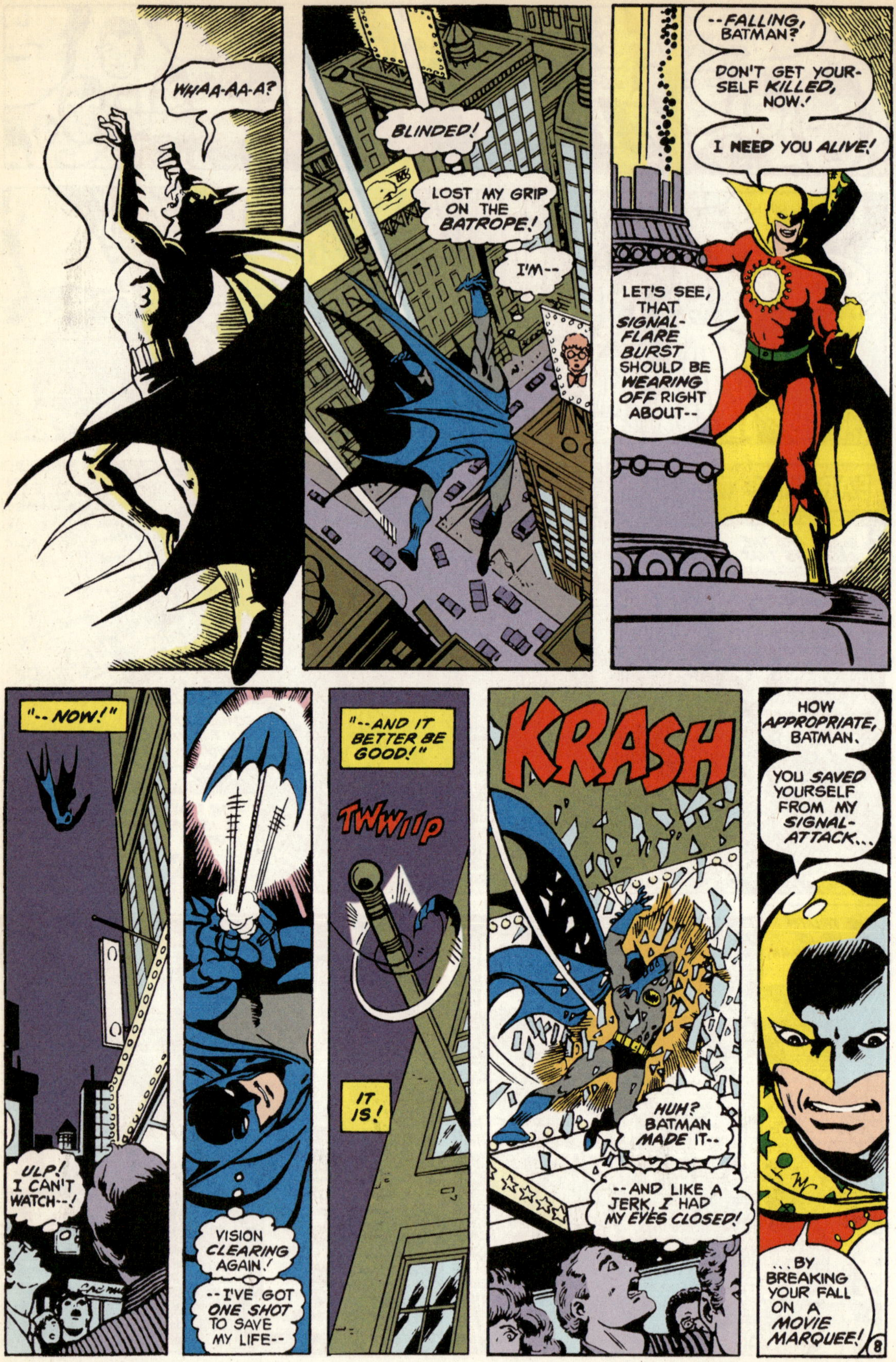

WHAA-AA-A?
BLINDED!
LOST MY GRIP ON THE BATROPE!
I'M--
--FALLING, BATMAN?
DON'T GET YOURSELF KILLED, NOW.!
I NEED YOU ALIVE!
LET'S SEE, THAT SIGNAL-FLARE BURST SHOULD BE WEARING OFF RIGHT ABOUT--
"--NOW!"
ULP! I CAN'T WATCH--!
VISION CLEARING AGAIN.!
--I'VE GOT ONE SHOT TO SAVE MY LIFE--
"--AND IT BETTER BE GOOD!"
TWWIIP
IT IS!
KRASH
HUH? BATMAN MADE IT--
--AND LIKE A JERK, I HAD MY EYES CLOSED!
HOW APPROPRIATE, BATMAN.
YOU SAVED YOURSELF FROM MY SIGNAL-ATTACK...
...BY BREAKING YOUR FALL ON A MOVIE MARQUEE!
8

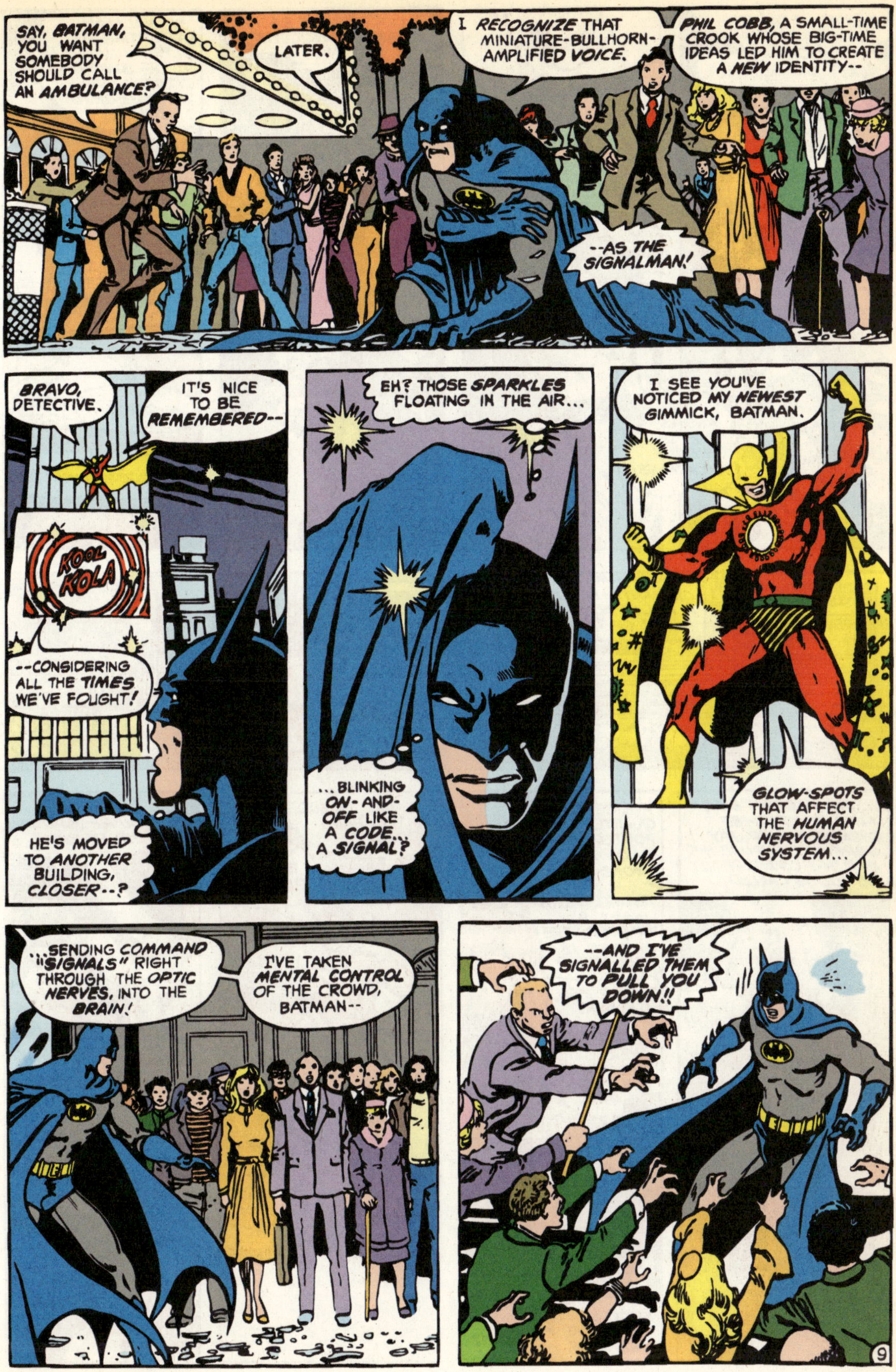
SAY, BATMAN, YOU WANT SOMEBODY SHOULD CALL AN AMBULANCE?
LATER.
I RECOGNIZE THAT MINIATURE-BULLHORN-AMPLIFIED VOICE.
PHIL COBB, A SMALL-TIME CROOK WHOSE BIG-TIME IDEAS LED HIM TO CREATE A NEW IDENTITY--
--AS THE SIGNALMAN!
BRAVO, DETECTIVE.
IT'S NICE TO BE REMEMBERED--
KOOL KOLA
--CONSIDERING ALL THE TIMES WE'VE FOUGHT!
HE'S MOVED TO ANOTHER BUILDING, CLOSER--?
EH? THOSE SPARKLES FLOATING IN THE AIR...
...BLINKING ON-AND-OFF LIKE A CODE... A SIGNAL?
I SEE YOU'VE NOTICED MY NEWEST GIMMICK, BATMAN.
GLOW-SPOTS THAT AFFECT THE HUMAN NERVOUS SYSTEM...
SENDING COMMAND "SIGNALS" RIGHT THROUGH THE OPTIC NERVES, INTO THE BRAIN!
I'VE TAKEN MENTAL CONTROL OF THE CROWD, BATMAN--
--AND I'VE SIGNALLED THEM TO PULL YOU DOWN!!
9

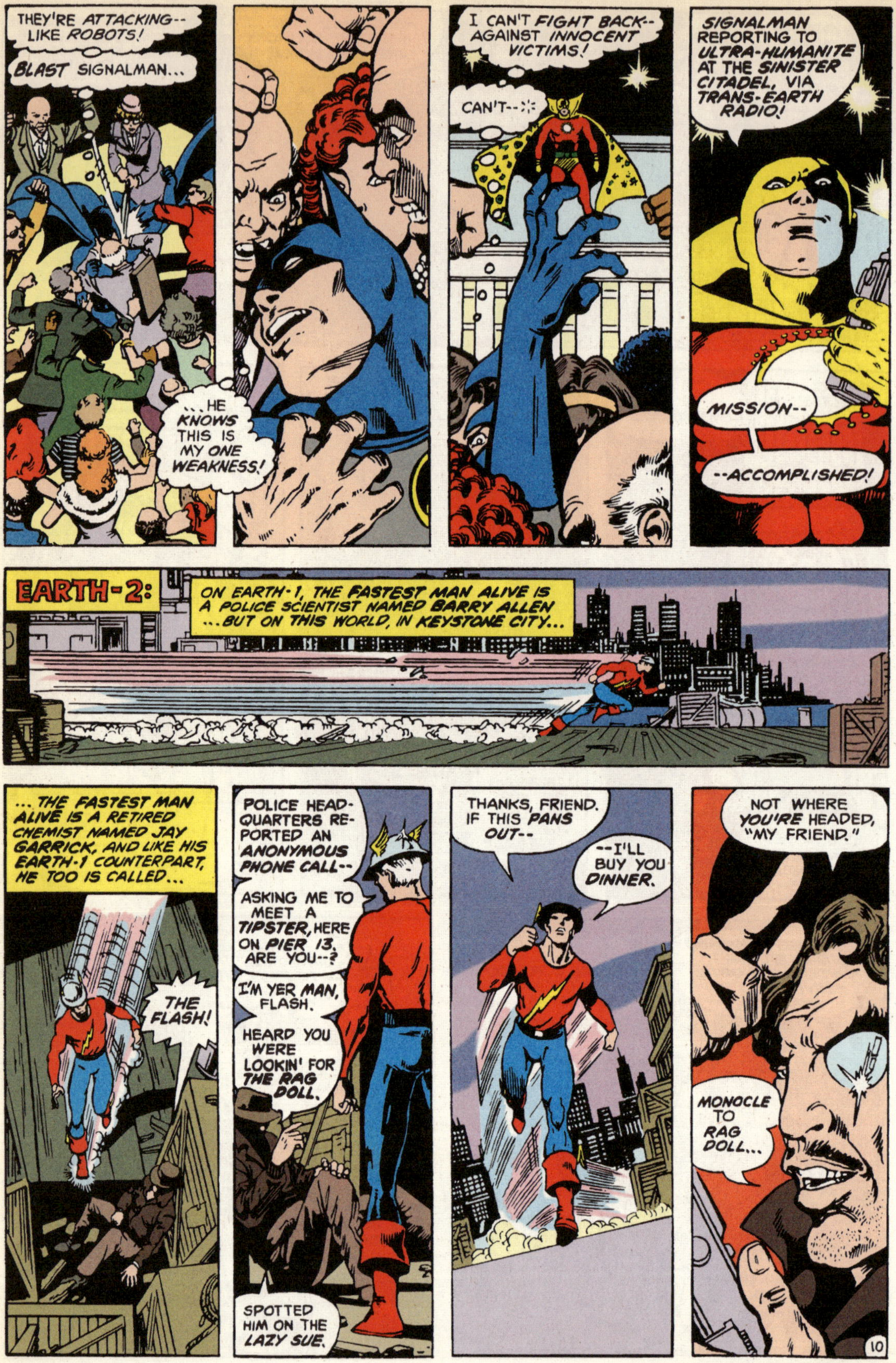
THEY'RE ATTACKING-- LIKE ROBOTS!
BLAST SIGNALMAN...
...HE KNOWS THIS IS MY ONE WEAKNESS!
I CAN'T FIGHT BACK-- AGAINST INNOCENT VICTIMS!
CAN'T--
SIGNALMAN REPORTING TO ULTRA-HUMANITE AT THE SINISTER CITADEL, VIA TRANS-EARTH RADIO!
MISSION--
--ACCOMPLISHED!
EARTH-2:
ON EARTH-1, THE FASTEST MAN ALIVE IS A POLICE SCIENTIST NAMED BARRY ALLEN ...BUT ON THIS WORLD, IN KEYSTONE CITY...
...THE FASTEST MAN ALIVE IS A RETIRED CHEMIST NAMED JAY GARRICK, AND LIKE HIS EARTH-1 COUNTERPART, HE TOO IS CALLED...
THE FLASH!
POLICE HEAD-QUARTERS RE-PORTED AN ANONYMOUS PHONE CALL--
ASKING ME TO MEET A TIPSTER, HERE ON PIER 13. ARE YOU--?
I'M YER MAN, FLASH.
HEARD YOU WERE LOOKIN' FOR THE RAG DOLL.
SPOTTED HIM ON THE LAZY SUE.
THANKS, FRIEND. IF THIS PANS OUT--
--I'LL BUY YOU DINNER.
NOT WHERE YOU'RE HEADED, "MY FRIEND."
MONOCLE TO RAG DOLL...
10

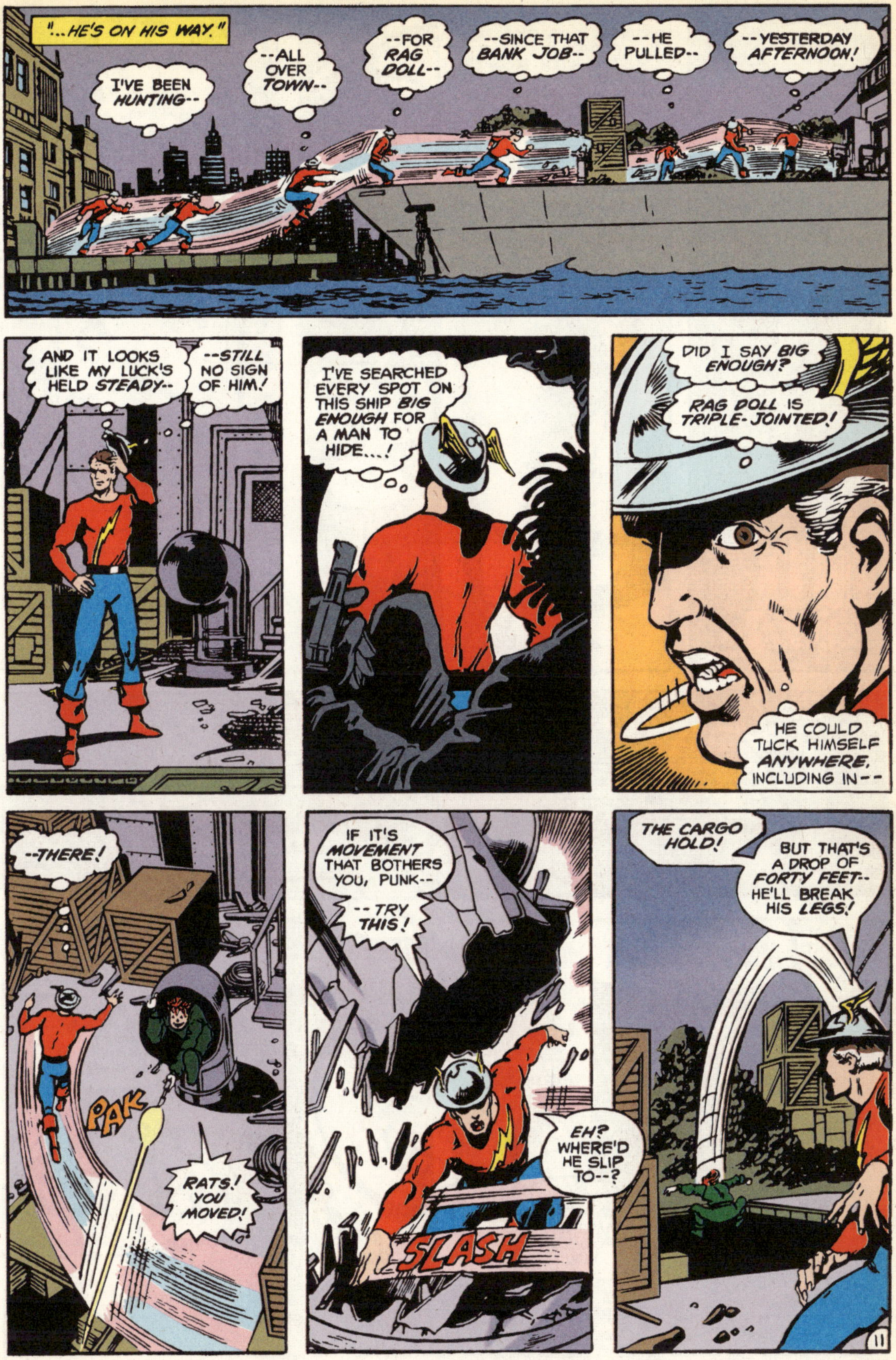
"...HE'S ON HIS WAY."
I'VE BEEN HUNTING--
--ALL OVER TOWN--
--FOR RAG DOLL--
--SINCE THAT BANK JOB--
--HE PULLED--
--YESTERDAY AFTERNOON!
AND IT LOOKS LIKE MY LUCK'S HELD STEADY--
--STILL NO SIGN OF HIM!
I'VE SEARCHED EVERY SPOT ON THIS SHIP BIG ENOUGH FOR A MAN TO HIDE...!
DID I SAY BIG ENOUGH?
RAG DOLL IS TRIPLE-JOINTED!
HE COULD TUCK HIMSELF ANYWHERE, INCLUDING IN--
--THERE!
PAK
RATS! YOU MOVED!
IF IT'S MOVEMENT THAT BOTHERS YOU, PUNK--
--TRY THIS!
EH? WHERE'D HE SLIP TO--?
SLASH
THE CARGO HOLD!
BUT THAT'S A DROP OF FORTY FEET-- HE'LL BREAK HIS LEGS!
11

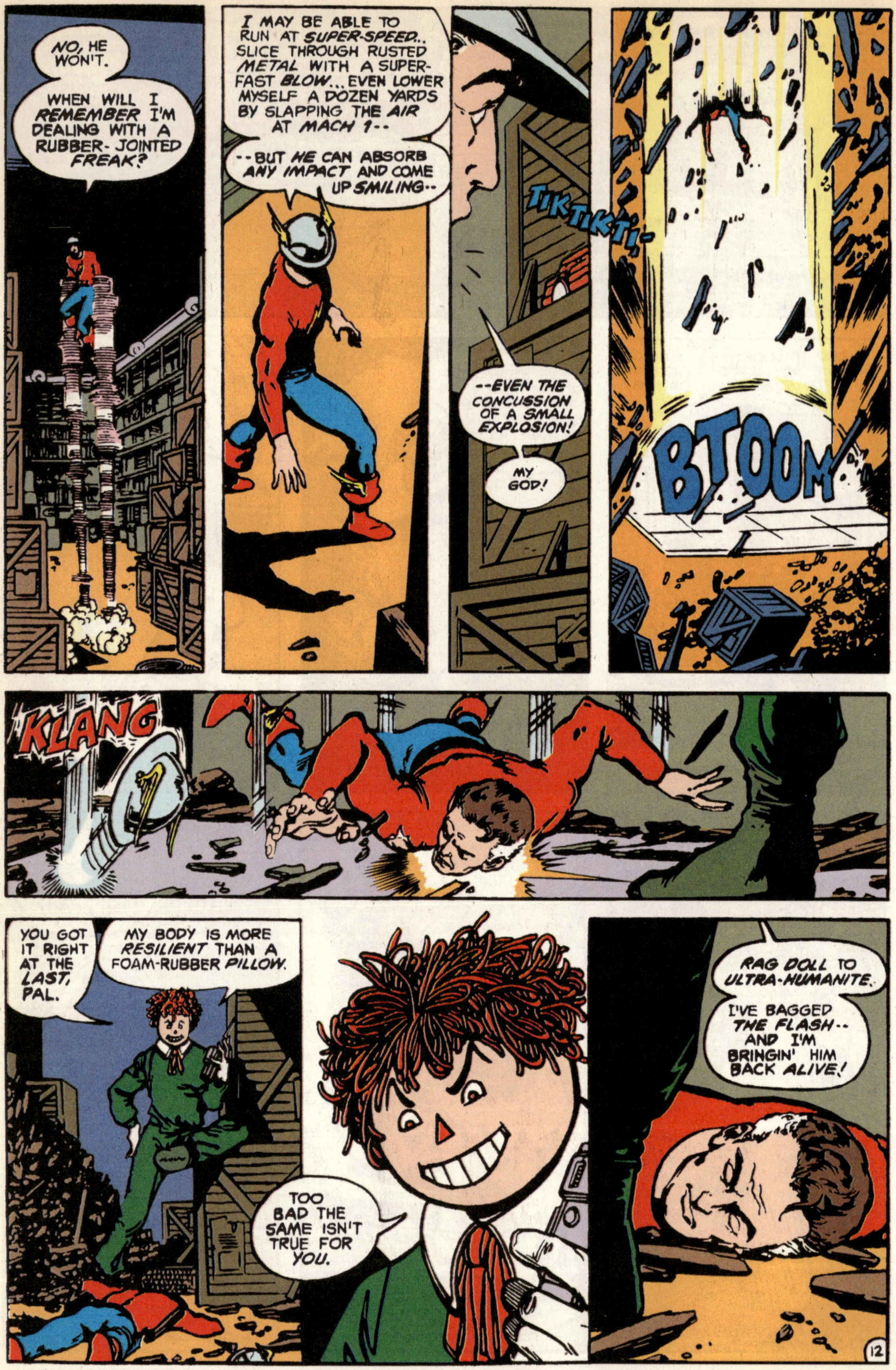
NO, HE WON'T.
WHEN WILL I REMEMBER I'M DEALING WITH A RUBBER-JOINTED FREAK?
I MAY BE ABLE TO RUN AT SUPER-SPEED.. SLICE THROUGH RUSTED METAL WITH A SUPER-FAST BLOW... EVEN LOWER MYSELF A DOZEN YARDS BY SLAPPING THE AIR AT MACH 1--
--BUT HE CAN ABSORB ANY IMPACT AND COME UP SMILING--
TIKTIKTI-
--EVEN THE CONCUSSION OF A SMALL EXPLOSION!
MY GOD!
BTOOM
KLANG
YOU GOT IT RIGHT AT THE LAST, PAL.
MY BODY IS MORE RESILIENT THAN A FOAM-RUBBER PILLOW.
TOO BAD THE SAME ISN'T TRUE FOR YOU.
RAG DOLL TO ULTRA-HUMANITE.
I'VE BAGGED THE FLASH-- AND I'M BRINGIN' HIM BACK ALIVE!
12

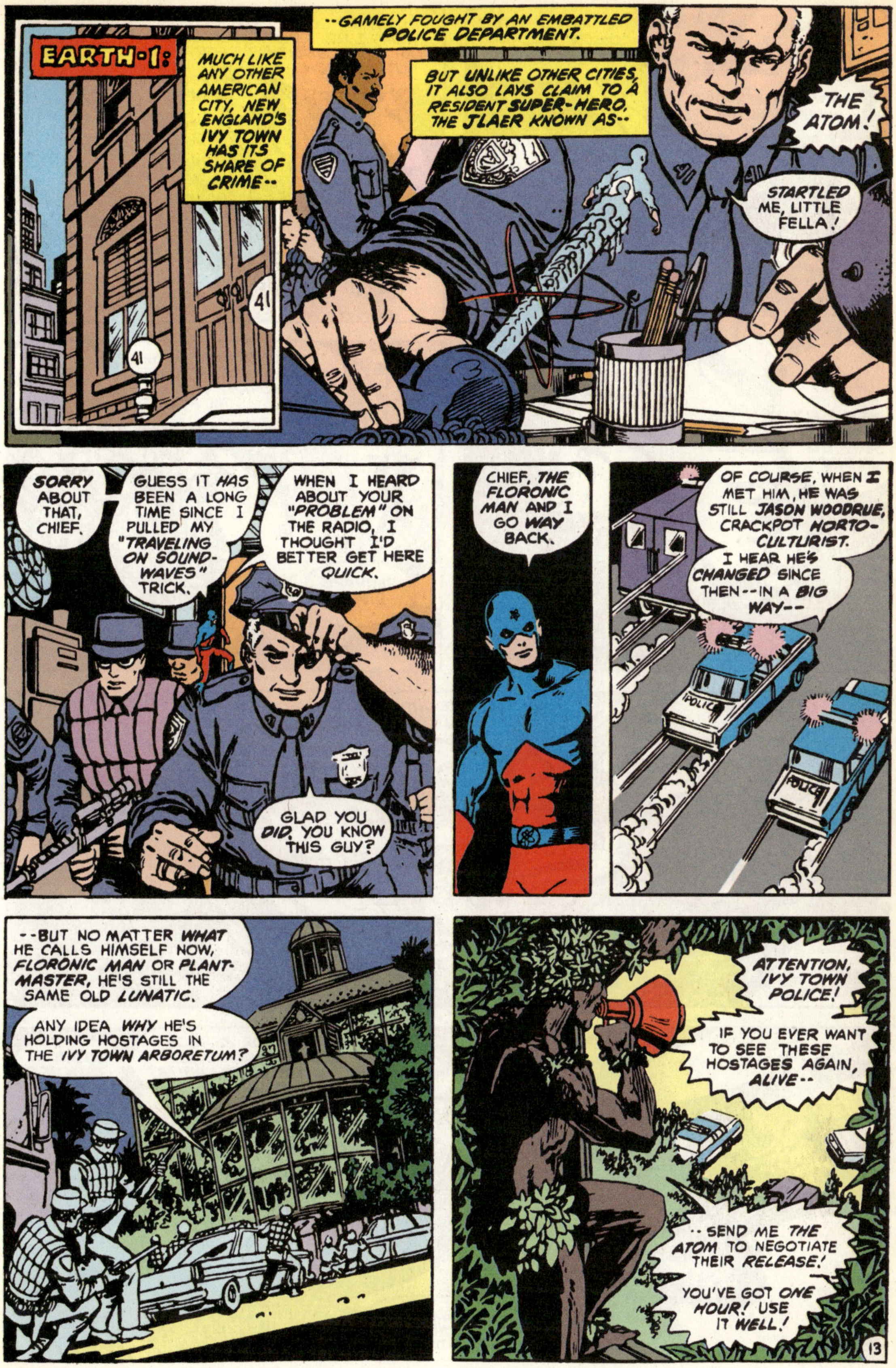
EARTH-1:
MUCH LIKE ANY OTHER AMERICAN CITY, NEW ENGLAND'S IVY TOWN HAS ITS SHARE OF CRIME--
--GAMELY FOUGHT BY AN EMBATTLED POLICE DEPARTMENT.
BUT UNLIKE OTHER CITIES, IT ALSO LAYS CLAIM TO A RESIDENT SUPER-HERO, THE JLAER KNOWN AS--
THE ATOM!
STARTLED ME, LITTLE FELLA!
41
41
SORRY ABOUT THAT, CHIEF.
GUESS IT HAS BEEN A LONG TIME SINCE I PULLED MY "TRAVELING ON SOUND-WAVES" TRICK.
WHEN I HEARD ABOUT YOUR "PROBLEM" ON THE RADIO, I THOUGHT I'D BETTER GET HERE QUICK.
GLAD YOU DID. YOU KNOW THIS GUY?
CHIEF, THE FLORONIC MAN AND I GO WAY BACK.
OF COURSE, WHEN I MET HIM, HE WAS STILL JASON WOODRUE, CRACKPOT HORTO-CULTURIST.
I HEAR HE'S CHANGED SINCE THEN--IN A BIG WAY--
POLICE
POLICE
--BUT NO MATTER WHAT HE CALLS HIMSELF NOW, FLORONIC MAN OR PLANT-MASTER, HE'S STILL THE SAME OLD LUNATIC.
ANY IDEA WHY HE'S HOLDING HOSTAGES IN THE IVY TOWN ARBORETUM?
ATTENTION, IVY TOWN POLICE!
IF YOU EVER WANT TO SEE THESE HOSTAGES AGAIN, ALIVE--
..SEND ME THE ATOM TO NEGOTIATE THEIR RELEASE!
YOU'VE GOT ONE HOUR! USE IT WELL!
13

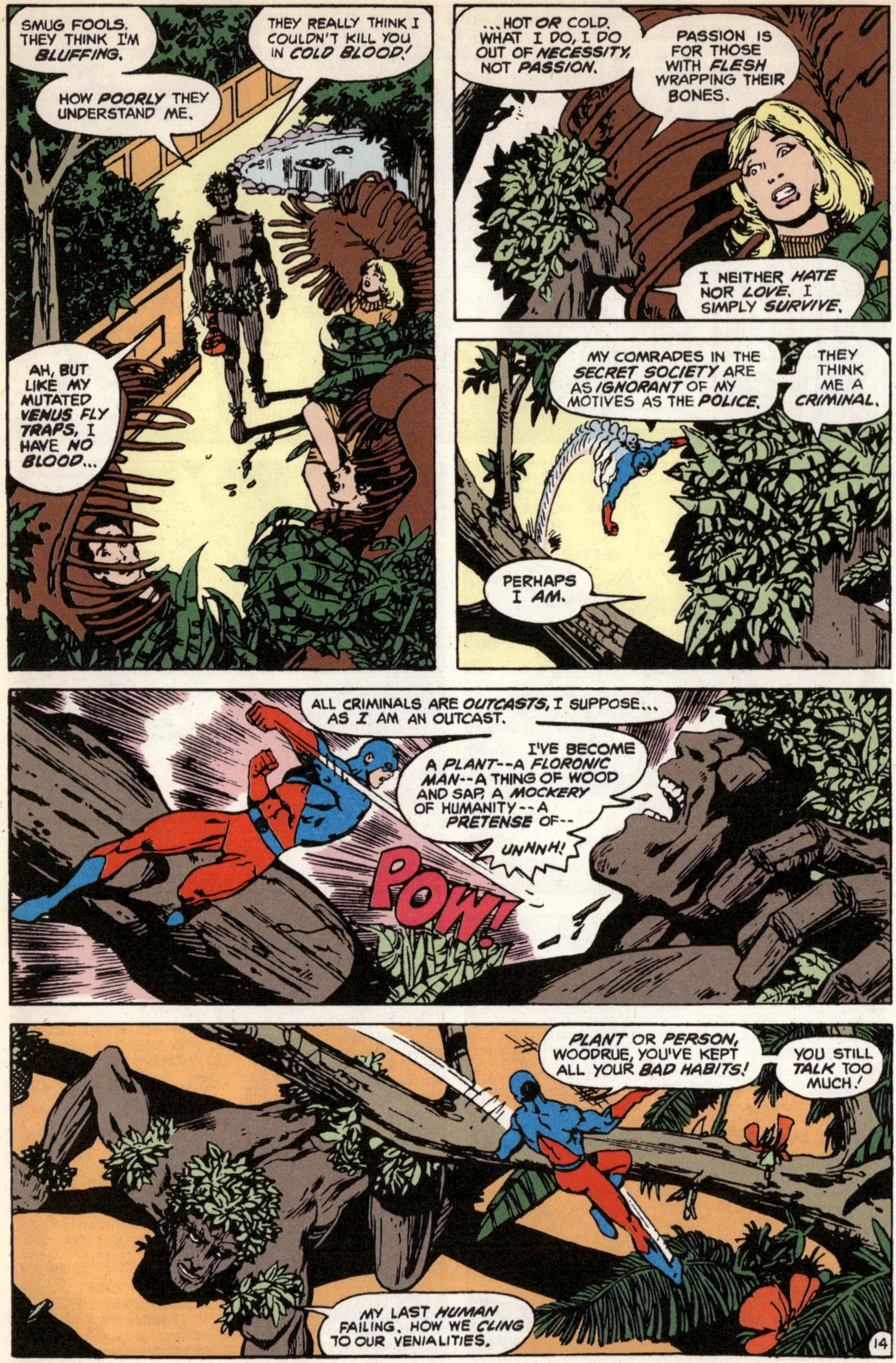
SMUG FOOLS. THEY THINK I'M BLUFFING.
HOW POORLY THEY UNDERSTAND ME.
THEY REALLY THINK I COULDN'T KILL YOU IN COLD BLOOD!
AH, BUT LIKE MY MUTATED VENUS FLY TRAPS, I HAVE NO BLOOD...
...HOT OR COLD. WHAT I DO, I DO OUT OF NECESSITY, NOT PASSION.
PASSION IS FOR THOSE WITH FLESH WRAPPING THEIR BONES.
I NEITHER HATE NOR LOVE. I SIMPLY SURVIVE.
MY COMRADES IN THE SECRET SOCIETY ARE AS IGNORANT OF MY MOTIVES AS THE POLICE.
THEY THINK ME A CRIMINAL.
PERHAPS I AM.
ALL CRIMINALS ARE OUTCASTS, I SUPPOSE... AS I AM AN OUTCAST.
I'VE BECOME A PLANT--A FLORONIC MAN--A THING OF WOOD AND SAP, A MOCKERY OF HUMANITY--A PRETENSE OF--
UNNNH!
POW!
PLANT OR PERSON, WOODRUE, YOU'VE KEPT ALL YOUR BAD HABITS!
YOU STILL TALK TOO MUCH!
MY LAST HUMAN FAILING. HOW WE CLING TO OUR VENIALITIES.
14

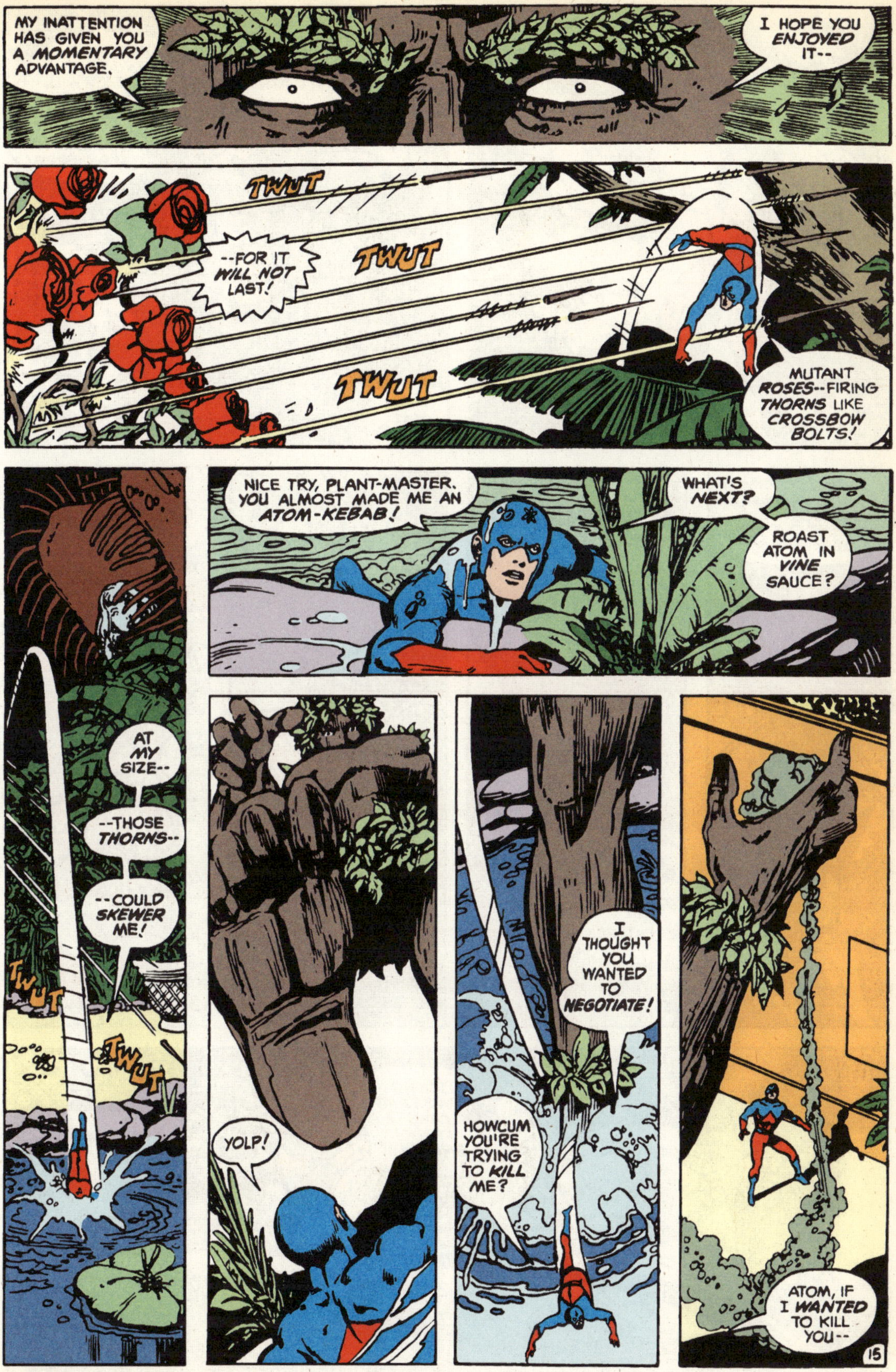
MY INATTENTION HAS GIVEN YOU A MOMENTARY ADVANTAGE.
I HOPE YOU ENJOYED IT--
TWUT
--FOR IT WILL NOT LAST!
TWUT
TWUT
MUTANT ROSES--FIRING THORNS LIKE CROSSBOW BOLTS!
AT MY SIZE--
--THOSE THORNS--
--COULD SKEWER ME!
TWUT
TWUT
NICE TRY, PLANT-MASTER. YOU ALMOST MADE ME AN ATOM-KEBAB!
WHAT'S NEXT?
ROAST ATOM IN VINE SAUCE?
YOLP!
I THOUGHT YOU WANTED TO NEGOTIATE!
HOWCUM YOU'RE TRYING TO KILL ME?
ATOM, IF I WANTED TO KILL YOU--
15

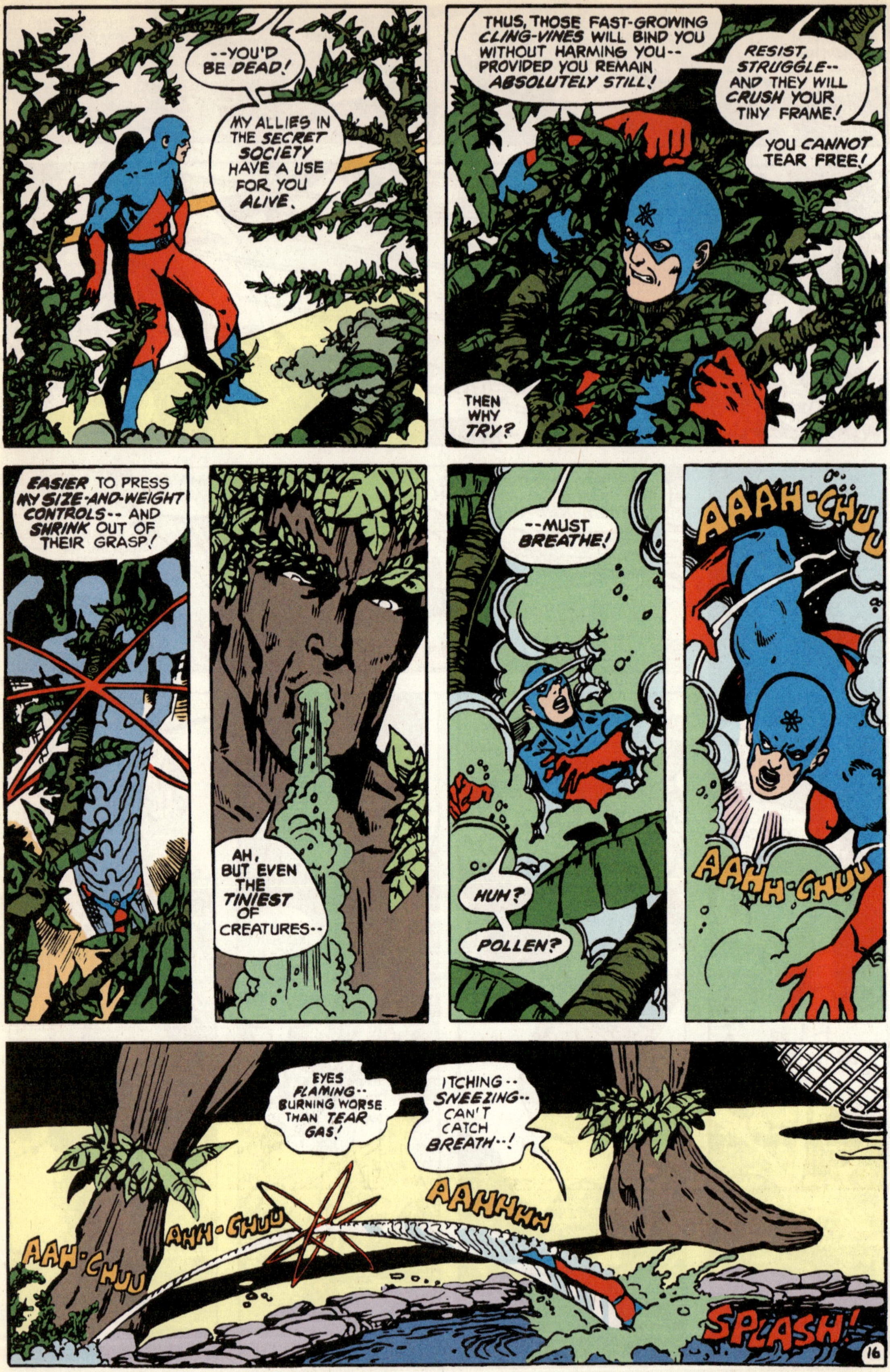

--YOU'D BE DEAD!
MY ALLIES IN THE SECRET SOCIETY HAVE A USE FOR YOU ALIVE.
THUS, THOSE FAST-GROWING CLING-VINES WILL BIND YOU WITHOUT HARMING YOU-- PROVIDED YOU REMAIN ABSOLUTELY STILL!
RESIST, STRUGGLE-- AND THEY WILL CRUSH YOUR TINY FRAME!
YOU CANNOT TEAR FREE!
THEN WHY TRY?
EASIER TO PRESS MY SIZE-AND-WEIGHT CONTROLS-- AND SHRINK OUT OF THEIR GRASP!
AH, BUT EVEN THE TINIEST OF CREATURES--
--MUST BREATHE!
HUH?
POLLEN?
AAAH-CHUU
AAHH-CHUU
EYES FLAMING-- BURNING WORSE THAN TEAR GAS!
ITCHING-- SNEEZING-- CAN'T CATCH BREATH--!
AAHHHH
AAH-CHUU
AHH-CHUU
SPLASH!
16

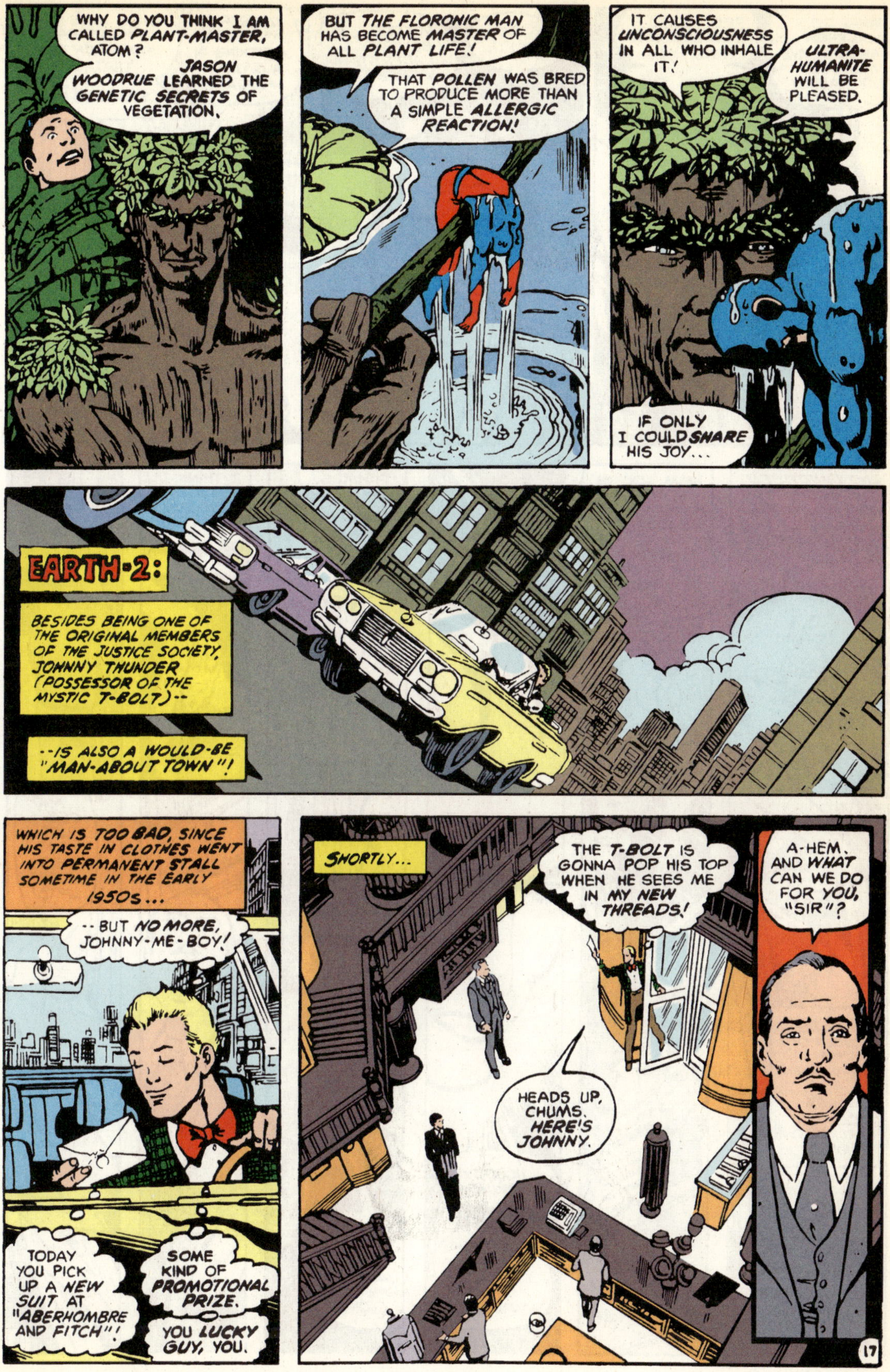
WHY DO YOU THINK I AM CALLED PLANT-MASTER, ATOM?
JASON WOODRUE LEARNED THE GENETIC SECRETS OF VEGETATION.
BUT THE FLORONIC MAN HAS BECOME MASTER OF ALL PLANT LIFE!
THAT POLLEN WAS BRED TO PRODUCE MORE THAN A SIMPLE ALLERGIC REACTION!
IT CAUSES UNCONSCIOUSNESS IN ALL WHO INHALE IT!
ULTRA-HUMANITE WILL BE PLEASED.
IF ONLY I COULD SHARE HIS JOY...
EARTH-2:
BESIDES BEING ONE OF THE ORIGINAL MEMBERS OF THE JUSTICE SOCIETY, JOHNNY THUNDER (POSSESSOR OF THE MYSTIC T-BOLT)--
--IS ALSO A WOULD-BE "MAN-ABOUT TOWN"!
WHICH IS TOO BAD, SINCE HIS TASTE IN CLOTHES WENT INTO PERMANENT STALL SOMETIME IN THE EARLY 1950s...
--BUT NO MORE, JOHNNY-ME-BOY!
TODAY YOU PICK UP A NEW SUIT AT "ABERHOMBRE AND FITCH"!
SOME KIND OF PROMOTIONAL PRIZE.
YOU LUCKY GUY, YOU.
SHORTLY...
THE T-BOLT IS GONNA POP HIS TOP WHEN HE SEES ME IN MY NEW THREADS!
HEADS UP, CHUMS. HERE'S JOHNNY.
A-HEM. AND WHAT CAN WE DO FOR YOU, "SIR"?
17

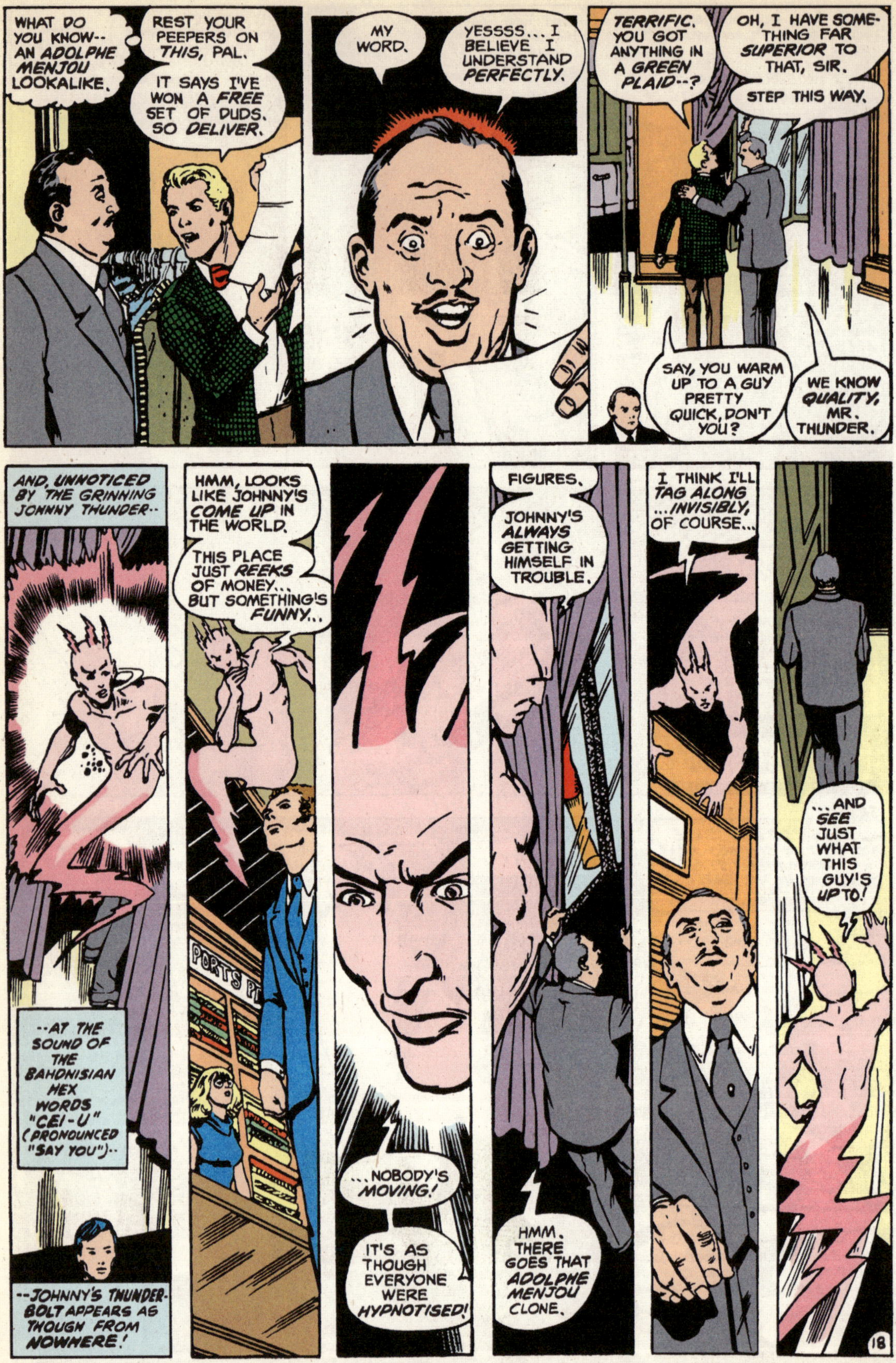
WHAT DO YOU KNOW-- AN ADOLPHE MENJOU LOOKALIKE.
REST YOUR PEEPERS ON THIS, PAL.
IT SAYS I'VE WON A FREE SET OF DUDS. SO DELIVER.
MY WORD.
YESSSS... I BELIEVE I UNDERSTAND PERFECTLY.
TERRIFIC. YOU GOT ANYTHING IN A GREEN PLAID--?
OH, I HAVE SOMETHING FAR SUPERIOR TO THAT, SIR.
STEP THIS WAY.
SAY, YOU WARM UP TO A GUY PRETTY QUICK, DON'T YOU?
WE KNOW QUALITY, MR. THUNDER.
AND, UNNOTICED BY THE GRINNING JOHNNY THUNDER--
--AT THE SOUND OF THE BAHDNISIAN HEX WORDS "CEI-U" (PRONOUNCED "SAY YOU")--
--JOHNNY'S THUNDERBOLT APPEARS AS THOUGH FROM NOWHERE!
HMM, LOOKS LIKE JOHNNY'S COME UP IN THE WORLD.
THIS PLACE JUST REEKS OF MONEY... BUT SOMETHING'S FUNNY...
...NOBODY'S MOVING!
IT'S AS THOUGH EVERYONE WERE HYPNOTISED!
FIGURES.
JOHNNY'S ALWAYS GETTING HIMSELF IN TROUBLE.
HMM. THERE GOES THAT ADOLPHE MENJOU CLONE.
I THINK I'LL TAG ALONG ...INVISIBLY, OF COURSE...
...AND SEE JUST WHAT THIS GUY'S UP TO!
18

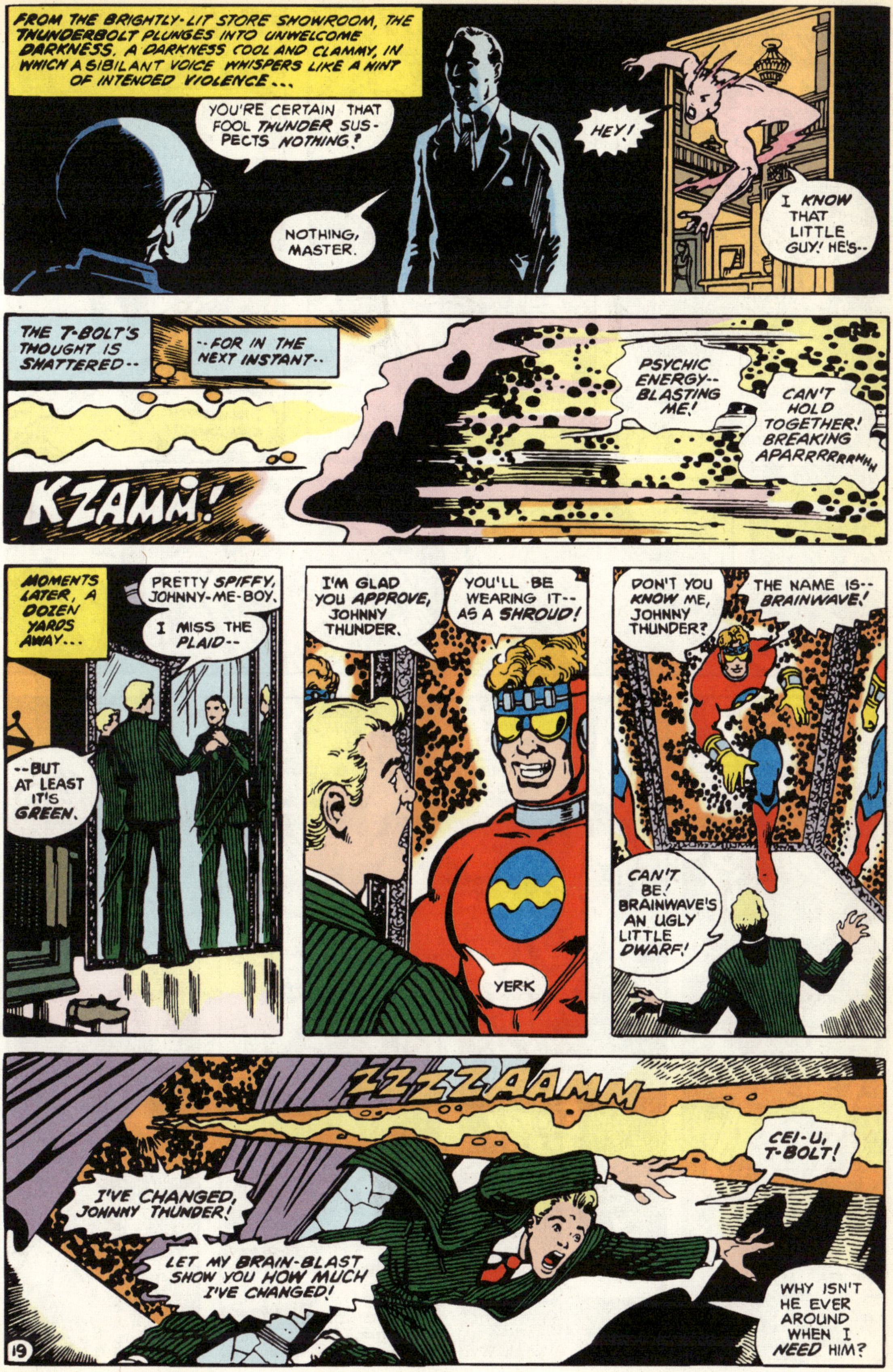
FROM THE BRIGHTLY-LIT STORE SHOWROOM, THE THUNDERBOLT PLUNGES INTO UNWELCOME DARKNESS. A DARKNESS COOL AND CLAMMY, IN WHICH A SIBILANT VOICE WHISPERS LIKE A HINT OF INTENDED VIOLENCE...
YOU'RE CERTAIN THAT FOOL THUNDER SUSPECTS NOTHING?
NOTHING, MASTER.
HEY!
I KNOW THAT LITTLE GUY! HE'S--
THE T-BOLT'S THOUGHT IS SHATTERED--
--FOR IN THE NEXT INSTANT--
KZAMM!
PSYCHIC ENERGY--BLASTING ME!
CAN'T HOLD TOGETHER! BREAKING APARRRRRRMHH
MOMENTS LATER, A DOZEN YARDS AWAY...
PRETTY SPIFFY, JOHNNY-ME-BOY.
I MISS THE PLAID--
--BUT AT LEAST IT'S GREEN.
I'M GLAD YOU APPROVE, JOHNNY THUNDER.
YOU'LL BE WEARING IT--AS A SHROUD!
YERK
DON'T YOU KNOW ME, JOHNNY THUNDER?
THE NAME IS--BRAINWAVE!
CAN'T BE! BRAINWAVE'S AN UGLY LITTLE DWARF!
ZZZZAAMM
I'VE CHANGED, JOHNNY THUNDER!
LET MY BRAIN-BLAST SHOW YOU HOW MUCH I'VE CHANGED!
CEI-U, T-BOLT!
WHY ISN'T HE EVER AROUND WHEN I NEED HIM?
19

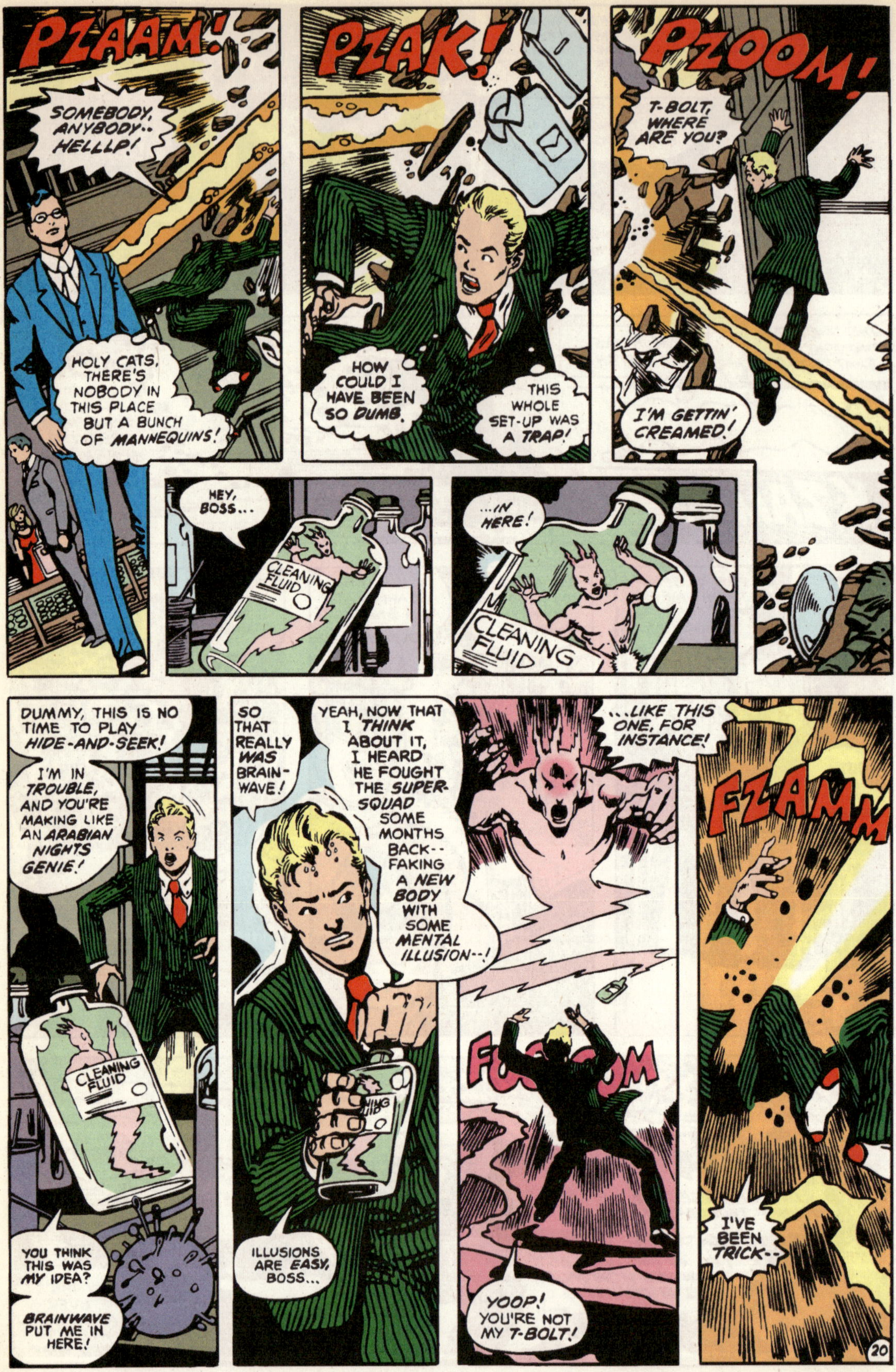
PZAAM!
SOMEBODY, ANYBODY-- HELLLP!
HOLY CATS, THERE'S NOBODY IN THIS PLACE BUT A BUNCH OF MANNEQUINS!
PZAK!
HOW COULD I HAVE BEEN SO DUMB.
THIS WHOLE SET-UP WAS A TRAP!
PZOOM!
T-BOLT, WHERE ARE YOU?
I'M GETTIN' CREAMED!
HEY, BOSS...
CLEANING FLUID
...IN HERE!
CLEANING FLUID
DUMMY, THIS IS NO TIME TO PLAY HIDE-AND-SEEK!
I'M IN TROUBLE, AND YOU'RE MAKING LIKE AN ARABIAN NIGHTS GENIE!
CLEANING FLUID
YOU THINK THIS WAS MY IDEA?
BRAINWAVE PUT ME IN HERE!
SO THAT REALLY WAS BRAIN-WAVE!
YEAH, NOW THAT I THINK ABOUT IT, I HEARD HE FOUGHT THE SUPER-SQUAD SOME MONTHS BACK-- FAKING A NEW BODY WITH SOME MENTAL ILLUSION--!
ILLUSIONS ARE EASY, BOSS...
...LIKE THIS ONE, FOR INSTANCE!
YOOP! YOU'RE NOT MY T-BOLT!
FZAMM
I'VE BEEN TRICK--
20

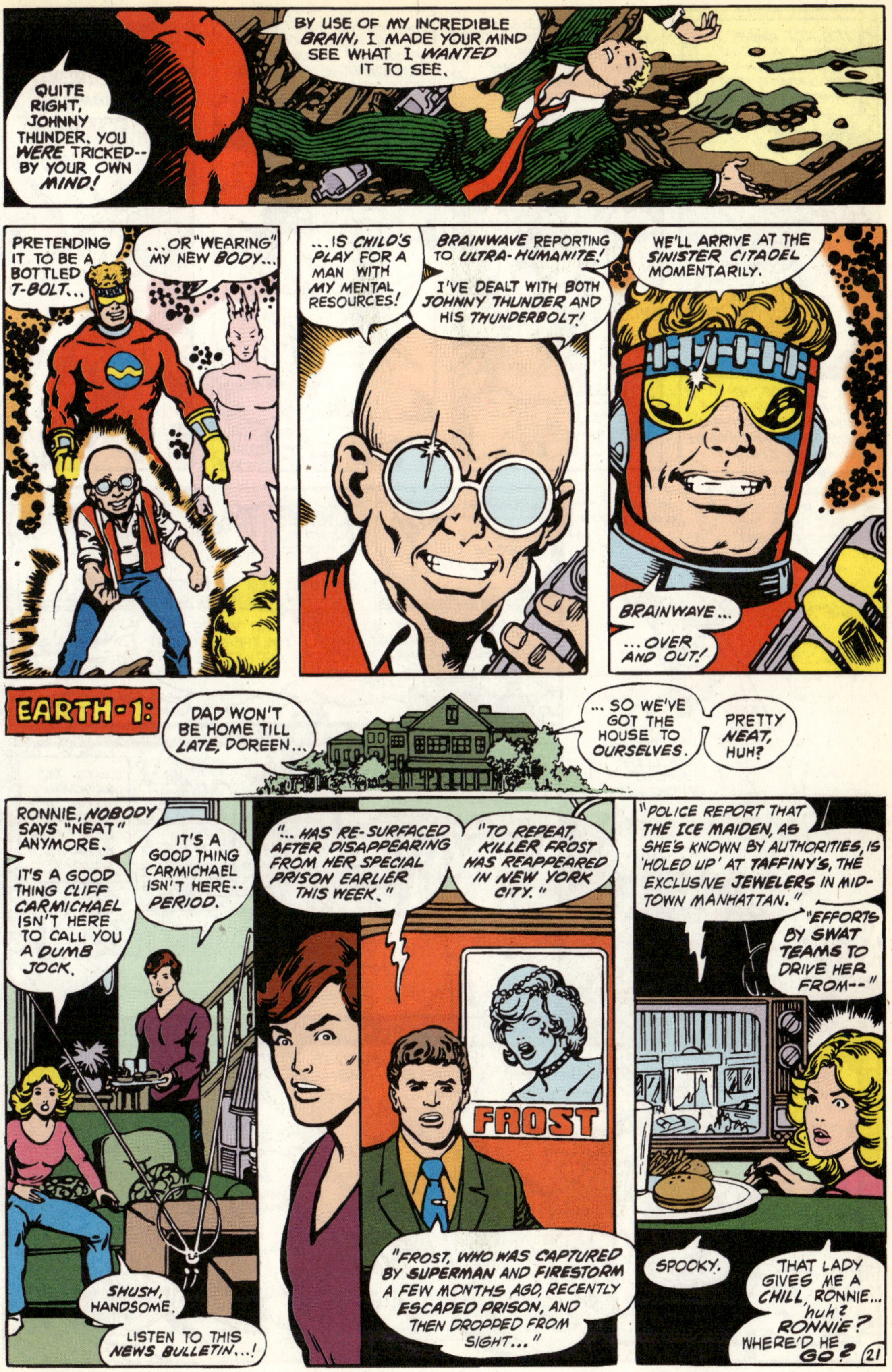
BY USE OF MY INCREDIBLE BRAIN, I MADE YOUR MIND SEE WHAT I WANTED IT TO SEE.
QUITE RIGHT, JOHNNY THUNDER. YOU WERE TRICKED-- BY YOUR OWN MIND!
PRETENDING IT TO BE A BOTTLED T-BOLT...
...OR "WEARING" MY NEW BODY...
...IS CHILD'S PLAY FOR A MAN WITH MY MENTAL RESOURCES!
BRAINWAVE REPORTING TO ULTRA-HUMANITE!
I'VE DEALT WITH BOTH JOHNNY THUNDER AND HIS THUNDERBOLT!
WE'LL ARRIVE AT THE SINISTER CITADEL MOMENTARILY.
BRAINWAVE...
...OVER AND OUT!
EARTH-1:
DAD WON'T BE HOME TILL LATE, DOREEN...
...SO WE'VE GOT THE HOUSE TO OURSELVES.
PRETTY NEAT, HUH?
RONNIE, NOBODY SAYS "NEAT" ANYMORE.
IT'S A GOOD THING CLIFF CARMICHAEL ISN'T HERE TO CALL YOU A DUMB JOCK.
IT'S A GOOD THING CARMICHAEL ISN'T HERE-- PERIOD.
SHUSH, HANDSOME.
LISTEN TO THIS NEWS BULLETIN...!
"...HAS RE-SURFACED AFTER DISAPPEARING FROM HER SPECIAL PRISON EARLIER THIS WEEK."
"TO REPEAT, KILLER FROST HAS REAPPEARED IN NEW YORK CITY."
FROST
"FROST, WHO WAS CAPTURED BY SUPERMAN AND FIRESTORM A FEW MONTHS AGO, RECENTLY ESCAPED PRISON, AND THEN DROPPED FROM SIGHT..."
"POLICE REPORT THAT THE ICE MAIDEN, AS SHE'S KNOWN BY AUTHORITIES, IS 'HOLED UP' AT TAFFINY'S, THE EXCLUSIVE JEWELERS IN MID-TOWN MANHATTAN."
"EFFORTS BY SWAT TEAMS TO DRIVE HER FROM--"
SPOOKY.
THAT LADY GIVES ME A CHILL, RONNIE... huh? RONNIE? WHERE'D HE GO?
21

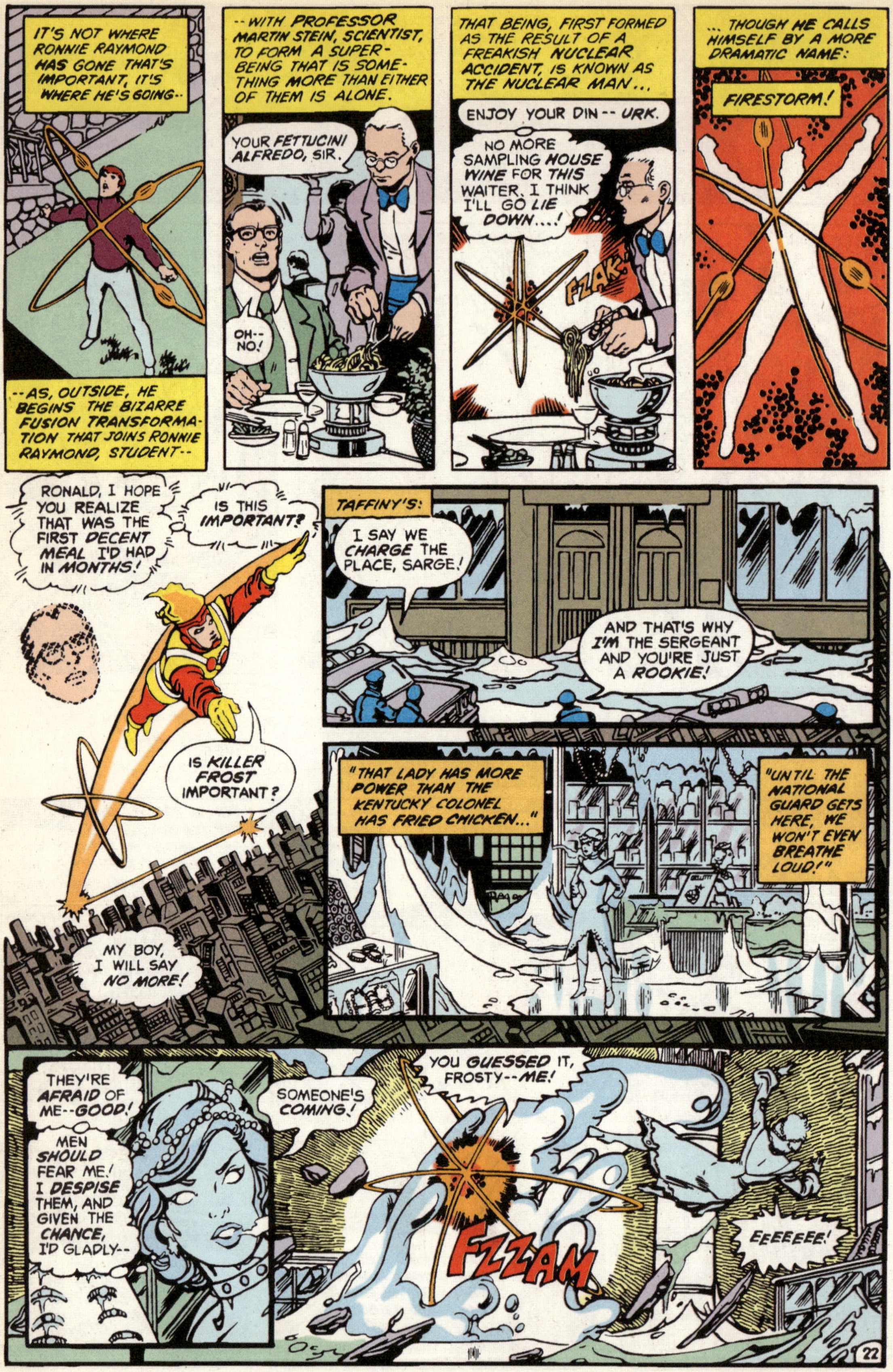
IT'S NOT WHERE RONNIE RAYMOND HAS GONE THAT'S IMPORTANT, IT'S WHERE HE'S GOING--
--AS, OUTSIDE, HE BEGINS THE BIZARRE FUSION TRANSFORMATION THAT JOINS RONNIE RAYMOND, STUDENT--
--WITH PROFESSOR MARTIN STEIN, SCIENTIST, TO FORM A SUPER-BEING THAT IS SOMETHING MORE THAN EITHER OF THEM IS ALONE.
YOUR FETTUCINI ALFREDO, SIR.
OH--NO!
THAT BEING, FIRST FORMED AS THE RESULT OF A FREAKISH NUCLEAR ACCIDENT, IS KNOWN AS THE NUCLEAR MAN...
ENJOY YOUR DIN--URK.
NO MORE SAMPLING HOUSE WINE FOR THIS WAITER, I THINK I'LL GO LIE DOWN...!
FZAK!
...THOUGH HE CALLS HIMSELF BY A MORE DRAMATIC NAME:
FIRESTORM!
RONALD, I HOPE YOU REALIZE THAT WAS THE FIRST DECENT MEAL I'D HAD IN MONTHS!
IS THIS IMPORTANT?
IS KILLER FROST IMPORTANT?
MY BOY, I WILL SAY NO MORE!
TAFFINY'S:
I SAY WE CHARGE THE PLACE, SARGE!
AND THAT'S WHY I'M THE SERGEANT AND YOU'RE JUST A ROOKIE!
"THAT LADY HAS MORE POWER THAN THE KENTUCKY COLONEL HAS FRIED CHICKEN..."
"UNTIL THE NATIONAL GUARD GETS HERE, WE WON'T EVEN BREATHE LOUD!"
THEY'RE AFRAID OF ME--GOOD!
MEN SHOULD FEAR ME! I DESPISE THEM, AND GIVEN THE CHANCE, I'D GLADLY--
SOMEONE'S COMING!
YOU GUESSED IT, FROSTY--ME!
FZZAM
EEEEEEE!
22

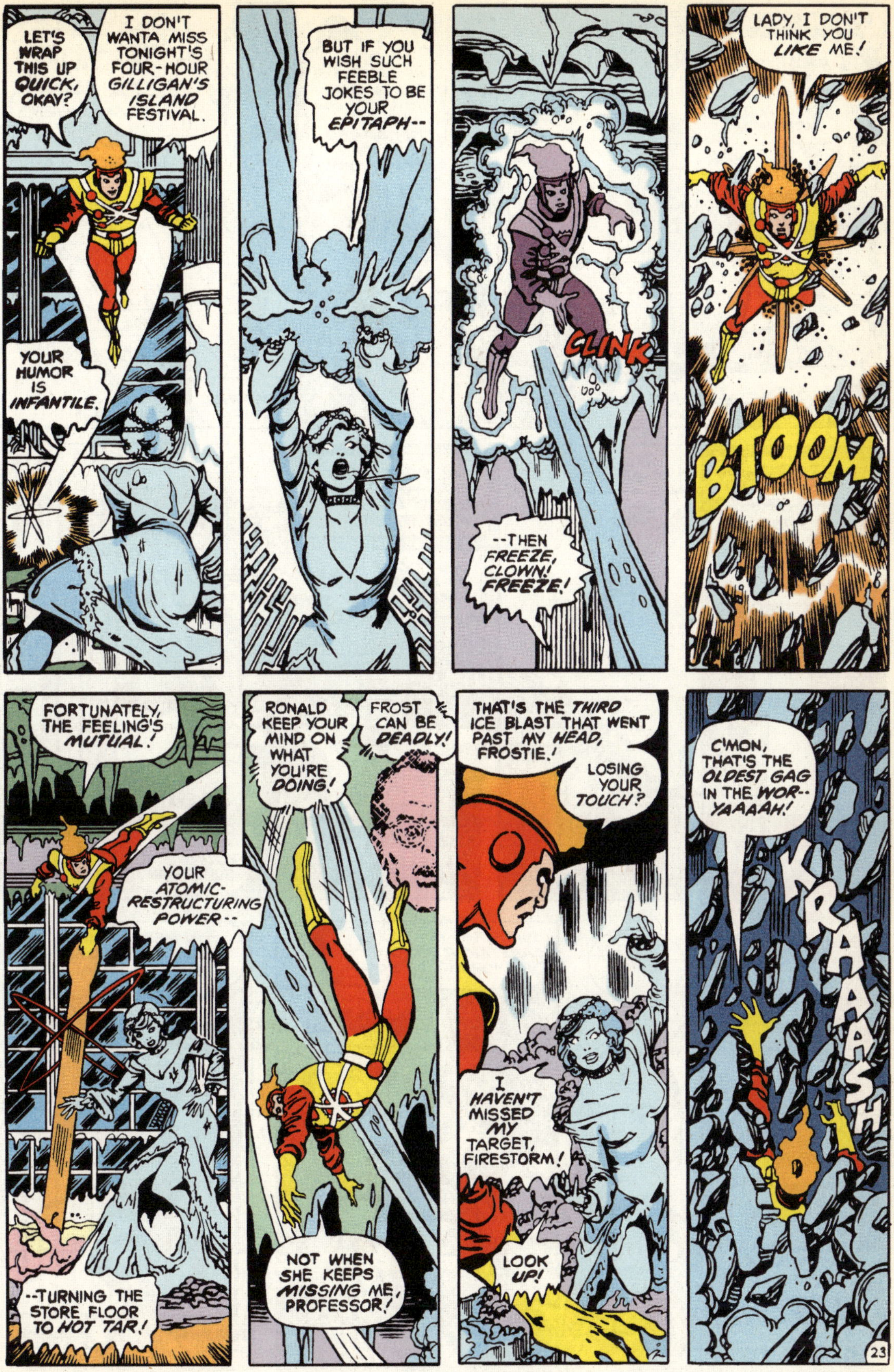
LET'S WRAP THIS UP QUICK, OKAY?
I DON'T WANTA MISS TONIGHT'S FOUR-HOUR GILLIGAN'S ISLAND FESTIVAL.
YOUR HUMOR IS INFANTILE.
BUT IF YOU WISH SUCH FEEBLE JOKES TO BE YOUR EPITAPH--
CLINK
--THEN FREEZE, CLOWN! FREEZE!
LADY, I DON'T THINK YOU LIKE ME!
BTOOM
FORTUNATELY, THE FEELING'S MUTUAL!
YOUR ATOMIC-RESTRUCTURING POWER--
--TURNING THE STORE FLOOR TO HOT TAR!
RONALD KEEP YOUR MIND ON WHAT YOU'RE DOING!
FROST CAN BE DEADLY!
NOT WHEN SHE KEEPS MISSING ME, PROFESSOR!
THAT'S THE THIRD ICE BLAST THAT WENT PAST MY HEAD, FROSTIE!
LOSING YOUR TOUCH?
I HAVEN'T MISSED MY TARGET, FIRESTORM!
LOOK UP!
C'MON, THAT'S THE OLDEST GAG IN THE WOR-- YAAAAH!
KRAAASH
23

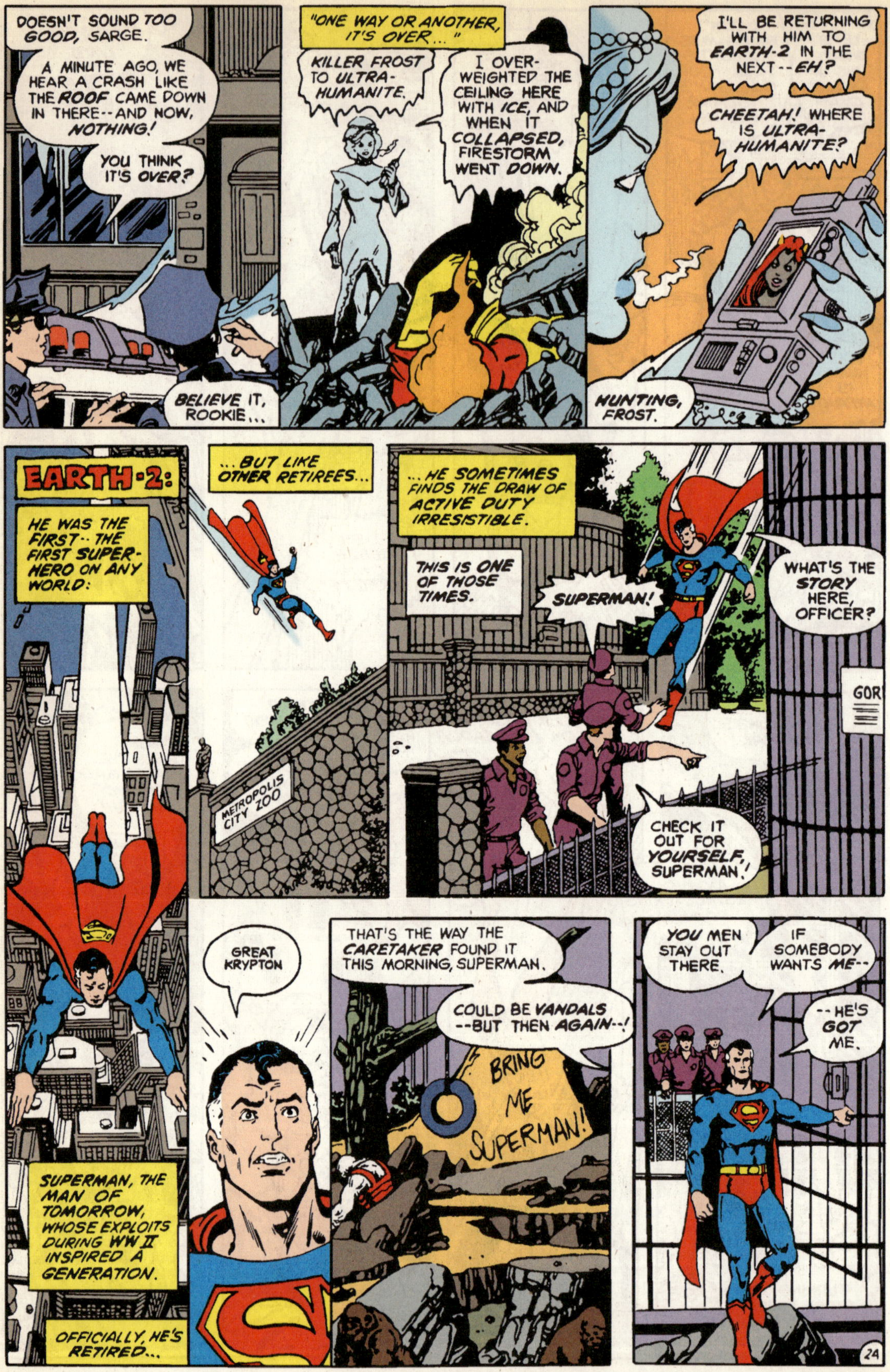

DOESN'T SOUND TOO GOOD, SARGE.
A MINUTE AGO, WE HEAR A CRASH LIKE THE ROOF CAME DOWN IN THERE--AND NOW, NOTHING!
YOU THINK IT'S OVER?
BELIEVE IT, ROOKIE...
"ONE WAY OR ANOTHER, IT'S OVER..."
KILLER FROST TO ULTRA-HUMANITE.
I OVER-WEIGHTED THE CEILING HERE WITH ICE, AND WHEN IT COLLAPSED, FIRESTORM WENT DOWN.
I'LL BE RETURNING WITH HIM TO EARTH-2 IN THE NEXT--EH?
CHEETAH! WHERE IS ULTRA-HUMANITE?
HUNTING, FROST.
EARTH-2:
HE WAS THE FIRST--THE FIRST SUPER-HERO ON ANY WORLD:
SUPERMAN, THE MAN OF TOMORROW, WHOSE EXPLOITS DURING WW II INSPIRED A GENERATION.
OFFICIALLY, HE'S RETIRED...
...BUT LIKE OTHER RETIREES...
METROPOLIS CITY ZOO
...HE SOMETIMES FINDS THE DRAW OF ACTIVE DUTY IRRESISTIBLE.
THIS IS ONE OF THOSE TIMES.
SUPERMAN!
WHAT'S THE STORY HERE, OFFICER?
GOR
CHECK IT OUT FOR YOURSELF, SUPERMAN!
GREAT KRYPTON
THAT'S THE WAY THE CARETAKER FOUND IT THIS MORNING, SUPERMAN.
COULD BE VANDALS --BUT THEN AGAIN--!
BRING ME SUPERMAN!
YOU MEN STAY OUT THERE.
IF SOMEBODY WANTS ME--
--HE'S GOT ME.
24

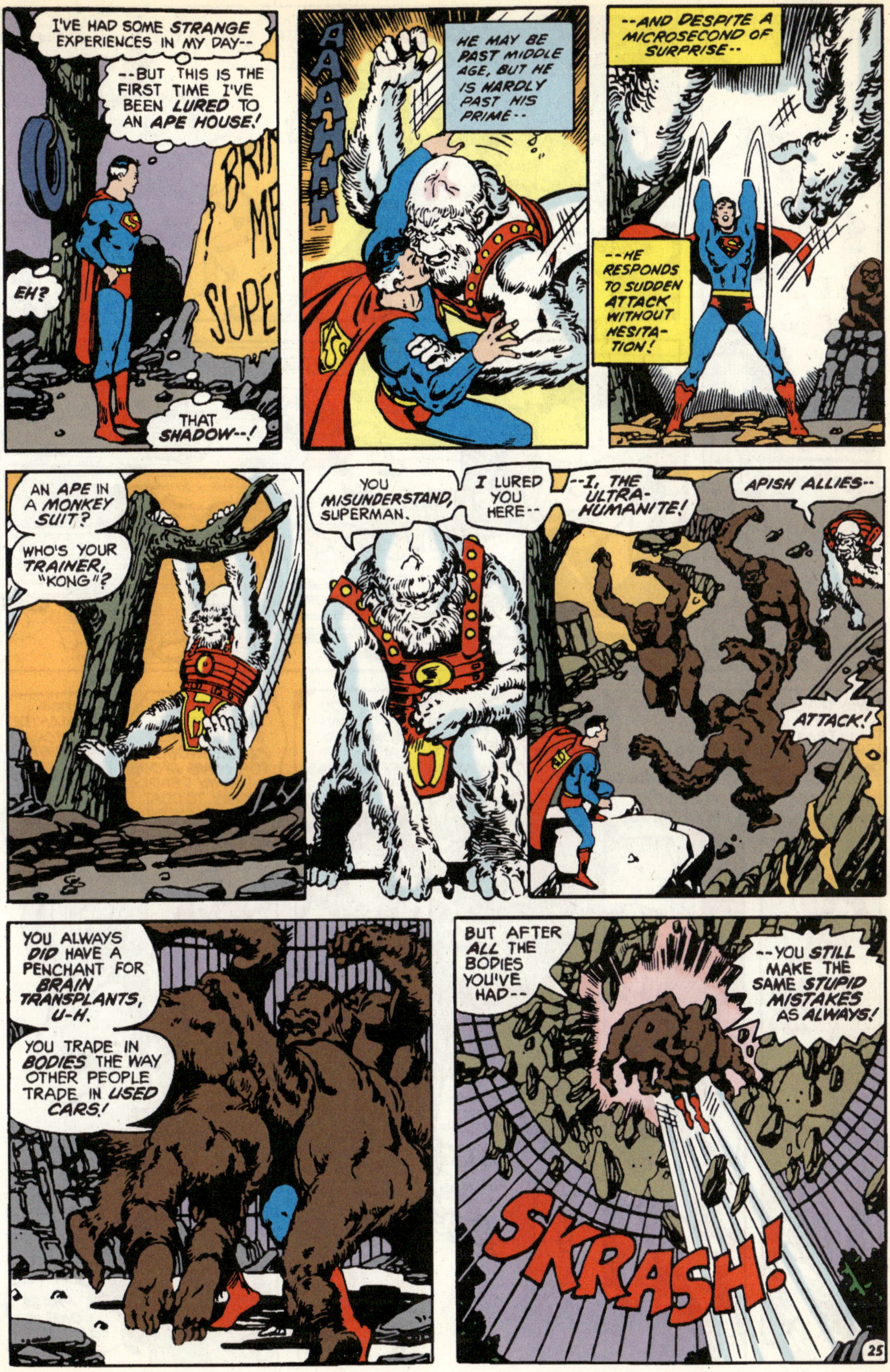

I'VE HAD SOME *STRANGE* EXPERIENCES IN MY DAY--
--BUT THIS IS THE FIRST TIME I'VE BEEN *LURED* TO AN *APE HOUSE!*
EH?
THAT *SHADOW*--!
HE MAY BE PAST MIDDLE AGE, BUT HE IS HARDLY PAST HIS PRIME--
--AND DESPITE A MICROSECOND OF SURPRISE--
--HE RESPONDS TO SUDDEN *ATTACK* WITHOUT HESITA-TION!
AN *APE* IN A *MONKEY SUIT?*
WHO'S YOUR *TRAINER,* "KONG"?
YOU *MISUNDERSTAND,* SUPERMAN.
I LURED YOU HERE--
--I, THE ULTRA-HUMANITE!
APISH ALLIES--
ATTACK!
YOU ALWAYS *DID* HAVE A PENCHANT FOR *BRAIN TRANSPLANTS,* U-H.
YOU TRADE IN *BODIES* THE WAY OTHER PEOPLE TRADE IN *USED CARS!*
BUT AFTER *ALL* THE BODIES YOU'VE HAD--
--YOU *STILL* MAKE THE SAME *STUPID MISTAKES* AS *ALWAYS!*
SKRASH!
25

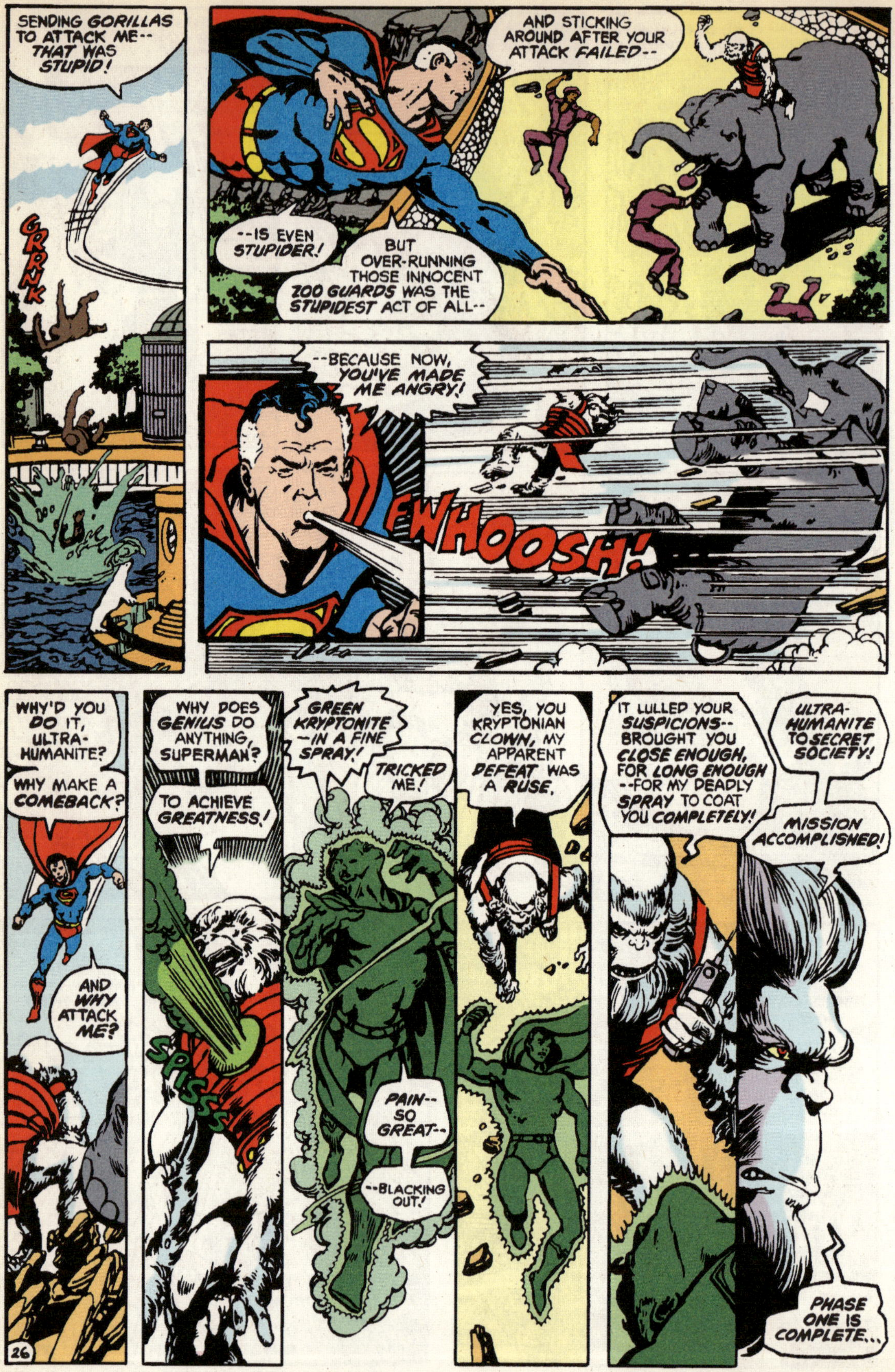

SENDING GORILLAS TO ATTACK ME-- THAT WAS STUPID!
GRRNK
AND STICKING AROUND AFTER YOUR ATTACK FAILED--
--IS EVEN STUPIDER!
BUT OVER-RUNNING THOSE INNOCENT ZOO GUARDS WAS THE STUPIDEST ACT OF ALL--
--BECAUSE NOW, YOU'VE MADE ME ANGRY!
WHOOSH!
WHY'D YOU DO IT, ULTRA-HUMANITE?
WHY MAKE A COMEBACK?
AND WHY ATTACK ME?
26
WHY DOES GENIUS DO ANYTHING, SUPERMAN?
TO ACHIEVE GREATNESS!
SPISSS
GREEN KRYPTONITE --IN A FINE SPRAY!
TRICKED ME!
PAIN-- SO GREAT--
--BLACKING OUT!
YES, YOU KRYPTONIAN CLOWN, MY APPARENT DEFEAT WAS A RUSE.
IT LULLED YOUR SUSPICIONS-- BROUGHT YOU CLOSE ENOUGH, FOR LONG ENOUGH --FOR MY DEADLY SPRAY TO COAT YOU COMPLETELY!
ULTRA-HUMANITE TO SECRET SOCIETY!
MISSION ACCOMPLISHED!
PHASE ONE IS COMPLETE...

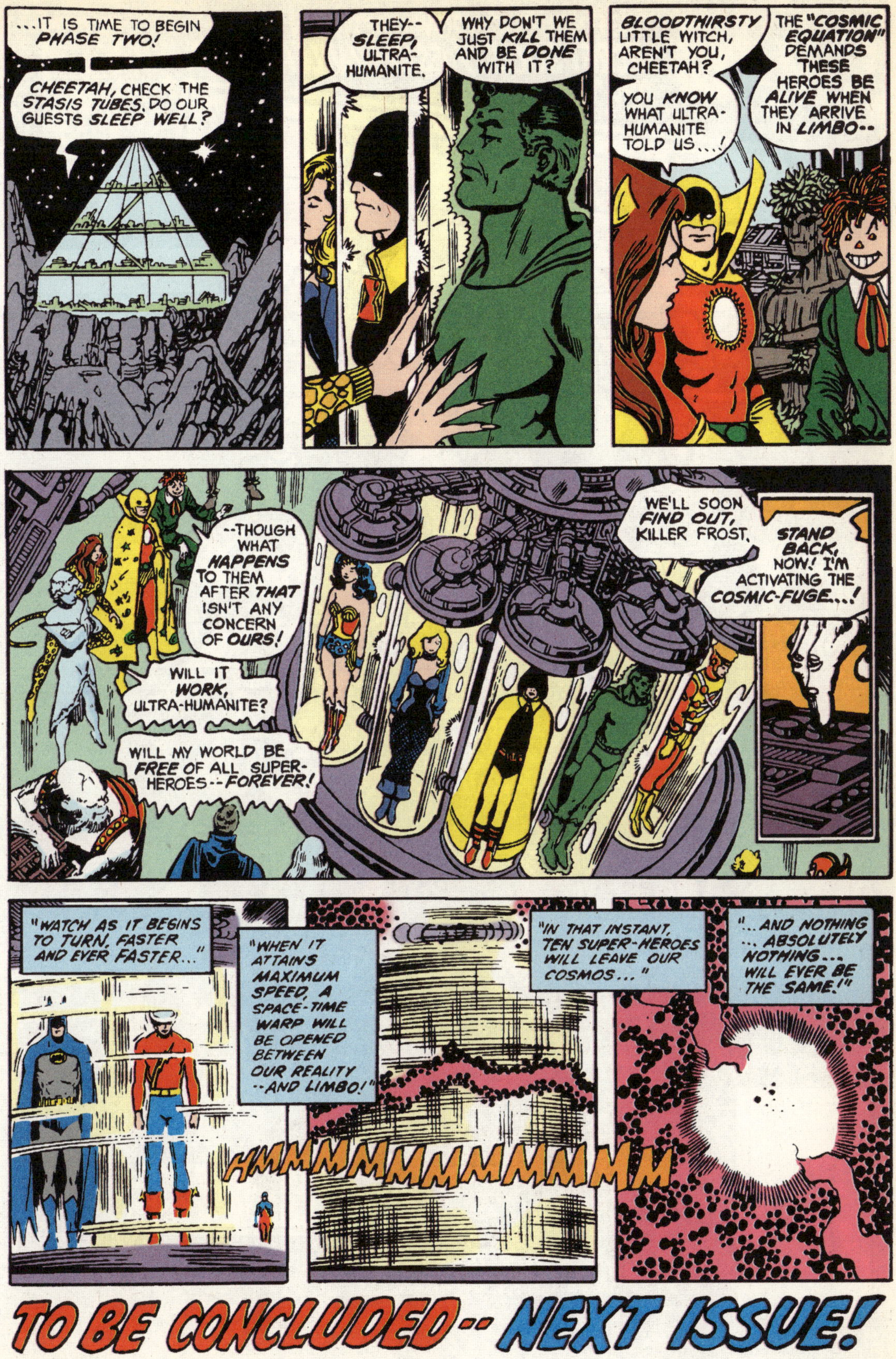
...IT IS TIME TO BEGIN PHASE TWO!
CHEETAH, CHECK THE STASIS TUBES. DO OUR GUESTS SLEEP WELL?
THEY--SLEEP, ULTRA-HUMANITE.
WHY DON'T WE JUST KILL THEM AND BE DONE WITH IT?
BLOODTHIRSTY LITTLE WITCH, AREN'T YOU, CHEETAH?
YOU KNOW WHAT ULTRA-HUMANITE TOLD US...!
THE "COSMIC EQUATION" DEMANDS THESE HEROES BE ALIVE WHEN THEY ARRIVE IN LIMBO--
--THOUGH WHAT HAPPENS TO THEM AFTER THAT ISN'T ANY CONCERN OF OURS!
WILL IT WORK, ULTRA-HUMANITE?
WILL MY WORLD BE FREE OF ALL SUPER-HEROES--FOREVER!
WE'LL SOON FIND OUT, KILLER FROST.
STAND BACK, NOW! I'M ACTIVATING THE COSMIC-FUGE...!
"WATCH AS IT BEGINS TO TURN, FASTER AND EVER FASTER..."
"WHEN IT ATTAINS MAXIMUM SPEED, A SPACE-TIME WARP WILL BE OPENED BETWEEN OUR REALITY --AND LIMBO!"
HMMMMMMMMMMMMMM
"IN THAT INSTANT, TEN SUPER-HEROES WILL LEAVE OUR COSMOS..."
"...AND NOTHING ... ABSOLUTELY NOTHING... WILL EVER BE THE SAME!"
TO BE CONCLUDED-- NEXT ISSUE!

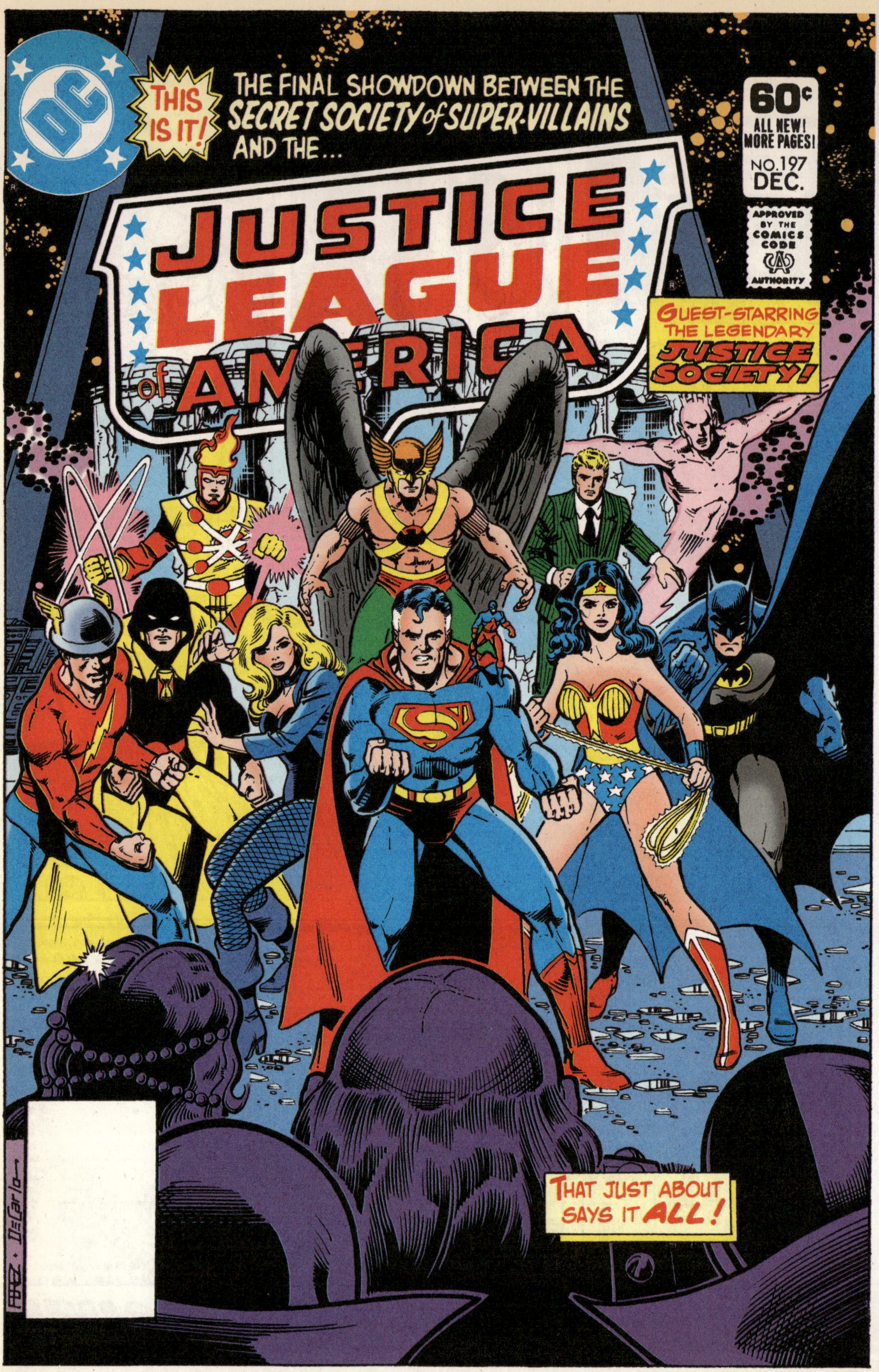
THIS IS IT!
THE FINAL SHOWDOWN BETWEEN THE SECRET SOCIETY of SUPER-VILLAINS AND THE...
JUSTICE LEAGUE of AMERICA
60¢ ALL NEW! MORE PAGES!
NO.197 DEC.
APPROVED BY THE COMICS CODE AUTHORITY
GUEST-STARRING THE LEGENDARY JUSTICE SOCIETY!
THAT JUST ABOUT SAYS IT ALL!

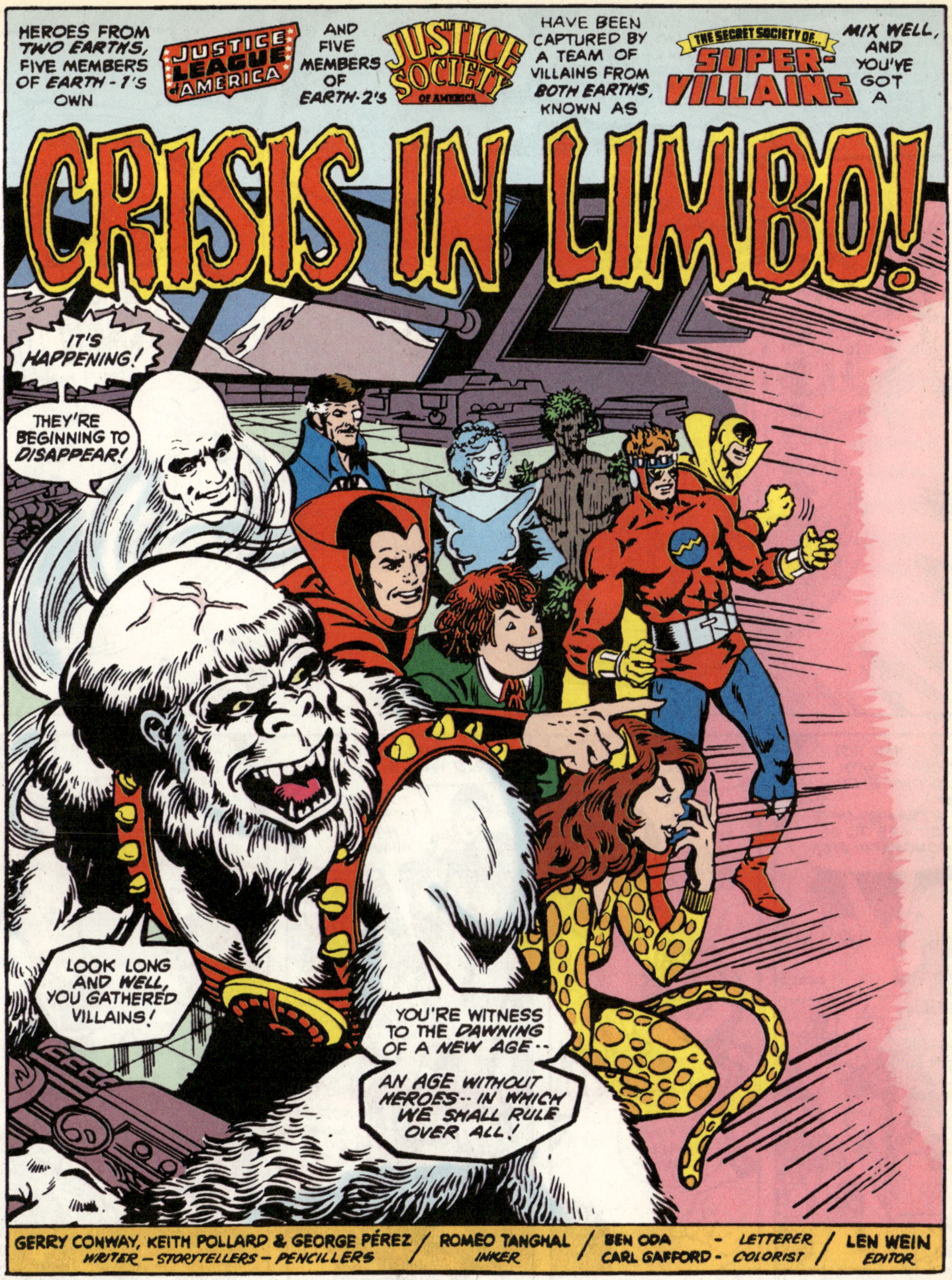
HEROES FROM TWO EARTHS, FIVE MEMBERS OF EARTH-1'S OWN
JUSTICE LEAGUE of AMERICA
AND FIVE MEMBERS OF EARTH-2'S
JUSTICE SOCIETY OF AMERICA
HAVE BEEN CAPTURED BY A TEAM OF VILLAINS FROM BOTH EARTHS, KNOWN AS
THE SECRET SOCIETY OF... SUPER-VILLAINS
MIX WELL, AND YOU'VE GOT A
CRISIS IN LIMBO!
IT'S HAPPENING!
THEY'RE BEGINNING TO DISAPPEAR!
LOOK LONG AND WELL, YOU GATHERED VILLAINS!
YOU'RE WITNESS TO THE DAWNING OF A NEW AGE --
AN AGE WITHOUT HEROES -- IN WHICH WE SHALL RULE OVER ALL!
GERRY CONWAY, KEITH POLLARD & GEORGE PÉREZ WRITER — STORYTELLERS — PENCILLERS / ROMEO TANGHAL INKER / BEN ODA - LETTERER CARL GAFFORD - COLORIST / LEN WEIN EDITOR

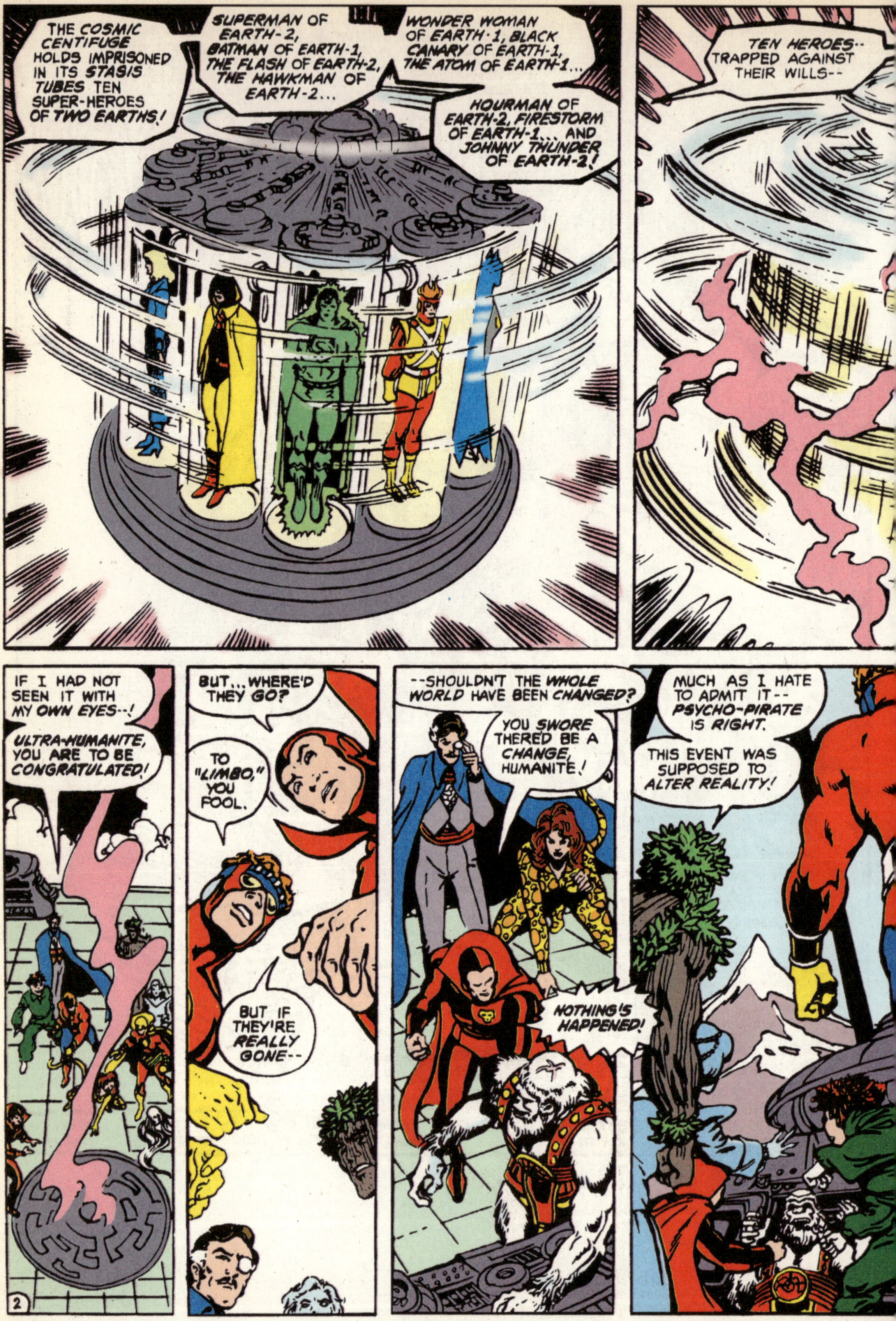
THE COSMIC CENTIFUGE HOLDS IMPRISONED IN ITS STASIS TUBES TEN SUPER-HEROES OF TWO EARTHS!
SUPERMAN OF EARTH-2, BATMAN OF EARTH-1, THE FLASH OF EARTH-2, THE HAWKMAN OF EARTH-2...
WONDER WOMAN OF EARTH-1, BLACK CANARY OF EARTH-1, THE ATOM OF EARTH-1...
HOURMAN OF EARTH-2, FIRESTORM OF EARTH-1... AND JOHNNY THUNDER OF EARTH-2!
TEN HEROES-- TRAPPED AGAINST THEIR WILLS--
IF I HAD NOT SEEN IT WITH MY OWN EYES--!
ULTRA-HUMANITE, YOU ARE TO BE CONGRATULATED!
2
BUT... WHERE'D THEY GO?
TO "LIMBO," YOU FOOL.
BUT IF THEY'RE REALLY GONE--
--SHOULDN'T THE WHOLE WORLD HAVE BEEN CHANGED?
YOU SWORE THERE'D BE A CHANGE, HUMANITE!
NOTHING'S HAPPENED!
MUCH AS I HATE TO ADMIT IT-- PSYCHO-PIRATE IS RIGHT.
THIS EVENT WAS SUPPOSED TO ALTER REALITY!

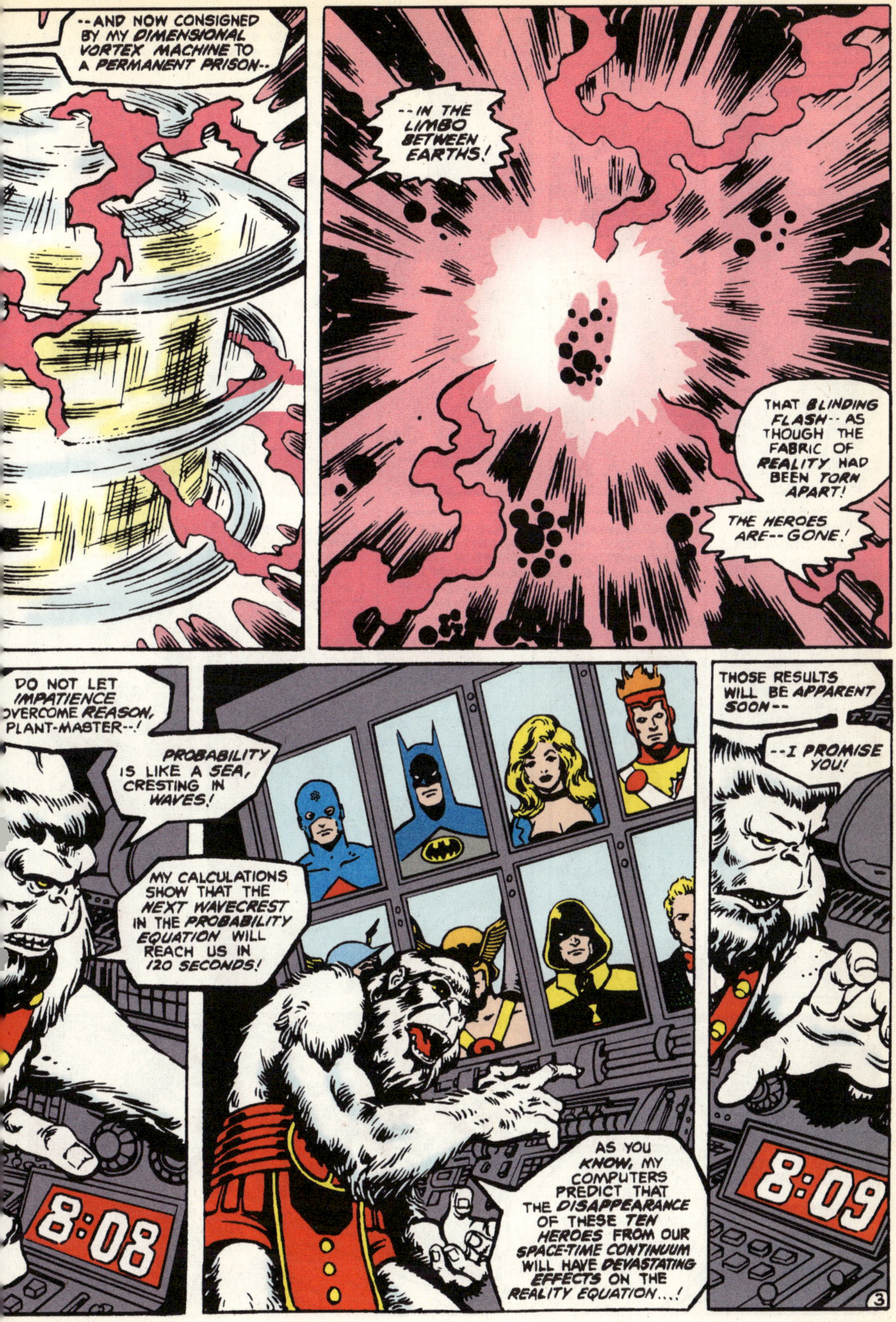
--AND NOW CONSIGNED BY MY DIMENSIONAL VORTEX MACHINE TO A PERMANENT PRISON--
--IN THE LIMBO BETWEEN EARTHS!
THAT BLINDING FLASH--AS THOUGH THE FABRIC OF REALITY HAD BEEN TORN APART!
THE HEROES ARE--GONE!
DO NOT LET IMPATIENCE OVERCOME REASON, PLANT-MASTER--!
PROBABILITY IS LIKE A SEA, CRESTING IN WAVES!
MY CALCULATIONS SHOW THAT THE NEXT WAVECREST IN THE PROBABILITY EQUATION WILL REACH US IN 120 SECONDS!
8:08
AS YOU KNOW, MY COMPUTERS PREDICT THAT THE DISAPPEARANCE OF THESE TEN HEROES FROM OUR SPACE-TIME CONTINUUM WILL HAVE DEVASTATING EFFECTS ON THE REALITY EQUATION...!
THOSE RESULTS WILL BE APPARENT SOON--
--I PROMISE YOU!
8:09
3

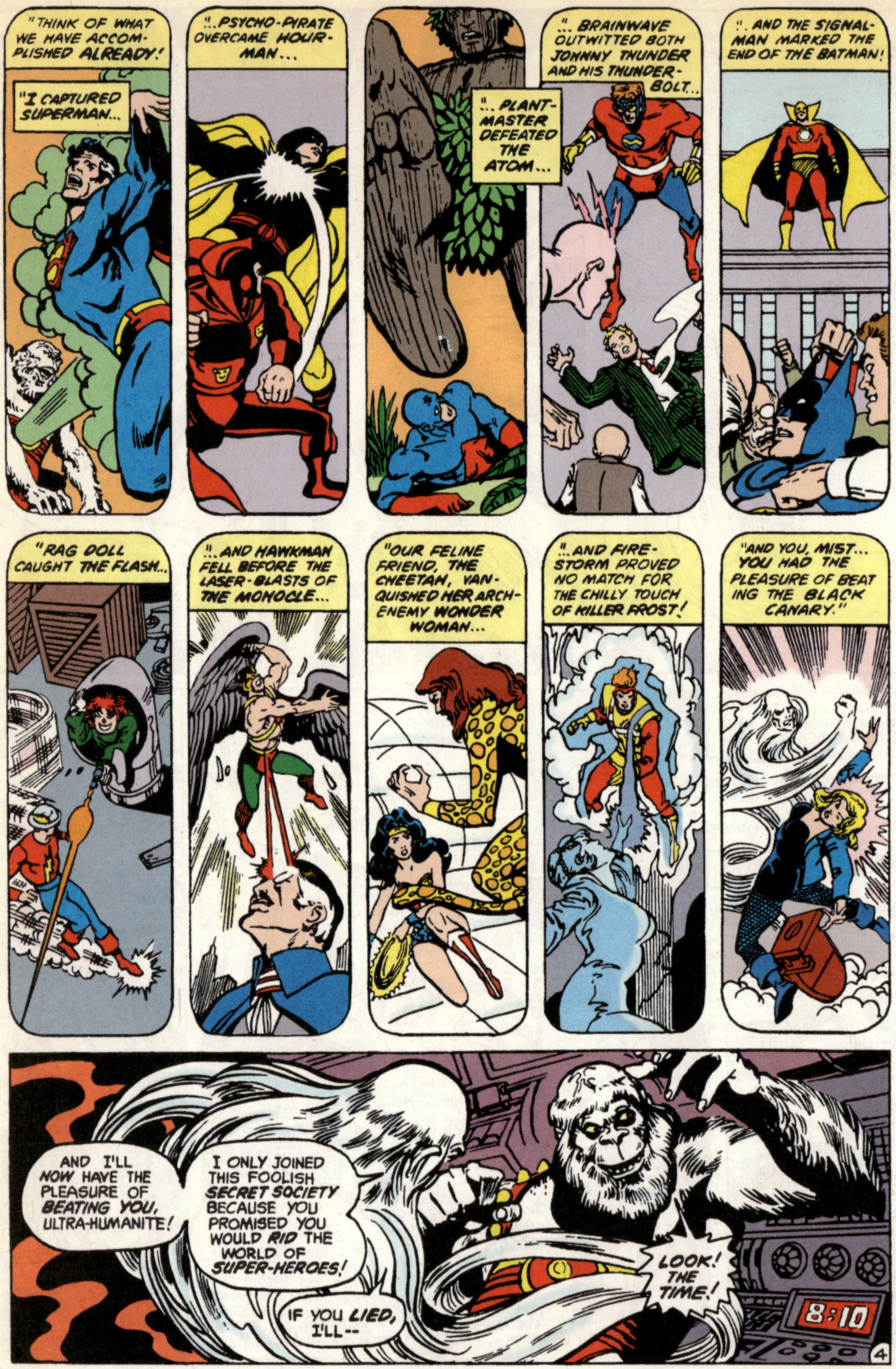
"THINK OF WHAT WE HAVE ACCOMPLISHED ALREADY!
"I CAPTURED SUPERMAN...
"...PSYCHO-PIRATE OVERCAME HOURMAN...
"...PLANT-MASTER DEFEATED THE ATOM...
"...BRAINWAVE OUTWITTED BOTH JOHNNY THUNDER AND HIS THUNDERBOLT...
"...AND THE SIGNALMAN MARKED THE END OF THE BATMAN!
"RAG DOLL CAUGHT THE FLASH...
"...AND HAWKMAN FELL BEFORE THE LASER-BLASTS OF THE MONOCLE...
"OUR FELINE FRIEND, THE CHEETAH, VANQUISHED HER ARCH-ENEMY WONDER WOMAN...
"...AND FIRESTORM PROVED NO MATCH FOR THE CHILLY TOUCH OF KILLER FROST!
"AND YOU, MIST... YOU HAD THE PLEASURE OF BEATING THE BLACK CANARY."
AND I'LL NOW HAVE THE PLEASURE OF BEATING YOU, ULTRA-HUMANITE!
I ONLY JOINED THIS FOOLISH SECRET SOCIETY BECAUSE YOU PROMISED YOU WOULD RID THE WORLD OF SUPER-HEROES!
IF YOU LIED, I'LL--
LOOK! THE TIME!
8:10
4

THE MOMENT OF CHANGE IS UPON US-- NOW!
YAAAHH
IMAGINE THE UNIVERSE--PLUCKED AND TORN ASUNDER LIKE SO MUCH PAPIER-MÂCHÉ...
IMAGINE A COSMOS GONE MAD...
...AND YOU WOULD BARELY BEGIN TO UNDERSTAND THE FORCES UNLEASHED THIS DAY...
ALL ACROSS THE FACE OF THE WORLD WE KNOW AS EARTH-2, THE RIPPLING WAVES OF CHANGE WREAK HAVOC ON REALITY...
PROBABILITY IS ITSELF DISTORTED... REALITY IS THROWN INTO DISARRAY... AND FOR ONE TIMELESS INSTANT A UNIVERSE TOTTERS ON THE BRINK OF INSANITY...
...ONLY TO SETTLE BACK, WITH AN ALMOST AUDIBLE "SIGH"...
THE COSMIC BALANCE HAS REASSERTED ITSELF.
THE MOMENT OF CHANGE HAS PASSED... AND ON BOTH EARTH-1 AND EARTH-2, IN TWO DIFFERENT THOUGH PARALLEL DIMENSIONS--
-- THE WORLD IS CALM ONCE MORE...
BEN'S
LIQUOR
5

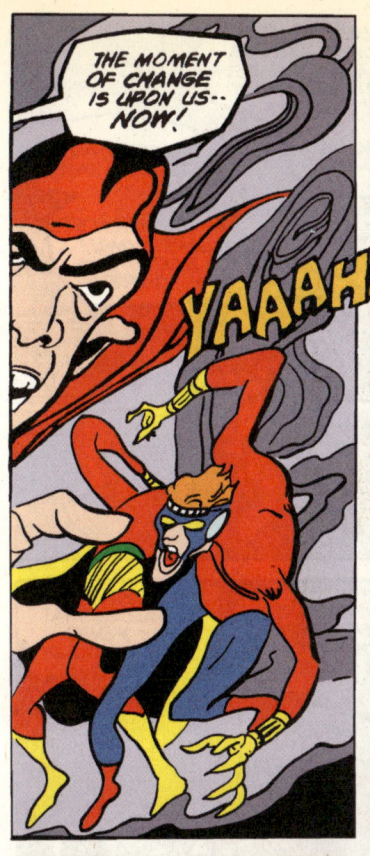

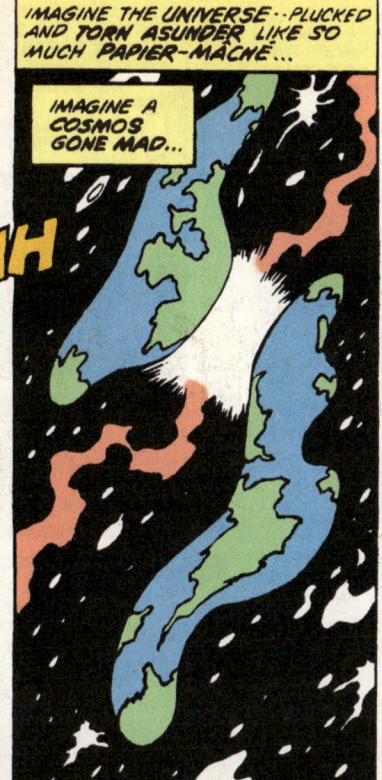

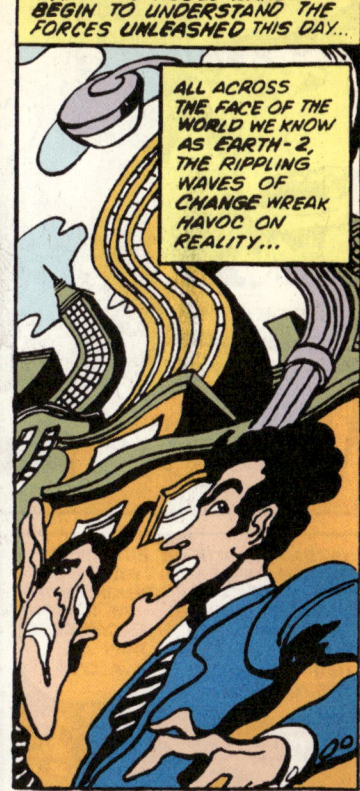

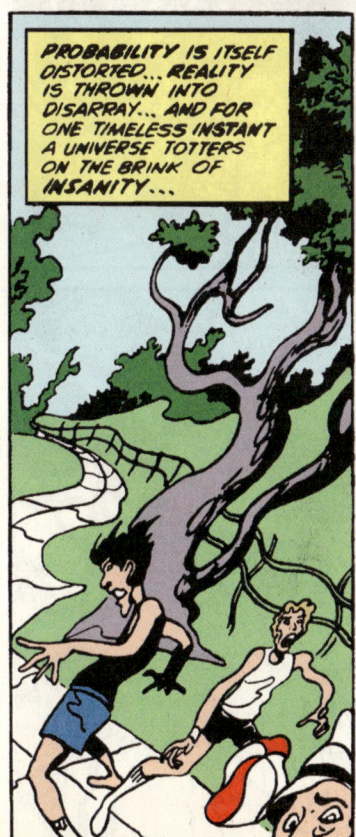

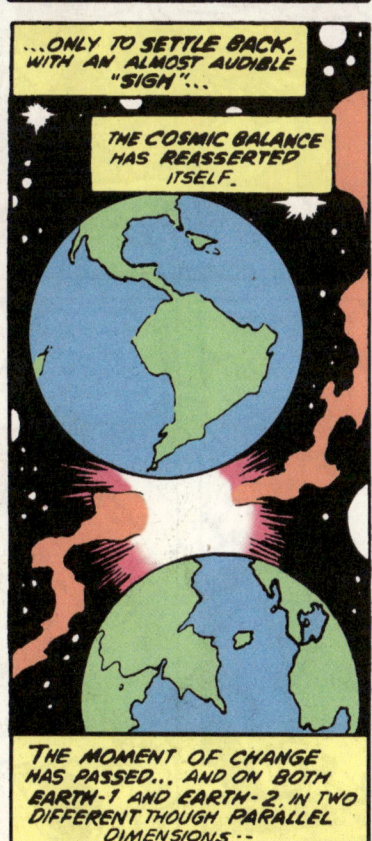

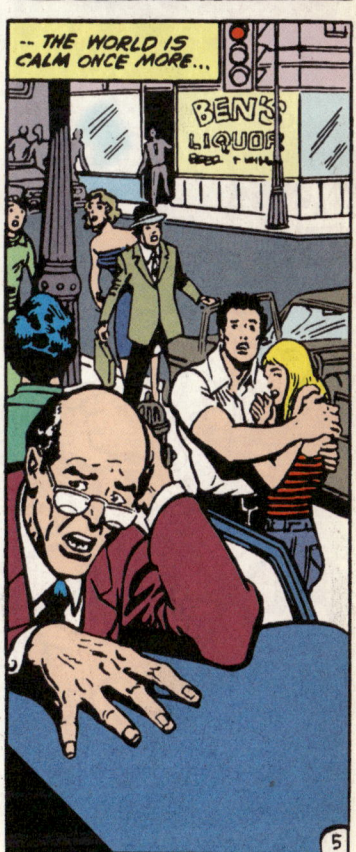

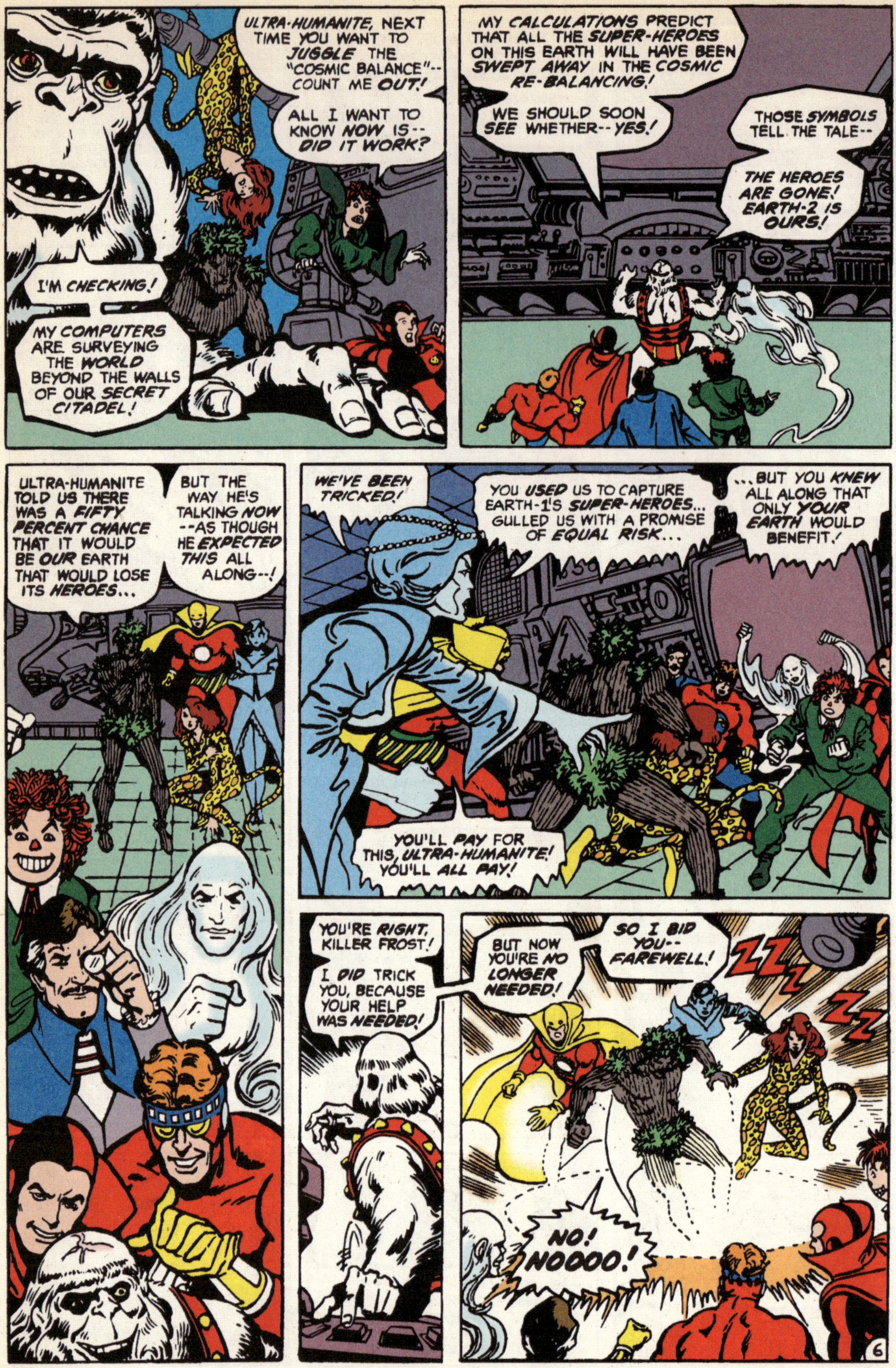
ULTRA-HUMANITE, NEXT TIME YOU WANT TO JUGGLE THE "COSMIC BALANCE"-- COUNT ME OUT!
ALL I WANT TO KNOW NOW IS-- DID IT WORK?
I'M CHECKING!
MY COMPUTERS ARE SURVEYING THE WORLD BEYOND THE WALLS OF OUR SECRET CITADEL!
MY CALCULATIONS PREDICT THAT ALL THE SUPER-HEROES ON THIS EARTH WILL HAVE BEEN SWEPT AWAY IN THE COSMIC RE-BALANCING!
WE SHOULD SOON SEE WHETHER-- YES.!
THOSE SYMBOLS TELL THE TALE--
THE HEROES ARE GONE! EARTH-2 IS OURS!
ULTRA-HUMANITE TOLD US THERE WAS A FIFTY PERCENT CHANCE THAT IT WOULD BE OUR EARTH THAT WOULD LOSE ITS HEROES...
BUT THE WAY HE'S TALKING NOW --AS THOUGH HE EXPECTED THIS ALL ALONG--!
WE'VE BEEN TRICKED!
YOU USED US TO CAPTURE EARTH-1'S SUPER-HEROES... GULLED US WITH A PROMISE OF EQUAL RISK...
...BUT YOU KNEW ALL ALONG THAT ONLY YOUR EARTH WOULD BENEFIT.!
YOU'LL PAY FOR THIS, ULTRA-HUMANITE! YOU'LL ALL PAY!
YOU'RE RIGHT, KILLER FROST! I DID TRICK YOU, BECAUSE YOUR HELP WAS NEEDED!
BUT NOW YOU'RE NO LONGER NEEDED!
SO I BID YOU-- FAREWELL!
ZZZ
ZZZ
NO! NOOOO!
6

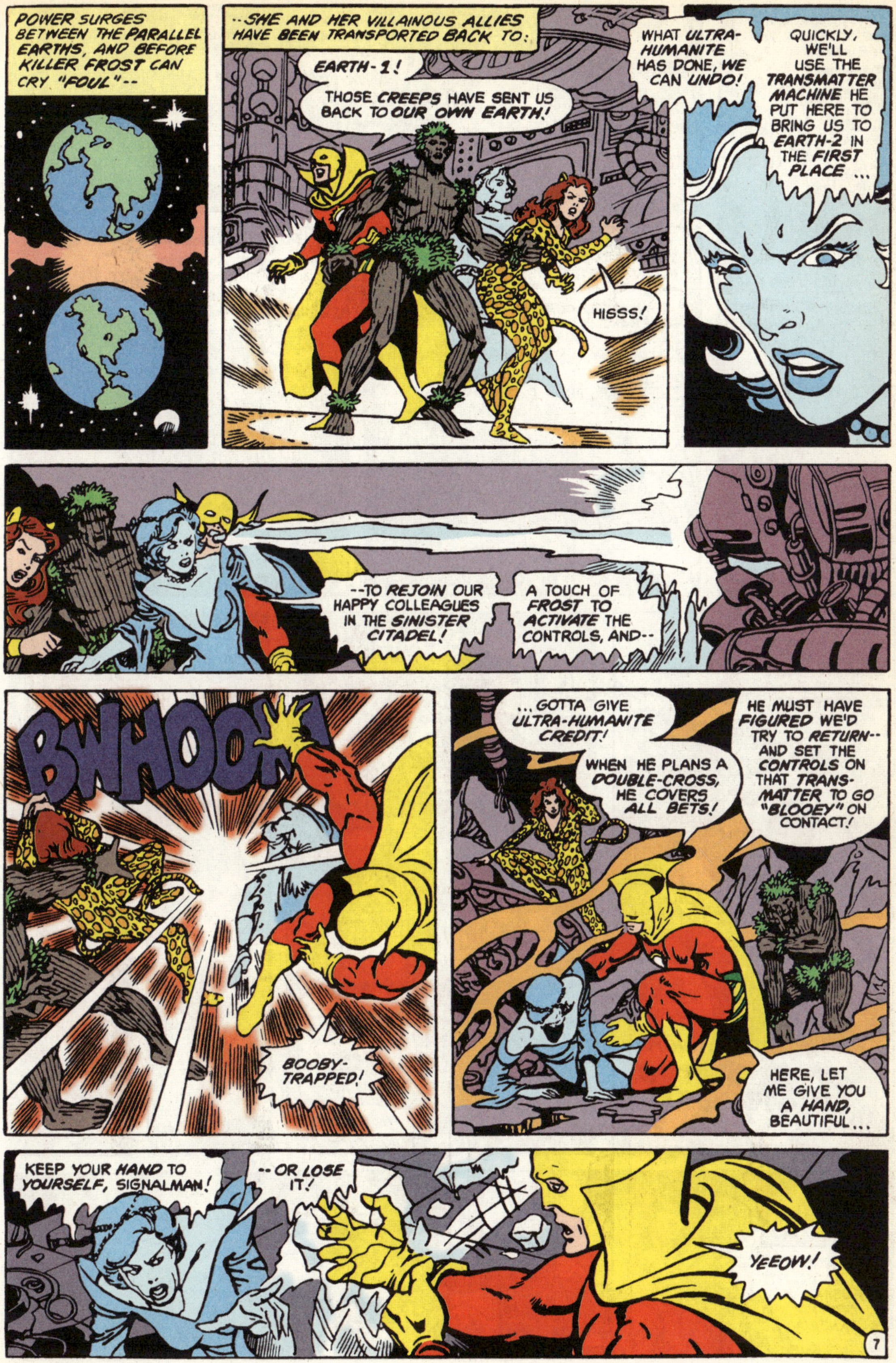
POWER SURGES BETWEEN THE PARALLEL EARTHS, AND BEFORE KILLER FROST CAN CRY "FOUL"--
--SHE AND HER VILLAINOUS ALLIES HAVE BEEN TRANSPORTED BACK TO:
EARTH-1!
THOSE CREEPS HAVE SENT US BACK TO OUR OWN EARTH!
HISSS!
WHAT ULTRA-HUMANITE HAS DONE, WE CAN UNDO!
QUICKLY, WE'LL USE THE TRANSMATTER MACHINE HE PUT HERE TO BRING US TO EARTH-2 IN THE FIRST PLACE...
--TO REJOIN OUR HAPPY COLLEAGUES IN THE SINISTER CITADEL!
A TOUCH OF FROST TO ACTIVATE THE CONTROLS, AND--
BWHOOM
BOOBY-TRAPPED!
...GOTTA GIVE ULTRA-HUMANITE CREDIT!
WHEN HE PLANS A DOUBLE-CROSS, HE COVERS ALL BETS!
HE MUST HAVE FIGURED WE'D TRY TO RETURN--AND SET THE CONTROLS ON THAT TRANS-MATTER TO GO "BLOOEY" ON CONTACT!
HERE, LET ME GIVE YOU A HAND, BEAUTIFUL...
KEEP YOUR HAND TO YOURSELF, SIGNALMAN!
--OR LOSE IT!
YEEOW!
7

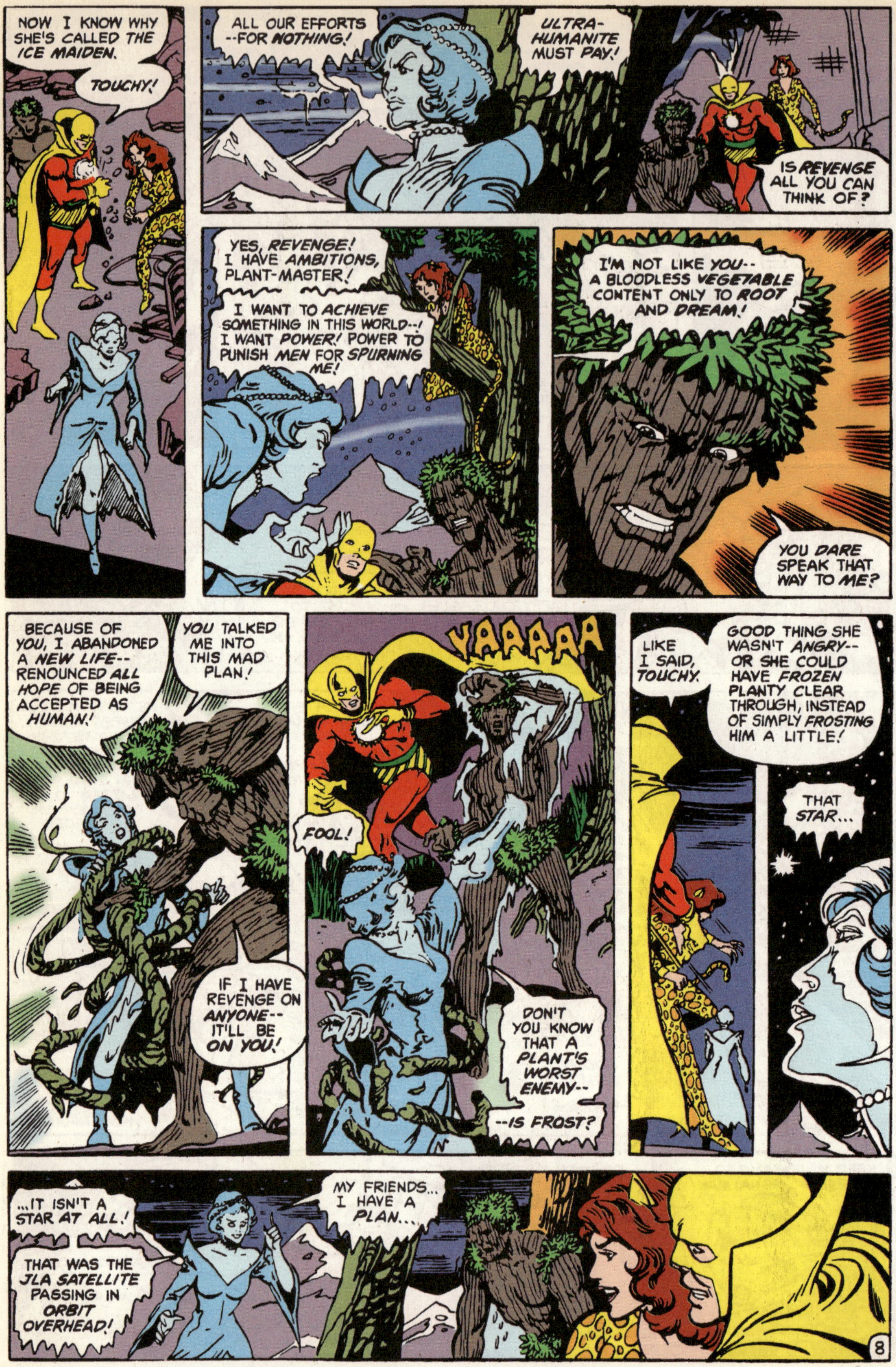

NOW I KNOW WHY SHE'S CALLED THE ICE MAIDEN.
TOUCHY!
ALL OUR EFFORTS --FOR NOTHING!
ULTRA-HUMANITE MUST PAY!
IS REVENGE ALL YOU CAN THINK OF?
YES, REVENGE! I HAVE AMBITIONS, PLANT-MASTER!
I WANT TO ACHIEVE SOMETHING IN THIS WORLD--! I WANT POWER! POWER TO PUNISH MEN FOR SPURNING ME!
I'M NOT LIKE YOU-- A BLOODLESS VEGETABLE CONTENT ONLY TO ROOT AND DREAM!
YOU DARE SPEAK THAT WAY TO ME?
BECAUSE OF YOU, I ABANDONED A NEW LIFE-- RENOUNCED ALL HOPE OF BEING ACCEPTED AS HUMAN!
YOU TALKED ME INTO THIS MAD PLAN!
IF I HAVE REVENGE ON ANYONE-- IT'LL BE ON YOU!
YAAAAA
FOOL!
DON'T YOU KNOW THAT A PLANT'S WORST ENEMY--
--IS FROST?
LIKE I SAID, TOUCHY.
GOOD THING SHE WASN'T ANGRY-- OR SHE COULD HAVE FROZEN PLANTY CLEAR THROUGH, INSTEAD OF SIMPLY FROSTING HIM A LITTLE!
THAT STAR...
...IT ISN'T A STAR AT ALL!
THAT WAS THE JLA SATELLITE PASSING IN ORBIT OVERHEAD!
MY FRIENDS... I HAVE A PLAN...
8

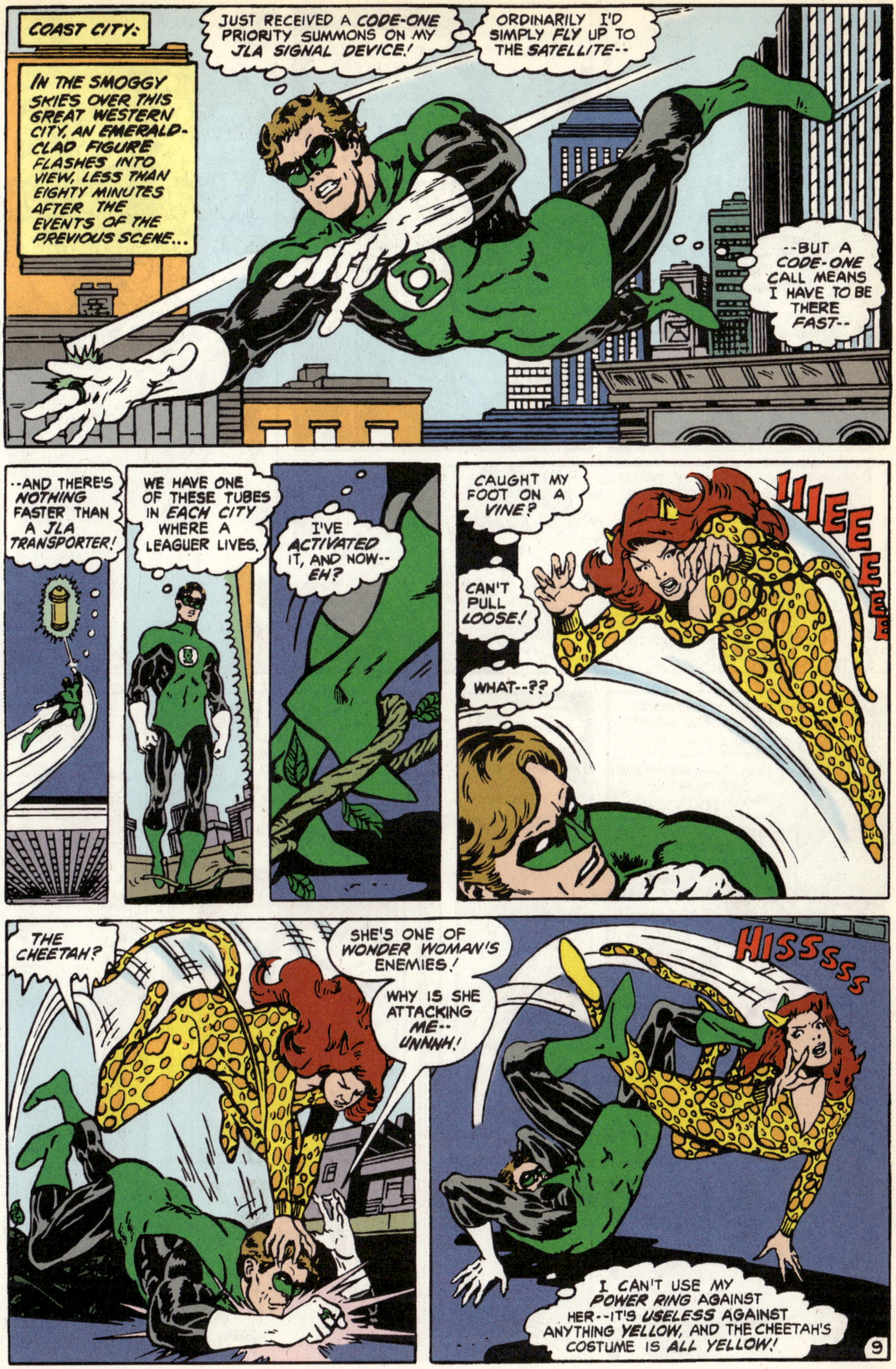
COAST CITY:
IN THE SMOGGY SKIES OVER THIS GREAT WESTERN CITY, AN EMERALD-CLAD FIGURE FLASHES INTO VIEW, LESS THAN EIGHTY MINUTES AFTER THE EVENTS OF THE PREVIOUS SCENE...
JUST RECEIVED A CODE-ONE PRIORITY SUMMONS ON MY JLA SIGNAL DEVICE!
ORDINARILY I'D SIMPLY FLY UP TO THE SATELLITE--
--BUT A CODE-ONE CALL MEANS I HAVE TO BE THERE FAST--
--AND THERE'S NOTHING FASTER THAN A JLA TRANSPORTER!
WE HAVE ONE OF THESE TUBES IN EACH CITY WHERE A LEAGUER LIVES.
I'VE ACTIVATED IT, AND NOW-- EH?
CAUGHT MY FOOT ON A VINE?
CAN'T PULL LOOSE!
WHAT--??
IIIEEEEE
THE CHEETAH?
SHE'S ONE OF WONDER WOMAN'S ENEMIES!
WHY IS SHE ATTACKING ME-- UNNNH!
HISSsss
I CAN'T USE MY POWER RING AGAINST HER--IT'S USELESS AGAINST ANYTHING YELLOW, AND THE CHEETAH'S COSTUME IS ALL YELLOW!
9

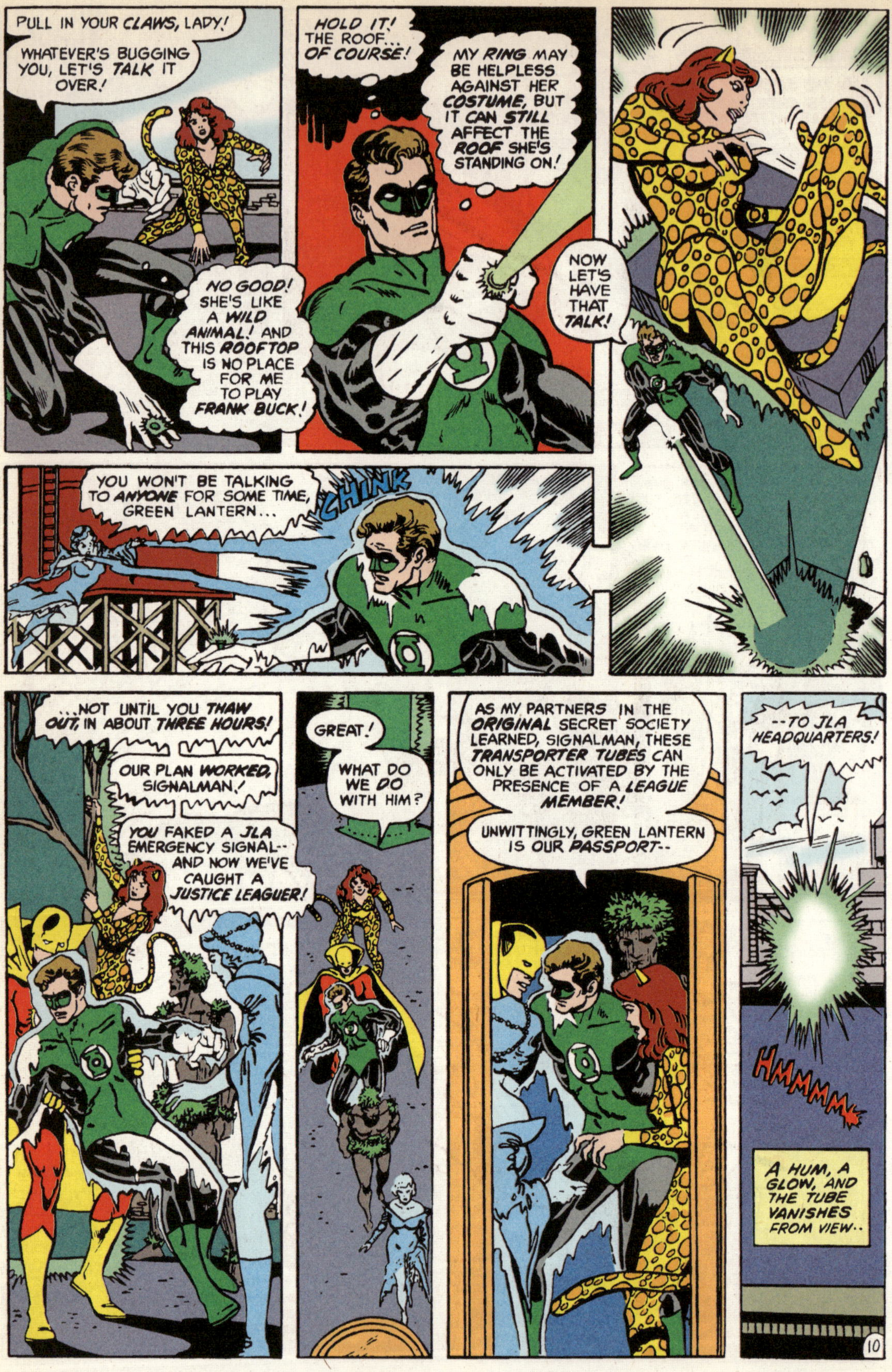
PULL IN YOUR CLAWS, LADY!
WHATEVER'S BUGGING YOU, LET'S TALK IT OVER!
NO GOOD! SHE'S LIKE A WILD ANIMAL! AND THIS ROOFTOP IS NO PLACE FOR ME TO PLAY FRANK BUCK!
HOLD IT! THE ROOF... OF COURSE!
MY RING MAY BE HELPLESS AGAINST HER COSTUME, BUT IT CAN STILL AFFECT THE ROOF SHE'S STANDING ON!
NOW LET'S HAVE THAT TALK!
YOU WON'T BE TALKING TO ANYONE FOR SOME TIME, GREEN LANTERN...
CHINK
...NOT UNTIL YOU THAW OUT, IN ABOUT THREE HOURS!
OUR PLAN WORKED, SIGNALMAN!
YOU FAKED A JLA EMERGENCY SIGNAL-- AND NOW WE'VE CAUGHT A JUSTICE LEAGUER!
GREAT!
WHAT DO WE DO WITH HIM?
AS MY PARTNERS IN THE ORIGINAL SECRET SOCIETY LEARNED, SIGNALMAN, THESE TRANSPORTER TUBES CAN ONLY BE ACTIVATED BY THE PRESENCE OF A LEAGUE MEMBER!
UNWITTINGLY, GREEN LANTERN IS OUR PASSPORT--
--TO JLA HEADQUARTERS!
HMMMM
A HUM, A GLOW, AND THE TUBE VANISHES FROM VIEW..
10

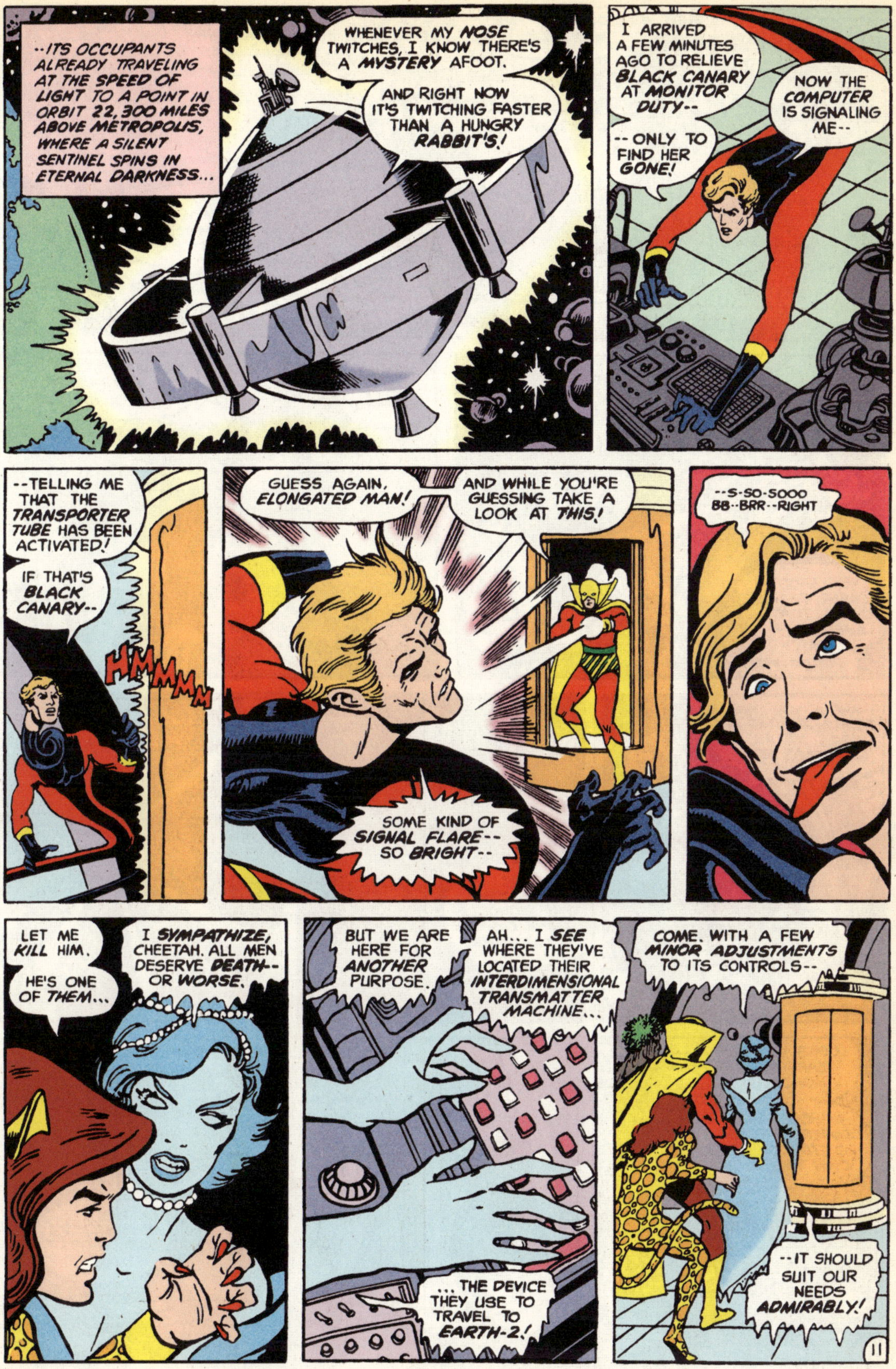

..ITS OCCUPANTS ALREADY TRAVELING AT THE SPEED OF LIGHT TO A POINT IN ORBIT 22,300 MILES ABOVE METROPOLIS, WHERE A SILENT SENTINEL SPINS IN ETERNAL DARKNESS...
WHENEVER MY NOSE TWITCHES, I KNOW THERE'S A MYSTERY AFOOT.
AND RIGHT NOW IT'S TWITCHING FASTER THAN A HUNGRY RABBIT'S!
I ARRIVED A FEW MINUTES AGO TO RELIEVE BLACK CANARY AT MONITOR DUTY--
-- ONLY TO FIND HER GONE!
NOW THE COMPUTER IS SIGNALING ME--
--TELLING ME THAT THE TRANSPORTER TUBE HAS BEEN ACTIVATED!
IF THAT'S BLACK CANARY--
HMMMM
GUESS AGAIN, ELONGATED MAN!
AND WHILE YOU'RE GUESSING TAKE A LOOK AT THIS!
SOME KIND OF SIGNAL FLARE-- SO BRIGHT--
--S-SO-SOOO BB--BRR--RIGHT
LET ME KILL HIM.
HE'S ONE OF THEM...
I SYMPATHIZE, CHEETAH. ALL MEN DESERVE DEATH-- OR WORSE.
BUT WE ARE HERE FOR ANOTHER PURPOSE.
AH... I SEE WHERE THEY'VE LOCATED THEIR INTERDIMENSIONAL TRANSMATTER MACHINE...
... THE DEVICE THEY USE TO TRAVEL TO EARTH-2!
COME. WITH A FEW MINOR ADJUSTMENTS TO ITS CONTROLS--
--IT SHOULD SUIT OUR NEEDS ADMIRABLY!
11

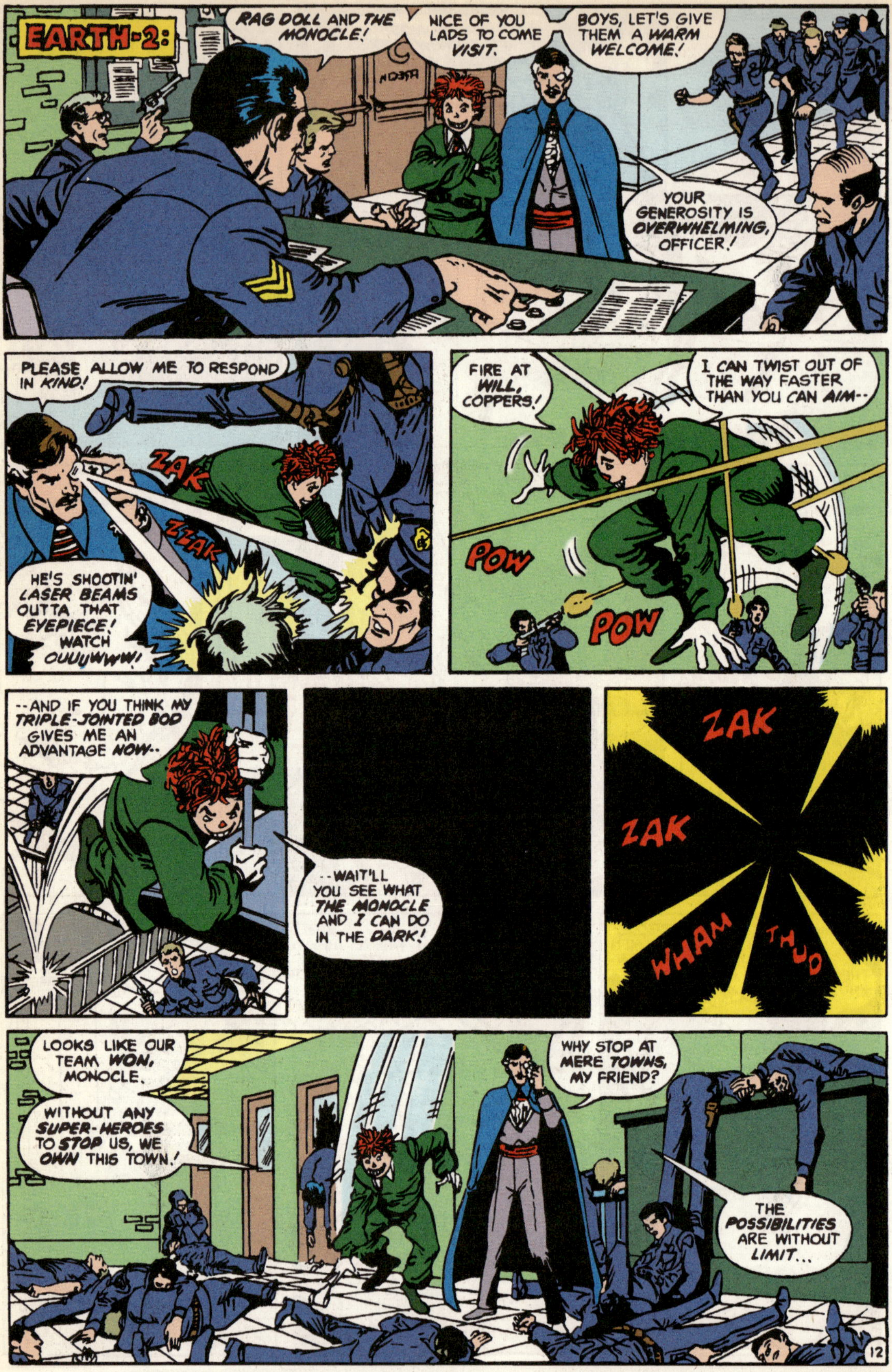
EARTH-2:
RAG DOLL AND THE MONOCLE!
NICE OF YOU LADS TO COME VISIT.
BOYS, LET'S GIVE THEM A WARM WELCOME!
YOUR GENEROSITY IS OVERWHELMING, OFFICER!
PLEASE ALLOW ME TO RESPOND IN KIND!
ZAK
ZZAK
HE'S SHOOTIN' LASER BEAMS OUTTA THAT EYEPIECE! WATCH OUUUWWW!
FIRE AT WILL, COPPERS!
I CAN TWIST OUT OF THE WAY FASTER THAN YOU CAN AIM--
POW
POW
--AND IF YOU THINK MY TRIPLE-JOINTED BOD GIVES ME AN ADVANTAGE NOW--
--WAIT'LL YOU SEE WHAT THE MONOCLE AND I CAN DO IN THE DARK!
ZAK
ZAK
WHAM
THUD
LOOKS LIKE OUR TEAM WON, MONOCLE.
WITHOUT ANY SUPER-HEROES TO STOP US, WE OWN THIS TOWN!
WHY STOP AT MERE TOWNS, MY FRIEND?
THE POSSIBILITIES ARE WITHOUT LIMIT...
12

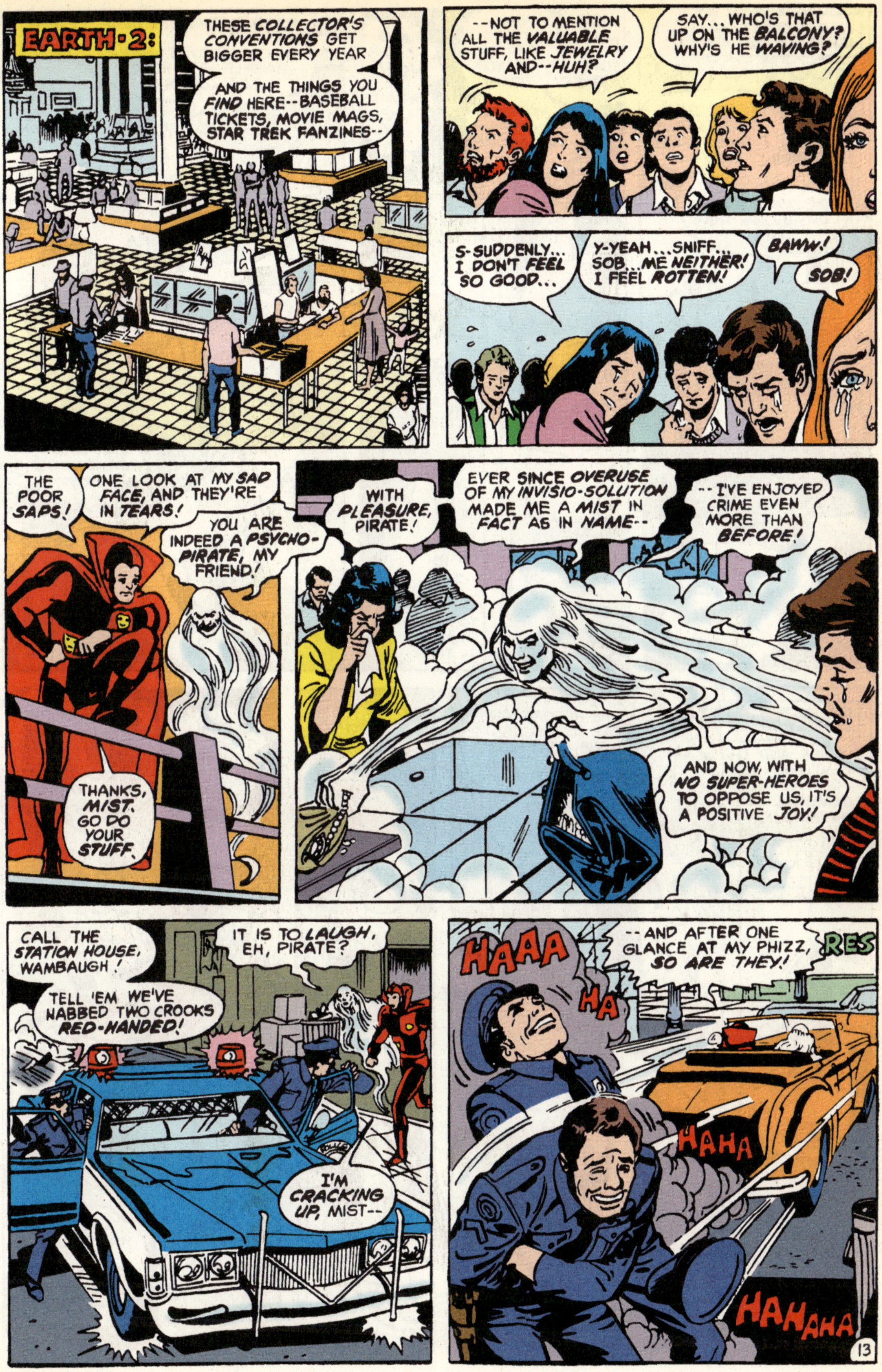
EARTH-2:
THESE COLLECTOR'S CONVENTIONS GET BIGGER EVERY YEAR
AND THE THINGS YOU FIND HERE--BASEBALL TICKETS, MOVIE MAGS, STAR TREK FANZINES--
--NOT TO MENTION ALL THE VALUABLE STUFF, LIKE JEWELRY AND--HUH?
SAY... WHO'S THAT UP ON THE BALCONY? WHY'S HE WAVING?
S-SUDDENLY... I DON'T FEEL SO GOOD...
Y-YEAH... SNIFF... SOB... ME NEITHER! I FEEL ROTTEN!
BAWW!
SOB!
THE POOR SAPS!
ONE LOOK AT MY SAD FACE, AND THEY'RE IN TEARS!
YOU ARE INDEED A PSYCHO-PIRATE, MY FRIEND!
THANKS, MIST. GO DO YOUR STUFF.
WITH PLEASURE, PIRATE!
EVER SINCE OVERUSE OF MY INVISIO-SOLUTION MADE ME A MIST IN FACT AS IN NAME--
--I'VE ENJOYED CRIME EVEN MORE THAN BEFORE!
AND NOW, WITH NO SUPER-HEROES TO OPPOSE US, IT'S A POSITIVE JOY!
CALL THE STATION HOUSE, WAMBAUGH!
TELL 'EM WE'VE NABBED TWO CROOKS RED-HANDED!
IT IS TO LAUGH, EH, PIRATE?
I'M CRACKING UP, MIST--
HAAAA
HA
--AND AFTER ONE GLANCE AT MY PHIZZ, SO ARE THEY!
RES
HAHA
HAHAHA
13

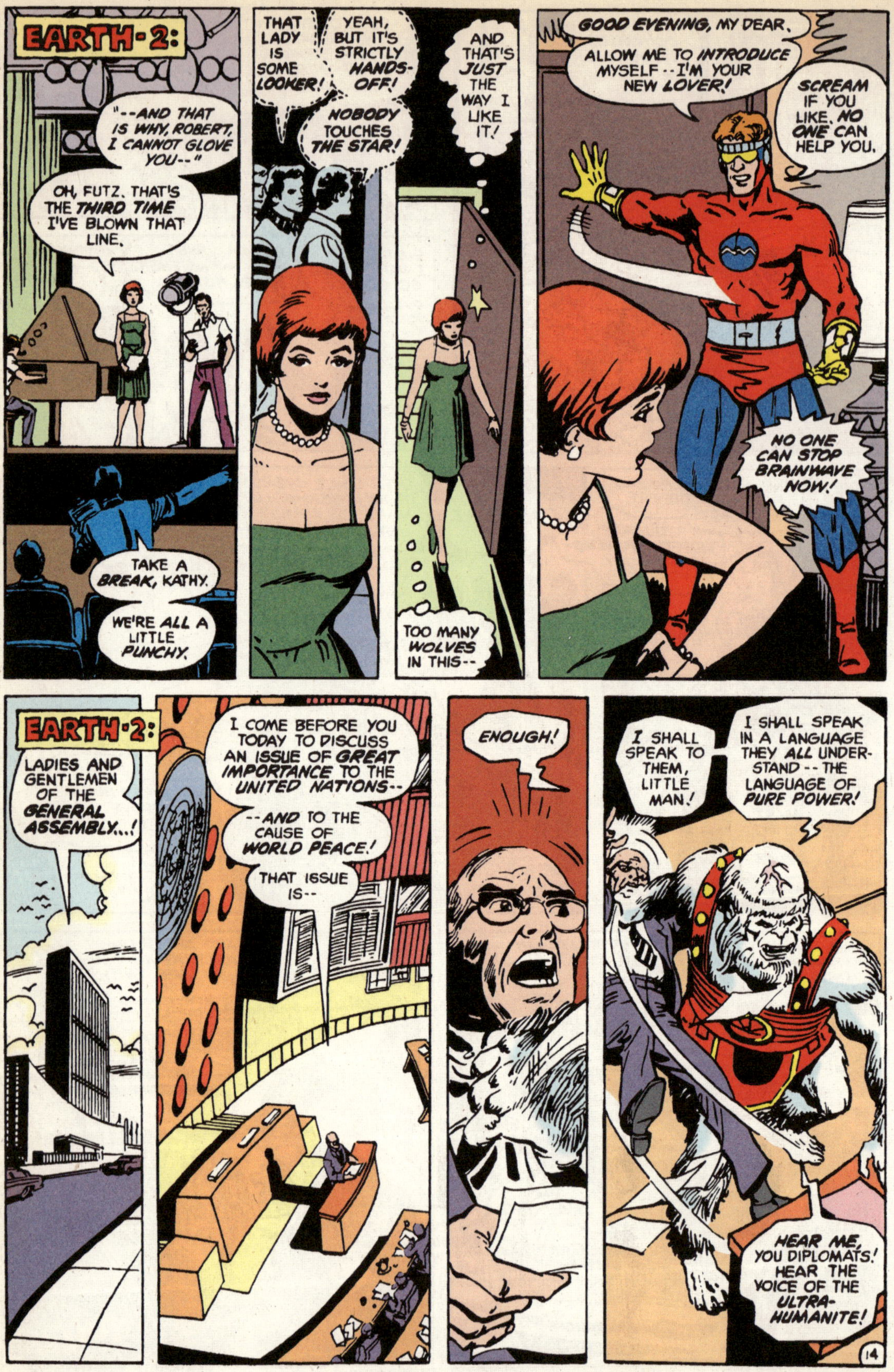

EARTH-2:
"--AND THAT IS WHY, ROBERT, I CANNOT GLOVE YOU--"
OH, FUTZ. THAT'S THE THIRD TIME I'VE BLOWN THAT LINE.
TAKE A BREAK, KATHY.
WE'RE ALL A LITTLE PUNCHY.
THAT LADY IS SOME LOOKER!
YEAH, BUT IT'S STRICTLY HANDS-OFF!
NOBODY TOUCHES THE STAR!
AND THAT'S JUST THE WAY I LIKE IT!
TOO MANY WOLVES IN THIS--
GOOD EVENING, MY DEAR.
ALLOW ME TO INTRODUCE MYSELF--I'M YOUR NEW LOVER!
SCREAM IF YOU LIKE. NO ONE CAN HELP YOU.
NO ONE CAN STOP BRAINWAVE NOW!
EARTH-2:
LADIES AND GENTLEMEN OF THE GENERAL ASSEMBLY...!
I COME BEFORE YOU TODAY TO DISCUSS AN ISSUE OF GREAT IMPORTANCE TO THE UNITED NATIONS--
--AND TO THE CAUSE OF WORLD PEACE!
THAT ISSUE IS--
ENOUGH!
I SHALL SPEAK TO THEM, LITTLE MAN!
I SHALL SPEAK IN A LANGUAGE THEY ALL UNDERSTAND -- THE LANGUAGE OF PURE POWER!
HEAR ME, YOU DIPLOMATS! HEAR THE VOICE OF THE ULTRA-HUMANITE!
14

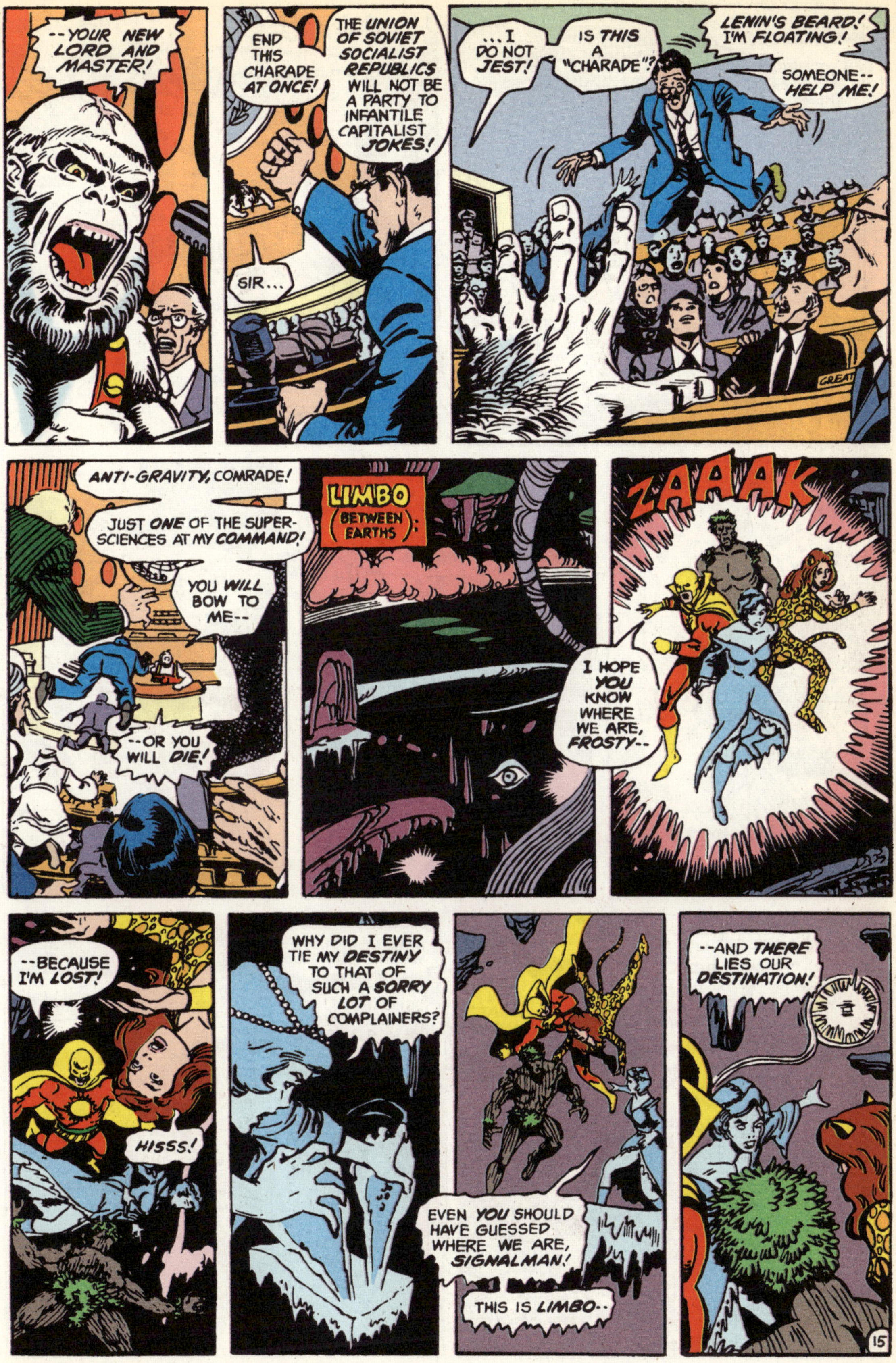
--YOUR NEW LORD AND MASTER!
END THIS CHARADE AT ONCE!
THE UNION OF SOVIET SOCIALIST REPUBLICS WILL NOT BE A PARTY TO INFANTILE CAPITALIST JOKES!
SIR...
...I DO NOT JEST!
IS THIS A "CHARADE"?
LENIN'S BEARD! I'M FLOATING!
SOMEONE-- HELP ME!
ANTI-GRAVITY, COMRADE!
JUST ONE OF THE SUPER-SCIENCES AT MY COMMAND!
YOU WILL BOW TO ME--
--OR YOU WILL DIE!
LIMBO (BETWEEN EARTHS):
ZAAAK
I HOPE YOU KNOW WHERE WE ARE, FROSTY--
--BECAUSE I'M LOST!
HISSS!
WHY DID I EVER TIE MY DESTINY TO THAT OF SUCH A SORRY LOT OF COMPLAINERS?
EVEN YOU SHOULD HAVE GUESSED WHERE WE ARE, SIGNALMAN!
THIS IS LIMBO--
--AND THERE LIES OUR DESTINATION!
15

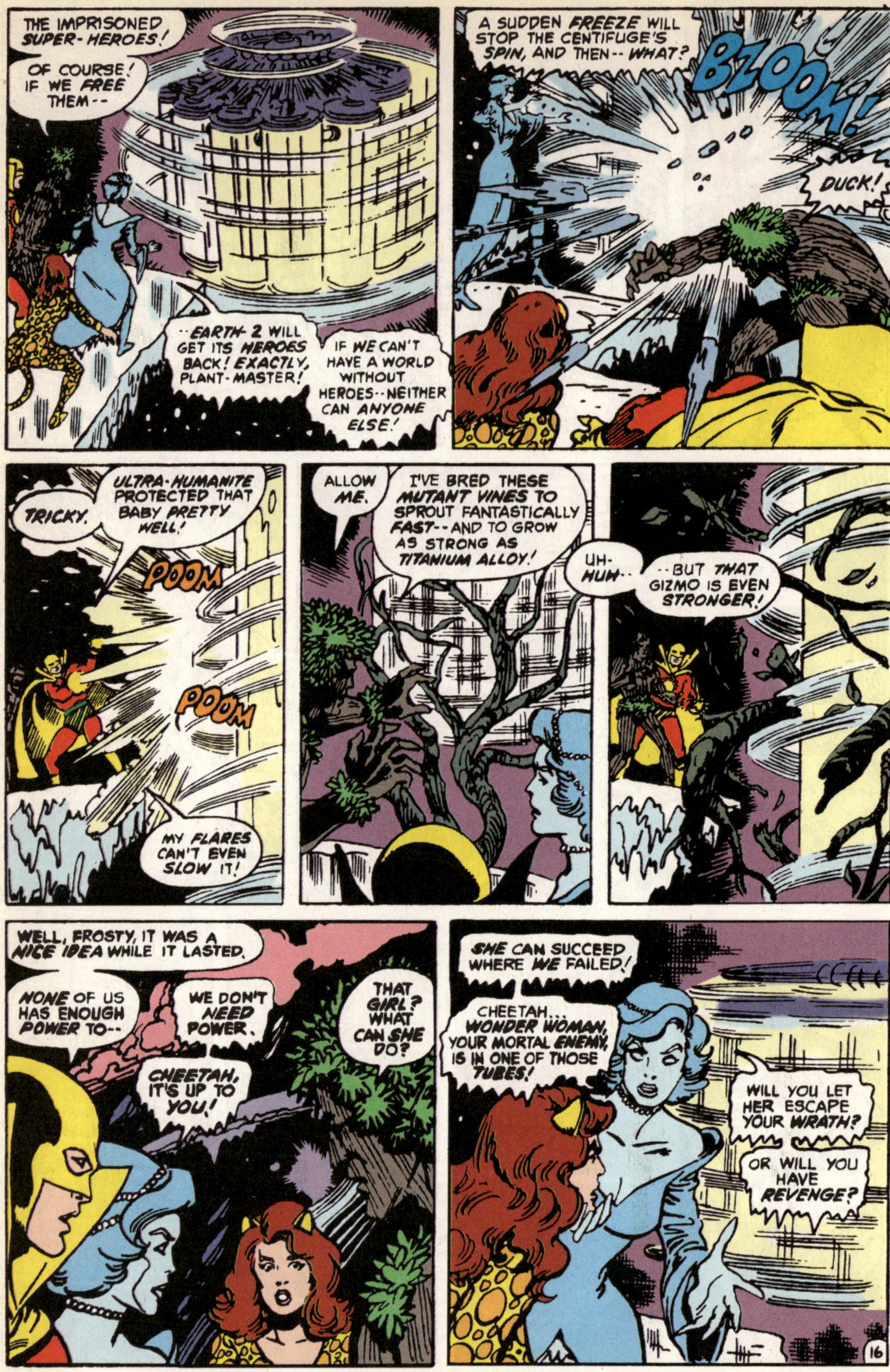
THE IMPRISONED SUPER-HEROES!
OF COURSE! IF WE FREE THEM--
--EARTH-2 WILL GET ITS HEROES BACK! EXACTLY, PLANT-MASTER!
IF WE CAN'T HAVE A WORLD WITHOUT HEROES--NEITHER CAN ANYONE ELSE!
A SUDDEN FREEZE WILL STOP THE CENTIFUGE'S SPIN, AND THEN-- WHAT?
BZOOM!
DUCK!
TRICKY.
ULTRA-HUMANITE PROTECTED THAT BABY PRETTY WELL!
POOM
POOM
MY FLARES CAN'T EVEN SLOW IT!
ALLOW ME.
I'VE BRED THESE MUTANT VINES TO SPROUT FANTASTICALLY FAST--AND TO GROW AS STRONG AS TITANIUM ALLOY!
UH-HUH--
--BUT THAT GIZMO IS EVEN STRONGER!
WELL, FROSTY, IT WAS A NICE IDEA WHILE IT LASTED.
NONE OF US HAS ENOUGH POWER TO--
WE DON'T NEED POWER.
THAT GIRL? WHAT CAN SHE DO?
CHEETAH, IT'S UP TO YOU!
SHE CAN SUCCEED WHERE WE FAILED!
CHEETAH... WONDER WOMAN, YOUR MORTAL ENEMY, IS IN ONE OF THOSE TUBES!
WILL YOU LET HER ESCAPE YOUR WRATH?
OR WILL YOU HAVE REVENGE?
16

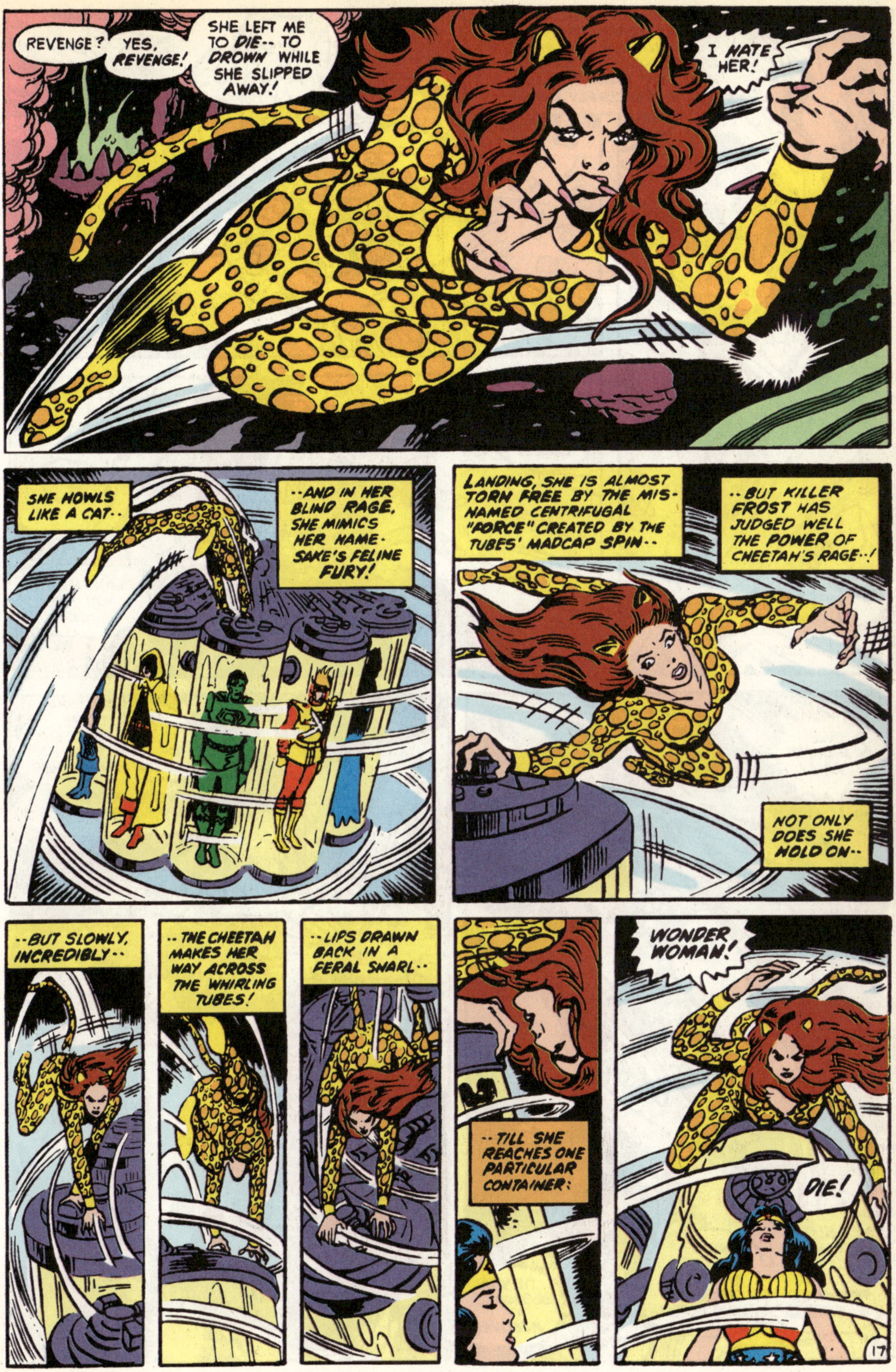

REVENGE?
YES, REVENGE!
SHE LEFT ME TO DIE-- TO DROWN WHILE SHE SLIPPED AWAY!
I HATE HER!
SHE HOWLS LIKE A CAT--
--AND IN HER BLIND RAGE, SHE MIMICS HER NAME-SAKE'S FELINE FURY!
LANDING, SHE IS ALMOST TORN FREE BY THE MIS-NAMED CENTRIFUGAL "FORCE" CREATED BY THE TUBES' MADCAP SPIN--
--BUT KILLER FROST HAS JUDGED WELL THE POWER OF CHEETAH'S RAGE--!
NOT ONLY DOES SHE HOLD ON--
--BUT SLOWLY, INCREDIBLY--
--THE CHEETAH MAKES HER WAY ACROSS THE WHIRLING TUBES!
--LIPS DRAWN BACK IN A FERAL SNARL--
--TILL SHE REACHES ONE PARTICULAR CONTAINER:
WONDER WOMAN!
DIE!
17

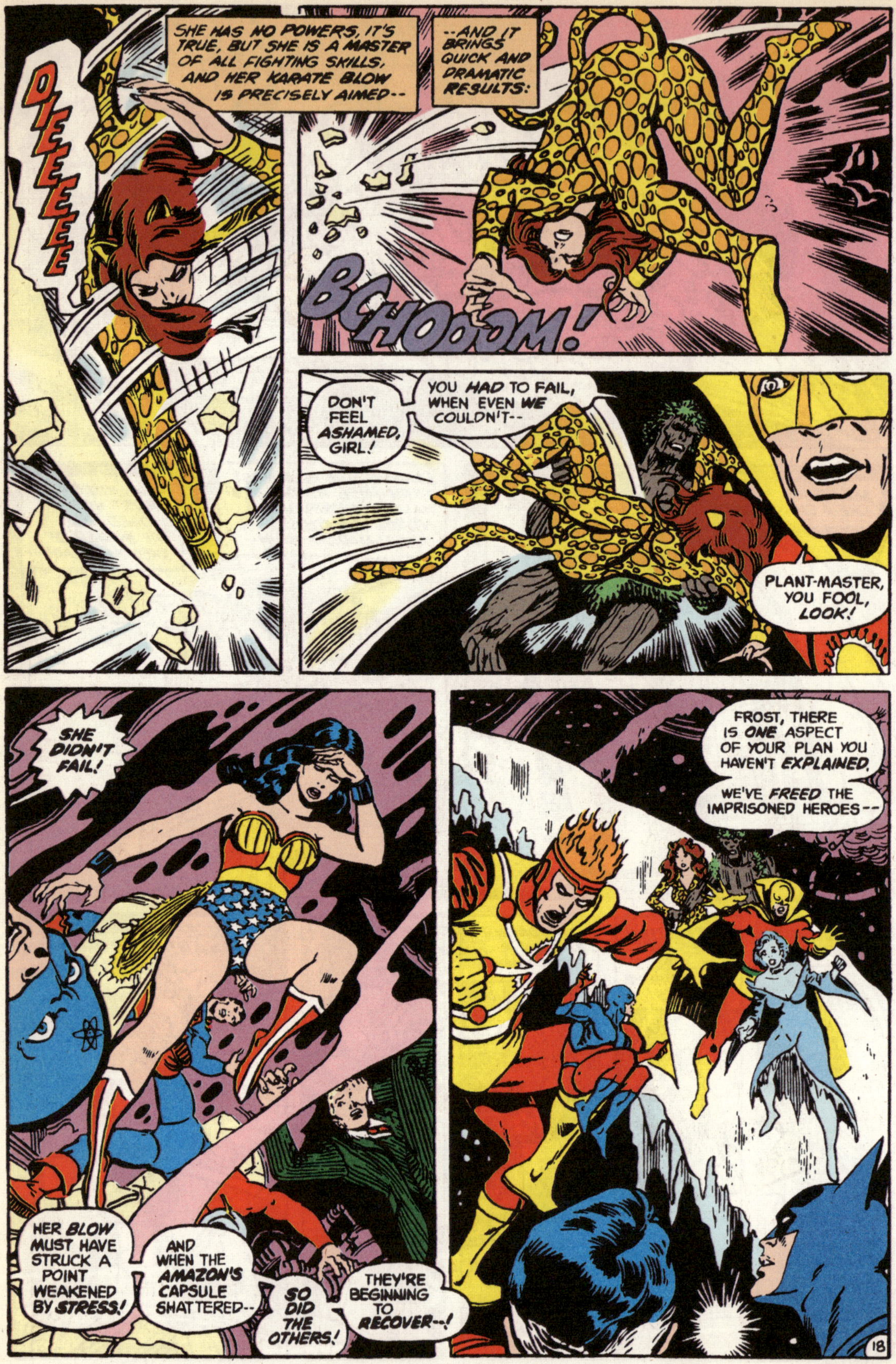
SHE HAS NO POWERS, IT'S TRUE, BUT SHE IS A MASTER OF ALL FIGHTING SKILLS, AND HER KARATE BLOW IS PRECISELY AIMED--
DIEEEEEE
--AND IT BRINGS QUICK AND DRAMATIC RESULTS:
BCHOOOM!
DON'T FEEL ASHAMED, GIRL!
YOU HAD TO FAIL, WHEN EVEN WE COULDN'T--
PLANT-MASTER, YOU FOOL, LOOK!
SHE DIDN'T FAIL!
HER BLOW MUST HAVE STRUCK A POINT WEAKENED BY STRESS!
AND WHEN THE AMAZON'S CAPSULE SHATTERED--
SO DID THE OTHERS!
THEY'RE BEGINNING TO RECOVER--!
FROST, THERE IS ONE ASPECT OF YOUR PLAN YOU HAVEN'T EXPLAINED.
WE'VE FREED THE IMPRISONED HEROES--
18

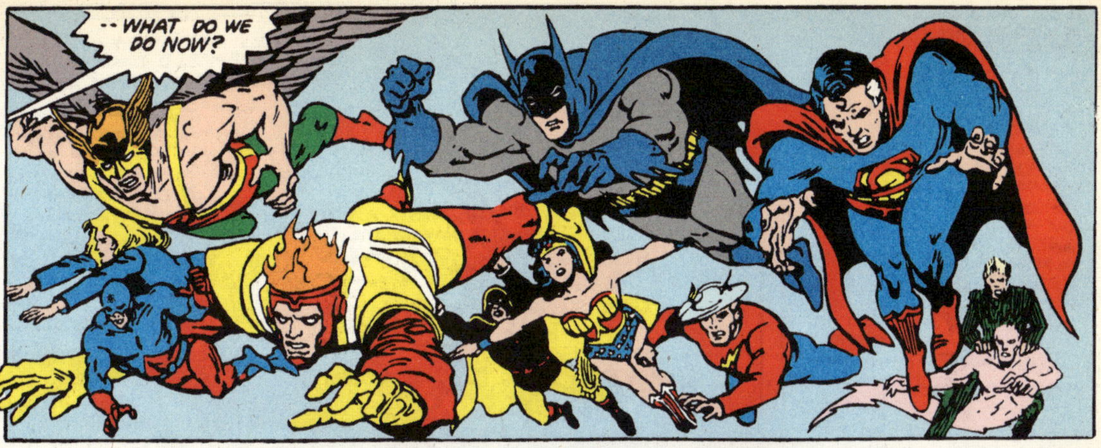
-- WHAT DO WE DO NOW?

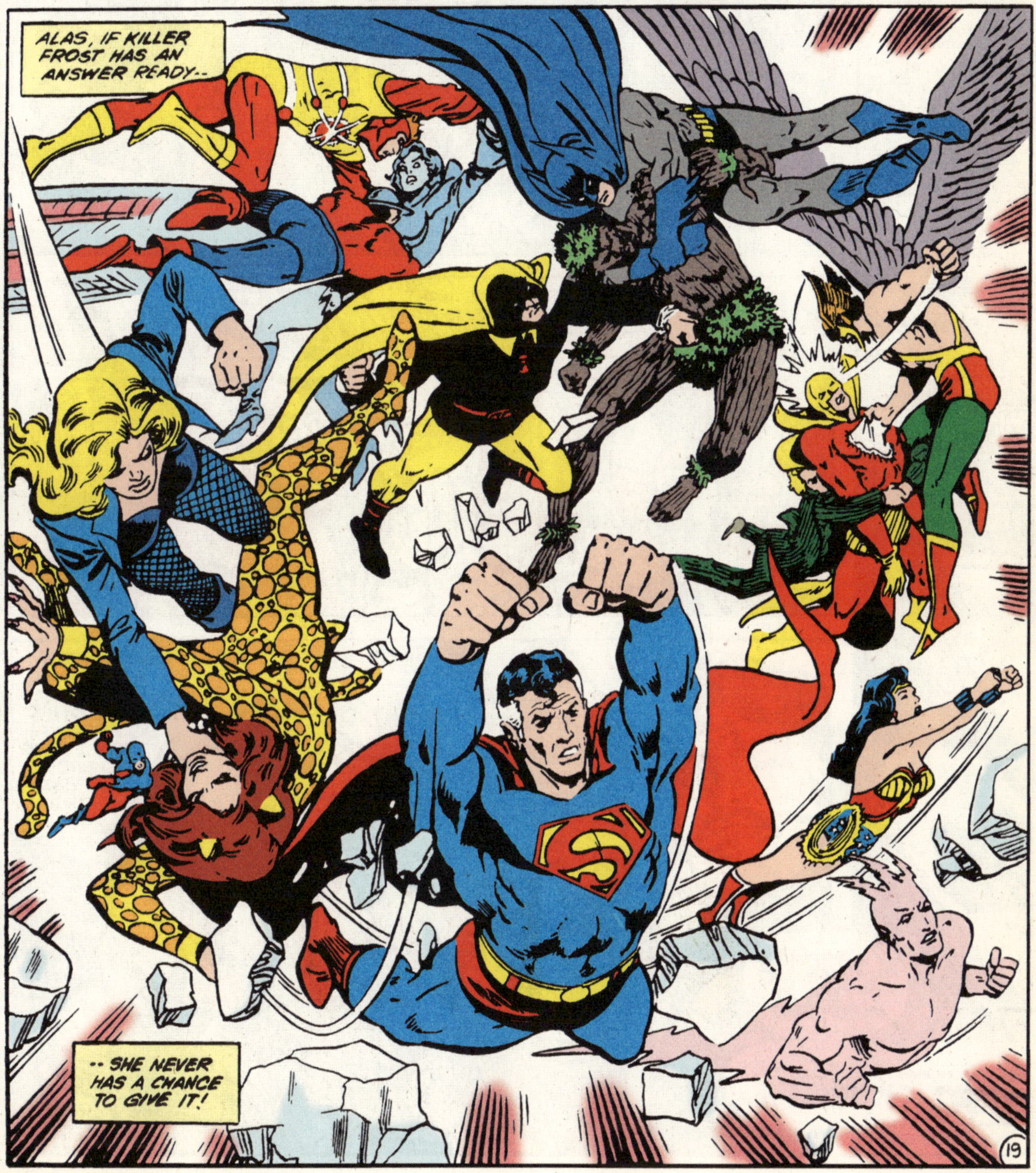
ALAS, IF KILLER FROST HAS AN ANSWER READY--
-- SHE NEVER HAS A CHANCE TO GIVE IT!
19

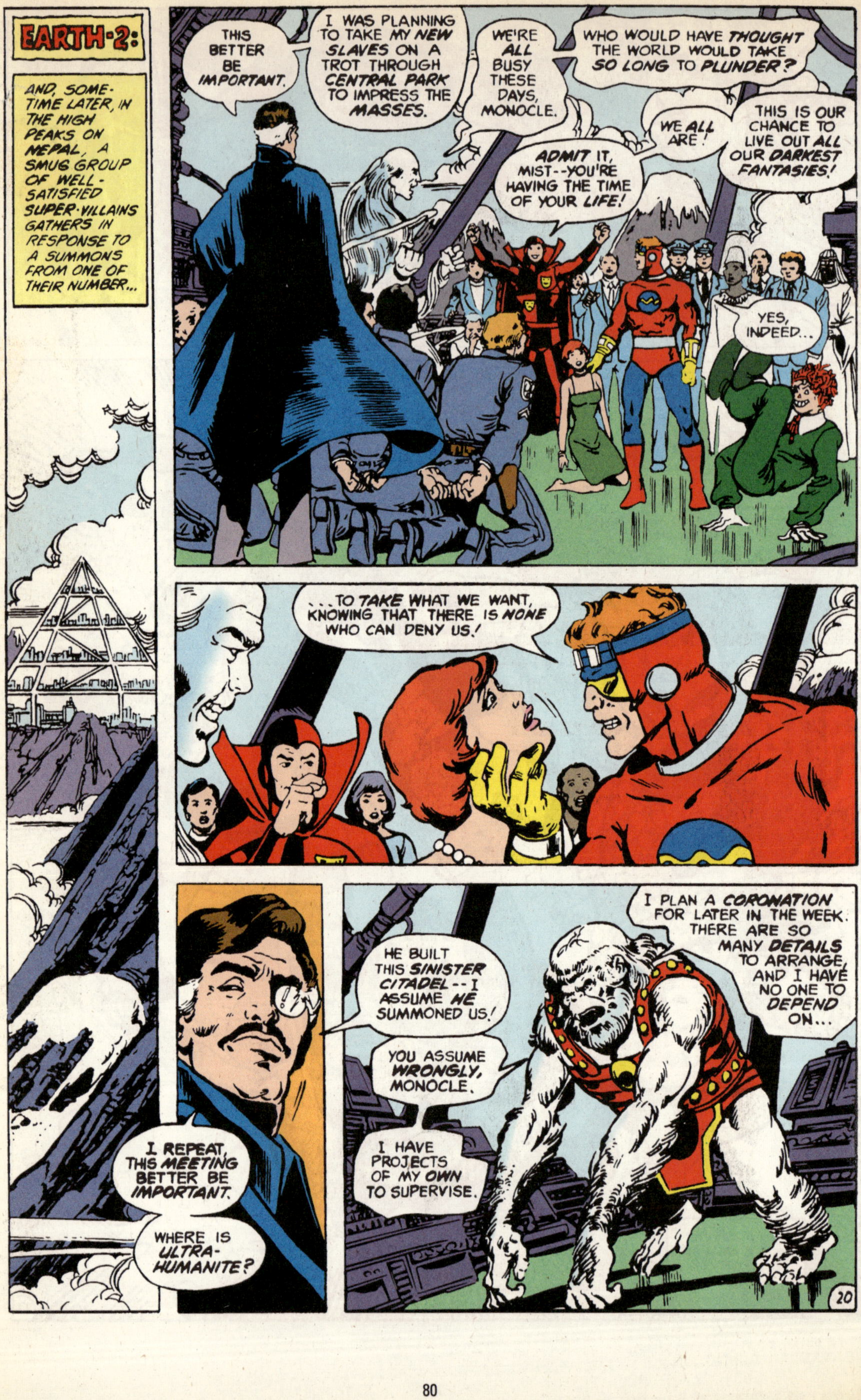
EARTH-2:
AND, SOME-TIME LATER, IN THE HIGH PEAKS ON NEPAL, A SMUG GROUP OF WELL-SATISFIED SUPER-VILLAINS GATHERS IN RESPONSE TO A SUMMONS FROM ONE OF THEIR NUMBER...
THIS BETTER BE IMPORTANT.
I WAS PLANNING TO TAKE MY NEW SLAVES ON A TROT THROUGH CENTRAL PARK TO IMPRESS THE MASSES.
WE'RE ALL BUSY THESE DAYS, MONOCLE.
WHO WOULD HAVE THOUGHT THE WORLD WOULD TAKE SO LONG TO PLUNDER?
WE ALL ARE!
THIS IS OUR CHANCE TO LIVE OUT ALL OUR DARKEST FANTASIES!
ADMIT IT, MIST--YOU'RE HAVING THE TIME OF YOUR LIFE!
YES, INDEED...
...TO TAKE WHAT WE WANT, KNOWING THAT THERE IS NONE WHO CAN DENY US!
I REPEAT, THIS MEETING BETTER BE IMPORTANT.
WHERE IS ULTRA-HUMANITE?
HE BUILT THIS SINISTER CITADEL--I ASSUME HE SUMMONED US!
YOU ASSUME WRONGLY, MONOCLE.
I HAVE PROJECTS OF MY OWN TO SUPERVISE.
I PLAN A CORONATION FOR LATER IN THE WEEK. THERE ARE SO MANY DETAILS TO ARRANGE, AND I HAVE NO ONE TO DEPEND ON...
20

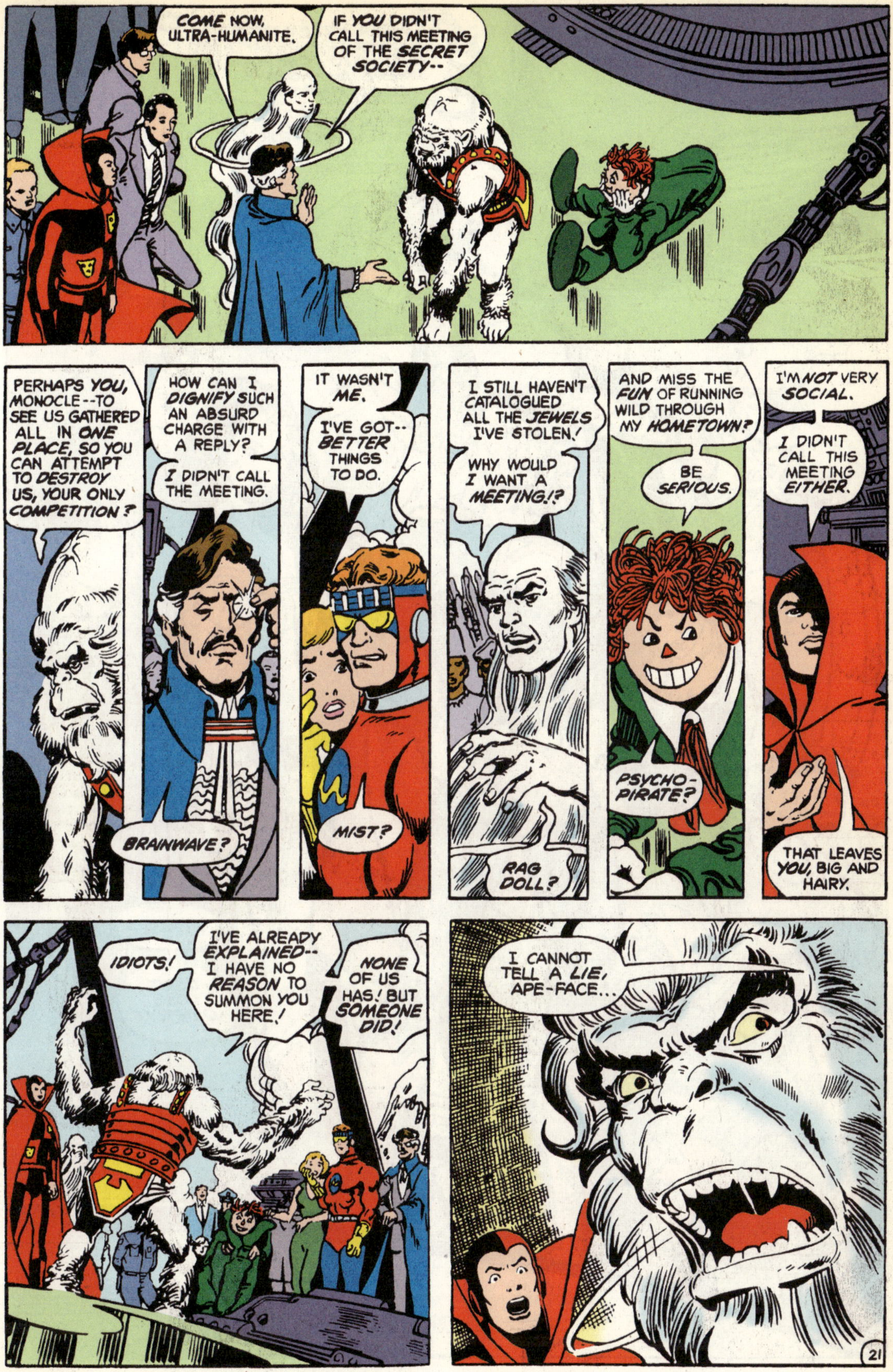

COME NOW, ULTRA-HUMANITE.
IF YOU DIDN'T CALL THIS MEETING OF THE SECRET SOCIETY--
PERHAPS YOU, MONOCLE--TO SEE US GATHERED ALL IN ONE PLACE, SO YOU CAN ATTEMPT TO DESTROY US, YOUR ONLY COMPETITION?
HOW CAN I DIGNIFY SUCH AN ABSURD CHARGE WITH A REPLY?
I DIDN'T CALL THE MEETING.
BRAINWAVE?
IT WASN'T ME.
I'VE GOT-- BETTER THINGS TO DO.
MIST?
I STILL HAVEN'T CATALOGUED ALL THE JEWELS I'VE STOLEN!
WHY WOULD I WANT A MEETING!?
RAG DOLL?
AND MISS THE FUN OF RUNNING WILD THROUGH MY HOMETOWN?
BE SERIOUS.
PSYCHO-PIRATE?
I'M NOT VERY SOCIAL.
I DIDN'T CALL THIS MEETING EITHER.
THAT LEAVES YOU, BIG AND HAIRY.
IDIOTS!
I'VE ALREADY EXPLAINED-- I HAVE NO REASON TO SUMMON YOU HERE!
NONE OF US HAS! BUT SOMEONE DID!
I CANNOT TELL A LIE, APE-FACE...
21

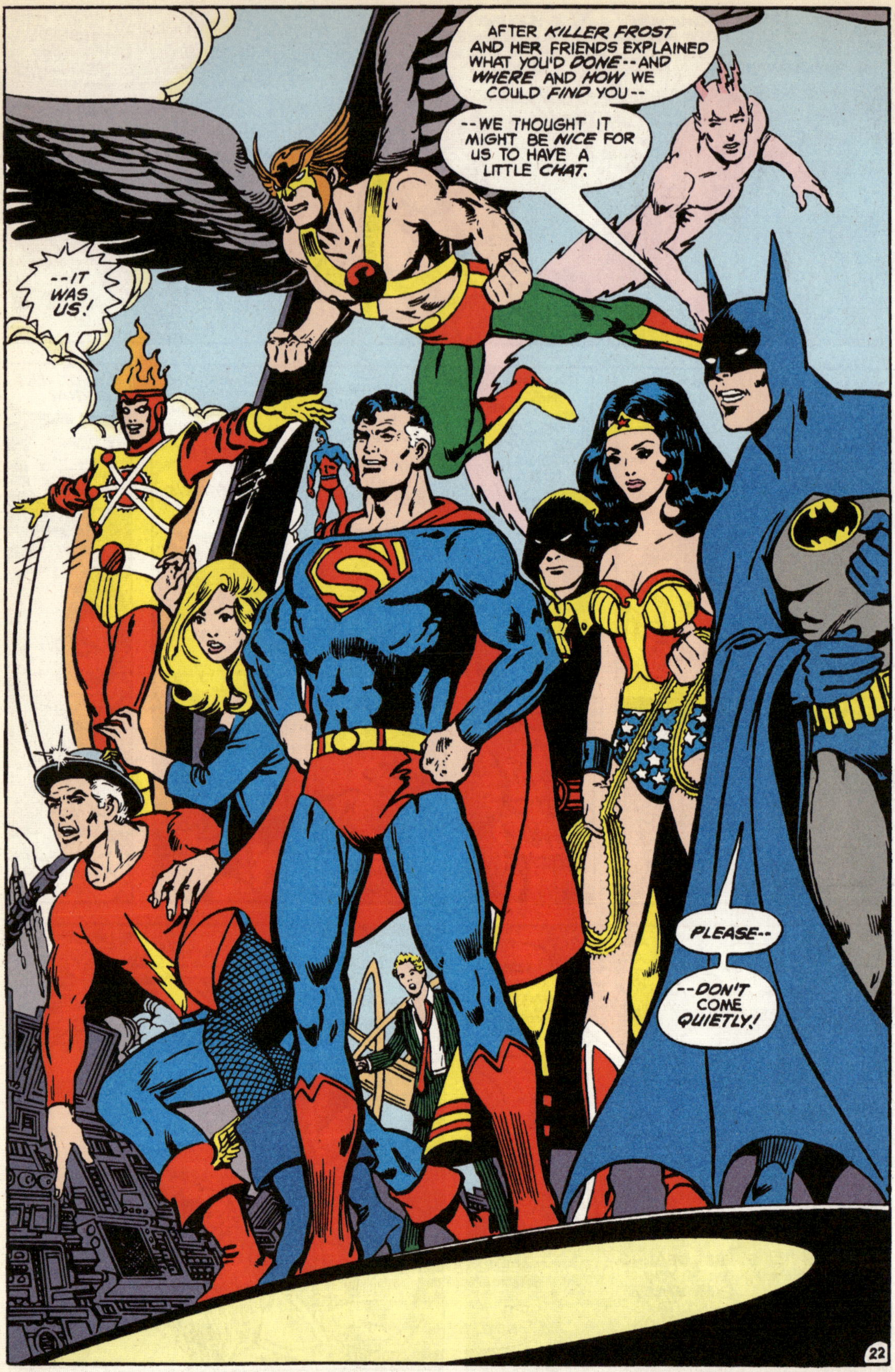
AFTER KILLER FROST AND HER FRIENDS EXPLAINED WHAT YOU'D DONE--AND WHERE AND HOW WE COULD FIND YOU--
--WE THOUGHT IT MIGHT BE NICE FOR US TO HAVE A LITTLE CHAT.
--IT WAS US!
PLEASE--
--DON'T COME QUIETLY!
22

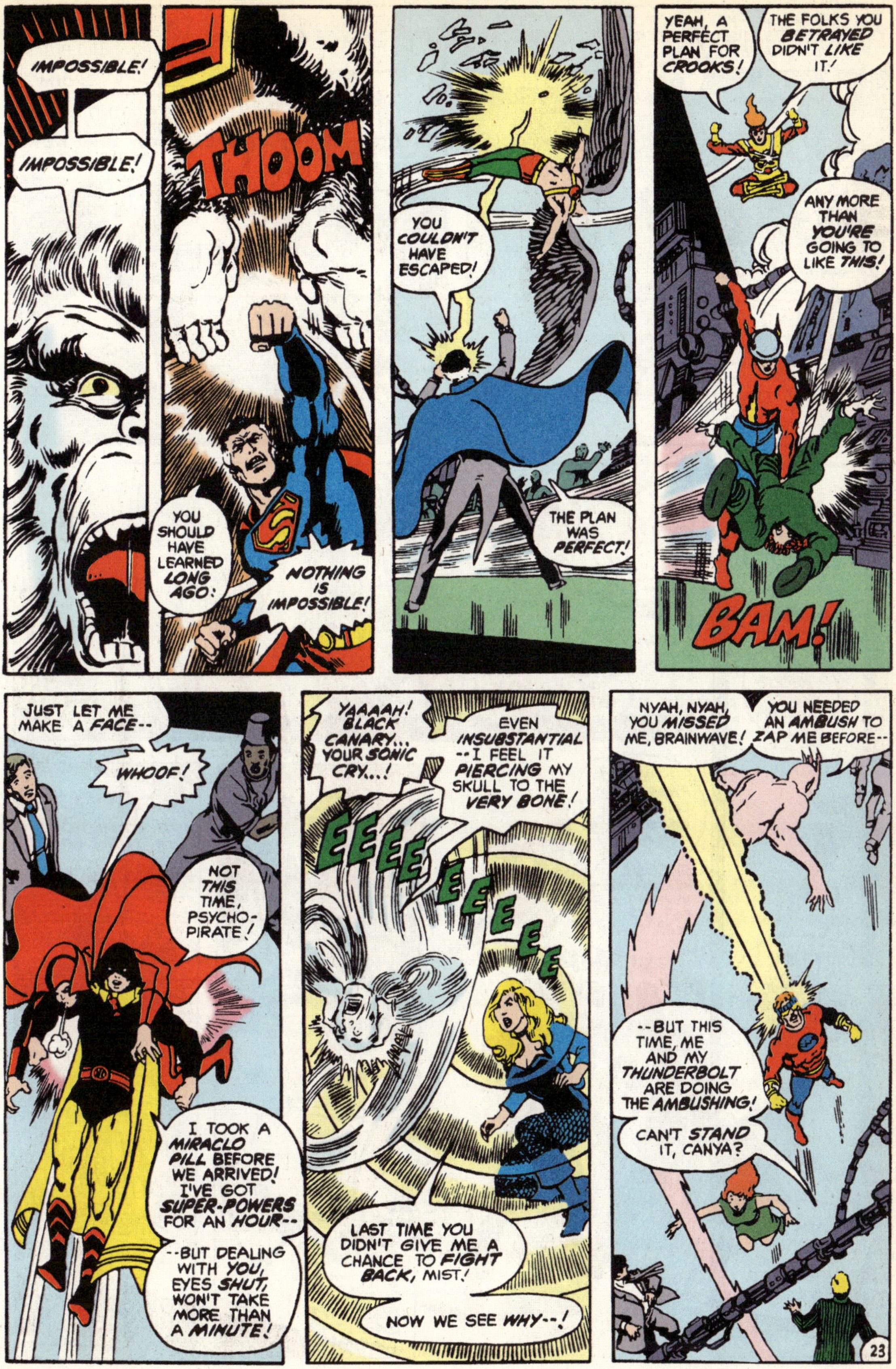
IMPOSSIBLE!
IMPOSSIBLE!
THOOM
YOU SHOULD HAVE LEARNED LONG AGO:
NOTHING IS IMPOSSIBLE!
YOU COULDN'T HAVE ESCAPED!
THE PLAN WAS PERFECT!
YEAH, A PERFECT PLAN FOR CROOKS!
THE FOLKS YOU BETRAYED DIDN'T LIKE IT.
ANY MORE THAN YOU'RE GOING TO LIKE THIS!
BAM!
JUST LET ME MAKE A FACE--
WHOOF!
NOT THIS TIME, PSYCHO-PIRATE!
I TOOK A MIRACLO PILL BEFORE WE ARRIVED! I'VE GOT SUPER-POWERS FOR AN HOUR--
--BUT DEALING WITH YOU, EYES SHUT, WON'T TAKE MORE THAN A MINUTE!
YAAAAH! BLACK CANARY... YOUR SONIC CRY...!
EVEN INSUBSTANTIAL --I FEEL IT PIERCING MY SKULL TO THE VERY BONE!
EEEEEEEEEE
LAST TIME YOU DIDN'T GIVE ME A CHANCE TO FIGHT BACK, MIST!
NOW WE SEE WHY--!
NYAH, NYAH, YOU MISSED ME, BRAINWAVE!
YOU NEEDED AN AMBUSH TO ZAP ME BEFORE--
--BUT THIS TIME, ME AND MY THUNDERBOLT ARE DOING THE AMBUSHING!
CAN'T STAND IT, CANYA?
23

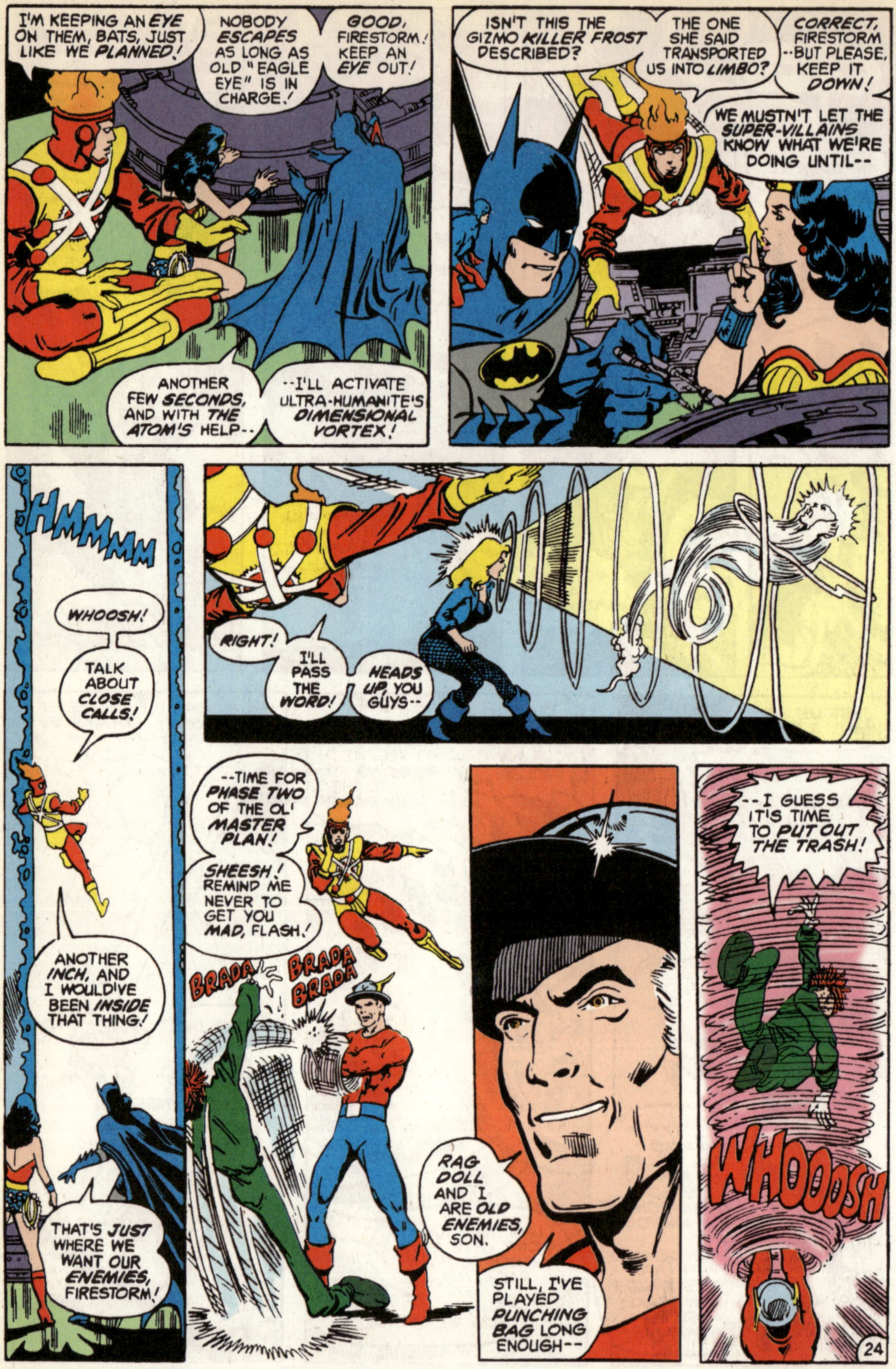
I'M KEEPING AN EYE ON THEM, BATS, JUST LIKE WE PLANNED!
NOBODY ESCAPES AS LONG AS OLD "EAGLE EYE" IS IN CHARGE!
GOOD, FIRESTORM! KEEP AN EYE OUT!
ANOTHER FEW SECONDS, AND WITH THE ATOM'S HELP--
--I'LL ACTIVATE ULTRA-HUMANITE'S DIMENSIONAL VORTEX!
ISN'T THIS THE GIZMO KILLER FROST DESCRIBED?
THE ONE SHE SAID TRANSPORTED US INTO LIMBO?
CORRECT, FIRESTORM --BUT PLEASE, KEEP IT DOWN!
WE MUSTN'T LET THE SUPER-VILLAINS KNOW WHAT WE'RE DOING UNTIL--
HMMMMM
WHOOSH!
TALK ABOUT CLOSE CALLS!
ANOTHER INCH, AND I WOULD'VE BEEN INSIDE THAT THING!
THAT'S JUST WHERE WE WANT OUR ENEMIES, FIRESTORM!
RIGHT!
I'LL PASS THE WORD!
HEADS UP, YOU GUYS--
--TIME FOR PHASE TWO OF THE OL' MASTER PLAN!
SHEESH! REMIND ME NEVER TO GET YOU MAD, FLASH!
BRADA
BRADA BRADA BRADA
RAG DOLL AND I ARE OLD ENEMIES, SON.
STILL, I'VE PLAYED PUNCHING BAG LONG ENOUGH--
--I GUESS IT'S TIME TO PUT OUT THE TRASH!
WHOOOSH
24

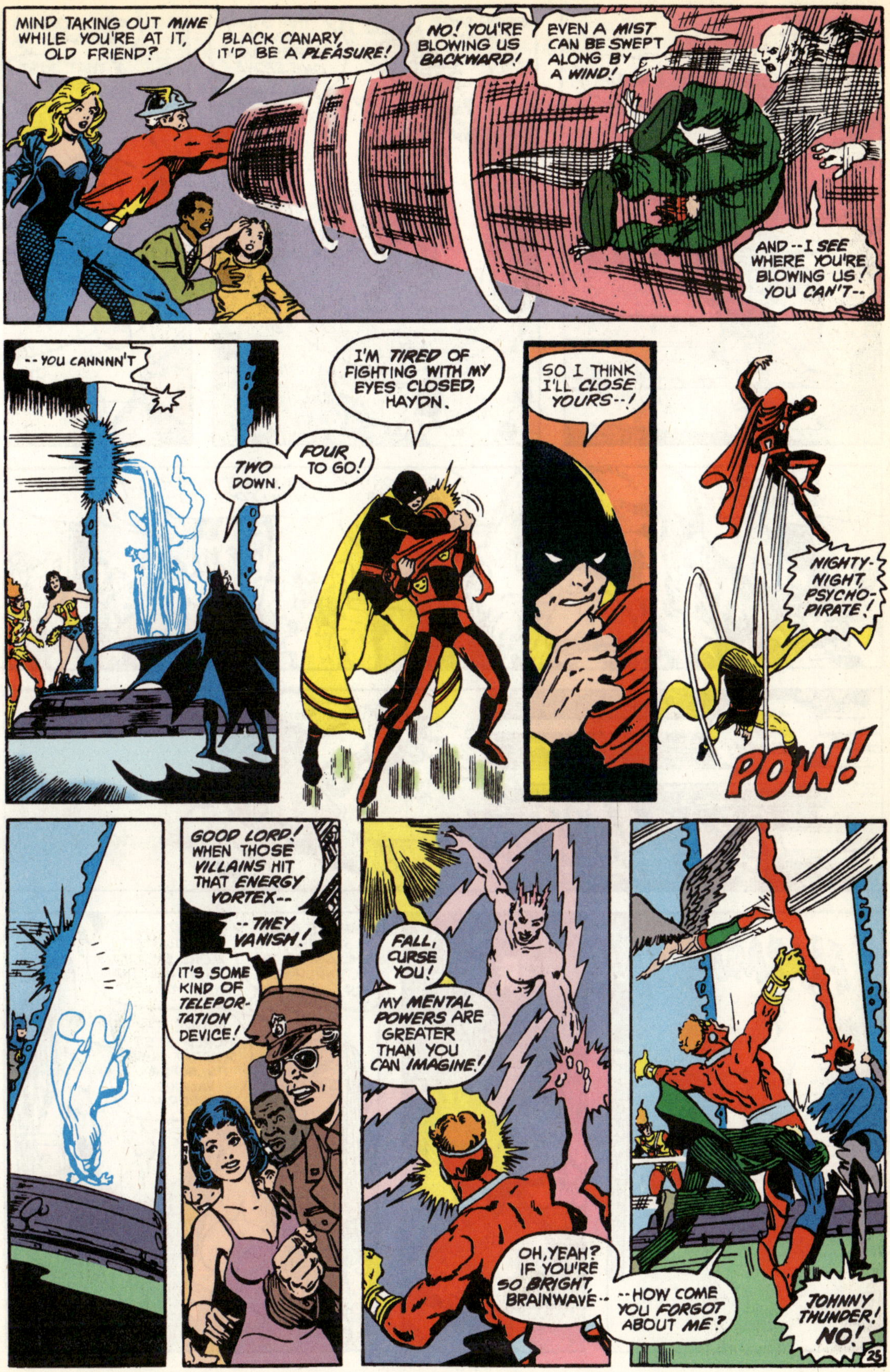
MIND TAKING OUT MINE WHILE YOU'RE AT IT, OLD FRIEND?
BLACK CANARY, IT'D BE A PLEASURE!
NO! YOU'RE BLOWING US BACKWARD!
EVEN A MIST CAN BE SWEPT ALONG BY A WIND!
AND -- I SEE WHERE YOU'RE BLOWING US! YOU CAN'T--
-- YOU CANNNN'T
TWO DOWN.
FOUR TO GO!
I'M TIRED OF FIGHTING WITH MY EYES CLOSED, HAYDN.
SO I THINK I'LL CLOSE YOURS--!
NIGHTY-NIGHT, PSYCHO-PIRATE!
POW!
GOOD LORD! WHEN THOSE VILLAINS HIT THAT ENERGY VORTEX--
-- THEY VANISH!
IT'S SOME KIND OF TELEPORTATION DEVICE!
FALL, CURSE YOU!
MY MENTAL POWERS ARE GREATER THAN YOU CAN IMAGINE!
OH, YEAH? IF YOU'RE SO BRIGHT, BRAINWAVE--
-- HOW COME YOU FORGOT ABOUT ME?
JOHNNY THUNDER! NO!
25

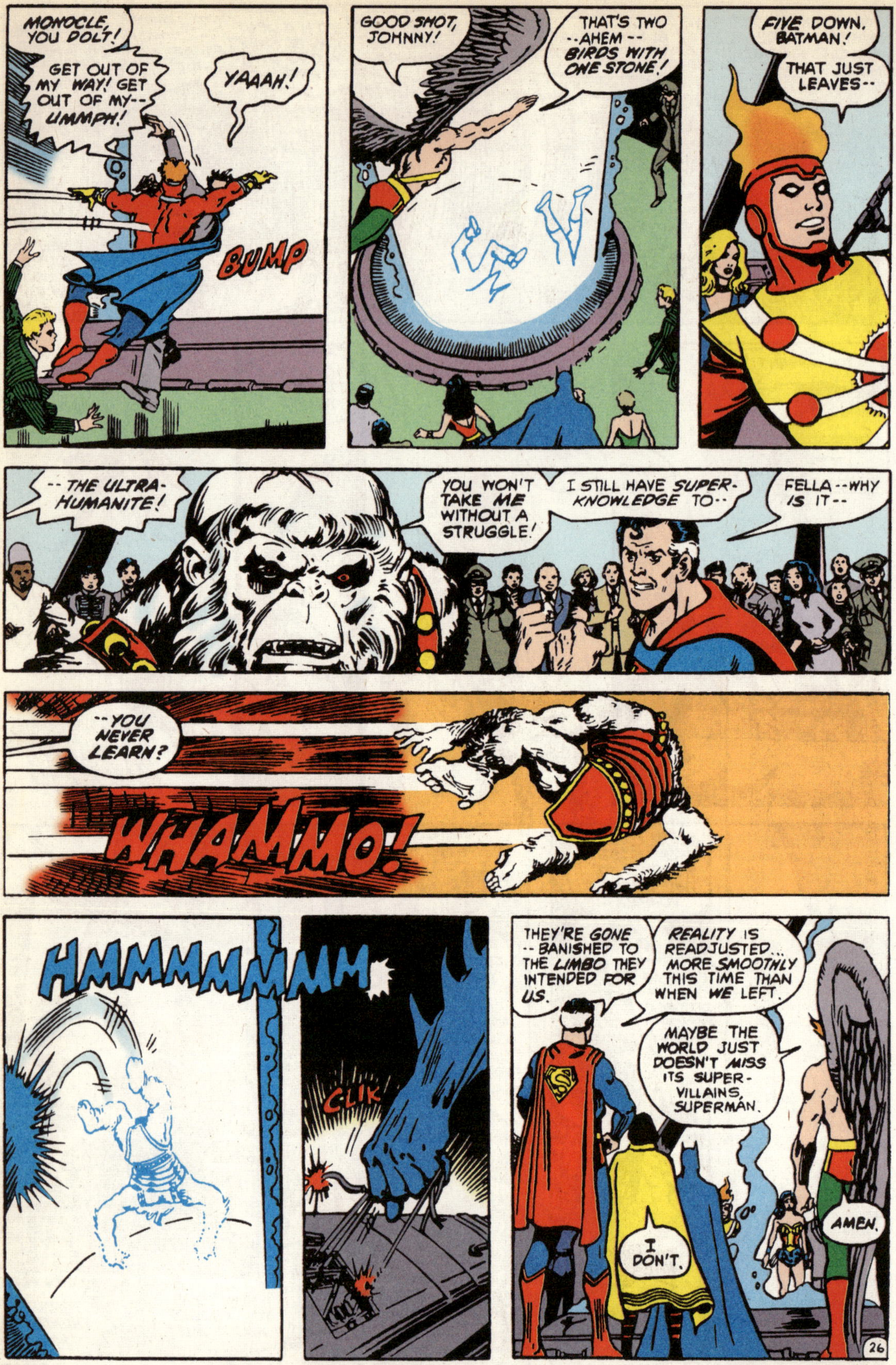
MONOCLE, YOU DOLT!
GET OUT OF MY WAY! GET OUT OF MY-- UMMPH!
YAAAH!
BUMP
GOOD SHOT, JOHNNY!
THAT'S TWO --AHEM-- BIRDS WITH ONE STONE!
FIVE DOWN, BATMAN!
THAT JUST LEAVES--
--THE ULTRA-HUMANITE!
YOU WON'T TAKE ME WITHOUT A STRUGGLE!
I STILL HAVE SUPER-KNOWLEDGE TO--
FELLA--WHY IS IT--
--YOU NEVER LEARN?
WHAMMO!
HMMMMMMMM
CLIK
THEY'RE GONE --BANISHED TO THE LIMBO THEY INTENDED FOR US.
REALITY IS READJUSTED... MORE SMOOTHLY THIS TIME THAN WHEN WE LEFT.
MAYBE THE WORLD JUST DOESN'T MISS ITS SUPER-VILLAINS, SUPERMAN.
I DON'T.
AMEN.
26

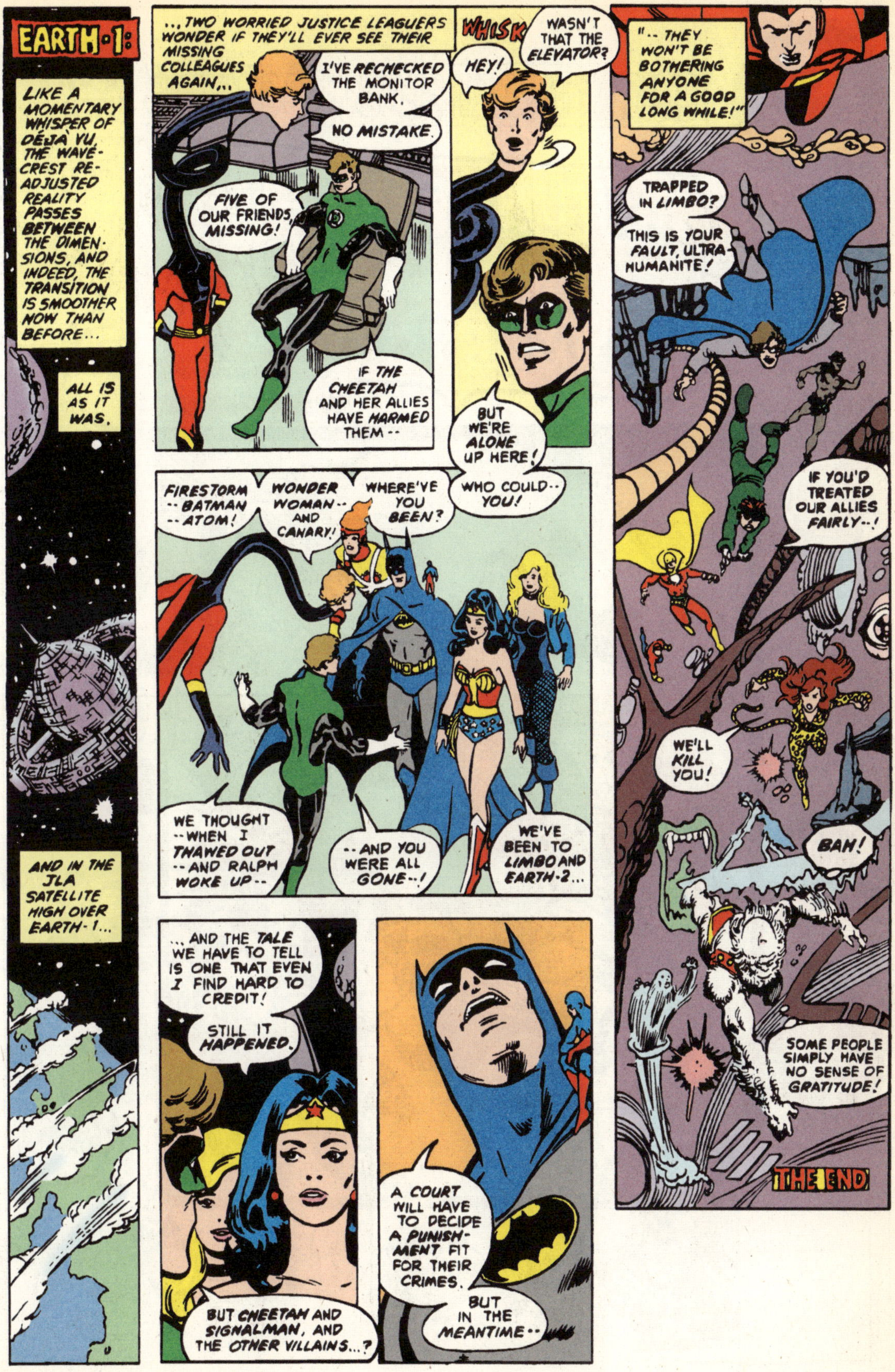
EARTH-1:
LIKE A MOMENTARY WHISPER OF DÉJÀ VU, THE WAVE-CREST RE-ADJUSTED REALITY PASSES BETWEEN THE DIMENSIONS, AND INDEED, THE TRANSITION IS SMOOTHER NOW THAN BEFORE...
ALL IS AS IT WAS.
AND IN THE JLA SATELLITE HIGH OVER EARTH-1...
..., TWO WORRIED JUSTICE LEAGUERS WONDER IF THEY'LL EVER SEE THEIR MISSING COLLEAGUES AGAIN,..
I'VE RECHECKED THE MONITOR BANK.
NO MISTAKE.
FIVE OF OUR FRIENDS, MISSING!
IF THE CHEETAH AND HER ALLIES HAVE HARMED THEM --
WHISK
HEY!
WASN'T THAT THE ELEVATOR?
BUT WE'RE ALONE UP HERE!
FIRESTORM -- BATMAN -- ATOM!
WONDER WOMAN -- AND CANARY!
WHERE'VE YOU BEEN?
WHO COULD -- YOU!
WE THOUGHT -- WHEN I THAWED OUT -- AND RALPH WOKE UP --
-- AND YOU WERE ALL GONE --!
WE'VE BEEN TO LIMBO AND EARTH-2...
... AND THE TALE WE HAVE TO TELL IS ONE THAT EVEN I FIND HARD TO CREDIT!
STILL IT HAPPENED.
BUT CHEETAH AND SIGNALMAN, AND THE OTHER VILLAINS...?
A COURT WILL HAVE TO DECIDE A PUNISHMENT FIT FOR THEIR CRIMES.
BUT IN THE MEANTIME --
"-- THEY WON'T BE BOTHERING ANYONE FOR A GOOD LONG WHILE!"
TRAPPED IN LIMBO?
THIS IS YOUR FAULT, ULTRA-HUMANITE!
IF YOU'D TREATED OUR ALLIES FAIRLY --!
WE'LL KILL YOU!
BAH!
SOME PEOPLE SIMPLY HAVE NO SENSE OF GRATITUDE!
THE END

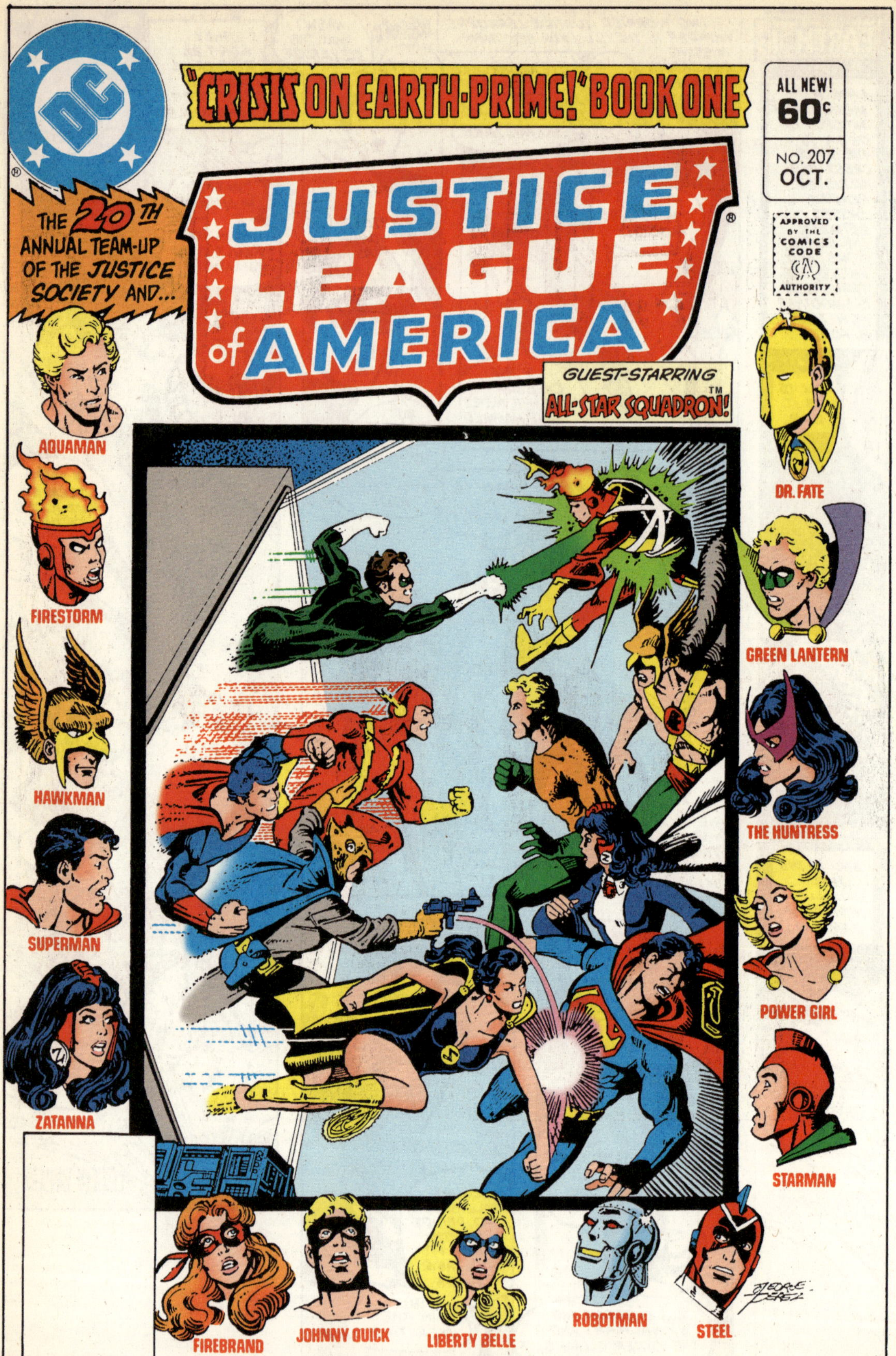
"CRISIS ON EARTH-PRIME!" BOOK ONE
ALL NEW! 60¢
NO. 207 OCT.
APPROVED BY THE COMICS CODE AUTHORITY
THE 20TH ANNUAL TEAM-UP OF THE JUSTICE SOCIETY AND...
JUSTICE LEAGUE of AMERICA
GUEST-STARRING ALL-STAR SQUADRON!
AQUAMAN
FIRESTORM
HAWKMAN
SUPERMAN
ZATANNA
DR. FATE
GREEN LANTERN
THE HUNTRESS
POWER GIRL
STARMAN
FIREBRAND
JOHNNY QUICK
LIBERTY BELLE
ROBOTMAN
STEEL

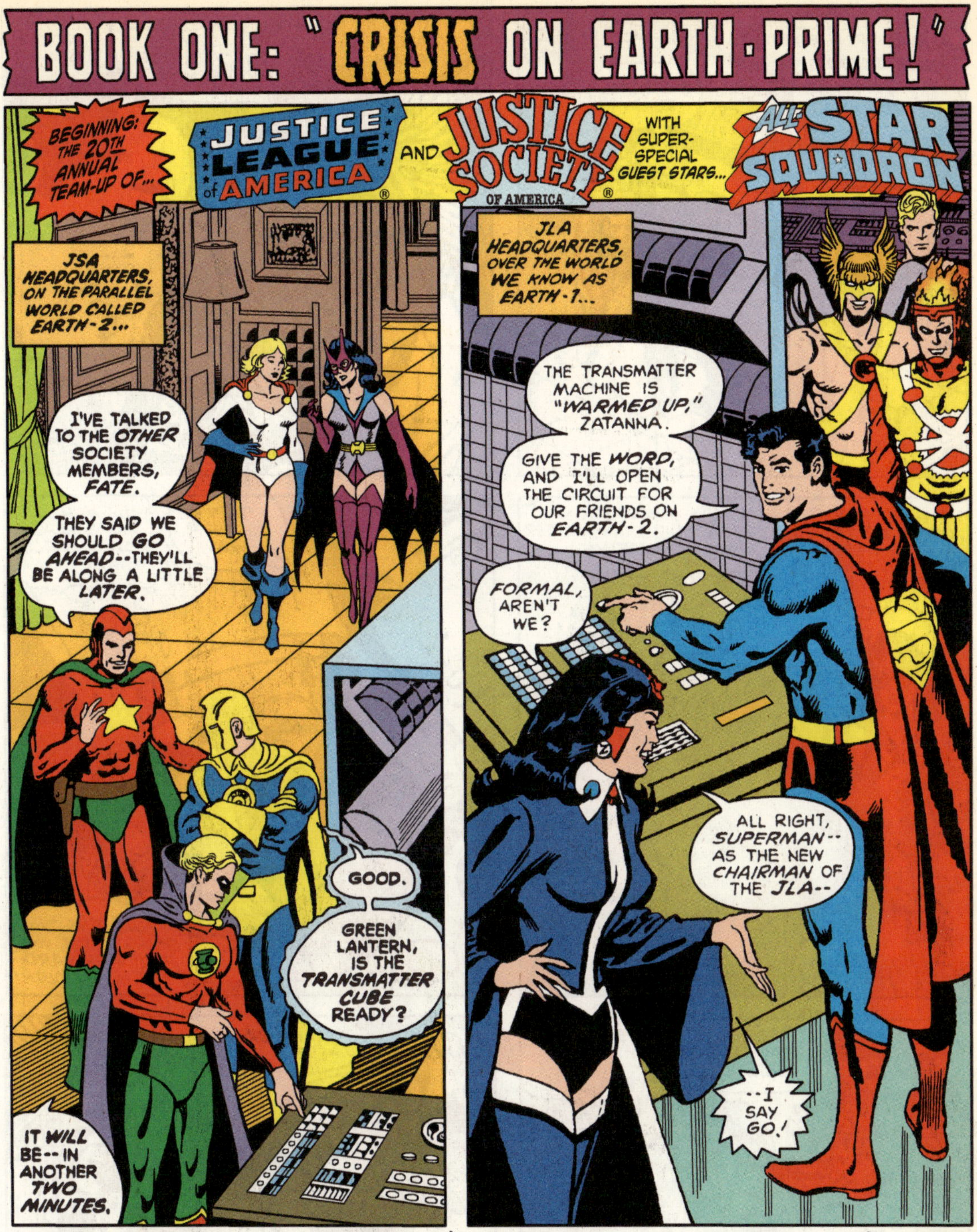
BOOK ONE: "CRISIS ON EARTH-PRIME!"
BEGINNING: THE 20TH ANNUAL TEAM-UP OF...
JUSTICE LEAGUE of AMERICA
AND
JUSTICE SOCIETY OF AMERICA
WITH SUPER-SPECIAL GUEST STARS...
ALL-STAR SQUADRON
JSA HEADQUARTERS, ON THE PARALLEL WORLD CALLED EARTH-2...
I'VE TALKED TO THE OTHER SOCIETY MEMBERS, FATE.
THEY SAID WE SHOULD GO AHEAD--THEY'LL BE ALONG A LITTLE LATER.
GOOD.
GREEN LANTERN, IS THE TRANSMATTER CUBE READY?
IT WILL BE--IN ANOTHER TWO MINUTES.
JLA HEADQUARTERS, OVER THE WORLD WE KNOW AS EARTH-1...
THE TRANSMATTER MACHINE IS "WARMED UP," ZATANNA.
GIVE THE WORD, AND I'LL OPEN THE CIRCUIT FOR OUR FRIENDS ON EARTH-2.
FORMAL, AREN'T WE?
ALL RIGHT, SUPERMAN--AS THE NEW CHAIRMAN OF THE JLA--
--I SAY GO!

GERRY CONWAY writer ✱ DON HECK & ROMEO TANGHAL artists ✱ BEN ODA letterer CARL GAFFORD colorist ✱ ROY THOMAS plot consultant ✱ LEN WEIN editor

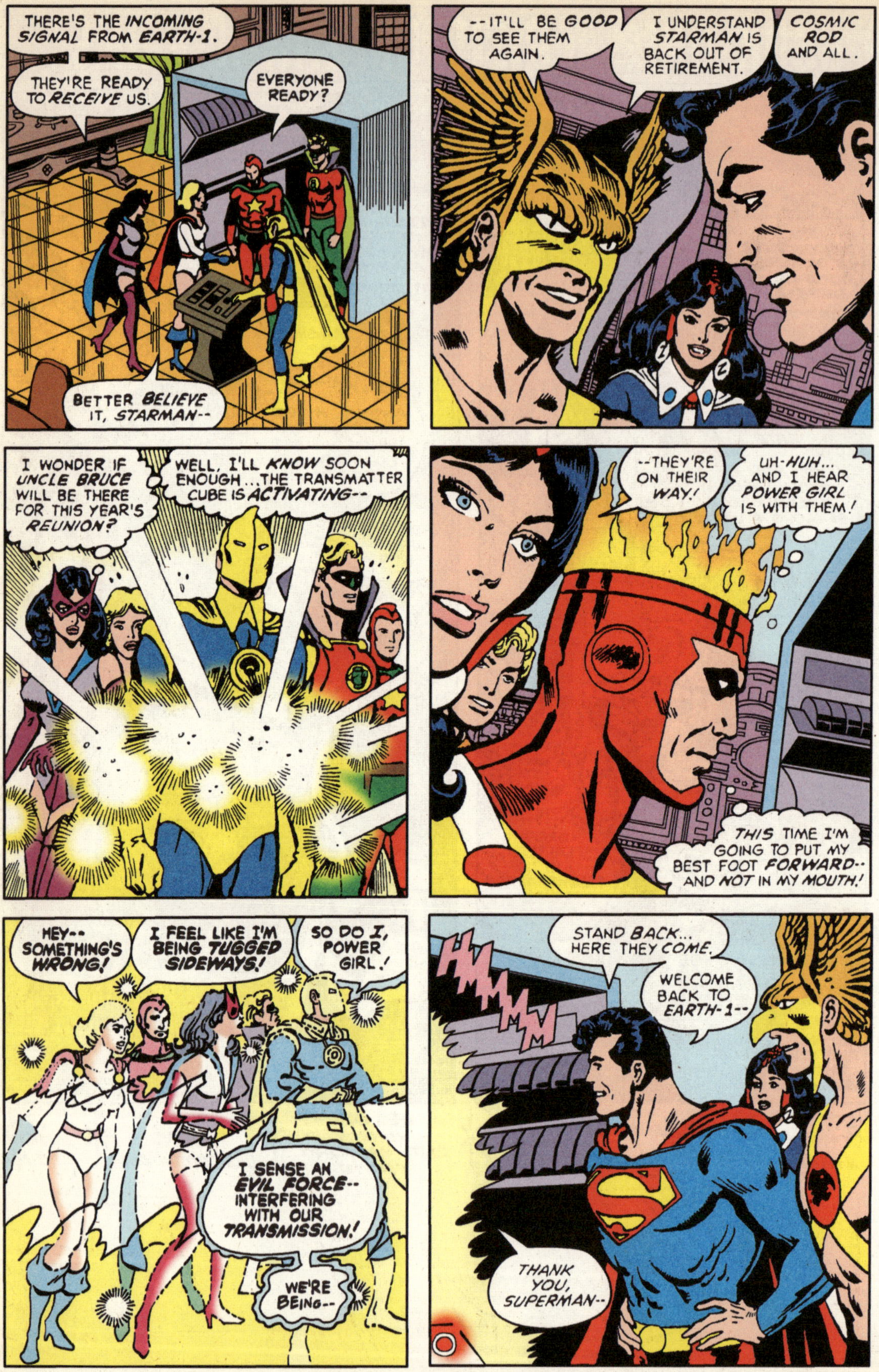
THERE'S THE INCOMING SIGNAL FROM EARTH-1.
THEY'RE READY TO RECEIVE US.
EVERYONE READY?
BETTER BELIEVE IT, STARMAN--
--IT'LL BE GOOD TO SEE THEM AGAIN.
I UNDERSTAND STARMAN IS BACK OUT OF RETIREMENT.
COSMIC ROD AND ALL.
I WONDER IF UNCLE BRUCE WILL BE THERE FOR THIS YEAR'S REUNION?
WELL, I'LL KNOW SOON ENOUGH...THE TRANSMATTER CUBE IS ACTIVATING--
--THEY'RE ON THEIR WAY!
UH-HUH... AND I HEAR POWER GIRL IS WITH THEM!
THIS TIME I'M GOING TO PUT MY BEST FOOT FORWARD-- AND NOT IN MY MOUTH!
HEY-- SOMETHING'S WRONG!
I FEEL LIKE I'M BEING TUGGED SIDEWAYS!
SO DO I, POWER GIRL!
I SENSE AN EVIL FORCE-- INTERFERING WITH OUR TRANSMISSION!
WE'RE BEING--
STAND BACK... HERE THEY COME.
WELCOME BACK TO EARTH-1--
HMMMM
THANK YOU, SUPERMAN--

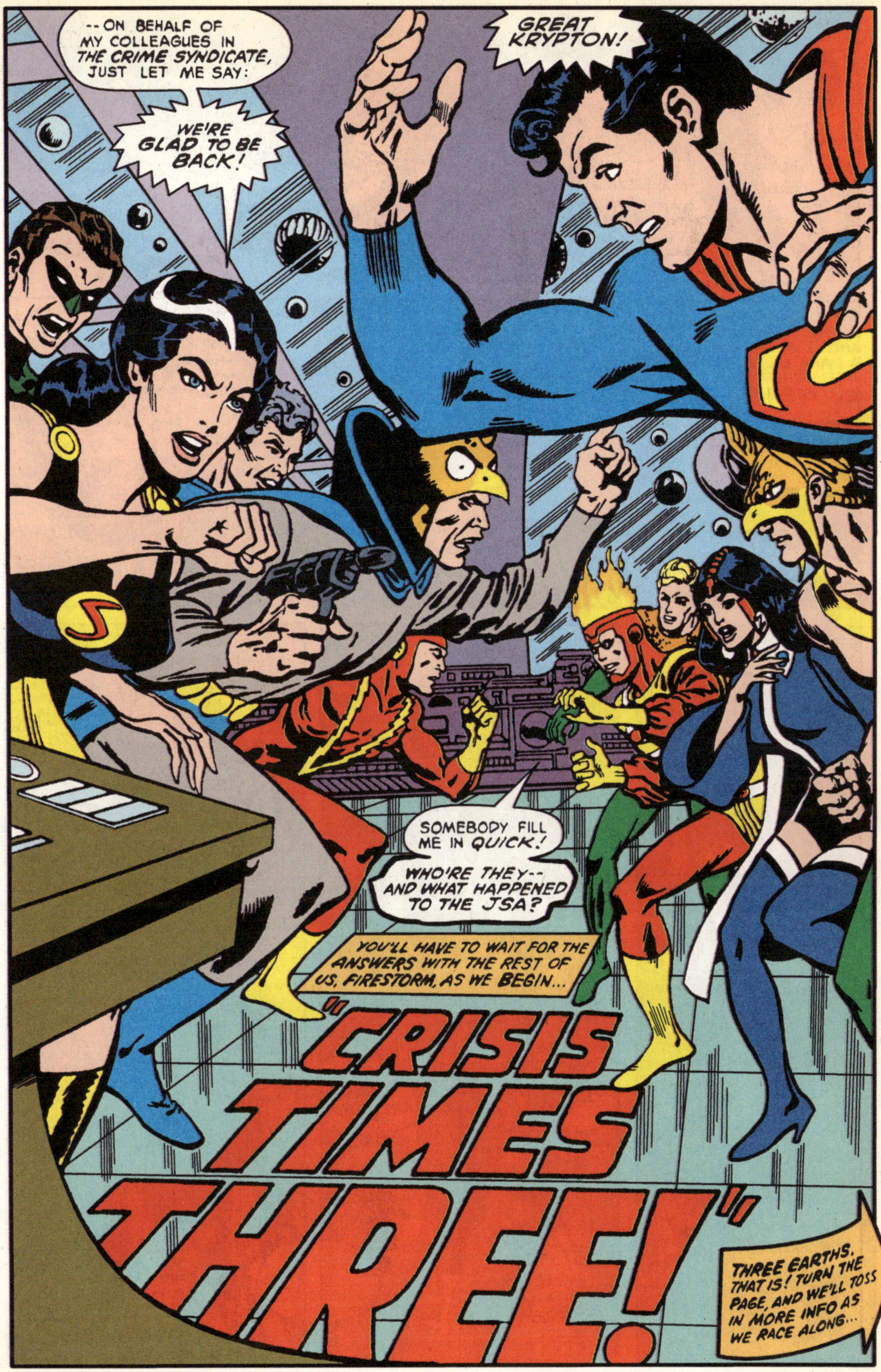
-- ON BEHALF OF MY COLLEAGUES IN THE CRIME SYNDICATE, JUST LET ME SAY:
WE'RE GLAD TO BE BACK!
GREAT KRYPTON!
SOMEBODY FILL ME IN QUICK!
WHO'RE THEY-- AND WHAT HAPPENED TO THE JSA?
YOU'LL HAVE TO WAIT FOR THE ANSWERS WITH THE REST OF US, FIRESTORM, AS WE BEGIN...
"CRISIS TIMES THREE!"
THREE EARTHS, THAT IS! TURN THE PAGE, AND WE'LL TOSS IN MORE INFO AS WE RACE ALONG...

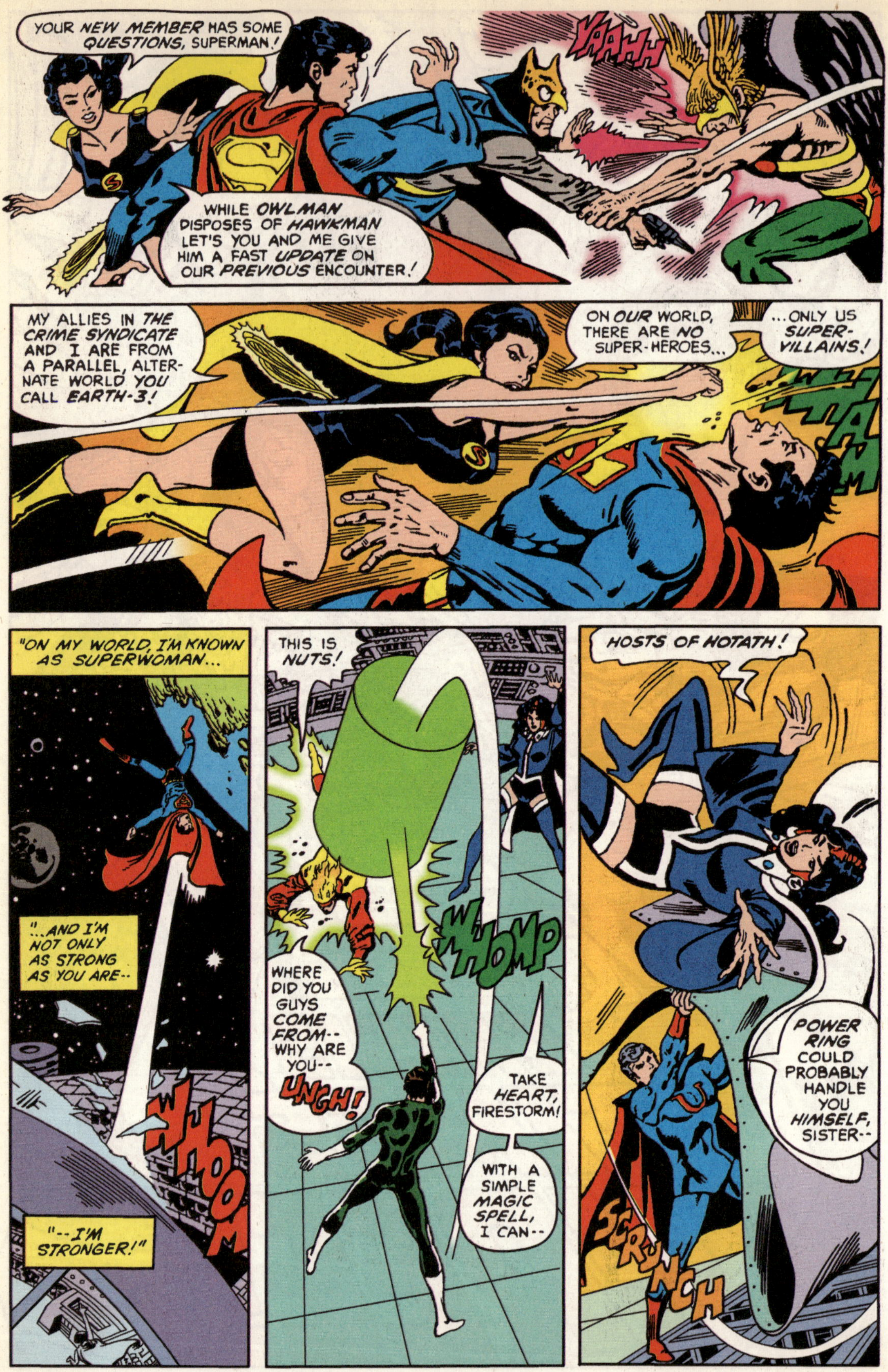

YOUR NEW MEMBER HAS SOME QUESTIONS, SUPERMAN!
YAAHH
WHILE OWLMAN DISPOSES OF HAWKMAN LET'S YOU AND ME GIVE HIM A FAST UPDATE ON OUR PREVIOUS ENCOUNTER!
MY ALLIES IN THE CRIME SYNDICATE AND I ARE FROM A PARALLEL, ALTERNATE WORLD YOU CALL EARTH-3!
ON OUR WORLD, THERE ARE NO SUPER-HEROES...
...ONLY US SUPER-VILLAINS!
WHAM
"ON MY WORLD, I'M KNOWN AS SUPERWOMAN...
"...AND I'M NOT ONLY AS STRONG AS YOU ARE--
WHOOM
"--I'M STRONGER!"
THIS IS NUTS!
WHOMP
WHERE DID YOU GUYS COME FROM-- WHY ARE YOU--
UNGH!
TAKE HEART, FIRESTORM!
WITH A SIMPLE MAGIC SPELL, I CAN--
HOSTS OF HOTATH!
POWER RING COULD PROBABLY HANDLE YOU HIMSELF, SISTER--
SCRUNCH

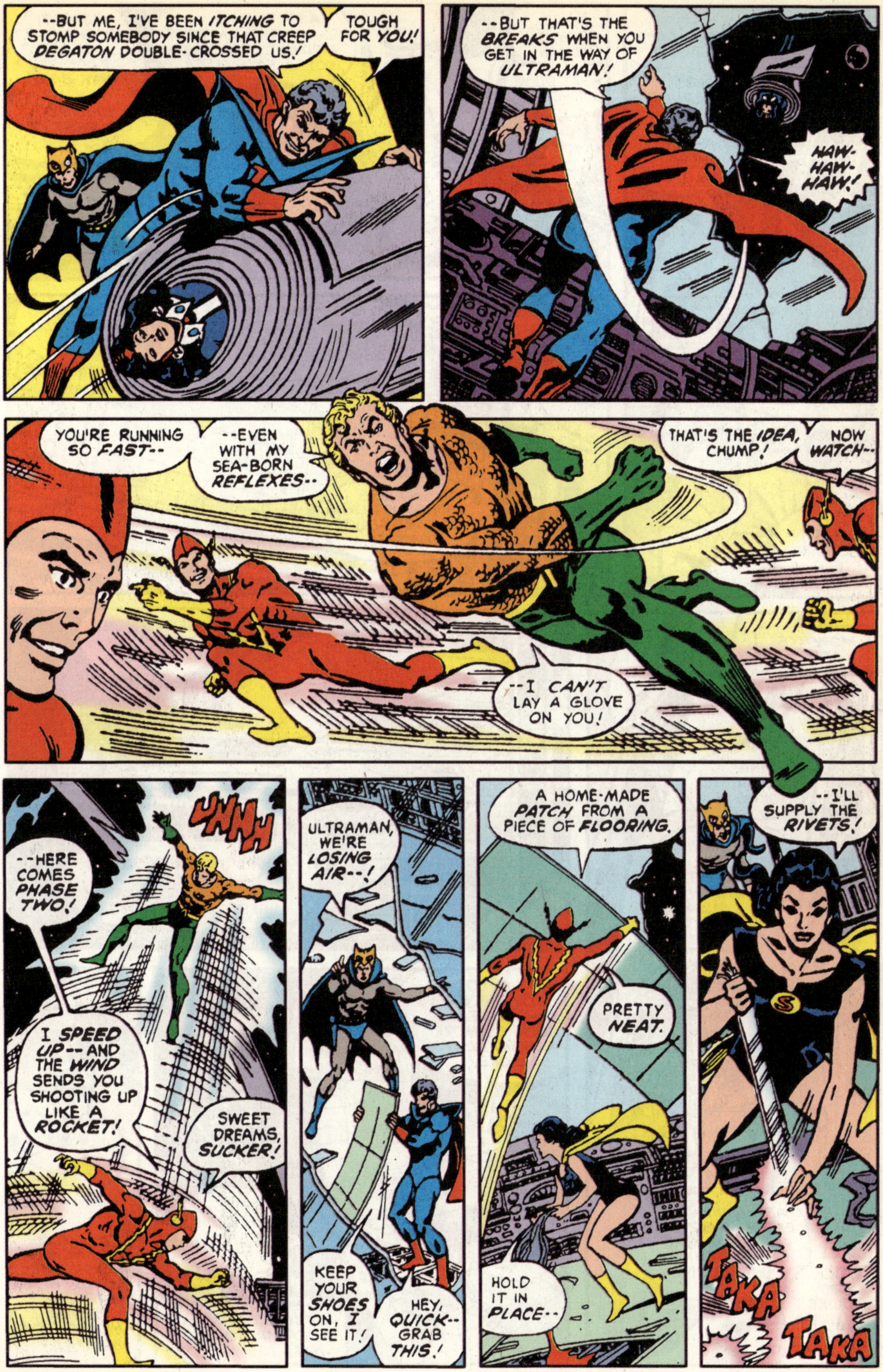
--BUT ME, I'VE BEEN ITCHING TO STOMP SOMEBODY SINCE THAT CREEP DEGATON DOUBLE-CROSSED US!
TOUGH FOR YOU!
--BUT THAT'S THE BREAKS WHEN YOU GET IN THE WAY OF ULTRAMAN!
HAW-HAW-HAW!
YOU'RE RUNNING SO FAST--
--EVEN WITH MY SEA-BORN REFLEXES--
--I CAN'T LAY A GLOVE ON YOU!
THAT'S THE IDEA, CHUMP!
NOW WATCH--
UNHH
--HERE COMES PHASE TWO!
I SPEED UP--AND THE WIND SENDS YOU SHOOTING UP LIKE A ROCKET!
SWEET DREAMS, SUCKER!
ULTRAMAN, WE'RE LOSING AIR--!
KEEP YOUR SHOES ON, I SEE IT!
HEY, QUICK--GRAB THIS!
A HOME-MADE PATCH FROM A PIECE OF FLOORING.
PRETTY NEAT.
HOLD IT IN PLACE--
--I'LL SUPPLY THE RIVETS!
TAKA
TAKA

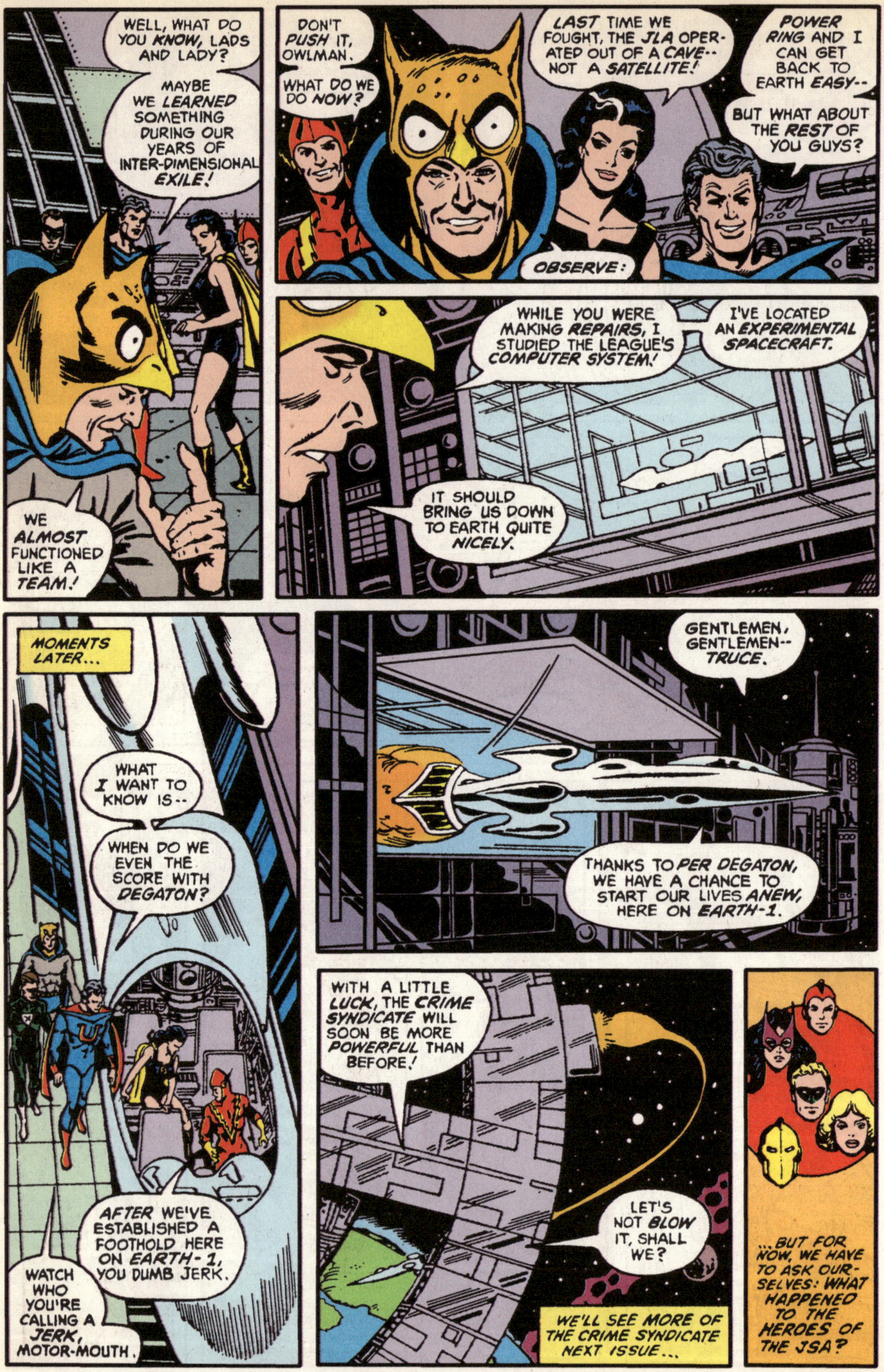
WELL, WHAT DO YOU KNOW, LADS AND LADY?
MAYBE WE LEARNED SOMETHING DURING OUR YEARS OF INTER-DIMENSIONAL EXILE!
WE ALMOST FUNCTIONED LIKE A TEAM!
DON'T PUSH IT, OWLMAN.
WHAT DO WE DO NOW?
LAST TIME WE FOUGHT, THE JLA OPERATED OUT OF A CAVE-- NOT A SATELLITE!
POWER RING AND I CAN GET BACK TO EARTH EASY--
BUT WHAT ABOUT THE REST OF YOU GUYS?
OBSERVE:
WHILE YOU WERE MAKING REPAIRS, I STUDIED THE LEAGUE'S COMPUTER SYSTEM!
I'VE LOCATED AN EXPERIMENTAL SPACECRAFT.
IT SHOULD BRING US DOWN TO EARTH QUITE NICELY.
MOMENTS LATER...
WHAT I WANT TO KNOW IS--
WHEN DO WE EVEN THE SCORE WITH DEGATON?
AFTER WE'VE ESTABLISHED A FOOTHOLD HERE ON EARTH-1, YOU DUMB JERK.
WATCH WHO YOU'RE CALLING A JERK, MOTOR-MOUTH.
GENTLEMEN, GENTLEMEN-- TRUCE.
THANKS TO PER DEGATON, WE HAVE A CHANCE TO START OUR LIVES ANEW, HERE ON EARTH-1.
WITH A LITTLE LUCK, THE CRIME SYNDICATE WILL SOON BE MORE POWERFUL THAN BEFORE!
LET'S NOT BLOW IT, SHALL WE?
WE'LL SEE MORE OF THE CRIME SYNDICATE NEXT ISSUE...
...BUT FOR NOW, WE HAVE TO ASK OURSELVES: WHAT HAPPENED TO THE HEROES OF THE JSA?

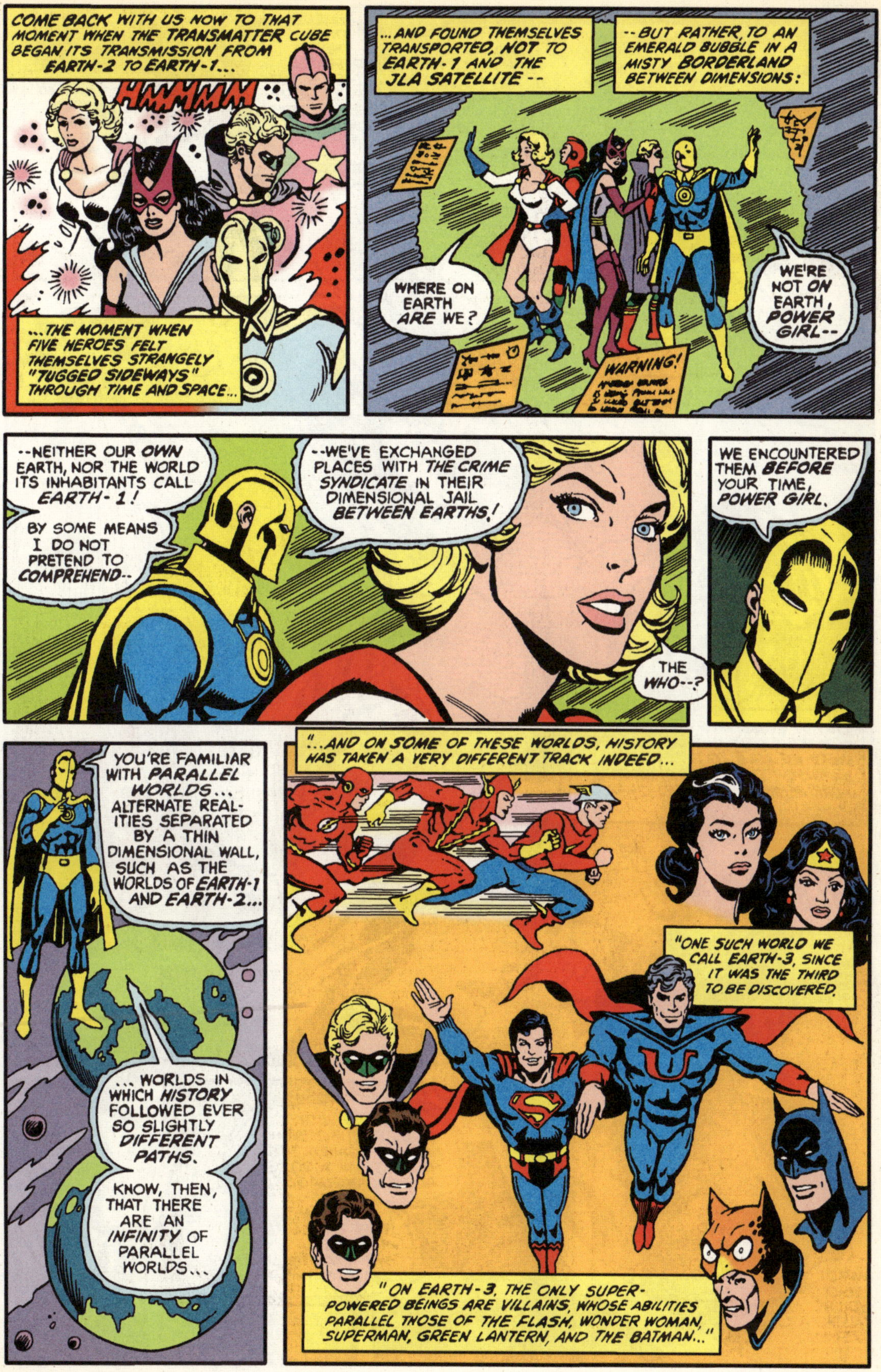
COME BACK WITH US NOW TO THAT MOMENT WHEN THE TRANSMATTER CUBE BEGAN ITS TRANSMISSION FROM EARTH-2 TO EARTH-1...
HMMMM
...THE MOMENT WHEN FIVE HEROES FELT THEMSELVES STRANGELY "TUGGED SIDEWAYS" THROUGH TIME AND SPACE...
...AND FOUND THEMSELVES TRANSPORTED, NOT TO EARTH-1 AND THE JLA SATELLITE --
--BUT RATHER, TO AN EMERALD BUBBLE IN A MISTY BORDERLAND BETWEEN DIMENSIONS:
WHERE ON EARTH ARE WE?
WE'RE NOT ON EARTH, POWER GIRL--
WARNING!
--NEITHER OUR OWN EARTH, NOR THE WORLD ITS INHABITANTS CALL EARTH-1!
BY SOME MEANS I DO NOT PRETEND TO COMPREHEND--
--WE'VE EXCHANGED PLACES WITH THE CRIME SYNDICATE IN THEIR DIMENSIONAL JAIL BETWEEN EARTHS!
THE WHO--?
WE ENCOUNTERED THEM BEFORE YOUR TIME, POWER GIRL.
YOU'RE FAMILIAR WITH PARALLEL WORLDS... ALTERNATE REALITIES SEPARATED BY A THIN DIMENSIONAL WALL, SUCH AS THE WORLDS OF EARTH-1 AND EARTH-2...
...WORLDS IN WHICH HISTORY FOLLOWED EVER SO SLIGHTLY DIFFERENT PATHS.
KNOW, THEN, THAT THERE ARE AN INFINITY OF PARALLEL WORLDS...
"...AND ON SOME OF THESE WORLDS, HISTORY HAS TAKEN A VERY DIFFERENT TRACK INDEED...
"ONE SUCH WORLD WE CALL EARTH-3, SINCE IT WAS THE THIRD TO BE DISCOVERED.
"ON EARTH-3, THE ONLY SUPER-POWERED BEINGS ARE VILLAINS, WHOSE ABILITIES PARALLEL THOSE OF THE FLASH, WONDER WOMAN, SUPERMAN, GREEN LANTERN, AND THE BATMAN..."

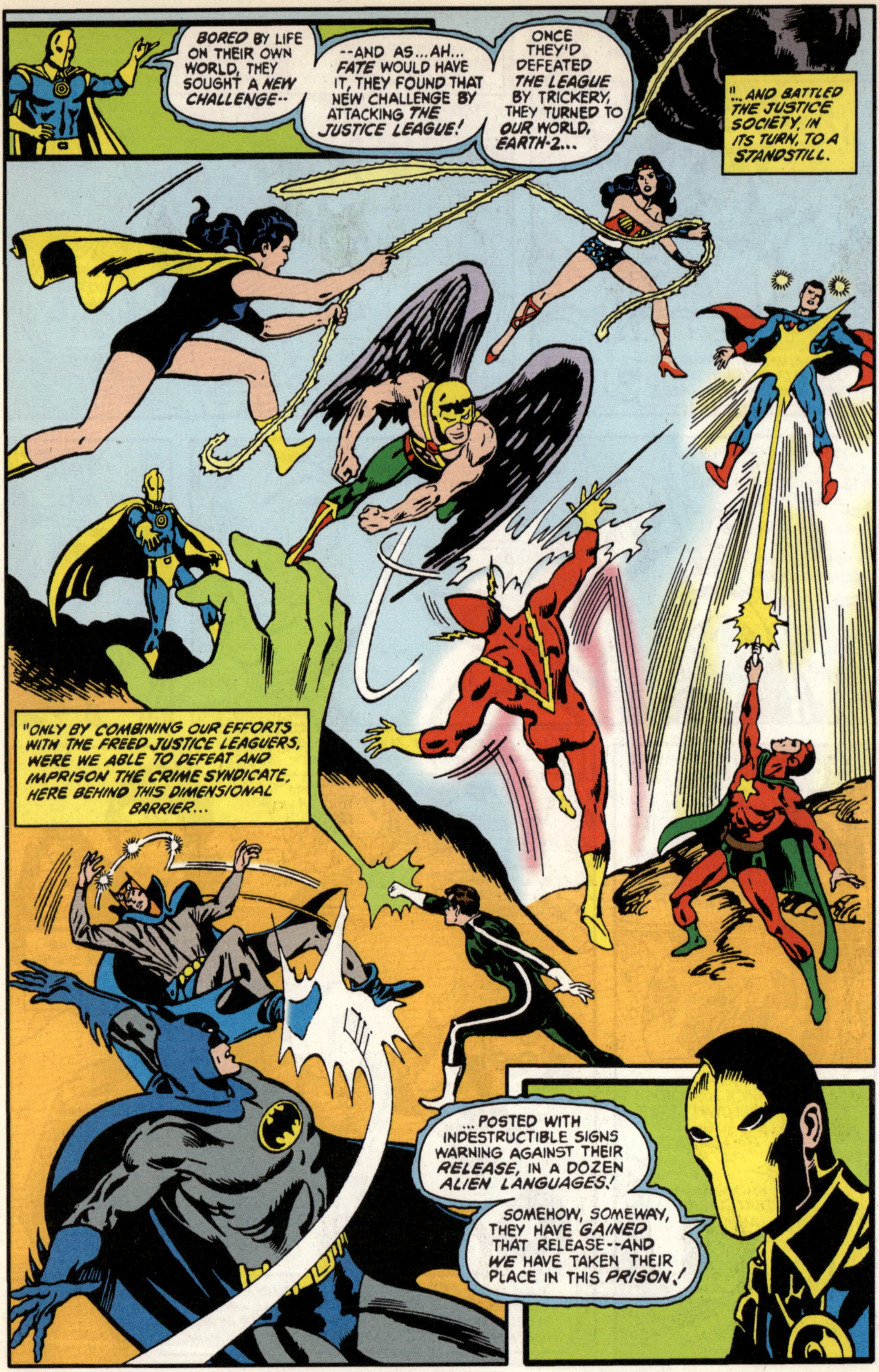

BORED BY LIFE ON THEIR OWN WORLD, THEY SOUGHT A NEW CHALLENGE--
--AND AS...AH... FATE WOULD HAVE IT, THEY FOUND THAT NEW CHALLENGE BY ATTACKING THE JUSTICE LEAGUE!
ONCE THEY'D DEFEATED THE LEAGUE BY TRICKERY, THEY TURNED TO OUR WORLD, EARTH-2...
"...AND BATTLED THE JUSTICE SOCIETY, IN ITS TURN, TO A STANDSTILL.
"ONLY BY COMBINING OUR EFFORTS WITH THE FREED JUSTICE LEAGUERS, WERE WE ABLE TO DEFEAT AND IMPRISON THE CRIME SYNDICATE, HERE BEHIND THIS DIMENSIONAL BARRIER...
...POSTED WITH INDESTRUCTIBLE SIGNS WARNING AGAINST THEIR RELEASE, IN A DOZEN ALIEN LANGUAGES!
SOMEHOW, SOMEWAY, THEY HAVE GAINED THAT RELEASE--AND WE HAVE TAKEN THEIR PLACE IN THIS PRISON!

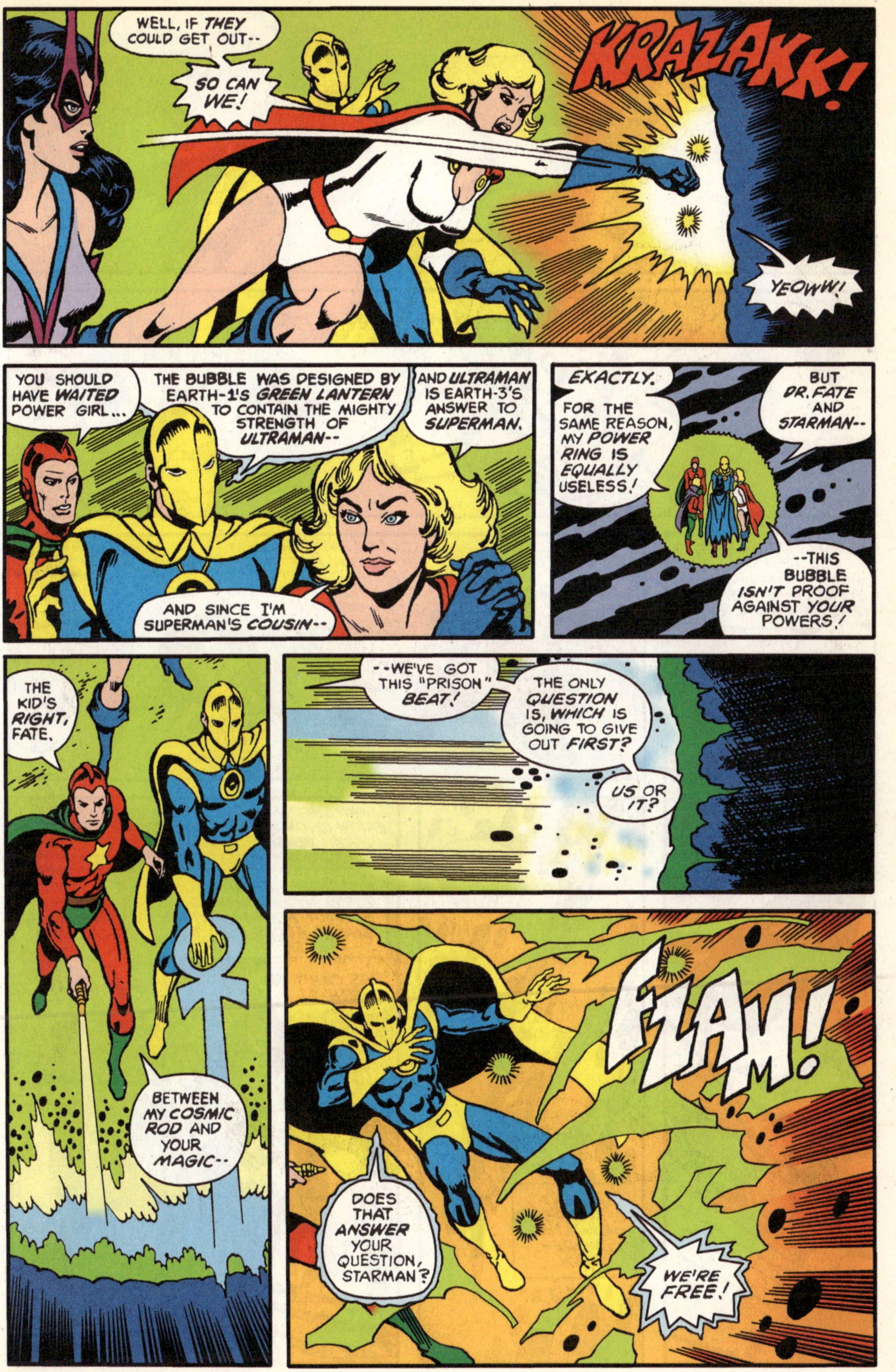
WELL, IF THEY COULD GET OUT--
SO CAN WE!
KRAZAKK!
YEOWW!
YOU SHOULD HAVE WAITED POWER GIRL...
THE BUBBLE WAS DESIGNED BY EARTH-1'S GREEN LANTERN TO CONTAIN THE MIGHTY STRENGTH OF ULTRAMAN--
AND ULTRAMAN IS EARTH-3'S ANSWER TO SUPERMAN.
AND SINCE I'M SUPERMAN'S COUSIN--
EXACTLY.
FOR THE SAME REASON, MY POWER RING IS EQUALLY USELESS!
BUT DR. FATE AND STARMAN--
--THIS BUBBLE ISN'T PROOF AGAINST YOUR POWERS!
THE KID'S RIGHT, FATE.
BETWEEN MY COSMIC ROD AND YOUR MAGIC--
--WE'VE GOT THIS "PRISON" BEAT!
THE ONLY QUESTION IS, WHICH IS GOING TO GIVE OUT FIRST?
US OR IT?
FLAM!
DOES THAT ANSWER YOUR QUESTION, STARMAN?
WE'RE FREE!

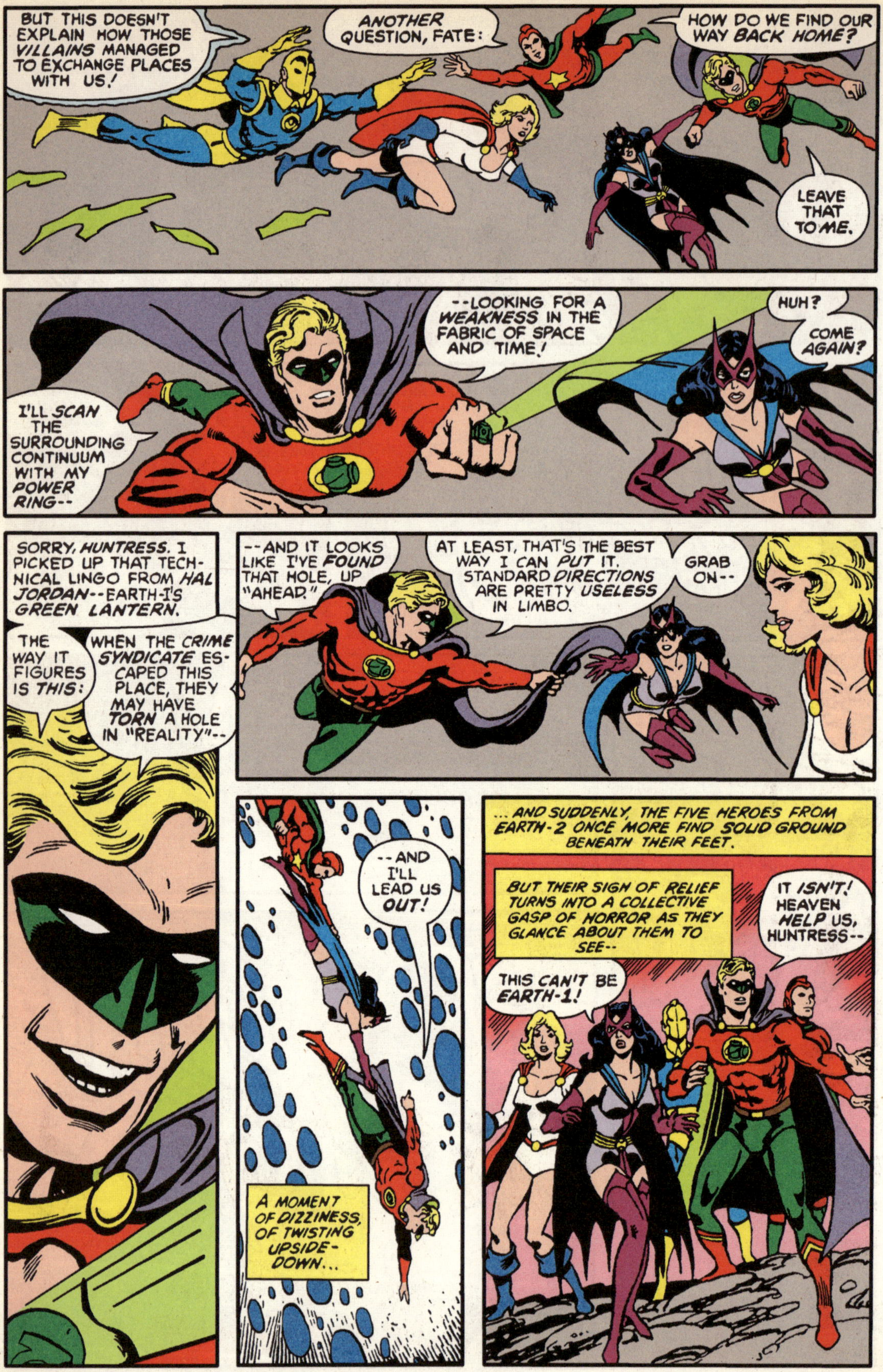
BUT THIS DOESN'T EXPLAIN HOW THOSE VILLAINS MANAGED TO EXCHANGE PLACES WITH US!
ANOTHER QUESTION, FATE:
HOW DO WE FIND OUR WAY BACK HOME?
LEAVE THAT TO ME.
I'LL SCAN THE SURROUNDING CONTINUUM WITH MY POWER RING--
--LOOKING FOR A WEAKNESS IN THE FABRIC OF SPACE AND TIME!
HUH?
COME AGAIN?
SORRY, HUNTRESS. I PICKED UP THAT TECHNICAL LINGO FROM HAL JORDAN--EARTH-1'S GREEN LANTERN.
THE WAY IT FIGURES IS THIS:
WHEN THE CRIME SYNDICATE ESCAPED THIS PLACE, THEY MAY HAVE TORN A HOLE IN "REALITY"--
--AND IT LOOKS LIKE I'VE FOUND THAT HOLE, UP "AHEAD."
AT LEAST, THAT'S THE BEST WAY I CAN PUT IT. STANDARD DIRECTIONS ARE PRETTY USELESS IN LIMBO.
GRAB ON--
--AND I'LL LEAD US OUT!
A MOMENT OF DIZZINESS, OF TWISTING UPSIDE-DOWN...
... AND SUDDENLY, THE FIVE HEROES FROM EARTH-2 ONCE MORE FIND SOLID GROUND BENEATH THEIR FEET.
BUT THEIR SIGH OF RELIEF TURNS INTO A COLLECTIVE GASP OF HORROR AS THEY GLANCE ABOUT THEM TO SEE--
THIS CAN'T BE EARTH-1!
IT ISN'T! HEAVEN HELP US, HUNTRESS--

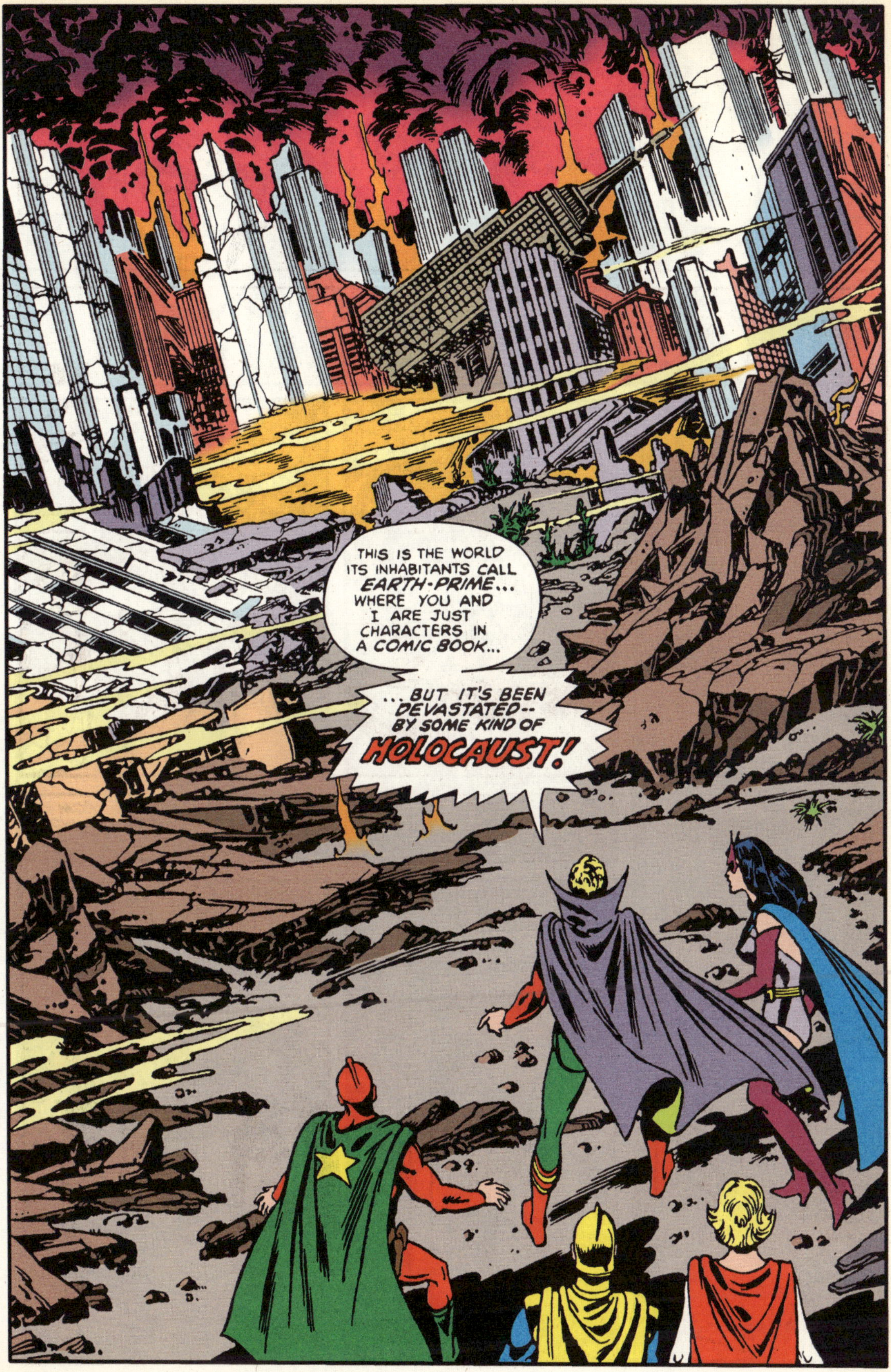
THIS IS THE WORLD ITS INHABITANTS CALL EARTH-PRIME... WHERE YOU AND I ARE JUST CHARACTERS IN A COMIC BOOK...
... BUT IT'S BEEN DEVASTATED-- BY SOME KIND OF HOLOCAUST!

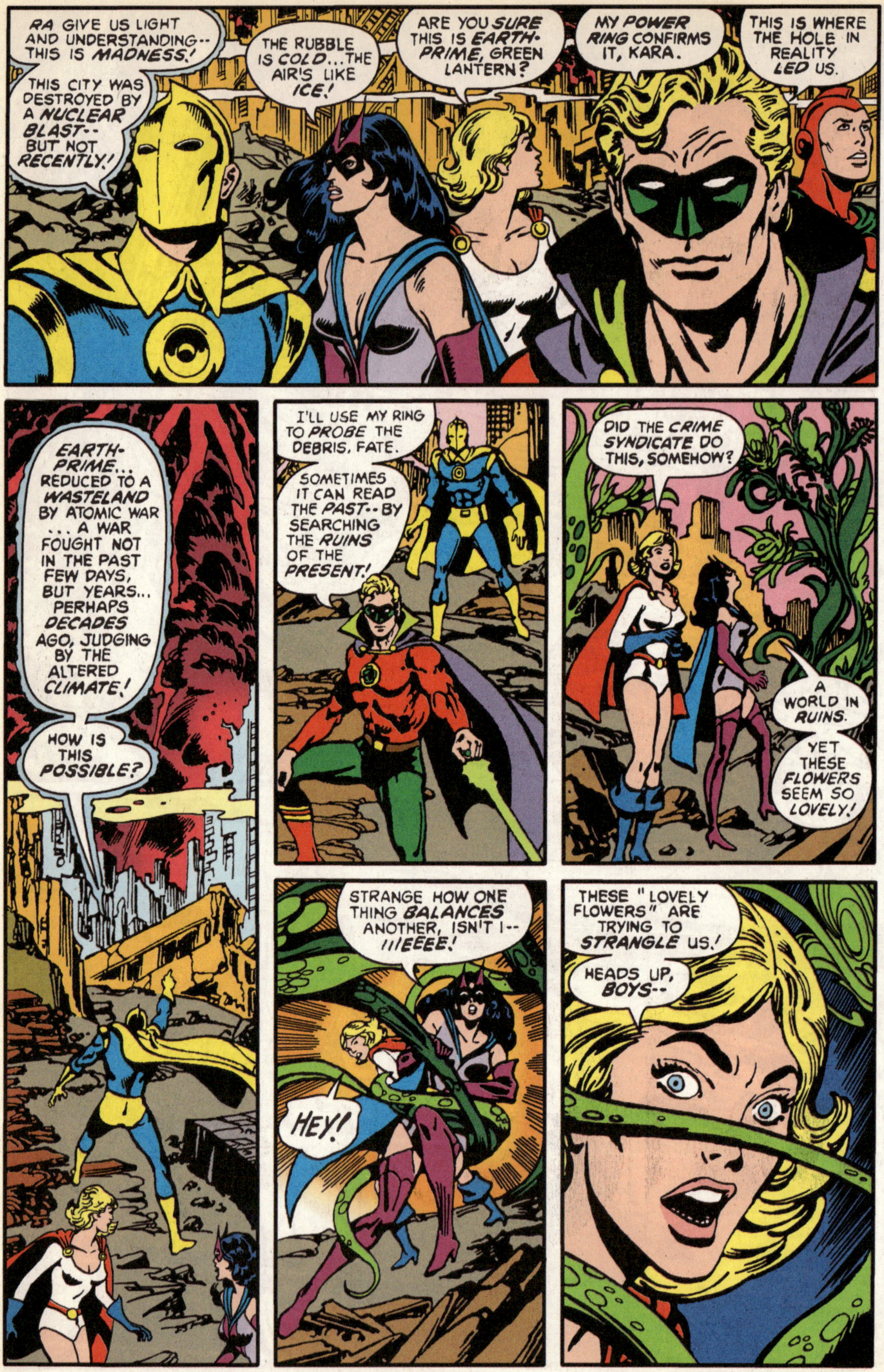
RA GIVE US LIGHT AND UNDERSTANDING-- THIS IS MADNESS!
THIS CITY WAS DESTROYED BY A NUCLEAR BLAST-- BUT NOT RECENTLY!
THE RUBBLE IS COLD... THE AIR'S LIKE ICE!
ARE YOU SURE THIS IS EARTH-PRIME, GREEN LANTERN?
MY POWER RING CONFIRMS IT, KARA.
THIS IS WHERE THE HOLE IN REALITY LED US.
EARTH-PRIME... REDUCED TO A WASTELAND BY ATOMIC WAR ... A WAR FOUGHT NOT IN THE PAST FEW DAYS, BUT YEARS... PERHAPS DECADES AGO, JUDGING BY THE ALTERED CLIMATE!
HOW IS THIS POSSIBLE?
I'LL USE MY RING TO PROBE THE DEBRIS, FATE.
SOMETIMES IT CAN READ THE PAST-- BY SEARCHING THE RUINS OF THE PRESENT!
DID THE CRIME SYNDICATE DO THIS, SOMEHOW?
A WORLD IN RUINS.
YET THESE FLOWERS SEEM SO LOVELY!
STRANGE HOW ONE THING BALANCES ANOTHER, ISN'T I-- IIIEEEE!
HEY!
THESE "LOVELY FLOWERS" ARE TRYING TO STRANGLE US!
HEADS UP, BOYS--

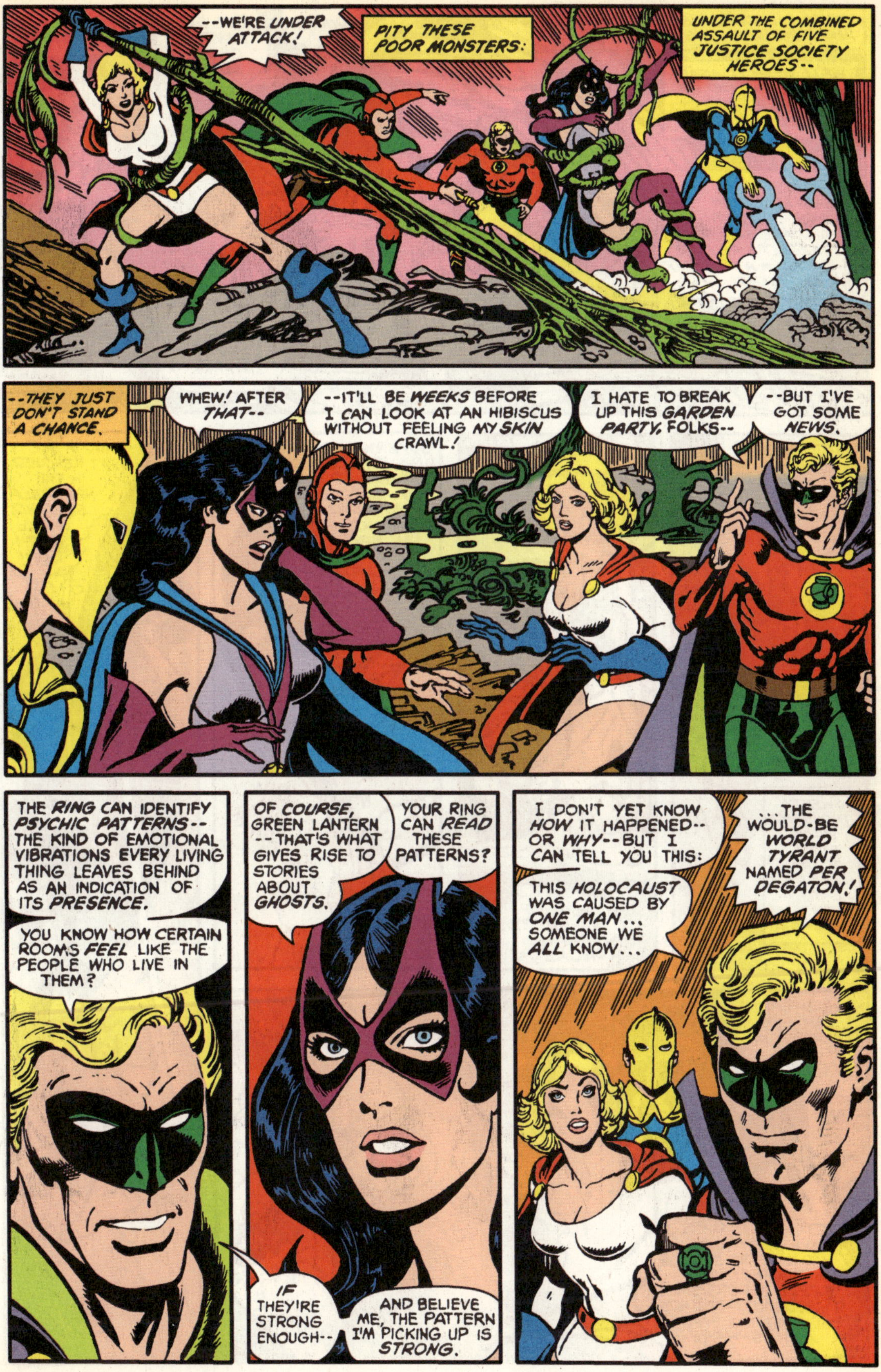
--WE'RE UNDER ATTACK!
PITY THESE POOR MONSTERS:
UNDER THE COMBINED ASSAULT OF FIVE JUSTICE SOCIETY HEROES--
--THEY JUST DON'T STAND A CHANCE.
WHEW! AFTER THAT--
--IT'LL BE WEEKS BEFORE I CAN LOOK AT AN HIBISCUS WITHOUT FEELING MY SKIN CRAWL!
I HATE TO BREAK UP THIS GARDEN PARTY, FOLKS--
--BUT I'VE GOT SOME NEWS.
THE RING CAN IDENTIFY PSYCHIC PATTERNS--THE KIND OF EMOTIONAL VIBRATIONS EVERY LIVING THING LEAVES BEHIND AS AN INDICATION OF ITS PRESENCE.
YOU KNOW HOW CERTAIN ROOMS FEEL LIKE THE PEOPLE WHO LIVE IN THEM?
IF THEY'RE STRONG ENOUGH--
OF COURSE, GREEN LANTERN--THAT'S WHAT GIVES RISE TO STORIES ABOUT GHOSTS.
YOUR RING CAN READ THESE PATTERNS?
AND BELIEVE ME, THE PATTERN I'M PICKING UP IS STRONG.
I DON'T YET KNOW HOW IT HAPPENED--OR WHY--BUT I CAN TELL YOU THIS:
THIS HOLOCAUST WAS CAUSED BY ONE MAN... SOMEONE WE ALL KNOW...
...THE WOULD-BE WORLD TYRANT NAMED PER DEGATON!

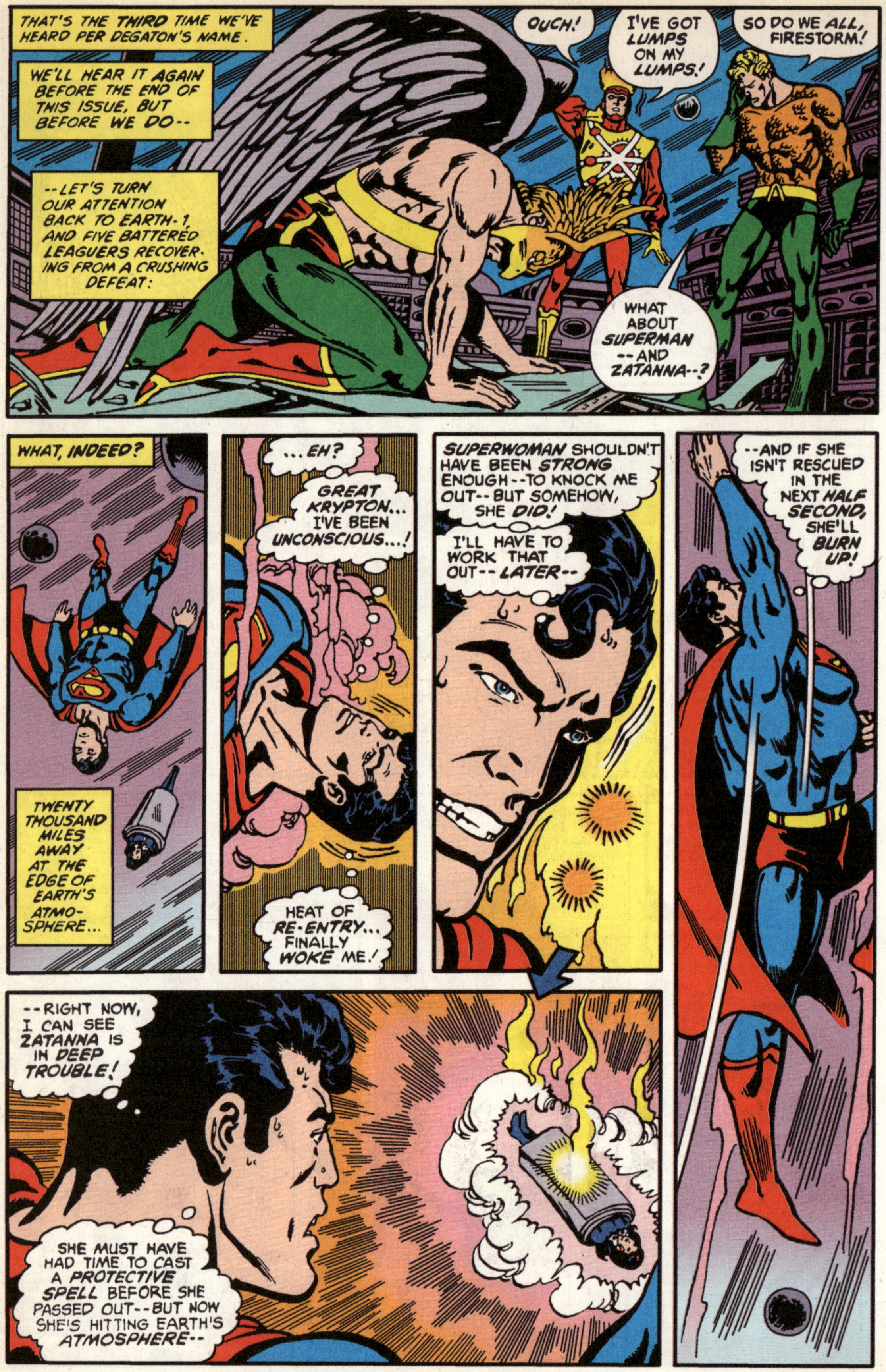
THAT'S THE THIRD TIME WE'VE HEARD PER DEGATON'S NAME.
WE'LL HEAR IT AGAIN BEFORE THE END OF THIS ISSUE, BUT BEFORE WE DO--
--LET'S TURN OUR ATTENTION BACK TO EARTH-1, AND FIVE BATTERED LEAGUERS RECOVERING FROM A CRUSHING DEFEAT:
OUCH!
I'VE GOT LUMPS ON MY LUMPS!
SO DO WE ALL, FIRESTORM!
WHAT ABOUT SUPERMAN --AND ZATANNA--?
WHAT, INDEED?
TWENTY THOUSAND MILES AWAY AT THE EDGE OF EARTH'S ATMOSPHERE...
...EH?
GREAT KRYPTON... I'VE BEEN UNCONSCIOUS...!
HEAT OF RE-ENTRY... FINALLY WOKE ME.!
SUPERWOMAN SHOULDN'T HAVE BEEN STRONG ENOUGH--TO KNOCK ME OUT--BUT SOMEHOW, SHE DID!
I'LL HAVE TO WORK THAT OUT--LATER--
--AND IF SHE ISN'T RESCUED IN THE NEXT HALF SECOND, SHE'LL BURN UP!
--RIGHT NOW, I CAN SEE ZATANNA IS IN DEEP TROUBLE!
SHE MUST HAVE HAD TIME TO CAST A PROTECTIVE SPELL BEFORE SHE PASSED OUT--BUT NOW SHE'S HITTING EARTH'S ATMOSPHERE--

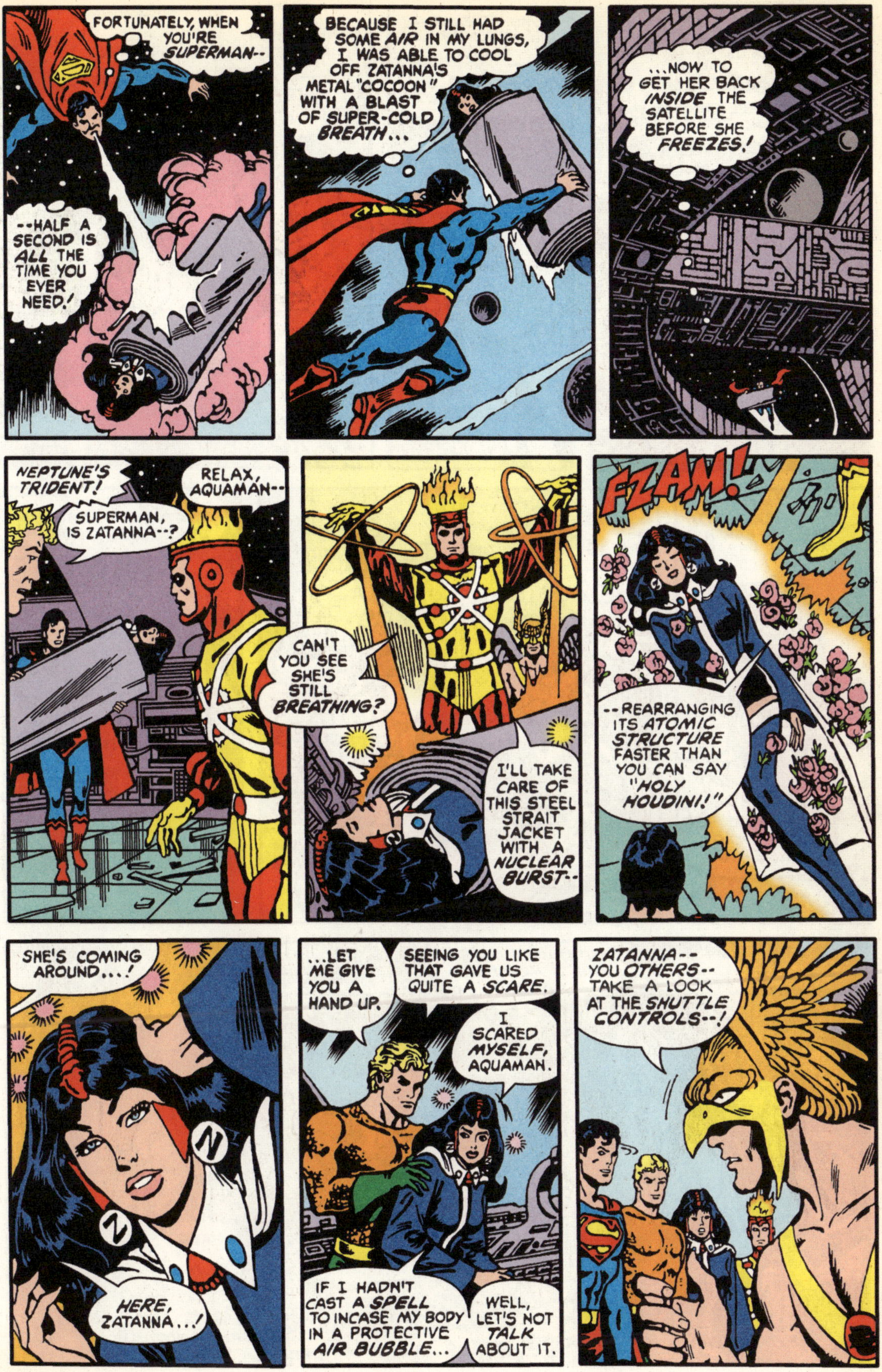
FORTUNATELY, WHEN YOU'RE SUPERMAN--
--HALF A SECOND IS ALL THE TIME YOU EVER NEED!
BECAUSE I STILL HAD SOME AIR IN MY LUNGS, I WAS ABLE TO COOL OFF ZATANNA'S METAL "COCOON" WITH A BLAST OF SUPER-COLD BREATH...
...NOW TO GET HER BACK INSIDE THE SATELLITE BEFORE SHE FREEZES!
NEPTUNE'S TRIDENT!
SUPERMAN, IS ZATANNA--?
RELAX, AQUAMAN--
CAN'T YOU SEE SHE'S STILL BREATHING?
I'LL TAKE CARE OF THIS STEEL STRAIT JACKET WITH A NUCLEAR BURST--
FZAM!
--REARRANGING ITS ATOMIC STRUCTURE FASTER THAN YOU CAN SAY "HOLY HOUDINI!"
SHE'S COMING AROUND...!
HERE, ZATANNA...!
...LET ME GIVE YOU A HAND UP.
SEEING YOU LIKE THAT GAVE US QUITE A SCARE.
I SCARED MYSELF, AQUAMAN.
IF I HADN'T CAST A SPELL TO INCASE MY BODY IN A PROTECTIVE AIR BUBBLE...
WELL, LET'S NOT TALK ABOUT IT.
ZATANNA-- YOU OTHERS-- TAKE A LOOK AT THE SHUTTLE CONTROLS--!

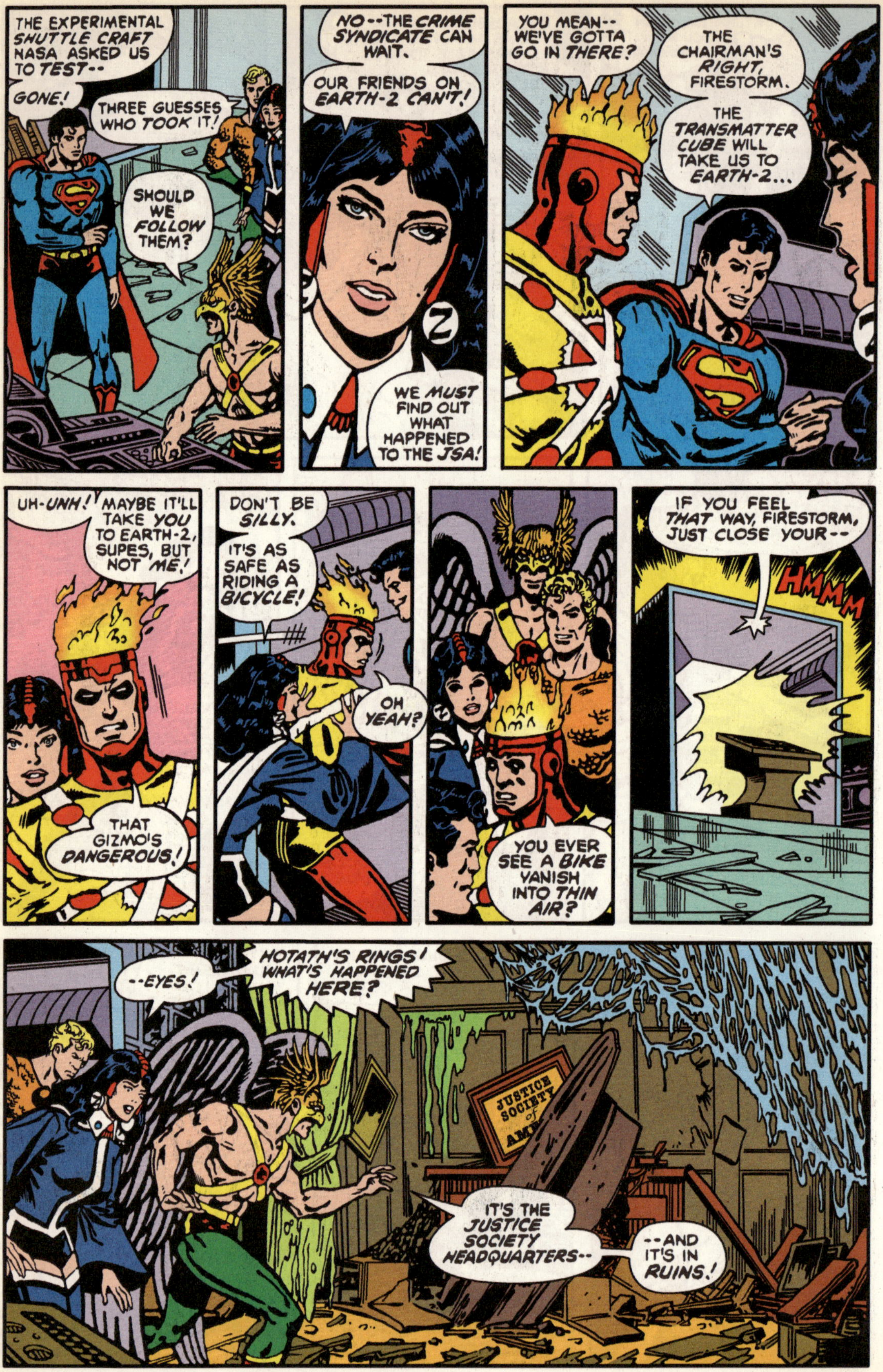

THE EXPERIMENTAL SHUTTLE CRAFT NASA ASKED US TO TEST--
GONE!
THREE GUESSES WHO TOOK IT!
SHOULD WE FOLLOW THEM?
NO--THE CRIME SYNDICATE CAN WAIT.
OUR FRIENDS ON EARTH-2 CAN'T!
WE MUST FIND OUT WHAT HAPPENED TO THE JSA!
YOU MEAN--WE'VE GOTTA GO IN THERE?
THE CHAIRMAN'S RIGHT, FIRESTORM.
THE TRANSMATTER CUBE WILL TAKE US TO EARTH-2...
UH-UNH!
MAYBE IT'LL TAKE YOU TO EARTH-2, SUPES, BUT NOT ME!
THAT GIZMO'S DANGEROUS!
DON'T BE SILLY.
IT'S AS SAFE AS RIDING A BICYCLE!
OH YEAH?
YOU EVER SEE A BIKE VANISH INTO THIN AIR?
IF YOU FEEL THAT WAY, FIRESTORM, JUST CLOSE YOUR--
HMMM
--EYES!
HOTATH'S RINGS! WHAT'S HAPPENED HERE?
JUSTICE SOCIETY of AM
IT'S THE JUSTICE SOCIETY HEADQUARTERS--
--AND IT'S IN RUINS!

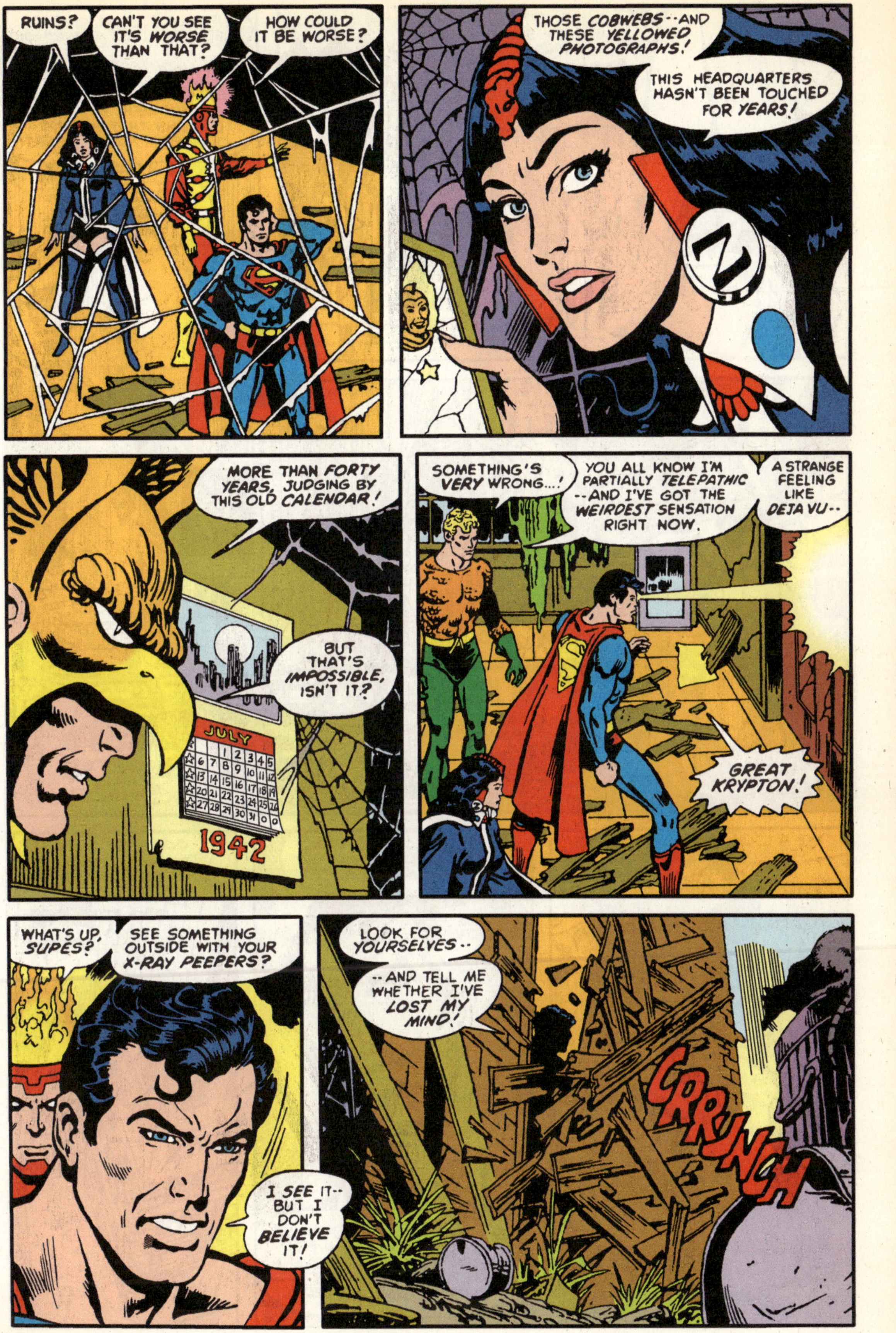
RUINS?
CAN'T YOU SEE IT'S WORSE THAN THAT?
HOW COULD IT BE WORSE?
THOSE COBWEBS--AND THESE YELLOWED PHOTOGRAPHS!
THIS HEADQUARTERS HASN'T BEEN TOUCHED FOR YEARS!
MORE THAN FORTY YEARS, JUDGING BY THIS OLD CALENDAR!
JULY
1942
BUT THAT'S IMPOSSIBLE, ISN'T IT?
SOMETHING'S VERY WRONG...!
YOU ALL KNOW I'M PARTIALLY TELEPATHIC --AND I'VE GOT THE WEIRDEST SENSATION RIGHT NOW.
A STRANGE FEELING LIKE DEJA VU--
GREAT KRYPTON!
WHAT'S UP, SUPES?
SEE SOMETHING OUTSIDE WITH YOUR X-RAY PEEPERS?
I SEE IT-- BUT I DON'T BELIEVE IT!
LOOK FOR YOURSELVES--
--AND TELL ME WHETHER I'VE LOST MY MIND!
CRRUNCH

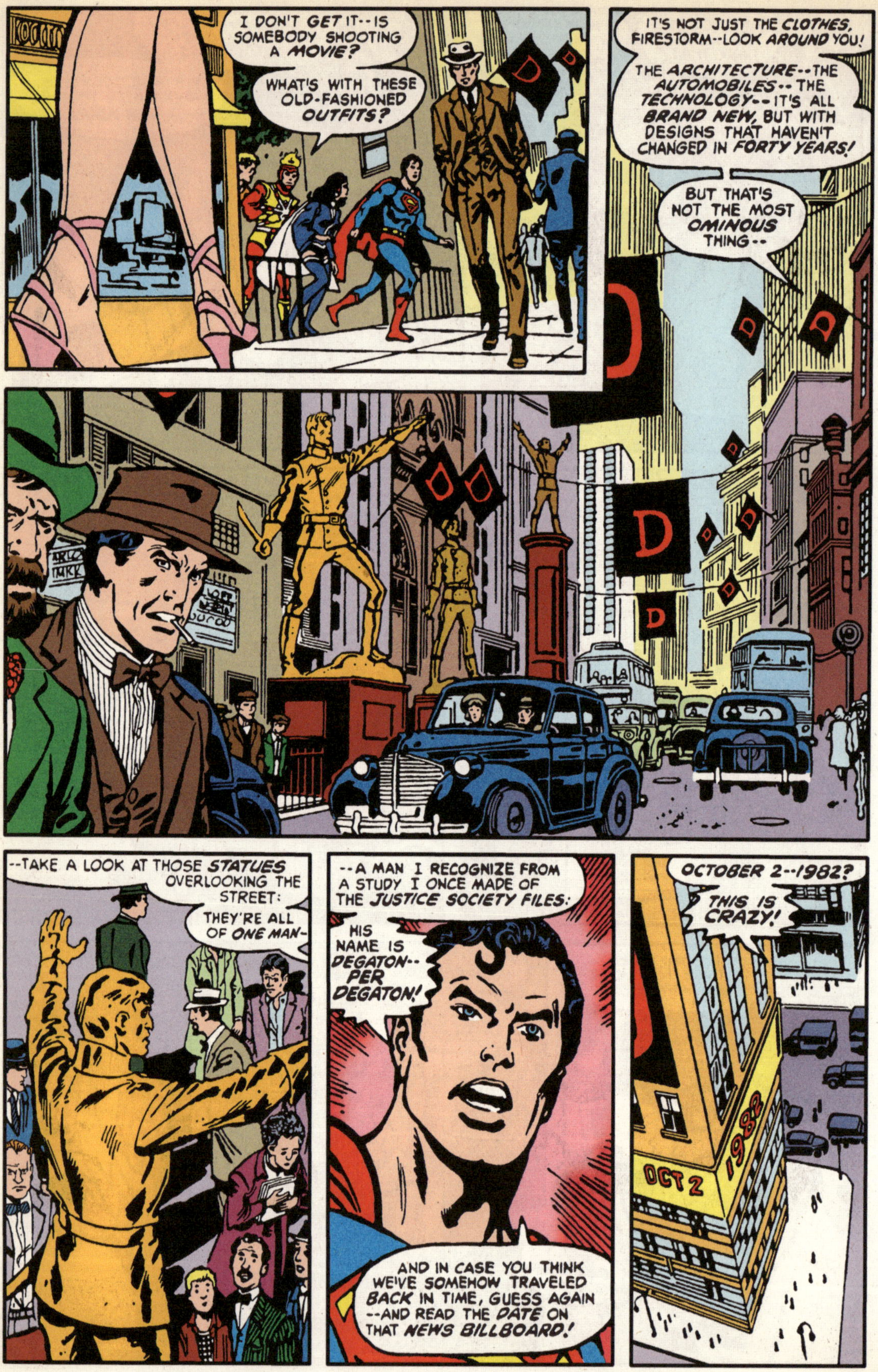

I DON'T GET IT--IS SOMEBODY SHOOTING A MOVIE?
WHAT'S WITH THESE OLD-FASHIONED OUTFITS?
IT'S NOT JUST THE CLOTHES, FIRESTORM--LOOK AROUND YOU!
THE ARCHITECTURE--THE AUTOMOBILES--THE TECHNOLOGY--IT'S ALL BRAND NEW, BUT WITH DESIGNS THAT HAVEN'T CHANGED IN FORTY YEARS!
BUT THAT'S NOT THE MOST OMINOUS THING--
--TAKE A LOOK AT THOSE STATUES OVERLOOKING THE STREET:
THEY'RE ALL OF ONE MAN-
--A MAN I RECOGNIZE FROM A STUDY I ONCE MADE OF THE JUSTICE SOCIETY FILES:
HIS NAME IS DEGATON--PER DEGATON!
AND IN CASE YOU THINK WE'VE SOMEHOW TRAVELED BACK IN TIME, GUESS AGAIN--AND READ THE DATE ON THAT NEWS BILLBOARD!
OCTOBER 2--1982?
THIS IS CRAZY!
OCT 2
1982

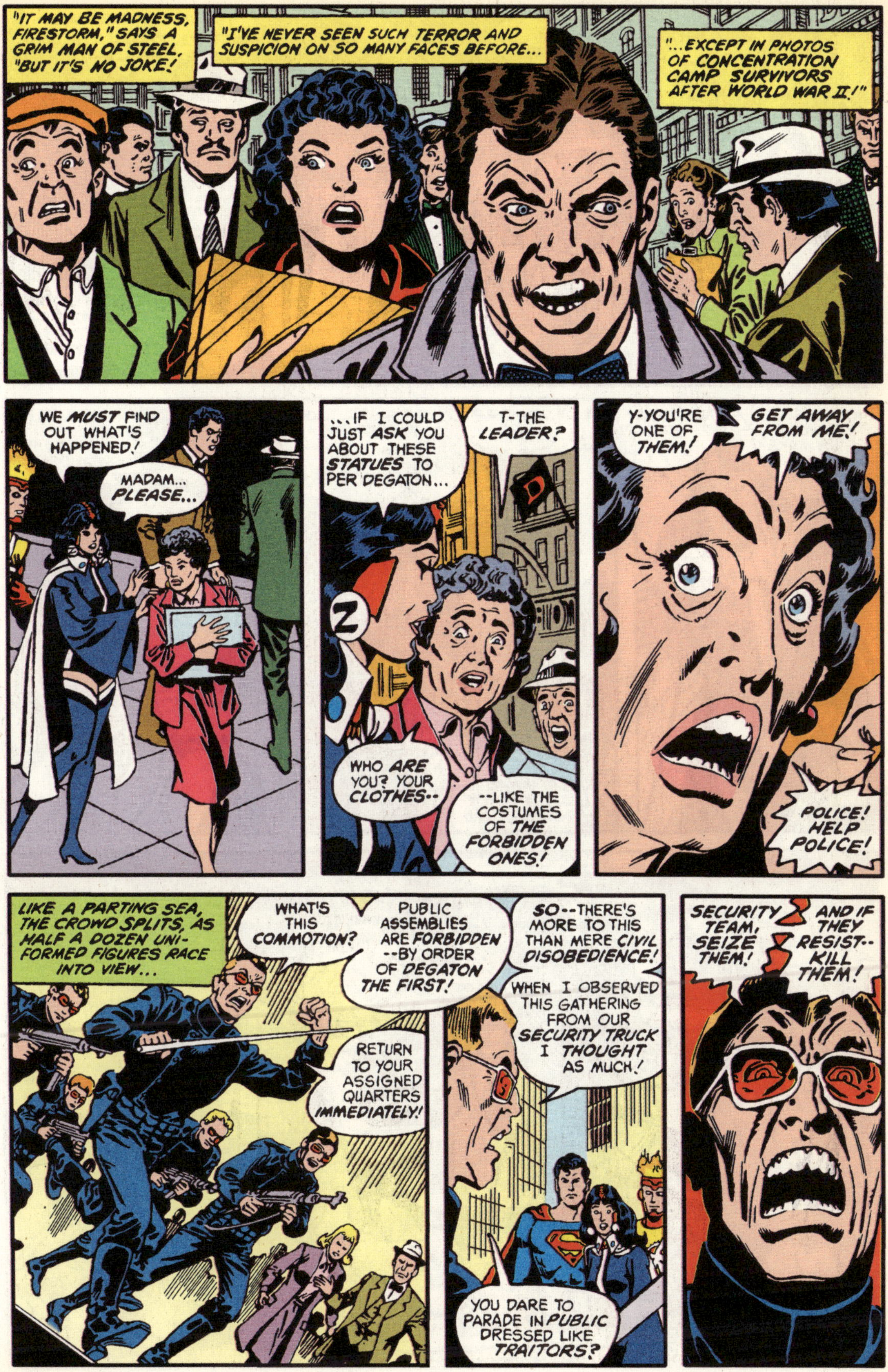
"IT MAY BE MADNESS, FIRESTORM," SAYS A GRIM MAN OF STEEL. "BUT IT'S NO JOKE!
"I'VE NEVER SEEN SUCH TERROR AND SUSPICION ON SO MANY FACES BEFORE...
"...EXCEPT IN PHOTOS OF CONCENTRATION CAMP SURVIVORS AFTER WORLD WAR II!"
WE MUST FIND OUT WHAT'S HAPPENED!
MADAM... PLEASE...
...IF I COULD JUST ASK YOU ABOUT THESE STATUES TO PER DEGATON...
T-THE LEADER?
WHO ARE YOU? YOUR CLOTHES--
--LIKE THE COSTUMES OF THE FORBIDDEN ONES!
Y-YOU'RE ONE OF THEM!
GET AWAY FROM ME!
POLICE! HELP POLICE!
LIKE A PARTING SEA, THE CROWD SPLITS, AS HALF A DOZEN UNIFORMED FIGURES RACE INTO VIEW...
WHAT'S THIS COMMOTION?
PUBLIC ASSEMBLIES ARE FORBIDDEN --BY ORDER OF DEGATON THE FIRST!
RETURN TO YOUR ASSIGNED QUARTERS IMMEDIATELY!
SO--THERE'S MORE TO THIS THAN MERE CIVIL DISOBEDIENCE!
WHEN I OBSERVED THIS GATHERING FROM OUR SECURITY TRUCK I THOUGHT AS MUCH!
YOU DARE TO PARADE IN PUBLIC DRESSED LIKE TRAITORS?
SECURITY TEAM, SEIZE THEM!
AND IF THEY RESIST-- KILL THEM!

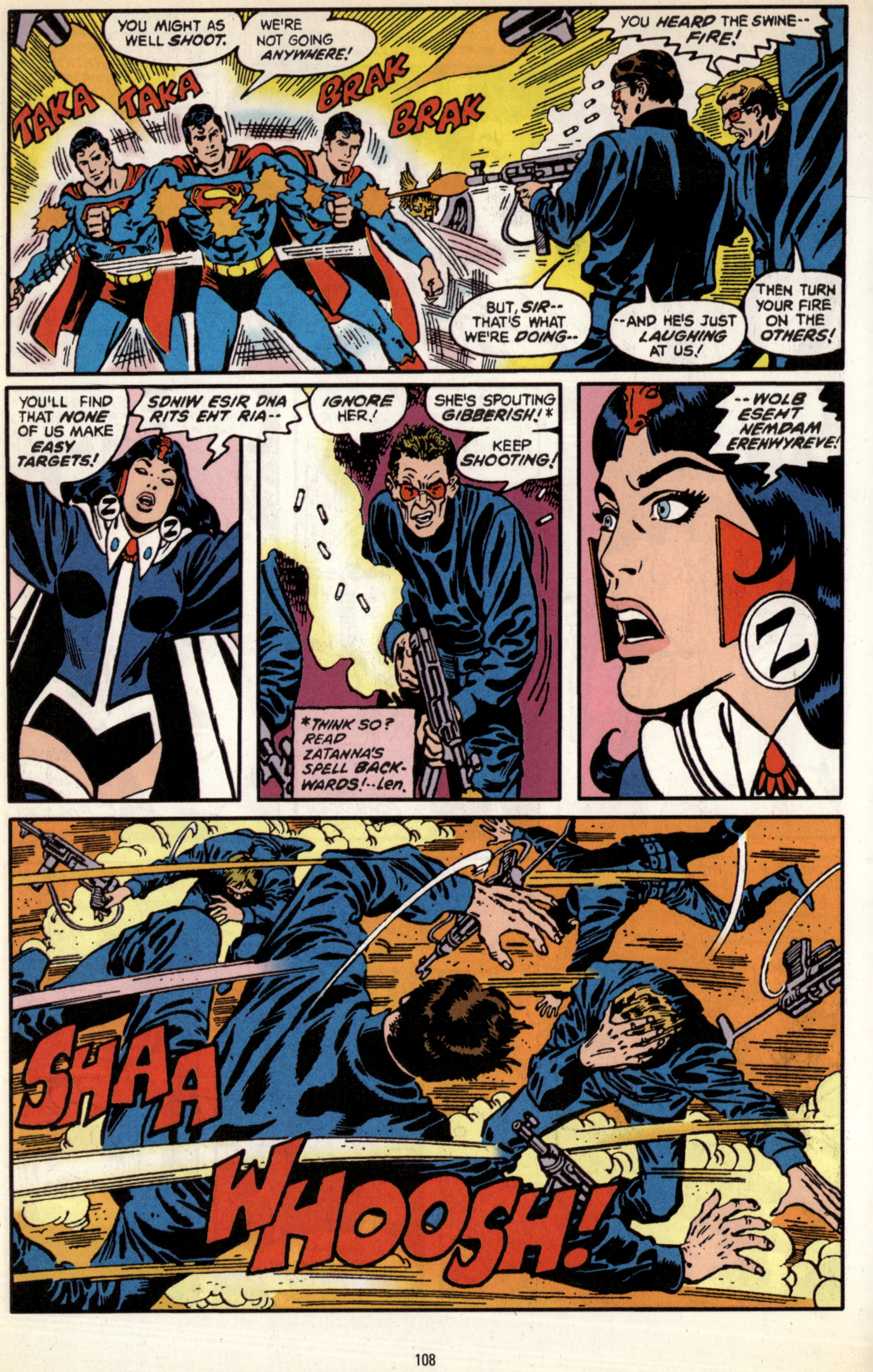
YOU MIGHT AS WELL SHOOT.
WE'RE NOT GOING ANYWHERE!
TAKA TAKA
BRAK BRAK
YOU HEARD THE SWINE-- FIRE!
BUT, SIR-- THAT'S WHAT WE'RE DOING--
--AND HE'S JUST LAUGHING AT US!
THEN TURN YOUR FIRE ON THE OTHERS!
YOU'LL FIND THAT NONE OF US MAKE EASY TARGETS!
SDNIW ESIR DNA RITS EHT RIA--
IGNORE HER!
SHE'S SPOUTING GIBBERISH!*
KEEP SHOOTING!
*THINK SO? READ ZATANNA'S SPELL BACKWARDS!--Len.
--WOLB ESENT NEMDAM ERENWYREVE!
SHAA
WHOOSH!

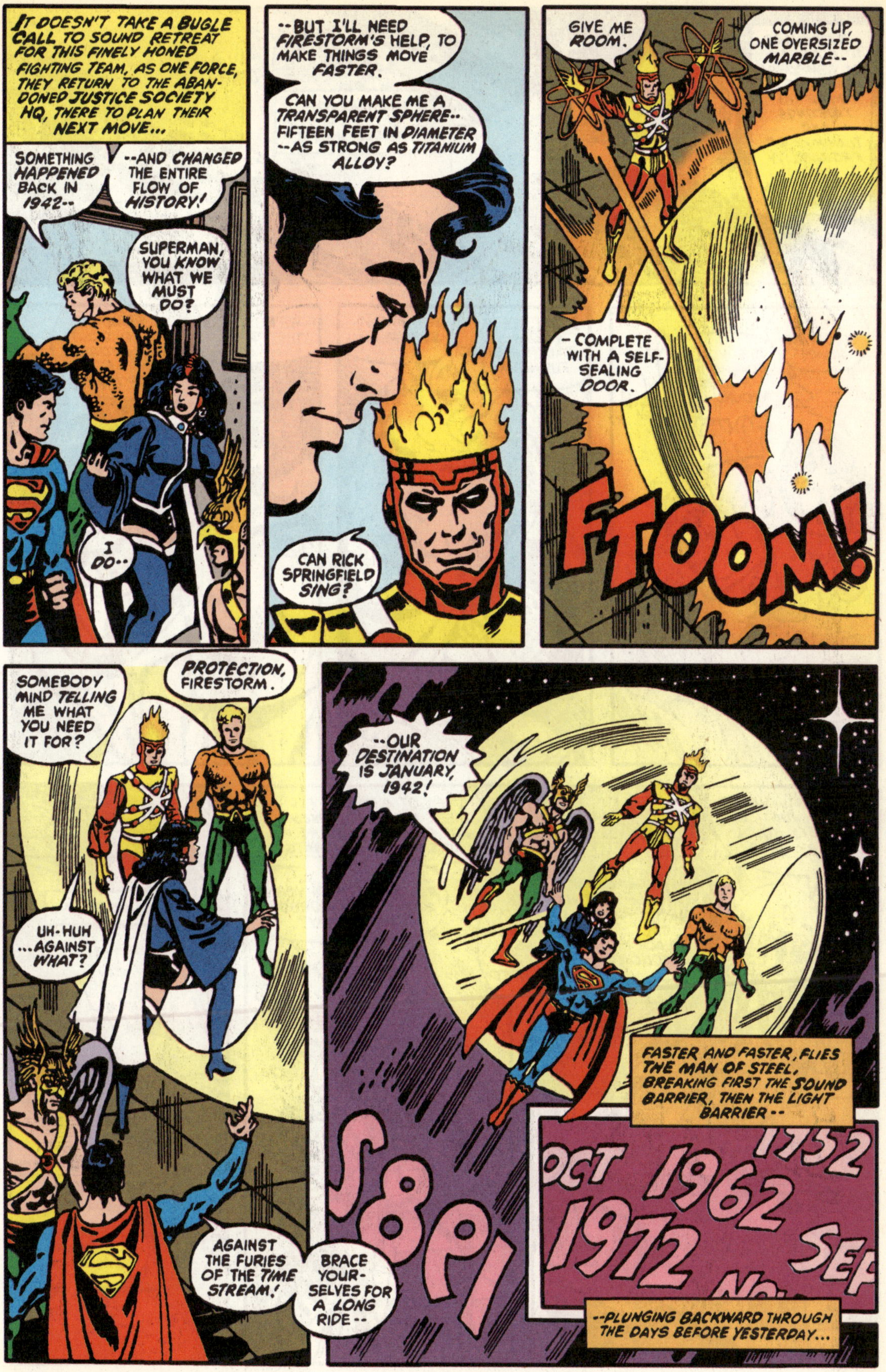

IT DOESN'T TAKE A BUGLE CALL TO SOUND RETREAT FOR THIS FINELY HONED FIGHTING TEAM. AS ONE FORCE, THEY RETURN TO THE ABANDONED JUSTICE SOCIETY HQ, THERE TO PLAN THEIR NEXT MOVE...
SOMETHING HAPPENED BACK IN 1942--
--AND CHANGED THE ENTIRE FLOW OF HISTORY!
SUPERMAN, YOU KNOW WHAT WE MUST DO?
I DO--
--BUT I'LL NEED FIRESTORM'S HELP, TO MAKE THINGS MOVE FASTER.
CAN YOU MAKE ME A TRANSPARENT SPHERE-- FIFTEEN FEET IN DIAMETER --AS STRONG AS TITANIUM ALLOY?
CAN RICK SPRINGFIELD SING?
GIVE ME ROOM.
COMING UP, ONE OVERSIZED MARBLE--
- COMPLETE WITH A SELF-SEALING DOOR.
FTOOM!
SOMEBODY MIND TELLING ME WHAT YOU NEED IT FOR?
PROTECTION, FIRESTORM.
UH-HUH ...AGAINST WHAT?
AGAINST THE FURIES OF THE TIME STREAM!
BRACE YOURSELVES FOR A LONG RIDE--
--OUR DESTINATION IS JANUARY, 1942!
FASTER AND FASTER, FLIES THE MAN OF STEEL, BREAKING FIRST THE SOUND BARRIER, THEN THE LIGHT BARRIER--
1952
OCT
1962
1972
SEP
--PLUNGING BACKWARD THROUGH THE DAYS BEFORE YESTERDAY...

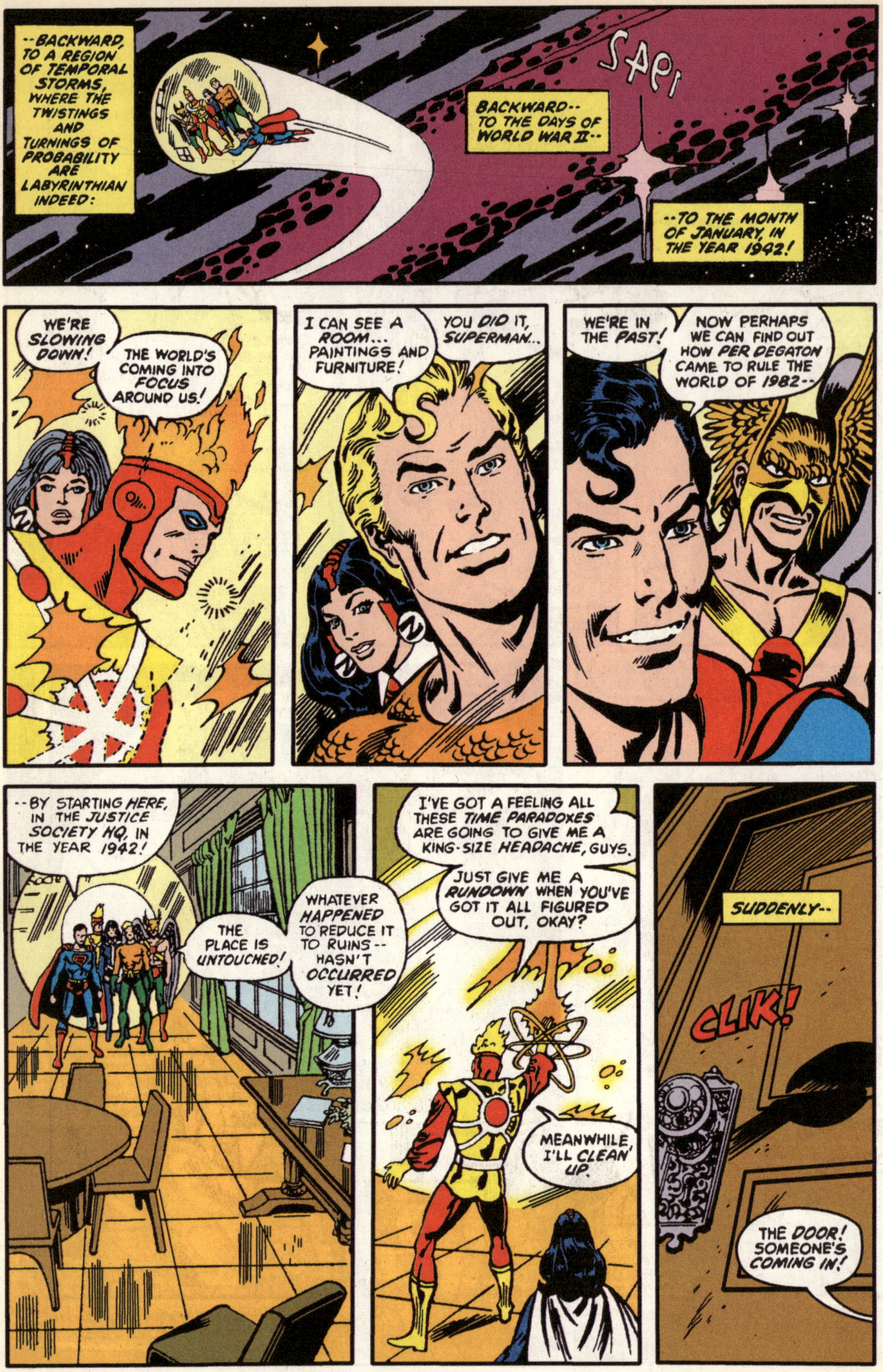
--BACKWARD, TO A REGION OF TEMPORAL STORMS, WHERE THE TWISTINGS AND TURNINGS OF PROBABILITY ARE LABYRINTHIAN INDEED:
BACKWARD-- TO THE DAYS OF WORLD WAR II--
--TO THE MONTH OF JANUARY, IN THE YEAR 1942!
WE'RE SLOWING DOWN!
THE WORLD'S COMING INTO FOCUS AROUND US!
I CAN SEE A ROOM... PAINTINGS AND FURNITURE!
YOU DID IT, SUPERMAN...
WE'RE IN THE PAST!
NOW PERHAPS WE CAN FIND OUT HOW PER DEGATON CAME TO RULE THE WORLD OF 1982--
--BY STARTING HERE, IN THE JUSTICE SOCIETY HQ, IN THE YEAR 1942!
THE PLACE IS UNTOUCHED!
WHATEVER HAPPENED TO REDUCE IT TO RUINS--HASN'T OCCURRED YET!
I'VE GOT A FEELING ALL THESE TIME PARADOXES ARE GOING TO GIVE ME A KING-SIZE HEADACHE, GUYS.
JUST GIVE ME A RUNDOWN WHEN YOU'VE GOT IT ALL FIGURED OUT, OKAY?
MEANWHILE, I'LL CLEAN UP.
SUDDENLY--
CLIK!
THE DOOR! SOMEONE'S COMING IN!

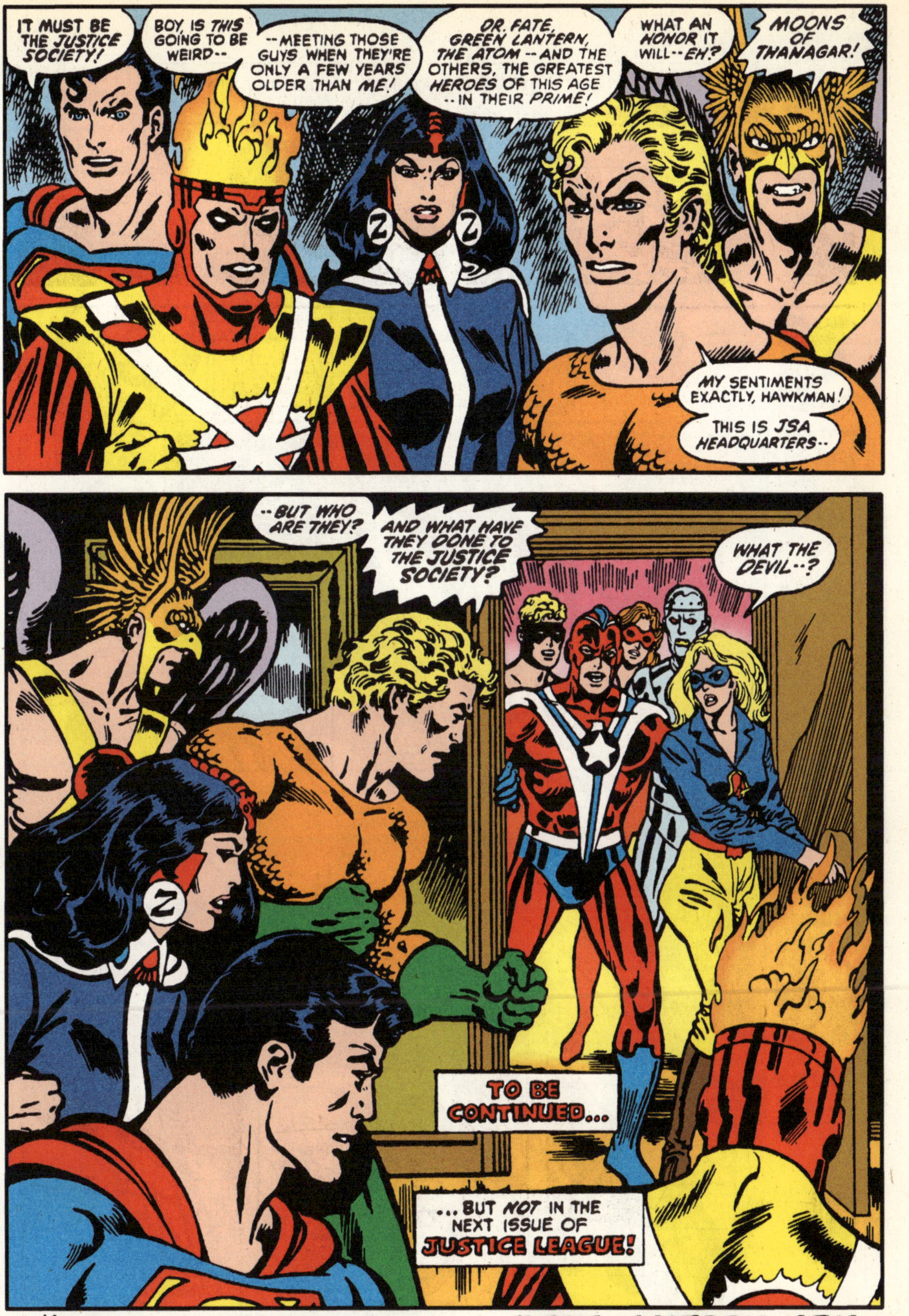
IT MUST BE THE JUSTICE SOCIETY!
BOY, IS THIS GOING TO BE WEIRD--
--MEETING THOSE GUYS WHEN THEY'RE ONLY A FEW YEARS OLDER THAN ME!
DR. FATE, GREEN LANTERN, THE ATOM -- AND THE OTHERS, THE GREATEST HEROES OF THIS AGE -- IN THEIR PRIME!
WHAT AN HONOR IT WILL -- EH?
MOONS OF THANAGAR!
MY SENTIMENTS EXACTLY, HAWKMAN!
THIS IS JSA HEADQUARTERS--
--BUT WHO ARE THEY?
AND WHAT HAVE THEY DONE TO THE JUSTICE SOCIETY?
WHAT THE DEVIL--?
TO BE CONTINUED...
...BUT NOT IN THE NEXT ISSUE OF JUSTICE LEAGUE!

YES, THIS IS A STORY SO BIG -- PAINTED ON SUCH A LARGE CANVAS -- THAT ONLY TWO BOOKS COULD CONTAIN IT! FOR BOOK TWO OF "CRISIS ON EARTH-PRIME" SEE ALL-STAR SQUADRON #14, AND A STORY TITLED... **"THE MYSTERY-MEN OF OCTOBER!"**

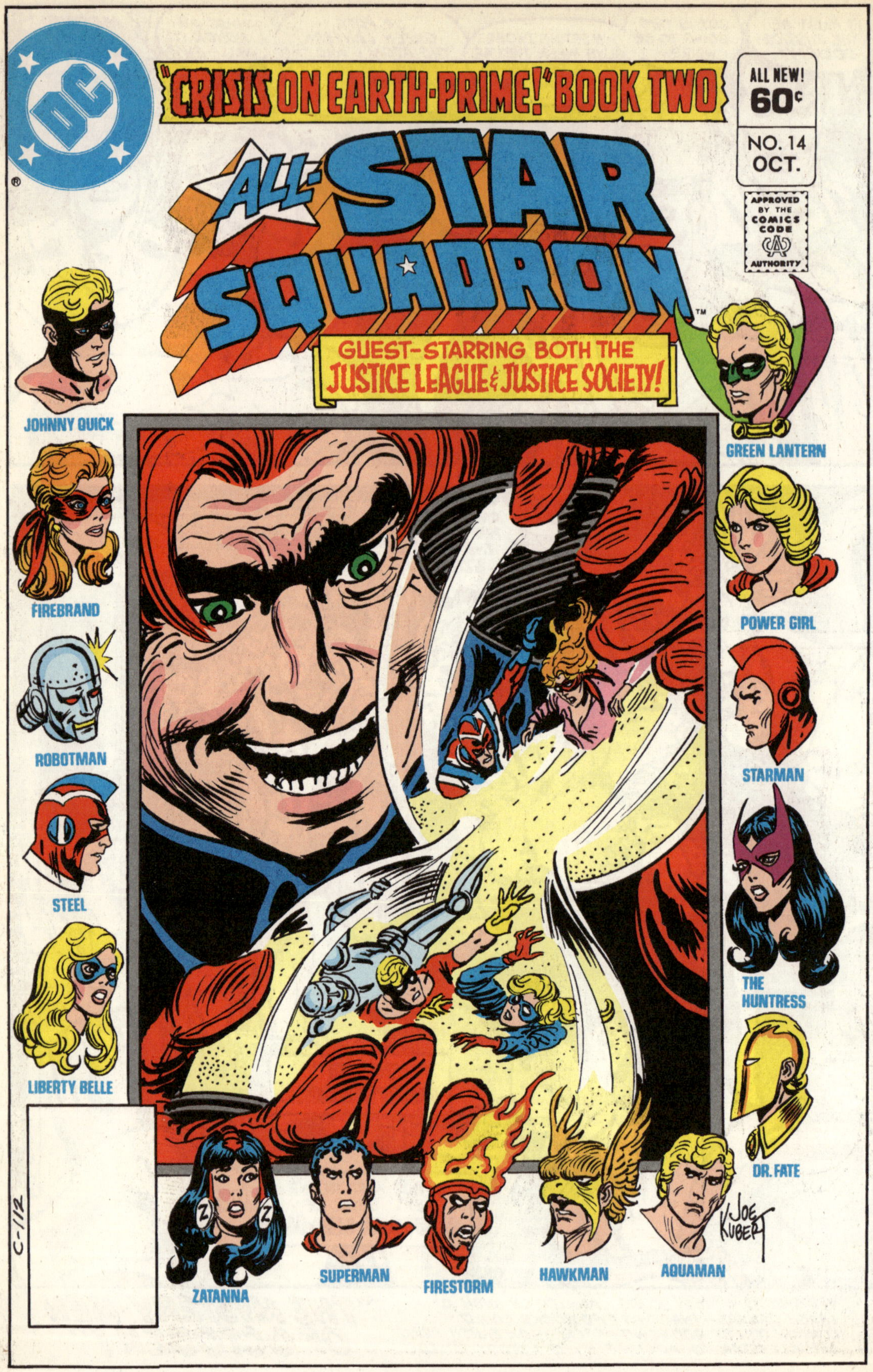
"CRISIS ON EARTH-PRIME!" BOOK TWO
ALL NEW! 60¢
NO. 14 OCT.
APPROVED BY THE COMICS CODE AUTHORITY
ALL-STAR SQUADRON
GUEST-STARRING BOTH THE JUSTICE LEAGUE & JUSTICE SOCIETY!
JOHNNY QUICK
FIREBRAND
ROBOTMAN
STEEL
LIBERTY BELLE
GREEN LANTERN
POWER GIRL
STARMAN
THE HUNTRESS
DR. FATE
ZATANNA
SUPERMAN
FIRESTORM
HAWKMAN
AQUAMAN
JOE KUBERT
C-112

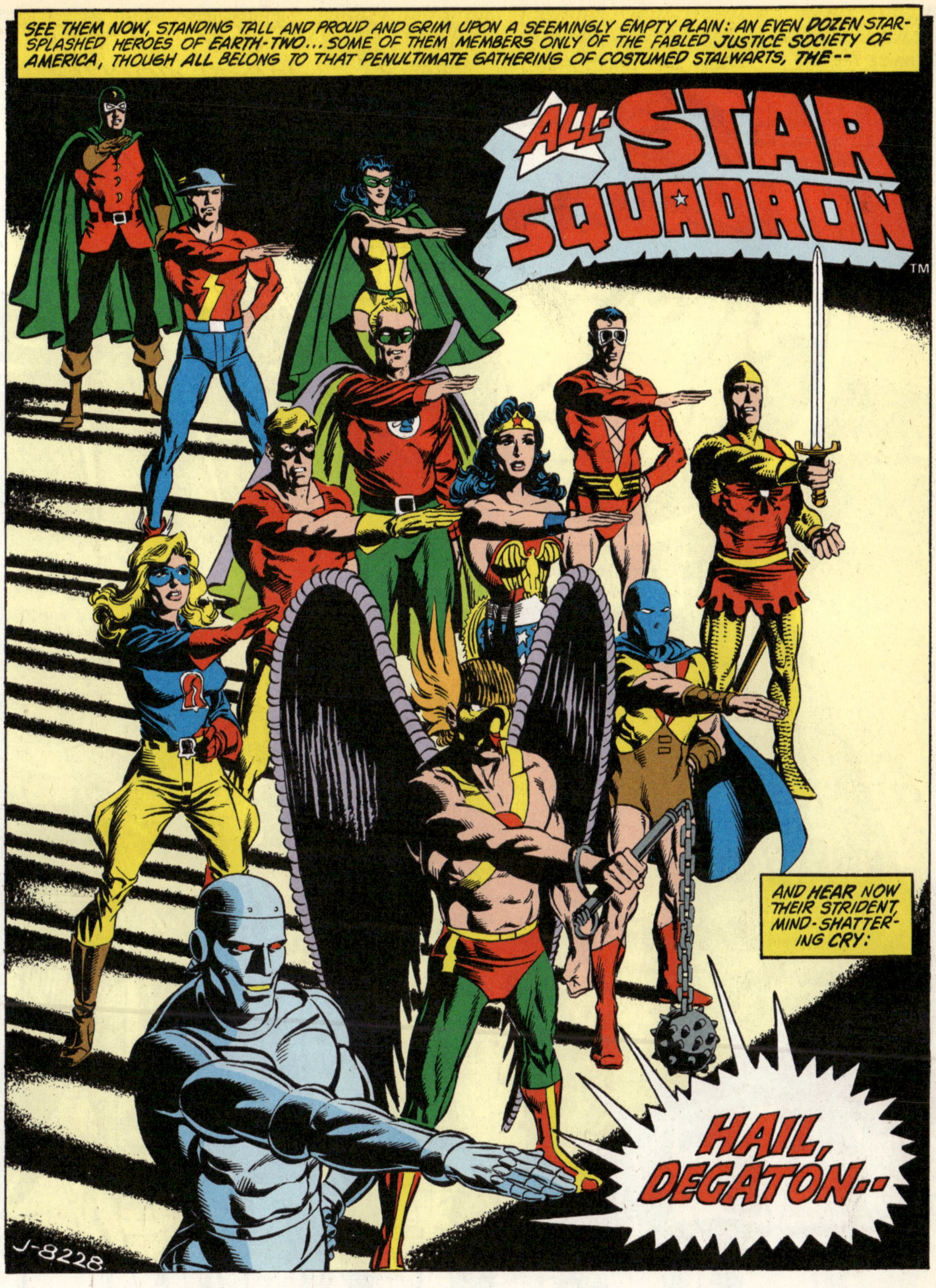
SEE THEM NOW, STANDING TALL AND PROUD AND GRIM UPON A SEEMINGLY EMPTY PLAIN: AN EVEN DOZEN STAR-SPLASHED HEROES OF EARTH-TWO... SOME OF THEM MEMBERS ONLY OF THE FABLED JUSTICE SOCIETY OF AMERICA, THOUGH ALL BELONG TO THAT PENULTIMATE GATHERING OF COSTUMED STALWARTS, THE--
ALL-STAR SQUADRON
TM
AND HEAR NOW THEIR STRIDENT, MIND-SHATTERING CRY:
HAIL, DEGATON..
J-8228

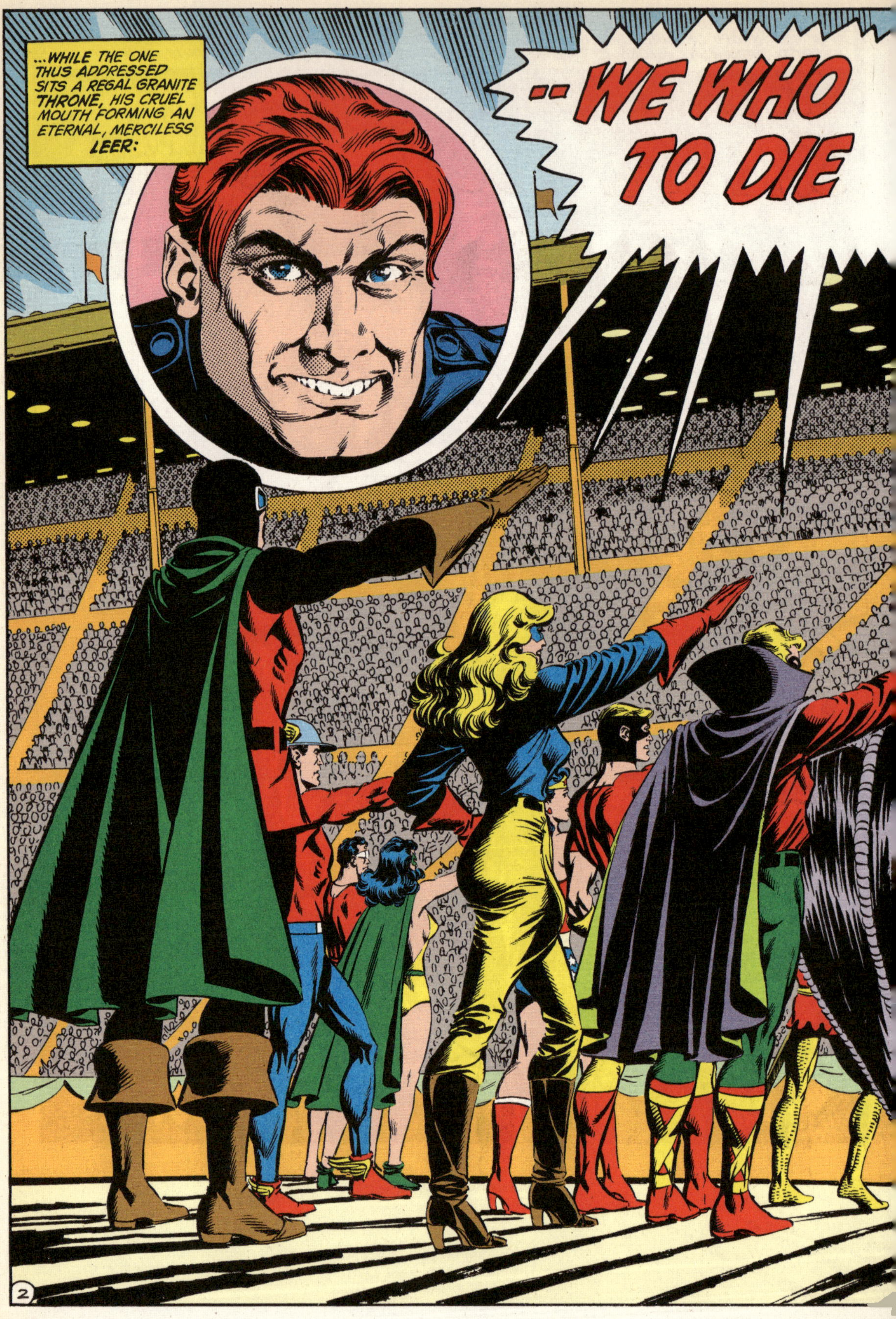
...WHILE THE ONE THUS ADDRESSED SITS A REGAL GRANITE THRONE, HIS CRUEL MOUTH FORMING AN ETERNAL, MERCILESS LEER:
-- WE WHO TO DIE
2

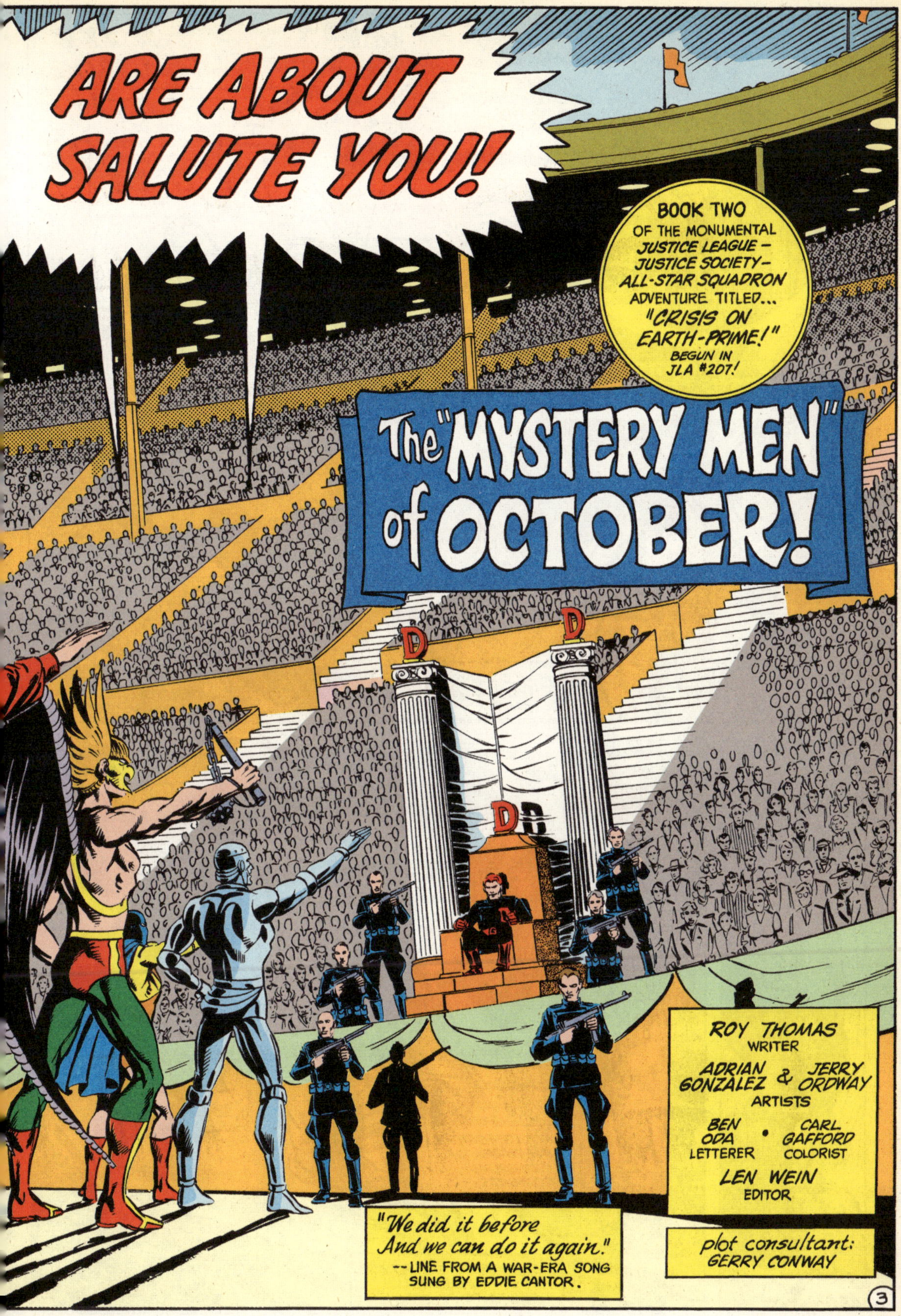

ARE ABOUT SALUTE YOU!
BOOK TWO OF THE MONUMENTAL JUSTICE LEAGUE — JUSTICE SOCIETY — ALL-STAR SQUADRON ADVENTURE TITLED... "CRISIS ON EARTH-PRIME!" BEGUN IN JLA #207!
The "MYSTERY MEN" of OCTOBER!
ROY THOMAS WRITER
ADRIAN GONZALEZ & JERRY ORDWAY ARTISTS
BEN ODA LETTERER • CARL GAFFORD COLORIST
LEN WEIN EDITOR
"We did it before And we can do it again." --LINE FROM A WAR-ERA SONG SUNG BY EDDIE CANTOR.
plot consultant: GERRY CONWAY
3

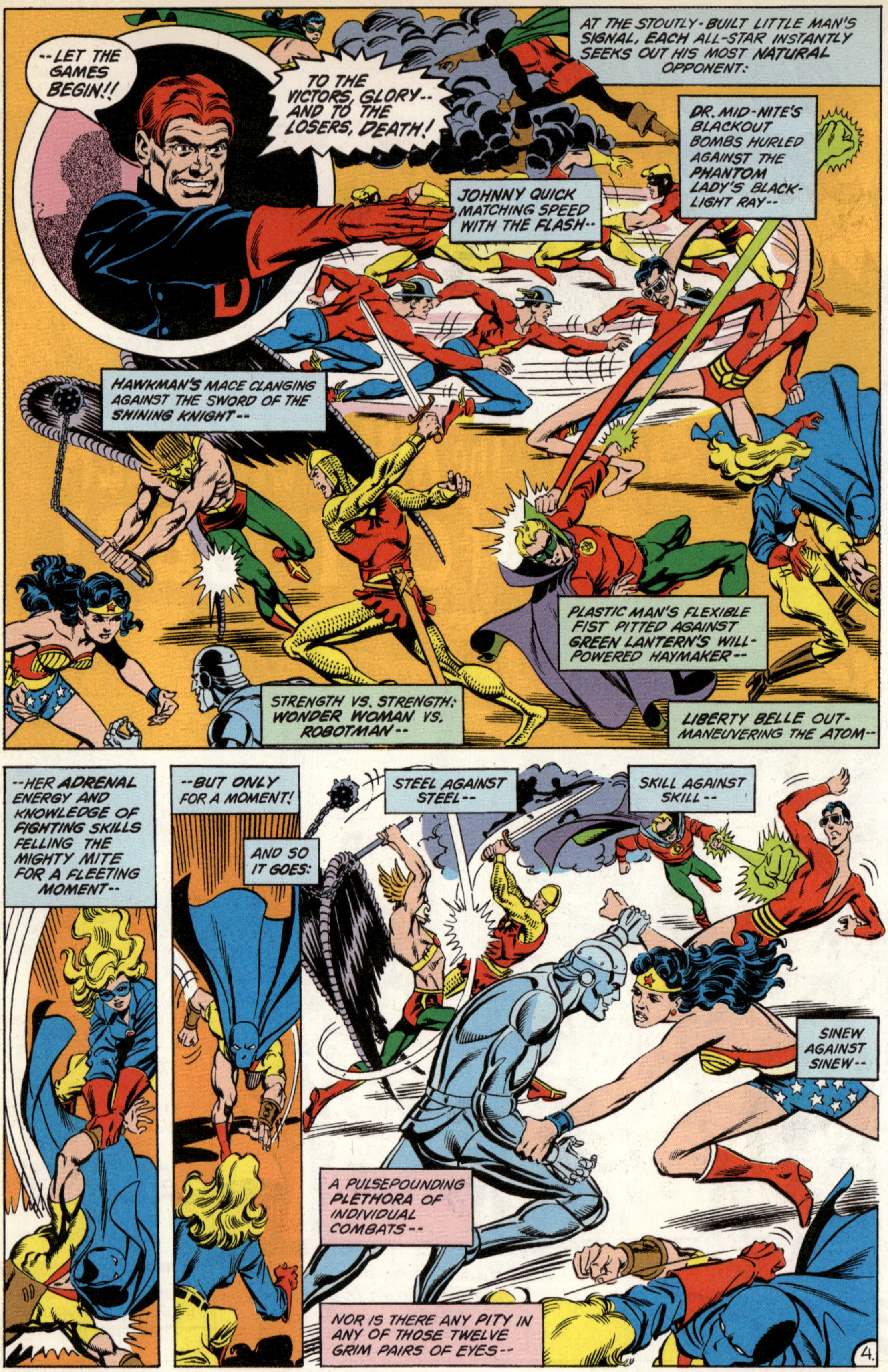
--LET THE GAMES BEGIN!!
TO THE VICTORS, GLORY-- AND TO THE LOSERS, DEATH!
AT THE STOUTLY-BUILT LITTLE MAN'S SIGNAL, EACH ALL-STAR INSTANTLY SEEKS OUT HIS MOST NATURAL OPPONENT:
DR. MID-NITE'S BLACKOUT BOMBS HURLED AGAINST THE PHANTOM LADY'S BLACK-LIGHT RAY--
JOHNNY QUICK MATCHING SPEED WITH THE FLASH--
HAWKMAN'S MACE CLANGING AGAINST THE SWORD OF THE SHINING KNIGHT--
PLASTIC MAN'S FLEXIBLE FIST PITTED AGAINST GREEN LANTERN'S WILL-POWERED HAYMAKER--
STRENGTH VS. STRENGTH: WONDER WOMAN VS. ROBOTMAN--
LIBERTY BELLE OUT-MANEUVERING THE ATOM--
--HER ADRENAL ENERGY AND KNOWLEDGE OF FIGHTING SKILLS FELLING THE MIGHTY MITE FOR A FLEETING MOMENT--
--BUT ONLY FOR A MOMENT!
AND SO IT GOES:
STEEL AGAINST STEEL--
SKILL AGAINST SKILL--
SINEW AGAINST SINEW--
A PULSEPOUNDING PLETHORA OF INDIVIDUAL COMBATS--
NOR IS THERE ANY PITY IN ANY OF THOSE TWELVE GRIM PAIRS OF EYES--
4.

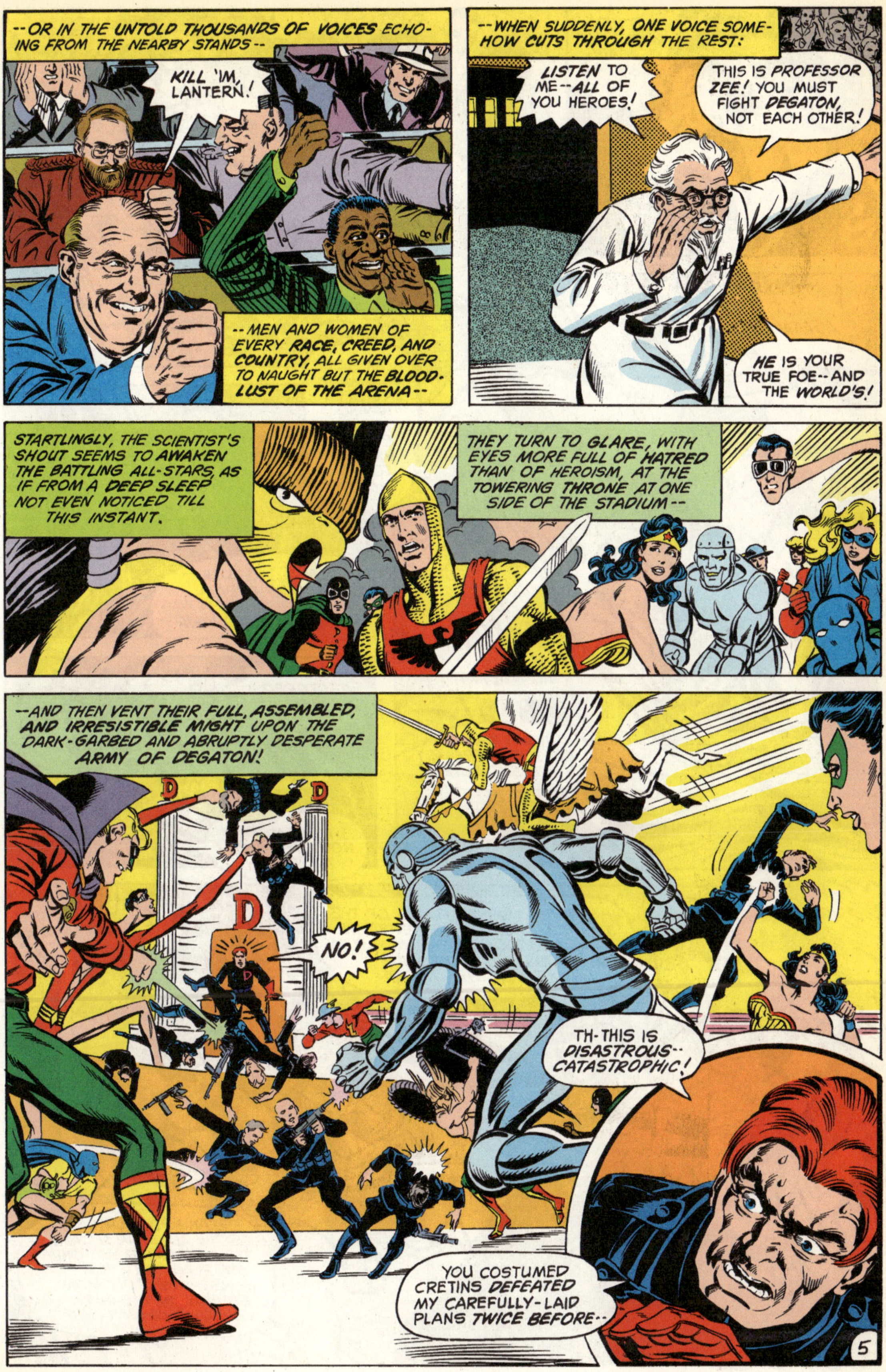
--OR IN THE UNTOLD THOUSANDS OF VOICES ECHOING FROM THE NEARBY STANDS--
KILL 'IM, LANTERN!
--MEN AND WOMEN OF EVERY RACE, CREED, AND COUNTRY, ALL GIVEN OVER TO NAUGHT BUT THE BLOOD-LUST OF THE ARENA--
--WHEN SUDDENLY, ONE VOICE SOMEHOW CUTS THROUGH THE REST:
LISTEN TO ME--ALL OF YOU HEROES!
THIS IS PROFESSOR ZEE! YOU MUST FIGHT DEGATON, NOT EACH OTHER!
HE IS YOUR TRUE FOE--AND THE WORLD'S!
STARTLINGLY, THE SCIENTIST'S SHOUT SEEMS TO AWAKEN THE BATTLING ALL-STARS, AS IF FROM A DEEP SLEEP NOT EVEN NOTICED TILL THIS INSTANT.
THEY TURN TO GLARE, WITH EYES MORE FULL OF HATRED THAN OF HEROISM, AT THE TOWERING THRONE AT ONE SIDE OF THE STADIUM--
--AND THEN VENT THEIR FULL, ASSEMBLED, AND IRRESISTIBLE MIGHT UPON THE DARK-GARBED AND ABRUPTLY DESPERATE ARMY OF DEGATON!
NO!
TH-THIS IS DISASTROUS--CATASTROPHIC!
YOU COSTUMED CRETINS DEFEATED MY CAREFULLY-LAID PLANS TWICE BEFORE--
5

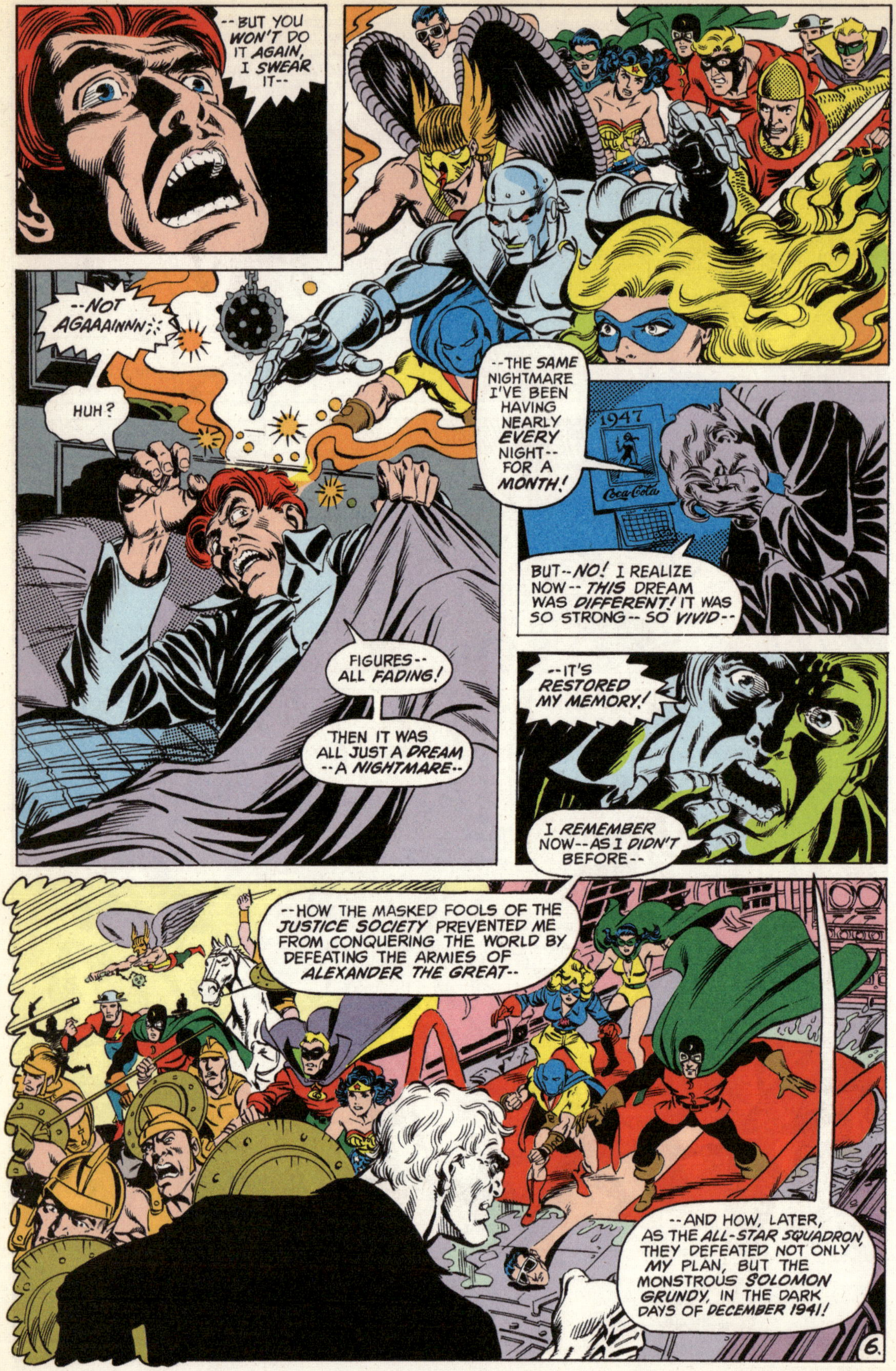
--BUT YOU WON'T DO IT AGAIN, I SWEAR IT--
--NOT AGAAAINNN!
HUH?
FIGURES--ALL FADING!
THEN IT WAS ALL JUST A DREAM --A NIGHTMARE--
--THE SAME NIGHTMARE I'VE BEEN HAVING NEARLY EVERY NIGHT--FOR A MONTH!
1947
Coca-Cola
BUT--NO! I REALIZE NOW--THIS DREAM WAS DIFFERENT! IT WAS SO STRONG--SO VIVID--
--IT'S RESTORED MY MEMORY!
I REMEMBER NOW--AS I DIDN'T BEFORE--
--HOW THE MASKED FOOLS OF THE JUSTICE SOCIETY PREVENTED ME FROM CONQUERING THE WORLD BY DEFEATING THE ARMIES OF ALEXANDER THE GREAT--
--AND HOW, LATER, AS THE ALL-STAR SQUADRON, THEY DEFEATED NOT ONLY MY PLAN, BUT THE MONSTROUS SOLOMON GRUNDY, IN THE DARK DAYS OF DECEMBER 1941!
6.

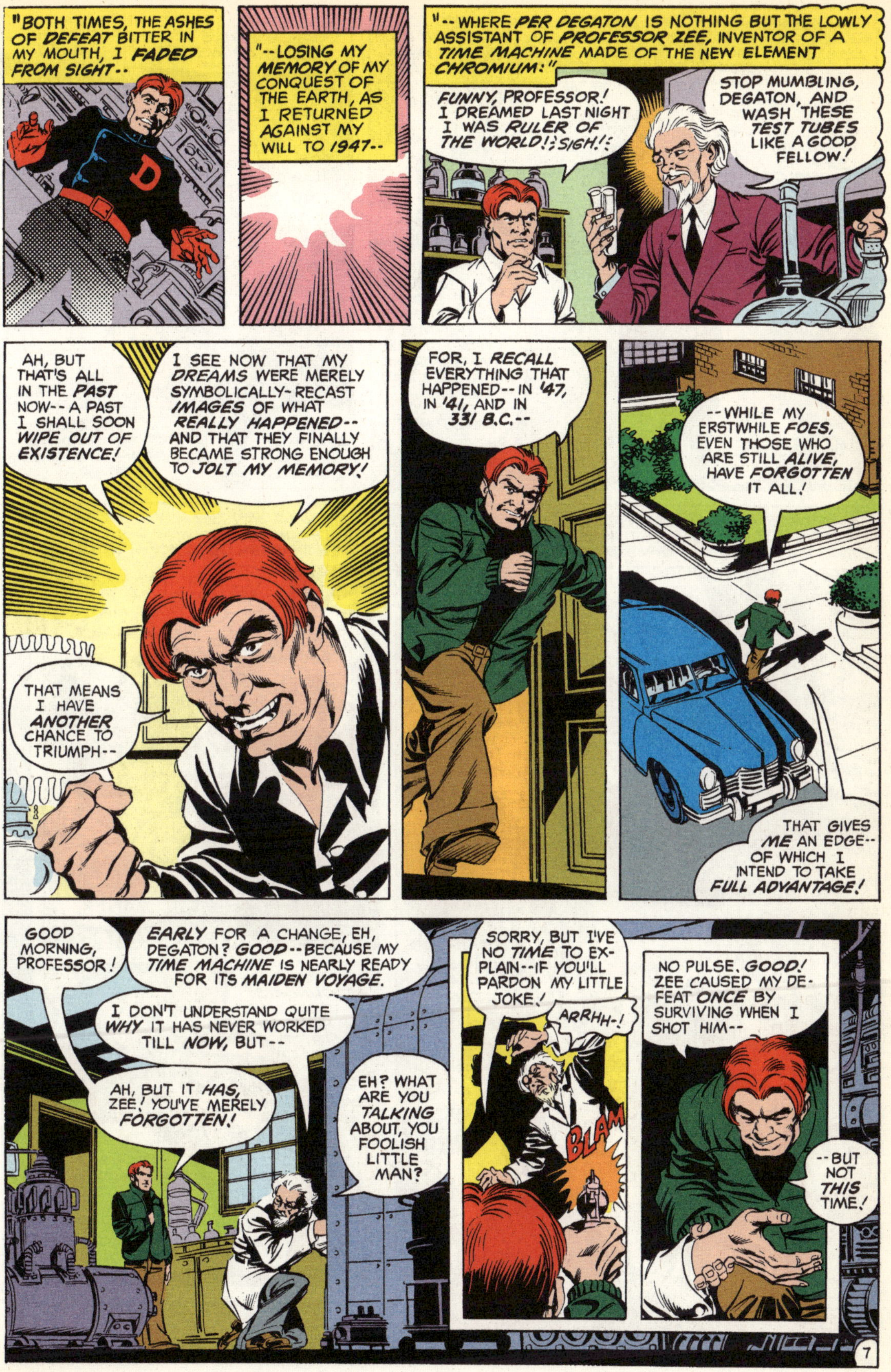
"BOTH TIMES, THE ASHES OF DEFEAT BITTER IN MY MOUTH, I FADED FROM SIGHT--
"--LOSING MY MEMORY OF MY CONQUEST OF THE EARTH, AS I RETURNED AGAINST MY WILL TO 1947--
"--WHERE PER DEGATON IS NOTHING BUT THE LOWLY ASSISTANT OF PROFESSOR ZEE, INVENTOR OF A TIME MACHINE MADE OF THE NEW ELEMENT CHROMIUM:"
FUNNY, PROFESSOR! I DREAMED LAST NIGHT I WAS RULER OF THE WORLD! :SIGH!:
STOP MUMBLING, DEGATON, AND WASH THESE TEST TUBES LIKE A GOOD FELLOW!
AH, BUT THAT'S ALL IN THE PAST NOW-- A PAST I SHALL SOON WIPE OUT OF EXISTENCE!
I SEE NOW THAT MY DREAMS WERE MERELY SYMBOLICALLY-RECAST IMAGES OF WHAT REALLY HAPPENED-- AND THAT THEY FINALLY BECAME STRONG ENOUGH TO JOLT MY MEMORY!
THAT MEANS I HAVE ANOTHER CHANCE TO TRIUMPH--
FOR, I RECALL EVERYTHING THAT HAPPENED-- IN '47, IN '41, AND IN 331 B.C.--
--WHILE MY ERSTWHILE FOES, EVEN THOSE WHO ARE STILL ALIVE, HAVE FORGOTTEN IT ALL!
THAT GIVES ME AN EDGE-- OF WHICH I INTEND TO TAKE FULL ADVANTAGE!
GOOD MORNING, PROFESSOR!
EARLY FOR A CHANGE, EH, DEGATON? GOOD-- BECAUSE MY TIME MACHINE IS NEARLY READY FOR ITS MAIDEN VOYAGE.
I DON'T UNDERSTAND QUITE WHY IT HAS NEVER WORKED TILL NOW, BUT--
AH, BUT IT HAS, ZEE! YOU'VE MERELY FORGOTTEN!
EH? WHAT ARE YOU TALKING ABOUT, YOU FOOLISH LITTLE MAN?
SORRY, BUT I'VE NO TIME TO EX-PLAIN--IF YOU'LL PARDON MY LITTLE JOKE!
ARRHH-!
BLAM
NO PULSE. GOOD! ZEE CAUSED MY DE-FEAT ONCE BY SURVIVING WHEN I SHOT HIM--
--BUT NOT THIS TIME!
7

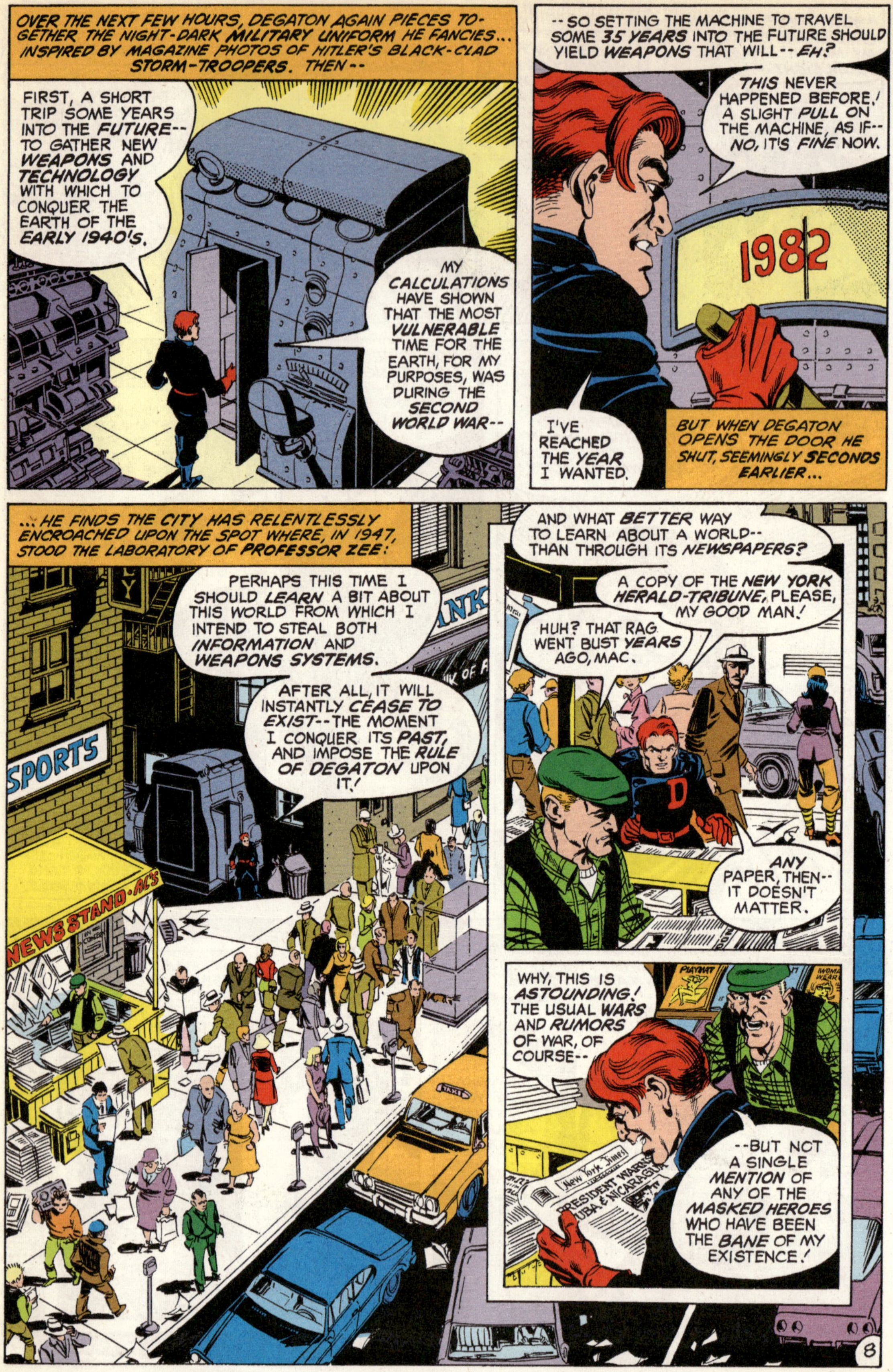
OVER THE NEXT FEW HOURS, DEGATON AGAIN PIECES TOGETHER THE NIGHT-DARK MILITARY UNIFORM HE FANCIES... INSPIRED BY MAGAZINE PHOTOS OF HITLER'S BLACK-CLAD STORM-TROOPERS. THEN--
FIRST, A SHORT TRIP SOME YEARS INTO THE FUTURE-- TO GATHER NEW WEAPONS AND TECHNOLOGY WITH WHICH TO CONQUER THE EARTH OF THE EARLY 1940'S.
MY CALCULATIONS HAVE SHOWN THAT THE MOST VULNERABLE TIME FOR THE EARTH, FOR MY PURPOSES, WAS DURING THE SECOND WORLD WAR--
--SO SETTING THE MACHINE TO TRAVEL SOME 35 YEARS INTO THE FUTURE SHOULD YIELD WEAPONS THAT WILL-- EH?
THIS NEVER HAPPENED BEFORE! A SLIGHT PULL ON THE MACHINE, AS IF-- NO, IT'S FINE NOW.
1982
I'VE REACHED THE YEAR I WANTED.
BUT WHEN DEGATON OPENS THE DOOR HE SHUT, SEEMINGLY SECONDS EARLIER...
...HE FINDS THE CITY HAS RELENTLESSLY ENCROACHED UPON THE SPOT WHERE, IN 1947, STOOD THE LABORATORY OF PROFESSOR ZEE:
PERHAPS THIS TIME I SHOULD LEARN A BIT ABOUT THIS WORLD FROM WHICH I INTEND TO STEAL BOTH INFORMATION AND WEAPONS SYSTEMS.
AFTER ALL, IT WILL INSTANTLY CEASE TO EXIST--THE MOMENT I CONQUER ITS PAST, AND IMPOSE THE RULE OF DEGATON UPON IT!
SPORTS
NEWS STAND - AL'S
TAXI
AND WHAT BETTER WAY TO LEARN ABOUT A WORLD-- THAN THROUGH ITS NEWSPAPERS?
A COPY OF THE NEW YORK HERALD-TRIBUNE, PLEASE, MY GOOD MAN!
HUH? THAT RAG WENT BUST YEARS AGO, MAC.
ANY PAPER, THEN-- IT DOESN'T MATTER.
WHY, THIS IS ASTOUNDING! THE USUAL WARS AND RUMORS OF WAR, OF COURSE--
New York Times
PRESIDENT WARNS CUBA & NICARAGUA
--BUT NOT A SINGLE MENTION OF ANY OF THE MASKED HEROES WHO HAVE BEEN THE BANE OF MY EXISTENCE!
8

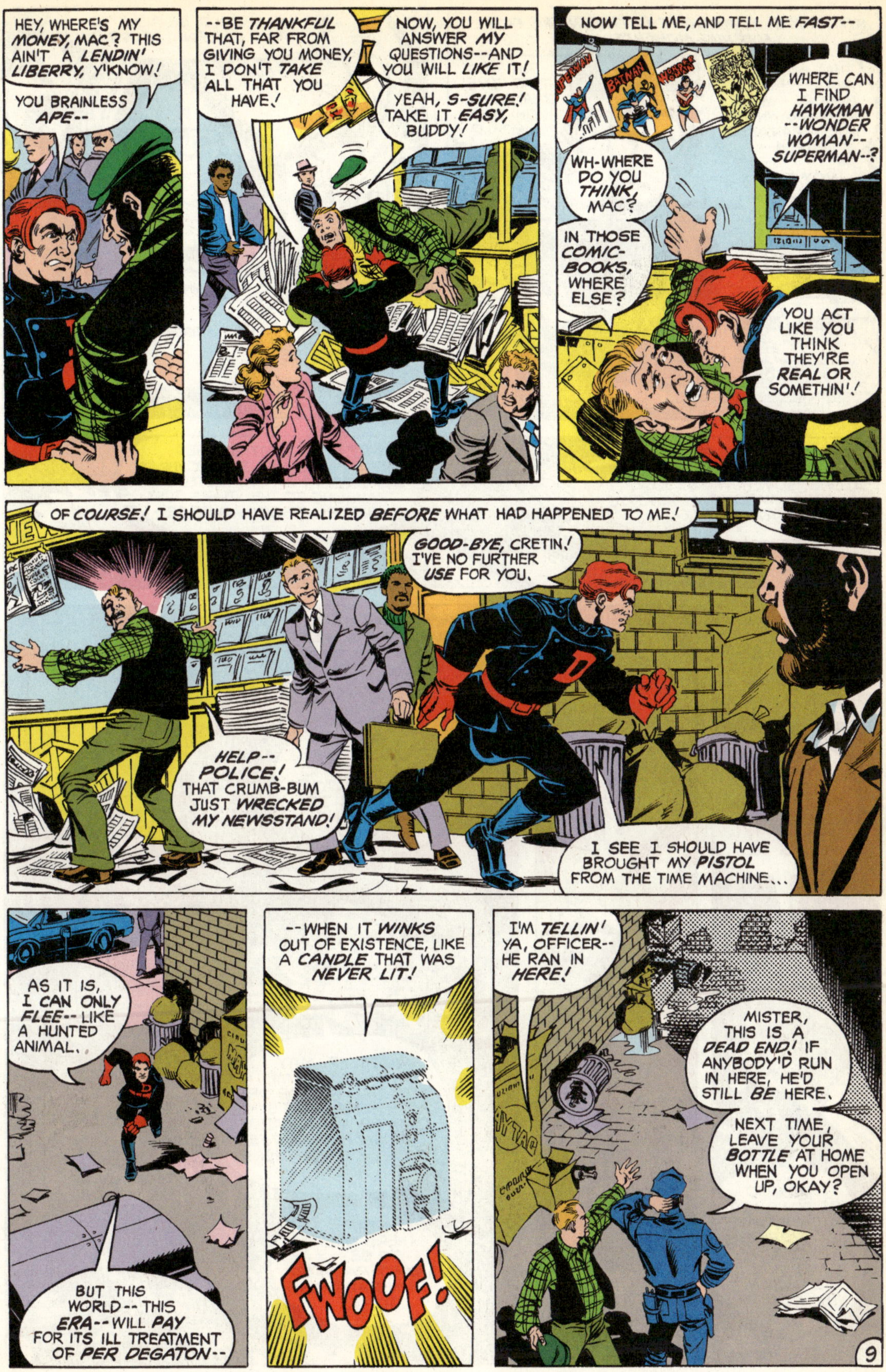
HEY, WHERE'S MY MONEY, MAC? THIS AIN'T A LENDIN' LIBERRY, Y'KNOW!
YOU BRAINLESS APE--
--BE THANKFUL THAT, FAR FROM GIVING YOU MONEY, I DON'T TAKE ALL THAT YOU HAVE!
NOW, YOU WILL ANSWER MY QUESTIONS--AND YOU WILL LIKE IT!
YEAH, S-SURE! TAKE IT EASY, BUDDY!
NOW TELL ME, AND TELL ME FAST--
SUPERMAN
BATMAN
WONDER
WHERE CAN I FIND HAWKMAN--WONDER WOMAN--SUPERMAN--?
WH-WHERE DO YOU THINK, MAC?
IN THOSE COMIC-BOOKS, WHERE ELSE?
YOU ACT LIKE YOU THINK THEY'RE REAL OR SOMETHIN'!
OF COURSE! I SHOULD HAVE REALIZED BEFORE WHAT HAD HAPPENED TO ME!
GOOD-BYE, CRETIN! I'VE NO FURTHER USE FOR YOU.
HELP--POLICE! THAT CRUMB-BUM JUST WRECKED MY NEWSSTAND!
I SEE I SHOULD HAVE BROUGHT MY PISTOL FROM THE TIME MACHINE...
AS IT IS, I CAN ONLY FLEE--LIKE A HUNTED ANIMAL.
BUT THIS WORLD--THIS ERA--WILL PAY FOR ITS ILL TREATMENT OF PER DEGATON--
--WHEN IT WINKS OUT OF EXISTENCE, LIKE A CANDLE THAT WAS NEVER LIT!
FWOOF!
I'M TELLIN' YA, OFFICER--HE RAN IN HERE!
MISTER, THIS IS A DEAD END! IF ANYBODY'D RUN IN HERE, HE'D STILL BE HERE.
NEXT TIME, LEAVE YOUR BOTTLE AT HOME WHEN YOU OPEN UP, OKAY?
9

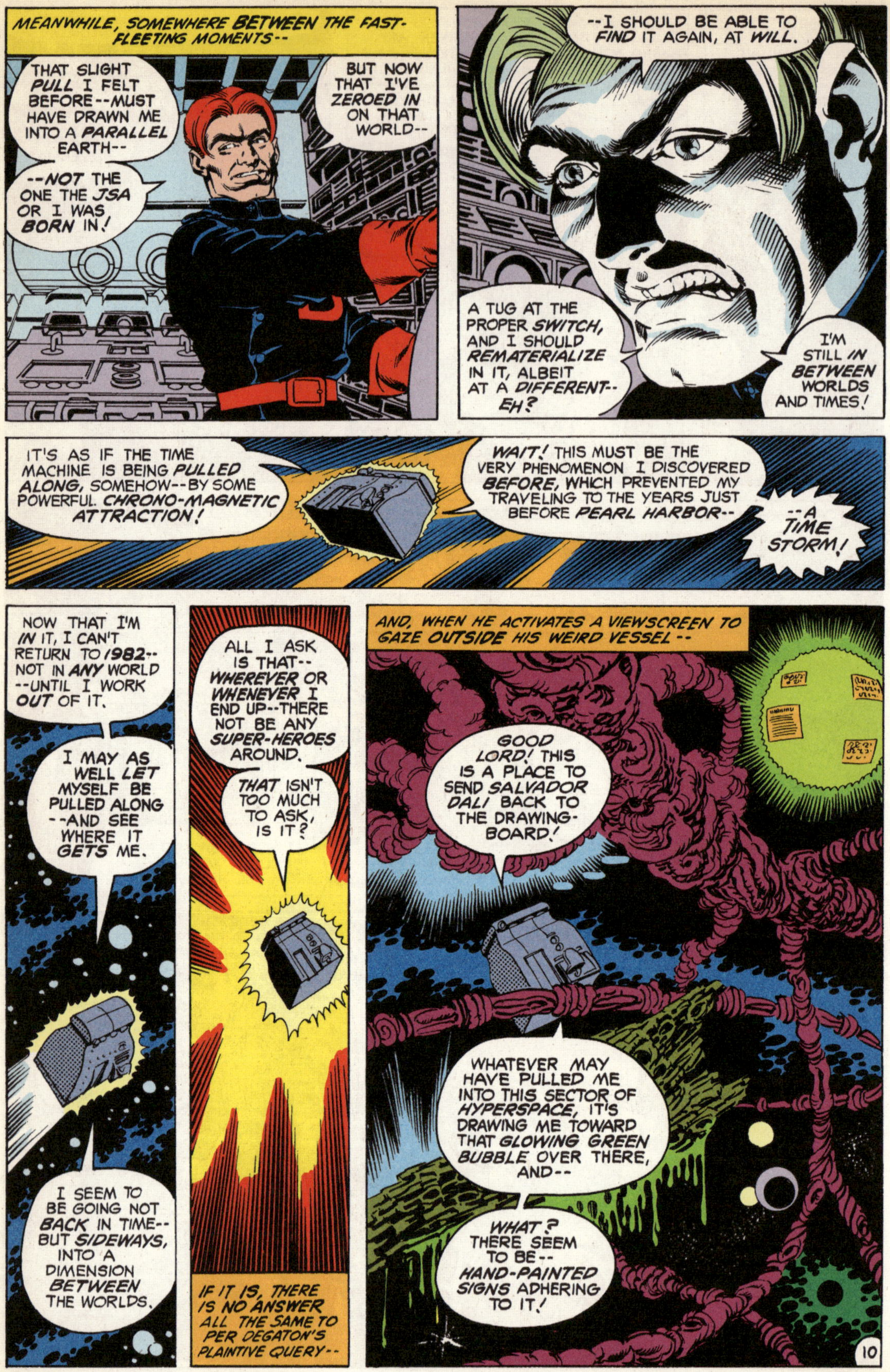
MEANWHILE, SOMEWHERE BETWEEN THE FAST-FLEETING MOMENTS--
THAT SLIGHT PULL I FELT BEFORE--MUST HAVE DRAWN ME INTO A PARALLEL EARTH--
--NOT THE ONE THE JSA OR I WAS BORN IN!
BUT NOW THAT I'VE ZEROED IN ON THAT WORLD--
--I SHOULD BE ABLE TO FIND IT AGAIN, AT WILL.
A TUG AT THE PROPER SWITCH, AND I SHOULD REMATERIALIZE IN IT, ALBEIT AT A DIFFERENT-- EH?
I'M STILL IN BETWEEN WORLDS AND TIMES!
IT'S AS IF THE TIME MACHINE IS BEING PULLED ALONG, SOMEHOW--BY SOME POWERFUL CHRONO-MAGNETIC ATTRACTION!
WAIT! THIS MUST BE THE VERY PHENOMENON I DISCOVERED BEFORE, WHICH PREVENTED MY TRAVELING TO THE YEARS JUST BEFORE PEARL HARBOR--
--A TIME STORM!
NOW THAT I'M IN IT, I CAN'T RETURN TO 1982-- NOT IN ANY WORLD --UNTIL I WORK OUT OF IT.
I MAY AS WELL LET MYSELF BE PULLED ALONG --AND SEE WHERE IT GETS ME.
I SEEM TO BE GOING NOT BACK IN TIME-- BUT SIDEWAYS, INTO A DIMENSION BETWEEN THE WORLDS.
ALL I ASK IS THAT--WHEREVER OR WHENEVER I END UP--THERE NOT BE ANY SUPER-HEROES AROUND.
THAT ISN'T TOO MUCH TO ASK, IS IT?
IF IT IS, THERE IS NO ANSWER ALL THE SAME TO PER DEGATON'S PLAINTIVE QUERY--
AND, WHEN HE ACTIVATES A VIEWSCREEN TO GAZE OUTSIDE HIS WEIRD VESSEL--
GOOD LORD! THIS IS A PLACE TO SEND SALVADOR DALI BACK TO THE DRAWING-BOARD!
WHATEVER MAY HAVE PULLED ME INTO THIS SECTOR OF HYPERSPACE, IT'S DRAWING ME TOWARD THAT GLOWING GREEN BUBBLE OVER THERE, AND--
WHAT? THERE SEEM TO BE--HAND-PAINTED SIGNS ADHERING TO IT!
10

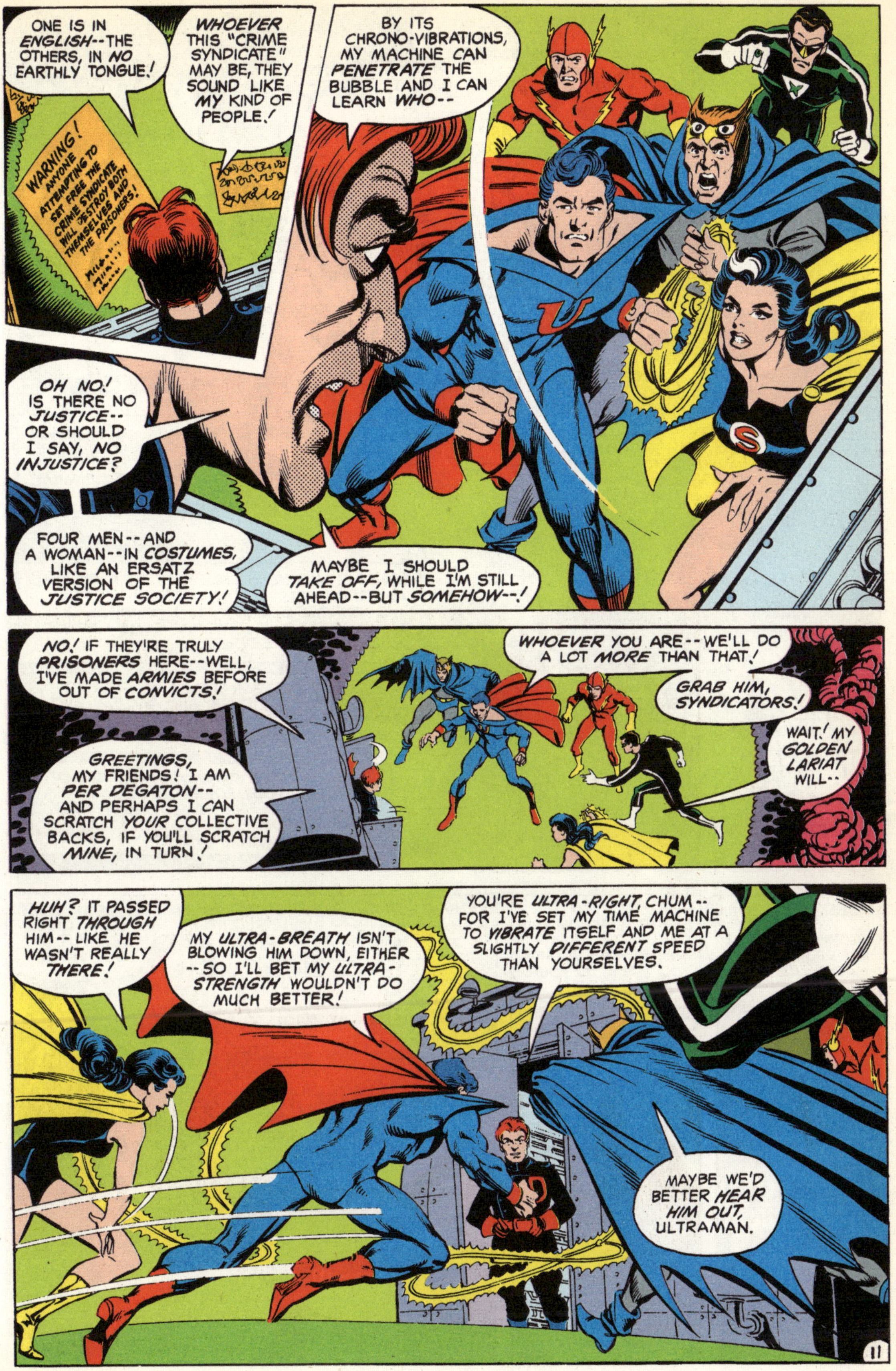
ONE IS IN ENGLISH--THE OTHERS, IN NO EARTHLY TONGUE!
WHOEVER THIS "CRIME SYNDICATE" MAY BE, THEY SOUND LIKE MY KIND OF PEOPLE!
WARNING! ANYONE ATTEMPTING TO SET FREE THE CRIME SYNDICATE WILL DESTROY BOTH THEMSELVES AND THE PRISONERS!
BY ITS CHRONO-VIBRATIONS, MY MACHINE CAN PENETRATE THE BUBBLE AND I CAN LEARN WHO--
OH NO! IS THERE NO JUSTICE--OR SHOULD I SAY, NO INJUSTICE?
FOUR MEN--AND A WOMAN--IN COSTUMES, LIKE AN ERSATZ VERSION OF THE JUSTICE SOCIETY!
MAYBE I SHOULD TAKE OFF, WHILE I'M STILL AHEAD--BUT SOMEHOW--!
NO! IF THEY'RE TRULY PRISONERS HERE--WELL, I'VE MADE ARMIES BEFORE OUT OF CONVICTS!
GREETINGS, MY FRIENDS! I AM PER DEGATON--AND PERHAPS I CAN SCRATCH YOUR COLLECTIVE BACKS, IF YOU'LL SCRATCH MINE, IN TURN!
WHOEVER YOU ARE--WE'LL DO A LOT MORE THAN THAT!
GRAB HIM, SYNDICATORS!
WAIT! MY GOLDEN LARIAT WILL--
HUH? IT PASSED RIGHT THROUGH HIM--LIKE HE WASN'T REALLY THERE!
MY ULTRA-BREATH ISN'T BLOWING HIM DOWN, EITHER--SO I'LL BET MY ULTRA-STRENGTH WOULDN'T DO MUCH BETTER!
YOU'RE ULTRA-RIGHT, CHUM--FOR I'VE SET MY TIME MACHINE TO VIBRATE ITSELF AND ME AT A SLIGHTLY DIFFERENT SPEED THAN YOURSELVES.
MAYBE WE'D BETTER HEAR HIM OUT, ULTRAMAN.
11

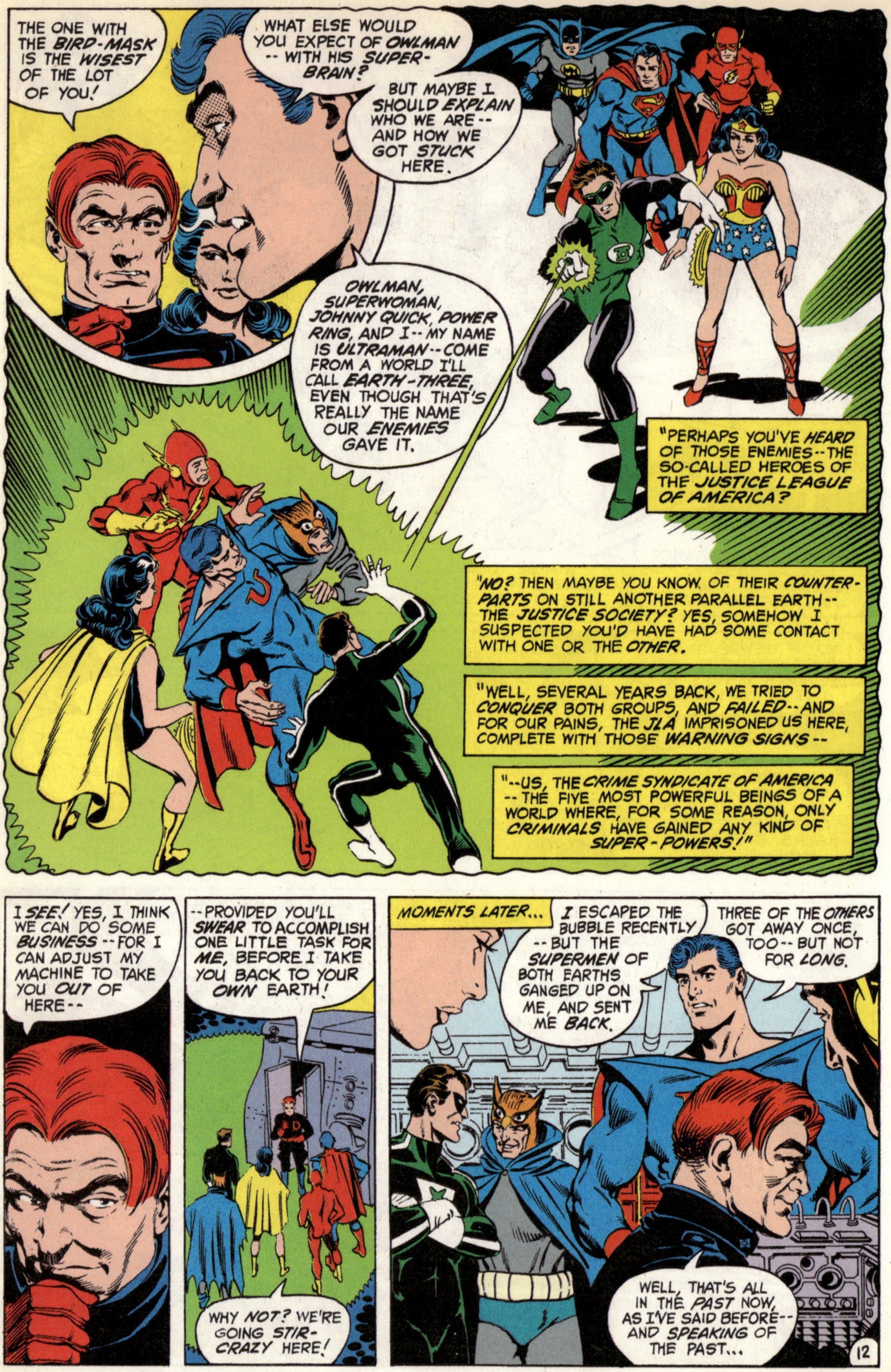
THE ONE WITH THE BIRD-MASK IS THE WISEST OF THE LOT OF YOU!
WHAT ELSE WOULD YOU EXPECT OF OWLMAN -- WITH HIS SUPER-BRAIN?
BUT MAYBE I SHOULD EXPLAIN WHO WE ARE -- AND HOW WE GOT STUCK HERE.
OWLMAN, SUPERWOMAN, JOHNNY QUICK, POWER RING, AND I -- MY NAME IS ULTRAMAN -- COME FROM A WORLD I'LL CALL EARTH-THREE, EVEN THOUGH THAT'S REALLY THE NAME OUR ENEMIES GAVE IT.
"PERHAPS YOU'VE HEARD OF THOSE ENEMIES -- THE SO-CALLED HEROES OF THE JUSTICE LEAGUE OF AMERICA?
"NO? THEN MAYBE YOU KNOW OF THEIR COUNTER-PARTS ON STILL ANOTHER PARALLEL EARTH -- THE JUSTICE SOCIETY? YES, SOMEHOW I SUSPECTED YOU'D HAVE HAD SOME CONTACT WITH ONE OR THE OTHER.
"WELL, SEVERAL YEARS BACK, WE TRIED TO CONQUER BOTH GROUPS, AND FAILED -- AND FOR OUR PAINS, THE JLA IMPRISONED US HERE, COMPLETE WITH THOSE WARNING SIGNS --
"-- US, THE CRIME SYNDICATE OF AMERICA -- THE FIVE MOST POWERFUL BEINGS OF A WORLD WHERE, FOR SOME REASON, ONLY CRIMINALS HAVE GAINED ANY KIND OF SUPER-POWERS!"
I SEE! YES, I THINK WE CAN DO SOME BUSINESS -- FOR I CAN ADJUST MY MACHINE TO TAKE YOU OUT OF HERE --
-- PROVIDED YOU'LL SWEAR TO ACCOMPLISH ONE LITTLE TASK FOR ME, BEFORE I TAKE YOU BACK TO YOUR OWN EARTH!
WHY NOT? WE'RE GOING STIR-CRAZY HERE!
MOMENTS LATER...
I ESCAPED THE BUBBLE RECENTLY -- BUT THE SUPERMEN OF BOTH EARTHS GANGED UP ON ME, AND SENT ME BACK.
THREE OF THE OTHERS GOT AWAY ONCE, TOO -- BUT NOT FOR LONG.
WELL, THAT'S ALL IN THE PAST NOW, AS I'VE SAID BEFORE -- AND SPEAKING OF THE PAST...
12

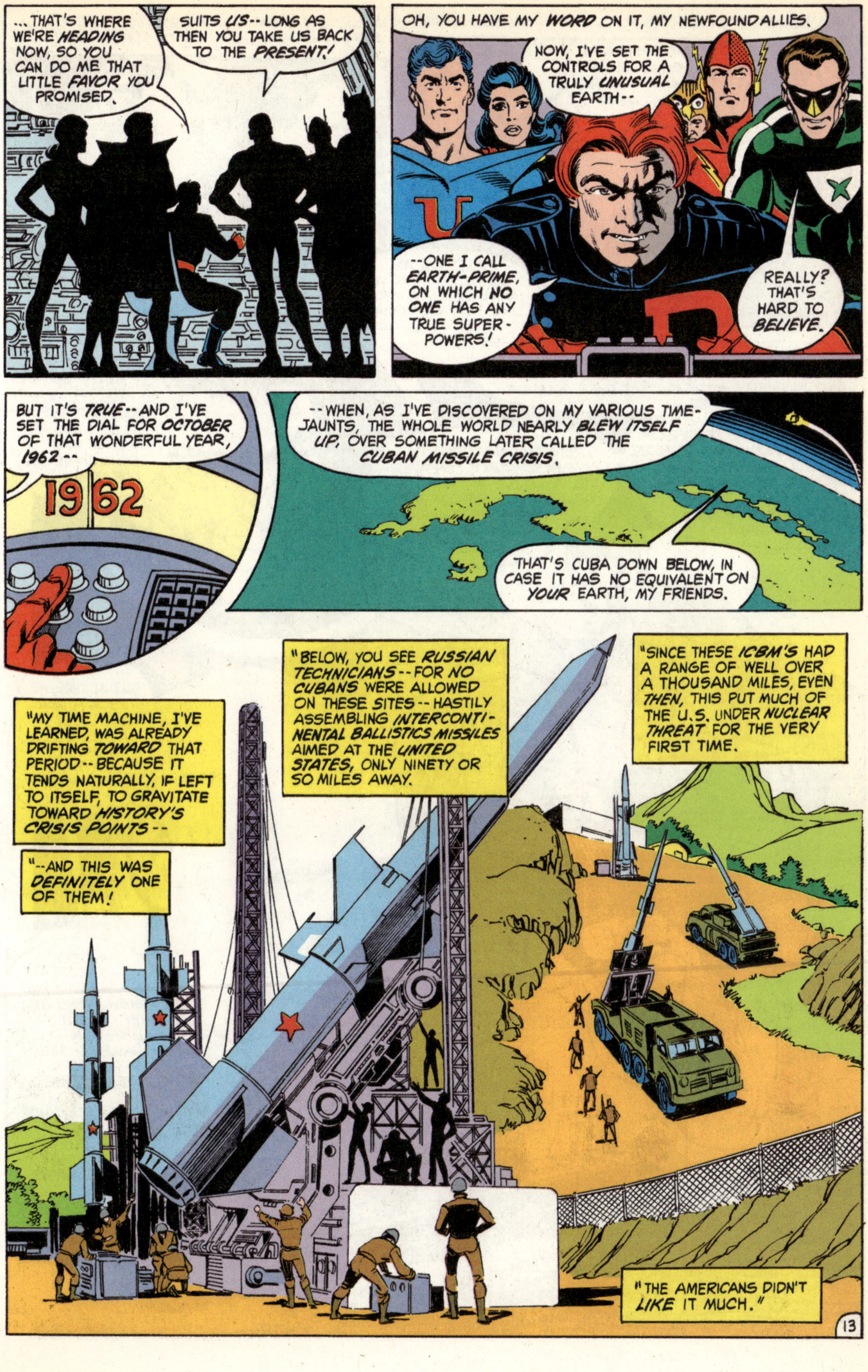
...THAT'S WHERE WE'RE HEADING NOW, SO YOU CAN DO ME THAT LITTLE FAVOR YOU PROMISED.
SUITS US-- LONG AS THEN YOU TAKE US BACK TO THE PRESENT!
OH, YOU HAVE MY WORD ON IT, MY NEWFOUND ALLIES.
NOW, I'VE SET THE CONTROLS FOR A TRULY UNUSUAL EARTH--
--ONE I CALL EARTH-PRIME, ON WHICH NO ONE HAS ANY TRUE SUPER-POWERS!
REALLY? THAT'S HARD TO BELIEVE.
BUT IT'S TRUE-- AND I'VE SET THE DIAL FOR OCTOBER OF THAT WONDERFUL YEAR, 1962--
1962
--WHEN, AS I'VE DISCOVERED ON MY VARIOUS TIME-JAUNTS, THE WHOLE WORLD NEARLY BLEW ITSELF UP, OVER SOMETHING LATER CALLED THE CUBAN MISSILE CRISIS.
THAT'S CUBA DOWN BELOW, IN CASE IT HAS NO EQUIVALENT ON YOUR EARTH, MY FRIENDS.
"MY TIME MACHINE, I'VE LEARNED, WAS ALREADY DRIFTING TOWARD THAT PERIOD-- BECAUSE IT TENDS NATURALLY, IF LEFT TO ITSELF, TO GRAVITATE TOWARD HISTORY'S CRISIS POINTS--
"--AND THIS WAS DEFINITELY ONE OF THEM!
"BELOW, YOU SEE RUSSIAN TECHNICIANS-- FOR NO CUBANS WERE ALLOWED ON THESE SITES-- HASTILY ASSEMBLING INTERCONTI-NENTAL BALLISTICS MISSILES AIMED AT THE UNITED STATES, ONLY NINETY OR SO MILES AWAY.
"SINCE THESE ICBM'S HAD A RANGE OF WELL OVER A THOUSAND MILES, EVEN THEN, THIS PUT MUCH OF THE U.S. UNDER NUCLEAR THREAT FOR THE VERY FIRST TIME.
"THE AMERICANS DIDN'T LIKE IT MUCH."
13

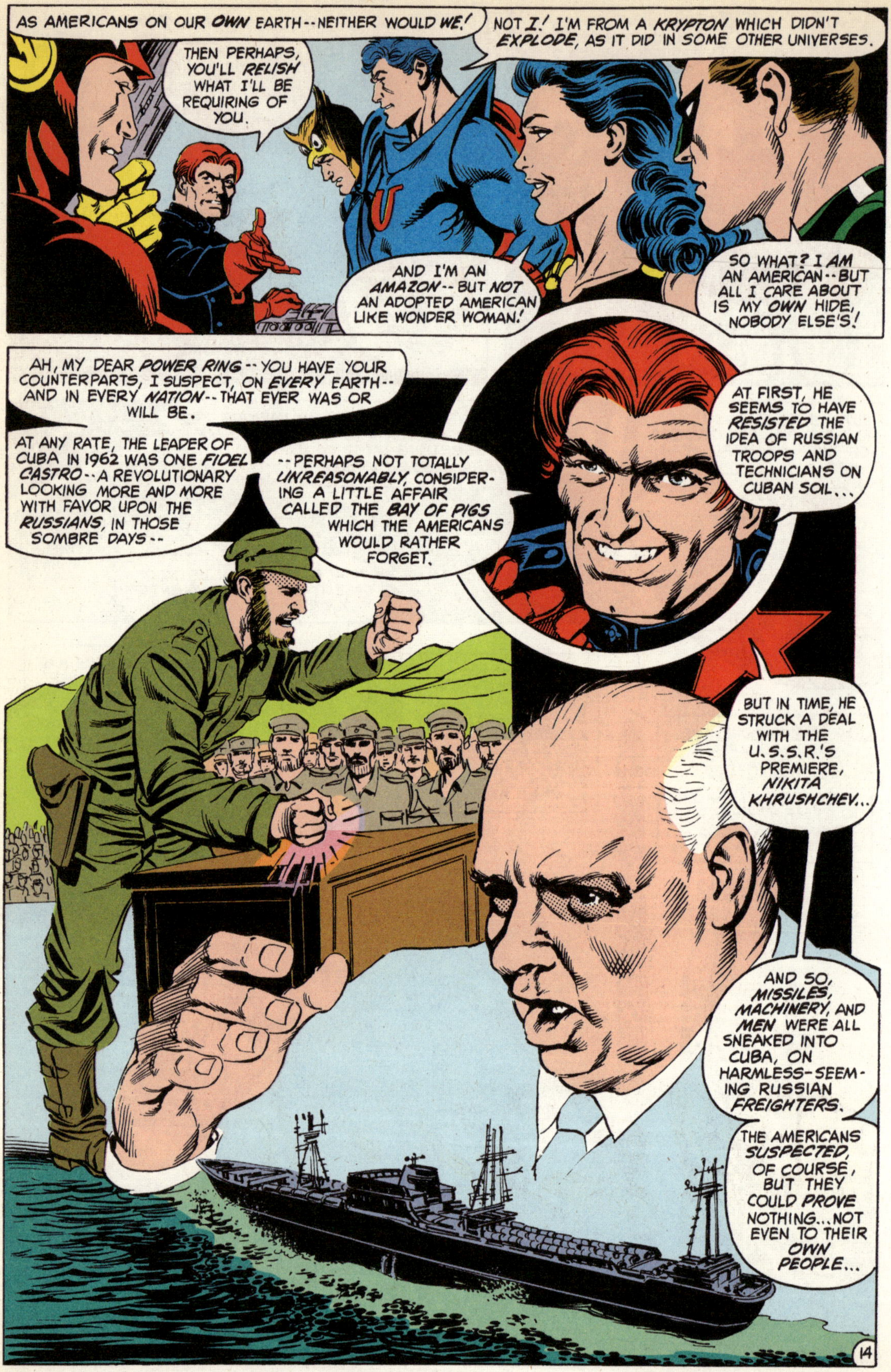
AS AMERICANS ON OUR OWN EARTH--NEITHER WOULD WE!
THEN PERHAPS, YOU'LL RELISH WHAT I'LL BE REQUIRING OF YOU.
NOT I! I'M FROM A KRYPTON WHICH DIDN'T EXPLODE, AS IT DID IN SOME OTHER UNIVERSES.
AND I'M AN AMAZON--BUT NOT AN ADOPTED AMERICAN LIKE WONDER WOMAN!
SO WHAT? I AM AN AMERICAN--BUT ALL I CARE ABOUT IS MY OWN HIDE, NOBODY ELSE'S!
AH, MY DEAR POWER RING--YOU HAVE YOUR COUNTERPARTS, I SUSPECT, ON EVERY EARTH--AND IN EVERY NATION--THAT EVER WAS OR WILL BE.
AT ANY RATE, THE LEADER OF CUBA IN 1962 WAS ONE FIDEL CASTRO--A REVOLUTIONARY LOOKING MORE AND MORE WITH FAVOR UPON THE RUSSIANS, IN THOSE SOMBRE DAYS--
--PERHAPS NOT TOTALLY UNREASONABLY, CONSIDERING A LITTLE AFFAIR CALLED THE BAY OF PIGS WHICH THE AMERICANS WOULD RATHER FORGET.
AT FIRST, HE SEEMS TO HAVE RESISTED THE IDEA OF RUSSIAN TROOPS AND TECHNICIANS ON CUBAN SOIL...
BUT IN TIME, HE STRUCK A DEAL WITH THE U.S.S.R.'S PREMIERE, NIKITA KHRUSHCHEV...
AND SO, MISSILES, MACHINERY, AND MEN WERE ALL SNEAKED INTO CUBA, ON HARMLESS-SEEMING RUSSIAN FREIGHTERS.
THE AMERICANS SUSPECTED, OF COURSE, BUT THEY COULD PROVE NOTHING...NOT EVEN TO THEIR OWN PEOPLE...
14

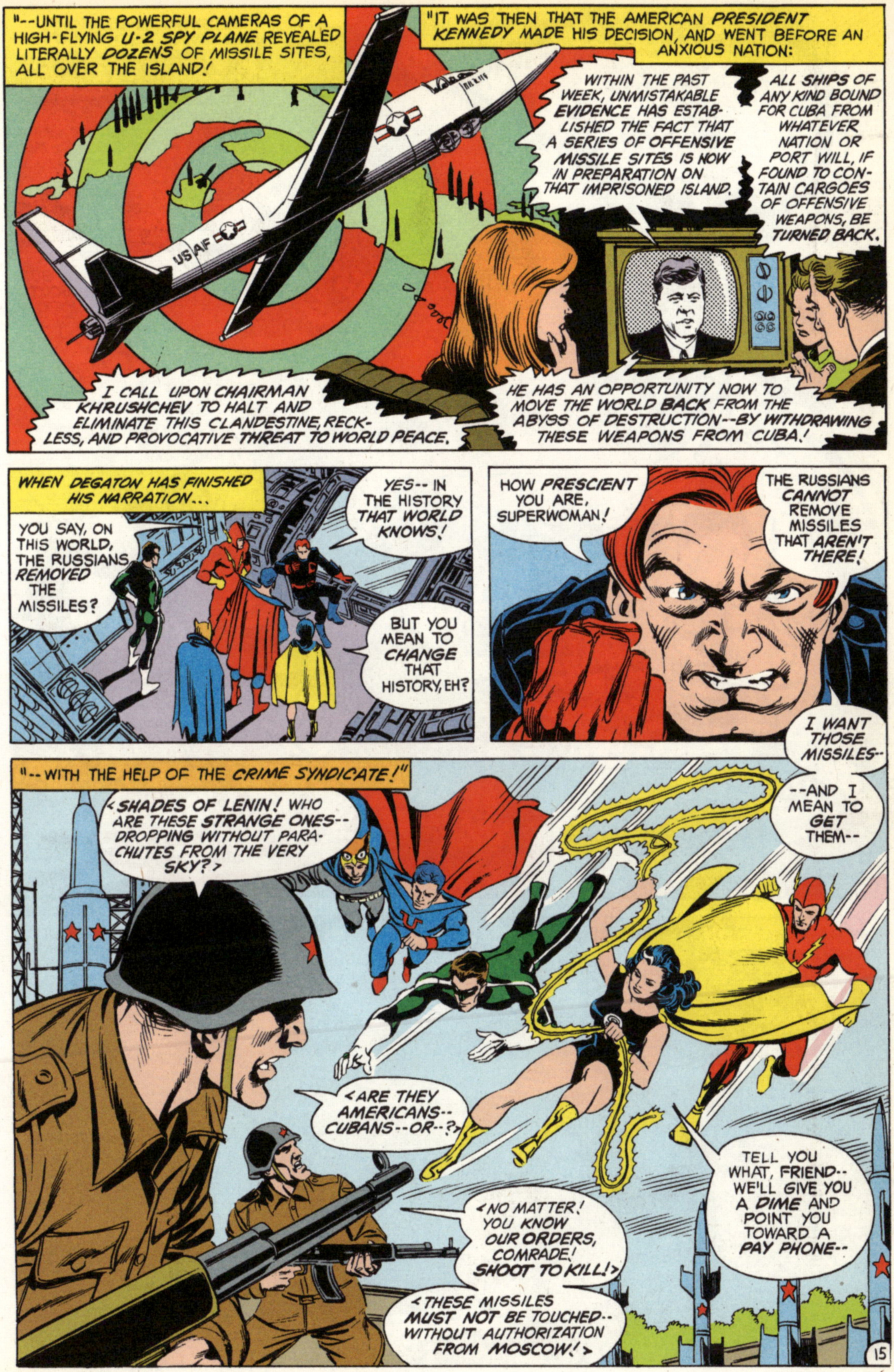
"--UNTIL THE POWERFUL CAMERAS OF A HIGH-FLYING U-2 SPY PLANE REVEALED LITERALLY DOZENS OF MISSILE SITES, ALL OVER THE ISLAND!
USAF
I CALL UPON CHAIRMAN KHRUSHCHEV TO HALT AND ELIMINATE THIS CLANDESTINE, RECKLESS, AND PROVOCATIVE THREAT TO WORLD PEACE.
"IT WAS THEN THAT THE AMERICAN PRESIDENT KENNEDY MADE HIS DECISION, AND WENT BEFORE AN ANXIOUS NATION:
WITHIN THE PAST WEEK, UNMISTAKABLE EVIDENCE HAS ESTABLISHED THE FACT THAT A SERIES OF OFFENSIVE MISSILE SITES IS NOW IN PREPARATION ON THAT IMPRISONED ISLAND.
ALL SHIPS OF ANY KIND BOUND FOR CUBA FROM WHATEVER NATION OR PORT WILL, IF FOUND TO CONTAIN CARGOES OF OFFENSIVE WEAPONS, BE TURNED BACK.
HE HAS AN OPPORTUNITY NOW TO MOVE THE WORLD BACK FROM THE ABYSS OF DESTRUCTION--BY WITHDRAWING THESE WEAPONS FROM CUBA!
WHEN DEGATON HAS FINISHED HIS NARRATION...
YOU SAY, ON THIS WORLD, THE RUSSIANS REMOVED THE MISSILES?
YES-- IN THE HISTORY THAT WORLD KNOWS!
BUT YOU MEAN TO CHANGE THAT HISTORY, EH?
HOW PRESCIENT YOU ARE, SUPERWOMAN!
THE RUSSIANS CANNOT REMOVE MISSILES THAT AREN'T THERE!
"--WITH THE HELP OF THE CRIME SYNDICATE!"
<SHADES OF LENIN! WHO ARE THESE STRANGE ONES-- DROPPING WITHOUT PARACHUTES FROM THE VERY SKY?>
I WANT THOSE MISSILES--
--AND I MEAN TO GET THEM--
<ARE THEY AMERICANS-- CUBANS--OR--?>
TELL YOU WHAT, FRIEND-- WE'LL GIVE YOU A DIME AND POINT YOU TOWARD A PAY PHONE--
<NO MATTER! YOU KNOW OUR ORDERS, COMRADE! SHOOT TO KILL!>
<THESE MISSILES MUST NOT BE TOUCHED-- WITHOUT AUTHORIZATION FROM MOSCOW!>
15

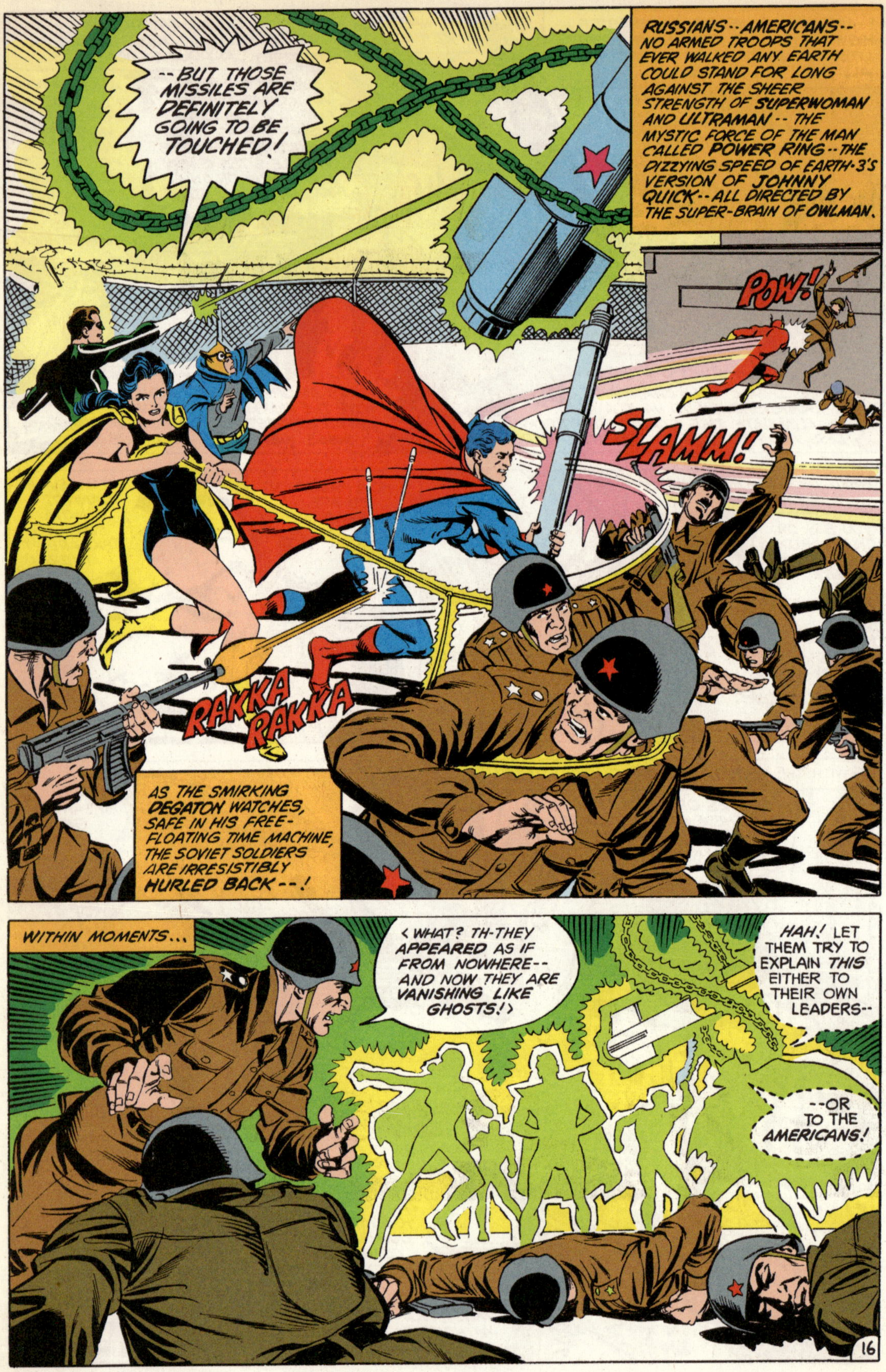
--BUT THOSE MISSILES ARE DEFINITELY GOING TO BE TOUCHED!
RUSSIANS--AMERICANS--NO ARMED TROOPS THAT EVER WALKED ANY EARTH COULD STAND FOR LONG AGAINST THE SHEER STRENGTH OF SUPERWOMAN AND ULTRAMAN--THE MYSTIC FORCE OF THE MAN CALLED POWER RING--THE DIZZYING SPEED OF EARTH-3'S VERSION OF JOHNNY QUICK--ALL DIRECTED BY THE SUPER-BRAIN OF OWLMAN.
POW!
SLAMM!
RAKKA RAKKA
AS THE SMIRKING DEGATON WATCHES, SAFE IN HIS FREE-FLOATING TIME MACHINE, THE SOVIET SOLDIERS ARE IRRESISTIBLY HURLED BACK--!
WITHIN MOMENTS...
<WHAT? TH-THEY APPEARED AS IF FROM NOWHERE--AND NOW THEY ARE VANISHING LIKE GHOSTS!>
HAH! LET THEM TRY TO EXPLAIN THIS EITHER TO THEIR OWN LEADERS--
--OR TO THE AMERICANS!
16

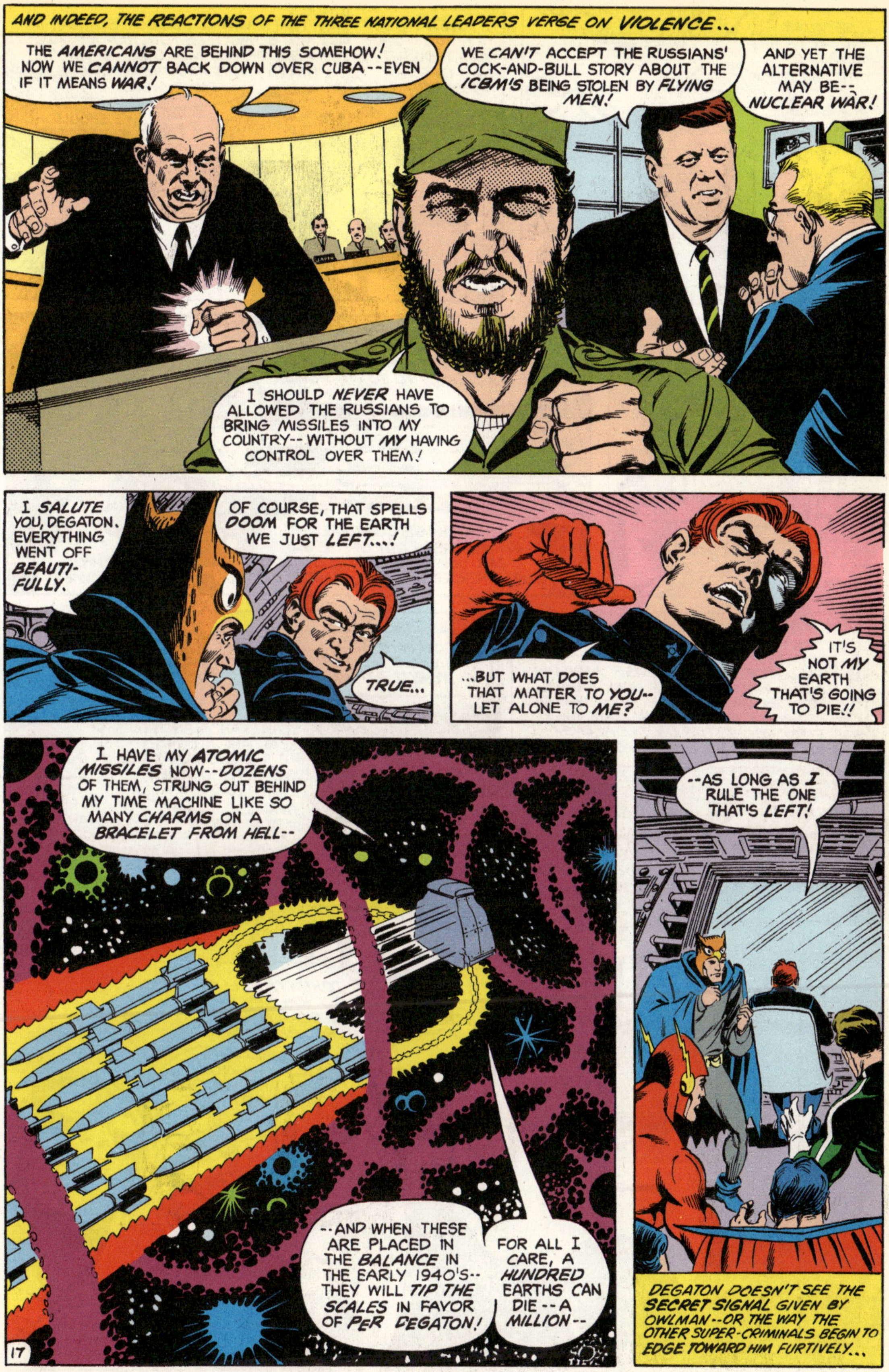
AND INDEED, THE REACTIONS OF THE THREE NATIONAL LEADERS VERGE ON VIOLENCE...
THE AMERICANS ARE BEHIND THIS SOMEHOW! NOW WE CANNOT BACK DOWN OVER CUBA--EVEN IF IT MEANS WAR!
WE CAN'T ACCEPT THE RUSSIANS' COCK-AND-BULL STORY ABOUT THE ICBM'S BEING STOLEN BY FLYING MEN!
AND YET THE ALTERNATIVE MAY BE--NUCLEAR WAR!
I SHOULD NEVER HAVE ALLOWED THE RUSSIANS TO BRING MISSILES INTO MY COUNTRY--WITHOUT MY HAVING CONTROL OVER THEM!
I SALUTE YOU, DEGATON. EVERYTHING WENT OFF BEAUTI-FULLY.
OF COURSE, THAT SPELLS DOOM FOR THE EARTH WE JUST LEFT...!
TRUE...
...BUT WHAT DOES THAT MATTER TO YOU--LET ALONE TO ME?
IT'S NOT MY EARTH THAT'S GOING TO DIE!!
I HAVE MY ATOMIC MISSILES NOW--DOZENS OF THEM, STRUNG OUT BEHIND MY TIME MACHINE LIKE SO MANY CHARMS ON A BRACELET FROM HELL--
--AND WHEN THESE ARE PLACED IN THE BALANCE IN THE EARLY 1940'S--THEY WILL TIP THE SCALES IN FAVOR OF PER DEGATON!
FOR ALL I CARE, A HUNDRED EARTHS CAN DIE--A MILLION--
17
--AS LONG AS I RULE THE ONE THAT'S LEFT!
DEGATON DOESN'T SEE THE SECRET SIGNAL GIVEN BY OWLMAN--OR THE WAY THE OTHER SUPER-CRIMINALS BEGIN TO EDGE TOWARD HIM FURTIVELY...

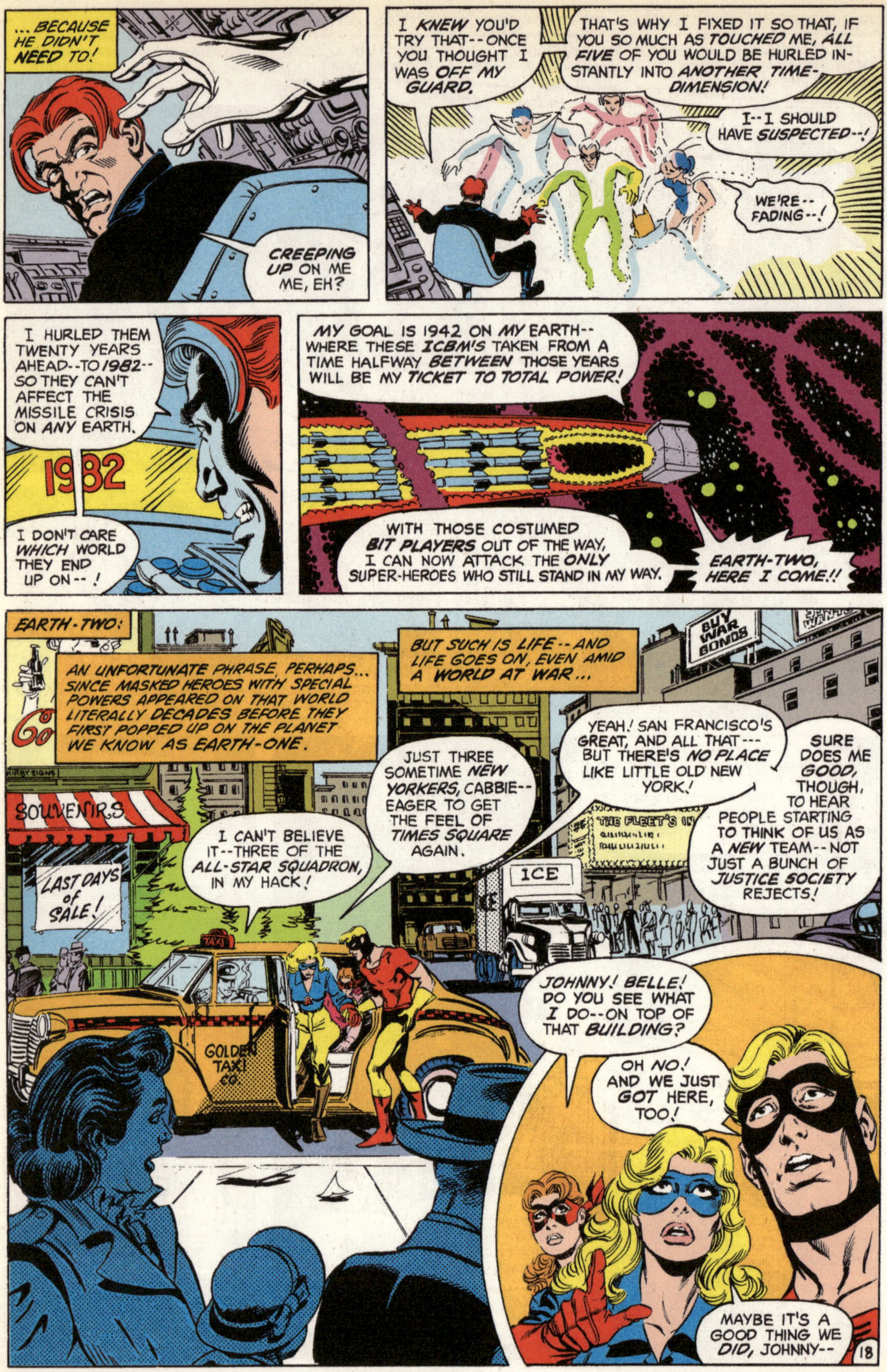
...BECAUSE HE DIDN'T NEED TO!
CREEPING UP ON ME ME, EH?
I KNEW YOU'D TRY THAT--ONCE YOU THOUGHT I WAS OFF MY GUARD.
THAT'S WHY I FIXED IT SO THAT, IF YOU SO MUCH AS TOUCHED ME, ALL FIVE OF YOU WOULD BE HURLED INSTANTLY INTO ANOTHER TIME-DIMENSION!
I--I SHOULD HAVE SUSPECTED--!
WE'RE--FADING--!
I HURLED THEM TWENTY YEARS AHEAD--TO 1982--SO THEY CAN'T AFFECT THE MISSILE CRISIS ON ANY EARTH.
1982
I DON'T CARE WHICH WORLD THEY END UP ON--!
MY GOAL IS 1942 ON MY EARTH--WHERE THESE ICBM'S TAKEN FROM A TIME HALFWAY BETWEEN THOSE YEARS WILL BE MY TICKET TO TOTAL POWER!
WITH THOSE COSTUMED BIT PLAYERS OUT OF THE WAY, I CAN NOW ATTACK THE ONLY SUPER-HEROES WHO STILL STAND IN MY WAY.
EARTH-TWO, HERE I COME!!
EARTH-TWO:
AN UNFORTUNATE PHRASE, PERHAPS... SINCE MASKED HEROES WITH SPECIAL POWERS APPEARED ON THAT WORLD LITERALLY DECADES BEFORE THEY FIRST POPPED UP ON THE PLANET WE KNOW AS EARTH-ONE.
BUT SUCH IS LIFE--AND LIFE GOES ON, EVEN AMID A WORLD AT WAR...
BUY WAR BONDS
SOUVENIRS
LAST DAYS of SALE!
I CAN'T BELIEVE IT--THREE OF THE ALL-STAR SQUADRON, IN MY HACK!
JUST THREE SOMETIME NEW YORKERS, CABBIE--EAGER TO GET THE FEEL OF TIMES SQUARE AGAIN.
YEAH! SAN FRANCISCO'S GREAT, AND ALL THAT---BUT THERE'S NO PLACE LIKE LITTLE OLD NEW YORK!
SURE DOES ME GOOD, THOUGH, TO HEAR PEOPLE STARTING TO THINK OF US AS A NEW TEAM--NOT JUST A BUNCH OF JUSTICE SOCIETY REJECTS!
THE FLEET'S IN
ICE
TAXI
GOLDEN TAXI CO.
JOHNNY! BELLE! DO YOU SEE WHAT I DO--ON TOP OF THAT BUILDING?
OH NO! AND WE JUST GOT HERE, TOO!
MAYBE IT'S A GOOD THING WE DID, JOHNNY--
18

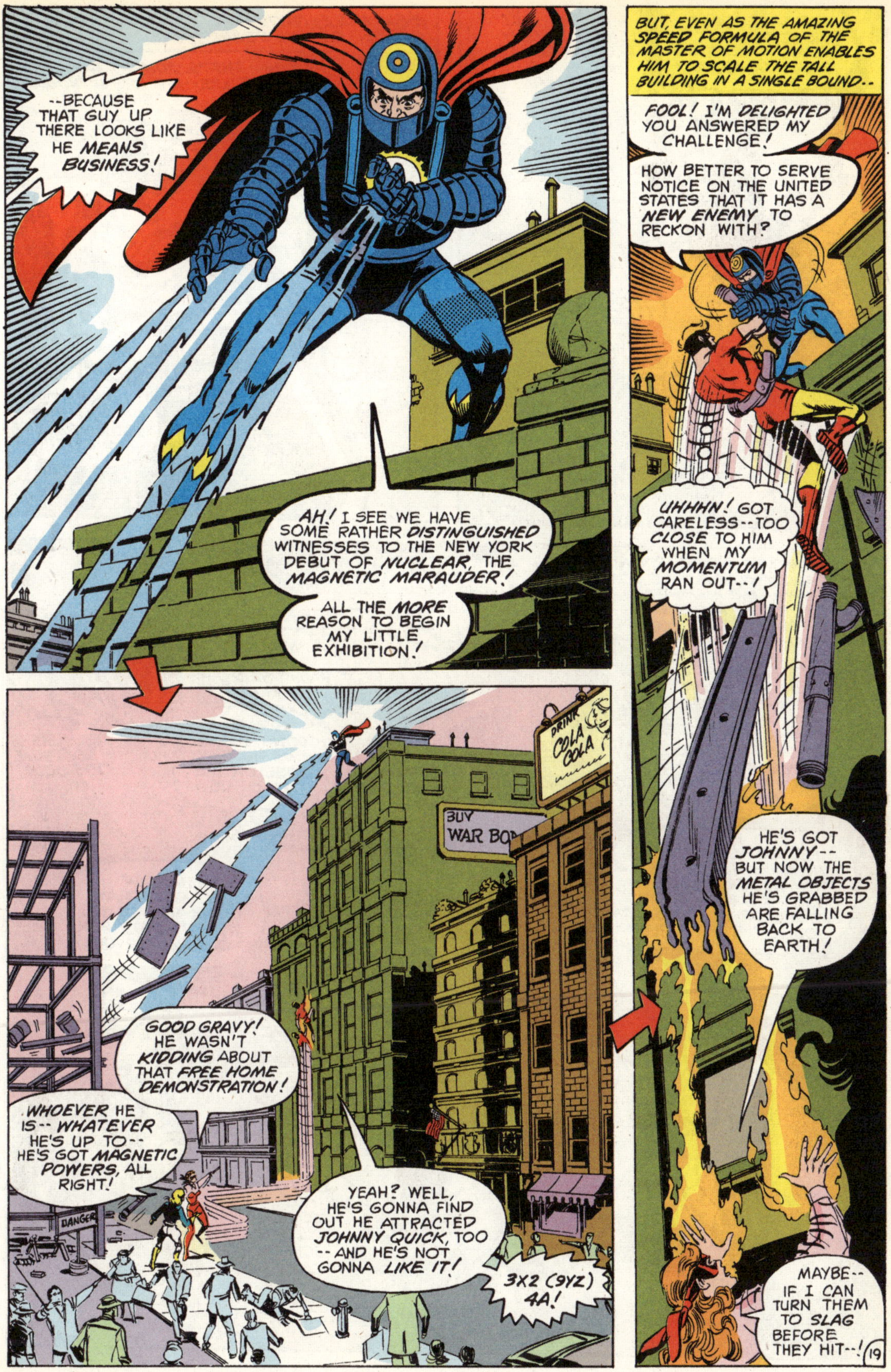
--BECAUSE THAT GUY UP THERE LOOKS LIKE HE MEANS BUSINESS!
AH! I SEE WE HAVE SOME RATHER DISTINGUISHED WITNESSES TO THE NEW YORK DEBUT OF NUCLEAR, THE MAGNETIC MARAUDER!
ALL THE MORE REASON TO BEGIN MY LITTLE EXHIBITION!
DRINK COLA COLA
BUY WAR BO
GOOD GRAVY! HE WASN'T KIDDING ABOUT THAT FREE HOME DEMONSTRATION!
WHOEVER HE IS-- WHATEVER HE'S UP TO-- HE'S GOT MAGNETIC POWERS, ALL RIGHT!
DANGER
YEAH? WELL, HE'S GONNA FIND OUT HE ATTRACTED JOHNNY QUICK, TOO --AND HE'S NOT GONNA LIKE IT!
3X2 (9YZ) 4A!
BUT, EVEN AS THE AMAZING SPEED FORMULA OF THE MASTER OF MOTION ENABLES HIM TO SCALE THE TALL BUILDING IN A SINGLE BOUND..
FOOL! I'M DELIGHTED YOU ANSWERED MY CHALLENGE!
HOW BETTER TO SERVE NOTICE ON THE UNITED STATES THAT IT HAS A NEW ENEMY TO RECKON WITH?
UHHHN! GOT CARELESS--TOO CLOSE TO HIM WHEN MY MOMENTUM RAN OUT--!
HE'S GOT JOHNNY-- BUT NOW THE METAL OBJECTS HE'S GRABBED ARE FALLING BACK TO EARTH!
MAYBE-- IF I CAN TURN THEM TO SLAG BEFORE THEY HIT--!
19

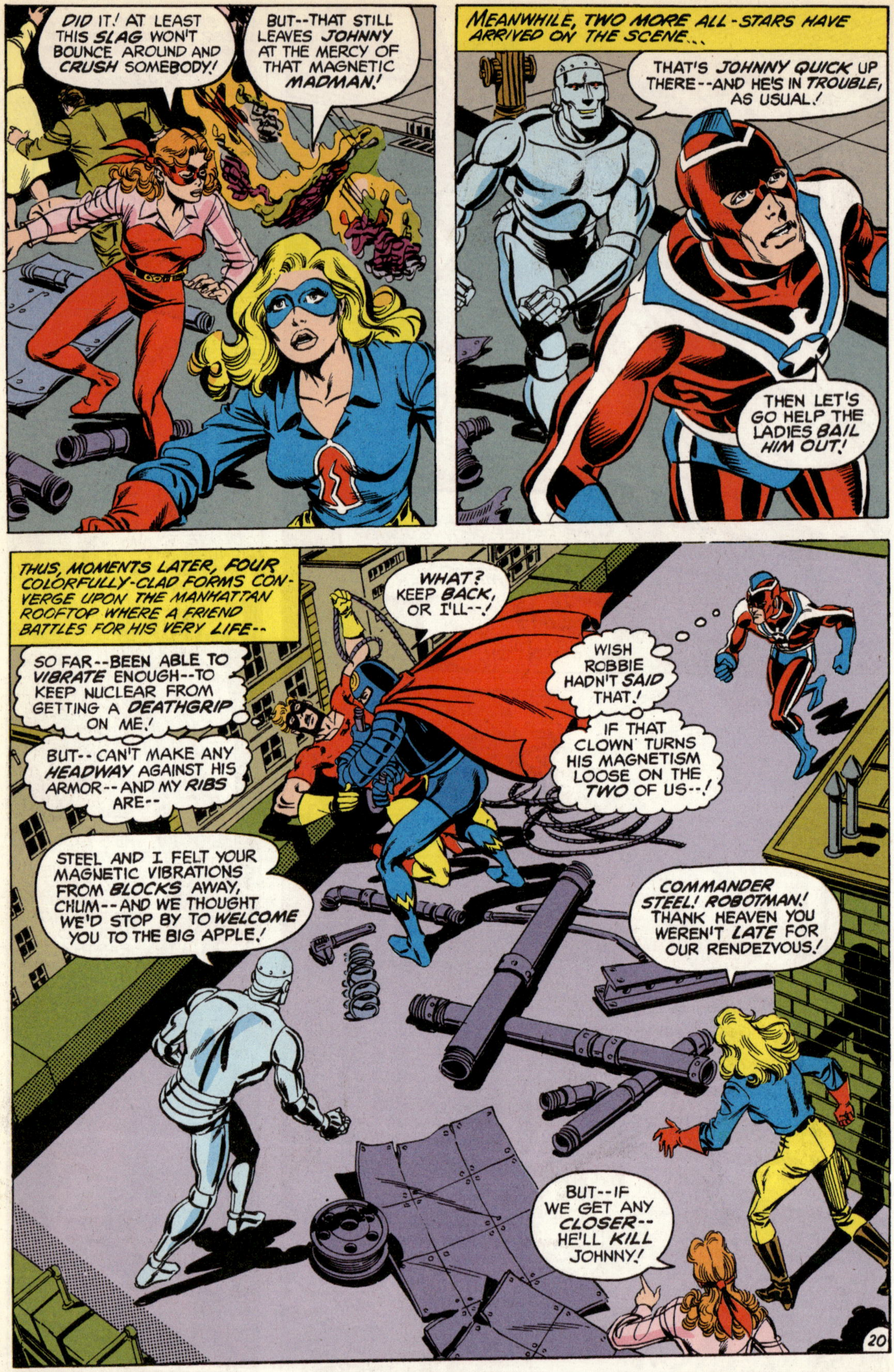

DID IT! AT LEAST THIS SLAG WON'T BOUNCE AROUND AND CRUSH SOMEBODY!
BUT--THAT STILL LEAVES JOHNNY AT THE MERCY OF THAT MAGNETIC MADMAN!
MEANWHILE, TWO MORE ALL-STARS HAVE ARRIVED ON THE SCENE...
THAT'S JOHNNY QUICK UP THERE--AND HE'S IN TROUBLE, AS USUAL!
THEN LET'S GO HELP THE LADIES BAIL HIM OUT!
THUS, MOMENTS LATER, FOUR COLORFULLY-CLAD FORMS CON-VERGE UPON THE MANHATTAN ROOFTOP WHERE A FRIEND BATTLES FOR HIS VERY LIFE--
SO FAR--BEEN ABLE TO VIBRATE ENOUGH--TO KEEP NUCLEAR FROM GETTING A DEATHGRIP ON ME.!
BUT--CAN'T MAKE ANY HEADWAY AGAINST HIS ARMOR--AND MY RIBS ARE--
WHAT? KEEP BACK, OR I'LL--!
WISH ROBBIE HADN'T SAID THAT!
IF THAT CLOWN TURNS HIS MAGNETISM LOOSE ON THE TWO OF US--!
STEEL AND I FELT YOUR MAGNETIC VIBRATIONS FROM BLOCKS AWAY, CHUM--AND WE THOUGHT WE'D STOP BY TO WELCOME YOU TO THE BIG APPLE!
COMMANDER STEEL! ROBOTMAN! THANK HEAVEN YOU WEREN'T LATE FOR OUR RENDEZVOUS!
BUT--IF WE GET ANY CLOSER--HE'LL KILL JOHNNY!
20

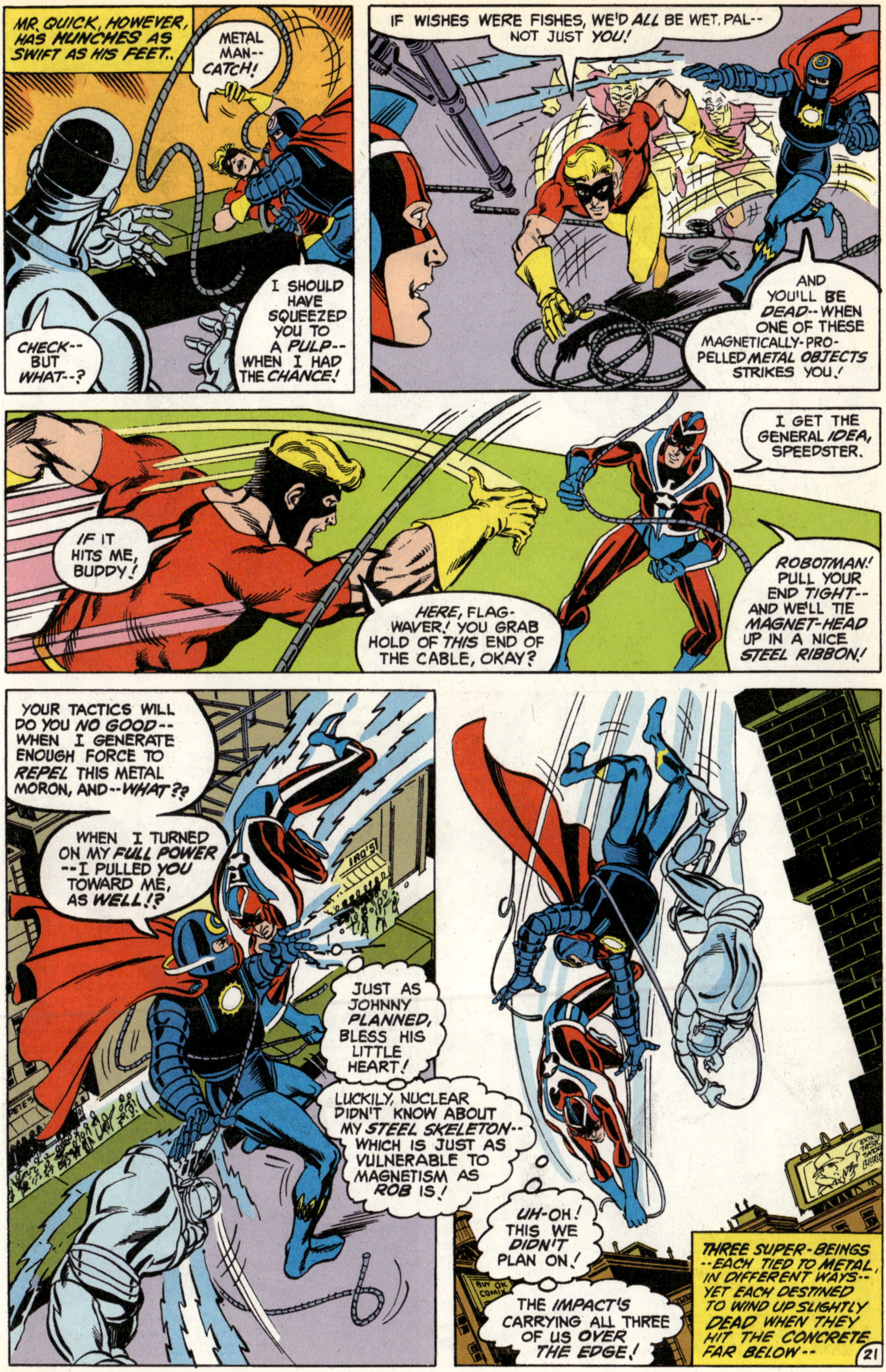

MR. QUICK, HOWEVER, HAS HUNCHES AS SWIFT AS HIS FEET..
METAL MAN-- CATCH!
I SHOULD HAVE SQUEEZED YOU TO A PULP-- WHEN I HAD THE CHANCE!
CHECK-- BUT WHAT--?
IF WISHES WERE FISHES, WE'D ALL BE WET, PAL-- NOT JUST YOU!
AND YOU'LL BE DEAD-- WHEN ONE OF THESE MAGNETICALLY-PROPELLED METAL OBJECTS STRIKES YOU!
IF IT HITS ME, BUDDY!
HERE, FLAG-WAVER! YOU GRAB HOLD OF THIS END OF THE CABLE, OKAY?
I GET THE GENERAL IDEA, SPEEDSTER.
ROBOTMAN! PULL YOUR END TIGHT-- AND WE'LL TIE MAGNET-HEAD UP IN A NICE STEEL RIBBON!
YOUR TACTICS WILL DO YOU NO GOOD-- WHEN I GENERATE ENOUGH FORCE TO REPEL THIS METAL MORON, AND--WHAT??
WHEN I TURNED ON MY FULL POWER --I PULLED YOU TOWARD ME, AS WELL!?
JUST AS JOHNNY PLANNED, BLESS HIS LITTLE HEART!
LUCKILY, NUCLEAR DIDN'T KNOW ABOUT MY STEEL SKELETON-- WHICH IS JUST AS VULNERABLE TO MAGNETISM AS ROB IS!
UH-OH! THIS WE DIDN'T PLAN ON!
THE IMPACT'S CARRYING ALL THREE OF US OVER THE EDGE!
THREE SUPER-BEINGS --EACH TIED TO METAL, IN DIFFERENT WAYS-- YET EACH DESTINED TO WIND UP SLIGHTLY DEAD WHEN THEY HIT THE CONCRETE FAR BELOW--
21

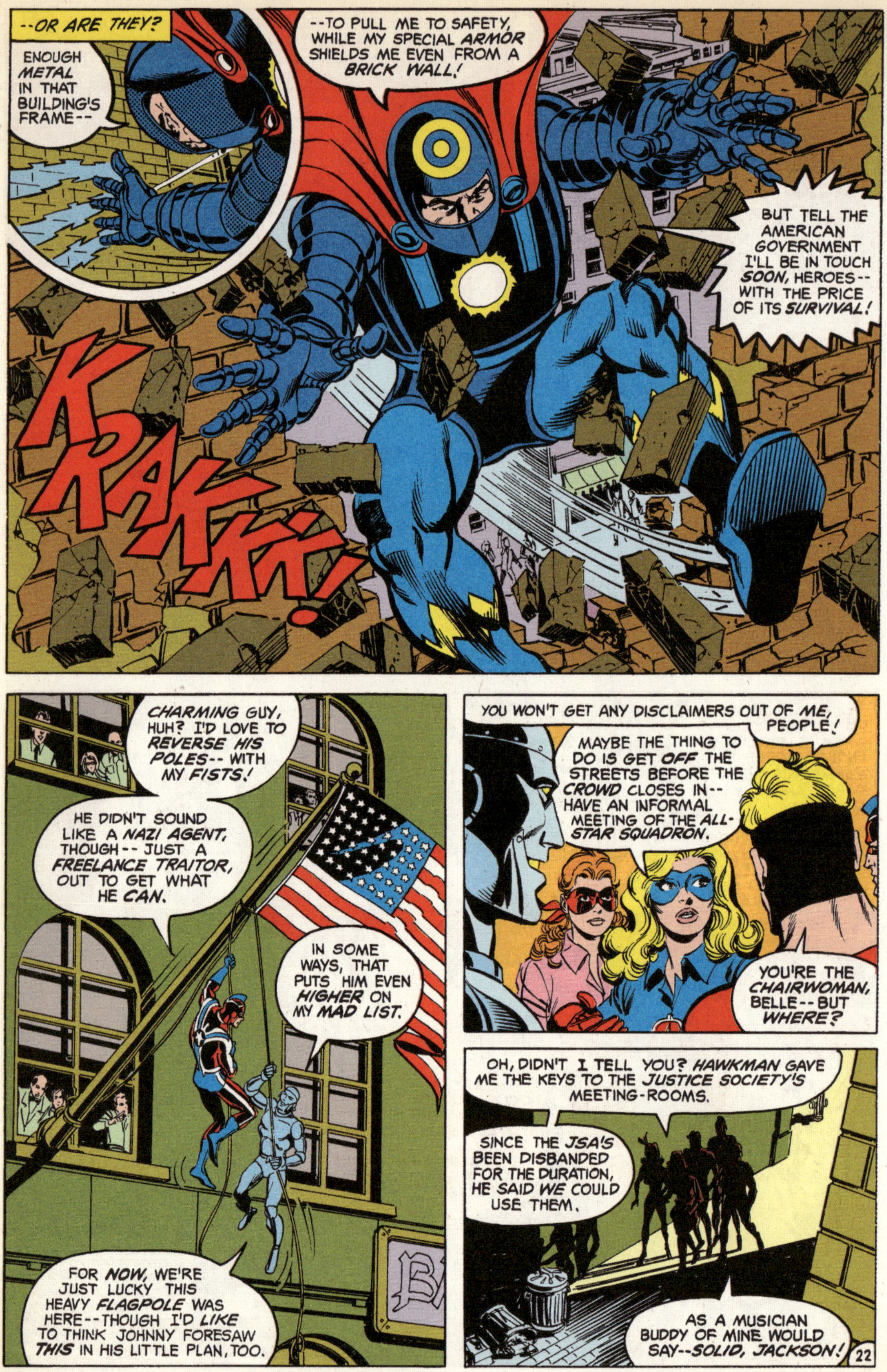
--OR ARE THEY?
ENOUGH METAL IN THAT BUILDING'S FRAME--
--TO PULL ME TO SAFETY, WHILE MY SPECIAL ARMOR SHIELDS ME EVEN FROM A BRICK WALL!
BUT TELL THE AMERICAN GOVERNMENT I'LL BE IN TOUCH SOON, HEROES--WITH THE PRICE OF ITS SURVIVAL!
KRAKKK!
CHARMING GUY, HUH? I'D LOVE TO REVERSE HIS POLES-- WITH MY FISTS!
HE DIDN'T SOUND LIKE A NAZI AGENT, THOUGH-- JUST A FREELANCE TRAITOR, OUT TO GET WHAT HE CAN.
IN SOME WAYS, THAT PUTS HIM EVEN HIGHER ON MY MAD LIST.
FOR NOW, WE'RE JUST LUCKY THIS HEAVY FLAGPOLE WAS HERE--THOUGH I'D LIKE TO THINK JOHNNY FORESAW THIS IN HIS LITTLE PLAN, TOO.
YOU WON'T GET ANY DISCLAIMERS OUT OF ME, PEOPLE!
MAYBE THE THING TO DO IS GET OFF THE STREETS BEFORE THE CROWD CLOSES IN--HAVE AN INFORMAL MEETING OF THE ALL-STAR SQUADRON.
YOU'RE THE CHAIRWOMAN, BELLE--BUT WHERE?
OH, DIDN'T I TELL YOU? HAWKMAN GAVE ME THE KEYS TO THE JUSTICE SOCIETY'S MEETING-ROOMS.
SINCE THE JSA'S BEEN DISBANDED FOR THE DURATION, HE SAID WE COULD USE THEM.
AS A MUSICIAN BUDDY OF MINE WOULD SAY--SOLID, JACKSON!
22

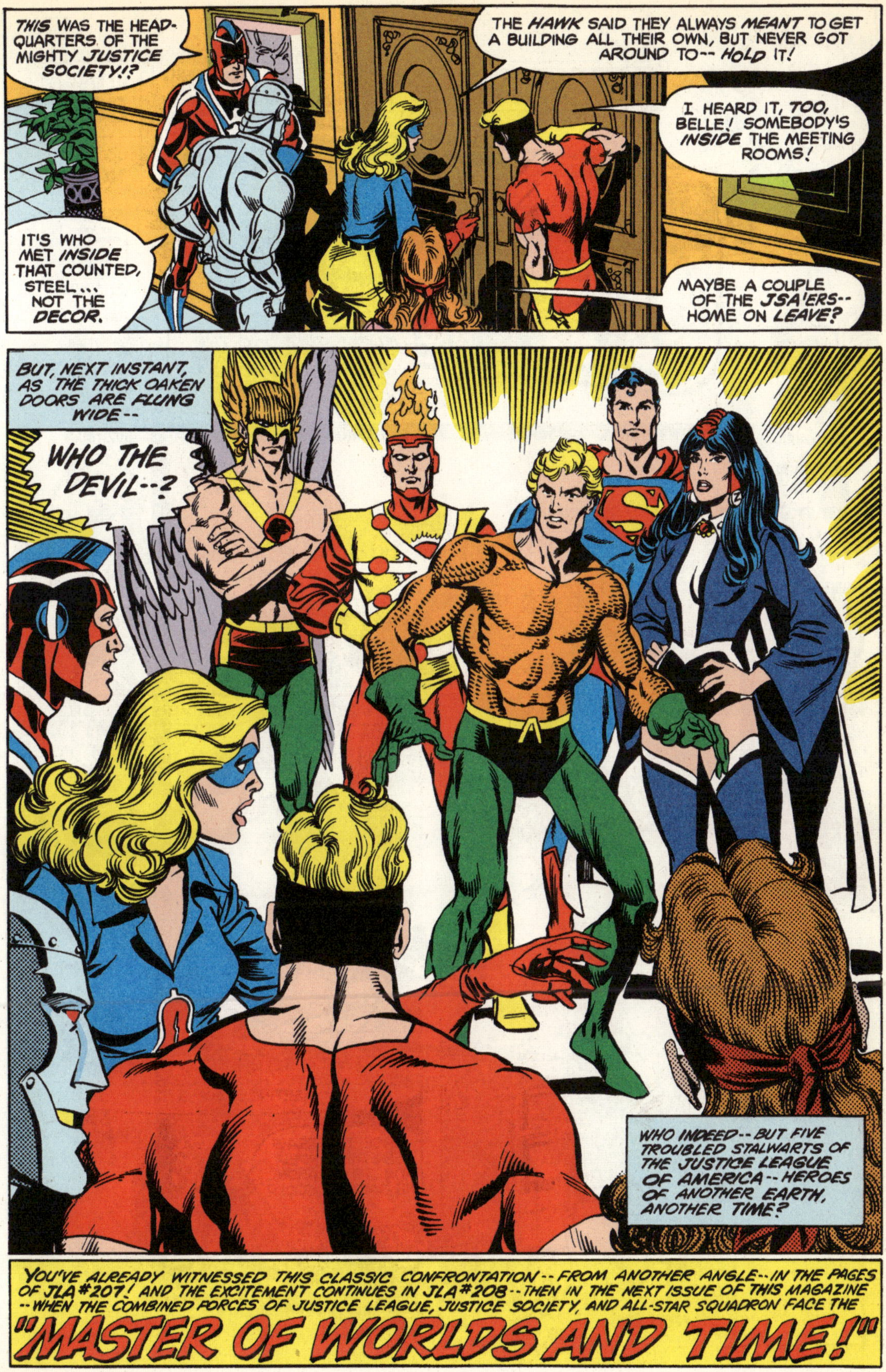
THIS WAS THE HEAD-QUARTERS OF THE MIGHTY JUSTICE SOCIETY!?
THE HAWK SAID THEY ALWAYS MEANT TO GET A BUILDING ALL THEIR OWN, BUT NEVER GOT AROUND TO-- HOLD IT!
I HEARD IT, TOO, BELLE! SOMEBODY'S INSIDE THE MEETING ROOMS!
IT'S WHO MET INSIDE THAT COUNTED, STEEL... NOT THE DECOR.
MAYBE A COUPLE OF THE JSA'ERS-- HOME ON LEAVE?
BUT, NEXT INSTANT, AS THE THICK OAKEN DOORS ARE FLUNG WIDE--
WHO THE DEVIL--?
WHO INDEED-- BUT FIVE TROUBLED STALWARTS OF THE JUSTICE LEAGUE OF AMERICA-- HEROES OF ANOTHER EARTH, ANOTHER TIME?
YOU'VE ALREADY WITNESSED THIS CLASSIC CONFRONTATION-- FROM ANOTHER ANGLE-- IN THE PAGES OF JLA #207! AND THE EXCITEMENT CONTINUES IN JLA #208-- THEN IN THE NEXT ISSUE OF THIS MAGAZINE -- WHEN THE COMBINED FORCES OF JUSTICE LEAGUE, JUSTICE SOCIETY, AND ALL-STAR SQUADRON FACE THE
"MASTER OF WORLDS AND TIME!"

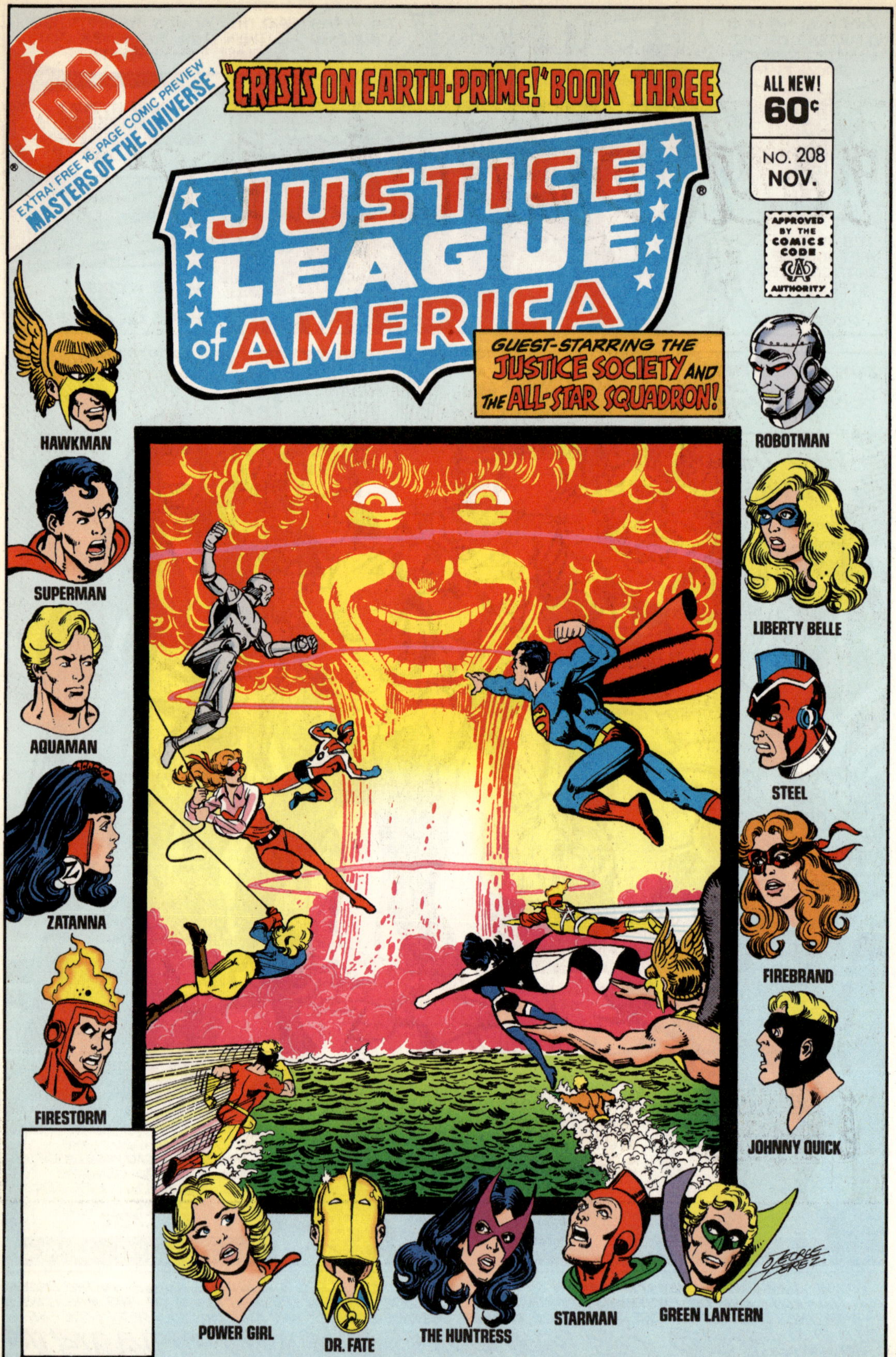
"CRISIS ON EARTH-PRIME!" BOOK THREE
ALL NEW! 60¢
NO. 208 NOV.
APPROVED BY THE COMICS CODE AUTHORITY
EXTRA! FREE 16-PAGE COMIC PREVIEW MASTERS OF THE UNIVERSE
JUSTICE LEAGUE of AMERICA
GUEST-STARRING THE JUSTICE SOCIETY AND THE ALL-STAR SQUADRON!
HAWKMAN
SUPERMAN
AQUAMAN
ZATANNA
FIRESTORM
ROBOTMAN
LIBERTY BELLE
STEEL
FIREBRAND
JOHNNY QUICK
POWER GIRL
DR. FATE
THE HUNTRESS
STARMAN
GREEN LANTERN
GEORGE PÉREZ

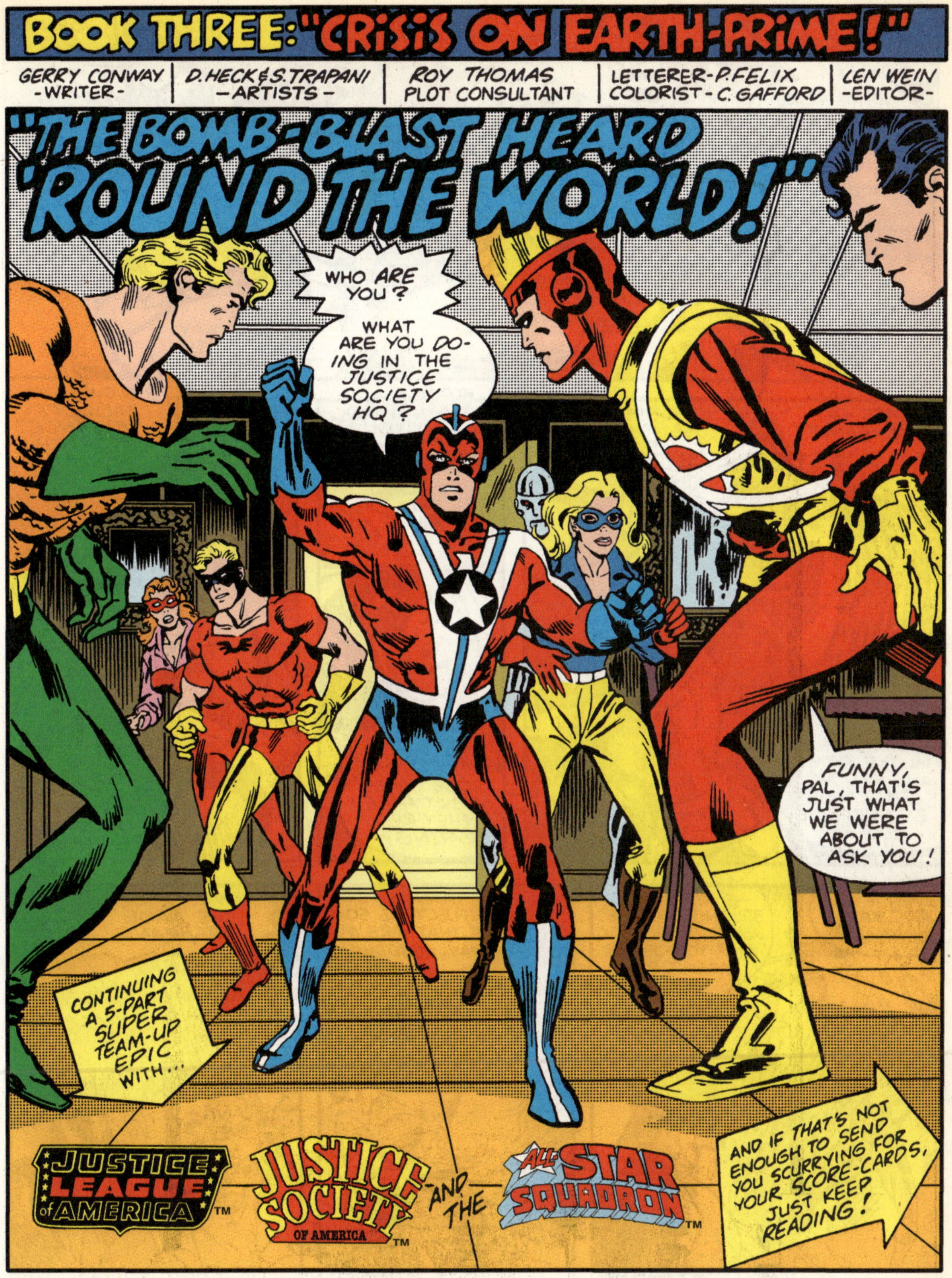
BOOK THREE: "CRISIS ON EARTH-PRIME!"
GERRY CONWAY -WRITER-
D. HECK & S. TRAPANI -ARTISTS-
ROY THOMAS PLOT CONSULTANT
LETTERER-P. FELIX COLORIST-C. GAFFORD
LEN WEIN -EDITOR-
"THE BOMB-BLAST HEARD 'ROUND THE WORLD!"
WHO ARE YOU? WHAT ARE YOU DOING IN THE JUSTICE SOCIETY HQ?
FUNNY, PAL, THAT'S JUST WHAT WE WERE ABOUT TO ASK YOU!
CONTINUING A 5-PART SUPER TEAM-UP EPIC WITH...
JUSTICE LEAGUE of AMERICA
JUSTICE SOCIETY OF AMERICA
AND THE
ALL-STAR SQUADRON
AND IF THAT'S NOT ENOUGH TO SEND YOU SCURRYING FOR YOUR SCORE-CARDS, JUST KEEP READING!

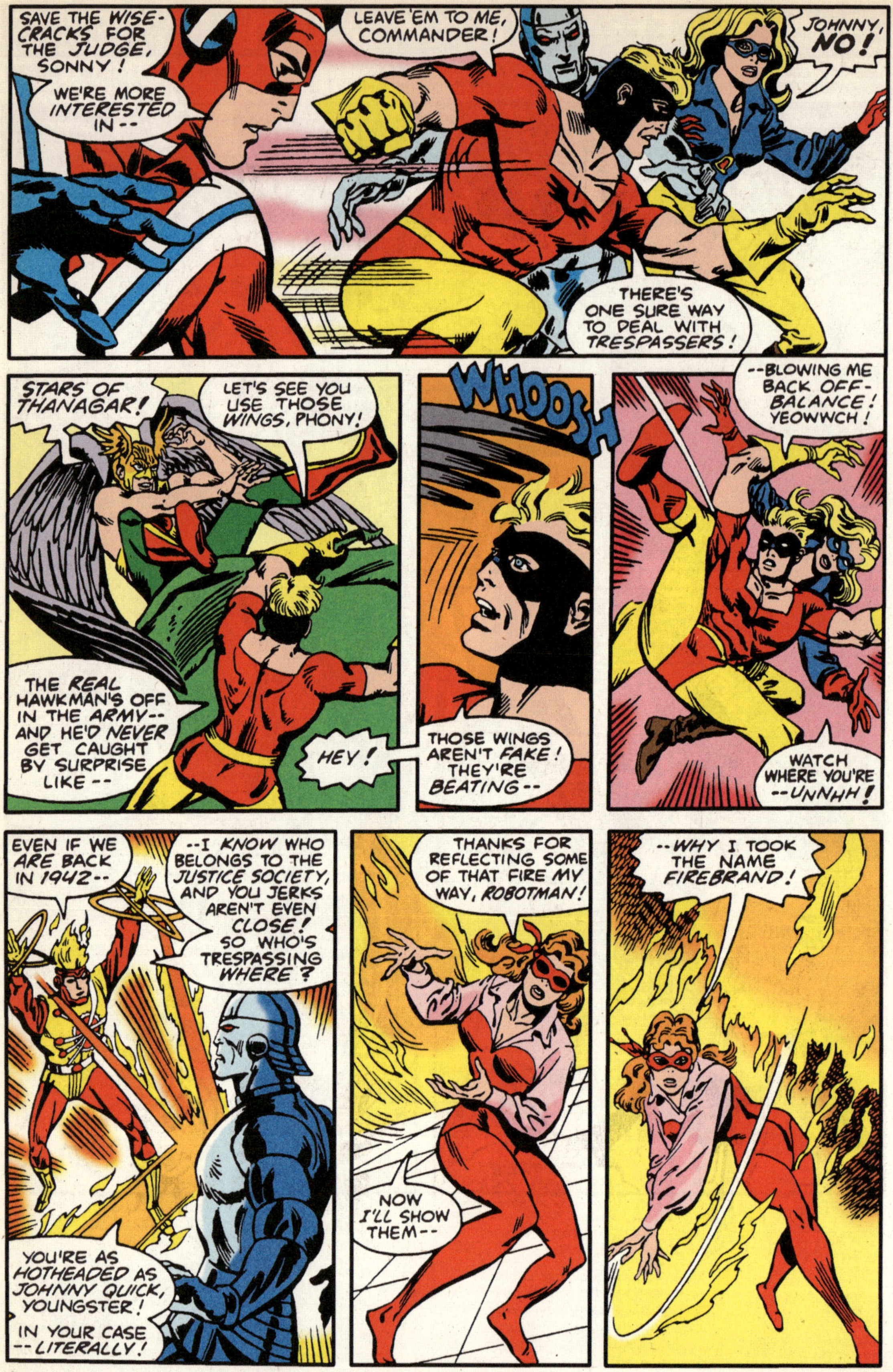
SAVE THE WISE-CRACKS FOR THE JUDGE, SONNY!
WE'RE MORE INTERESTED IN--
LEAVE 'EM TO ME, COMMANDER!
JOHNNY, NO!
THERE'S ONE SURE WAY TO DEAL WITH TRESPASSERS!
STARS OF THANAGAR!
LET'S SEE YOU USE THOSE WINGS, PHONY!
THE REAL HAWKMAN'S OFF IN THE ARMY-- AND HE'D NEVER GET CAUGHT BY SURPRISE LIKE--
HEY!
WHOOSH
THOSE WINGS AREN'T FAKE! THEY'RE BEATING--
--BLOWING ME BACK OFF-BALANCE! YEOWWCH!
WATCH WHERE YOU'RE --UNNHH!
EVEN IF WE ARE BACK IN 1942--
--I KNOW WHO BELONGS TO THE JUSTICE SOCIETY, AND YOU JERKS AREN'T EVEN CLOSE! SO WHO'S TRESPASSING WHERE?
YOU'RE AS HOTHEADED AS JOHNNY QUICK, YOUNGSTER!
IN YOUR CASE --LITERALLY!
THANKS FOR REFLECTING SOME OF THAT FIRE MY WAY, ROBOTMAN!
NOW I'LL SHOW THEM--
--WHY I TOOK THE NAME FIREBRAND!

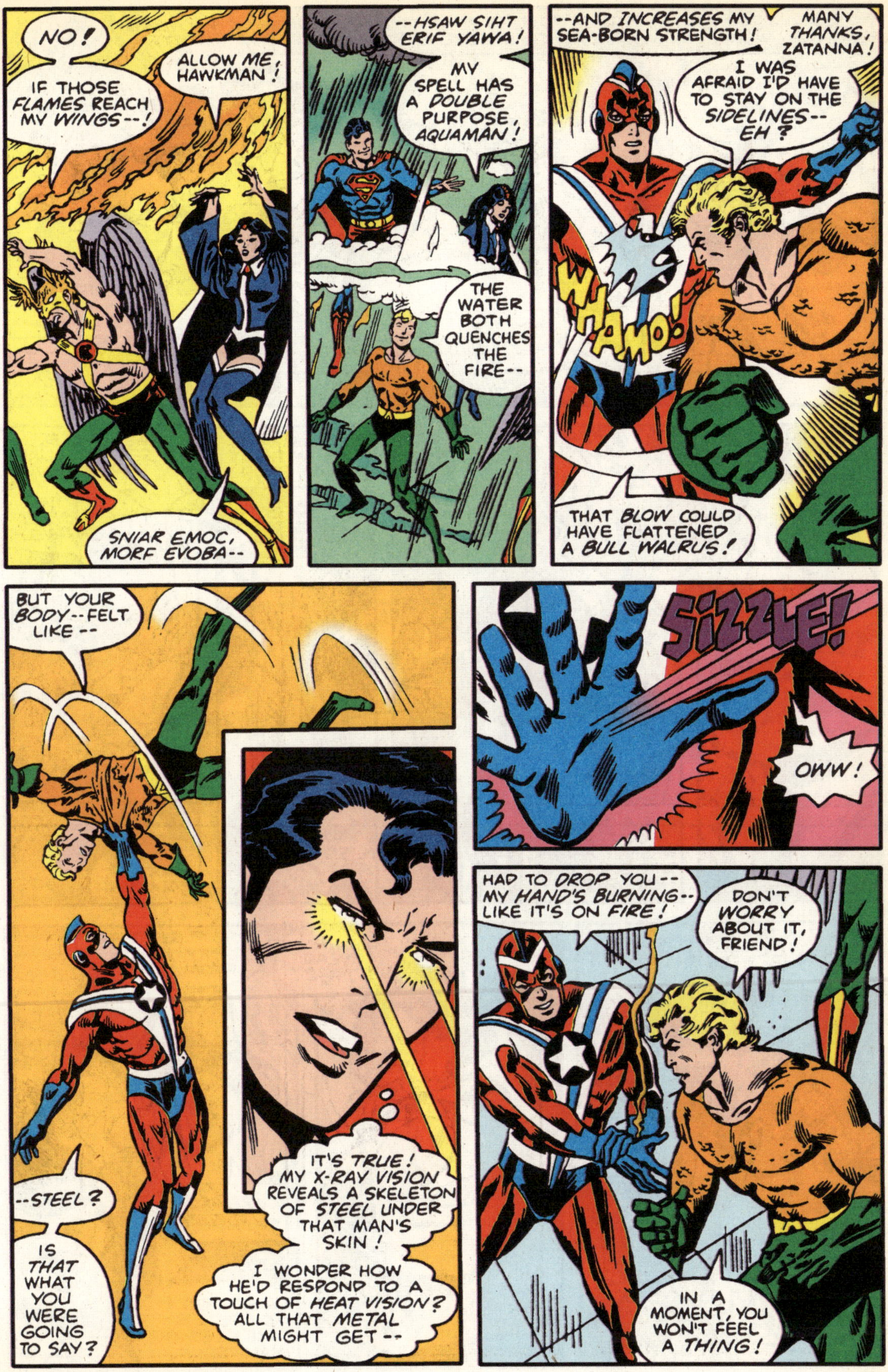
NO!
IF THOSE FLAMES REACH MY WINGS--!
ALLOW ME, HAWKMAN!
SNIAR EMOC, MORF EVOBA--
--HSAW SIHT ERIF YAWA!
MY SPELL HAS A DOUBLE PURPOSE, AQUAMAN!
THE WATER BOTH QUENCHES THE FIRE--
--AND INCREASES MY SEA-BORN STRENGTH!
MANY THANKS, ZATANNA!
I WAS AFRAID I'D HAVE TO STAY ON THE SIDELINES-- EH?
WHAMO!
THAT BLOW COULD HAVE FLATTENED A BULL WALRUS!
BUT YOUR BODY--FELT LIKE--
--STEEL?
IS THAT WHAT YOU WERE GOING TO SAY?
IT'S TRUE! MY X-RAY VISION REVEALS A SKELETON OF STEEL UNDER THAT MAN'S SKIN!
I WONDER HOW HE'D RESPOND TO A TOUCH OF HEAT VISION? ALL THAT METAL MIGHT GET--
SIZZLE!
OWW!
HAD TO DROP YOU-- MY HAND'S BURNING-- LIKE IT'S ON FIRE!
DON'T WORRY ABOUT IT, FRIEND!
IN A MOMENT, YOU WON'T FEEL A THING!

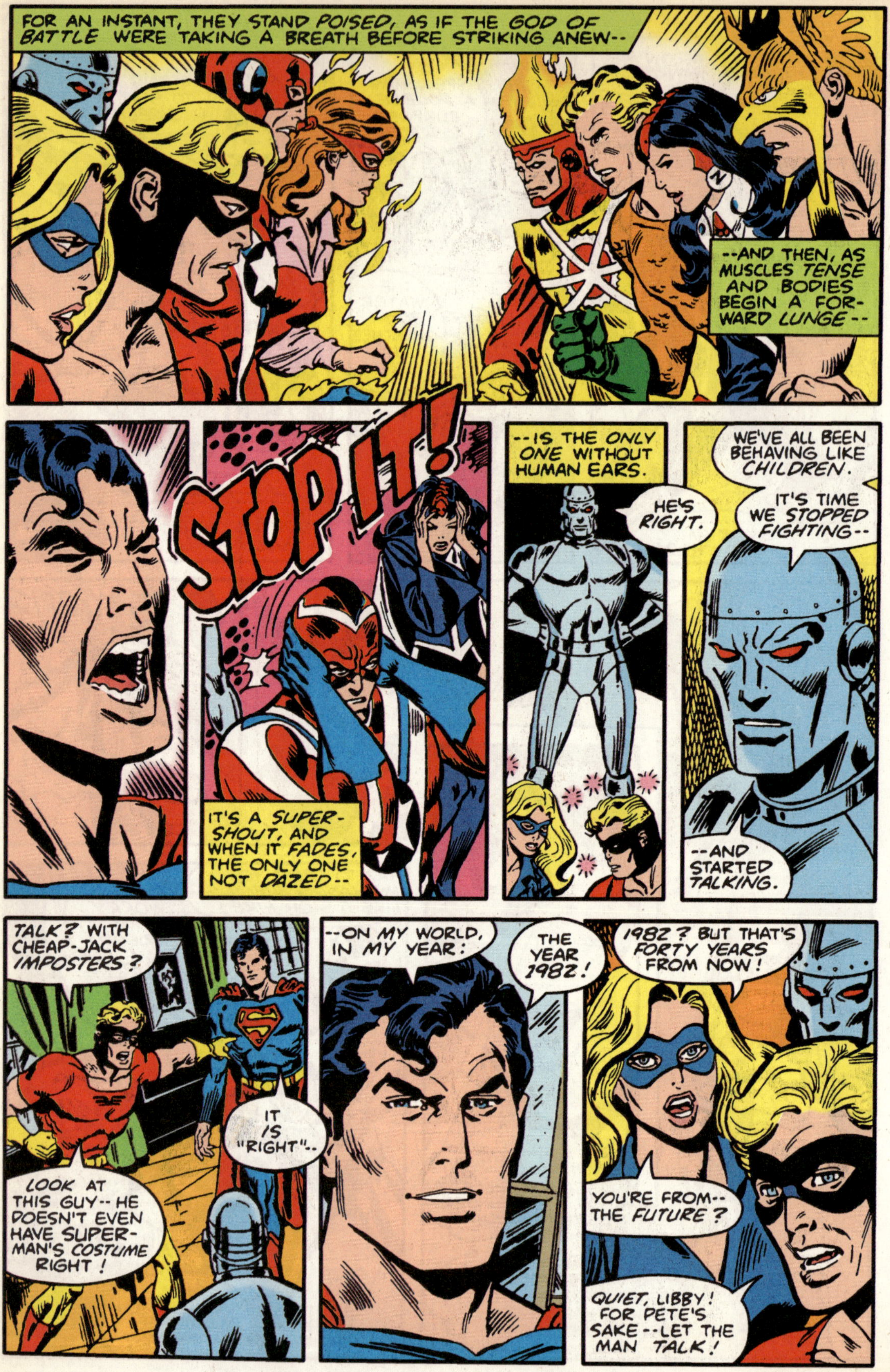
FOR AN INSTANT, THEY STAND POISED, AS IF THE GOD OF BATTLE WERE TAKING A BREATH BEFORE STRIKING ANEW--
--AND THEN, AS MUSCLES TENSE AND BODIES BEGIN A FORWARD LUNGE--
STOP IT!
IT'S A SUPER-SHOUT, AND WHEN IT FADES, THE ONLY ONE NOT DAZED--
--IS THE ONLY ONE WITHOUT HUMAN EARS.
HE'S RIGHT.
WE'VE ALL BEEN BEHAVING LIKE CHILDREN.
IT'S TIME WE STOPPED FIGHTING--
--AND STARTED TALKING.
TALK? WITH CHEAP-JACK IMPOSTERS?
IT IS "RIGHT"--
LOOK AT THIS GUY--HE DOESN'T EVEN HAVE SUPERMAN'S COSTUME RIGHT!
--ON MY WORLD, IN MY YEAR:
THE YEAR 1982!
1982? BUT THAT'S FORTY YEARS FROM NOW!
YOU'RE FROM--THE FUTURE?
QUIET, LIBBY! FOR PETE'S SAKE--LET THE MAN TALK!

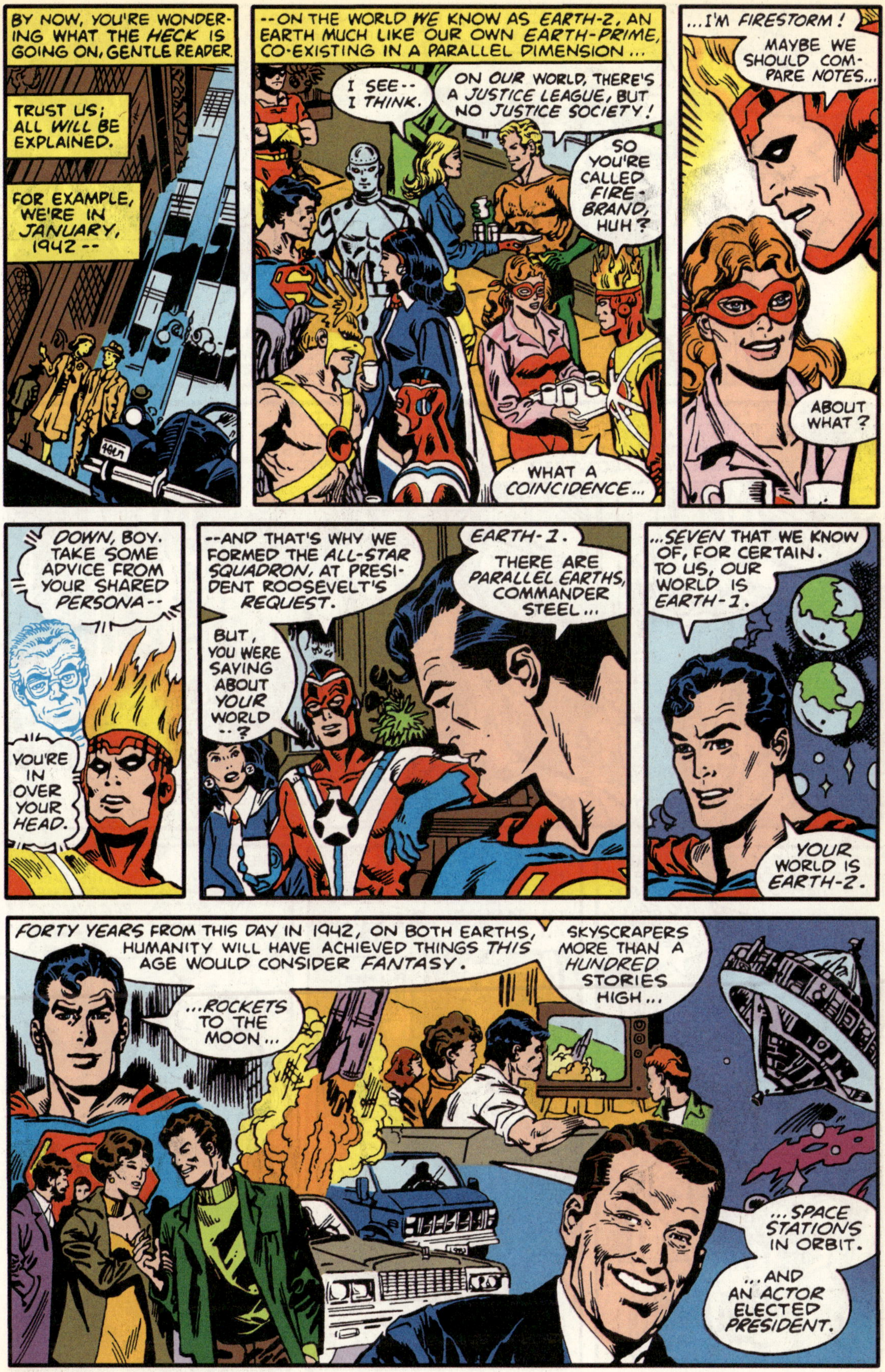
BY NOW, YOU'RE WONDERING WHAT THE HECK IS GOING ON, GENTLE READER.
TRUST US; ALL WILL BE EXPLAINED.
FOR EXAMPLE, WE'RE IN JANUARY, 1942 --
--ON THE WORLD WE KNOW AS EARTH-2, AN EARTH MUCH LIKE OUR OWN EARTH-PRIME, CO-EXISTING IN A PARALLEL DIMENSION ...
I SEE-- I THINK.
ON OUR WORLD, THERE'S A JUSTICE LEAGUE, BUT NO JUSTICE SOCIETY!
SO YOU'RE CALLED FIRE-BRAND, HUH?
WHAT A COINCIDENCE...
...I'M FIRESTORM!
MAYBE WE SHOULD COMPARE NOTES...
ABOUT WHAT?
DOWN, BOY. TAKE SOME ADVICE FROM YOUR SHARED PERSONA--
YOU'RE IN OVER YOUR HEAD.
--AND THAT'S WHY WE FORMED THE ALL-STAR SQUADRON, AT PRESIDENT ROOSEVELT'S REQUEST.
BUT, YOU WERE SAYING ABOUT YOUR WORLD --?
EARTH-1.
THERE ARE PARALLEL EARTHS, COMMANDER STEEL...
...SEVEN THAT WE KNOW OF, FOR CERTAIN. TO US, OUR WORLD IS EARTH-1.
YOUR WORLD IS EARTH-2.
FORTY YEARS FROM THIS DAY IN 1942, ON BOTH EARTHS, HUMANITY WILL HAVE ACHIEVED THINGS THIS AGE WOULD CONSIDER FANTASY.
SKYSCRAPERS MORE THAN A HUNDRED STORIES HIGH...
...ROCKETS TO THE MOON...
...SPACE STATIONS IN ORBIT.
...AND AN ACTOR ELECTED PRESIDENT.

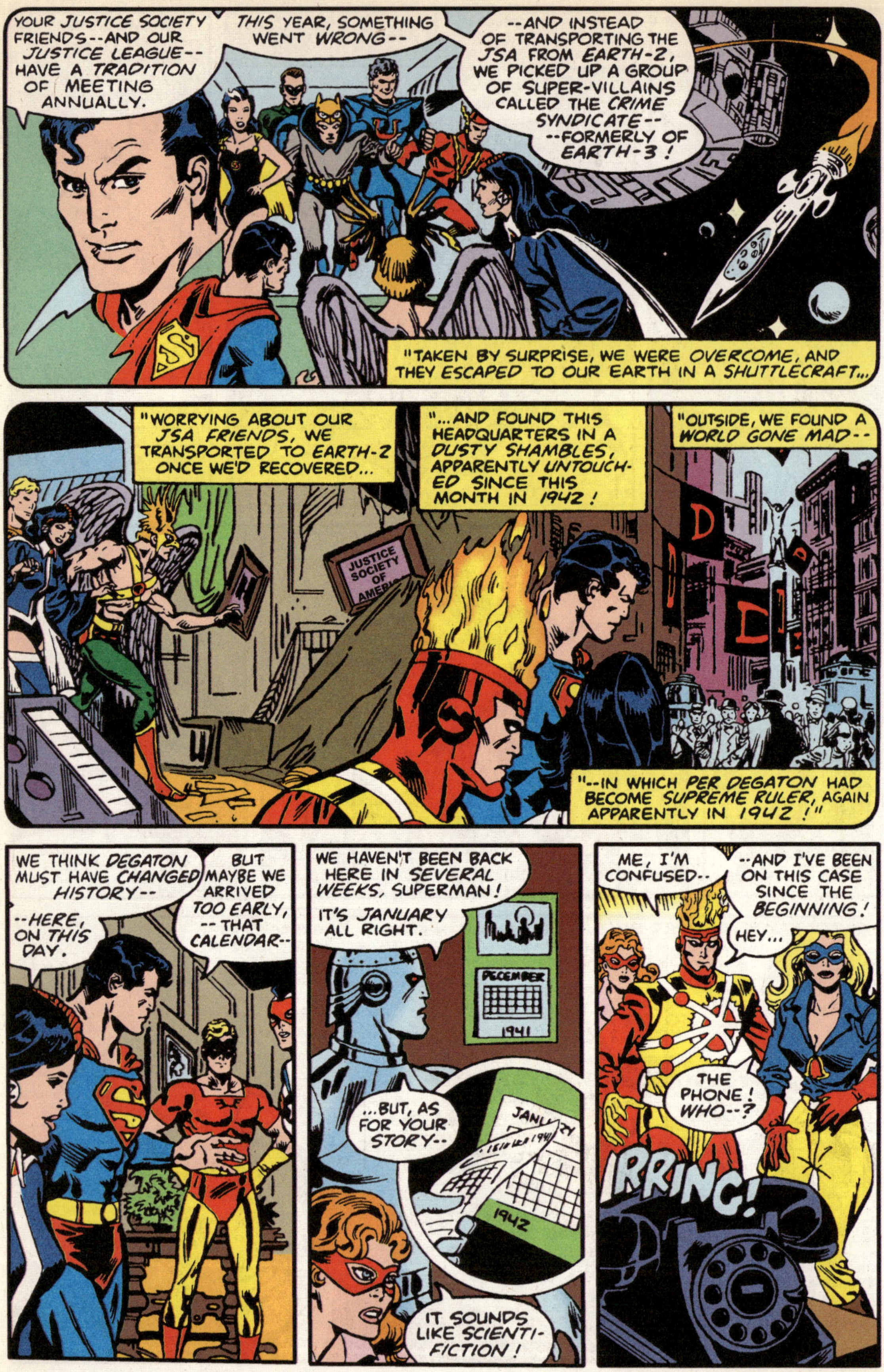
YOUR *JUSTICE SOCIETY* FRIENDS--AND OUR *JUSTICE LEAGUE*--HAVE A *TRADITION* OF MEETING ANNUALLY.
THIS YEAR, SOMETHING WENT *WRONG*--
--AND INSTEAD OF TRANSPORTING THE *JSA* FROM *EARTH-2*, WE PICKED UP A GROUP OF SUPER-VILLAINS CALLED THE *CRIME SYNDICATE*--
--FORMERLY OF *EARTH-3*!
"TAKEN BY SURPRISE, WE WERE *OVERCOME*, AND THEY ESCAPED TO OUR EARTH IN A *SHUTTLECRAFT*...
"WORRYING ABOUT OUR *JSA FRIENDS*, WE TRANSPORTED TO *EARTH-2* ONCE WE'D RECOVERED...
"...AND FOUND THIS HEADQUARTERS IN A *DUSTY SHAMBLES*, APPARENTLY *UNTOUCHED* SINCE THIS MONTH IN *1942*!
JUSTICE SOCIETY OF
"OUTSIDE, WE FOUND A *WORLD GONE MAD*--
"--IN WHICH *PER DEGATON* HAD BECOME *SUPREME RULER*, AGAIN APPARENTLY IN *1942*!"
WE THINK *DEGATON* MUST HAVE *CHANGED HISTORY*--
--HERE, ON *THIS* DAY.
BUT MAYBE WE ARRIVED TOO EARLY, --THAT CALENDAR--
WE HAVEN'T BEEN BACK HERE IN *SEVERAL WEEKS*, SUPERMAN!
IT'S *JANUARY* ALL RIGHT.
DECEMBER
1941
...BUT, AS FOR YOUR STORY--
JANUARY
1942
IT SOUNDS LIKE SCIENTI-FICTION!
ME, I'M CONFUSED--
--AND I'VE BEEN ON THIS CASE SINCE THE *BEGINNING*!
HEY...
THE PHONE! WHO--?
RRING!

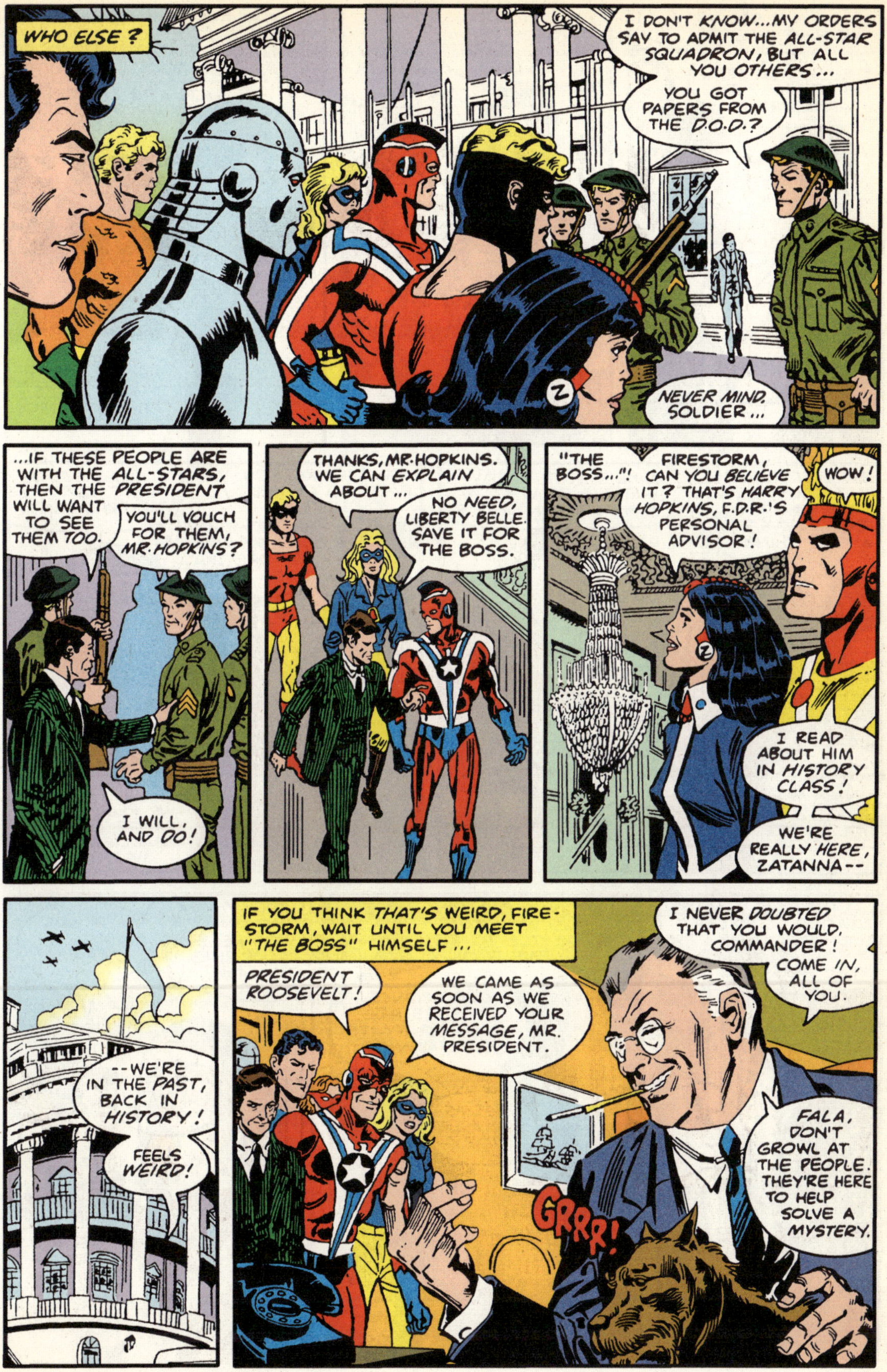
WHO ELSE?
I DON'T KNOW... MY ORDERS SAY TO ADMIT THE ALL-STAR SQUADRON, BUT ALL YOU OTHERS...
YOU GOT PAPERS FROM THE D.O.D.?
NEVER MIND, SOLDIER...
...IF THESE PEOPLE ARE WITH THE ALL-STARS, THEN THE PRESIDENT WILL WANT TO SEE THEM TOO.
YOU'LL VOUCH FOR THEM, MR. HOPKINS?
I WILL, AND DO!
THANKS, MR. HOPKINS. WE CAN EXPLAIN ABOUT...
NO NEED, LIBERTY BELLE. SAVE IT FOR THE BOSS.
"THE BOSS..."!
FIRESTORM, CAN YOU BELIEVE IT? THAT'S HARRY HOPKINS, F.D.R.'S PERSONAL ADVISOR!
WOW!
I READ ABOUT HIM IN HISTORY CLASS!
WE'RE REALLY HERE, ZATANNA--
--WE'RE IN THE PAST, BACK IN HISTORY!
FEELS WEIRD!
IF YOU THINK THAT'S WEIRD, FIRESTORM, WAIT UNTIL YOU MEET "THE BOSS" HIMSELF...
PRESIDENT ROOSEVELT!
WE CAME AS SOON AS WE RECEIVED YOUR MESSAGE, MR. PRESIDENT.
I NEVER DOUBTED THAT YOU WOULD, COMMANDER!
COME IN, ALL OF YOU.
GRRRR!
FALA, DON'T GROWL AT THE PEOPLE. THEY'RE HERE TO HELP SOLVE A MYSTERY.

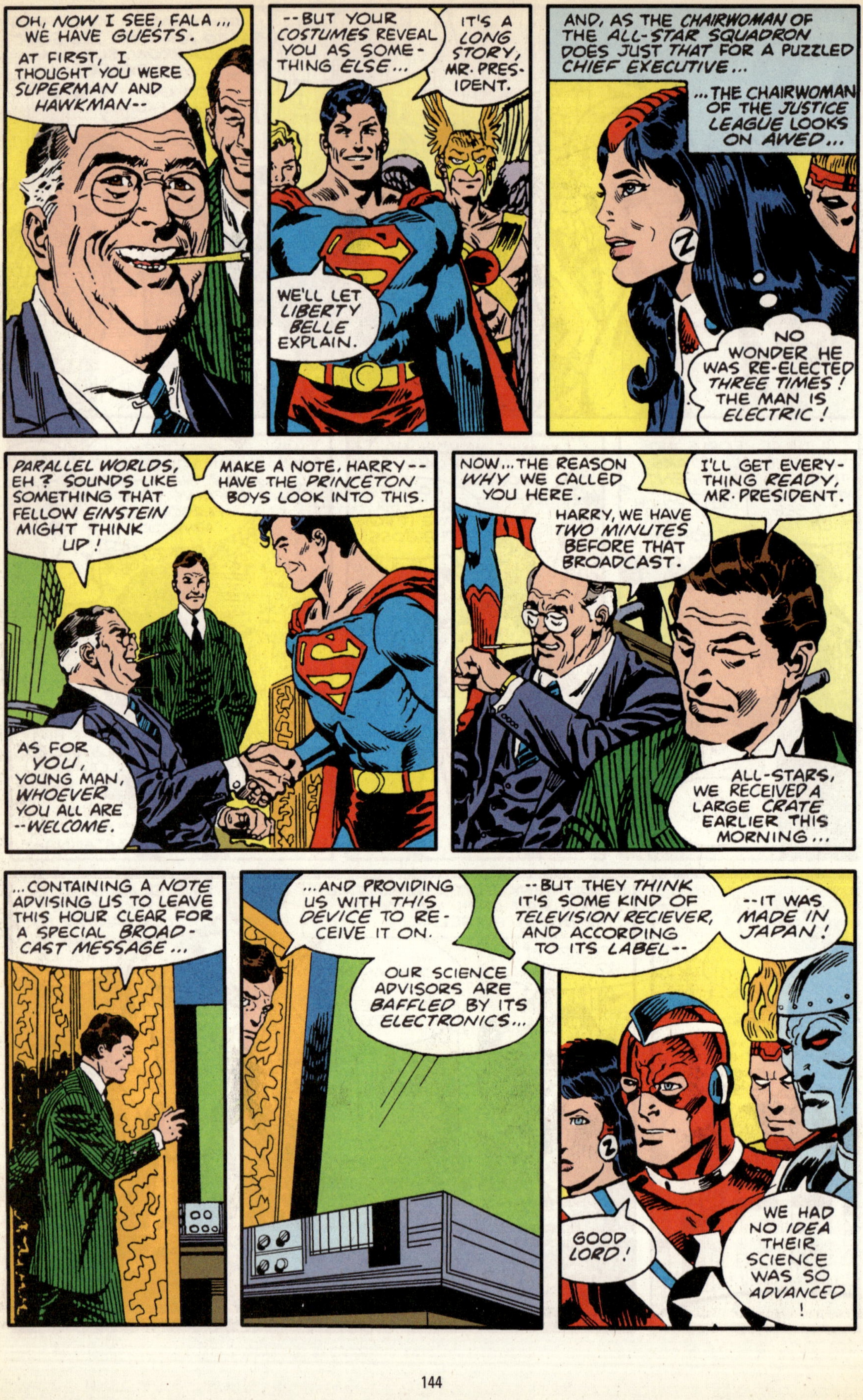

OH, NOW I SEE, FALA... WE HAVE GUESTS.
AT FIRST, I THOUGHT YOU WERE SUPERMAN AND HAWKMAN--
--BUT YOUR COSTUMES REVEAL YOU AS SOMETHING ELSE...
IT'S A LONG STORY, MR. PRESIDENT.
WE'LL LET LIBERTY BELLE EXPLAIN.
AND, AS THE CHAIRWOMAN OF THE ALL-STAR SQUADRON DOES JUST THAT FOR A PUZZLED CHIEF EXECUTIVE...
...THE CHAIRWOMAN OF THE JUSTICE LEAGUE LOOKS ON AWED...
NO WONDER HE WAS RE-ELECTED THREE TIMES! THE MAN IS ELECTRIC!
PARALLEL WORLDS, EH? SOUNDS LIKE SOMETHING THAT FELLOW EINSTEIN MIGHT THINK UP!
MAKE A NOTE, HARRY-- HAVE THE PRINCETON BOYS LOOK INTO THIS.
AS FOR YOU, YOUNG MAN, WHOEVER YOU ALL ARE --WELCOME.
NOW... THE REASON WHY WE CALLED YOU HERE.
HARRY, WE HAVE TWO MINUTES BEFORE THAT BROADCAST.
I'LL GET EVERYTHING READY, MR. PRESIDENT.
ALL-STARS, WE RECEIVED A LARGE CRATE EARLIER THIS MORNING...
...CONTAINING A NOTE ADVISING US TO LEAVE THIS HOUR CLEAR FOR A SPECIAL BROADCAST MESSAGE...
...AND PROVIDING US WITH THIS DEVICE TO RECEIVE IT ON.
OUR SCIENCE ADVISORS ARE BAFFLED BY ITS ELECTRONICS...
--BUT THEY THINK IT'S SOME KIND OF TELEVISION RECIEVER, AND ACCORDING TO ITS LABEL--
--IT WAS MADE IN JAPAN!
GOOD LORD!
WE HAD NO IDEA THEIR SCIENCE WAS SO ADVANCED!

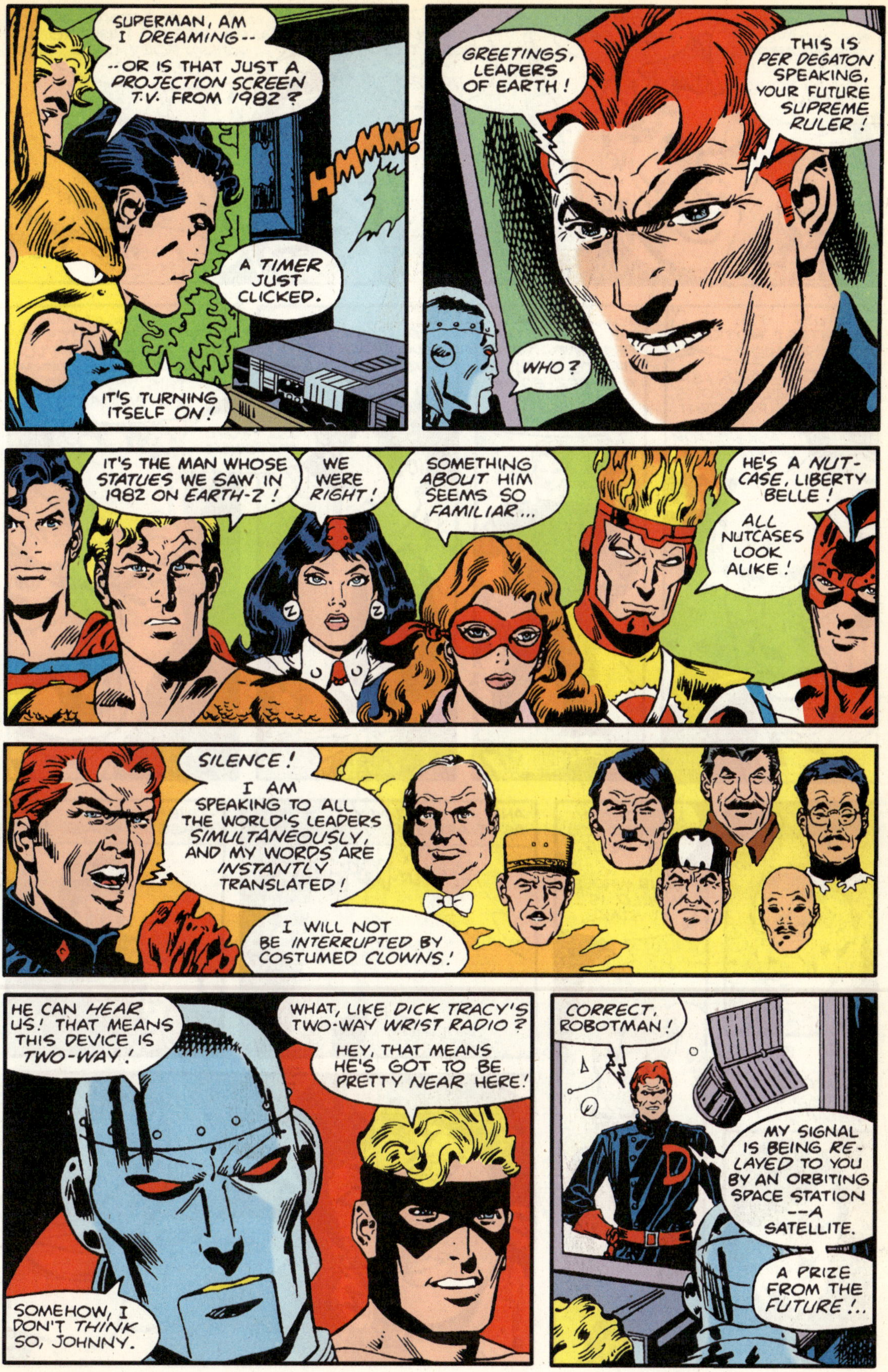
SUPERMAN, AM I DREAMING--
--OR IS THAT JUST A PROJECTION SCREEN T.V. FROM 1982 ?
HMMM!
A TIMER JUST CLICKED.
IT'S TURNING ITSELF ON!
GREETINGS, LEADERS OF EARTH!
THIS IS PER DEGATON SPEAKING, YOUR FUTURE SUPREME RULER!
WHO?
IT'S THE MAN WHOSE STATUES WE SAW IN 1982 ON EARTH-2!
WE WERE RIGHT!
SOMETHING ABOUT HIM SEEMS SO FAMILIAR...
HE'S A NUT-CASE, LIBERTY BELLE!
ALL NUTCASES LOOK ALIKE!
SILENCE!
I AM SPEAKING TO ALL THE WORLD'S LEADERS SIMULTANEOUSLY, AND MY WORDS ARE INSTANTLY TRANSLATED!
I WILL NOT BE INTERRUPTED BY COSTUMED CLOWNS!
HE CAN HEAR US! THAT MEANS THIS DEVICE IS TWO-WAY!
WHAT, LIKE DICK TRACY'S TWO-WAY WRIST RADIO?
HEY, THAT MEANS HE'S GOT TO BE PRETTY NEAR HERE!
SOMEHOW, I DON'T THINK SO, JOHNNY.
CORRECT, ROBOTMAN!
MY SIGNAL IS BEING RE-LAYED TO YOU BY AN ORBITING SPACE STATION --A SATELLITE.
A PRIZE FROM THE FUTURE!..

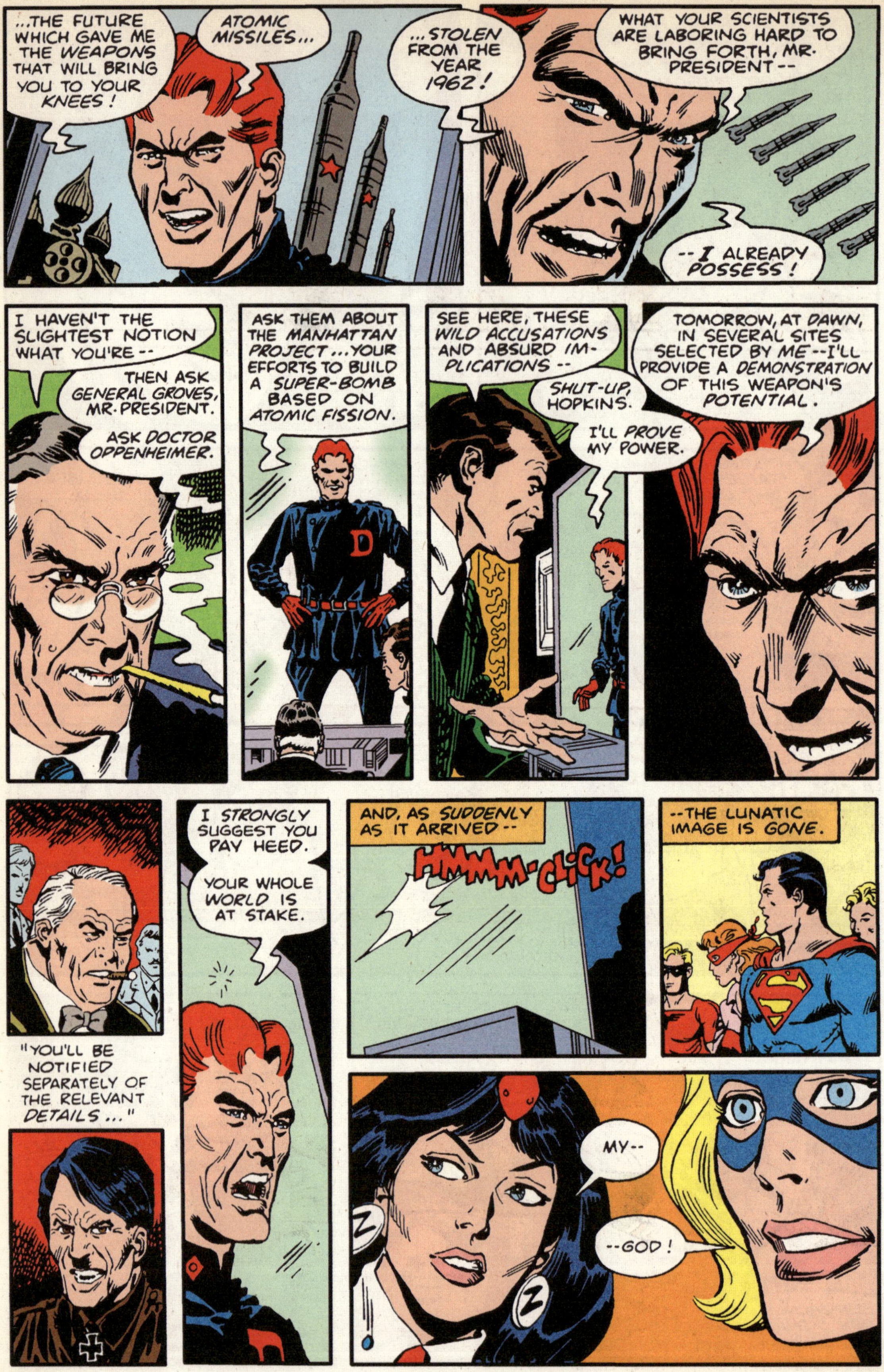
...THE FUTURE WHICH GAVE ME THE WEAPONS THAT WILL BRING YOU TO YOUR KNEES!
ATOMIC MISSILES...
...STOLEN FROM THE YEAR 1962!
WHAT YOUR SCIENTISTS ARE LABORING HARD TO BRING FORTH, MR. PRESIDENT--
--I ALREADY POSSESS!
I HAVEN'T THE SLIGHTEST NOTION WHAT YOU'RE--
THEN ASK GENERAL GROVES, MR. PRESIDENT.
ASK DOCTOR OPPENHEIMER.
ASK THEM ABOUT THE MANHATTAN PROJECT...YOUR EFFORTS TO BUILD A SUPER-BOMB BASED ON ATOMIC FISSION.
SEE HERE, THESE WILD ACCUSATIONS AND ABSURD IMPLICATIONS--
SHUT-UP, HOPKINS.
I'LL PROVE MY POWER.
TOMORROW, AT DAWN, IN SEVERAL SITES SELECTED BY ME--I'LL PROVIDE A DEMONSTRATION OF THIS WEAPON'S POTENTIAL.
"YOU'LL BE NOTIFIED SEPARATELY OF THE RELEVANT DETAILS..."
I STRONGLY SUGGEST YOU PAY HEED.
YOUR WHOLE WORLD IS AT STAKE.
AND, AS SUDDENLY AS IT ARRIVED--
HMMM-CLICK!
--THE LUNATIC IMAGE IS GONE.
MY--
--GOD!

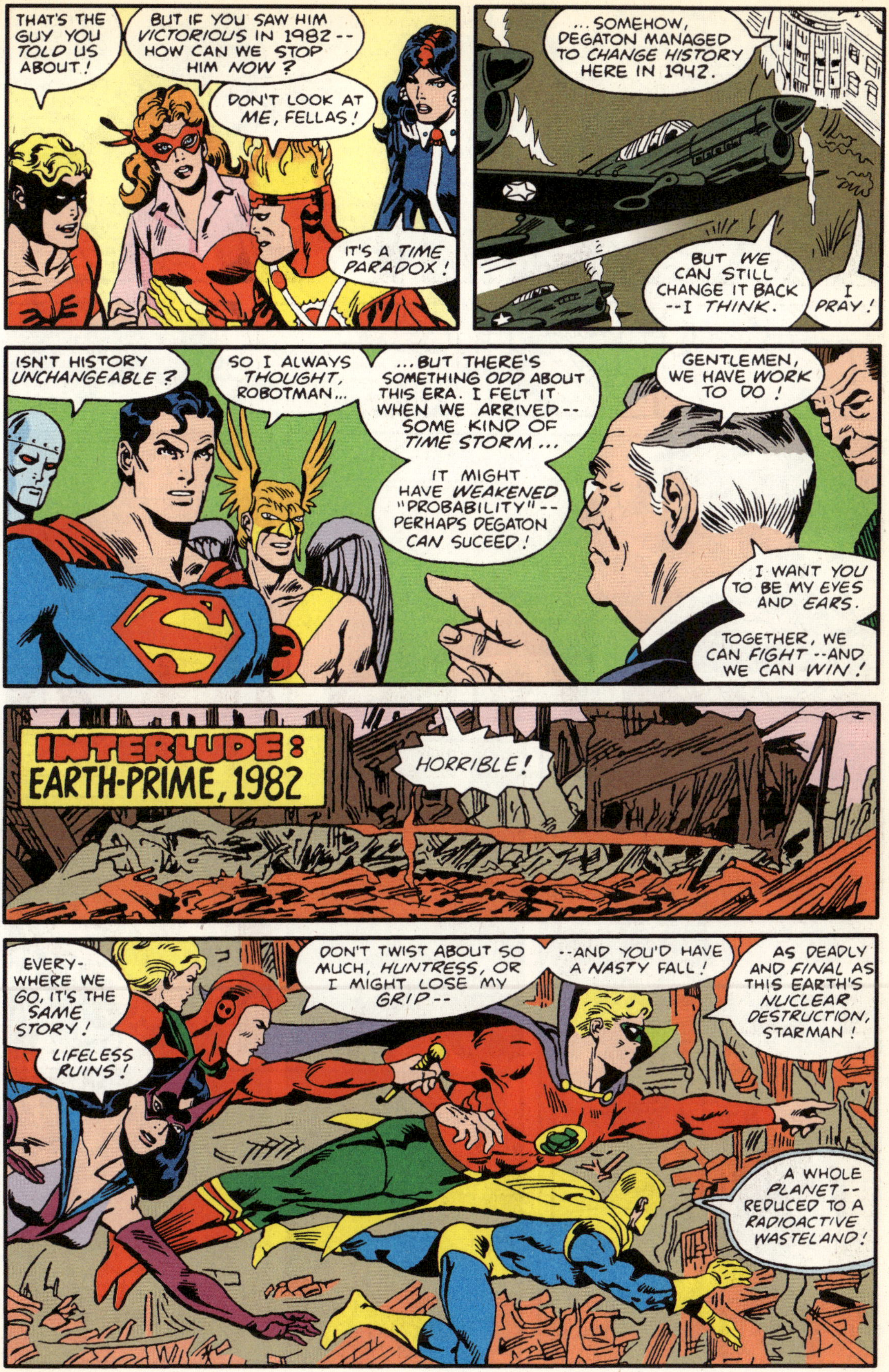
THAT'S THE GUY YOU TOLD US ABOUT!
BUT IF YOU SAW HIM VICTORIOUS IN 1982 -- HOW CAN WE STOP HIM NOW?
DON'T LOOK AT ME, FELLAS!
IT'S A TIME PARADOX!
... SOMEHOW, DEGATON MANAGED TO CHANGE HISTORY HERE IN 1942.
BUT WE CAN STILL CHANGE IT BACK --I THINK.
I PRAY!
ISN'T HISTORY UNCHANGEABLE?
SO I ALWAYS THOUGHT, ROBOTMAN...
...BUT THERE'S SOMETHING ODD ABOUT THIS ERA. I FELT IT WHEN WE ARRIVED -- SOME KIND OF TIME STORM ...
IT MIGHT HAVE WEAKENED "PROBABILITY" -- PERHAPS DEGATON CAN SUCEED!
GENTLEMEN, WE HAVE WORK TO DO!
I WANT YOU TO BE MY EYES AND EARS.
TOGETHER, WE CAN FIGHT --AND WE CAN WIN!
INTERLUDE: EARTH-PRIME, 1982
HORRIBLE!
EVERY-WHERE WE GO, IT'S THE SAME STORY!
LIFELESS RUINS!
DON'T TWIST ABOUT SO MUCH, HUNTRESS, OR I MIGHT LOSE MY GRIP --
--AND YOU'D HAVE A NASTY FALL!
AS DEADLY AND FINAL AS THIS EARTH'S NUCLEAR DESTRUCTION, STARMAN!
A WHOLE PLANET -- REDUCED TO A RADIOACTIVE WASTELAND!

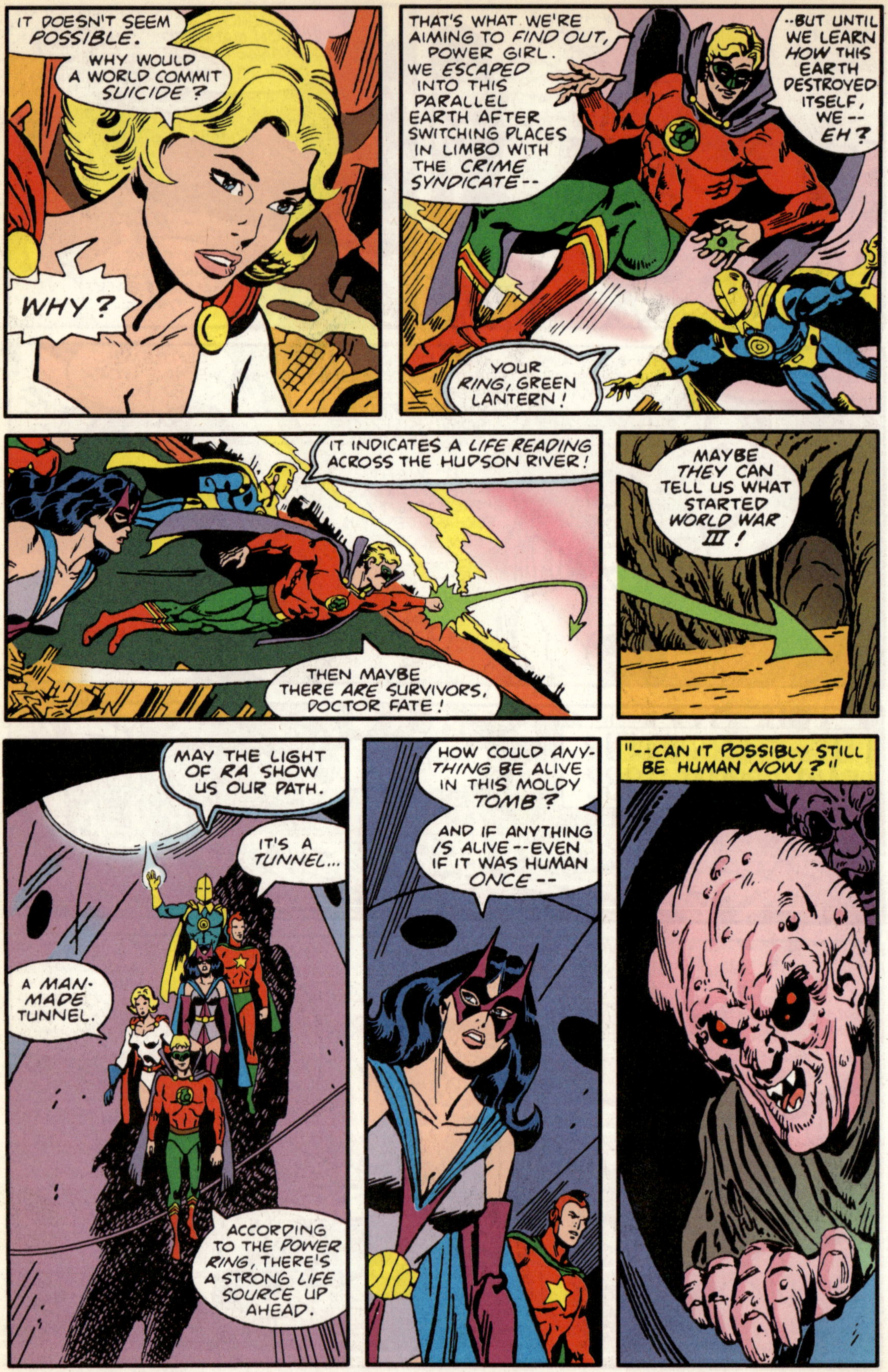
IT DOESN'T SEEM POSSIBLE.
WHY WOULD A WORLD COMMIT SUICIDE?
WHY?
THAT'S WHAT WE'RE AIMING TO FIND OUT, POWER GIRL. WE ESCAPED INTO THIS PARALLEL EARTH AFTER SWITCHING PLACES IN LIMBO WITH THE CRIME SYNDICATE--
..BUT UNTIL WE LEARN HOW THIS EARTH DESTROYED ITSELF, WE-- EH?
YOUR RING, GREEN LANTERN!
IT INDICATES A LIFE READING ACROSS THE HUDSON RIVER!
THEN MAYBE THERE ARE SURVIVORS, DOCTOR FATE!
MAYBE THEY CAN TELL US WHAT STARTED WORLD WAR III!
MAY THE LIGHT OF RA SHOW US OUR PATH.
IT'S A TUNNEL...
A MAN-MADE TUNNEL.
ACCORDING TO THE POWER RING, THERE'S A STRONG LIFE SOURCE UP AHEAD.
HOW COULD ANYTHING BE ALIVE IN THIS MOLDY TOMB?
AND IF ANYTHING IS ALIVE--EVEN IF IT WAS HUMAN ONCE--
"--CAN IT POSSIBLY STILL BE HUMAN NOW?"

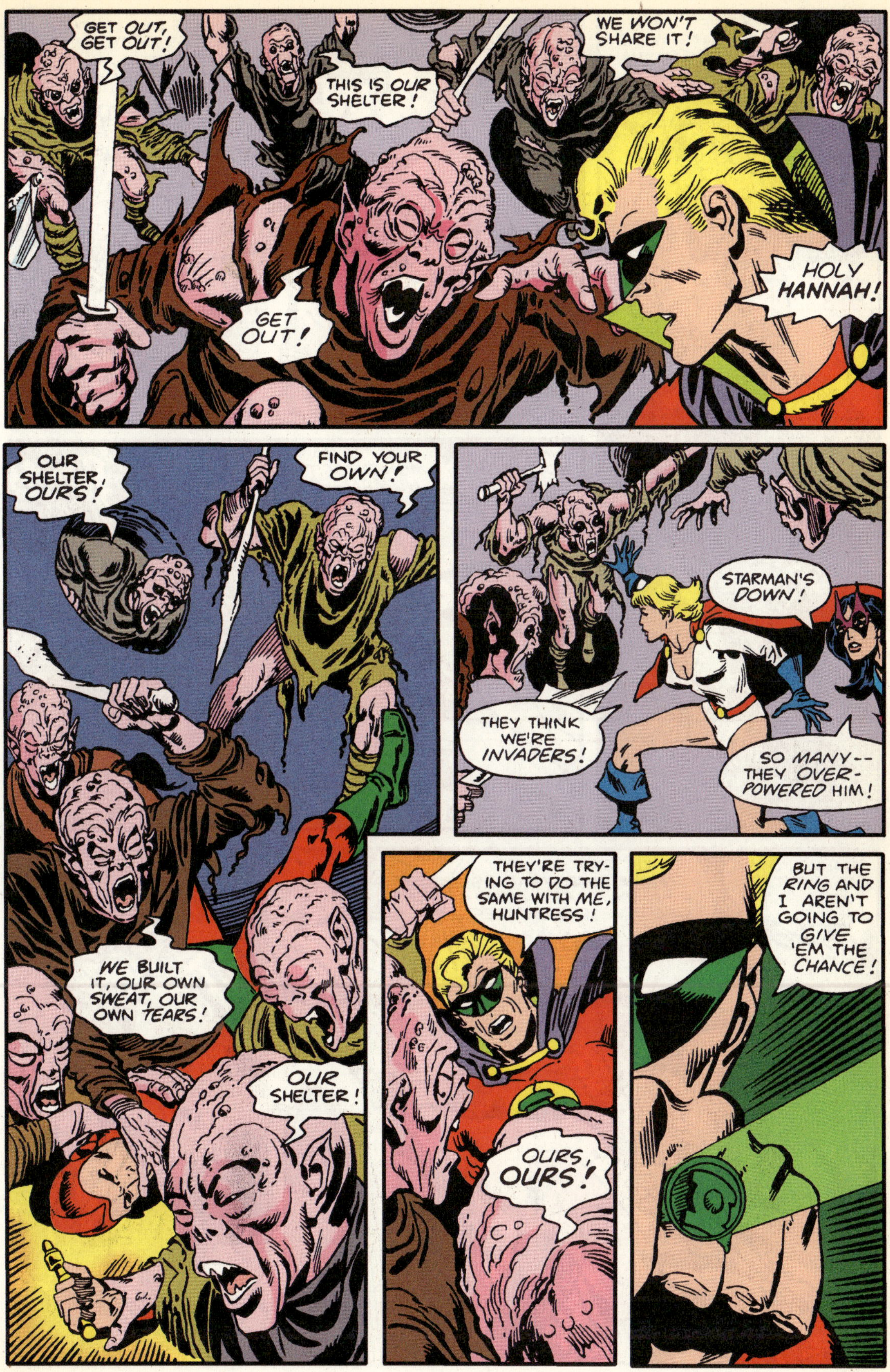
GET OUT, GET OUT!
THIS IS OUR SHELTER!
WE WON'T SHARE IT!
GET OUT!
HOLY HANNAH!
OUR SHELTER, OURS!
FIND YOUR OWN!
WE BUILT IT, OUR OWN SWEAT, OUR OWN TEARS!
OUR SHELTER!
STARMAN'S DOWN!
THEY THINK WE'RE INVADERS!
SO MANY--THEY OVER-POWERED HIM!
THEY'RE TRY-ING TO DO THE SAME WITH ME, HUNTRESS!
OURS, OURS!
BUT THE RING AND I AREN'T GOING TO GIVE 'EM THE CHANCE!

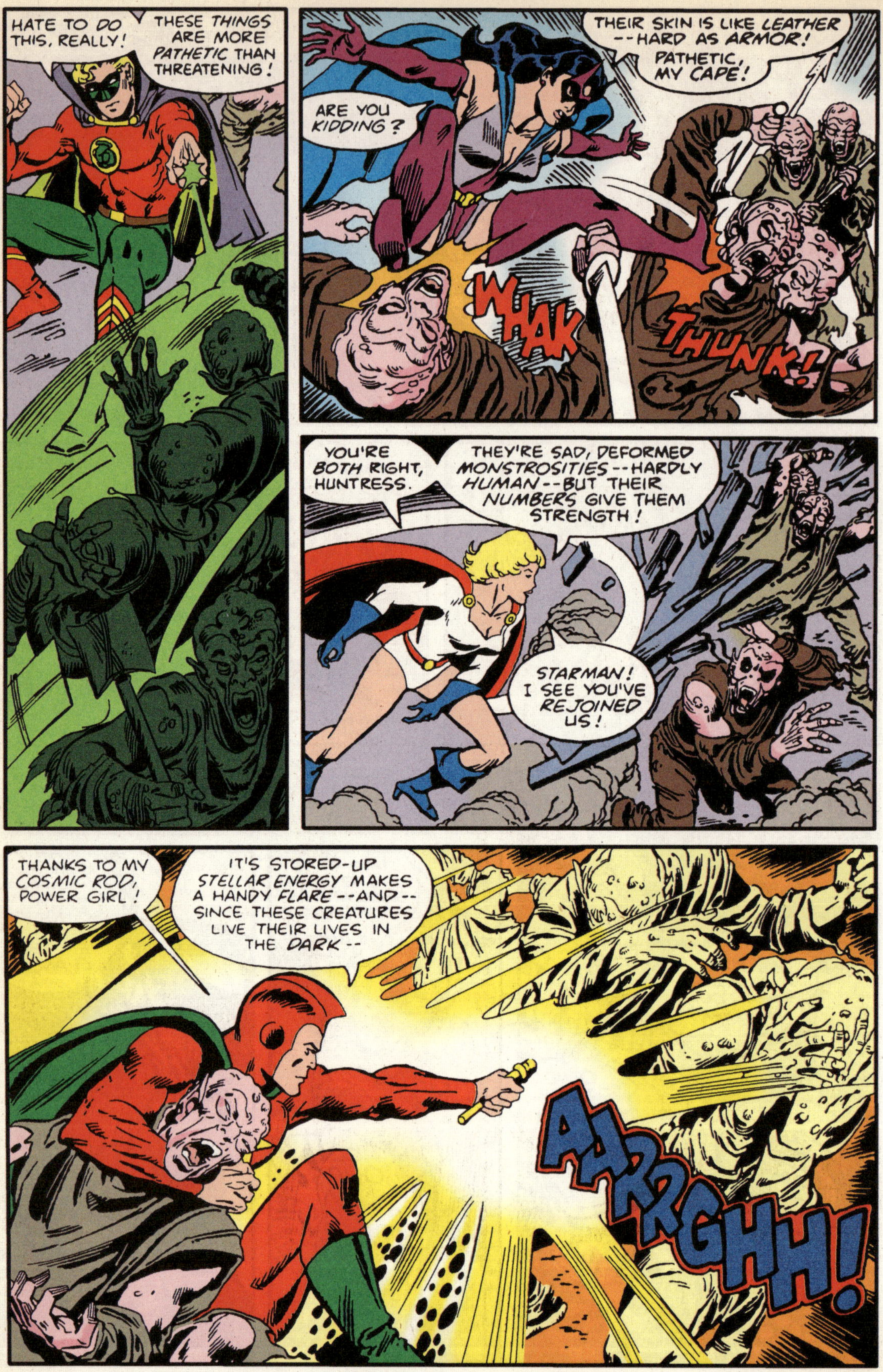
HATE TO DO THIS, REALLY!
THESE THINGS ARE MORE PATHETIC THAN THREATENING!
ARE YOU KIDDING?
THEIR SKIN IS LIKE LEATHER--HARD AS ARMOR!
PATHETIC, MY CAPE!
WHAK
THUNK!
YOU'RE BOTH RIGHT, HUNTRESS.
THEY'RE SAD, DEFORMED MONSTROSITIES--HARDLY HUMAN--BUT THEIR NUMBERS GIVE THEM STRENGTH!
STARMAN! I SEE YOU'VE REJOINED US!
THANKS TO MY COSMIC ROD, POWER GIRL!
IT'S STORED-UP STELLAR ENERGY MAKES A HANDY FLARE--AND--SINCE THESE CREATURES LIVE THEIR LIVES IN THE DARK--
AARRGHH!

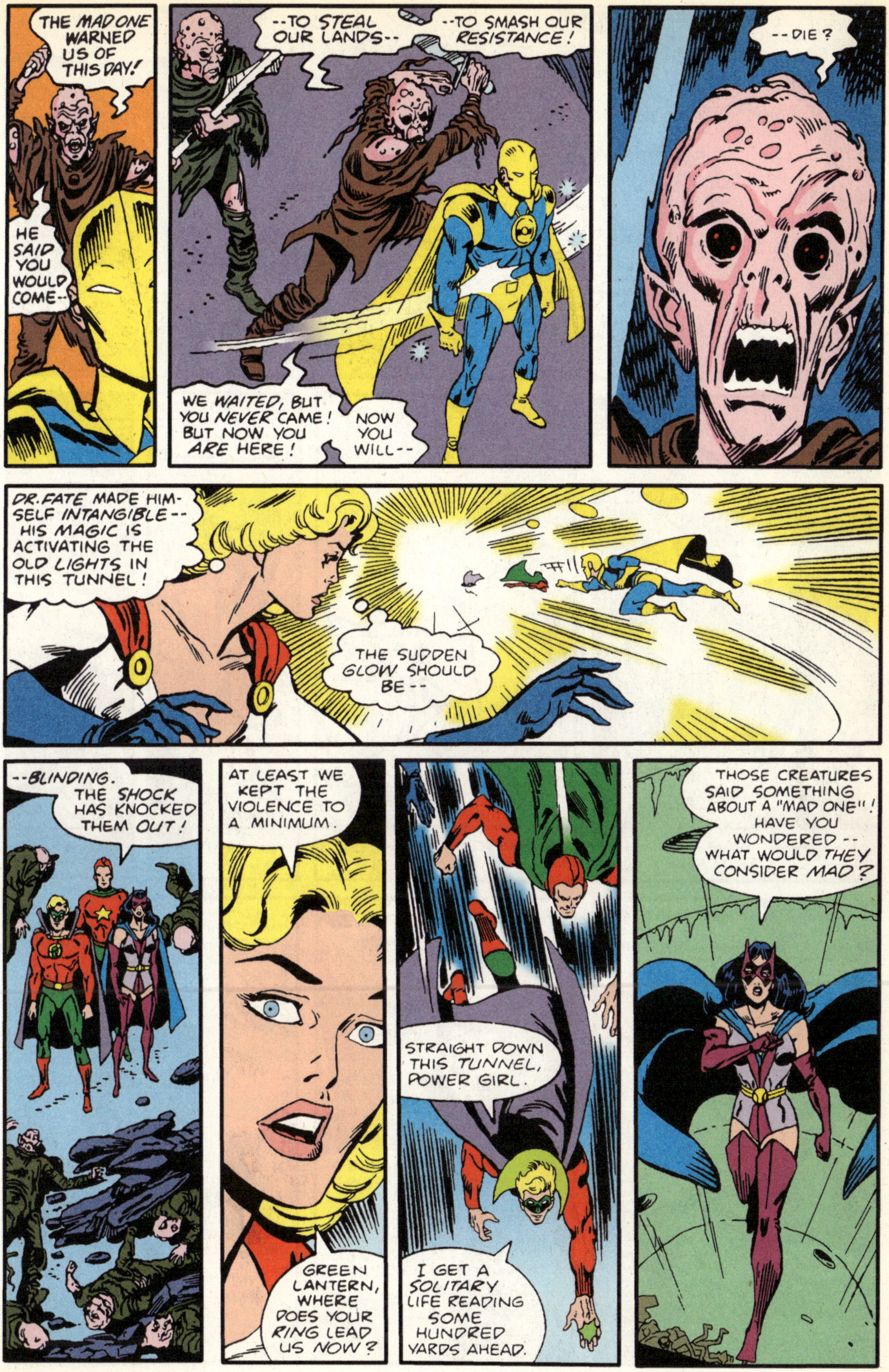
THE MAD ONE WARNED US OF THIS DAY!
HE SAID YOU WOULD COME--
--TO STEAL OUR LANDS--
--TO SMASH OUR RESISTANCE!
WE WAITED, BUT YOU NEVER CAME! BUT NOW YOU ARE HERE!
NOW YOU WILL--
--DIE?
DR. FATE MADE HIMSELF INTANGIBLE--HIS MAGIC IS ACTIVATING THE OLD LIGHTS IN THIS TUNNEL!
THE SUDDEN GLOW SHOULD BE--
--BLINDING. THE SHOCK HAS KNOCKED THEM OUT!
AT LEAST WE KEPT THE VIOLENCE TO A MINIMUM.
GREEN LANTERN, WHERE DOES YOUR RING LEAD US NOW?
STRAIGHT DOWN THIS TUNNEL, POWER GIRL.
I GET A SOLITARY LIFE READING SOME HUNDRED YARDS AHEAD.
THOSE CREATURES SAID SOMETHING ABOUT A "MAD ONE"! HAVE YOU WONDERED--WHAT WOULD THEY CONSIDER MAD?

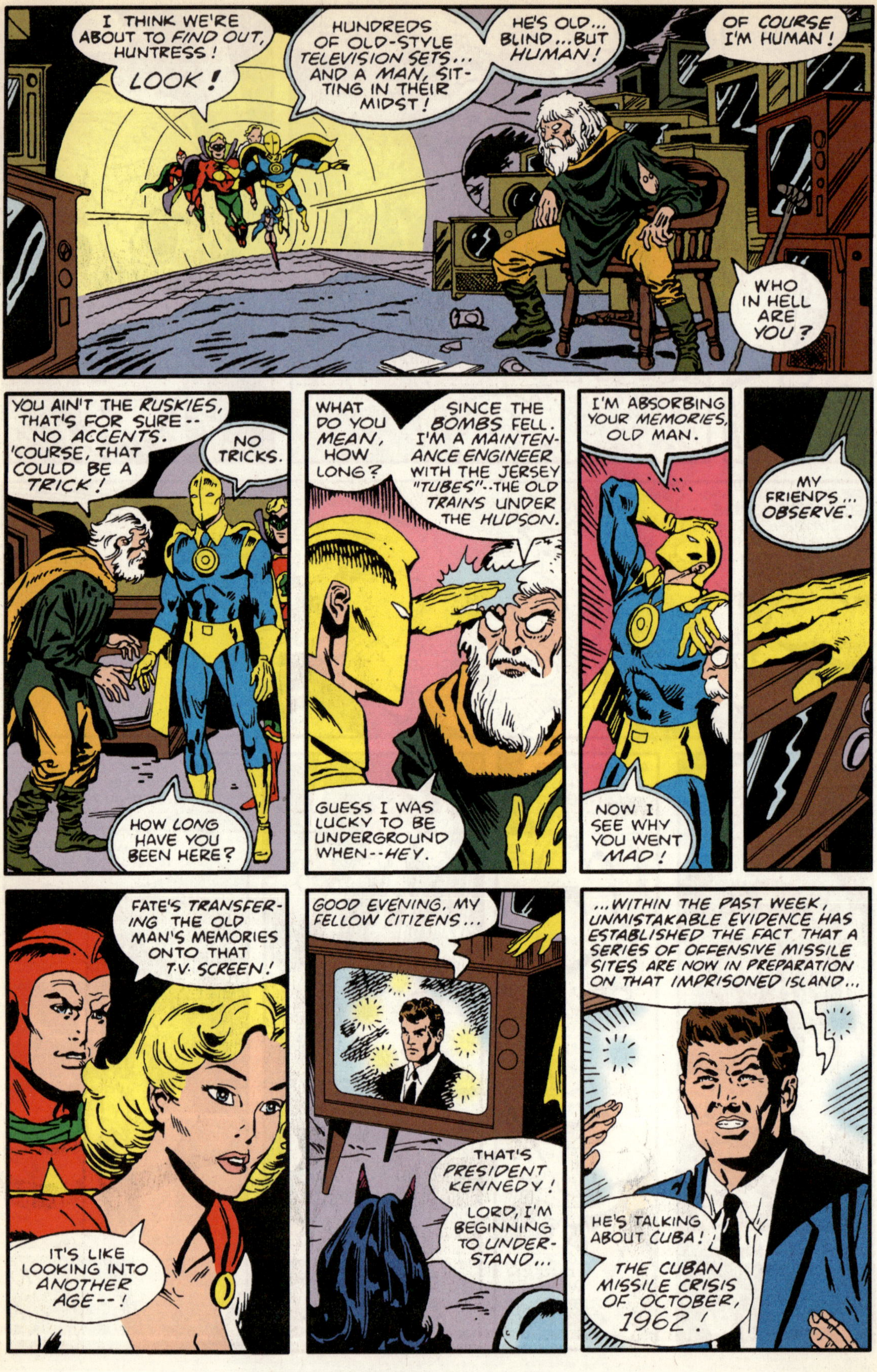
I THINK WE'RE ABOUT TO FIND OUT, HUNTRESS! LOOK!
HUNDREDS OF OLD-STYLE TELEVISION SETS... AND A MAN, SITTING IN THEIR MIDST!
HE'S OLD... BLIND... BUT HUMAN!
OF COURSE I'M HUMAN!
WHO IN HELL ARE YOU?
YOU AIN'T THE RUSKIES, THAT'S FOR SURE -- NO ACCENTS. 'COURSE, THAT COULD BE A TRICK!
NO TRICKS.
HOW LONG HAVE YOU BEEN HERE?
WHAT DO YOU MEAN, HOW LONG?
SINCE THE BOMBS FELL. I'M A MAINTENANCE ENGINEER WITH THE JERSEY "TUBES"--THE OLD TRAINS UNDER THE HUDSON.
GUESS I WAS LUCKY TO BE UNDERGROUND WHEN--HEY.
I'M ABSORBING YOUR MEMORIES, OLD MAN.
NOW I SEE WHY YOU WENT MAD!
MY FRIENDS... OBSERVE.
FATE'S TRANSFERING THE OLD MAN'S MEMORIES ONTO THAT T.V. SCREEN!
IT'S LIKE LOOKING INTO ANOTHER AGE--!
GOOD EVENING, MY FELLOW CITIZENS...
THAT'S PRESIDENT KENNEDY!
LORD, I'M BEGINNING TO UNDERSTAND...
...WITHIN THE PAST WEEK, UNMISTAKABLE EVIDENCE HAS ESTABLISHED THE FACT THAT A SERIES OF OFFENSIVE MISSILE SITES ARE NOW IN PREPARATION ON THAT IMPRISONED ISLAND...
HE'S TALKING ABOUT CUBA!
THE CUBAN MISSILE CRISIS OF OCTOBER, 1962!

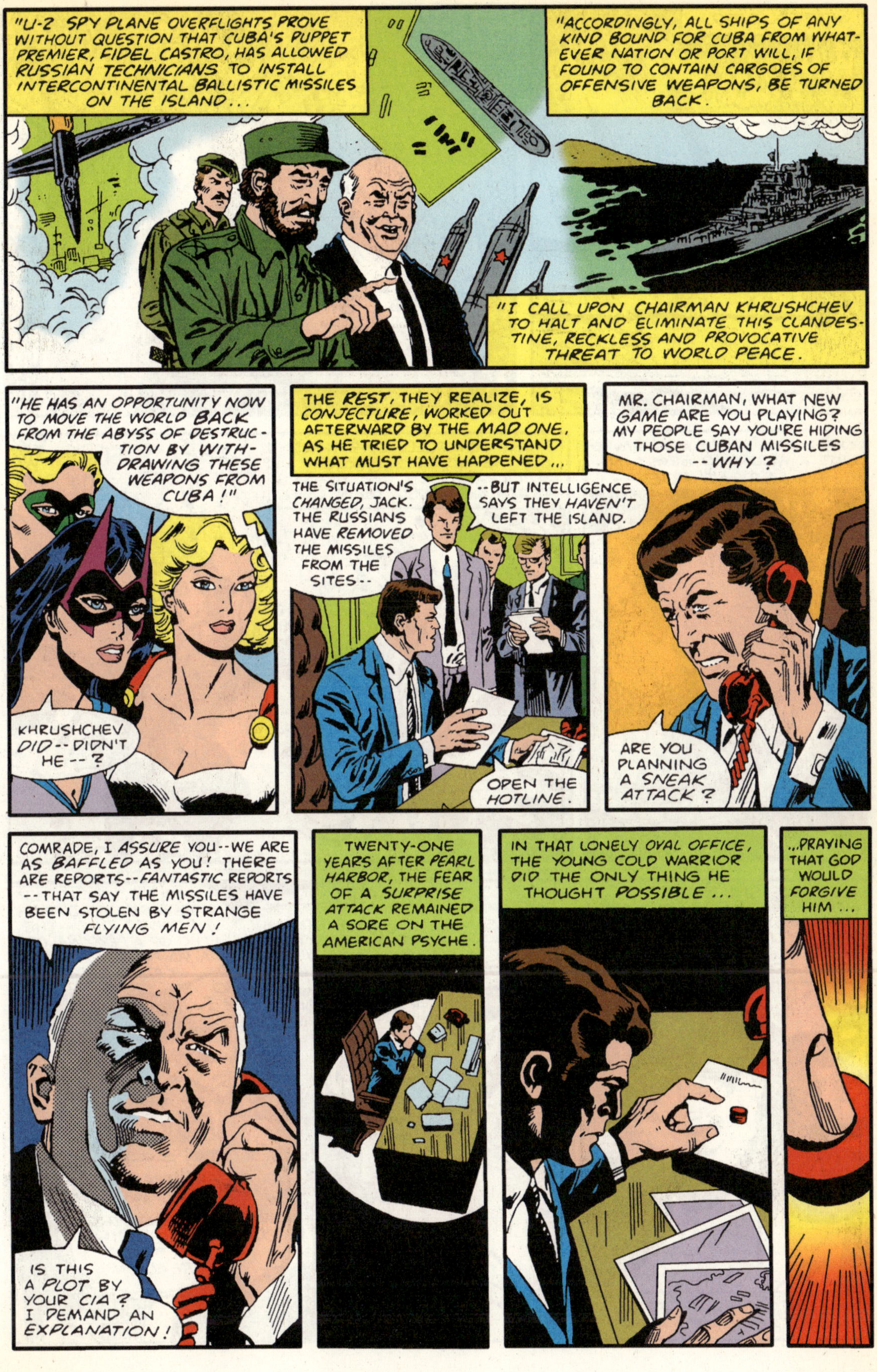
"U-2 SPY PLANE OVERFLIGHTS PROVE WITHOUT QUESTION THAT CUBA'S PUPPET PREMIER, FIDEL CASTRO, HAS ALLOWED RUSSIAN TECHNICIANS TO INSTALL INTERCONTINENTAL BALLISTIC MISSILES ON THE ISLAND...
"ACCORDINGLY, ALL SHIPS OF ANY KIND BOUND FOR CUBA FROM WHATEVER NATION OR PORT WILL, IF FOUND TO CONTAIN CARGOES OF OFFENSIVE WEAPONS, BE TURNED BACK.
"I CALL UPON CHAIRMAN KHRUSHCHEV TO HALT AND ELIMINATE THIS CLANDESTINE, RECKLESS AND PROVOCATIVE THREAT TO WORLD PEACE.
"HE HAS AN OPPORTUNITY NOW TO MOVE THE WORLD BACK FROM THE ABYSS OF DESTRUCTION BY WITHDRAWING THESE WEAPONS FROM CUBA!"
KHRUSHCHEV DID--DIDN'T HE--?
THE REST, THEY REALIZE, IS CONJECTURE, WORKED OUT AFTERWARD BY THE MAD ONE, AS HE TRIED TO UNDERSTAND WHAT MUST HAVE HAPPENED...
THE SITUATION'S CHANGED, JACK. THE RUSSIANS HAVE REMOVED THE MISSILES FROM THE SITES--
--BUT INTELLIGENCE SAYS THEY HAVEN'T LEFT THE ISLAND.
OPEN THE HOTLINE.
MR. CHAIRMAN, WHAT NEW GAME ARE YOU PLAYING? MY PEOPLE SAY YOU'RE HIDING THOSE CUBAN MISSILES --WHY?
ARE YOU PLANNING A SNEAK ATTACK?
COMRADE, I ASSURE YOU--WE ARE AS BAFFLED AS YOU! THERE ARE REPORTS--FANTASTIC REPORTS--THAT SAY THE MISSILES HAVE BEEN STOLEN BY STRANGE FLYING MEN!
IS THIS A PLOT BY YOUR CIA? I DEMAND AN EXPLANATION!
TWENTY-ONE YEARS AFTER PEARL HARBOR, THE FEAR OF A SURPRISE ATTACK REMAINED A SORE ON THE AMERICAN PSYCHE.
IN THAT LONELY OVAL OFFICE, THE YOUNG COLD WARRIOR DID THE ONLY THING HE THOUGHT POSSIBLE...
...PRAYING THAT GOD WOULD FORGIVE HIM...

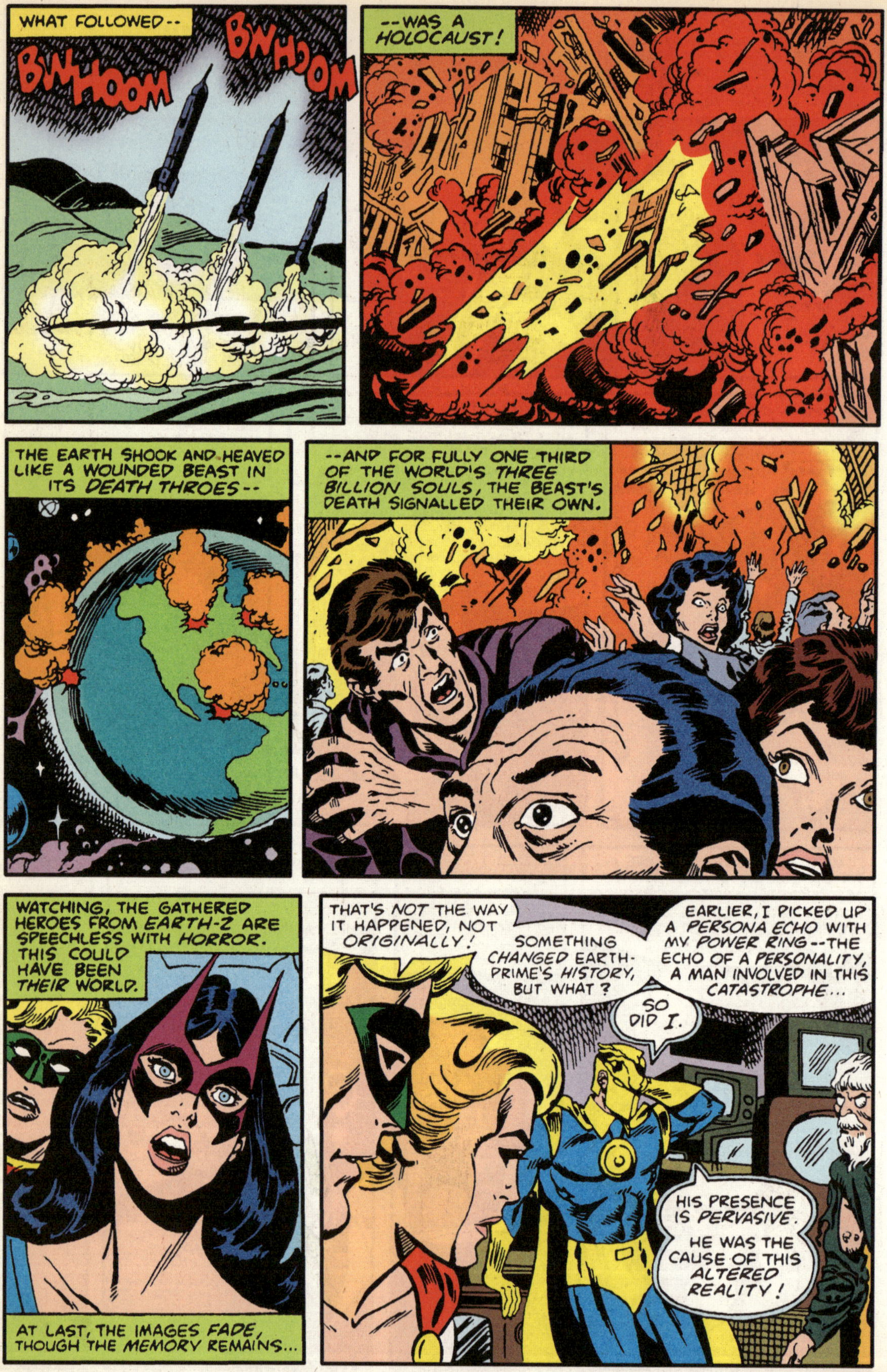
WHAT FOLLOWED--
BWHOOM
BWHOOM
--WAS A HOLOCAUST!
THE EARTH SHOOK AND HEAVED LIKE A WOUNDED BEAST IN ITS DEATH THROES--
--AND FOR FULLY ONE THIRD OF THE WORLD'S THREE BILLION SOULS, THE BEAST'S DEATH SIGNALLED THEIR OWN.
WATCHING, THE GATHERED HEROES FROM EARTH-2 ARE SPEECHLESS WITH HORROR. THIS COULD HAVE BEEN THEIR WORLD.
AT LAST, THE IMAGES FADE, THOUGH THE MEMORY REMAINS...
THAT'S NOT THE WAY IT HAPPENED, NOT ORIGINALLY!
SOMETHING CHANGED EARTH-PRIME'S HISTORY, BUT WHAT?
EARLIER, I PICKED UP A PERSONA ECHO WITH MY POWER RING--THE ECHO OF A PERSONALITY, A MAN INVOLVED IN THIS CATASTROPHE...
SO DID I.
HIS PRESENCE IS PERVASIVE.
HE WAS THE CAUSE OF THIS ALTERED REALITY!

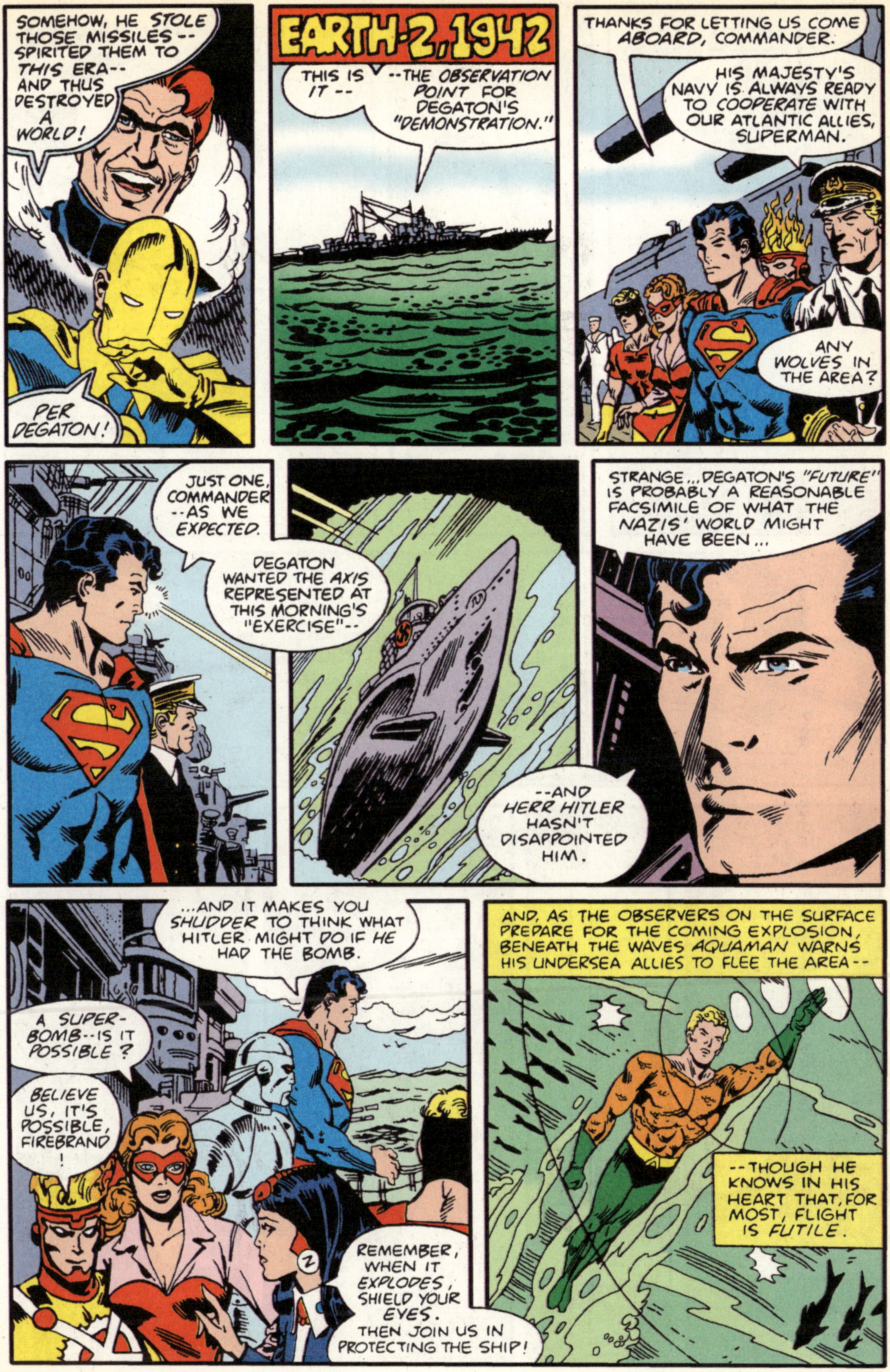
SOMEHOW, HE STOLE THOSE MISSILES -- SPIRITED THEM TO THIS ERA -- AND THUS DESTROYED A WORLD!
PER DEGATON!
EARTH-2, 1942
THIS IS IT --
--THE OBSERVATION POINT FOR DEGATON'S "DEMONSTRATION."
THANKS FOR LETTING US COME ABOARD, COMMANDER.
HIS MAJESTY'S NAVY IS ALWAYS READY TO COOPERATE WITH OUR ATLANTIC ALLIES, SUPERMAN.
ANY WOLVES IN THE AREA?
JUST ONE, COMMANDER --AS WE EXPECTED.
DEGATON WANTED THE AXIS REPRESENTED AT THIS MORNING'S "EXERCISE"--
--AND HERR HITLER HASN'T DISAPPOINTED HIM.
STRANGE... DEGATON'S "FUTURE" IS PROBABLY A REASONABLE FACSIMILE OF WHAT THE NAZIS' WORLD MIGHT HAVE BEEN...
...AND IT MAKES YOU SHUDDER TO THINK WHAT HITLER MIGHT DO IF HE HAD THE BOMB.
A SUPER-BOMB--IS IT POSSIBLE?
BELIEVE US, IT'S POSSIBLE, FIREBRAND!
REMEMBER, WHEN IT EXPLODES, SHIELD YOUR EYES. THEN JOIN US IN PROTECTING THE SHIP!
AND, AS THE OBSERVERS ON THE SURFACE PREPARE FOR THE COMING EXPLOSION, BENEATH THE WAVES AQUAMAN WARNS HIS UNDERSEA ALLIES TO FLEE THE AREA--
--THOUGH HE KNOWS IN HIS HEART THAT, FOR MOST, FLIGHT IS FUTILE.

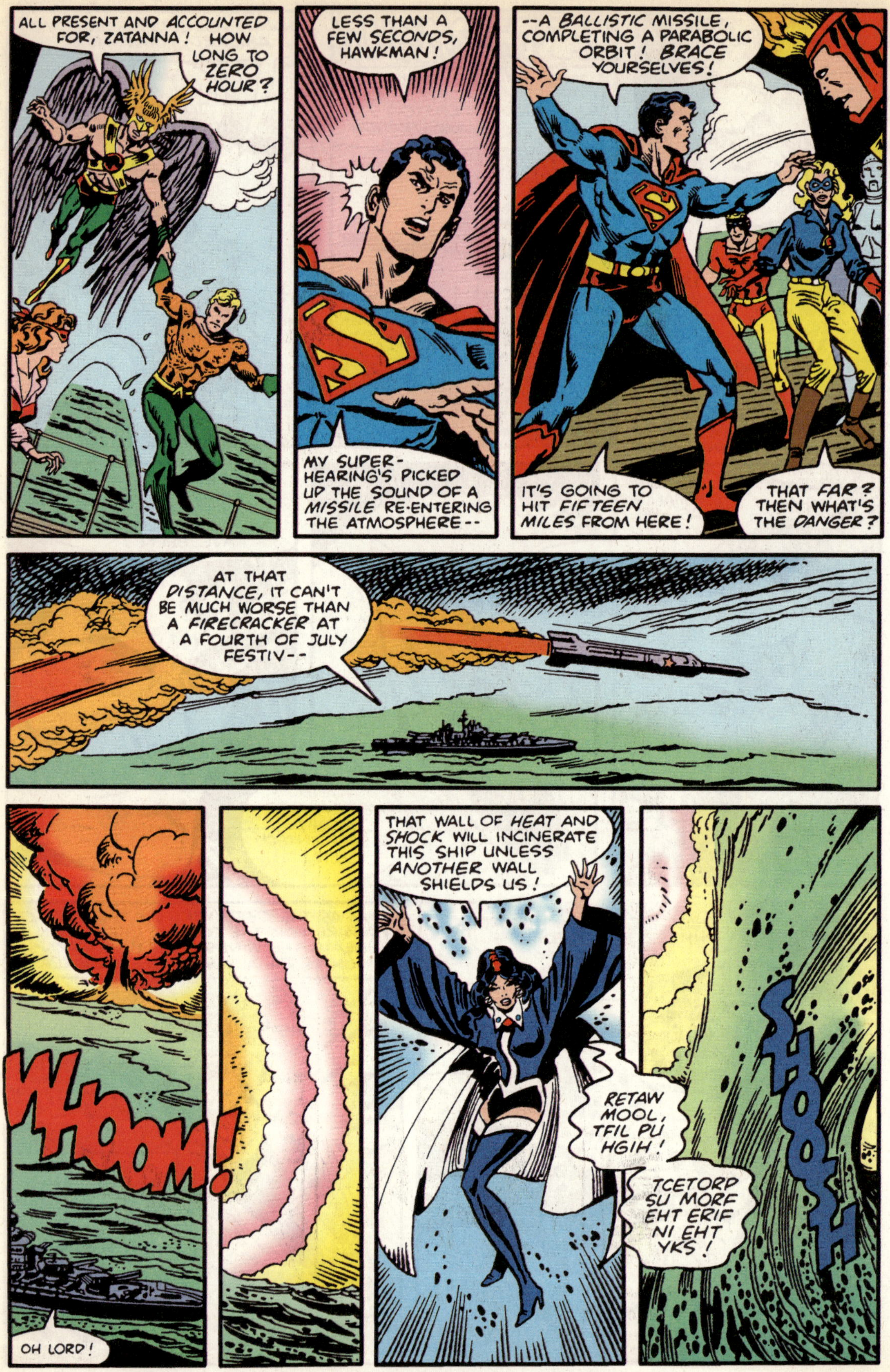
ALL PRESENT AND ACCOUNTED FOR, ZATANNA! HOW LONG TO ZERO HOUR?
LESS THAN A FEW SECONDS, HAWKMAN!
MY SUPER-HEARING'S PICKED UP THE SOUND OF A MISSILE RE-ENTERING THE ATMOSPHERE--
--A BALLISTIC MISSILE, COMPLETING A PARABOLIC ORBIT! BRACE YOURSELVES!
IT'S GOING TO HIT FIFTEEN MILES FROM HERE!
THAT FAR? THEN WHAT'S THE DANGER?
AT THAT DISTANCE, IT CAN'T BE MUCH WORSE THAN A FIRECRACKER AT A FOURTH OF JULY FESTIV--
WHOOM!
OH LORD!
THAT WALL OF HEAT AND SHOCK WILL INCINERATE THIS SHIP UNLESS ANOTHER WALL SHIELDS US!
RETAW MOOL, TFIL PU HGIH!
TCETORP SU MORF EHT ERIF NI EHT YKS!
SHOOSH

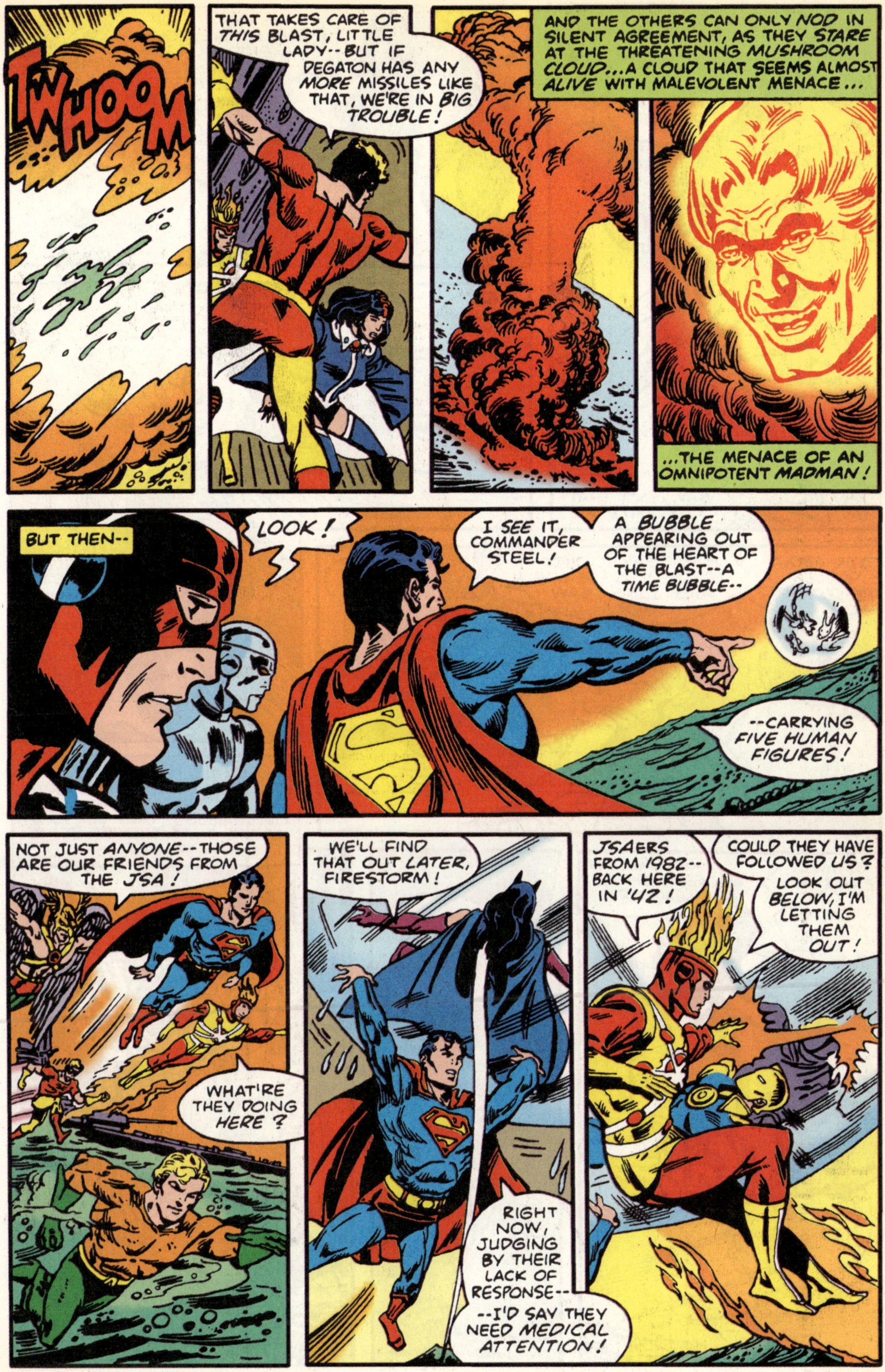
TWHOOM
THAT TAKES CARE OF THIS BLAST, LITTLE LADY-- BUT IF DEGATON HAS ANY MORE MISSILES LIKE THAT, WE'RE IN BIG TROUBLE!
AND THE OTHERS CAN ONLY NOD IN SILENT AGREEMENT, AS THEY STARE AT THE THREATENING MUSHROOM CLOUD... A CLOUD THAT SEEMS ALMOST ALIVE WITH MALEVOLENT MENACE...
...THE MENACE OF AN OMNIPOTENT MADMAN!
BUT THEN--
LOOK!
I SEE IT, COMMANDER STEEL!
A BUBBLE APPEARING OUT OF THE HEART OF THE BLAST--A TIME BUBBLE--
--CARRYING FIVE HUMAN FIGURES!
NOT JUST ANYONE--THOSE ARE OUR FRIENDS FROM THE JSA!
WHAT'RE THEY DOING HERE?
WE'LL FIND THAT OUT LATER, FIRESTORM!
RIGHT NOW, JUDGING BY THEIR LACK OF RESPONSE--
--I'D SAY THEY NEED MEDICAL ATTENTION!
JSAERS FROM 1982-- BACK HERE IN '42!
COULD THEY HAVE FOLLOWED US?
LOOK OUT BELOW, I'M LETTING THEM OUT!

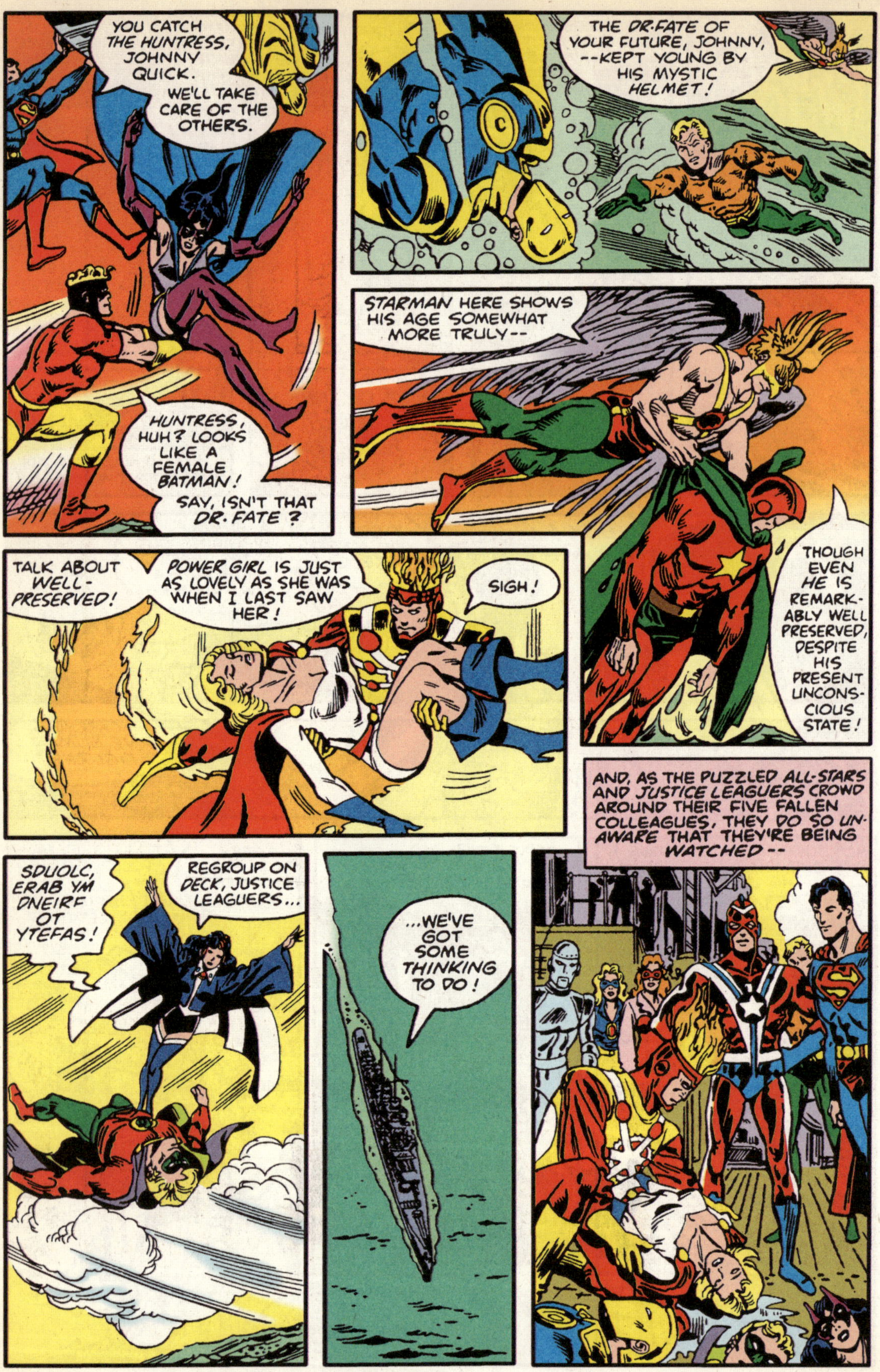

YOU CATCH THE HUNTRESS, JOHNNY QUICK.
WE'LL TAKE CARE OF THE OTHERS.
HUNTRESS, HUH? LOOKS LIKE A FEMALE BATMAN!
SAY, ISN'T THAT DR. FATE?
THE DR. FATE OF YOUR FUTURE, JOHNNY, --KEPT YOUNG BY HIS MYSTIC HELMET!
STARMAN HERE SHOWS HIS AGE SOMEWHAT MORE TRULY--
THOUGH EVEN HE IS REMARKABLY WELL PRESERVED, DESPITE HIS PRESENT UNCONSCIOUS STATE!
TALK ABOUT WELL-PRESERVED!
POWER GIRL IS JUST AS LOVELY AS SHE WAS WHEN I LAST SAW HER!
SIGH!
SDUOLC, ERAB YM DNEIRF OT YTEFAS!
REGROUP ON DECK, JUSTICE LEAGUERS...
...WE'VE GOT SOME THINKING TO DO!
AND, AS THE PUZZLED ALL-STARS AND JUSTICE LEAGUERS CROWD AROUND THEIR FIVE FALLEN COLLEAGUES, THEY DO SO UNAWARE THAT THEY'RE BEING WATCHED--

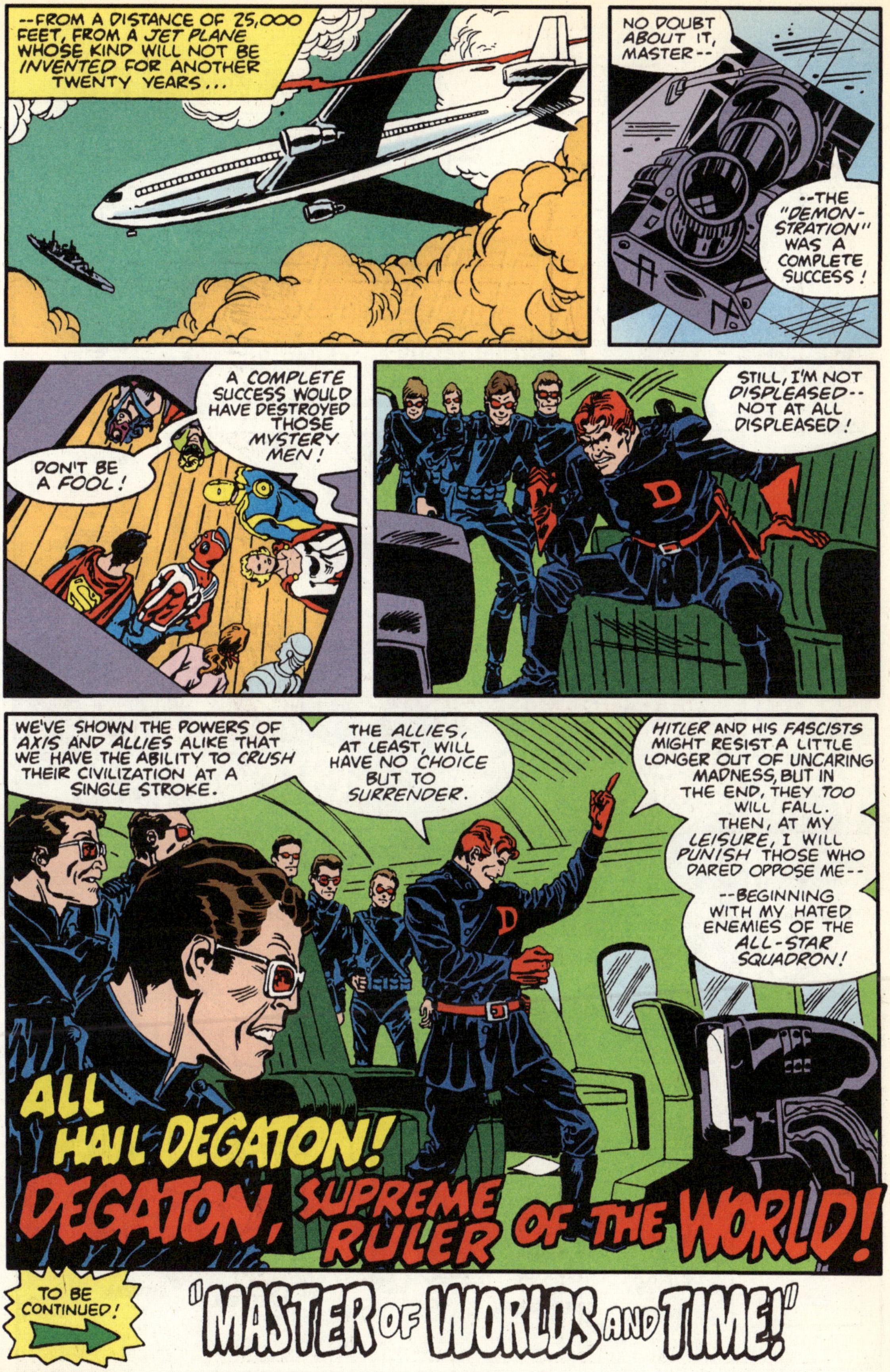
--FROM A DISTANCE OF 25,000 FEET, FROM A JET PLANE WHOSE KIND WILL NOT BE INVENTED FOR ANOTHER TWENTY YEARS...
NO DOUBT ABOUT IT, MASTER--
--THE "DEMON-STRATION" WAS A COMPLETE SUCCESS!
A COMPLETE SUCCESS WOULD HAVE DESTROYED THOSE MYSTERY MEN!
DON'T BE A FOOL!
STILL, I'M NOT DISPLEASED--NOT AT ALL DISPLEASED!
WE'VE SHOWN THE POWERS OF AXIS AND ALLIES ALIKE THAT WE HAVE THE ABILITY TO CRUSH THEIR CIVILIZATION AT A SINGLE STROKE.
THE ALLIES, AT LEAST, WILL HAVE NO CHOICE BUT TO SURRENDER.
HITLER AND HIS FASCISTS MIGHT RESIST A LITTLE LONGER OUT OF UNCARING MADNESS, BUT IN THE END, THEY TOO WILL FALL. THEN, AT MY LEISURE, I WILL PUNISH THOSE WHO DARED OPPOSE ME--
--BEGINNING WITH MY HATED ENEMIES OF THE ALL-STAR SQUADRON!
ALL HAIL DEGATON!
DEGATON, SUPREME RULER OF THE WORLD!
TO BE CONTINUED!
"MASTER OF WORLDS AND TIME!"

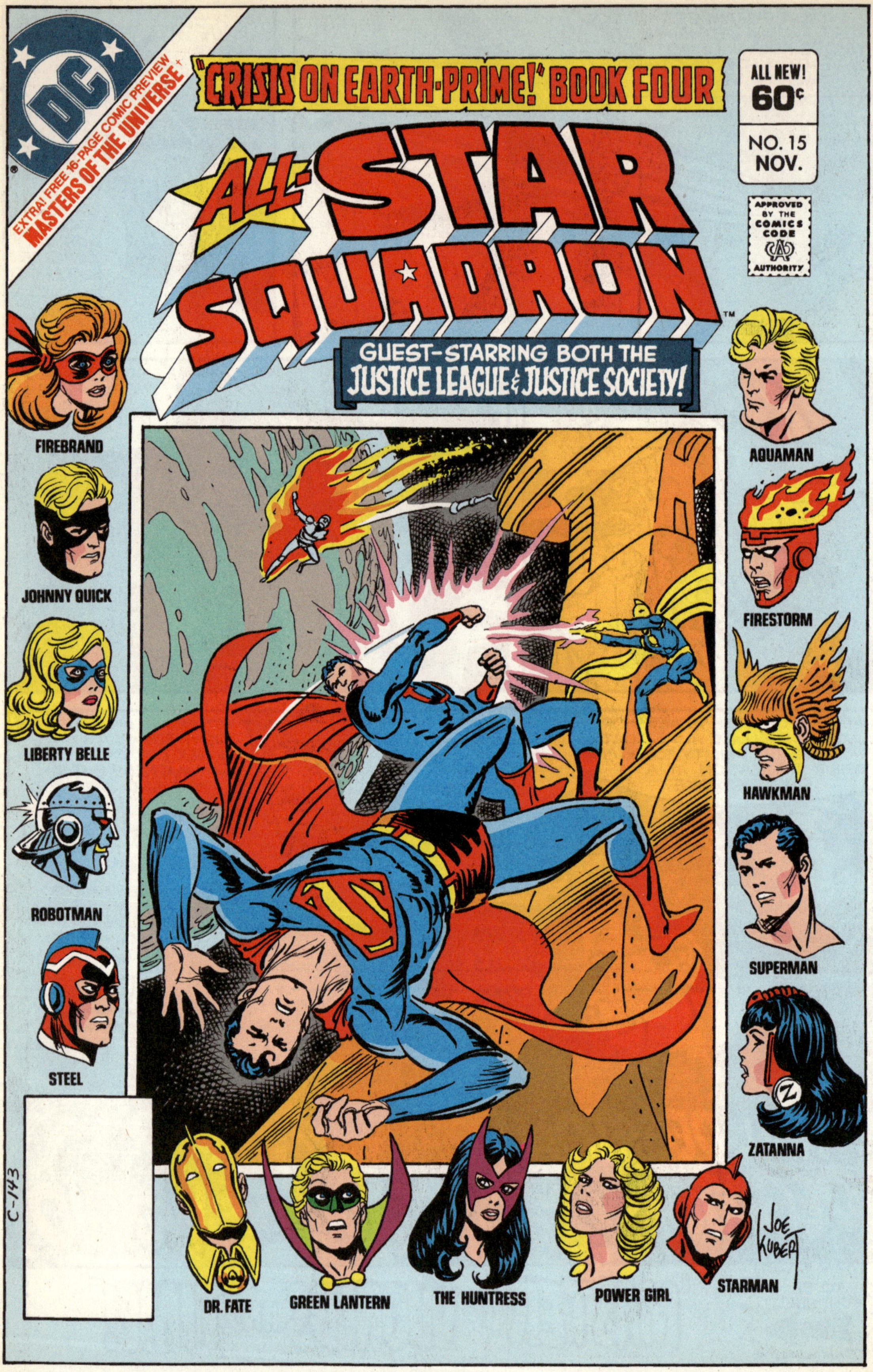

DC
EXTRA! FREE 16-PAGE COMIC PREVIEW
MASTERS OF THE UNIVERSE
"CRISIS ON EARTH-PRIME!" BOOK FOUR
ALL NEW! 60¢
NO. 15 NOV.
APPROVED BY THE COMICS CODE AUTHORITY
ALL-STAR SQUADRON
GUEST-STARRING BOTH THE JUSTICE LEAGUE & JUSTICE SOCIETY!
FIREBRAND
JOHNNY QUICK
LIBERTY BELLE
ROBOTMAN
STEEL
AQUAMAN
FIRESTORM
HAWKMAN
SUPERMAN
ZATANNA
DR. FATE
GREEN LANTERN
THE HUNTRESS
POWER GIRL
STARMAN
JOE KUBERT
C-143

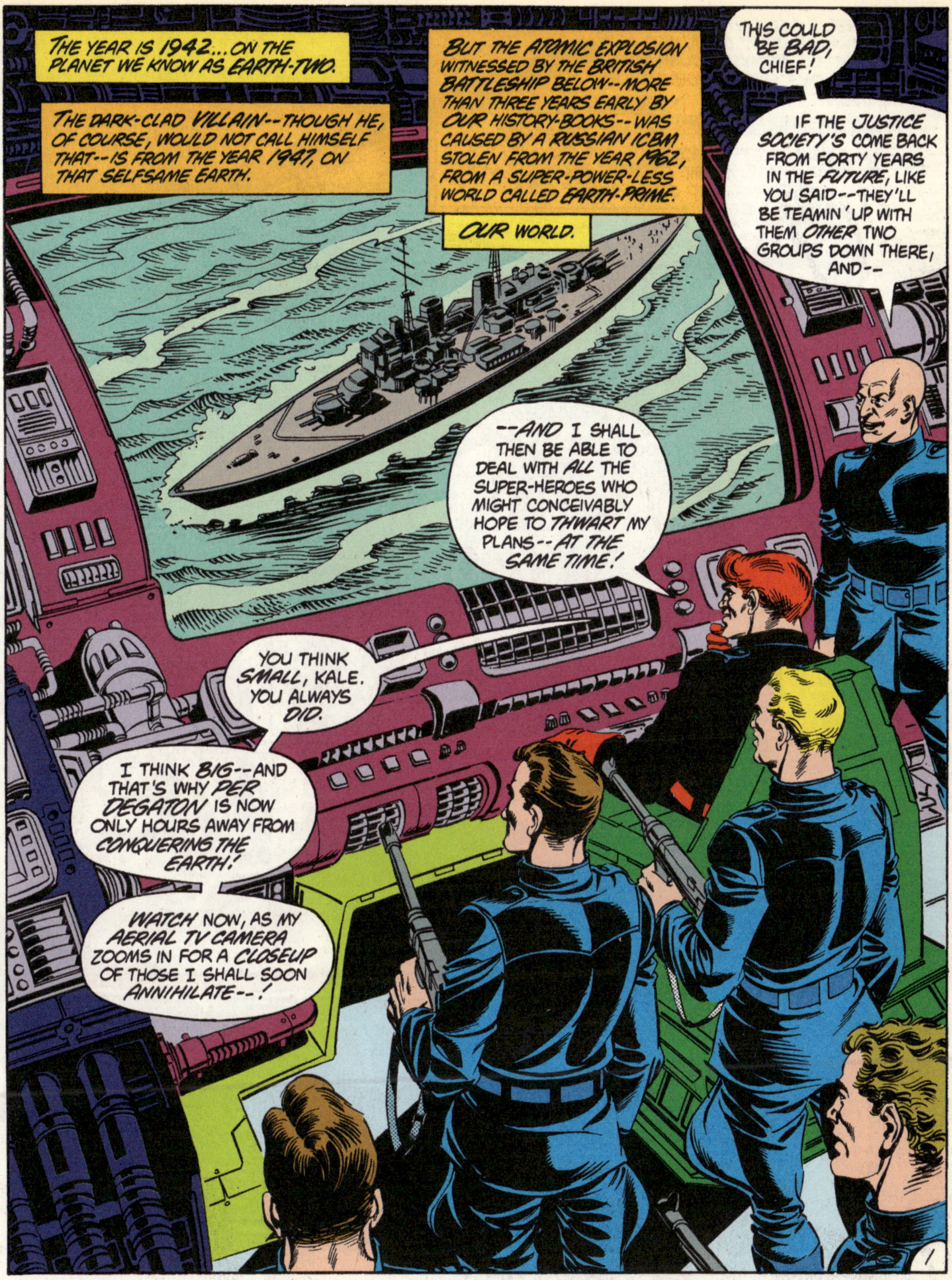

THE YEAR IS 1942...ON THE PLANET WE KNOW AS EARTH-TWO.
THE DARK-CLAD VILLAIN--THOUGH HE, OF COURSE, WOULD NOT CALL HIMSELF THAT--IS FROM THE YEAR 1947, ON THAT SELFSAME EARTH.
BUT THE ATOMIC EXPLOSION WITNESSED BY THE BRITISH BATTLESHIP BELOW--MORE THAN THREE YEARS EARLY BY OUR HISTORY-BOOKS--WAS CAUSED BY A RUSSIAN ICBM STOLEN FROM THE YEAR 1962, FROM A SUPER-POWER-LESS WORLD CALLED EARTH-PRIME.
OUR WORLD.
THIS COULD BE BAD, CHIEF!
IF THE JUSTICE SOCIETY'S COME BACK FROM FORTY YEARS IN THE FUTURE, LIKE YOU SAID--THEY'LL BE TEAMIN' UP WITH THEM OTHER TWO GROUPS DOWN THERE, AND--
--AND I SHALL THEN BE ABLE TO DEAL WITH ALL THE SUPER-HEROES WHO MIGHT CONCEIVABLY HOPE TO THWART MY PLANS--AT THE SAME TIME!
YOU THINK SMALL, KALE. YOU ALWAYS DID.
I THINK BIG--AND THAT'S WHY PER DEGATON IS NOW ONLY HOURS AWAY FROM CONQUERING THE EARTH!
WATCH NOW, AS MY AERIAL TV CAMERA ZOOMS IN FOR A CLOSEUP OF THOSE I SHALL SOON ANNIHILATE--!
1

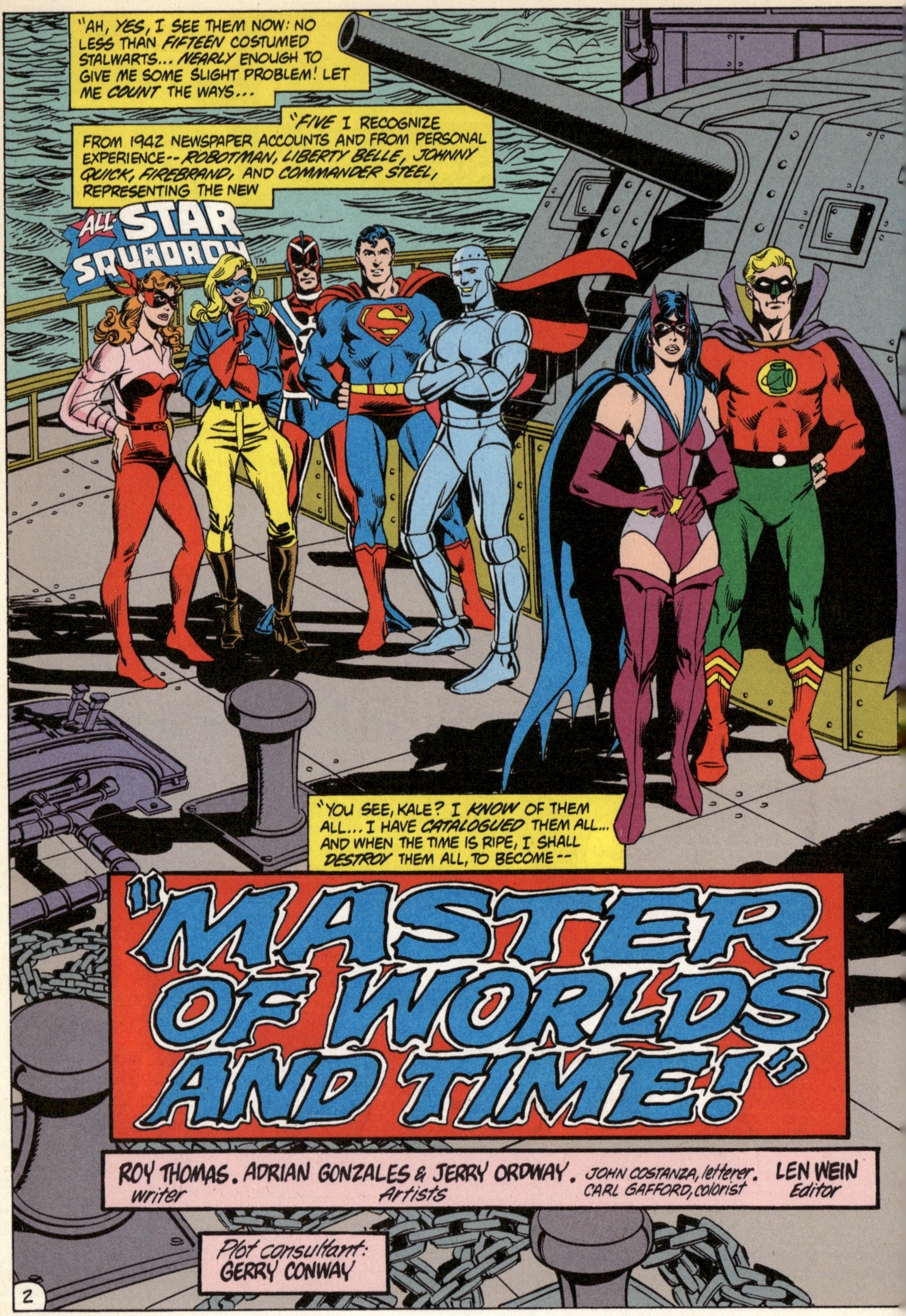
"AH, YES, I SEE THEM NOW: NO LESS THAN FIFTEEN COSTUMED STALWARTS... NEARLY ENOUGH TO GIVE ME SOME SLIGHT PROBLEM! LET ME COUNT THE WAYS...
"FIVE I RECOGNIZE FROM 1942 NEWSPAPER ACCOUNTS AND FROM PERSONAL EXPERIENCE--ROBOTMAN, LIBERTY BELLE, JOHNNY QUICK, FIREBRAND, AND COMMANDER STEEL, REPRESENTING THE NEW
ALL-STAR SQUADRON TM
"YOU SEE, KALE? I KNOW OF THEM ALL... I HAVE CATALOGUED THEM ALL... AND WHEN THE TIME IS RIPE, I SHALL DESTROY THEM ALL, TO BECOME--
"MASTER OF WORLDS AND TIME!"
ROY THOMAS. writer ADRIAN GONZALES & JERRY ORDWAY. Artists JOHN COSTANZA, letterer. CARL GAFFORD, colorist LEN WEIN Editor
Plot consultant: GERRY CONWAY
2

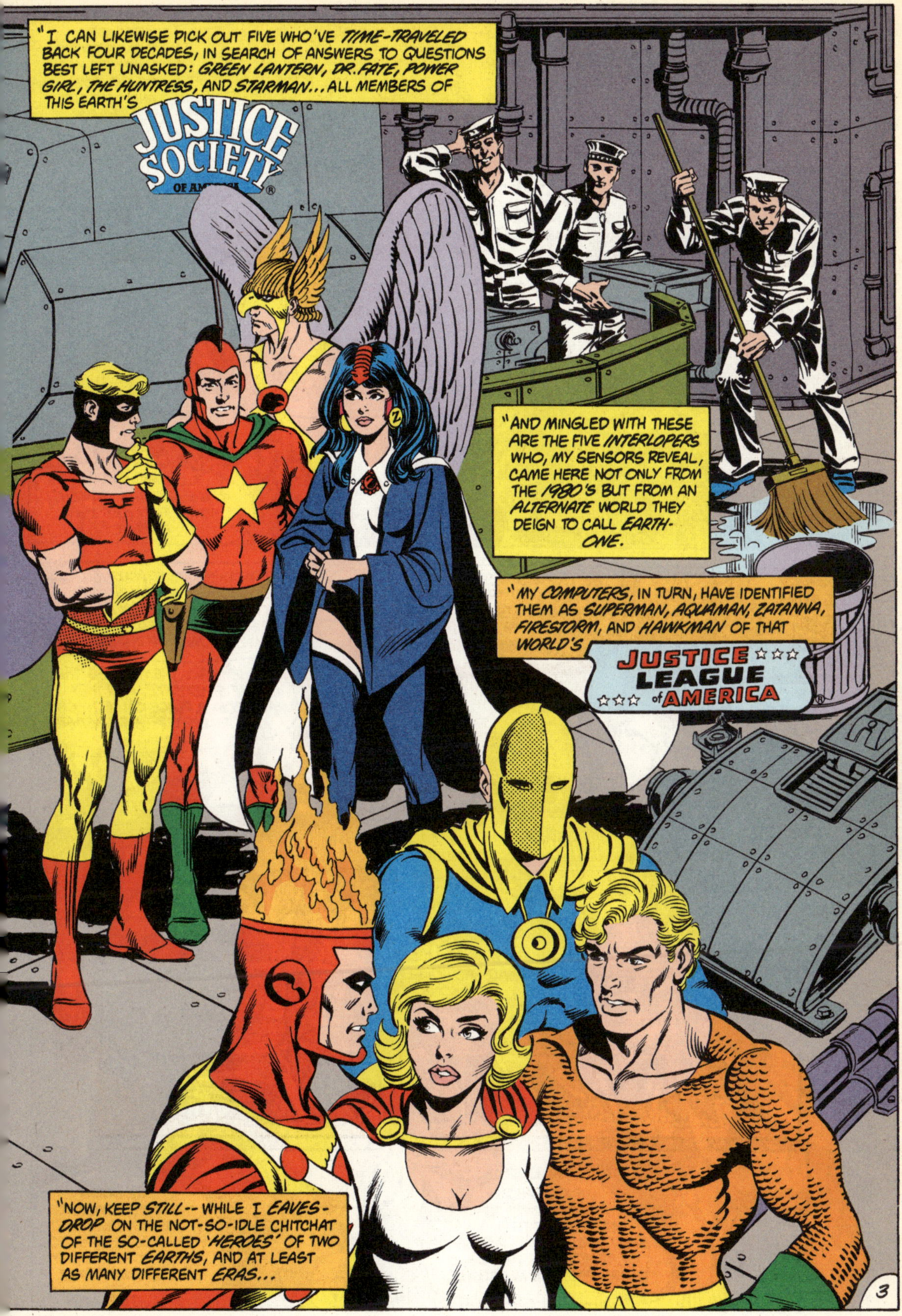
"I CAN LIKEWISE PICK OUT FIVE WHO'VE TIME-TRAVELED BACK FOUR DECADES, IN SEARCH OF ANSWERS TO QUESTIONS BEST LEFT UNASKED: GREEN LANTERN, DR. FATE, POWER GIRL, THE HUNTRESS, AND STARMAN... ALL MEMBERS OF THIS EARTH'S
JUSTICE SOCIETY
"AND MINGLED WITH THESE ARE THE FIVE INTERLOPERS WHO, MY SENSORS REVEAL, CAME HERE NOT ONLY FROM THE 1980'S BUT FROM AN ALTERNATE WORLD THEY DEIGN TO CALL EARTH-ONE.
"MY COMPUTERS, IN TURN, HAVE IDENTIFIED THEM AS SUPERMAN, AQUAMAN, ZATANNA, FIRESTORM, AND HAWKMAN OF THAT WORLD'S
JUSTICE LEAGUE of AMERICA
"NOW, KEEP STILL -- WHILE I EAVES-DROP ON THE NOT-SO-IDLE CHITCHAT OF THE SO-CALLED 'HEROES' OF TWO DIFFERENT EARTHS, AND AT LEAST AS MANY DIFFERENT ERAS...
3

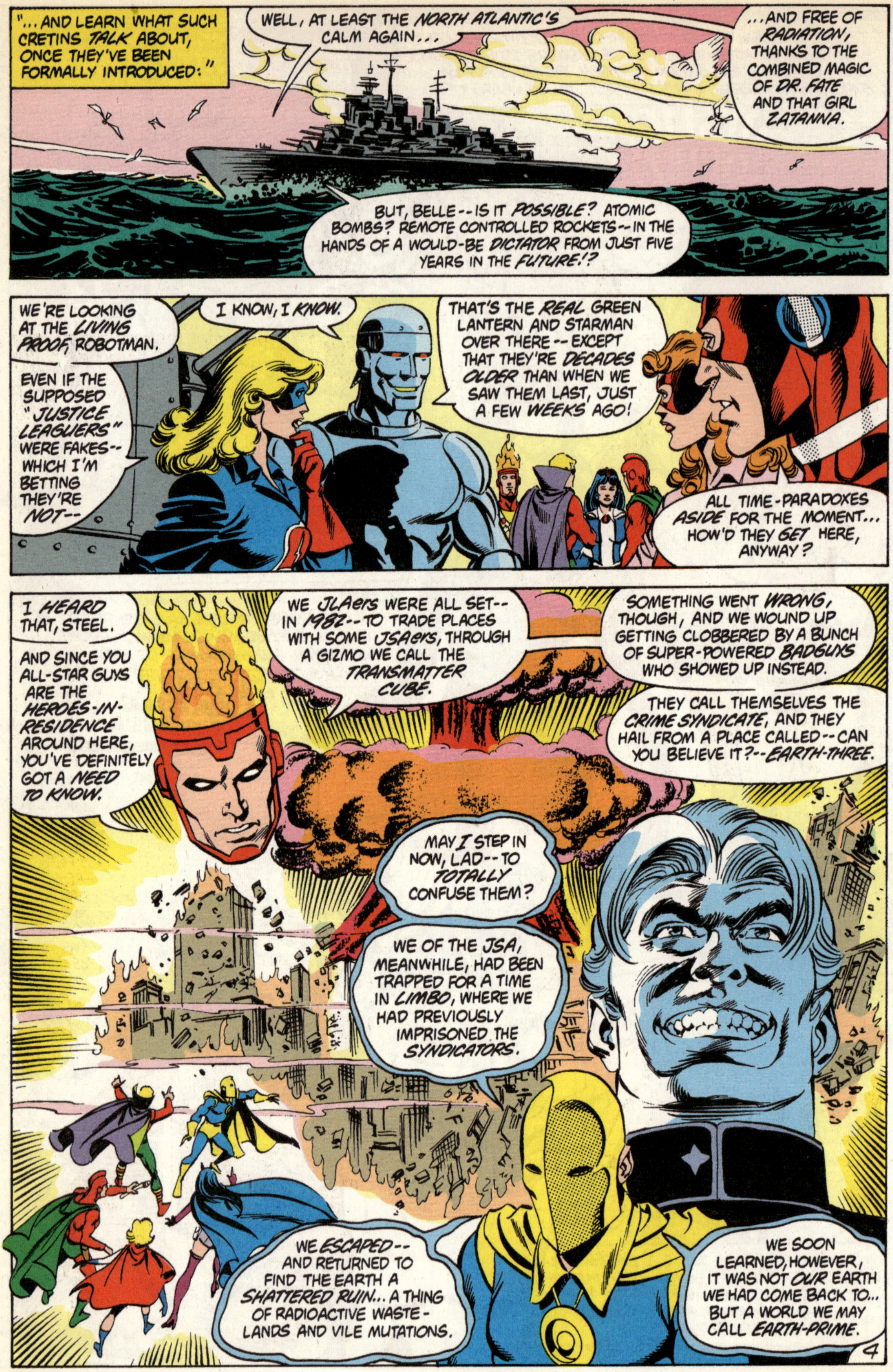

"...AND LEARN WHAT SUCH CRETINS TALK ABOUT, ONCE THEY'VE BEEN FORMALLY INTRODUCED:"
WELL, AT LEAST THE NORTH ATLANTIC'S CALM AGAIN...
...AND FREE OF RADIATION, THANKS TO THE COMBINED MAGIC OF DR. FATE AND THAT GIRL ZATANNA.
BUT, BELLE--IS IT POSSIBLE? ATOMIC BOMBS? REMOTE CONTROLLED ROCKETS--IN THE HANDS OF A WOULD-BE DICTATOR FROM JUST FIVE YEARS IN THE FUTURE!?
WE'RE LOOKING AT THE LIVING PROOF, ROBOTMAN.
EVEN IF THE SUPPOSED "JUSTICE LEAGUERS" WERE FAKES--WHICH I'M BETTING THEY'RE NOT--
I KNOW, I KNOW.
THAT'S THE REAL GREEN LANTERN AND STARMAN OVER THERE--EXCEPT THAT THEY'RE DECADES OLDER THAN WHEN WE SAW THEM LAST, JUST A FEW WEEKS AGO!
ALL TIME-PARADOXES ASIDE FOR THE MOMENT... HOW'D THEY GET HERE, ANYWAY?
I HEARD THAT, STEEL.
AND SINCE YOU ALL-STAR GUYS ARE THE HEROES-IN-RESIDENCE AROUND HERE, YOU'VE DEFINITELY GOT A NEED TO KNOW.
WE JLAers WERE ALL SET--IN 1982--TO TRADE PLACES WITH SOME JSAers, THROUGH A GIZMO WE CALL THE TRANSMATTER CUBE.
SOMETHING WENT WRONG, THOUGH, AND WE WOUND UP GETTING CLOBBERED BY A BUNCH OF SUPER-POWERED BADGUYS WHO SHOWED UP INSTEAD.
THEY CALL THEMSELVES THE CRIME SYNDICATE, AND THEY HAIL FROM A PLACE CALLED--CAN YOU BELIEVE IT?--EARTH-THREE.
MAY I STEP IN NOW, LAD--TO TOTALLY CONFUSE THEM?
WE OF THE JSA, MEANWHILE, HAD BEEN TRAPPED FOR A TIME IN LIMBO, WHERE WE HAD PREVIOUSLY IMPRISONED THE SYNDICATORS.
WE ESCAPED--AND RETURNED TO FIND THE EARTH A SHATTERED RUIN... A THING OF RADIOACTIVE WASTE-LANDS AND VILE MUTATIONS.
WE SOON LEARNED, HOWEVER, IT WAS NOT OUR EARTH WE HAD COME BACK TO... BUT A WORLD WE MAY CALL EARTH-PRIME.
4

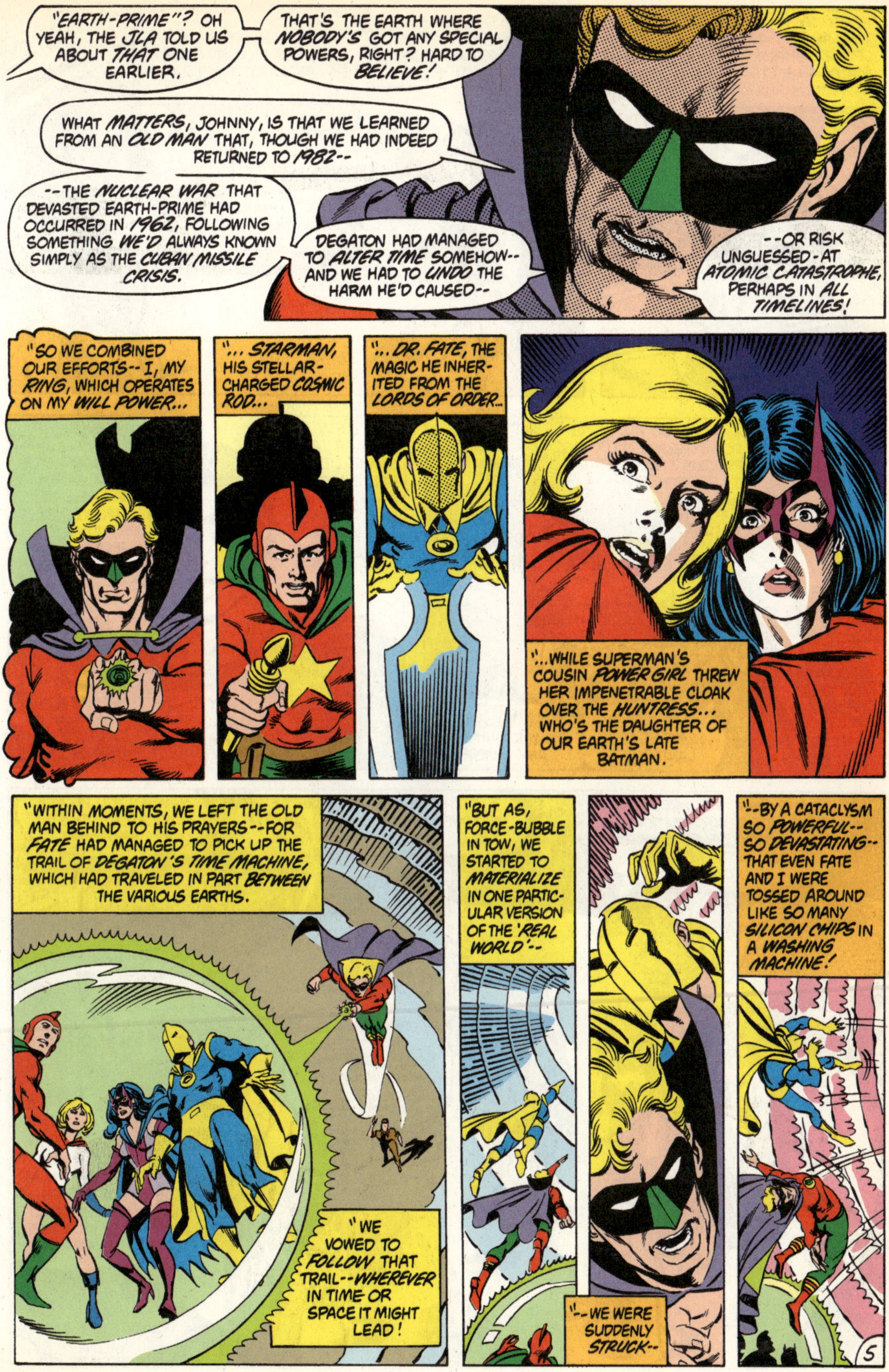

"EARTH-PRIME"? OH YEAH, THE JLA TOLD US ABOUT THAT ONE EARLIER.
THAT'S THE EARTH WHERE NOBODY'S GOT ANY SPECIAL POWERS, RIGHT? HARD TO BELIEVE!
WHAT MATTERS, JOHNNY, IS THAT WE LEARNED FROM AN OLD MAN THAT, THOUGH WE HAD INDEED RETURNED TO 1982--
--THE NUCLEAR WAR THAT DEVASTED EARTH-PRIME HAD OCCURRED IN 1962, FOLLOWING SOMETHING WE'D ALWAYS KNOWN SIMPLY AS THE CUBAN MISSILE CRISIS.
DEGATON HAD MANAGED TO ALTER TIME SOMEHOW-- AND WE HAD TO UNDO THE HARM HE'D CAUSED--
--OR RISK UNGUESSED-AT ATOMIC CATASTROPHE, PERHAPS IN ALL TIMELINES!
"SO WE COMBINED OUR EFFORTS-- I, MY RING, WHICH OPERATES ON MY WILL POWER...
"... STARMAN, HIS STELLAR-CHARGED COSMIC ROD...
"... DR. FATE, THE MAGIC HE INHERITED FROM THE LORDS OF ORDER...
"...WHILE SUPERMAN'S COUSIN POWER GIRL THREW HER IMPENETRABLE CLOAK OVER THE HUNTRESS... WHO'S THE DAUGHTER OF OUR EARTH'S LATE BATMAN.
"WITHIN MOMENTS, WE LEFT THE OLD MAN BEHIND TO HIS PRAYERS--FOR FATE HAD MANAGED TO PICK UP THE TRAIL OF DEGATON'S TIME MACHINE, WHICH HAD TRAVELED IN PART BETWEEN THE VARIOUS EARTHS.
"WE VOWED TO FOLLOW THAT TRAIL--WHEREVER IN TIME OR SPACE IT MIGHT LEAD!
"BUT AS, FORCE-BUBBLE IN TOW, WE STARTED TO MATERIALIZE IN ONE PARTICULAR VERSION OF THE 'REAL WORLD'--
"--WE WERE SUDDENLY STRUCK--
"--BY A CATACLYSM SO POWERFUL-- SO DEVASTATING-- THAT EVEN FATE AND I WERE TOSSED AROUND LIKE SO MANY SILICON CHIPS IN A WASHING MACHINE!
5

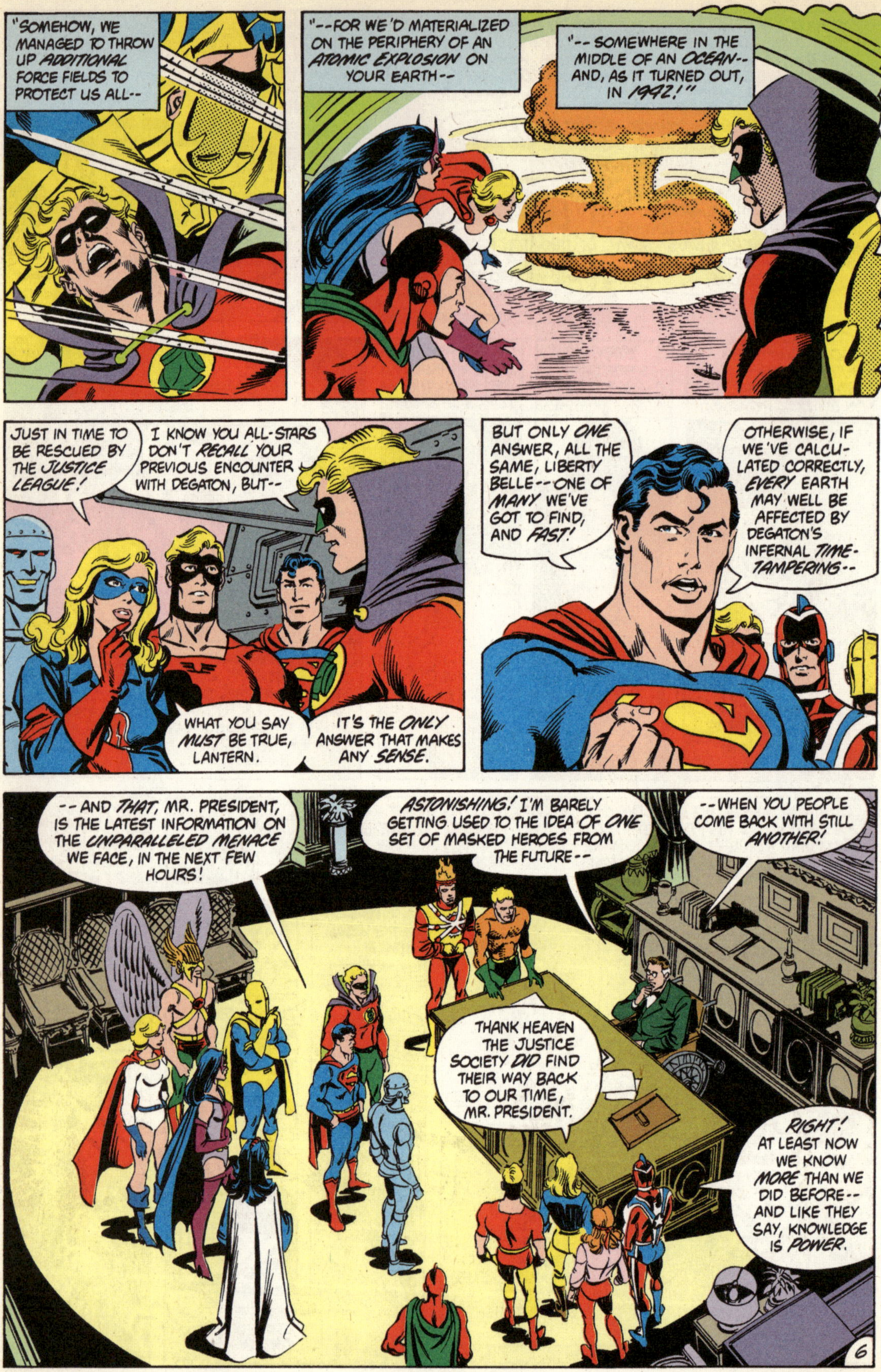
"SOMEHOW, WE MANAGED TO THROW UP ADDITIONAL FORCE FIELDS TO PROTECT US ALL--
"--FOR WE'D MATERIALIZED ON THE PERIPHERY OF AN ATOMIC EXPLOSION ON YOUR EARTH--
"--SOMEWHERE IN THE MIDDLE OF AN OCEAN--AND, AS IT TURNED OUT, IN 1942!"
JUST IN TIME TO BE RESCUED BY THE JUSTICE LEAGUE!
I KNOW YOU ALL-STARS DON'T RECALL YOUR PREVIOUS ENCOUNTER WITH DEGATON, BUT--
WHAT YOU SAY MUST BE TRUE, LANTERN.
IT'S THE ONLY ANSWER THAT MAKES ANY SENSE.
BUT ONLY ONE ANSWER, ALL THE SAME, LIBERTY BELLE--ONE OF MANY WE'VE GOT TO FIND, AND FAST!
OTHERWISE, IF WE'VE CALCULATED CORRECTLY, EVERY EARTH MAY WELL BE AFFECTED BY DEGATON'S INFERNAL TIME-TAMPERING--
--AND THAT, MR. PRESIDENT, IS THE LATEST INFORMATION ON THE UNPARALLELED MENACE WE FACE, IN THE NEXT FEW HOURS!
ASTONISHING! I'M BARELY GETTING USED TO THE IDEA OF ONE SET OF MASKED HEROES FROM THE FUTURE--
--WHEN YOU PEOPLE COME BACK WITH STILL ANOTHER!
THANK HEAVEN THE JUSTICE SOCIETY DID FIND THEIR WAY BACK TO OUR TIME, MR. PRESIDENT.
RIGHT! AT LEAST NOW WE KNOW MORE THAN WE DID BEFORE--AND LIKE THEY SAY, KNOWLEDGE IS POWER.
6

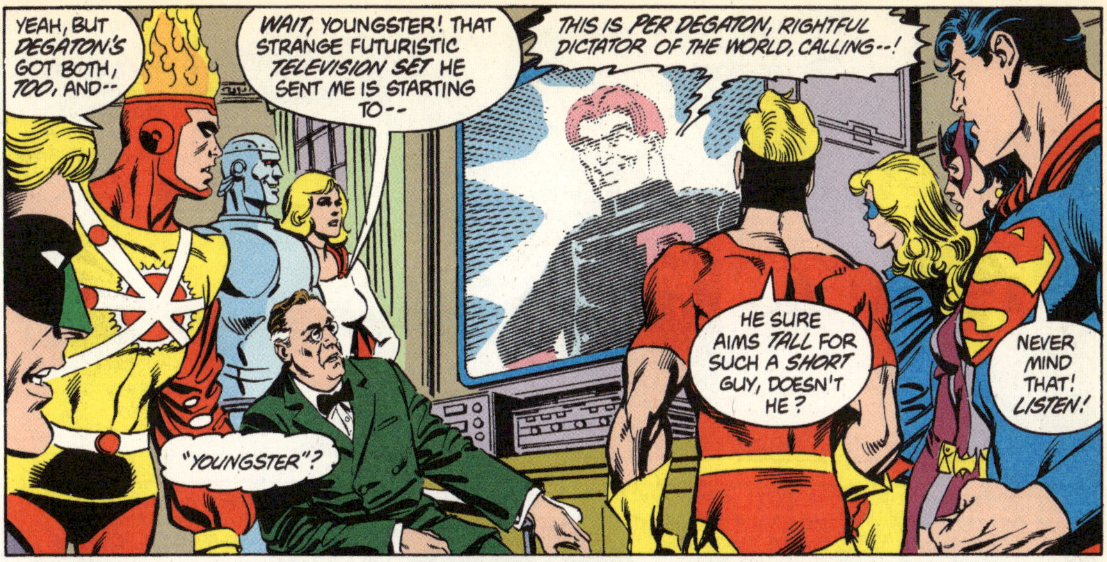
YEAH, BUT DEGATON'S GOT BOTH, TOO, AND--
WAIT, YOUNGSTER! THAT STRANGE FUTURISTIC TELEVISION SET HE SENT ME IS STARTING TO--
"YOUNGSTER"?
THIS IS PER DEGATON, RIGHTFUL DICTATOR OF THE WORLD, CALLING--!
HE SURE AIMS TALL FOR SUCH A SHORT GUY, DOESN'T HE?
NEVER MIND THAT! LISTEN!

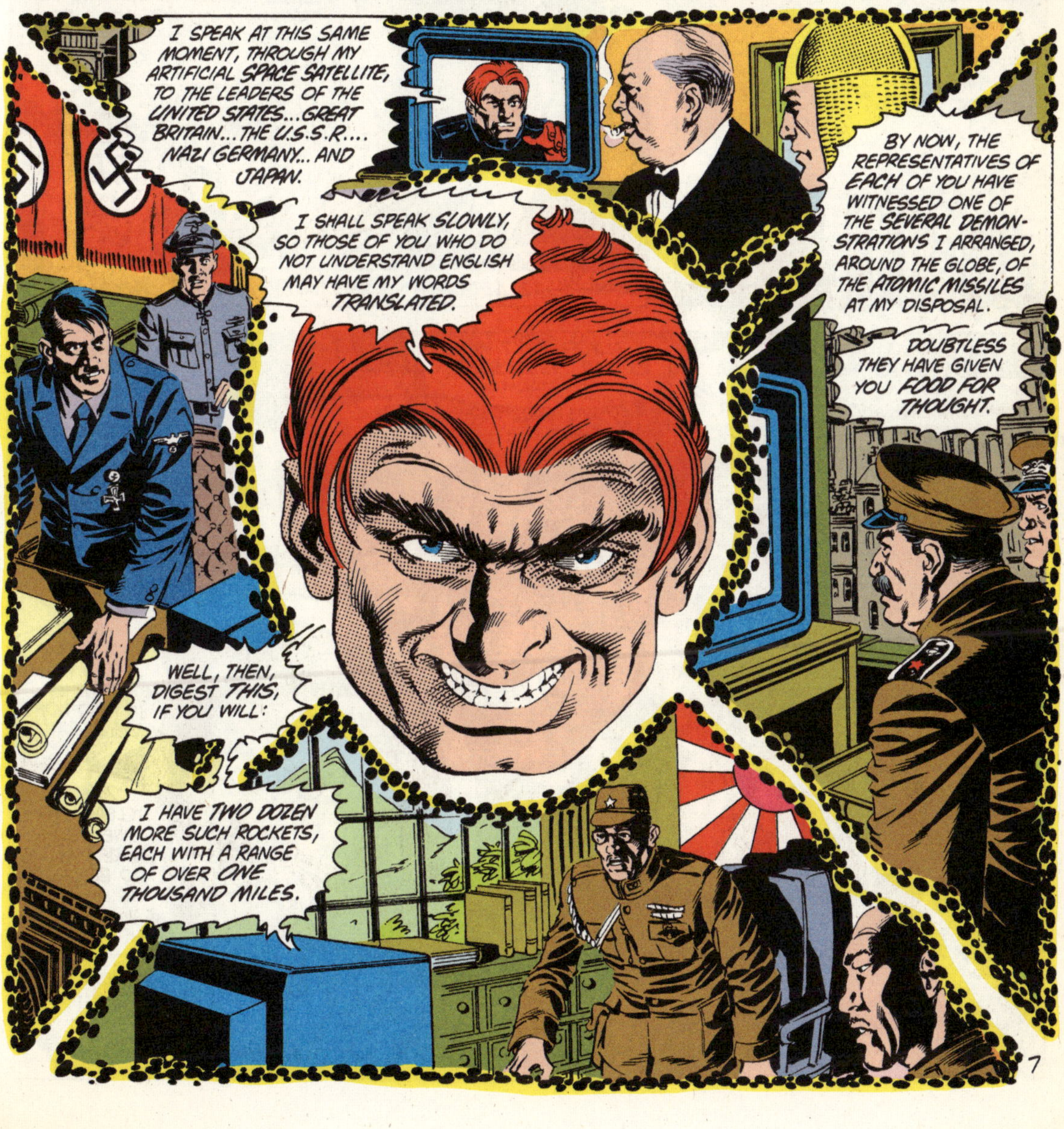
I SPEAK AT THIS SAME MOMENT, THROUGH MY ARTIFICIAL SPACE SATELLITE, TO THE LEADERS OF THE UNITED STATES...GREAT BRITAIN...THE U.S.S.R....NAZI GERMANY...AND JAPAN.
I SHALL SPEAK SLOWLY, SO THOSE OF YOU WHO DO NOT UNDERSTAND ENGLISH MAY HAVE MY WORDS TRANSLATED.
BY NOW, THE REPRESENTATIVES OF EACH OF YOU HAVE WITNESSED ONE OF THE SEVERAL DEMON-STRATIONS I ARRANGED, AROUND THE GLOBE, OF THE ATOMIC MISSILES AT MY DISPOSAL.
DOUBTLESS THEY HAVE GIVEN YOU FOOD FOR THOUGHT.
WELL, THEN, DIGEST THIS, IF YOU WILL:
I HAVE TWO DOZEN MORE SUCH ROCKETS, EACH WITH A RANGE OF OVER ONE THOUSAND MILES.
7

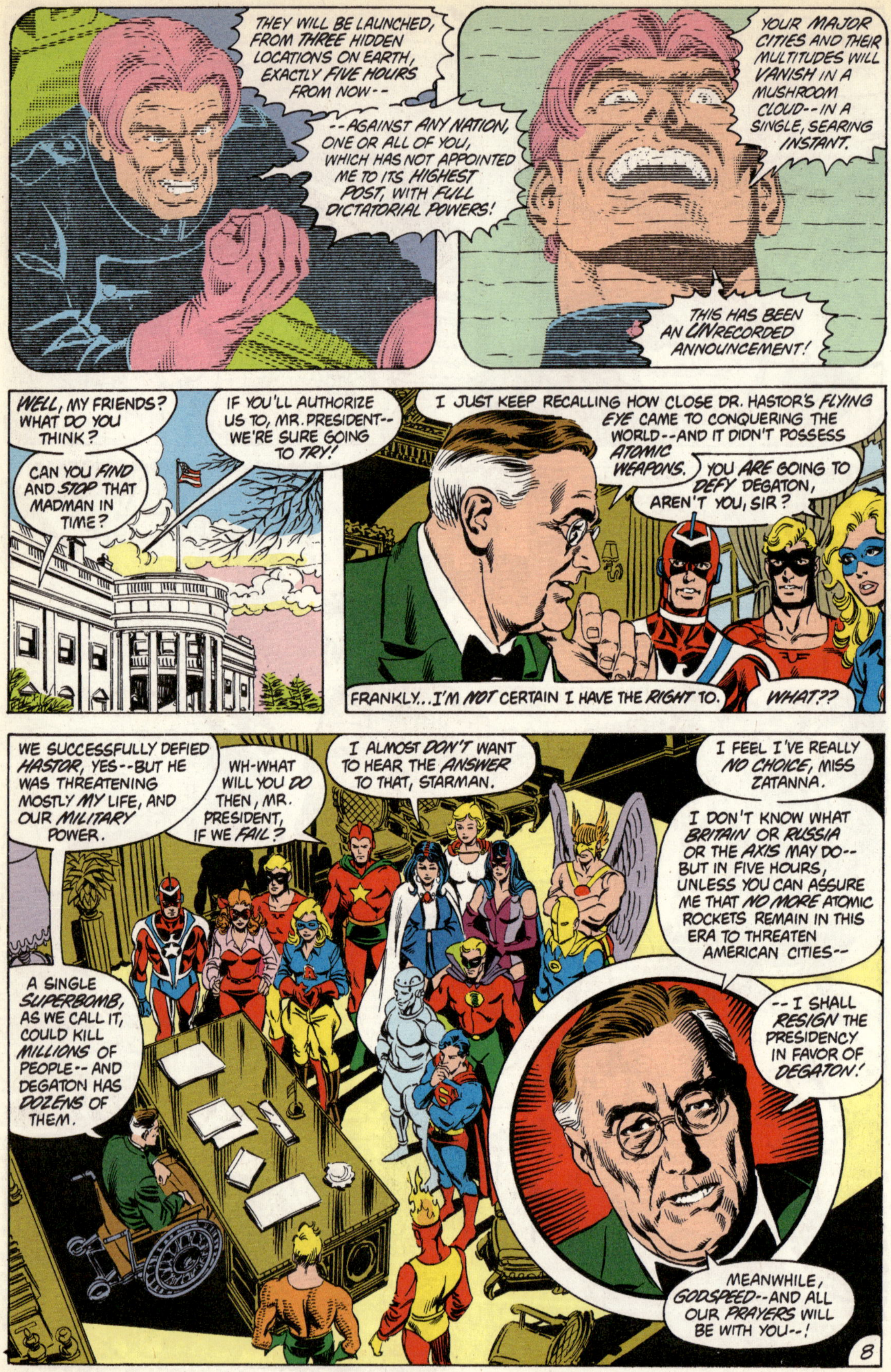

THEY WILL BE LAUNCHED, FROM THREE HIDDEN LOCATIONS ON EARTH, EXACTLY FIVE HOURS FROM NOW--
--AGAINST ANY NATION, ONE OR ALL OF YOU, WHICH HAS NOT APPOINTED ME TO ITS HIGHEST POST, WITH FULL DICTATORIAL POWERS!
YOUR MAJOR CITIES AND THEIR MULTITUDES WILL VANISH IN A MUSHROOM CLOUD--IN A SINGLE, SEARING INSTANT.
THIS HAS BEEN AN UNRECORDED ANNOUNCEMENT!
WELL, MY FRIENDS? WHAT DO YOU THINK?
CAN YOU FIND AND STOP THAT MADMAN IN TIME?
IF YOU'LL AUTHORIZE US TO, MR. PRESIDENT--WE'RE SURE GOING TO TRY!
I JUST KEEP RECALLING HOW CLOSE DR. HASTOR'S FLYING EYE CAME TO CONQUERING THE WORLD--AND IT DIDN'T POSSESS ATOMIC WEAPONS.
YOU ARE GOING TO DEFY DEGATON, AREN'T YOU, SIR?
FRANKLY...I'M NOT CERTAIN I HAVE THE RIGHT TO.
WHAT??
WE SUCCESSFULLY DEFIED HASTOR, YES--BUT HE WAS THREATENING MOSTLY MY LIFE, AND OUR MILITARY POWER.
WH-WHAT WILL YOU DO THEN, MR. PRESIDENT, IF WE FAIL?
I ALMOST DON'T WANT TO HEAR THE ANSWER TO THAT, STARMAN.
I FEEL I'VE REALLY NO CHOICE, MISS ZATANNA.
I DON'T KNOW WHAT BRITAIN OR RUSSIA OR THE AXIS MAY DO--BUT IN FIVE HOURS, UNLESS YOU CAN ASSURE ME THAT NO MORE ATOMIC ROCKETS REMAIN IN THIS ERA TO THREATEN AMERICAN CITIES--
A SINGLE SUPERBOMB, AS WE CALL IT, COULD KILL MILLIONS OF PEOPLE--AND DEGATON HAS DOZENS OF THEM.
--I SHALL RESIGN THE PRESIDENCY IN FAVOR OF DEGATON!
MEANWHILE, GODSPEED--AND ALL OUR PRAYERS WILL BE WITH YOU--!
8

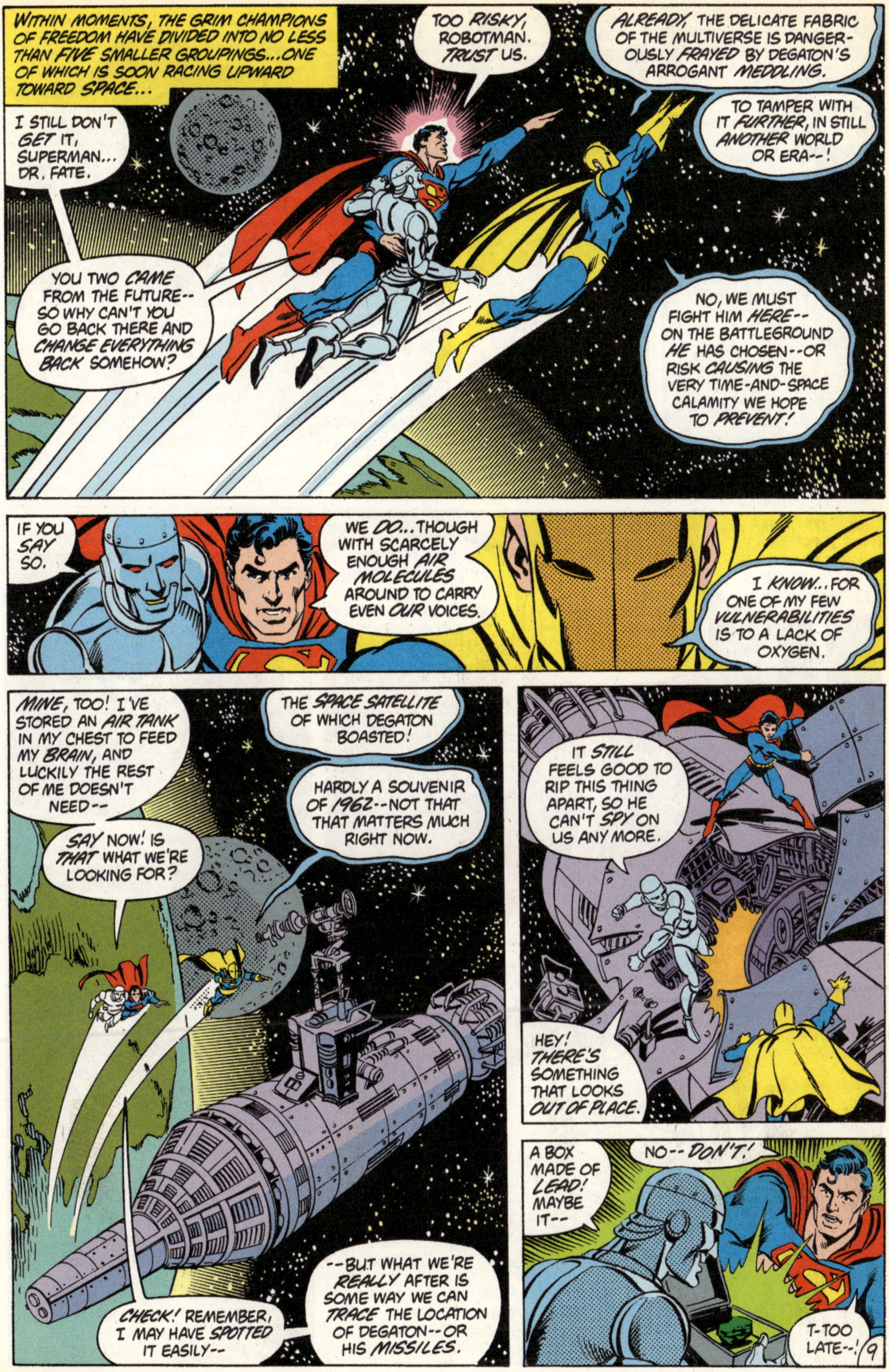
WITHIN MOMENTS, THE GRIM CHAMPIONS OF FREEDOM HAVE DIVIDED INTO NO LESS THAN FIVE SMALLER GROUPINGS...ONE OF WHICH IS SOON RACING UPWARD TOWARD SPACE...
I STILL DON'T GET IT, SUPERMAN... DR. FATE.
YOU TWO CAME FROM THE FUTURE-- SO WHY CAN'T YOU GO BACK THERE AND CHANGE EVERYTHING BACK SOMEHOW?
TOO RISKY, ROBOTMAN. TRUST US.
ALREADY, THE DELICATE FABRIC OF THE MULTIVERSE IS DANGEROUSLY FRAYED BY DEGATON'S ARROGANT MEDDLING.
TO TAMPER WITH IT FURTHER, IN STILL ANOTHER WORLD OR ERA--!
NO, WE MUST FIGHT HIM HERE-- ON THE BATTLEGROUND HE HAS CHOSEN--OR RISK CAUSING THE VERY TIME-AND-SPACE CALAMITY WE HOPE TO PREVENT!
IF YOU SAY SO.
WE DO...THOUGH WITH SCARCELY ENOUGH AIR MOLECULES AROUND TO CARRY EVEN OUR VOICES.
I KNOW...FOR ONE OF MY FEW VULNERABILITIES IS TO A LACK OF OXYGEN.
MINE, TOO! I'VE STORED AN AIR TANK IN MY CHEST TO FEED MY BRAIN, AND LUCKILY THE REST OF ME DOESN'T NEED--
SAY NOW! IS THAT WHAT WE'RE LOOKING FOR?
THE SPACE SATELLITE OF WHICH DEGATON BOASTED!
HARDLY A SOUVENIR OF 1962--NOT THAT THAT MATTERS MUCH RIGHT NOW.
CHECK! REMEMBER, I MAY HAVE SPOTTED IT EASILY--
--BUT WHAT WE'RE REALLY AFTER IS SOME WAY WE CAN TRACE THE LOCATION OF DEGATON--OR HIS MISSILES.
IT STILL FEELS GOOD TO RIP THIS THING APART, SO HE CAN'T SPY ON US ANY MORE.
HEY! THERE'S SOMETHING THAT LOOKS OUT OF PLACE.
A BOX MADE OF LEAD! MAYBE IT--
NO--DON'T!
T-TOO LATE--!
9

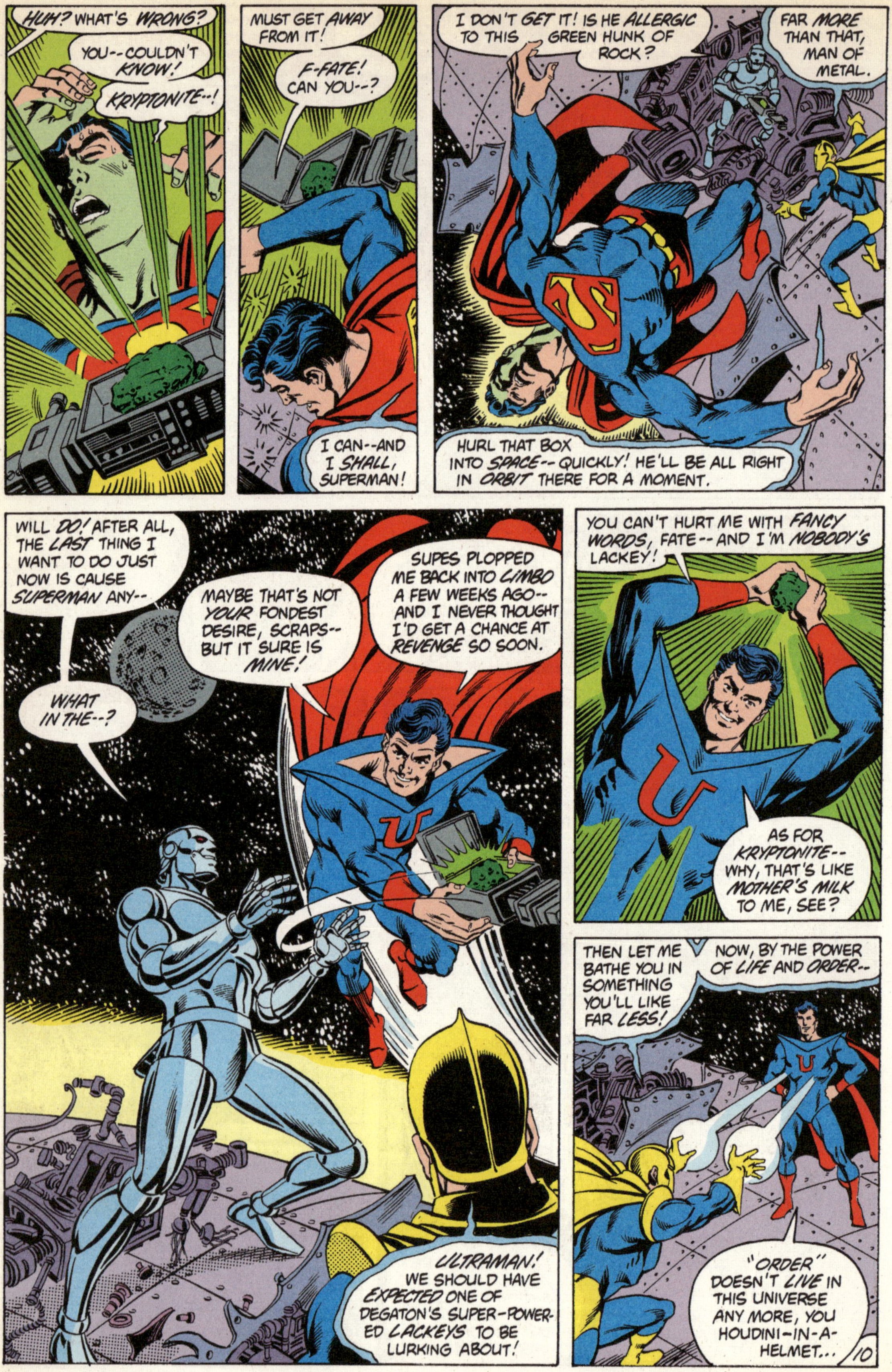
HUH? WHAT'S WRONG?
YOU--COULDN'T KNOW!
KRYPTONITE--!
MUST GET AWAY FROM IT!
F-FATE! CAN YOU--?
I CAN--AND I SHALL, SUPERMAN!
I DON'T GET IT! IS HE ALLERGIC TO THIS GREEN HUNK OF ROCK?
FAR MORE THAN THAT, MAN OF METAL.
HURL THAT BOX INTO SPACE--QUICKLY! HE'LL BE ALL RIGHT IN ORBIT THERE FOR A MOMENT.
WILL DO! AFTER ALL, THE LAST THING I WANT TO DO JUST NOW IS CAUSE SUPERMAN ANY--
WHAT IN THE--?
MAYBE THAT'S NOT YOUR FONDEST DESIRE, SCRAPS--BUT IT SURE IS MINE!
SUPES PLOPPED ME BACK INTO LIMBO A FEW WEEKS AGO--AND I NEVER THOUGHT I'D GET A CHANCE AT REVENGE SO SOON.
ULTRAMAN! WE SHOULD HAVE EXPECTED ONE OF DEGATON'S SUPER-POWERED LACKEYS TO BE LURKING ABOUT!
YOU CAN'T HURT ME WITH FANCY WORDS, FATE--AND I'M NOBODY'S LACKEY!
AS FOR KRYPTONITE--WHY, THAT'S LIKE MOTHER'S MILK TO ME, SEE?
THEN LET ME BATHE YOU IN SOMETHING YOU'LL LIKE FAR LESS!
NOW, BY THE POWER OF LIFE AND ORDER--
"ORDER" DOESN'T LIVE IN THIS UNIVERSE ANY MORE, YOU HOUDINI-IN-A-HELMET...
10

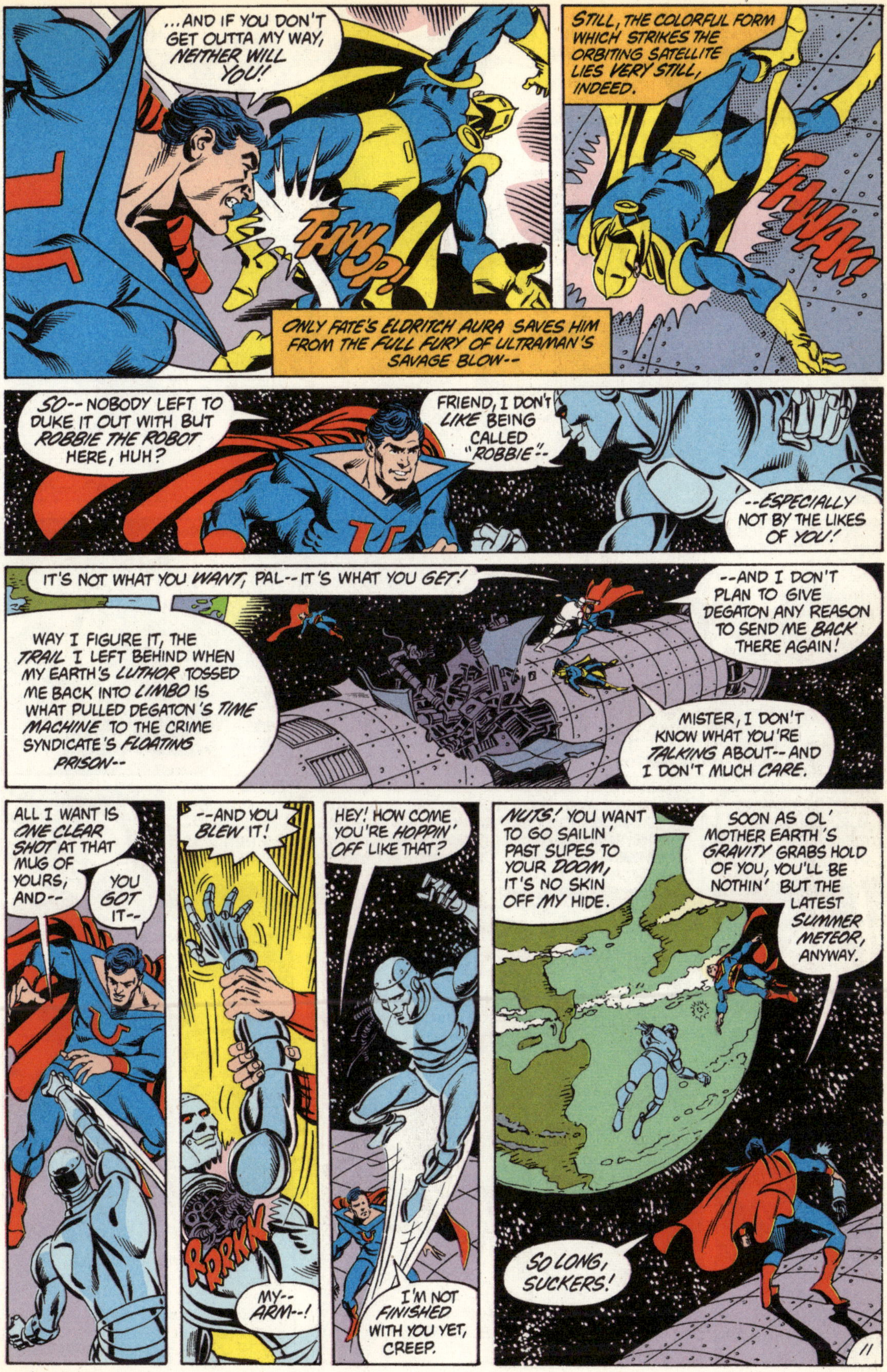
...AND IF YOU DON'T GET OUTTA MY WAY, NEITHER WILL YOU!
THWOP!
ONLY FATE'S ELDRITCH AURA SAVES HIM FROM THE FULL FURY OF ULTRAMAN'S SAVAGE BLOW--
STILL, THE COLORFUL FORM WHICH STRIKES THE ORBITING SATELLITE LIES VERY STILL, INDEED.
THWAK!
SO-- NOBODY LEFT TO DUKE IT OUT WITH BUT ROBBIE THE ROBOT HERE, HUH?
FRIEND, I DON'T LIKE BEING CALLED "ROBBIE"--
--ESPECIALLY NOT BY THE LIKES OF YOU!
IT'S NOT WHAT YOU WANT, PAL-- IT'S WHAT YOU GET!
WAY I FIGURE IT, THE TRAIL I LEFT BEHIND WHEN MY EARTH'S LUTHOR TOSSED ME BACK INTO LIMBO IS WHAT PULLED DEGATON'S TIME MACHINE TO THE CRIME SYNDICATE'S FLOATING PRISON--
--AND I DON'T PLAN TO GIVE DEGATON ANY REASON TO SEND ME BACK THERE AGAIN!
MISTER, I DON'T KNOW WHAT YOU'RE TALKING ABOUT-- AND I DON'T MUCH CARE.
ALL I WANT IS ONE CLEAR SHOT AT THAT MUG OF YOURS, AND--
YOU GOT IT--
--AND YOU BLEW IT!
RRRKK
MY-- ARM--!
HEY! HOW COME YOU'RE HOPPIN' OFF LIKE THAT?
I'M NOT FINISHED WITH YOU YET, CREEP.
NUTS! YOU WANT TO GO SAILIN' PAST SUPES TO YOUR DOOM, IT'S NO SKIN OFF MY HIDE.
SOON AS OL' MOTHER EARTH'S GRAVITY GRABS HOLD OF YOU, YOU'LL BE NOTHIN' BUT THE LATEST SUMMER METEOR, ANYWAY.
SO LONG, SUCKERS!
11

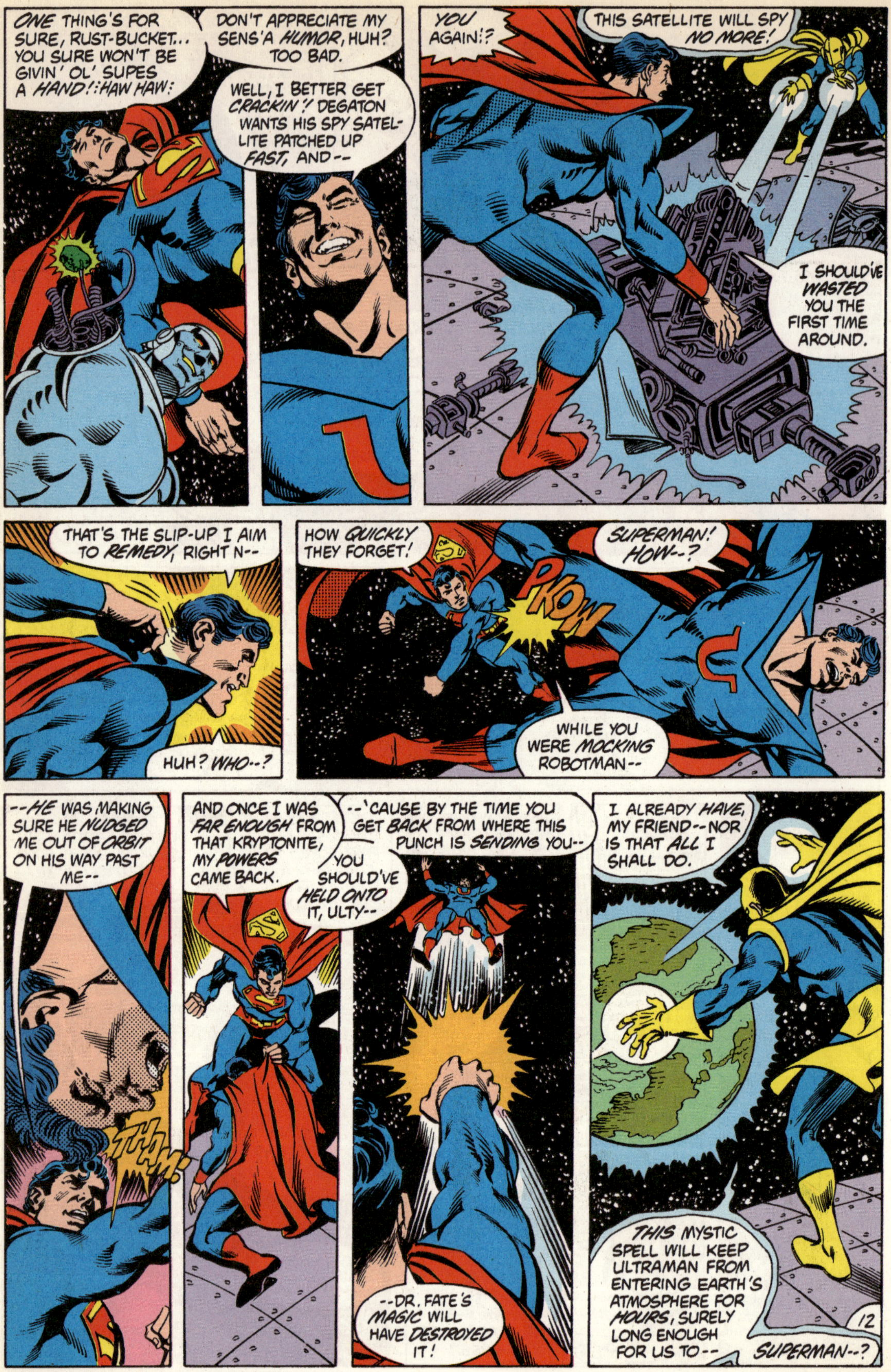
ONE THING'S FOR SURE, RUST-BUCKET... YOU SURE WON'T BE GIVIN' OL' SUPES A HAND! HAW HAW!
DON'T APPRECIATE MY SENS'A HUMOR, HUH? TOO BAD.
WELL, I BETTER GET CRACKIN'! DEGATON WANTS HIS SPY SATELLITE PATCHED UP FAST, AND--
YOU AGAIN!?
THIS SATELLITE WILL SPY NO MORE!
I SHOULD'VE WASTED YOU THE FIRST TIME AROUND.
THAT'S THE SLIP-UP I AIM TO REMEDY, RIGHT N--
HUH? WHO--?
HOW QUICKLY THEY FORGET!
SUPERMAN! HOW--?
POW
WHILE YOU WERE MOCKING ROBOTMAN--
--HE WAS MAKING SURE HE NUDGED ME OUT OF ORBIT ON HIS WAY PAST ME--
THAM!
AND ONCE I WAS FAR ENOUGH FROM THAT KRYPTONITE, MY POWERS CAME BACK.
YOU SHOULD'VE HELD ONTO IT, ULTY--
--'CAUSE BY THE TIME YOU GET BACK FROM WHERE THIS PUNCH IS SENDING YOU--
--DR. FATE'S MAGIC WILL HAVE DESTROYED IT!
I ALREADY HAVE, MY FRIEND--NOR IS THAT ALL I SHALL DO.
THIS MYSTIC SPELL WILL KEEP ULTRAMAN FROM ENTERING EARTH'S ATMOSPHERE FOR HOURS, SURELY LONG ENOUGH FOR US TO--
SUPERMAN--?
12

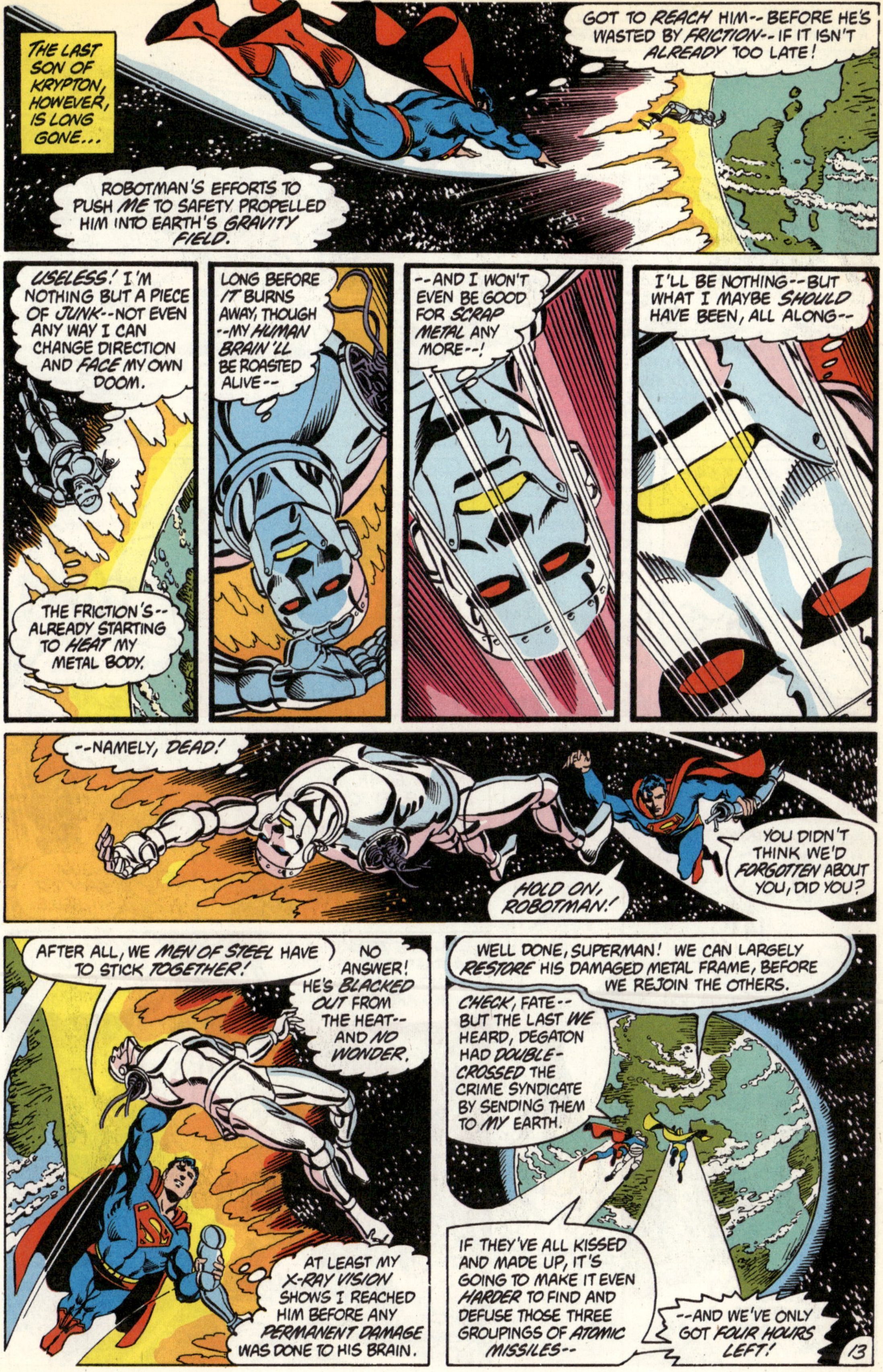
THE LAST SON OF KRYPTON, HOWEVER, IS LONG GONE...
GOT TO REACH HIM--BEFORE HE'S WASTED BY FRICTION--IF IT ISN'T ALREADY TOO LATE!
ROBOTMAN'S EFFORTS TO PUSH ME TO SAFETY PROPELLED HIM INTO EARTH'S GRAVITY FIELD.
USELESS! I'M NOTHING BUT A PIECE OF JUNK--NOT EVEN ANY WAY I CAN CHANGE DIRECTION AND FACE MY OWN DOOM.
THE FRICTION'S--ALREADY STARTING TO HEAT MY METAL BODY.
LONG BEFORE IT BURNS AWAY, THOUGH --MY HUMAN BRAIN'LL BE ROASTED ALIVE--
--AND I WON'T EVEN BE GOOD FOR SCRAP METAL ANY MORE--!
I'LL BE NOTHING--BUT WHAT I MAYBE SHOULD HAVE BEEN, ALL ALONG--
--NAMELY, DEAD!
HOLD ON, ROBOTMAN!
YOU DIDN'T THINK WE'D FORGOTTEN ABOUT YOU, DID YOU?
AFTER ALL, WE MEN OF STEEL HAVE TO STICK TOGETHER!
NO ANSWER! HE'S BLACKED OUT FROM THE HEAT--AND NO WONDER.
AT LEAST MY X-RAY VISION SHOWS I REACHED HIM BEFORE ANY PERMANENT DAMAGE WAS DONE TO HIS BRAIN.
WELL DONE, SUPERMAN! WE CAN LARGELY RESTORE HIS DAMAGED METAL FRAME, BEFORE WE REJOIN THE OTHERS.
CHECK, FATE--BUT THE LAST WE HEARD, DEGATON HAD DOUBLE-CROSSED THE CRIME SYNDICATE BY SENDING THEM TO MY EARTH.
IF THEY'VE ALL KISSED AND MADE UP, IT'S GOING TO MAKE IT EVEN HARDER TO FIND AND DEFUSE THOSE THREE GROUPINGS OF ATOMIC MISSILES--
--AND WE'VE ONLY GOT FOUR HOURS LEFT!
13

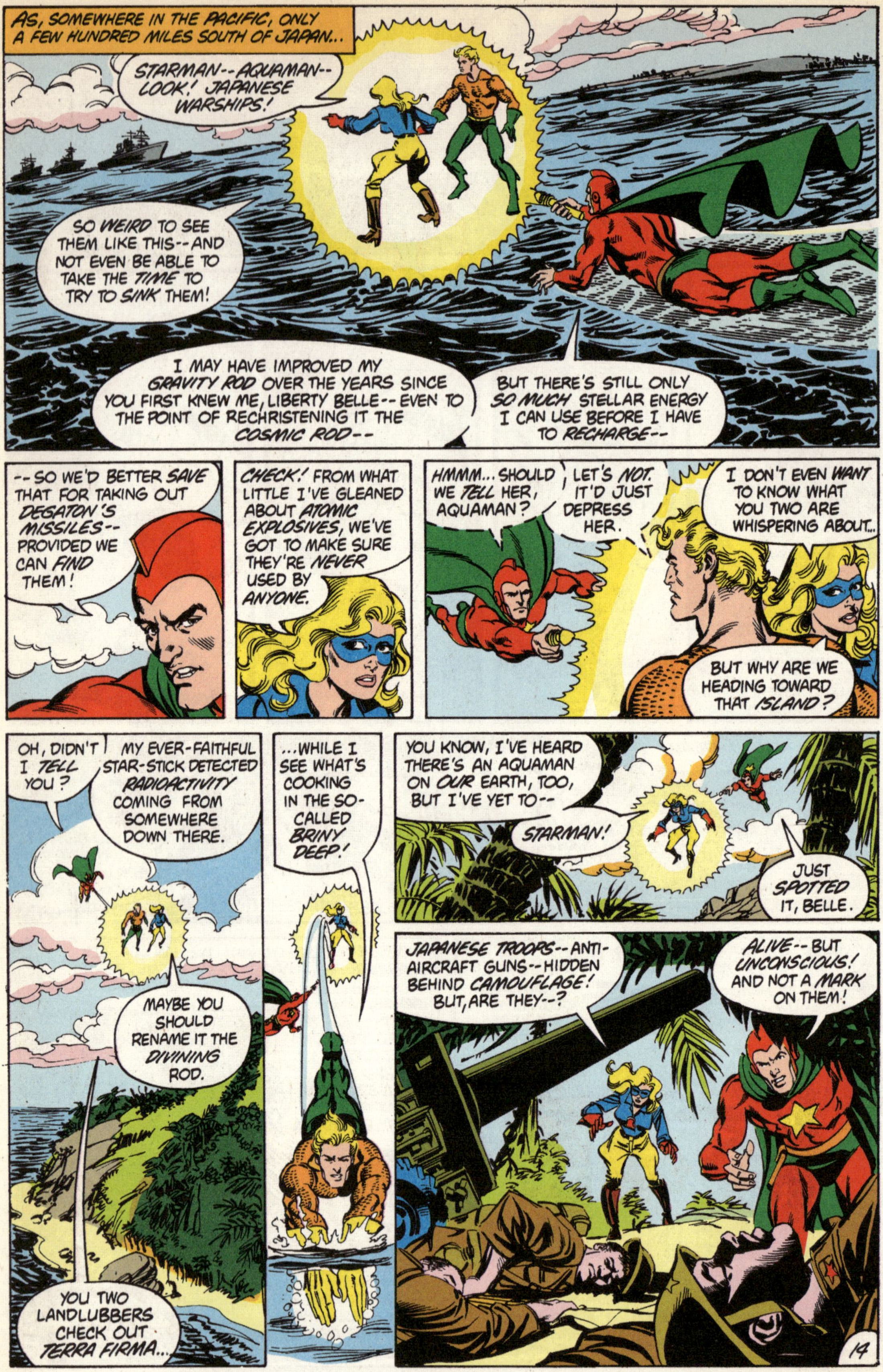
AS, SOMEWHERE IN THE PACIFIC, ONLY A FEW HUNDRED MILES SOUTH OF JAPAN...
STARMAN--AQUAMAN--LOOK! JAPANESE WARSHIPS!
SO WEIRD TO SEE THEM LIKE THIS--AND NOT EVEN BE ABLE TO TAKE THE TIME TO TRY TO SINK THEM!
I MAY HAVE IMPROVED MY GRAVITY ROD OVER THE YEARS SINCE YOU FIRST KNEW ME, LIBERTY BELLE--EVEN TO THE POINT OF RECHRISTENING IT THE COSMIC ROD--
BUT THERE'S STILL ONLY SO MUCH STELLAR ENERGY I CAN USE BEFORE I HAVE TO RECHARGE--
--SO WE'D BETTER SAVE THAT FOR TAKING OUT DEGATON'S MISSILES--PROVIDED WE CAN FIND THEM!
CHECK! FROM WHAT LITTLE I'VE GLEANED ABOUT ATOMIC EXPLOSIVES, WE'VE GOT TO MAKE SURE THEY'RE NEVER USED BY ANYONE.
HMMM... SHOULD WE TELL HER, AQUAMAN?
LET'S NOT. IT'D JUST DEPRESS HER.
I DON'T EVEN WANT TO KNOW WHAT YOU TWO ARE WHISPERING ABOUT...
BUT WHY ARE WE HEADING TOWARD THAT ISLAND?
OH, DIDN'T I TELL YOU?
MY EVER-FAITHFUL STAR-STICK DETECTED RADIOACTIVITY COMING FROM SOMEWHERE DOWN THERE.
MAYBE YOU SHOULD RENAME IT THE DIVINING ROD.
YOU TWO LANDLUBBERS CHECK OUT TERRA FIRMA...
...WHILE I SEE WHAT'S COOKING IN THE SO-CALLED BRINY DEEP!
YOU KNOW, I'VE HEARD THERE'S AN AQUAMAN ON OUR EARTH, TOO, BUT I'VE YET TO--
STARMAN!
JUST SPOTTED IT, BELLE.
JAPANESE TROOPS--ANTI-AIRCRAFT GUNS--HIDDEN BEHIND CAMOUFLAGE! BUT, ARE THEY--?
ALIVE--BUT UNCONSCIOUS! AND NOT A MARK ON THEM!
14

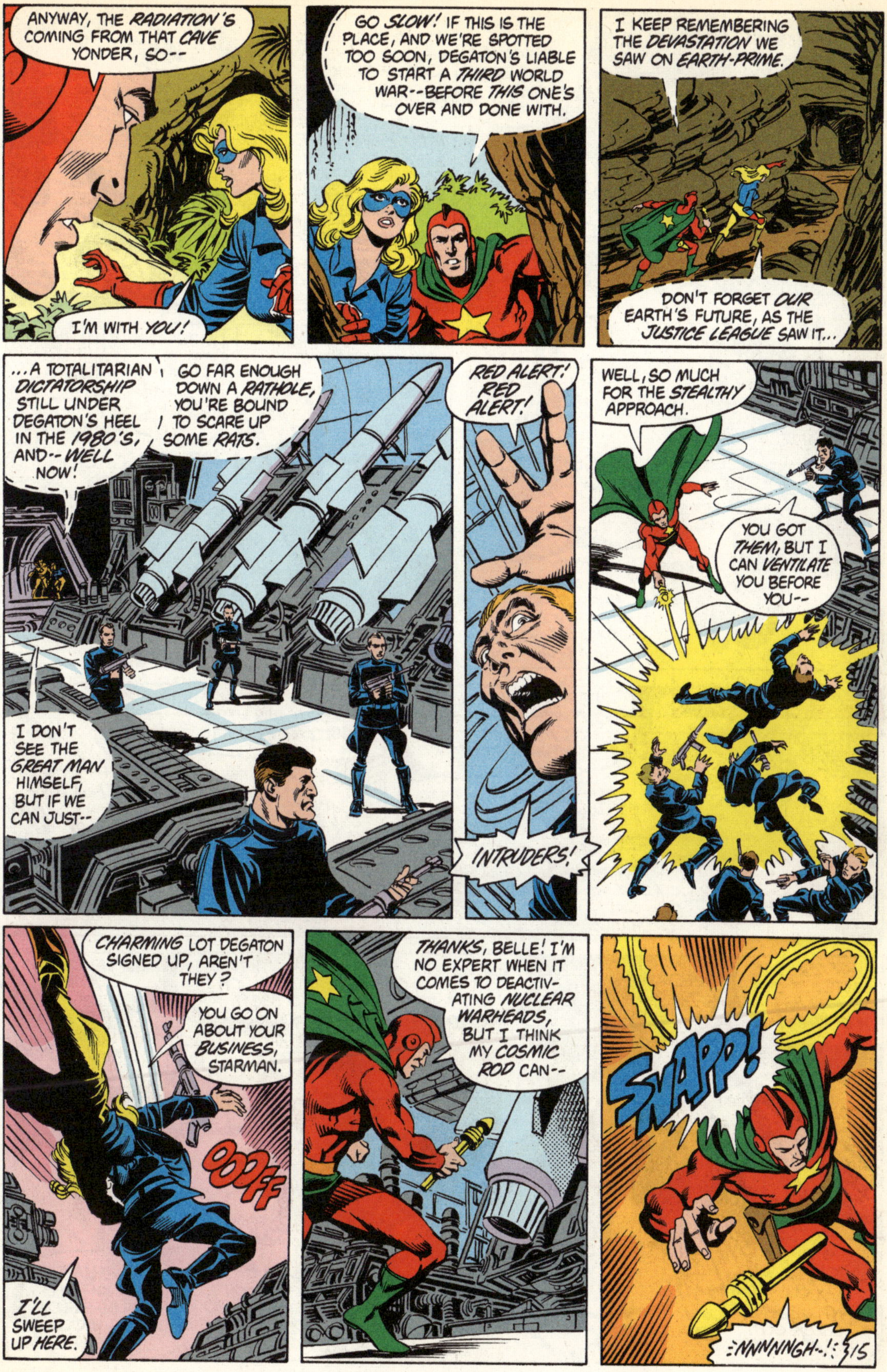
ANYWAY, THE RADIATION'S COMING FROM THAT CAVE YONDER, SO--
I'M WITH YOU!
GO SLOW! IF THIS IS THE PLACE, AND WE'RE SPOTTED TOO SOON, DEGATON'S LIABLE TO START A THIRD WORLD WAR--BEFORE THIS ONE'S OVER AND DONE WITH.
I KEEP REMEMBERING THE DEVASTATION WE SAW ON EARTH-PRIME.
DON'T FORGET OUR EARTH'S FUTURE, AS THE JUSTICE LEAGUE SAW IT...
...A TOTALITARIAN DICTATORSHIP STILL UNDER DEGATON'S HEEL IN THE 1980'S, AND--WELL NOW!
GO FAR ENOUGH DOWN A RATHOLE, YOU'RE BOUND TO SCARE UP SOME RATS.
I DON'T SEE THE GREAT MAN HIMSELF, BUT IF WE CAN JUST--
RED ALERT! RED ALERT!
INTRUDERS!
WELL, SO MUCH FOR THE STEALTHY APPROACH.
YOU GOT THEM, BUT I CAN VENTILATE YOU BEFORE YOU--
CHARMING LOT DEGATON SIGNED UP, AREN'T THEY?
YOU GO ON ABOUT YOUR BUSINESS, STARMAN.
OOOFF
I'LL SWEEP UP HERE.
THANKS, BELLE! I'M NO EXPERT WHEN IT COMES TO DEACTIV-ATING NUCLEAR WARHEADS, BUT I THINK MY COSMIC ROD CAN--
SNAPP!
NNNNNGH--!
15

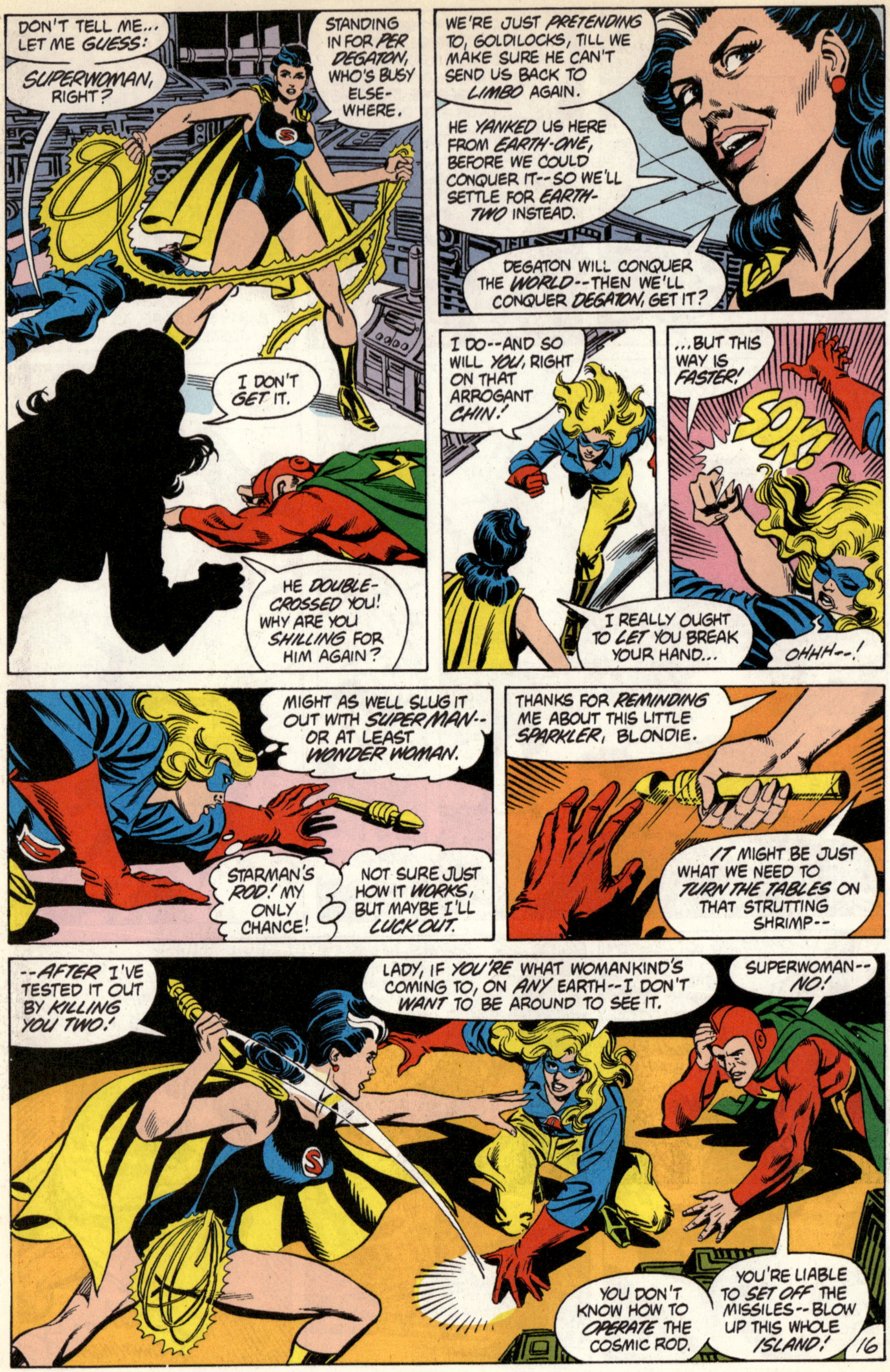

DON'T TELL ME... LET ME GUESS:
SUPERWOMAN, RIGHT?
STANDING IN FOR PER DEGATON, WHO'S BUSY ELSE-WHERE.
I DON'T GET IT.
HE DOUBLE-CROSSED YOU! WHY ARE YOU SHILLING FOR HIM AGAIN?
WE'RE JUST PRETENDING TO, GOLDILOCKS, TILL WE MAKE SURE HE CAN'T SEND US BACK TO LIMBO AGAIN.
HE YANKED US HERE FROM EARTH-ONE, BEFORE WE COULD CONQUER IT--SO WE'LL SETTLE FOR EARTH-TWO INSTEAD.
DEGATON WILL CONQUER THE WORLD--THEN WE'LL CONQUER DEGATON, GET IT?
I DO--AND SO WILL YOU, RIGHT ON THAT ARROGANT CHIN!
...BUT THIS WAY IS FASTER!
SOK!
I REALLY OUGHT TO LET YOU BREAK YOUR HAND...
OHHH--!
MIGHT AS WELL SLUG IT OUT WITH SUPERMAN--OR AT LEAST WONDER WOMAN.
STARMAN'S ROD! MY ONLY CHANCE!
NOT SURE JUST HOW IT WORKS, BUT MAYBE I'LL LUCK OUT.
THANKS FOR REMINDING ME ABOUT THIS LITTLE SPARKLER, BLONDIE.
IT MIGHT BE JUST WHAT WE NEED TO TURN THE TABLES ON THAT STRUTTING SHRIMP--
--AFTER I'VE TESTED IT OUT BY KILLING YOU TWO!
LADY, IF YOU'RE WHAT WOMANKIND'S COMING TO, ON ANY EARTH--I DON'T WANT TO BE AROUND TO SEE IT.
SUPERWOMAN--NO!
YOU DON'T KNOW HOW TO OPERATE THE COSMIC ROD.
YOU'RE LIABLE TO SET OFF THE MISSILES--BLOW UP THIS WHOLE ISLAND!
16

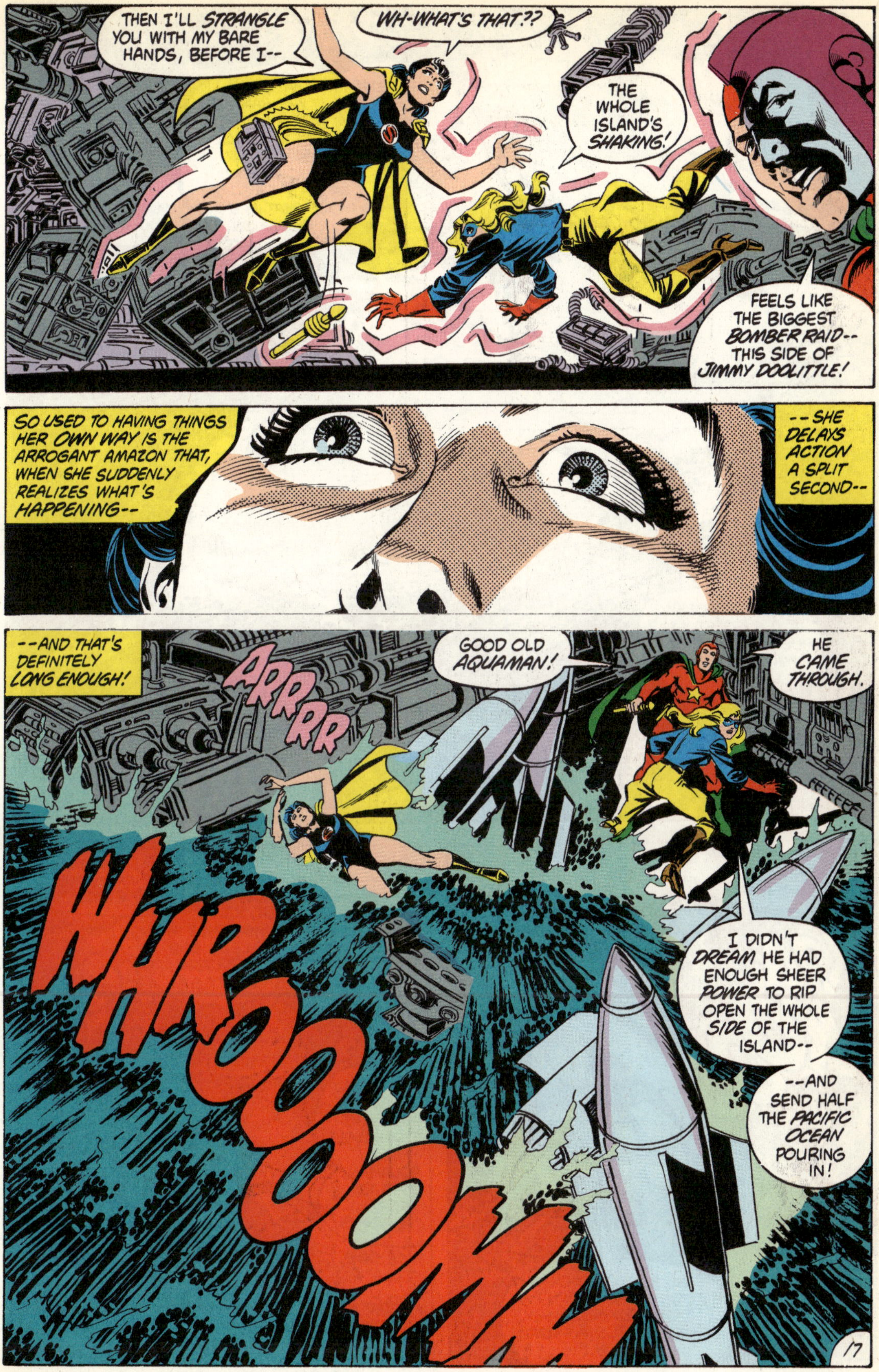
THEN I'LL STRANGLE YOU WITH MY BARE HANDS, BEFORE I--
WH-WHAT'S THAT??
THE WHOLE ISLAND'S SHAKING!
FEELS LIKE THE BIGGEST BOMBER RAID-- THIS SIDE OF JIMMY DOOLITTLE!
SO USED TO HAVING THINGS HER OWN WAY IS THE ARROGANT AMAZON THAT, WHEN SHE SUDDENLY REALIZES WHAT'S HAPPENING--
--SHE DELAYS ACTION A SPLIT SECOND--
--AND THAT'S DEFINITELY LONG ENOUGH!
ARRRR
GOOD OLD AQUAMAN!
HE CAME THROUGH.
WHROOOOMM
I DIDN'T DREAM HE HAD ENOUGH SHEER POWER TO RIP OPEN THE WHOLE SIDE OF THE ISLAND--
--AND SEND HALF THE PACIFIC OCEAN POURING IN!
17

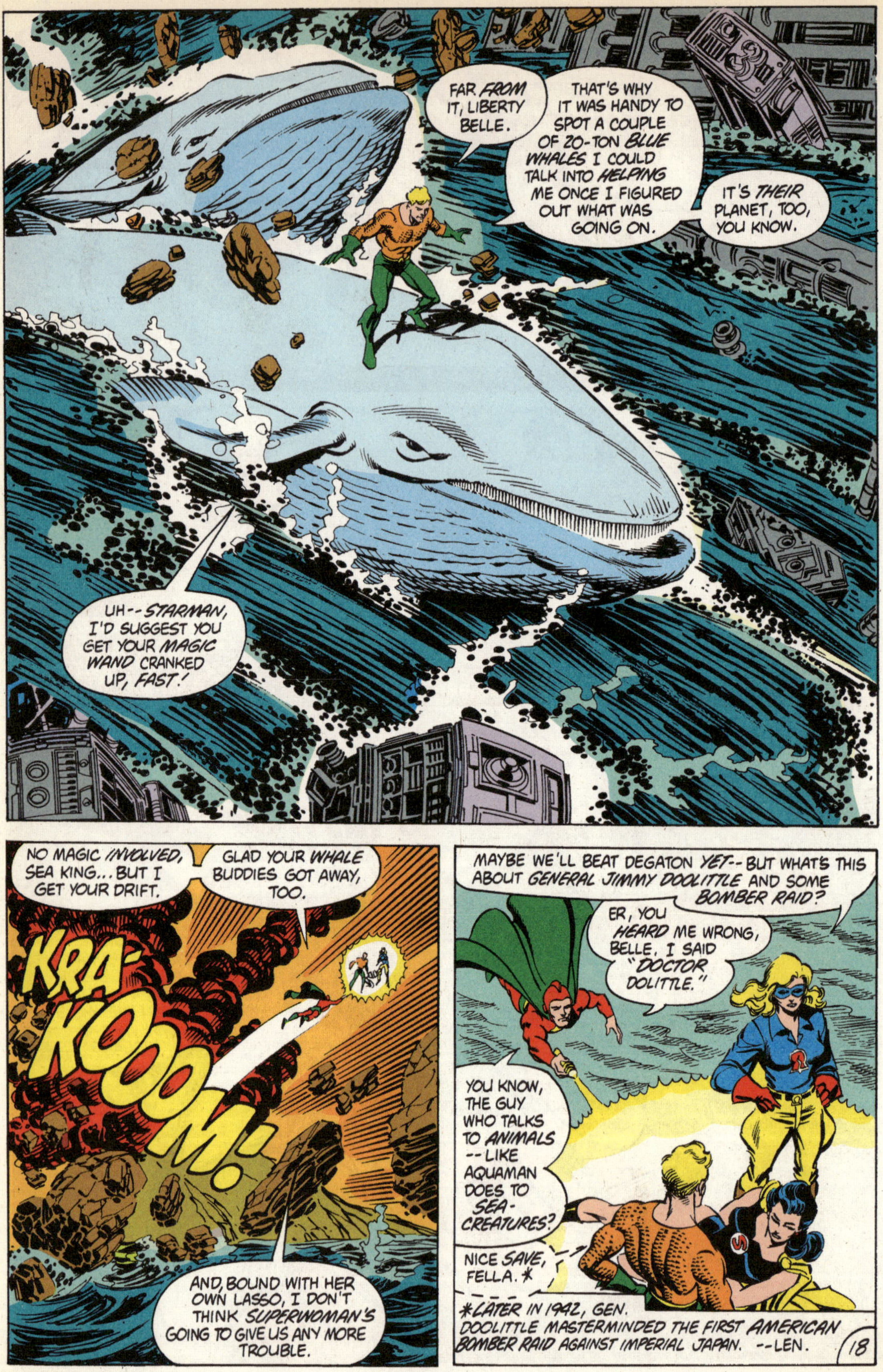
FAR FROM IT, LIBERTY BELLE.
THAT'S WHY IT WAS HANDY TO SPOT A COUPLE OF 20-TON BLUE WHALES I COULD TALK INTO HELPING ME ONCE I FIGURED OUT WHAT WAS GOING ON.
IT'S THEIR PLANET, TOO, YOU KNOW.
UH-- STARMAN, I'D SUGGEST YOU GET YOUR MAGIC WAND CRANKED UP, FAST!
NO MAGIC INVOLVED, SEA KING... BUT I GET YOUR DRIFT.
GLAD YOUR WHALE BUDDIES GOT AWAY, TOO.
KRA-KOOOM!
AND, BOUND WITH HER OWN LASSO, I DON'T THINK SUPERWOMAN'S GOING TO GIVE US ANY MORE TROUBLE.
MAYBE WE'LL BEAT DEGATON YET-- BUT WHAT'S THIS ABOUT GENERAL JIMMY DOOLITTLE AND SOME BOMBER RAID?
ER, YOU HEARD ME WRONG, BELLE. I SAID "DOCTOR DOLITTLE."
YOU KNOW, THE GUY WHO TALKS TO ANIMALS --LIKE AQUAMAN DOES TO SEA-CREATURES?
NICE SAVE, FELLA.*
*LATER IN 1942, GEN. DOOLITTLE MASTERMINDED THE FIRST AMERICAN BOMBER RAID AGAINST IMPERIAL JAPAN. --LEN.
18

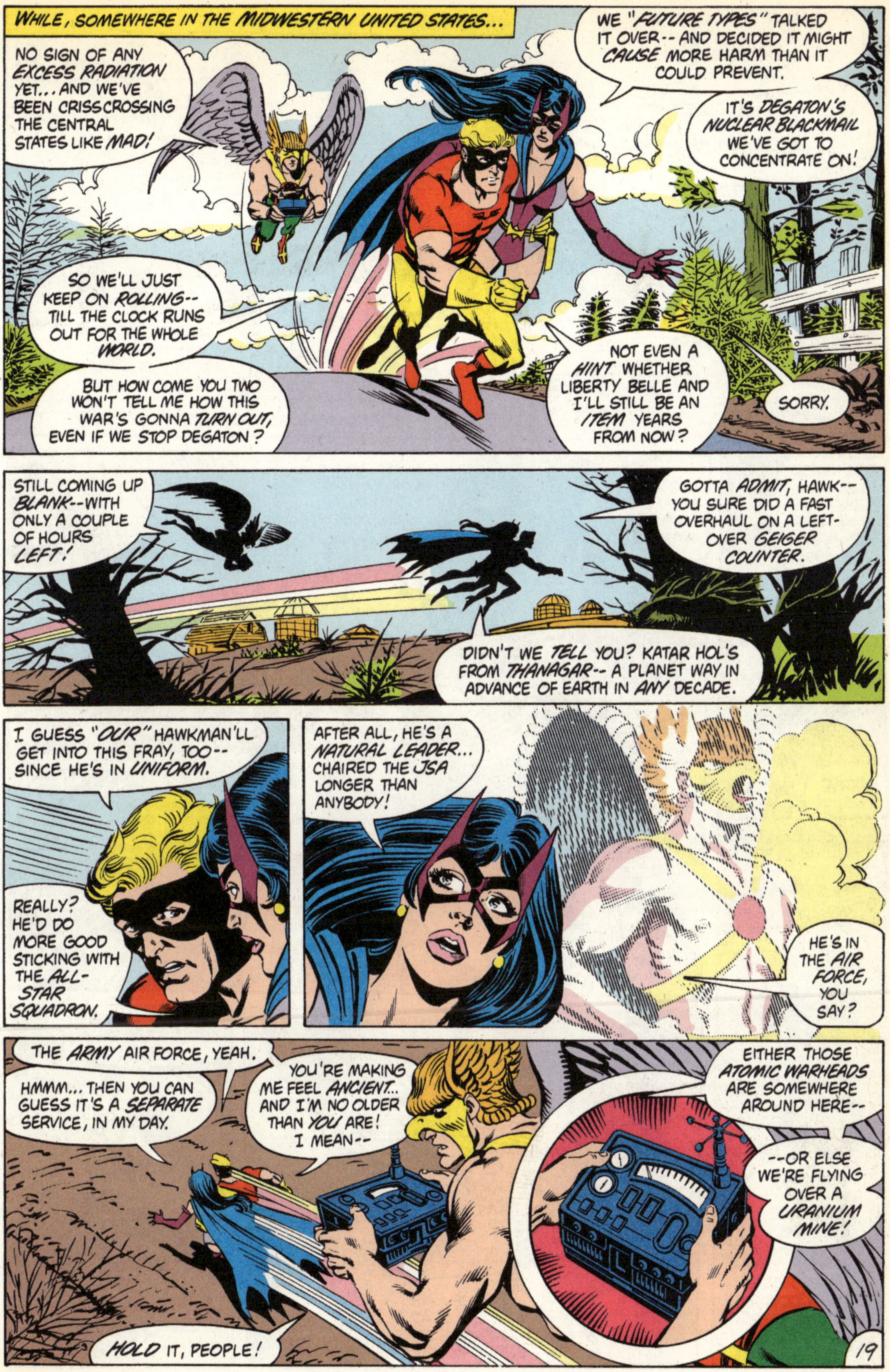
WHILE, SOMEWHERE IN THE MIDWESTERN UNITED STATES...
NO SIGN OF ANY EXCESS RADIATION YET... AND WE'VE BEEN CRISSCROSSING THE CENTRAL STATES LIKE MAD!
SO WE'LL JUST KEEP ON ROLLING-- TILL THE CLOCK RUNS OUT FOR THE WHOLE WORLD.
BUT HOW COME YOU TWO WON'T TELL ME HOW THIS WAR'S GONNA TURN OUT, EVEN IF WE STOP DEGATON?
NOT EVEN A HINT WHETHER LIBERTY BELLE AND I'LL STILL BE AN ITEM YEARS FROM NOW?
WE "FUTURE TYPES" TALKED IT OVER-- AND DECIDED IT MIGHT CAUSE MORE HARM THAN IT COULD PREVENT.
IT'S DEGATON'S NUCLEAR BLACKMAIL WE'VE GOT TO CONCENTRATE ON!
SORRY.
STILL COMING UP BLANK--WITH ONLY A COUPLE OF HOURS LEFT!
GOTTA ADMIT, HAWK-- YOU SURE DID A FAST OVERHAUL ON A LEFT-OVER GEIGER COUNTER.
DIDN'T WE TELL YOU? KATAR HOL'S FROM THANAGAR-- A PLANET WAY IN ADVANCE OF EARTH IN ANY DECADE.
I GUESS "OUR" HAWKMAN'LL GET INTO THIS FRAY, TOO-- SINCE HE'S IN UNIFORM.
REALLY? HE'D DO MORE GOOD STICKING WITH THE ALL-STAR SQUADRON.
AFTER ALL, HE'S A NATURAL LEADER... CHAIRED THE JSA LONGER THAN ANYBODY!
HE'S IN THE AIR FORCE, YOU SAY?
THE ARMY AIR FORCE, YEAH.
HMMM... THEN YOU CAN GUESS IT'S A SEPARATE SERVICE, IN MY DAY.
YOU'RE MAKING ME FEEL ANCIENT... AND I'M NO OLDER THAN YOU ARE! I MEAN--
EITHER THOSE ATOMIC WARHEADS ARE SOMEWHERE AROUND HERE--
--OR ELSE WE'RE FLYING OVER A URANIUM MINE!
HOLD IT, PEOPLE!
19

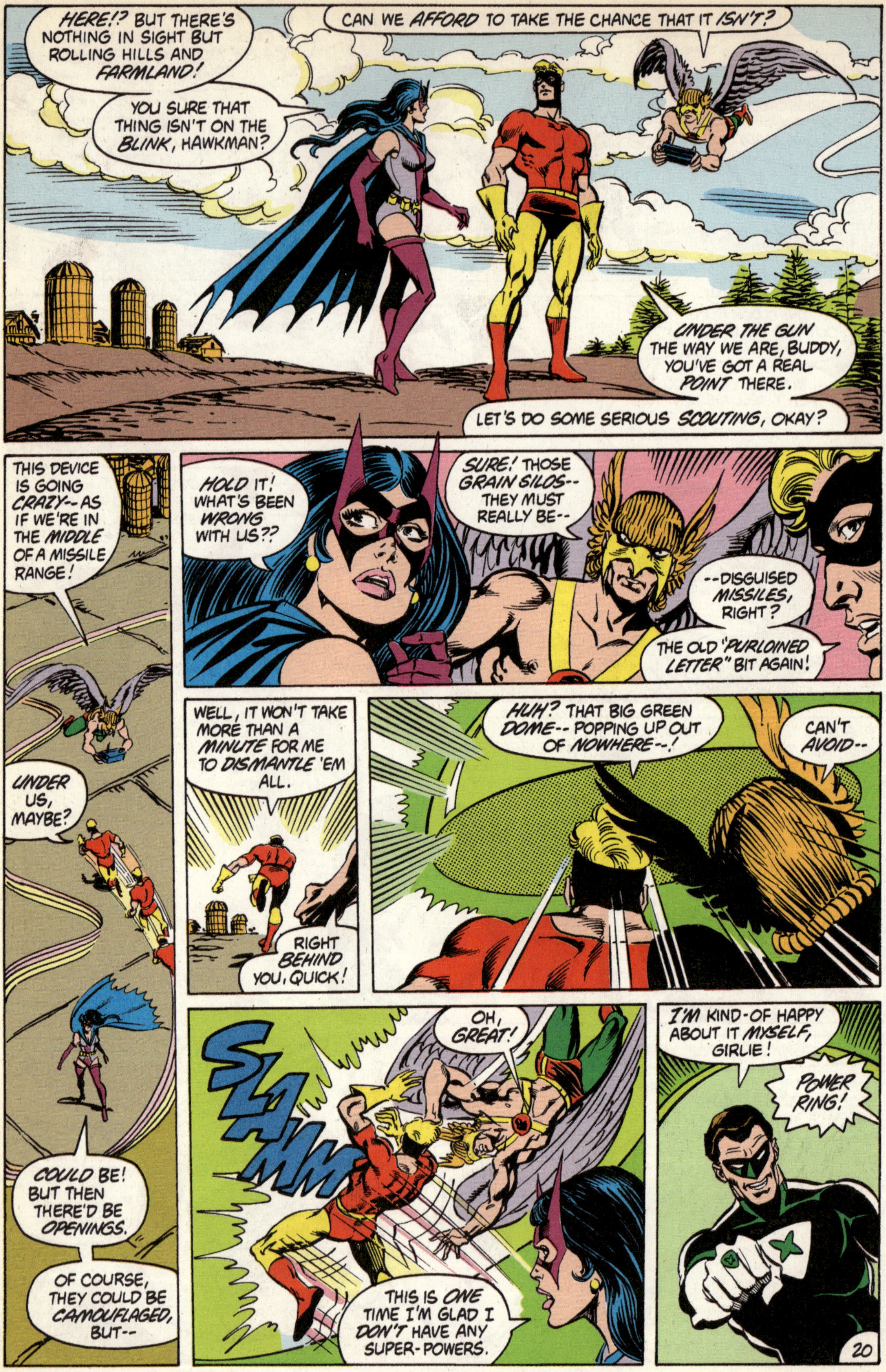
HERE!? BUT THERE'S NOTHING IN SIGHT BUT ROLLING HILLS AND FARMLAND!
YOU SURE THAT THING ISN'T ON THE BLINK, HAWKMAN?
CAN WE AFFORD TO TAKE THE CHANCE THAT IT ISN'T?
UNDER THE GUN THE WAY WE ARE, BUDDY, YOU'VE GOT A REAL POINT THERE.
LET'S DO SOME SERIOUS SCOUTING, OKAY?
THIS DEVICE IS GOING CRAZY--AS IF WE'RE IN THE MIDDLE OF A MISSILE RANGE!
UNDER US, MAYBE?
COULD BE! BUT THEN THERE'D BE OPENINGS.
OF COURSE, THEY COULD BE CAMOUFLAGED, BUT--
HOLD IT! WHAT'S BEEN WRONG WITH US??
SURE! THOSE GRAIN SILOS-- THEY MUST REALLY BE--
--DISGUISED MISSILES, RIGHT?
THE OLD "PURLOINED LETTER" BIT AGAIN!
WELL, IT WON'T TAKE MORE THAN A MINUTE FOR ME TO DISMANTLE 'EM ALL.
RIGHT BEHIND YOU, QUICK!
HUH? THAT BIG GREEN DOME-- POPPING UP OUT OF NOWHERE--!
CAN'T AVOID--
SLAMM
OH, GREAT!
THIS IS ONE TIME I'M GLAD I DON'T HAVE ANY SUPER-POWERS.
I'M KIND-OF HAPPY ABOUT IT MYSELF, GIRLIE!
POWER RING!
20

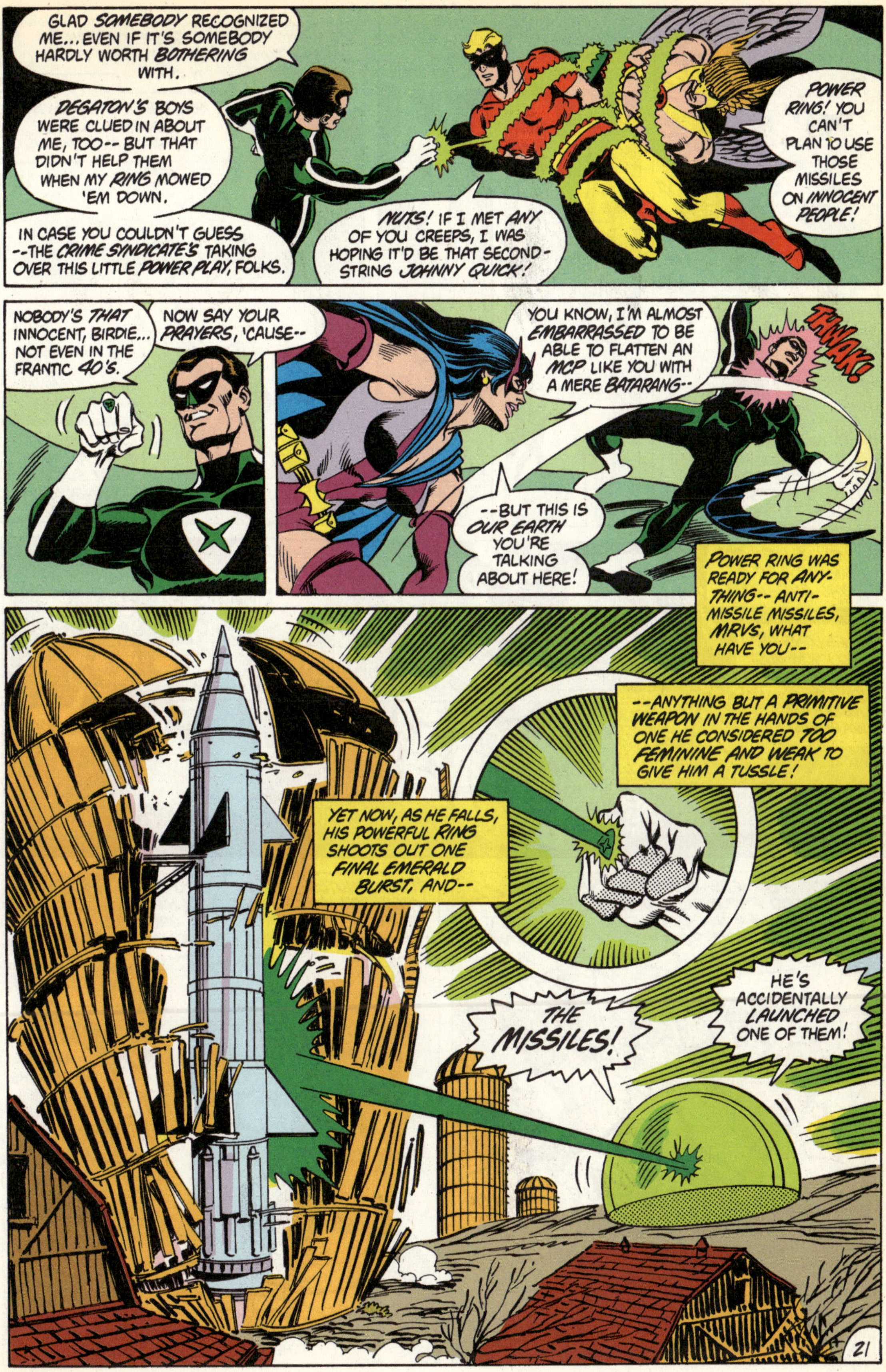
GLAD SOMEBODY RECOGNIZED ME... EVEN IF IT'S SOMEBODY HARDLY WORTH BOTHERING WITH.
DEGATON'S BOYS WERE CLUED IN ABOUT ME, TOO-- BUT THAT DIDN'T HELP THEM WHEN MY RING MOWED 'EM DOWN.
IN CASE YOU COULDN'T GUESS --THE CRIME SYNDICATE'S TAKING OVER THIS LITTLE POWER PLAY, FOLKS.
NUTS! IF I MET ANY OF YOU CREEPS, I WAS HOPING IT'D BE THAT SECOND-STRING JOHNNY QUICK!
POWER RING! YOU CAN'T PLAN TO USE THOSE MISSILES ON INNOCENT PEOPLE!
NOBODY'S THAT INNOCENT, BIRDIE... NOT EVEN IN THE FRANTIC 40'S.
NOW SAY YOUR PRAYERS, 'CAUSE--
YOU KNOW, I'M ALMOST EMBARRASSED TO BE ABLE TO FLATTEN AN MCP LIKE YOU WITH A MERE BATARANG--
THWAK!
--BUT THIS IS OUR EARTH YOU'RE TALKING ABOUT HERE!
POWER RING WAS READY FOR ANY-THING-- ANTI-MISSILE MISSILES, MRVS, WHAT HAVE YOU--
--ANYTHING BUT A PRIMITIVE WEAPON IN THE HANDS OF ONE HE CONSIDERED TOO FEMININE AND WEAK TO GIVE HIM A TUSSLE!
YET NOW, AS HE FALLS, HIS POWERFUL RING SHOOTS OUT ONE FINAL EMERALD BURST, AND--
THE MISSILES!
HE'S ACCIDENTALLY LAUNCHED ONE OF THEM!
21

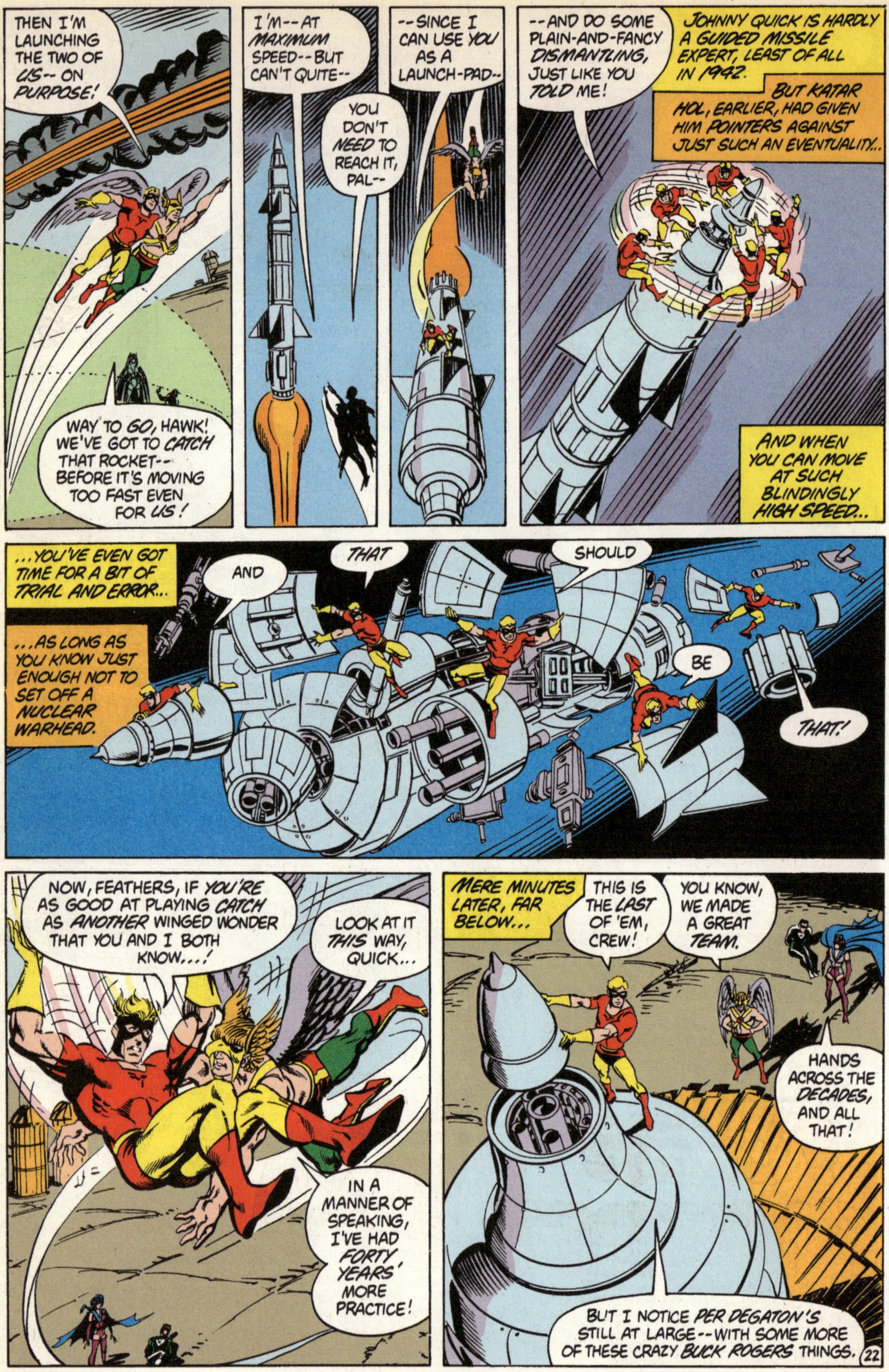
THEN I'M LAUNCHING THE TWO OF US-- ON PURPOSE!
WAY TO GO, HAWK! WE'VE GOT TO CATCH THAT ROCKET-- BEFORE IT'S MOVING TOO FAST EVEN FOR US!
I'M--AT MAXIMUM SPEED--BUT CAN'T QUITE--
YOU DON'T NEED TO REACH IT, PAL--
--SINCE I CAN USE YOU AS A LAUNCH-PAD--
--AND DO SOME PLAIN-AND-FANCY DISMANTLING, JUST LIKE YOU TOLD ME!
JOHNNY QUICK IS HARDLY A GUIDED MISSILE EXPERT, LEAST OF ALL IN 1942.
BUT KATAR HOL, EARLIER, HAD GIVEN HIM POINTERS AGAINST JUST SUCH AN EVENTUALITY...
AND WHEN YOU CAN MOVE AT SUCH BLINDINGLY HIGH SPEED...
...YOU'VE EVEN GOT TIME FOR A BIT OF TRIAL AND ERROR...
...AS LONG AS YOU KNOW JUST ENOUGH NOT TO SET OFF A NUCLEAR WARHEAD.
AND
THAT
SHOULD
BE
THAT!
NOW, FEATHERS, IF YOU'RE AS GOOD AT PLAYING CATCH AS ANOTHER WINGED WONDER THAT YOU AND I BOTH KNOW...!
LOOK AT IT THIS WAY, QUICK...
IN A MANNER OF SPEAKING, I'VE HAD FORTY YEARS' MORE PRACTICE!
MERE MINUTES LATER, FAR BELOW...
THIS IS THE LAST OF 'EM, CREW!
YOU KNOW, WE MADE A GREAT TEAM.
HANDS ACROSS THE DECADES, AND ALL THAT!
BUT I NOTICE PER DEGATON'S STILL AT LARGE--WITH SOME MORE OF THESE CRAZY BUCK ROGERS THINGS.
22

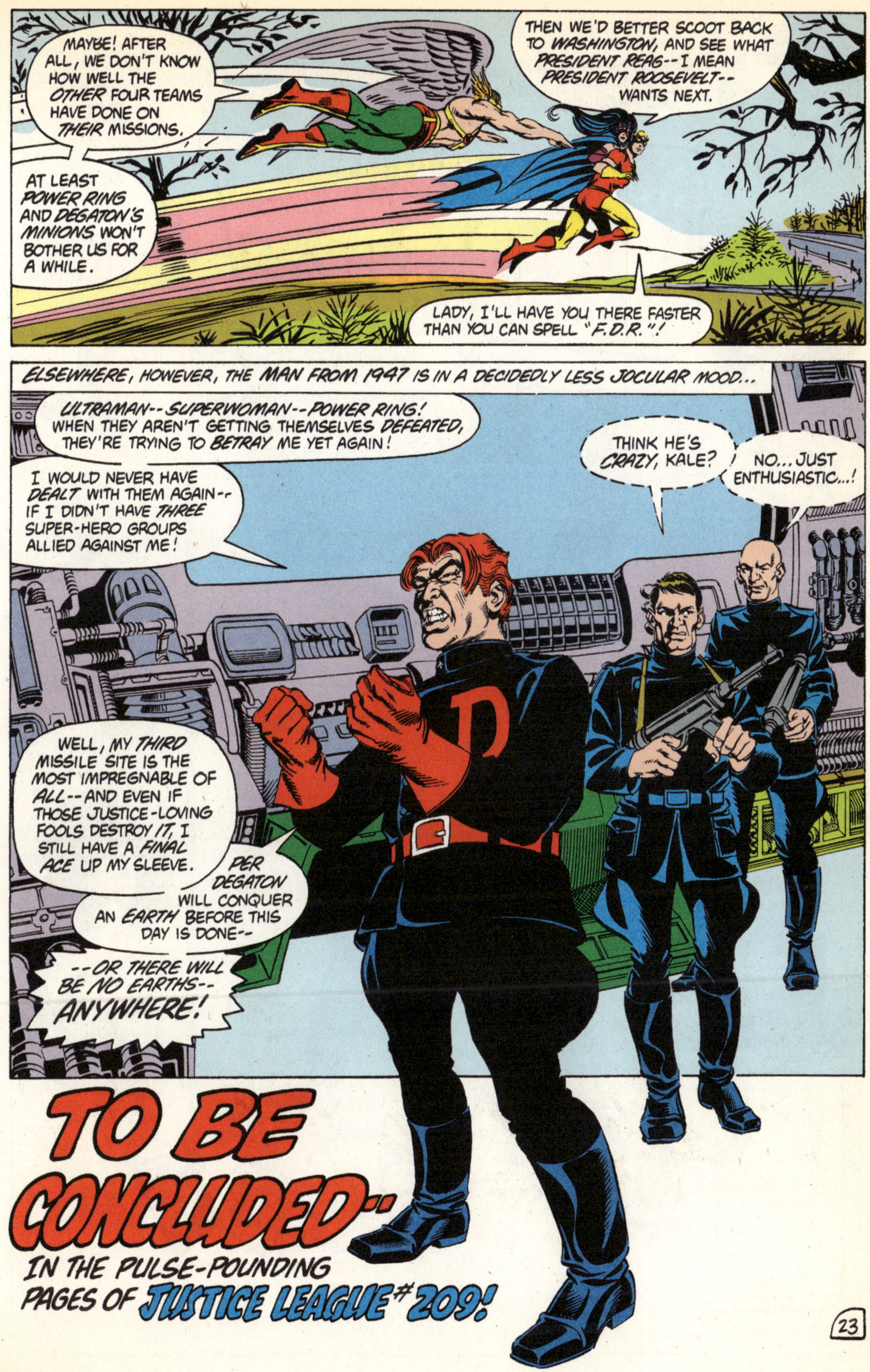
MAYBE! AFTER ALL, WE DON'T KNOW HOW WELL THE OTHER FOUR TEAMS HAVE DONE ON THEIR MISSIONS.
AT LEAST POWER RING AND DEGATON'S MINIONS WON'T BOTHER US FOR A WHILE.
THEN WE'D BETTER SCOOT BACK TO WASHINGTON, AND SEE WHAT PRESIDENT REAG--I MEAN PRESIDENT ROOSEVELT--WANTS NEXT.
LADY, I'LL HAVE YOU THERE FASTER THAN YOU CAN SPELL "F.D.R."!
ELSEWHERE, HOWEVER, THE MAN FROM 1947 IS IN A DECIDEDLY LESS JOCULAR MOOD...
ULTRAMAN--SUPERWOMAN--POWER RING! WHEN THEY AREN'T GETTING THEMSELVES DEFEATED, THEY'RE TRYING TO BETRAY ME YET AGAIN!
I WOULD NEVER HAVE DEALT WITH THEM AGAIN--IF I DIDN'T HAVE THREE SUPER-HERO GROUPS ALLIED AGAINST ME!
THINK HE'S CRAZY, KALE?
NO... JUST ENTHUSIASTIC...!
WELL, MY THIRD MISSILE SITE IS THE MOST IMPREGNABLE OF ALL--AND EVEN IF THOSE JUSTICE-LOVING FOOLS DESTROY IT, I STILL HAVE A FINAL ACE UP MY SLEEVE.
PER DEGATON WILL CONQUER AN EARTH BEFORE THIS DAY IS DONE--
--OR THERE WILL BE NO EARTHS--ANYWHERE!
TO BE CONCLUDED--
IN THE PULSE-POUNDING PAGES OF JUSTICE LEAGUE #209!
23

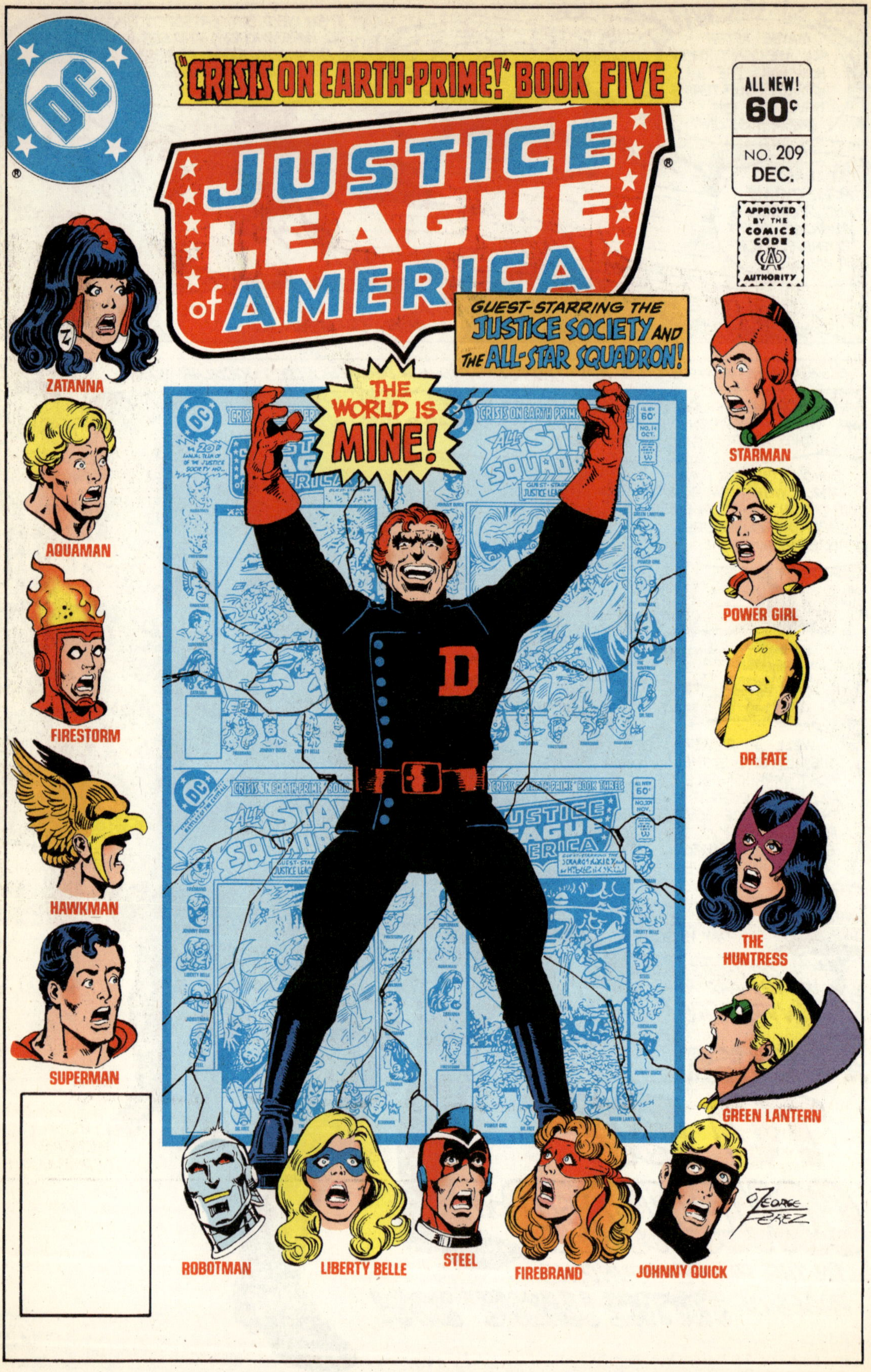
"CRISIS ON EARTH-PRIME!" BOOK FIVE
JUSTICE LEAGUE of AMERICA
ALL NEW! 60¢
NO. 209 DEC.
APPROVED BY THE COMICS CODE AUTHORITY
GUEST-STARRING THE JUSTICE SOCIETY AND THE ALL-STAR SQUADRON!
THE WORLD IS MINE!
ZATANNA
AQUAMAN
FIRESTORM
HAWKMAN
SUPERMAN
STARMAN
POWER GIRL
DR. FATE
THE HUNTRESS
GREEN LANTERN
ROBOTMAN
LIBERTY BELLE
STEEL
FIREBRAND
JOHNNY QUICK

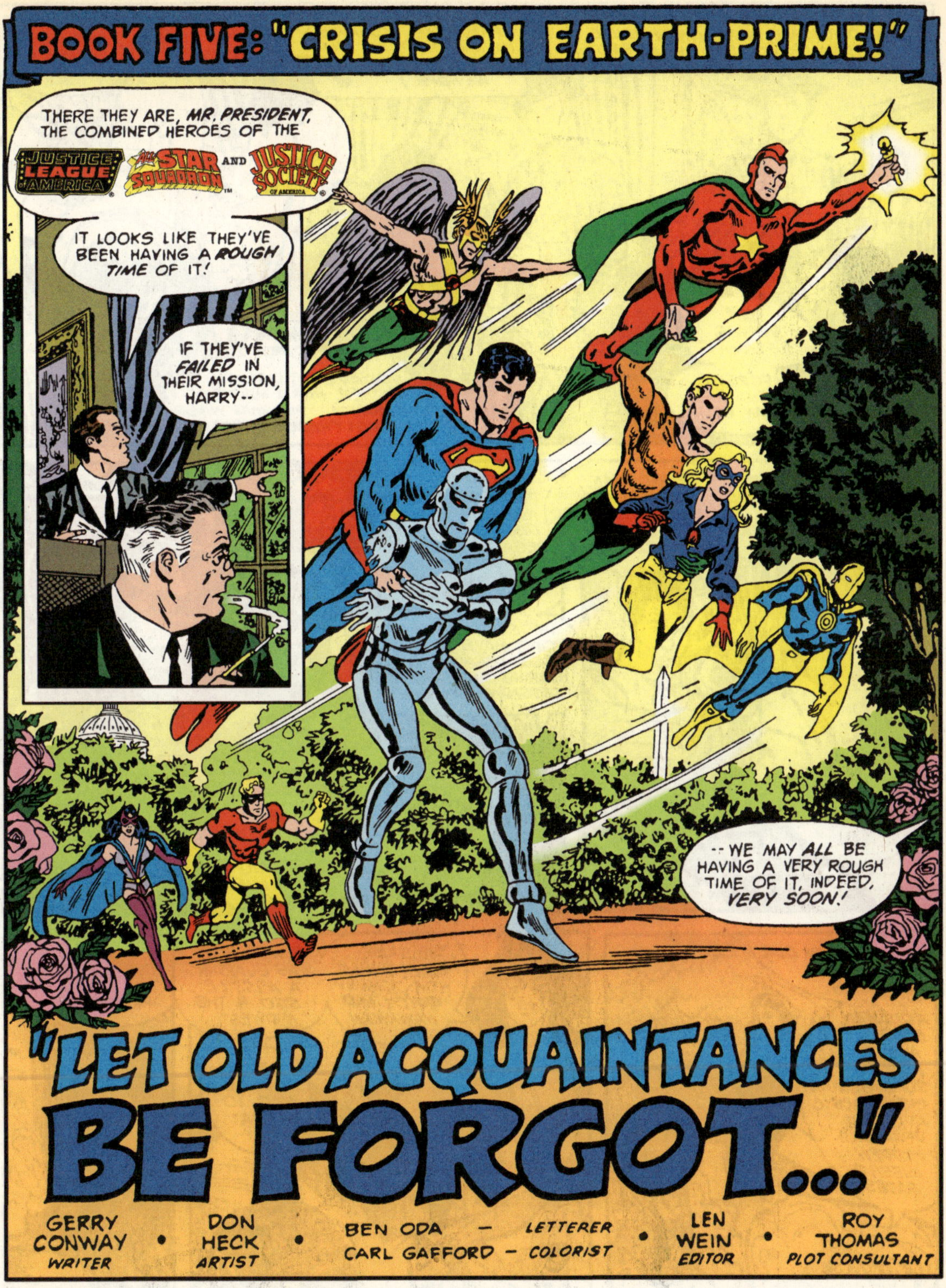
BOOK FIVE: "CRISIS ON EARTH-PRIME!"
THERE THEY ARE, MR. PRESIDENT, THE COMBINED HEROES OF THE JUSTICE LEAGUE OF AMERICA ALL-STAR SQUADRON AND JUSTICE SOCIETY OF AMERICA
IT LOOKS LIKE THEY'VE BEEN HAVING A ROUGH TIME OF IT!
IF THEY'VE FAILED IN THEIR MISSION, HARRY--
--WE MAY ALL BE HAVING A VERY ROUGH TIME OF IT, INDEED, VERY SOON!
"LET OLD ACQUAINTANCES BE FORGOT..."
GERRY CONWAY WRITER • DON HECK ARTIST • BEN ODA - LETTERER CARL GAFFORD - COLORIST • LEN WEIN EDITOR • ROY THOMAS PLOT CONSULTANT

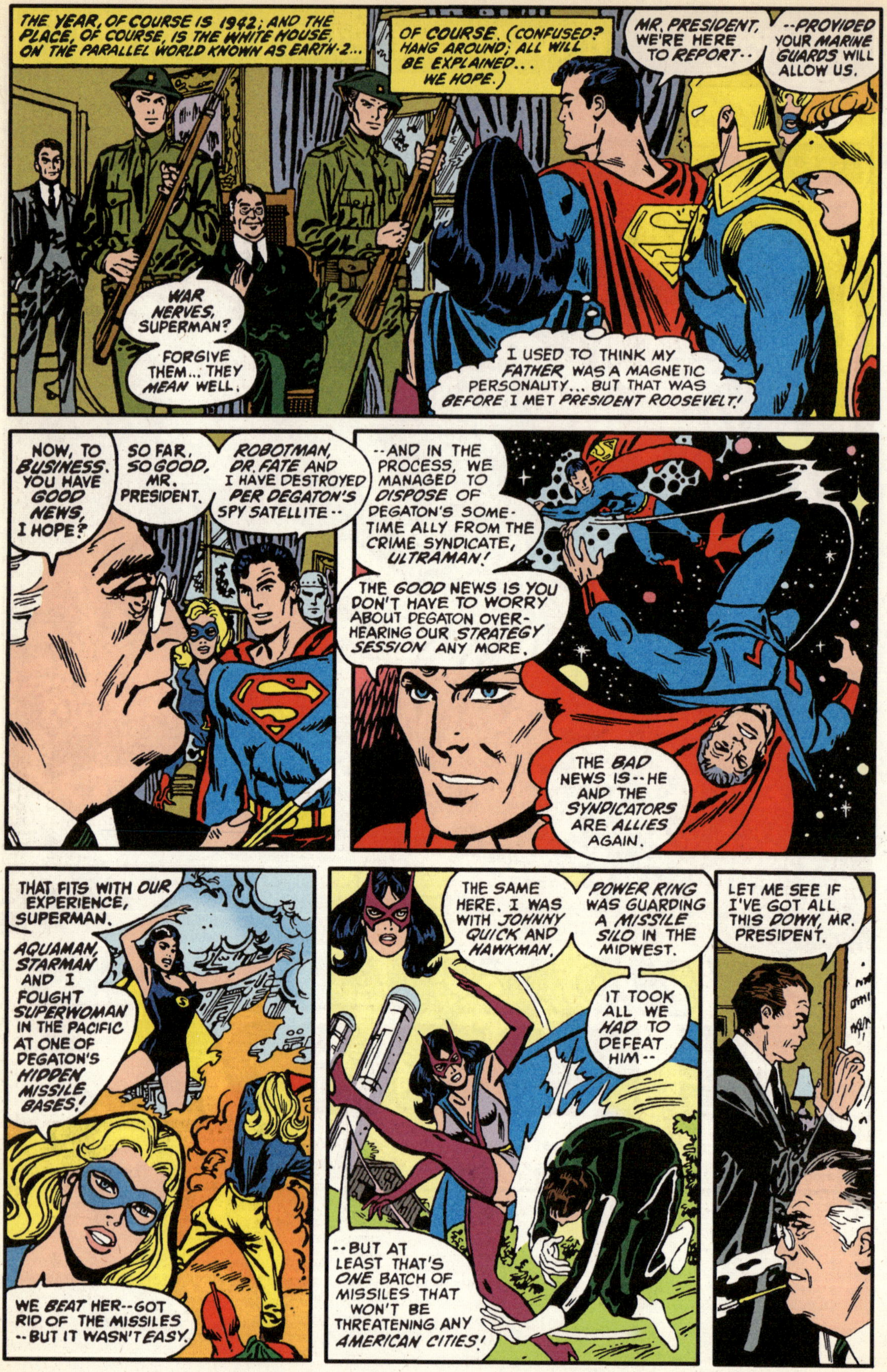
THE YEAR, OF COURSE IS 1942; AND THE PLACE, OF COURSE, IS THE WHITE HOUSE, ON THE PARALLEL WORLD KNOWN AS EARTH-2...
OF COURSE. (CONFUSED? HANG AROUND; ALL WILL BE EXPLAINED... WE HOPE.)
MR. PRESIDENT, WE'RE HERE TO REPORT--
--PROVIDED YOUR MARINE GUARDS WILL ALLOW US.
WAR NERVES, SUPERMAN?
FORGIVE THEM... THEY MEAN WELL.
I USED TO THINK MY FATHER WAS A MAGNETIC PERSONALITY... BUT THAT WAS BEFORE I MET PRESIDENT ROOSEVELT!
NOW, TO BUSINESS. YOU HAVE GOOD NEWS, I HOPE?
SO FAR, SO GOOD, MR. PRESIDENT.
ROBOTMAN, DR. FATE AND I HAVE DESTROYED PER DEGATON'S SPY SATELLITE--
--AND IN THE PROCESS, WE MANAGED TO DISPOSE OF DEGATON'S SOME-TIME ALLY FROM THE CRIME SYNDICATE, ULTRAMAN!
THE GOOD NEWS IS YOU DON'T HAVE TO WORRY ABOUT DEGATON OVER-HEARING OUR STRATEGY SESSION ANY MORE.
THE BAD NEWS IS--HE AND THE SYNDICATORS ARE ALLIES AGAIN.
THAT FITS WITH OUR EXPERIENCE, SUPERMAN.
AQUAMAN, STARMAN AND I FOUGHT SUPERWOMAN IN THE PACIFIC AT ONE OF DEGATON'S HIDDEN MISSILE BASES!
WE BEAT HER--GOT RID OF THE MISSILES --BUT IT WASN'T EASY.
THE SAME HERE. I WAS WITH JOHNNY QUICK AND HAWKMAN.
POWER RING WAS GUARDING A MISSILE SILO IN THE MIDWEST.
IT TOOK ALL WE HAD TO DEFEAT HIM--
--BUT AT LEAST THAT'S ONE BATCH OF MISSILES THAT WON'T BE THREATENING ANY AMERICAN CITIES!
LET ME SEE IF I'VE GOT ALL THIS DOWN, MR. PRESIDENT.

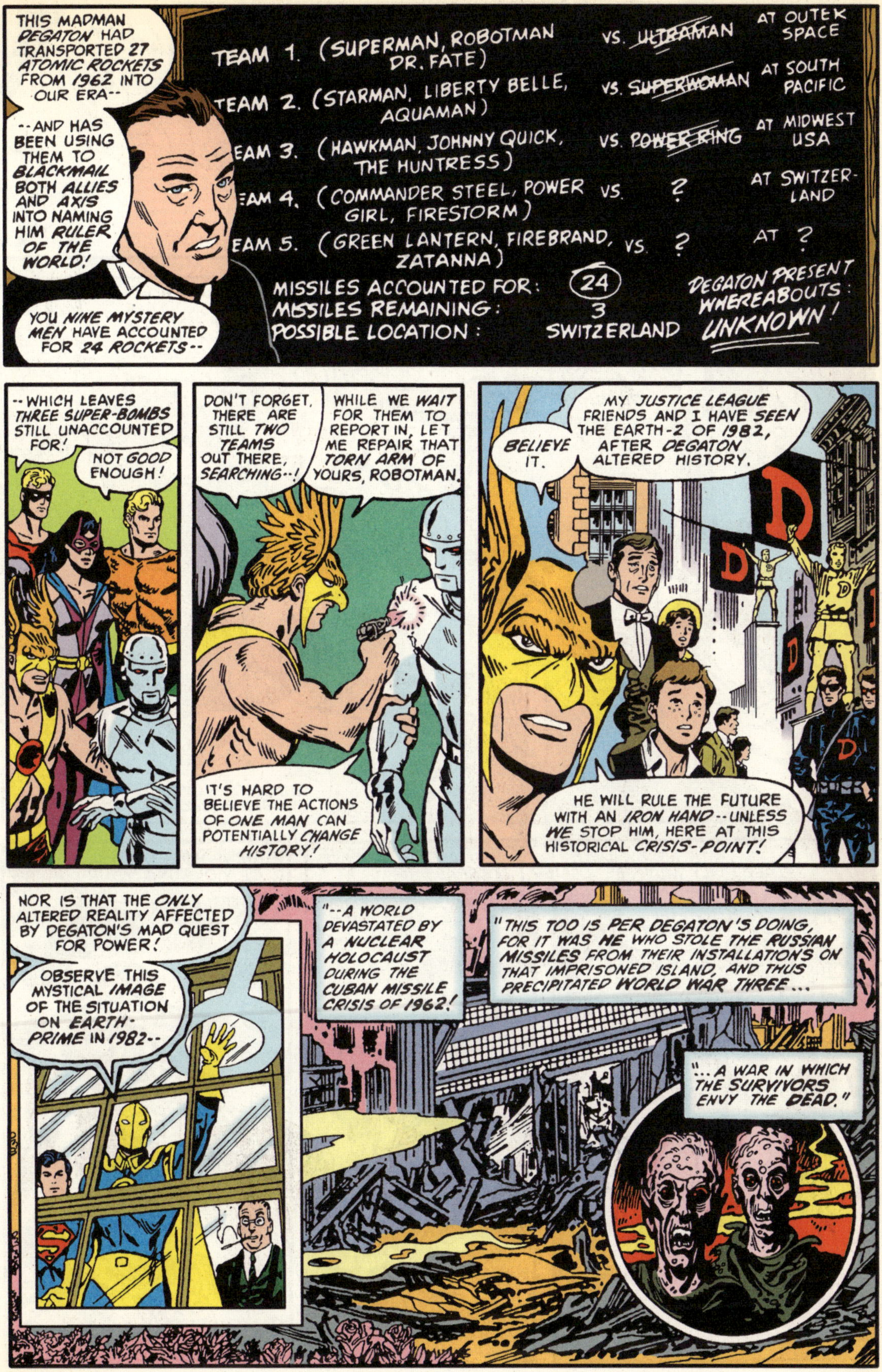
THIS MADMAN DEGATON HAD TRANSPORTED 27 ATOMIC ROCKETS FROM 1962 INTO OUR ERA--
--AND HAS BEEN USING THEM TO BLACKMAIL BOTH ALLIES AND AXIS INTO NAMING HIM RULER OF THE WORLD!
TEAM 1. (SUPERMAN, ROBOTMAN DR. FATE) VS. ULTRAMAN AT OUTER SPACE
TEAM 2. (STARMAN, LIBERTY BELLE, AQUAMAN) VS. SUPERWOMAN AT SOUTH PACIFIC
TEAM 3. (HAWKMAN, JOHNNY QUICK, THE HUNTRESS) VS. POWER RING AT MIDWEST USA
TEAM 4. (COMMANDER STEEL, POWER GIRL, FIRESTORM) VS. ? AT SWITZERLAND
TEAM 5. (GREEN LANTERN, FIREBRAND, ZATANNA) VS. ? AT ?
MISSILES ACCOUNTED FOR: 24
MISSILES REMAINING: 3
POSSIBLE LOCATION: SWITZERLAND
DEGATON PRESENT WHEREABOUTS: UNKNOWN!
YOU NINE MYSTERY MEN HAVE ACCOUNTED FOR 24 ROCKETS--
--WHICH LEAVES THREE SUPER-BOMBS STILL UNACCOUNTED FOR!
NOT GOOD ENOUGH!
DON'T FORGET, THERE ARE STILL TWO TEAMS OUT THERE, SEARCHING--!
WHILE WE WAIT FOR THEM TO REPORT IN, LET ME REPAIR THAT TORN ARM OF YOURS, ROBOTMAN.
IT'S HARD TO BELIEVE THE ACTIONS OF ONE MAN CAN POTENTIALLY CHANGE HISTORY!
BELIEVE IT.
MY JUSTICE LEAGUE FRIENDS AND I HAVE SEEN THE EARTH-2 OF 1982, AFTER DEGATON ALTERED HISTORY.
HE WILL RULE THE FUTURE WITH AN IRON HAND--UNLESS WE STOP HIM, HERE AT THIS HISTORICAL CRISIS-POINT!
NOR IS THAT THE ONLY ALTERED REALITY AFFECTED BY DEGATON'S MAD QUEST FOR POWER!
OBSERVE THIS MYSTICAL IMAGE OF THE SITUATION ON EARTH-PRIME IN 1982--
"--A WORLD DEVASTATED BY A NUCLEAR HOLOCAUST DURING THE CUBAN MISSILE CRISIS OF 1962!
"THIS TOO IS PER DEGATON'S DOING, FOR IT WAS HE WHO STOLE THE RUSSIAN MISSILES FROM THEIR INSTALLATIONS ON THAT IMPRISONED ISLAND, AND THUS PRECIPITATED WORLD WAR THREE...
"...A WAR IN WHICH THE SURVIVORS ENVY THE DEAD."

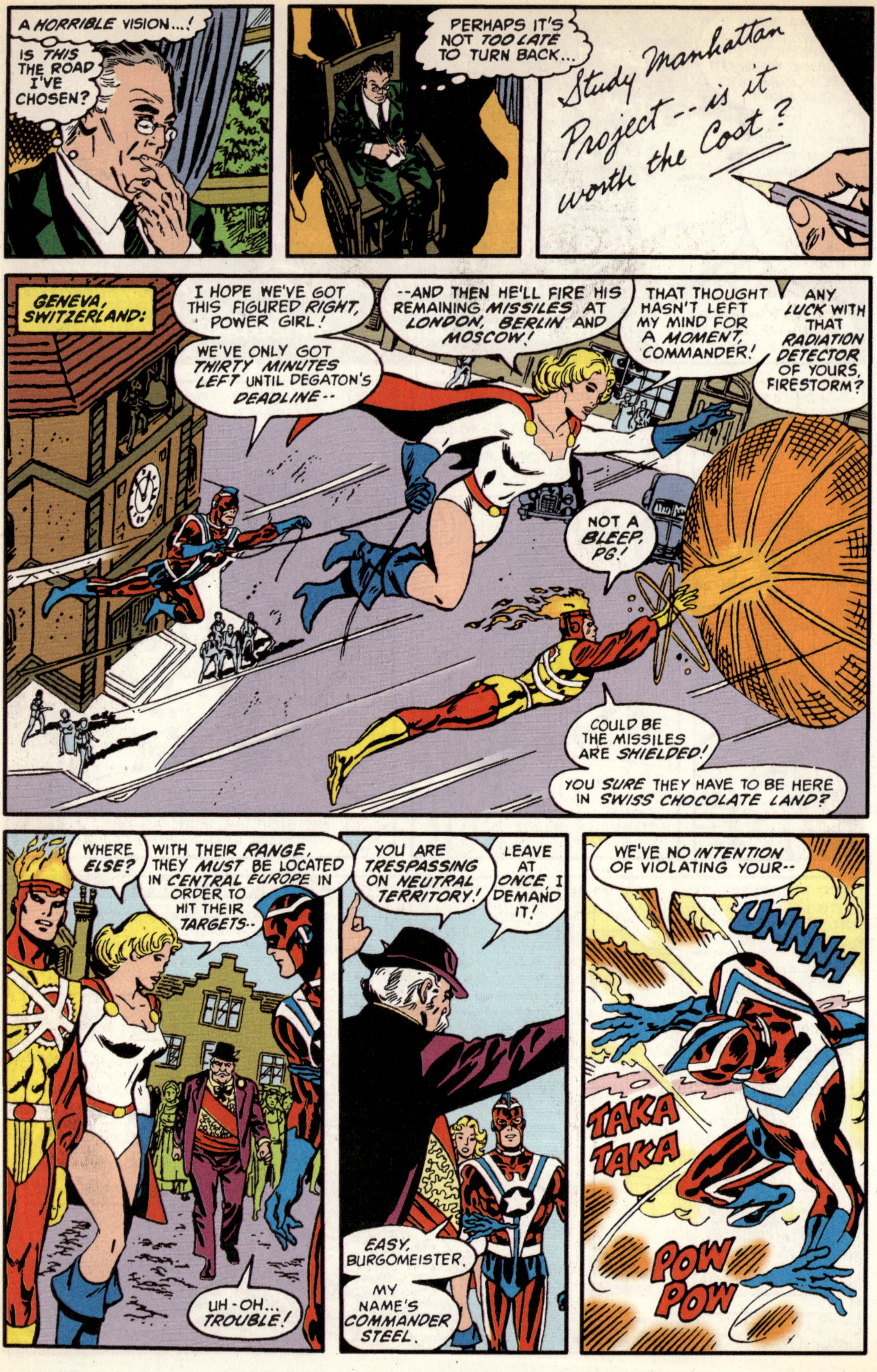
A HORRIBLE VISION...!
IS THIS THE ROAD I'VE CHOSEN?
PERHAPS IT'S NOT TOO LATE TO TURN BACK...
Study Manhattan Project -- is it worth the Cost?
GENEVA, SWITZERLAND:
I HOPE WE'VE GOT THIS FIGURED RIGHT, POWER GIRL!
WE'VE ONLY GOT THIRTY MINUTES LEFT UNTIL DEGATON'S DEADLINE--
--AND THEN HE'LL FIRE HIS REMAINING MISSILES AT LONDON, BERLIN AND MOSCOW!
THAT THOUGHT HASN'T LEFT MY MIND FOR A MOMENT, COMMANDER!
ANY LUCK WITH THAT RADIATION DETECTOR OF YOURS, FIRESTORM?
NOT A BLEEP, PG!
COULD BE THE MISSILES ARE SHIELDED!
YOU SURE THEY HAVE TO BE HERE IN SWISS CHOCOLATE LAND?
WHERE ELSE?
WITH THEIR RANGE, THEY MUST BE LOCATED IN CENTRAL EUROPE IN ORDER TO HIT THEIR TARGETS..
UH-OH... TROUBLE!
YOU ARE TRESPASSING ON NEUTRAL TERRITORY!
LEAVE AT ONCE, I DEMAND IT!
EASY, BURGOMEISTER.
MY NAME'S COMMANDER STEEL.
WE'VE NO INTENTION OF VIOLATING YOUR--
UNNNH
TAKA TAKA
POW POW

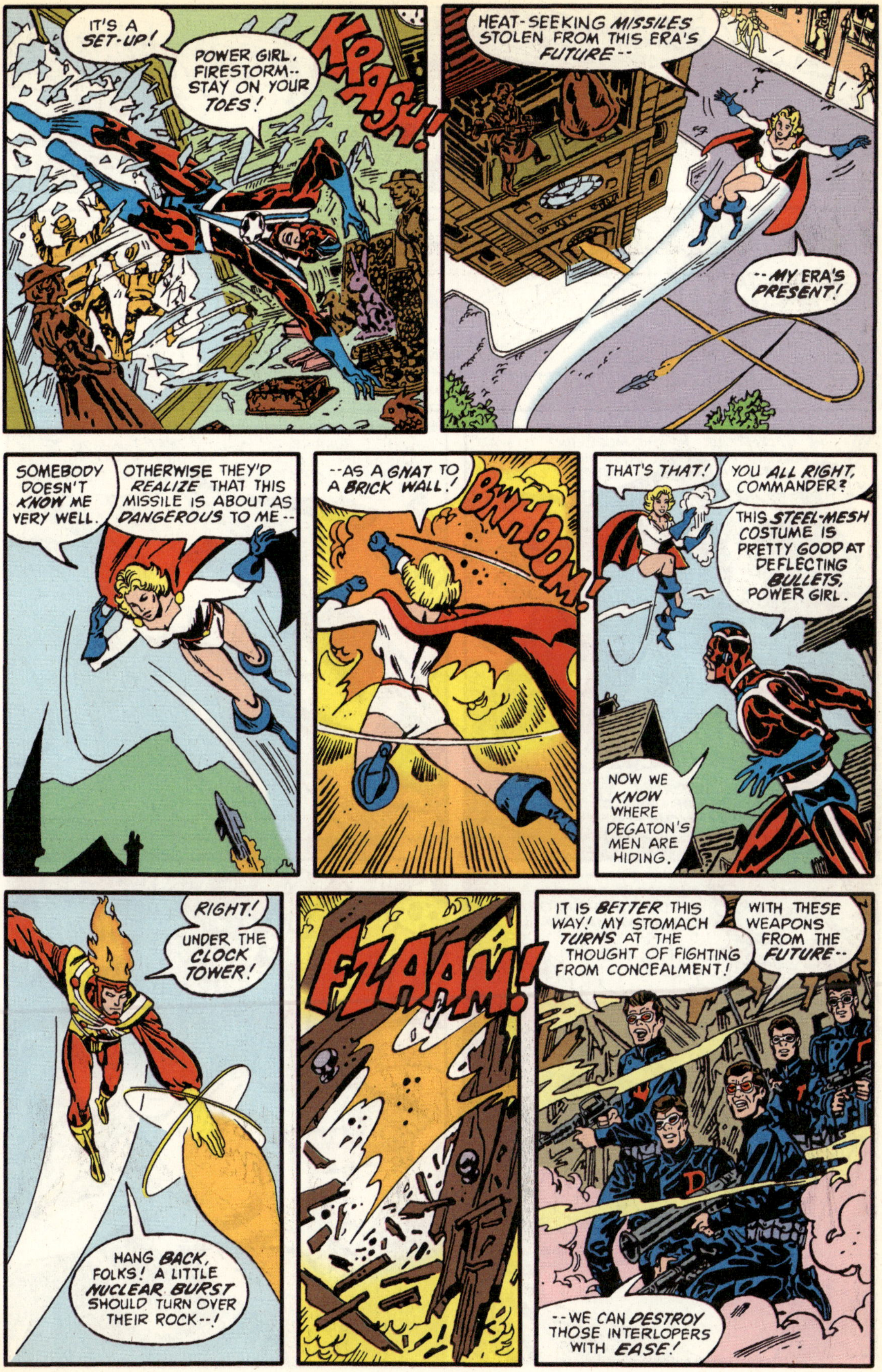

IT'S A SET-UP!
POWER GIRL, FIRESTORM-- STAY ON YOUR TOES!
KRASH!
HEAT-SEEKING MISSILES STOLEN FROM THIS ERA'S FUTURE--
--MY ERA'S PRESENT!
SOMEBODY DOESN'T KNOW ME VERY WELL.
OTHERWISE THEY'D REALIZE THAT THIS MISSILE IS ABOUT AS DANGEROUS TO ME--
--AS A GNAT TO A BRICK WALL!
BWHOOM!
THAT'S THAT!
YOU ALL RIGHT, COMMANDER?
THIS STEEL-MESH COSTUME IS PRETTY GOOD AT DEFLECTING BULLETS, POWER GIRL.
NOW WE KNOW WHERE DEGATON'S MEN ARE HIDING.
RIGHT!
UNDER THE CLOCK TOWER!
HANG BACK, FOLKS! A LITTLE NUCLEAR BURST SHOULD TURN OVER THEIR ROCK--!
FZAAM!
IT IS BETTER THIS WAY! MY STOMACH TURNS AT THE THOUGHT OF FIGHTING FROM CONCEALMENT!
WITH THESE WEAPONS FROM THE FUTURE--
--WE CAN DESTROY THOSE INTERLOPERS WITH EASE!

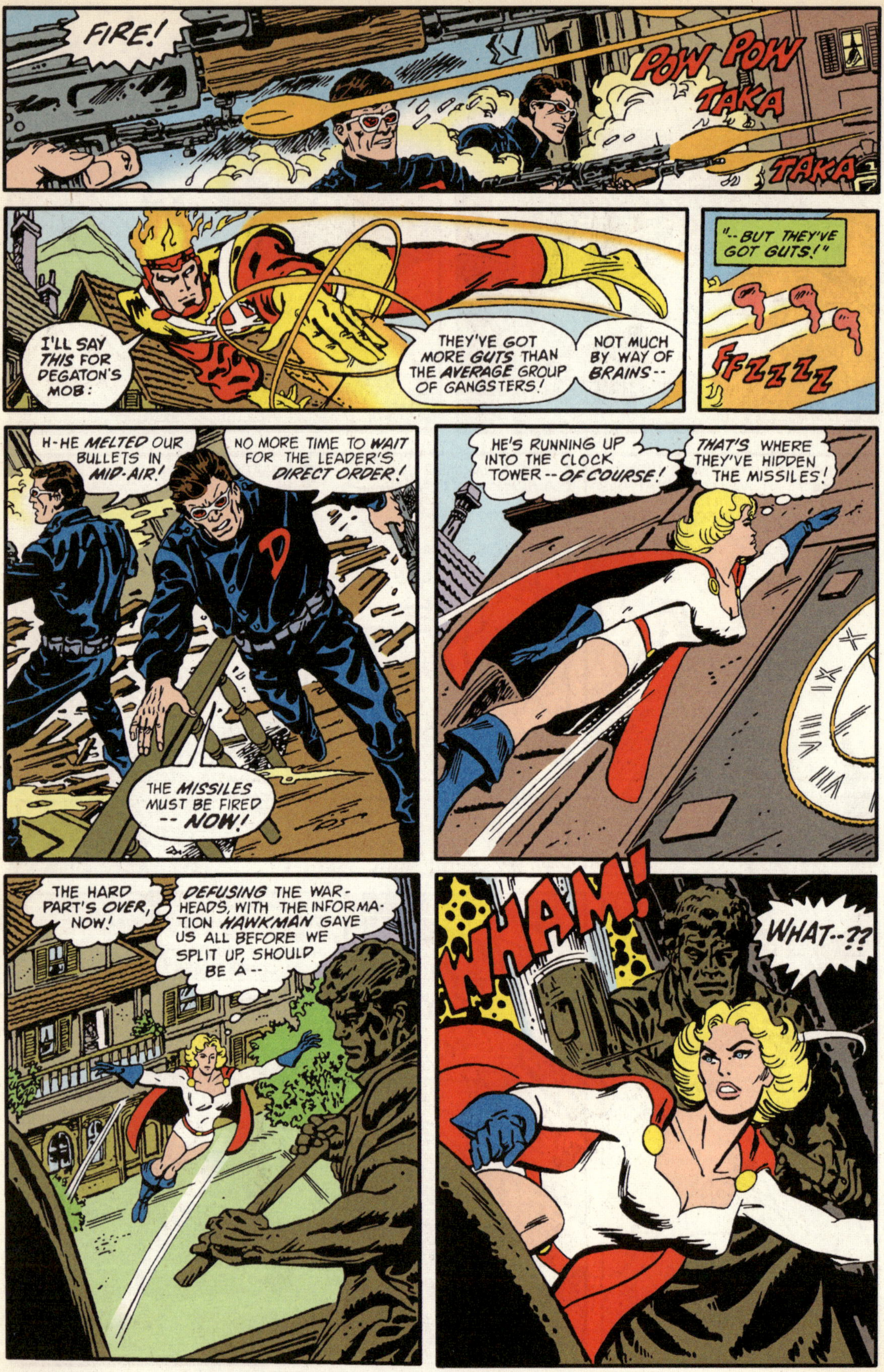
FIRE!
POW POW
TAKA
TAKA
I'LL SAY THIS FOR DEGATON'S MOB:
THEY'VE GOT MORE GUTS THAN THE AVERAGE GROUP OF GANGSTERS!
NOT MUCH BY WAY OF BRAINS--
"--BUT THEY'VE GOT GUTS!"
FFZZZZZ
H-HE MELTED OUR BULLETS IN MID-AIR!
NO MORE TIME TO WAIT FOR THE LEADER'S DIRECT ORDER!
THE MISSILES MUST BE FIRED -- NOW!
HE'S RUNNING UP INTO THE CLOCK TOWER -- OF COURSE!
THAT'S WHERE THEY'VE HIDDEN THE MISSILES!
THE HARD PART'S OVER, NOW!
DEFUSING THE WAR-HEADS, WITH THE INFORMATION HAWKMAN GAVE US ALL BEFORE WE SPLIT UP, SHOULD BE A--
WHAM!
WHAT--??

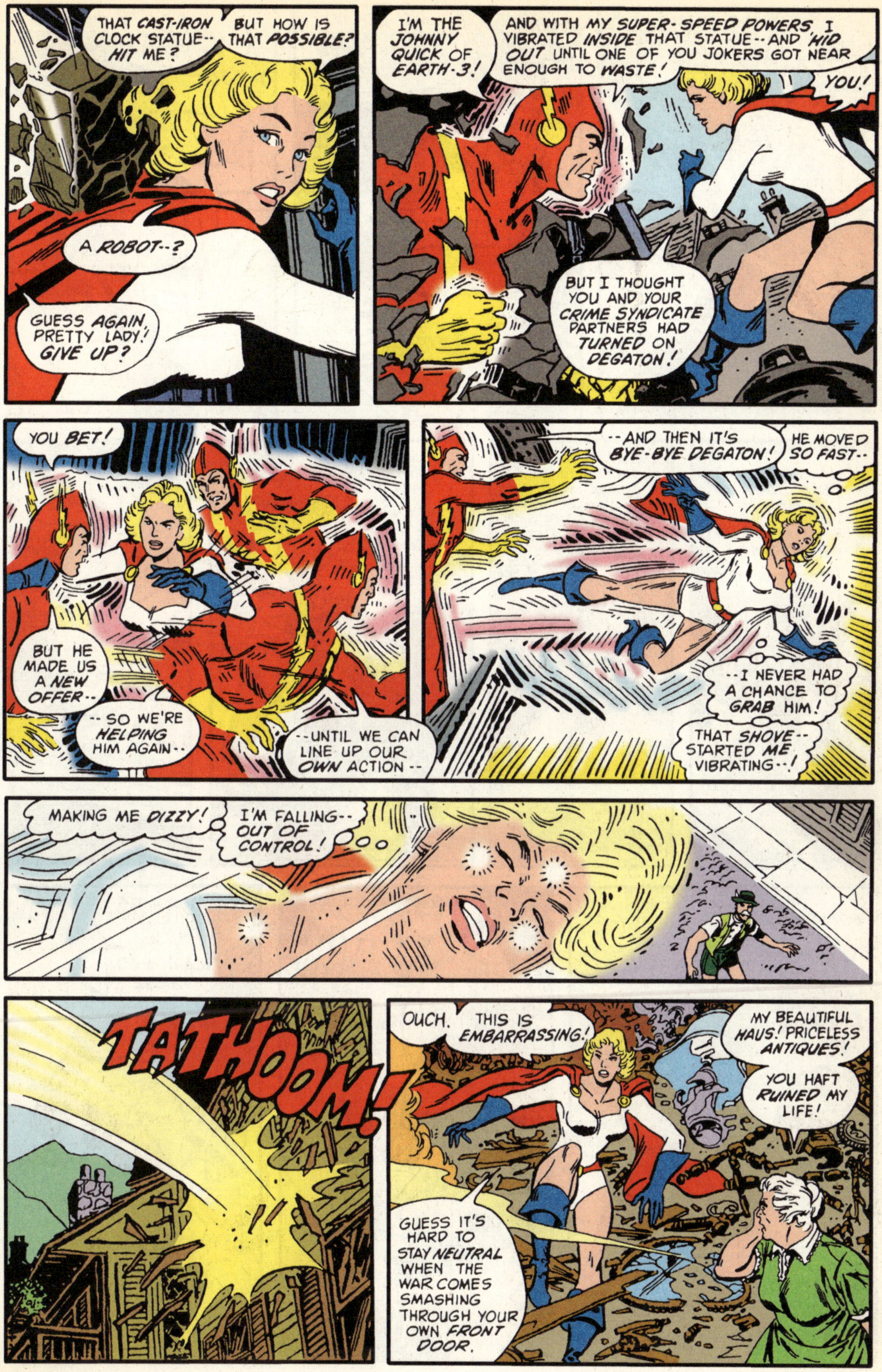

THAT CAST-IRON CLOCK STATUE-- HIT ME?
BUT HOW IS THAT POSSIBLE?
A ROBOT--?
GUESS AGAIN, PRETTY LADY! GIVE UP?
I'M THE JOHNNY QUICK OF EARTH-3!
AND WITH MY SUPER-SPEED POWERS, I VIBRATED INSIDE THAT STATUE--AND 'HID OUT' UNTIL ONE OF YOU JOKERS GOT NEAR ENOUGH TO WASTE!
YOU!
BUT I THOUGHT YOU AND YOUR CRIME SYNDICATE PARTNERS HAD TURNED ON DEGATON!
YOU BET!
BUT HE MADE US A NEW OFFER--
--SO WE'RE HELPING HIM AGAIN--
--UNTIL WE CAN LINE UP OUR OWN ACTION--
--AND THEN IT'S BYE-BYE DEGATON!
HE MOVED SO FAST--
--I NEVER HAD A CHANCE TO GRAB HIM!
THAT SHOVE--STARTED ME VIBRATING--!
MAKING ME DIZZY!
I'M FALLING--OUT OF CONTROL!
TATHOOM!
OUCH. THIS IS EMBARRASSING!
MY BEAUTIFUL HAUS! PRICELESS ANTIQUES!
YOU HAFT RUINED MY LIFE!
GUESS IT'S HARD TO STAY NEUTRAL WHEN THE WAR COMES SMASHING THROUGH YOUR OWN FRONT DOOR.

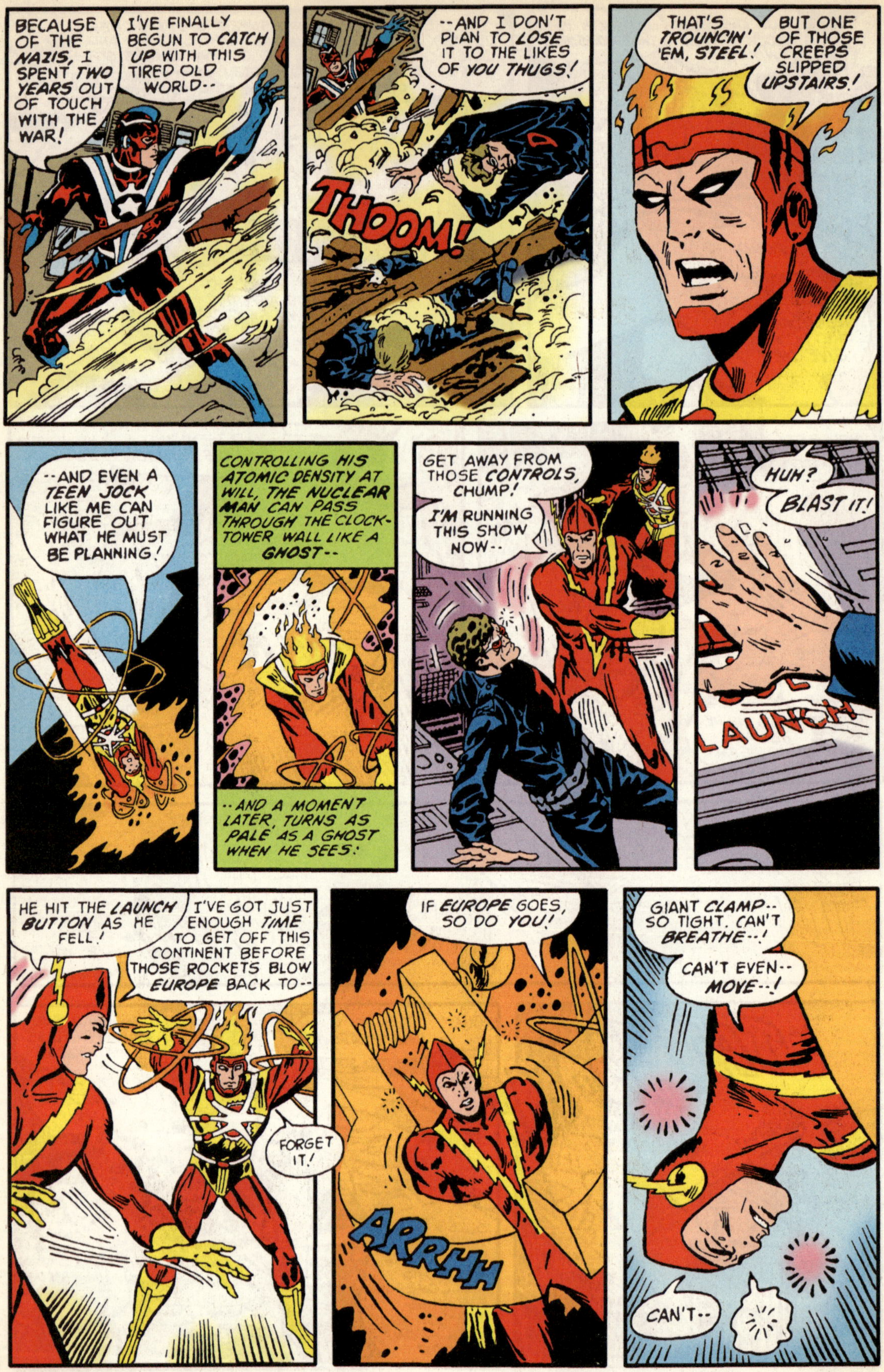
BECAUSE OF THE NAZIS, I SPENT TWO YEARS OUT OF TOUCH WITH THE WAR!
I'VE FINALLY BEGUN TO CATCH UP WITH THIS TIRED OLD WORLD--
--AND I DON'T PLAN TO LOSE IT TO THE LIKES OF YOU THUGS!
THOOM!
THAT'S TROUNCIN' 'EM, STEEL!
BUT ONE OF THOSE CREEPS SLIPPED UPSTAIRS!
--AND EVEN A TEEN JOCK LIKE ME CAN FIGURE OUT WHAT HE MUST BE PLANNING!
CONTROLLING HIS ATOMIC DENSITY AT WILL, THE NUCLEAR MAN CAN PASS THROUGH THE CLOCK-TOWER WALL LIKE A GHOST--
--AND A MOMENT LATER, TURNS AS PALE AS A GHOST WHEN HE SEES:
GET AWAY FROM THOSE CONTROLS, CHUMP!
I'M RUNNING THIS SHOW NOW--
HUH?
BLAST IT!
LAUNCH
HE HIT THE LAUNCH BUTTON AS HE FELL!
I'VE GOT JUST ENOUGH TIME TO GET OFF THIS CONTINENT BEFORE THOSE ROCKETS BLOW EUROPE BACK TO--
FORGET IT!
IF EUROPE GOES, SO DO YOU!
ARRHH
GIANT CLAMP-- SO TIGHT. CAN'T BREATHE--!
CAN'T EVEN-- MOVE--!
CAN'T--

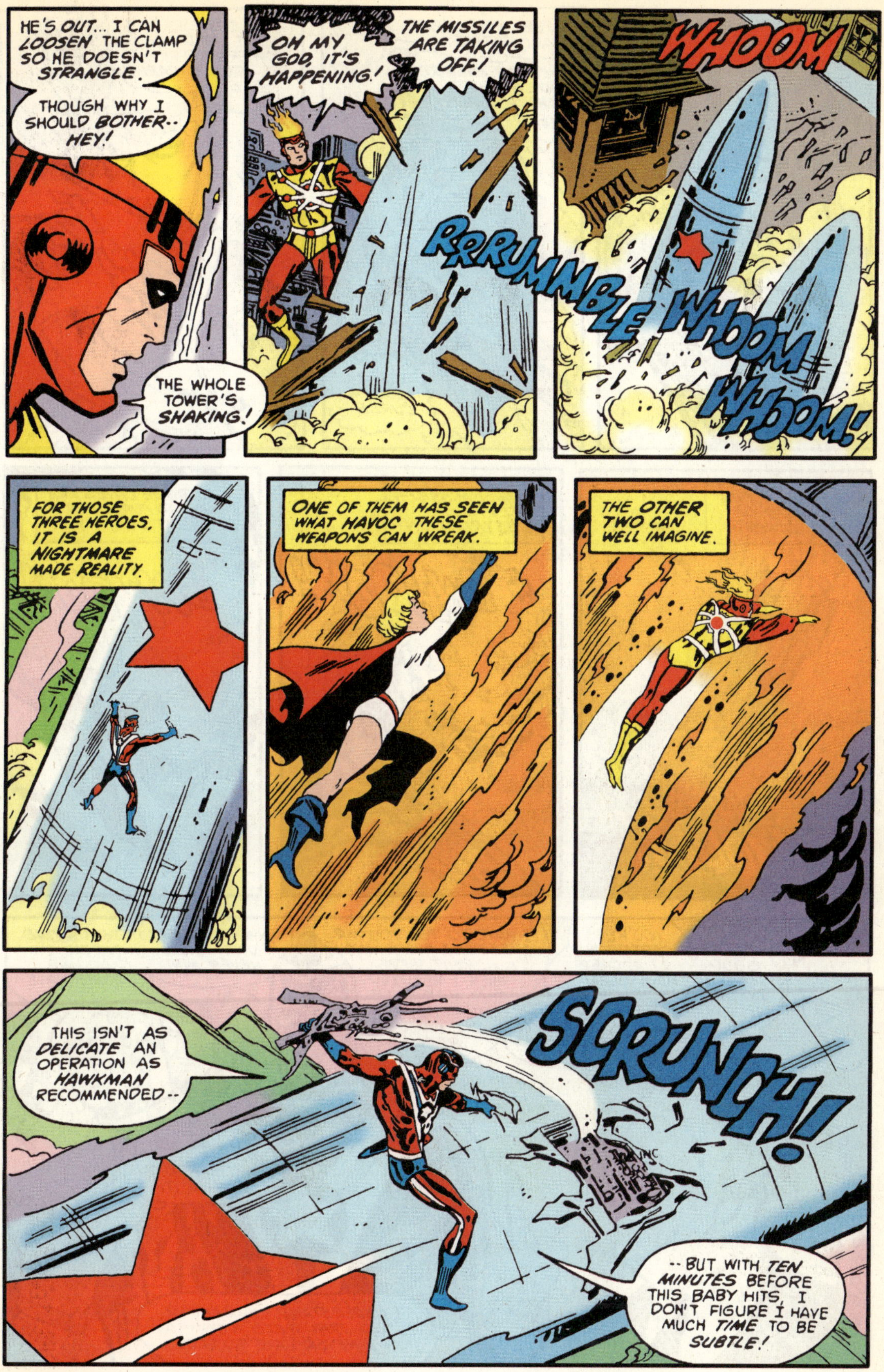

HE'S OUT... I CAN LOOSEN THE CLAMP SO HE DOESN'T STRANGLE.
THOUGH WHY I SHOULD BOTHER-- HEY!
THE WHOLE TOWER'S SHAKING!
OH MY GOD, IT'S HAPPENING!
THE MISSILES ARE TAKING OFF!
WHOOM
RRRUMMBLE
WHOOM
WHOOM!
FOR THOSE THREE HEROES, IT IS A NIGHTMARE MADE REALITY.
ONE OF THEM HAS SEEN WHAT HAVOC THESE WEAPONS CAN WREAK.
THE OTHER TWO CAN WELL IMAGINE.
THIS ISN'T AS DELICATE AN OPERATION AS HAWKMAN RECOMMENDED--
SCRUNCH!
--BUT WITH TEN MINUTES BEFORE THIS BABY HITS, I DON'T FIGURE I HAVE MUCH TIME TO BE SUBTLE!

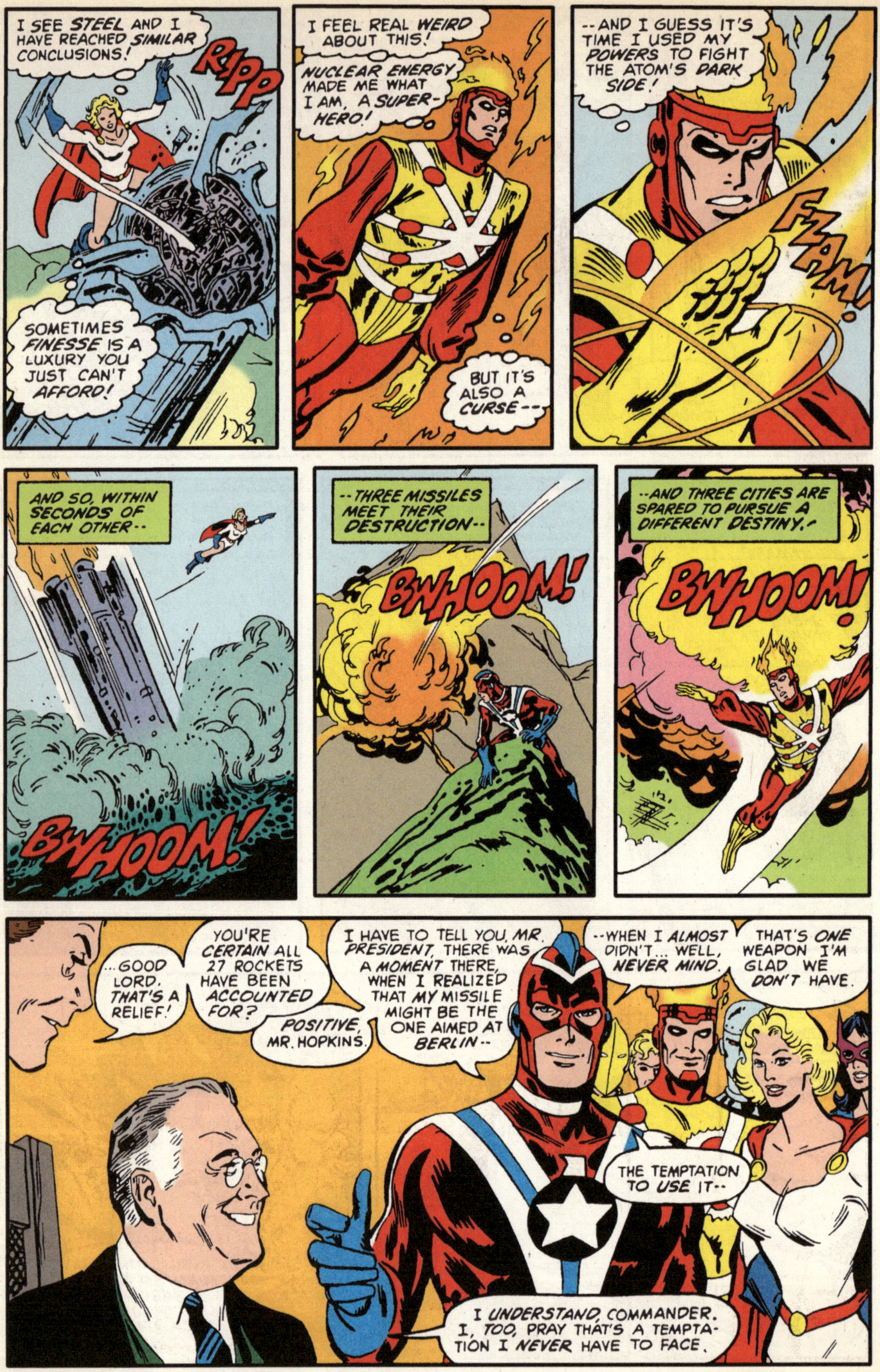
I SEE STEEL AND I HAVE REACHED SIMILAR CONCLUSIONS!
RIPP
SOMETIMES FINESSE IS A LUXURY YOU JUST CAN'T AFFORD!
I FEEL REAL WEIRD ABOUT THIS!
NUCLEAR ENERGY MADE ME WHAT I AM, A SUPER-HERO!
BUT IT'S ALSO A CURSE--
--AND I GUESS IT'S TIME I USED MY POWERS TO FIGHT THE ATOM'S DARK SIDE!
FZAM!
AND SO, WITHIN SECONDS OF EACH OTHER--
BWHOOM!
--THREE MISSILES MEET THEIR DESTRUCTION--
BWHOOM!
--AND THREE CITIES ARE SPARED TO PURSUE A DIFFERENT DESTINY.
BWHOOM!
...GOOD LORD. THAT'S A RELIEF!
YOU'RE CERTAIN ALL 27 ROCKETS HAVE BEEN ACCOUNTED FOR?
POSITIVE, MR. HOPKINS.
I HAVE TO TELL YOU, MR. PRESIDENT, THERE WAS A MOMENT THERE, WHEN I REALIZED THAT MY MISSILE MIGHT BE THE ONE AIMED AT BERLIN--
--WHEN I ALMOST DIDN'T... WELL, NEVER MIND.
THAT'S ONE WEAPON I'M GLAD WE DON'T HAVE.
THE TEMPTATION TO USE IT--
I UNDERSTAND, COMMANDER. I, TOO, PRAY THAT'S A TEMPTATION I NEVER HAVE TO FACE.

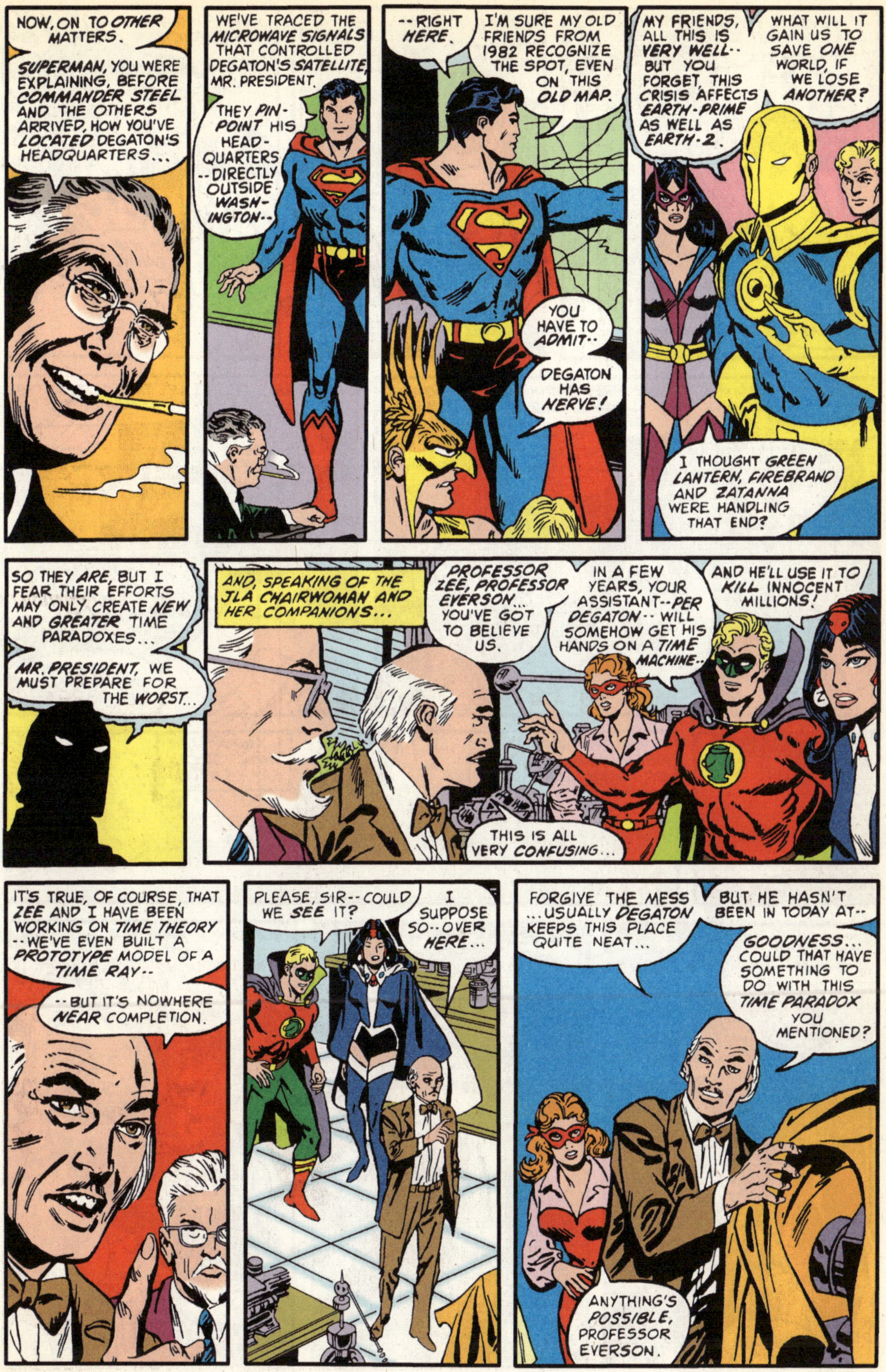
NOW, ON TO OTHER MATTERS.
SUPERMAN, YOU WERE EXPLAINING, BEFORE COMMANDER STEEL AND THE OTHERS ARRIVED, HOW YOU'VE LOCATED DEGATON'S HEADQUARTERS...
WE'VE TRACED THE MICROWAVE SIGNALS THAT CONTROLLED DEGATON'S SATELLITE, MR. PRESIDENT.
THEY PIN-POINT HIS HEAD-QUARTERS --DIRECTLY OUTSIDE WASH-INGTON--
--RIGHT HERE.
I'M SURE MY OLD FRIENDS FROM 1982 RECOGNIZE THE SPOT, EVEN ON THIS OLD MAP.
YOU HAVE TO ADMIT--
DEGATON HAS NERVE!
MY FRIENDS, ALL THIS IS VERY WELL-- BUT YOU FORGET, THIS CRISIS AFFECTS EARTH-PRIME AS WELL AS EARTH-2.
WHAT WILL IT GAIN US TO SAVE ONE WORLD, IF WE LOSE ANOTHER?
I THOUGHT GREEN LANTERN, FIREBRAND AND ZATANNA WERE HANDLING THAT END?
SO THEY ARE, BUT I FEAR THEIR EFFORTS MAY ONLY CREATE NEW AND GREATER TIME PARADOXES...
MR. PRESIDENT, WE MUST PREPARE FOR THE WORST...
AND, SPEAKING OF THE JLA CHAIRWOMAN AND HER COMPANIONS...
PROFESSOR ZEE, PROFESSOR EVERSON... YOU'VE GOT TO BELIEVE US.
IN A FEW YEARS, YOUR ASSISTANT--PER DEGATON-- WILL SOMEHOW GET HIS HANDS ON A TIME MACHINE...
AND HE'LL USE IT TO KILL INNOCENT MILLIONS!
THIS IS ALL VERY CONFUSING...
IT'S TRUE, OF COURSE, THAT ZEE AND I HAVE BEEN WORKING ON TIME THEORY --WE'VE EVEN BUILT A PROTOTYPE MODEL OF A TIME RAY--
--BUT IT'S NOWHERE NEAR COMPLETION.
PLEASE, SIR-- COULD WE SEE IT?
I SUPPOSE SO-- OVER HERE...
FORGIVE THE MESS ...USUALLY DEGATON KEEPS THIS PLACE QUITE NEAT...
BUT HE HASN'T BEEN IN TODAY AT--
GOODNESS... COULD THAT HAVE SOMETHING TO DO WITH THIS TIME PARADOX YOU MENTIONED?
ANYTHING'S POSSIBLE, PROFESSOR EVERSON.

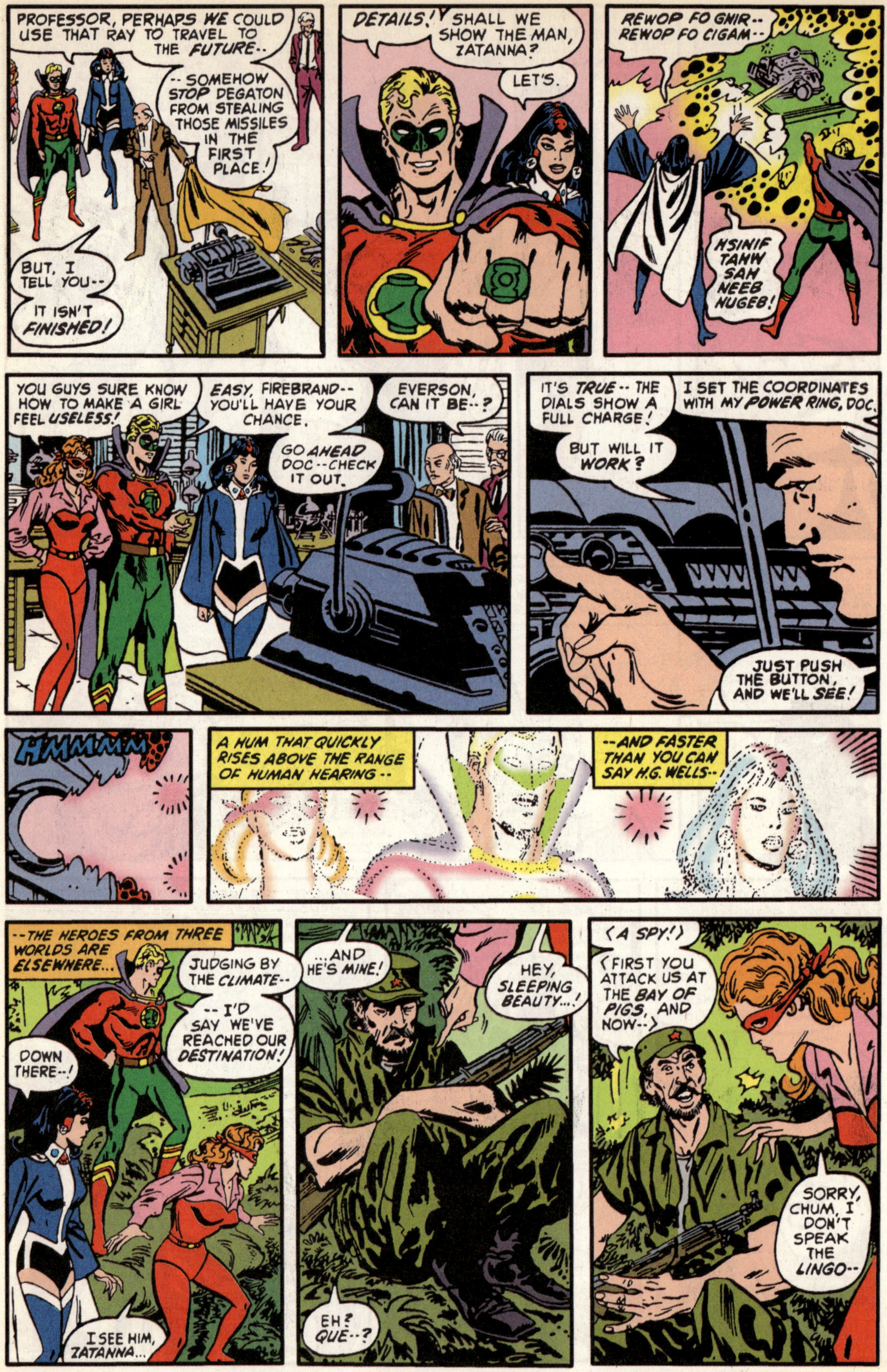

PROFESSOR, PERHAPS WE COULD USE THAT RAY TO TRAVEL TO THE FUTURE--
--SOMEHOW STOP DEGATON FROM STEALING THOSE MISSILES IN THE FIRST PLACE!
BUT, I TELL YOU--
IT ISN'T FINISHED!
DETAILS!
SHALL WE SHOW THE MAN, ZATANNA?
LET'S.
REWOP FO GNIR-- REWOP FO CIGAM--
HSINIF TAHW SAH NEEB NUGEB!
YOU GUYS SURE KNOW HOW TO MAKE A GIRL FEEL USELESS!
EASY, FIREBRAND-- YOU'LL HAVE YOUR CHANCE.
GO AHEAD DOC--CHECK IT OUT.
EVERSON, CAN IT BE--?
IT'S TRUE-- THE DIALS SHOW A FULL CHARGE!
I SET THE COORDINATES WITH MY POWER RING, DOC.
BUT WILL IT WORK?
JUST PUSH THE BUTTON, AND WE'LL SEE!
HMMMMM
A HUM THAT QUICKLY RISES ABOVE THE RANGE OF HUMAN HEARING--
--AND FASTER THAN YOU CAN SAY H.G. WELLS--
--THE HEROES FROM THREE WORLDS ARE ELSEWHERE...
JUDGING BY THE CLIMATE--
--I'D SAY WE'VE REACHED OUR DESTINATION!
DOWN THERE--!
I SEE HIM, ZATANNA...
...AND HE'S MINE!
HEY, SLEEPING BEAUTY...!
EH? QUE--?
(A SPY!)
(FIRST YOU ATTACK US AT THE BAY OF PIGS, AND NOW--)
SORRY, CHUM, I DON'T SPEAK THE LINGO--

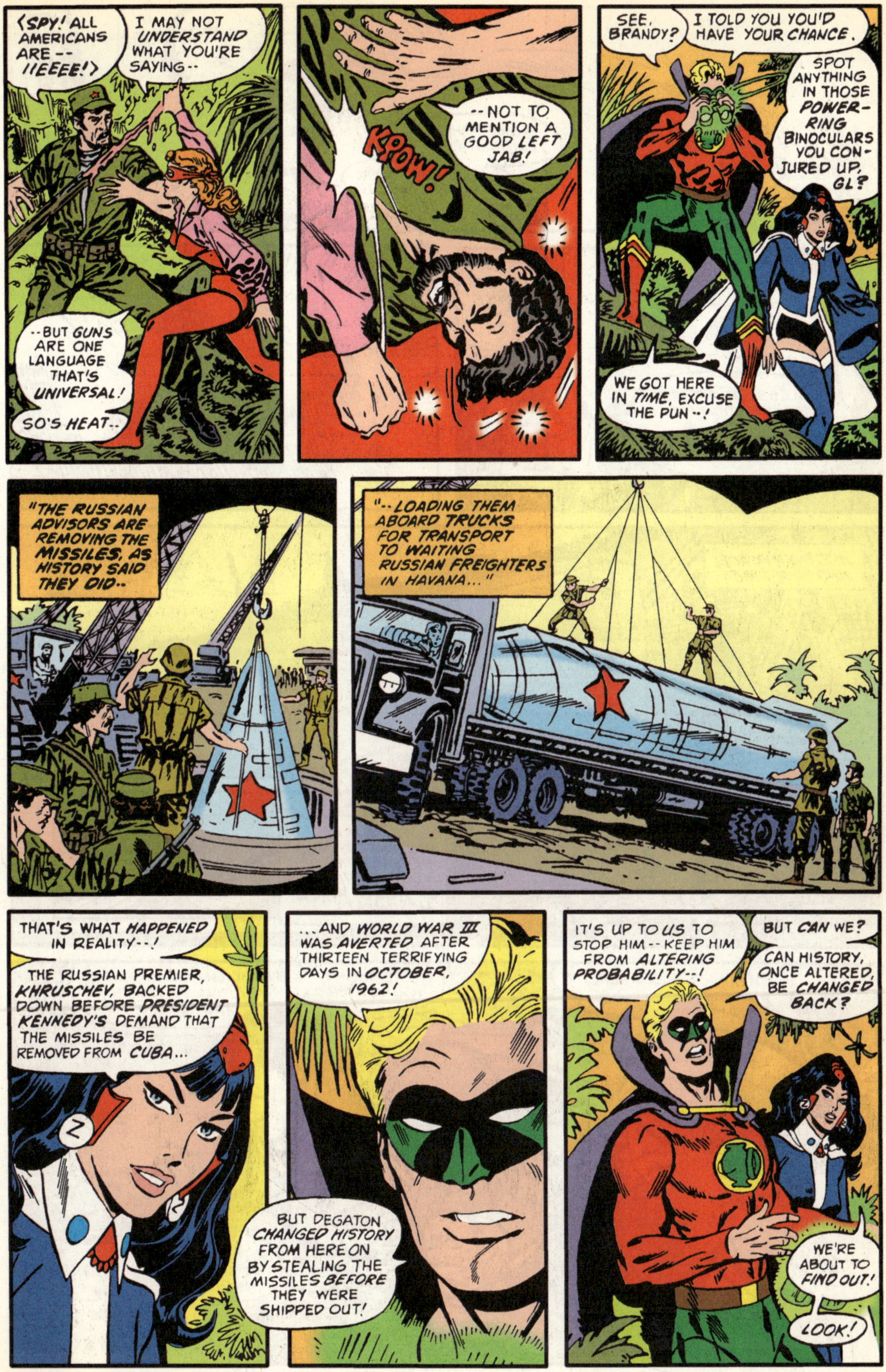

‹SPY! ALL AMERICANS ARE -- IIEEEE!›
I MAY NOT UNDERSTAND WHAT YOU'RE SAYING --
-- BUT GUNS ARE ONE LANGUAGE THAT'S UNIVERSAL!
SO'S HEAT..
-- NOT TO MENTION A GOOD LEFT JAB!
KPOW!
SEE, BRANDY?
I TOLD YOU YOU'D HAVE YOUR CHANCE.
SPOT ANYTHING IN THOSE POWER-RING BINOCULARS YOU CONJURED UP, GL?
WE GOT HERE IN TIME, EXCUSE THE PUN --!
"THE RUSSIAN ADVISORS ARE REMOVING THE MISSILES, AS HISTORY SAID THEY DID..
"..LOADING THEM ABOARD TRUCKS FOR TRANSPORT TO WAITING RUSSIAN FREIGHTERS IN HAVANA..."
THAT'S WHAT HAPPENED IN REALITY--!
THE RUSSIAN PREMIER, KHRUSCHEV, BACKED DOWN BEFORE PRESIDENT KENNEDY'S DEMAND THAT THE MISSILES BE REMOVED FROM CUBA...
...AND WORLD WAR III WAS AVERTED AFTER THIRTEEN TERRIFYING DAYS IN OCTOBER, 1962!
BUT DEGATON CHANGED HISTORY FROM HERE ON BY STEALING THE MISSILES BEFORE THEY WERE SHIPPED OUT!
IT'S UP TO US TO STOP HIM -- KEEP HIM FROM ALTERING PROBABILITY--!
BUT CAN WE?
CAN HISTORY, ONCE ALTERED, BE CHANGED BACK?
WE'RE ABOUT TO FIND OUT!
LOOK!

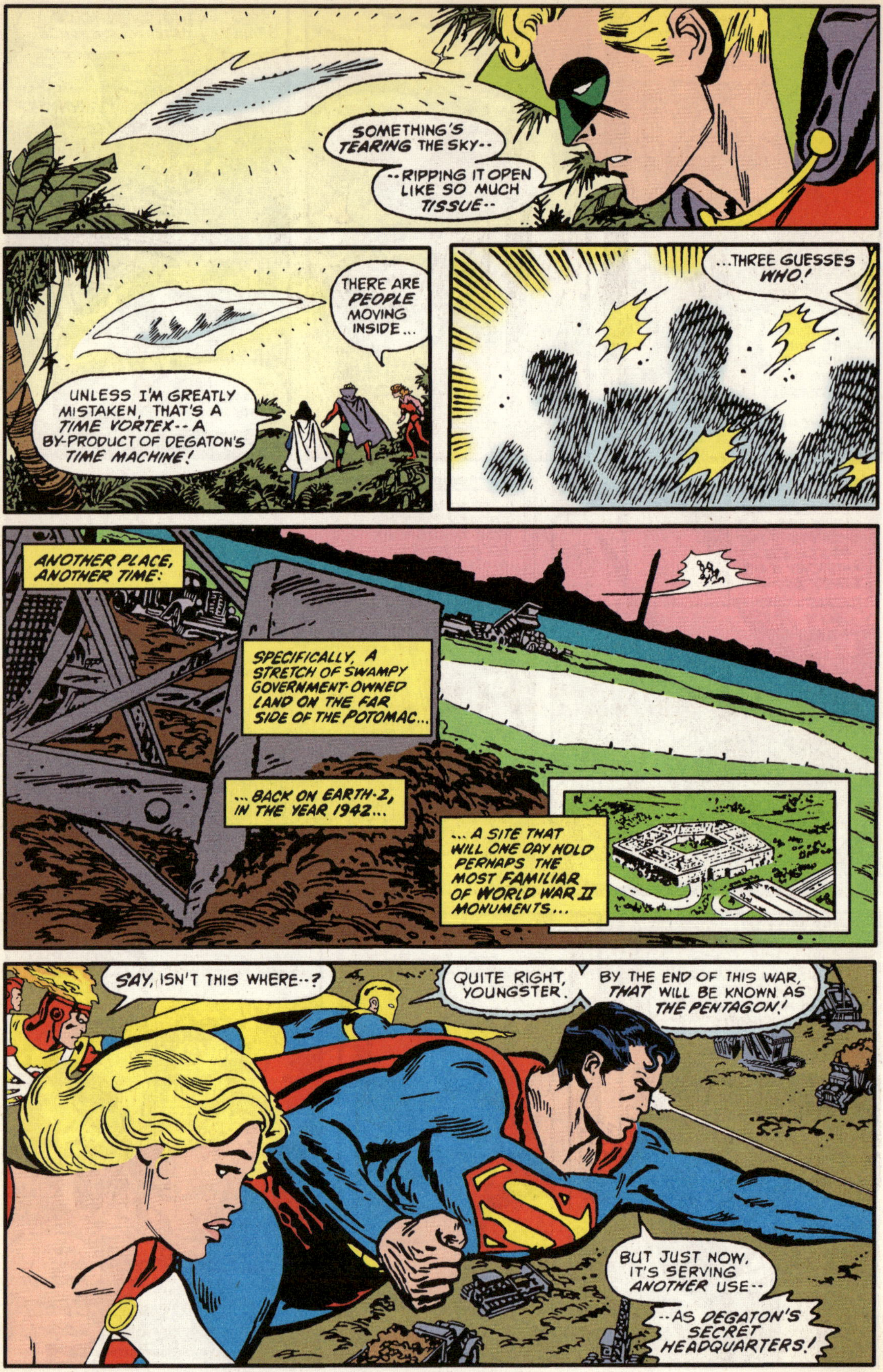
SOMETHING'S TEARING THE SKY--
--RIPPING IT OPEN LIKE SO MUCH TISSUE--
THERE ARE PEOPLE MOVING INSIDE...
UNLESS I'M GREATLY MISTAKEN, THAT'S A TIME VORTEX-- A BY-PRODUCT OF DEGATON'S TIME MACHINE!
...THREE GUESSES WHO!
ANOTHER PLACE, ANOTHER TIME:
SPECIFICALLY, A STRETCH OF SWAMPY GOVERNMENT-OWNED LAND ON THE FAR SIDE OF THE POTOMAC...
...BACK ON EARTH-2, IN THE YEAR 1942...
...A SITE THAT WILL ONE DAY HOLD PERHAPS THE MOST FAMILIAR OF WORLD WAR II MONUMENTS...
SAY, ISN'T THIS WHERE--?
QUITE RIGHT, YOUNGSTER.
BY THE END OF THIS WAR, THAT WILL BE KNOWN AS THE PENTAGON!
BUT JUST NOW, IT'S SERVING ANOTHER USE--
--AS DEGATON'S SECRET HEADQUARTERS!

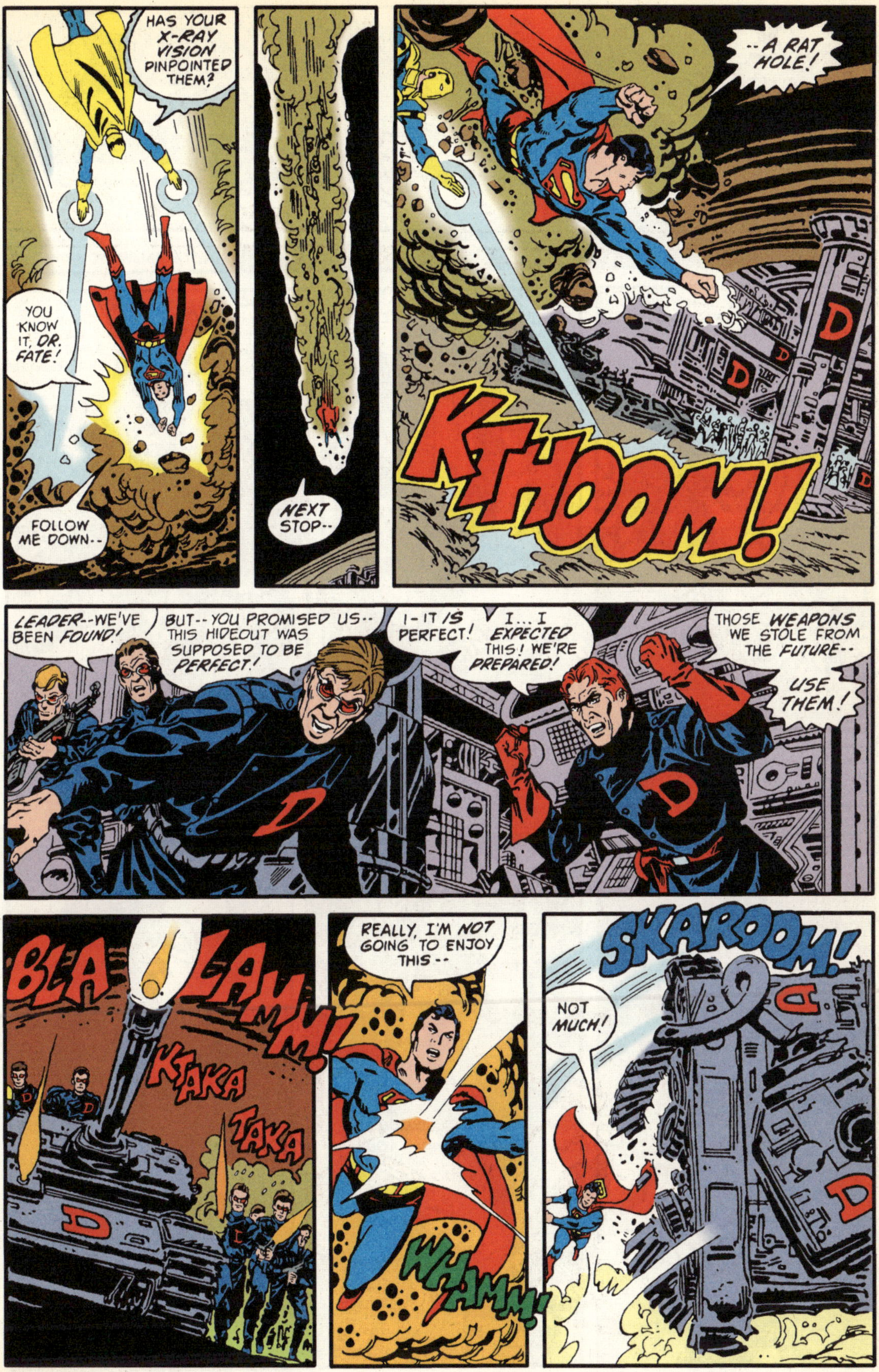
HAS YOUR X-RAY VISION PINPOINTED THEM?
YOU KNOW IT, DR. FATE!
FOLLOW ME DOWN--
NEXT STOP--
--A RAT HOLE!
KTHOOM!
LEADER--WE'VE BEEN FOUND!
BUT--YOU PROMISED US--THIS HIDEOUT WAS SUPPOSED TO BE PERFECT!
I-IT IS PERFECT!
I...I EXPECTED THIS! WE'RE PREPARED!
THOSE WEAPONS WE STOLE FROM THE FUTURE--
USE THEM!
BLA LAMM!
KTAKA TAKA
REALLY, I'M NOT GOING TO ENJOY THIS--
WHAMM!
SKAROOM!
NOT MUCH!

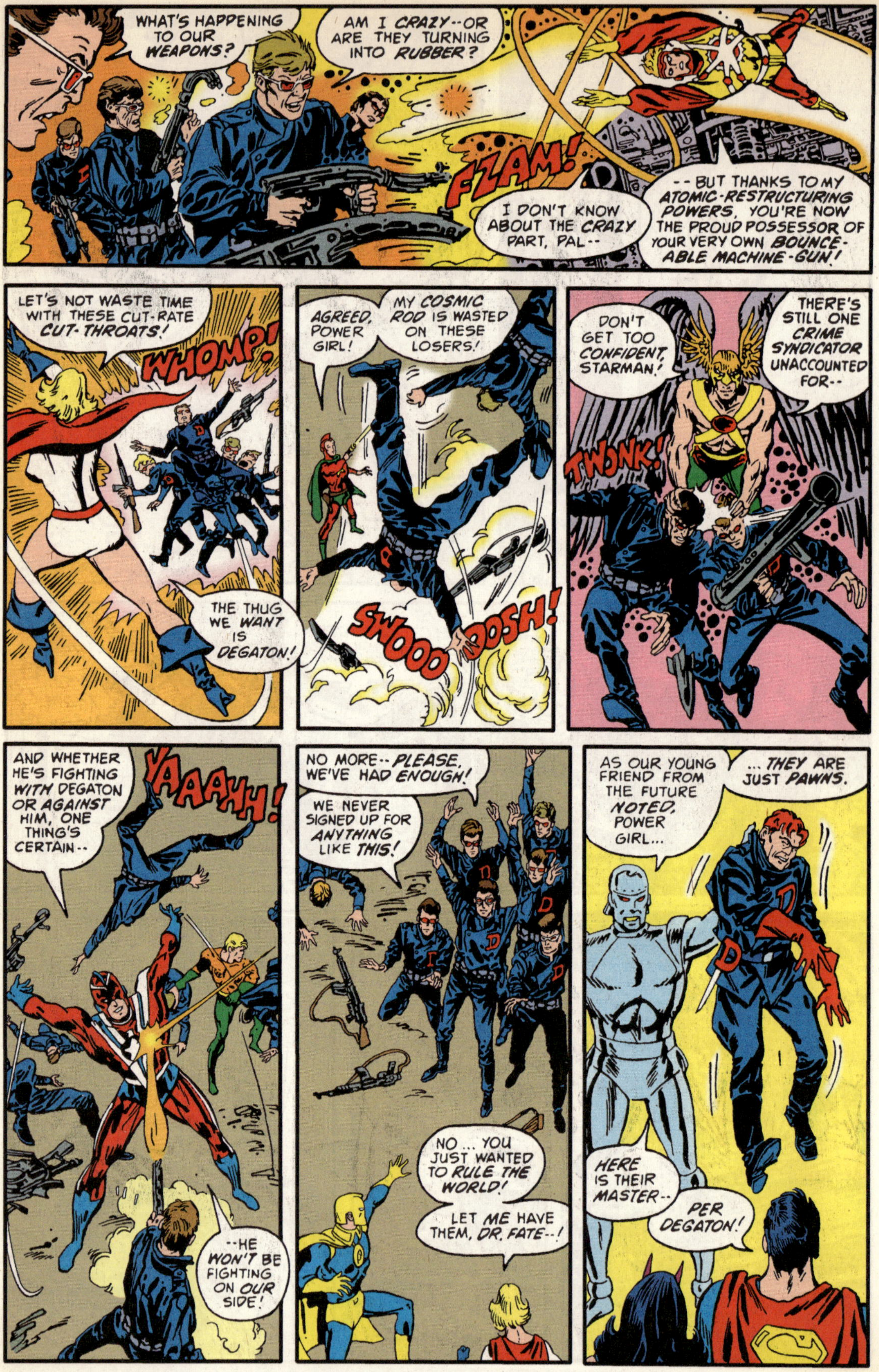
WHAT'S HAPPENING TO OUR WEAPONS?
AM I CRAZY--OR ARE THEY TURNING INTO RUBBER?
FZAM!
I DON'T KNOW ABOUT THE CRAZY PART, PAL--
--BUT THANKS TO MY ATOMIC-RESTRUCTURING POWERS, YOU'RE NOW THE PROUD POSSESSOR OF YOUR VERY OWN BOUNCE-ABLE MACHINE-GUN!
LET'S NOT WASTE TIME WITH THESE CUT-RATE CUT-THROATS!
WHOMP!
THE THUG WE WANT IS DEGATON!
AGREED, POWER GIRL!
MY COSMIC ROD IS WASTED ON THESE LOSERS!
SWOOOOOSH!
DON'T GET TOO CONFIDENT, STARMAN!
THERE'S STILL ONE CRIME SYNDICATOR UNACCOUNTED FOR--
TWONK!
AND WHETHER HE'S FIGHTING WITH DEGATON OR AGAINST HIM, ONE THING'S CERTAIN--
YAAAHH!
--HE WON'T BE FIGHTING ON OUR SIDE!
NO MORE--PLEASE. WE'VE HAD ENOUGH!
WE NEVER SIGNED UP FOR ANYTHING LIKE THIS!
NO ... YOU JUST WANTED TO RULE THE WORLD!
LET ME HAVE THEM, DR. FATE--!
AS OUR YOUNG FRIEND FROM THE FUTURE NOTED, POWER GIRL...
... THEY ARE JUST PAWNS.
HERE IS THEIR MASTER--
PER DEGATON!

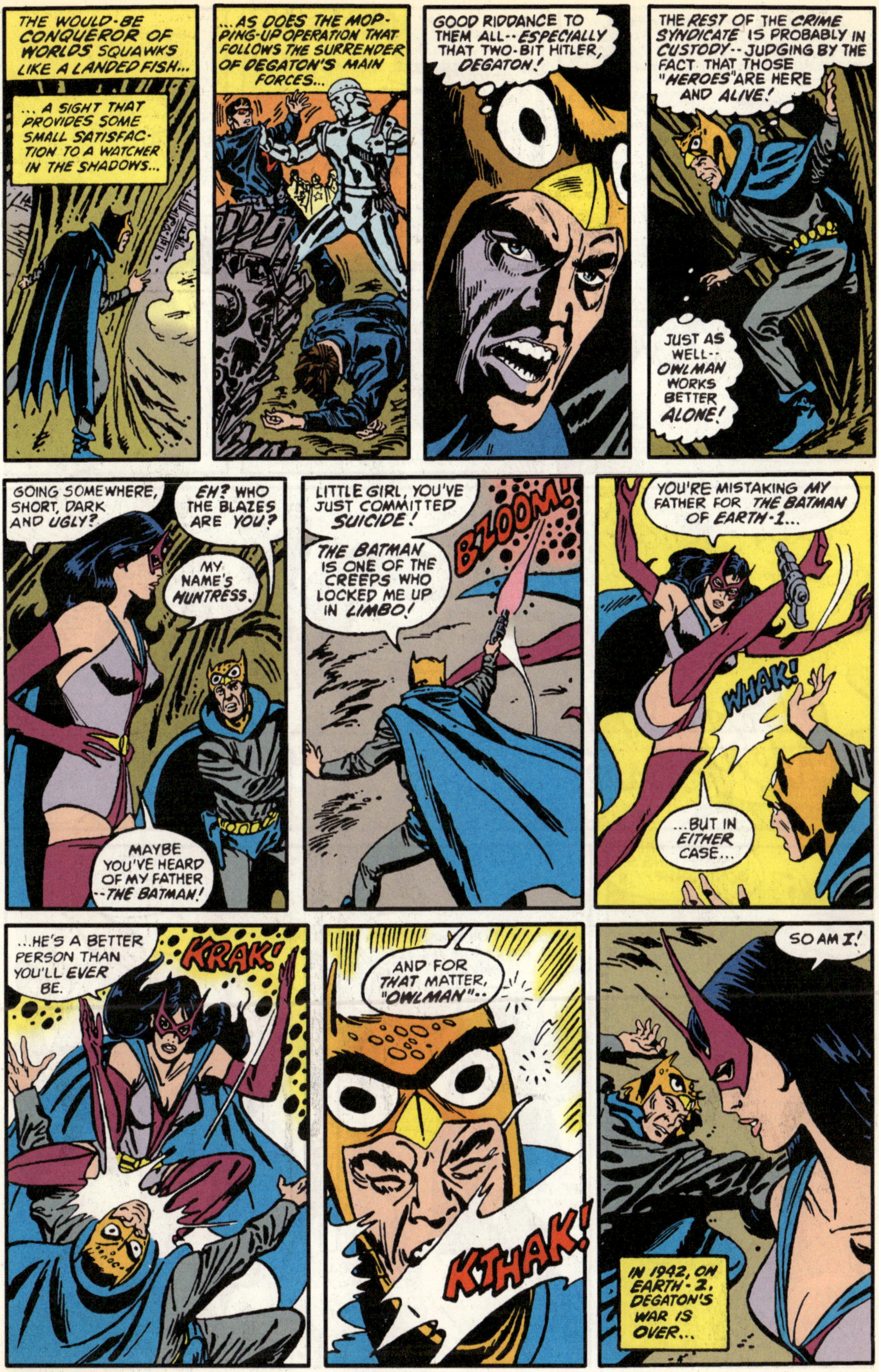
THE WOULD-BE CONQUEROR OF WORLDS SQUAWKS LIKE A LANDED FISH...
...A SIGHT THAT PROVIDES SOME SMALL SATISFACTION TO A WATCHER IN THE SHADOWS...
...AS DOES THE MOPPING-UP OPERATION THAT FOLLOWS THE SURRENDER OF DEGATON'S MAIN FORCES...
GOOD RIDDANCE TO THEM ALL--ESPECIALLY THAT TWO-BIT HITLER, DEGATON!
THE REST OF THE CRIME SYNDICATE IS PROBABLY IN CUSTODY--JUDGING BY THE FACT THAT THOSE "HEROES" ARE HERE AND ALIVE!
JUST AS WELL--OWLMAN WORKS BETTER ALONE!
GOING SOMEWHERE, SHORT, DARK AND UGLY?
EH? WHO THE BLAZES ARE YOU?
MY NAME'S HUNTRESS.
MAYBE YOU'VE HEARD OF MY FATHER--THE BATMAN!
LITTLE GIRL, YOU'VE JUST COMMITTED SUICIDE!
THE BATMAN IS ONE OF THE CREEPS WHO LOCKED ME UP IN LIMBO!
BZOOM!
YOU'RE MISTAKING MY FATHER FOR THE BATMAN OF EARTH-1...
WHAK!
...BUT IN EITHER CASE...
...HE'S A BETTER PERSON THAN YOU'LL EVER BE.
KRAK!
AND FOR THAT MATTER, "OWLMAN"--
KTHAK!
SO AM I!
IN 1942, ON EARTH-2, DEGATON'S WAR IS OVER...

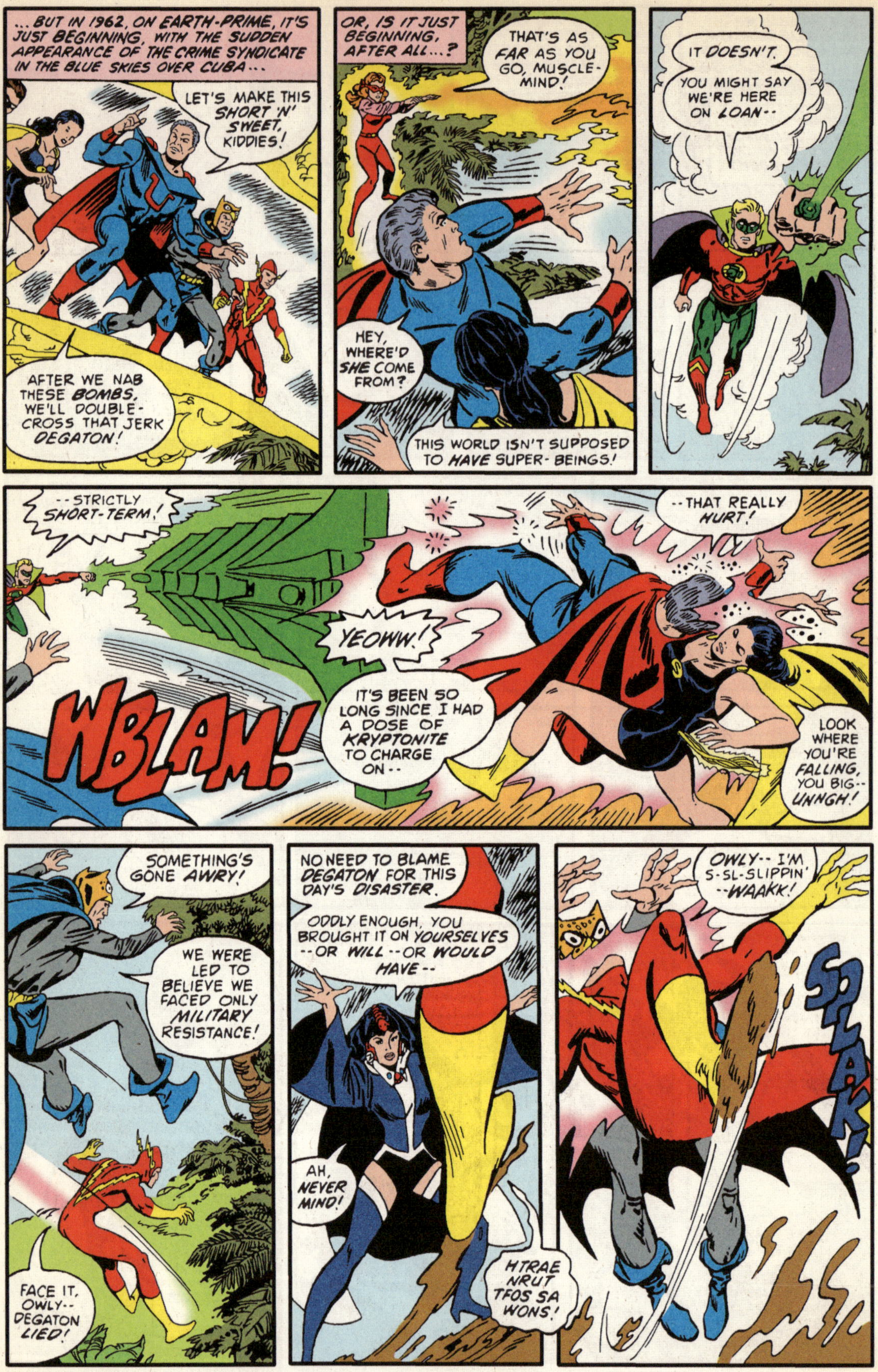
...BUT IN 1962, ON EARTH-PRIME, IT'S JUST BEGINNING, WITH THE SUDDEN APPEARANCE OF THE CRIME SYNDICATE IN THE BLUE SKIES OVER CUBA...
LET'S MAKE THIS SHORT 'N' SWEET, KIDDIES!
AFTER WE NAB THESE BOMBS, WE'LL DOUBLE-CROSS THAT JERK DEGATON!
OR, IS IT JUST BEGINNING, AFTER ALL...?
THAT'S AS FAR AS YOU GO, MUSCLE-MIND!
HEY, WHERE'D SHE COME FROM?
THIS WORLD ISN'T SUPPOSED TO HAVE SUPER-BEINGS!
IT DOESN'T.
YOU MIGHT SAY WE'RE HERE ON LOAN--
--STRICTLY SHORT-TERM!
WBLAM!
YEOWW!
IT'S BEEN SO LONG SINCE I HAD A DOSE OF KRYPTONITE TO CHARGE ON--
--THAT REALLY HURT!
LOOK WHERE YOU'RE FALLING, YOU BIG-- UNNGH!
SOMETHING'S GONE AWRY!
WE WERE LED TO BELIEVE WE FACED ONLY MILITARY RESISTANCE!
FACE IT, OWLY-- DEGATON LIED!
NO NEED TO BLAME DEGATON FOR THIS DAY'S DISASTER.
ODDLY ENOUGH, YOU BROUGHT IT ON YOURSELVES --OR WILL --OR WOULD HAVE--
AH, NEVER MIND!
HTRAE NRUT TFOS SA WONS!
OWLY-- I'M S-SL-SLIPPIN' --WAAKK!
SPLAK!

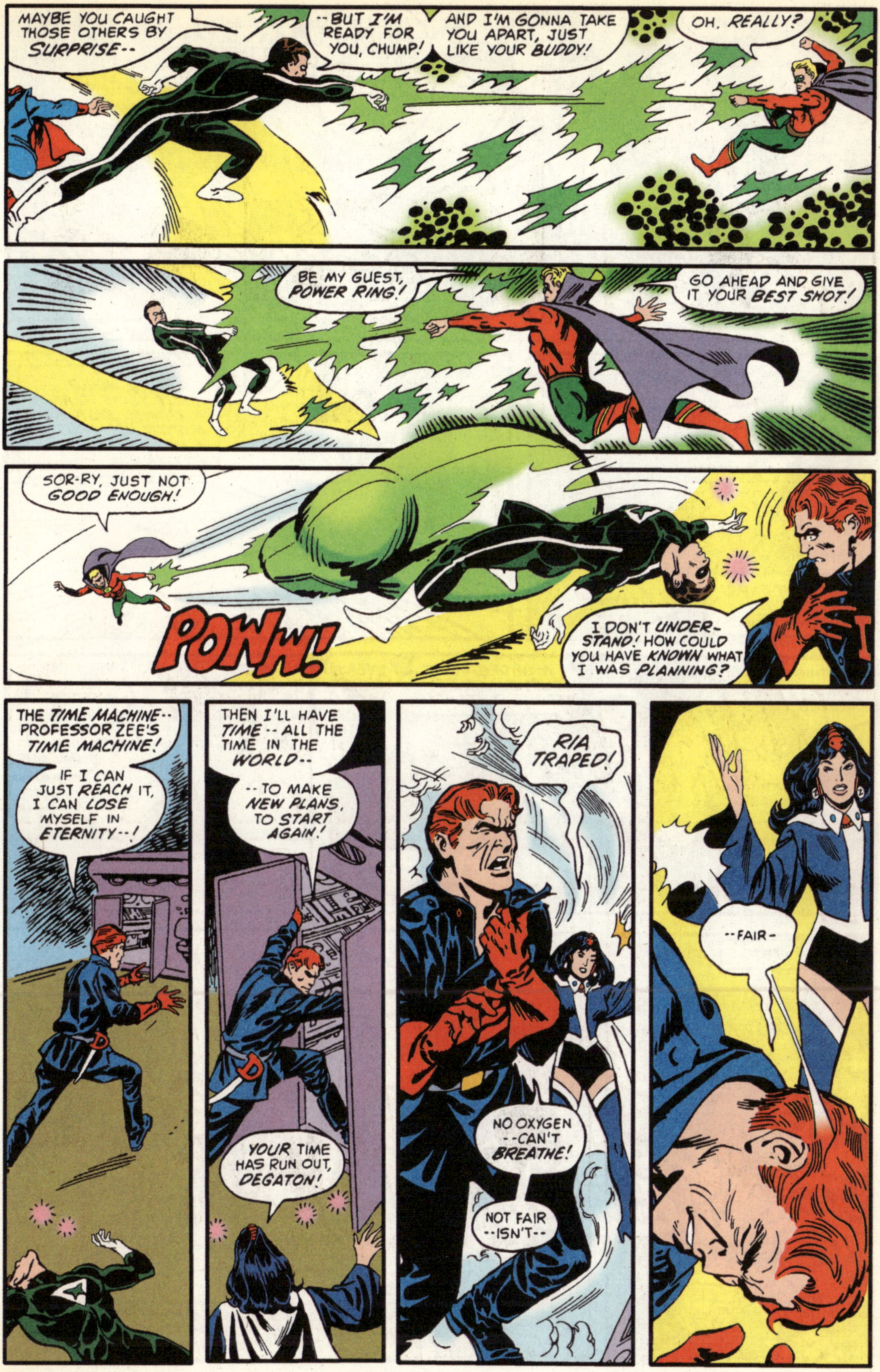
MAYBE YOU CAUGHT THOSE OTHERS BY SURPRISE--
--BUT I'M READY FOR YOU, CHUMP!
AND I'M GONNA TAKE YOU APART, JUST LIKE YOUR BUDDY!
OH, REALLY?
BE MY GUEST, POWER RING!
GO AHEAD AND GIVE IT YOUR BEST SHOT!
SOR-RY, JUST NOT GOOD ENOUGH!
POWW!
I DON'T UNDERSTAND! HOW COULD YOU HAVE KNOWN WHAT I WAS PLANNING?
THE TIME MACHINE-- PROFESSOR ZEE'S TIME MACHINE!
IF I CAN JUST REACH IT, I CAN LOSE MYSELF IN ETERNITY--!
THEN I'LL HAVE TIME -- ALL THE TIME IN THE WORLD--
--TO MAKE NEW PLANS, TO START AGAIN!
YOUR TIME HAS RUN OUT, DEGATON!
RIA TRAPED!
NO OXYGEN --CAN'T BREATHE!
NOT FAIR --ISN'T--
--FAIR--

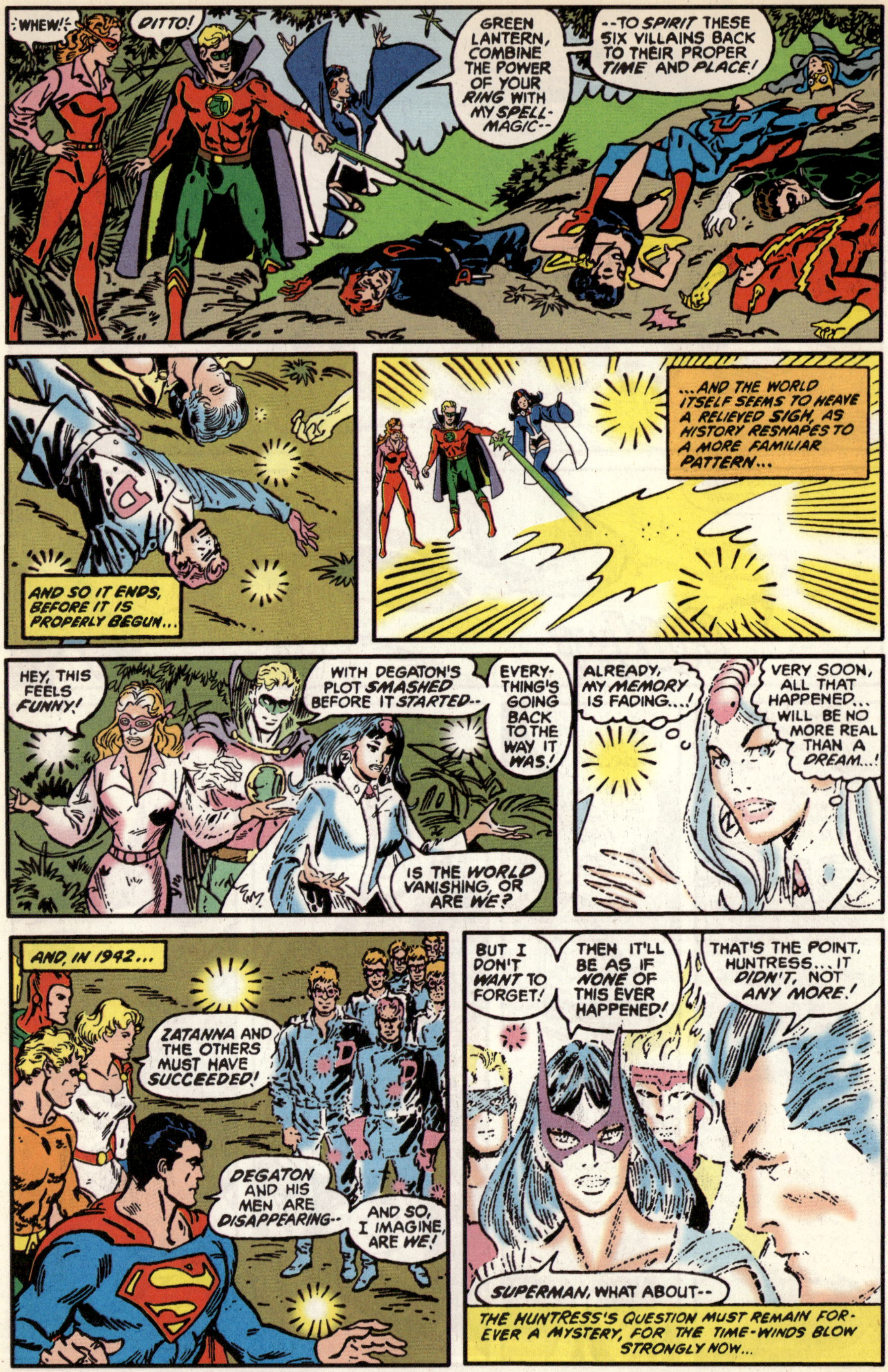
WHEW!
DITTO!
GREEN LANTERN, COMBINE THE POWER OF YOUR RING WITH MY SPELL-MAGIC--
--TO SPIRIT THESE SIX VILLAINS BACK TO THEIR PROPER TIME AND PLACE!
AND SO IT ENDS, BEFORE IT IS PROPERLY BEGUN...
...AND THE WORLD ITSELF SEEMS TO HEAVE A RELIEVED SIGH, AS HISTORY RESHAPES TO A MORE FAMILIAR PATTERN...
HEY, THIS FEELS FUNNY!
WITH DEGATON'S PLOT SMASHED BEFORE IT STARTED--
EVERY-THING'S GOING BACK TO THE WAY IT WAS!
IS THE WORLD VANISHING, OR ARE WE?
ALREADY, MY MEMORY IS FADING...!
VERY SOON, ALL THAT HAPPENED... WILL BE NO MORE REAL THAN A DREAM...!
AND, IN 1942...
ZATANNA AND THE OTHERS MUST HAVE SUCCEEDED!
DEGATON AND HIS MEN ARE DISAPPEARING--
AND SO, I IMAGINE, ARE WE!
BUT I DON'T WANT TO FORGET!
THEN IT'LL BE AS IF NONE OF THIS EVER HAPPENED!
THAT'S THE POINT, HUNTRESS... IT DIDN'T, NOT ANY MORE!
SUPERMAN, WHAT ABOUT--
THE HUNTRESS'S QUESTION MUST REMAIN FOR-EVER A MYSTERY, FOR THE TIME-WINDS BLOW STRONGLY NOW...

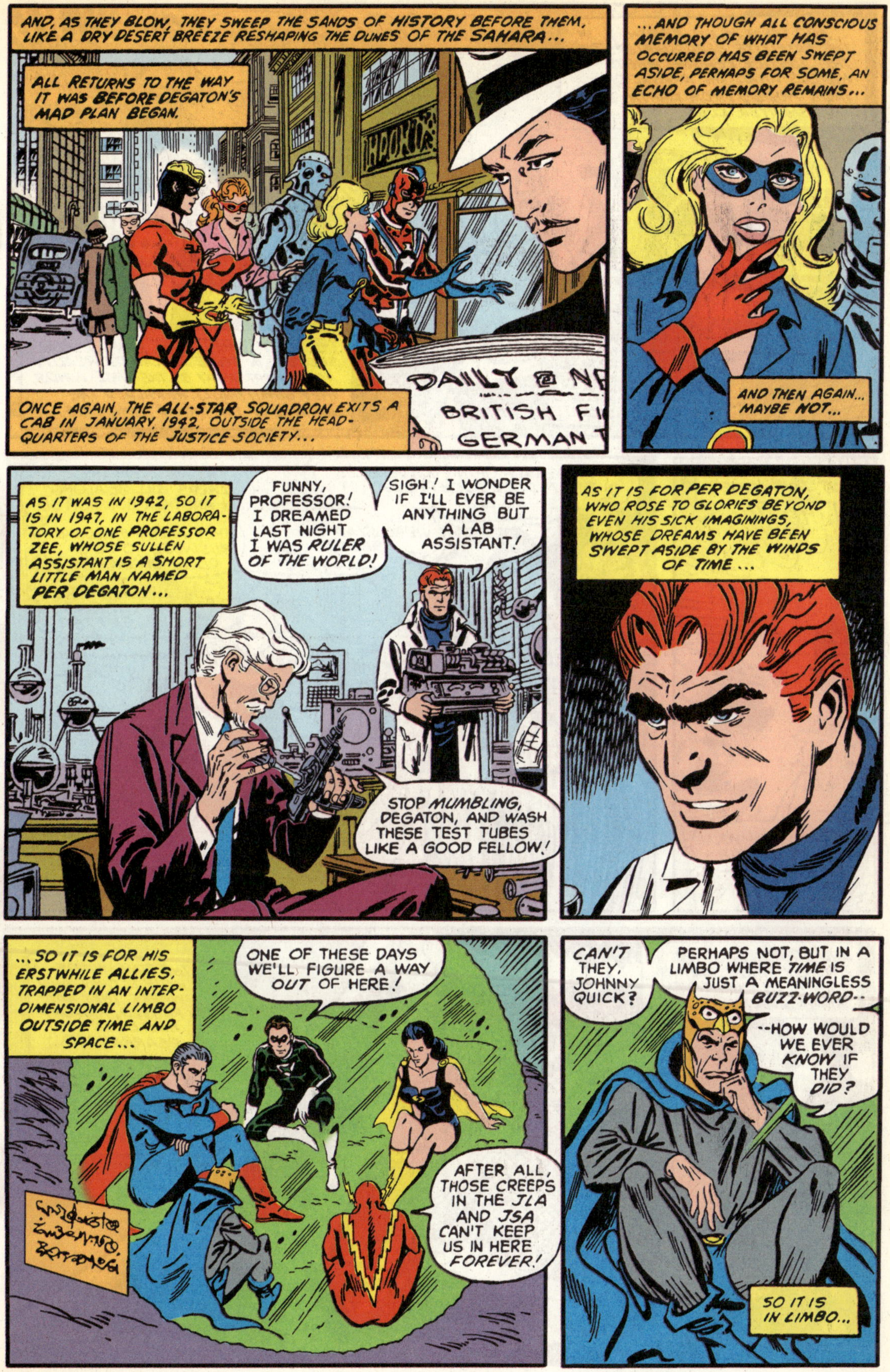

AND, AS THEY BLOW, THEY SWEEP THE SANDS OF HISTORY BEFORE THEM, LIKE A DRY DESERT BREEZE RESHAPING THE DUNES OF THE SAHARA...
ALL RETURNS TO THE WAY IT WAS BEFORE DEGATON'S MAD PLAN BEGAN.
ONCE AGAIN, THE ALL-STAR SQUADRON EXITS A CAB IN JANUARY, 1942, OUTSIDE THE HEAD-QUARTERS OF THE JUSTICE SOCIETY...
DAILY @ NE
BRITISH FI
GERMAN
...AND THOUGH ALL CONSCIOUS MEMORY OF WHAT HAS OCCURRED HAS BEEN SWEPT ASIDE, PERHAPS FOR SOME, AN ECHO OF MEMORY REMAINS...
AND THEN AGAIN... MAYBE NOT...
AS IT WAS IN 1942, SO IT IS IN 1947, IN THE LABORATORY OF ONE PROFESSOR ZEE, WHOSE SULLEN ASSISTANT IS A SHORT LITTLE MAN NAMED PER DEGATON...
FUNNY, PROFESSOR! I DREAMED LAST NIGHT I WAS RULER OF THE WORLD!
SIGH! I WONDER IF I'LL EVER BE ANYTHING BUT A LAB ASSISTANT!
STOP MUMBLING, DEGATON, AND WASH THESE TEST TUBES LIKE A GOOD FELLOW!
AS IT IS FOR PER DEGATON, WHO ROSE TO GLORIES BEYOND EVEN HIS SICK IMAGININGS, WHOSE DREAMS HAVE BEEN SWEPT ASIDE BY THE WINDS OF TIME...
...SO IT IS FOR HIS ERSTWHILE ALLIES, TRAPPED IN AN INTER-DIMENSIONAL LIMBO OUTSIDE TIME AND SPACE...
ONE OF THESE DAYS WE'LL FIGURE A WAY OUT OF HERE!
AFTER ALL, THOSE CREEPS IN THE JLA AND JSA CAN'T KEEP US IN HERE FOREVER!
CAN'T THEY, JOHNNY QUICK?
PERHAPS NOT, BUT IN A LIMBO WHERE TIME IS JUST A MEANINGLESS BUZZ-WORD--
--HOW WOULD WE EVER KNOW IF THEY DID?
SO IT IS IN LIMBO...

...AND SO IT IS ON EARTH-1, IN THE SATELLITE HEADQUARTERS OF THE JUSTICE LEAGUE, WHERE FIVE HEROES AWAIT THE ARRIVAL OF THEIR FRIENDS FROM EARTH-2 VIA TRANSMATTER CUBE...

STAND BACK... HERE THEY COME.

WELCOME BACK TO EARTH-1--

THE LAST "TIME" THOSE WORDS WERE SPOKEN, IN SOME ALTERNATE REALITY NOW SWEPT AWAY BY THE TIME-WINDS, THEY UNWITTINGLY HERALDED THE ARRIVAL OF THE CRIME SYNDICATE...

BUT THIS "TIME"...

THANK YOU, SUPERMAN--

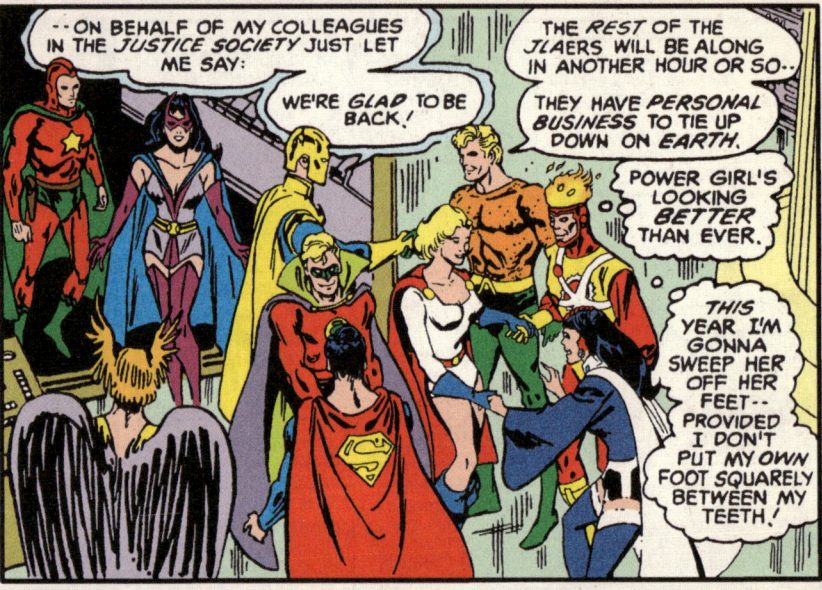

--ON BEHALF OF MY COLLEAGUES IN THE JUSTICE SOCIETY JUST LET ME SAY:

WE'RE GLAD TO BE BACK!

THE REST OF THE JLAERS WILL BE ALONG IN ANOTHER HOUR OR SO-- THEY HAVE PERSONAL BUSINESS TO TIE UP DOWN ON EARTH.

POWER GIRL'S LOOKING BETTER THAN EVER.

THIS YEAR I'M GONNA SWEEP HER OFF HER FEET-- PROVIDED I DON'T PUT MY OWN FOOT SQUARELY BETWEEN MY TEETH!

AND SO IT GOES: AS IT IS ON THREE EARTHS, SO IT IS IN THE HEAVENS ABOVE EARTH-1...

THE TIME-WINDS HAVE BLOWN, AND WHERE THEY HAVE PASSED, HISTORY HAS BEEN REARRANGED...

...AND WHAT HAS NEVER BEEN, OF COURSE, CANNOT BE REMEMBERED.

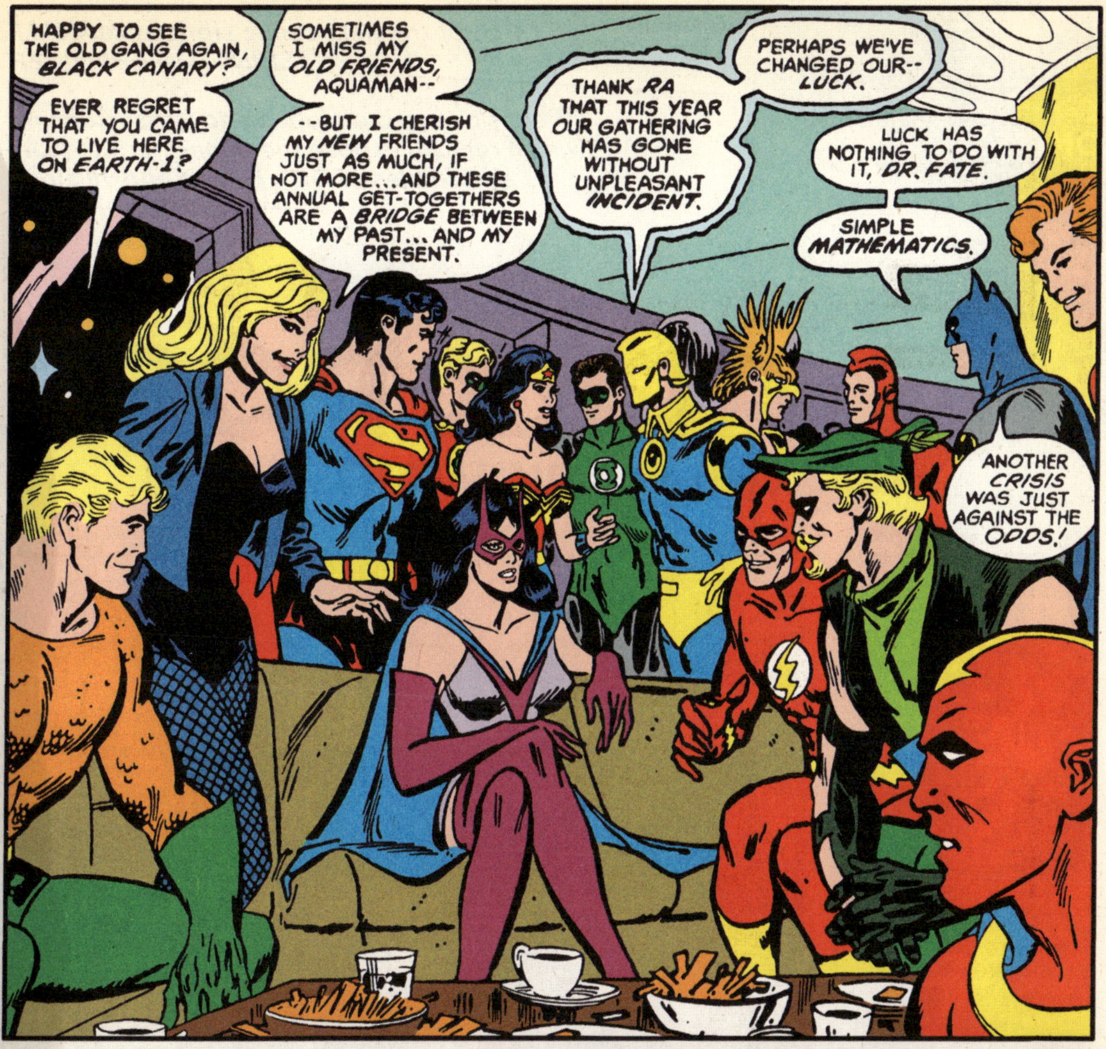
HAPPY TO SEE THE OLD GANG AGAIN, BLACK CANARY?
EVER REGRET THAT YOU CAME TO LIVE HERE ON EARTH-1?
SOMETIMES I MISS MY OLD FRIENDS, AQUAMAN--
--BUT I CHERISH MY NEW FRIENDS JUST AS MUCH, IF NOT MORE... AND THESE ANNUAL GET-TOGETHERS ARE A BRIDGE BETWEEN MY PAST... AND MY PRESENT.
THANK RA THAT THIS YEAR OUR GATHERING HAS GONE WITHOUT UNPLEASANT INCIDENT.
PERHAPS WE'VE CHANGED OUR-- LUCK.
LUCK HAS NOTHING TO DO WITH IT, DR. FATE.
SIMPLE MATHEMATICS.
ANOTHER CRISIS WAS JUST AGAINST THE ODDS!
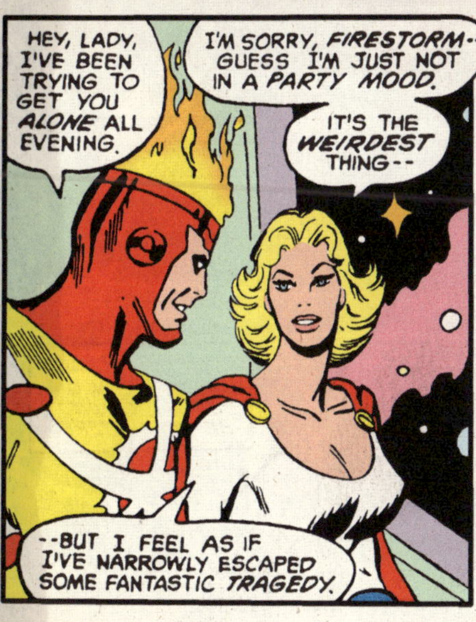
HEY, LADY, I'VE BEEN TRYING TO GET YOU ALONE ALL EVENING.
I'M SORRY, FIRESTORM-- GUESS I'M JUST NOT IN A PARTY MOOD.
IT'S THE WEIRDEST THING--
--BUT I FEEL AS IF I'VE NARROWLY ESCAPED SOME FANTASTIC TRAGEDY.
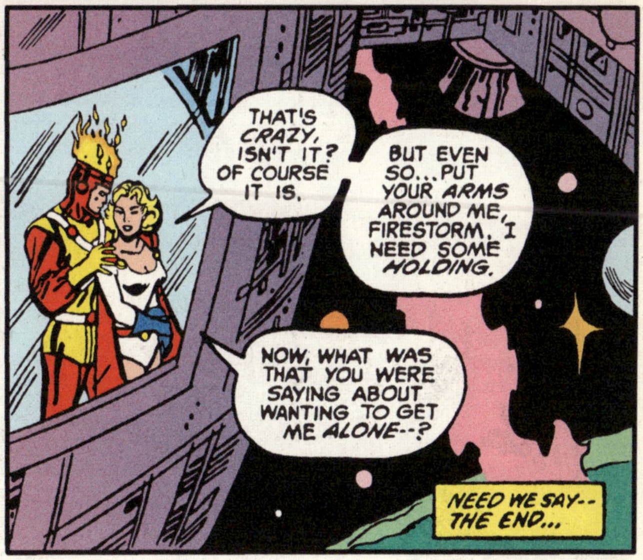
THAT'S CRAZY, ISN'T IT? OF COURSE IT IS.
BUT EVEN SO... PUT YOUR ARMS AROUND ME, FIRESTORM. I NEED SOME HOLDING.
NOW, WHAT WAS THAT YOU WERE SAYING ABOUT WANTING TO GET ME ALONE--?
NEED WE SAY-- THE END...

DC COMICS™

"One of the best comic stories ever told."
—WASHINGTON EXAMINER

"Waid's charged dialogue and Ross' stunning visual realism expose the genius, pride, fears and foibles of DC's heroes and villains."
—WASHINGTON POST

ALEX ROSS
with MARK WAID

JUSTICE

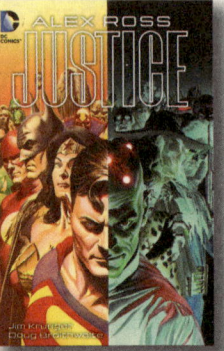

with JIM KRUEGER
& DOUG BRAITHWAITE

WORLD'S GREATEST SUPER-HEROES

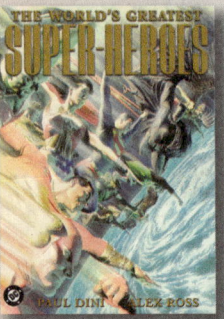

with PAUL DINI

JUSTICE SOCIETY OF AMERICA: THY KINGDOM COME PARTS 1-3

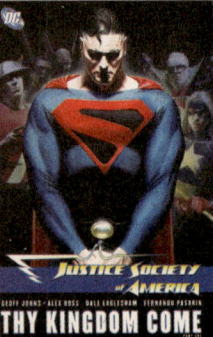

with GEOFF JOHNS and DALE EAGLESHAM

THE GREATEST SUPER-HERO EPIC OF TOMORROW!

KINGDOM COME

MARK WAID ALEX ROSS